Unbound by Shadowspire

Tracey Canole

Korben Skies Publishing

Contents

Contents

Acknowledgements

The lost.

The stuck.

The bound.

Forever Constricted

BEING ALONE WITH ONE'S thoughts is a necessity. Them leaving a mark on the soul because the owner knows that something is missing is precursor to the future. As is the bouncing knee. The prickle of electricity in the veins. The inadequacy.

Myrna pushes it back. It's in her head. This sense she does not belong.

It might be her severe lack of skill with beauty tools or her odd cadence of speech. At least one will lead to the grilling she'll receive when that door opens. A normality to the day she's not yet used to. Another reminder of their differences.

"Whoa! Did you get in a fight with your curling iron?"

Yes, Samantha. And what a wonderful sentiment to start the day.

Like the morning hasn't been a hard enough. Starting off with the screeching alarm set to ungodly levels, urging Myrna to destroy it upon its first trill. She fell out of bed and slammed her elbow on the side table. Then the water turned ice cold with an unexpected flash of hot. Note, third degree burns on one's butt *are* a thing. All followed by the neighbor next door blasting music at six in the morning. Which leaves little patience for the woman in front of her.

"Gee. Thanks, Sam." Myrna goes to slam the door in her best friend's face, but the little ball of sass has the gall to laugh. Of course she does.

"Is somebody cranky?" Sam asks, pouting her bottom lip. Those long lashed, deep blue eyes flutter at Myrna comically before Samantha Merance—trouble on four-inch red stiletto heels—sing-songs, "Even so, you look hot. Plus, I've got coffee!"

Myrna hesitates as the scent of almond, milk, and espresso wafts in. With a frustrated sigh, she swings the door open to find Sam blowing on the top of the cup so the smell moves toward the door. Even while being ridiculous, Sam's hair is perfect, pulled up in a classy updo. One Myrna could never replicate.

"You can stop that now," Myrna says, refusing to let her friend's antics amuse her. Sam grins, sashaying past Myrna and into her small one-bedroom apartment. "I assume those are why you're late?"

Sam gasps dramatically. "Oh my gosh, you used a contraction!"

Sam struts over to the counter and sets the cups down. She's wearing a too-tight pencil skirt and a hot red blouse that accentuates every curve. The purse she carries is half her size. How it doesn't cause her to trip, Myrna will never know.

"I happen to use contractions regularly now, thank you."

"Yeah...okay. Well, if you're just going to lie, I will, too." Her eyes widen as she says, "No, this is not why I'm late. But if I can't fix your hair..."

Myrna blanches. *Is it really that bad?*

"Don't worry. It's not like that one time," Sam says, reading her expression. She walks over and wraps individual curls around her finger, laying Myrna's stretched curls in a more organized manner.

"I tried," Myrna says with a pout.

"You weren't supposed to wrestle the damn thing, Myr."

Myrna shoots her an annoyed glare.

Sam laughs. "Well, at least those lessons on work attire worked. You look adorable. Of course, I'll take any excuse to go shopping. I do regret not getting that blue cashmere sweater, and I still think you should've gone with a smaller size for your skirts."

Chapter One

Myrna shakes her head at the continuous flow of words invading her peaceful home. The home that ten minutes ago she'd wished wasn't so quiet. It's odd, the longer Myrna's here, the more she doesn't feel comfortable. It's only when Sam, her mother, or childhood caretaker, Theia, is around that Myrna feels settled.

That's not completely true and you know it. Because moments before Myrna sat, feeling like an intruder in her own life urging her to leave and head to the one place that feels natural. Where she's safe and the weight of the world no longer is upon her.

Work. It is strange. Myrna's aware. Haszwalds Elite is just an office building, and she is but an intern—someone who, ninety percent of the time, sits at the welcome desk. Yet, walking into Haszwalds is like coming home. Warmth spreads through, providing a calmness and joy she rarely experiences.

Thank the heavens, Myrna's phone chimes, pulling her attention back to this time and space.

Theia: *Good morning, Darling. Have you packed your lunch? Do remember we have training tonight at six. Is Sam joining us?*

Myrna smiles. Theia approved of Sam, too. Mostly...

Tonight, Myrna works late, but it is also weapons training at the gym Theia set Myrna up with. It closes early so they can spar in private. Myrna wonders why Tomas is so willing to do this for them when he isn't willing to do it for anyone else.

Theia: *Will you be coming straight from campus?*

Myrna's stomach drops.

Sam notices instantly. "Hey, what's wrong?"

Myrna shakes her head and carefully chooses her words as she types out her response to Theia.

Myrna: *Do not worry, I have my lunch and workout bag ready for the day. I will meet you at the gym at our assigned time. Tomas has our normal room reserved, but Sam has a date. So, it will be us alone.*

Those little dots appear instantly, then Theia's reply comes: I *look forward to the retelling of Sam's date later. Oh, and tonight will be staffs. See you then.*

Myrna snorts. Sam has an interesting history with men, and they all know it. The stories are amazing. Her focus moves to the word "staffs" and excitement replaces the amusement, causing Myrna to bounce on her toes. That will be fun.

Her next thought suddenly has her feeling exhausted. Theia does not know the truth, and it's a problem. "A *lie to those you love cuts deeper than all others.*" Myrna raises her gaze to her friend as Theia's teachings whisper in her mind.

Knowing she is the single person who might understand, Myrna tells Sam, "I haven't told Theia about the internship yet."

Sam's mouth drops open. "What? It's been forever. How could you wait? I mean...you can tell her tonight, but..."

"Yeah...She asked if I was coming to training from classes today, and I realized I hadn't told her. She's going to be furious." Myrna paces across to the kitchen and back. It takes far less energy than she needs to release. "Both Theia and Mother are going to freak. They'll think it's a security risk, and I didn't tell them on purpose. That I'm in danger."

"Okay, first, did you? And two, what are you in danger from?"

"I didn't want them snooping around work. You know them. As for the second question...I don't know!" Myrna throws her hands up in the air and continues her pacing around the apartment. "Your guess is as good as mine. From the imaginary attackers that have been after us all my life? A paper cut? Men?"

"And you've asked?"

"Of course I have, but..." Myrna's voice trails off as memories of how the questioning of her mother has gone. Theia wasn't much better.

Sam approaches Myrna and rests her hands on the girl's shoulders. "But it didn't go well."

Myrna shakes her head.

Sam nods. "Theia loves you. She'll be excited you got the internship you wanted, and she'll help break the news to Laoise. You need this for your degree."

"Is your mother in town?" Sam asks, and Myrna shrugs. "Then maybe you worry for nothing. We haven't seen Laoise in a few months. It'll be all right."

But that means we're due for a visit. And when Mother finds out, she will be volatile. "Yeah. I guess."

Sam drops her arms to her sides. "I still think she's an assassin for hire."

Myrna snorts. "And yet you taunt her."

CHAPTER TWO

Energized Relief

"ALL RIGHT, LADY, WE got to get going." Sam grabs Myrna's lunch box from the counter and hurries to the small gym bag by the door. "Mrs. Smith is going to kill me if I'm late again. So, move your ass. You know I'll throw you under the bus and blame you for our tardiness!"

Chuckling, Myrna grabs her much more sedate one-inch pumps, slipping them on as they rush for the door, as Sam scoops up Myrna's pale pink backpack purse. The door nearly swings shut as the tiny fireball of energy flies through it and toward the elevator. Making quick work of the lock, Myrna jogs to catch up with her friend.

"She wouldn't believe you, and you know it. Cindy likes me," she says, taking her items from Sam. Myrna stands tall, almost regal compared to the sassy way Samantha does in her skintight skirt—hand on hip, shoulders back, heel cocked to the side.

"I don't get it. I work as hard as you do. She just hates me."

"You do. Perhaps it's your flirtatious ways? Or the way you ogle all the men when you should be working."

Sam gasps, her hand flying to her chest. "Hey, I get all my work done and on time!" She pouts. "And there are just so many pretty ones at Haszwalds. Especially on the fourth floor. Ugh."

Sam wiggles her eyebrows and shimmies her shoulders in a manner that sets Myrna to laughing.

She is ridiculous. One of the most hardworking individuals Myrna's ever met and loyal to a fault, but that outrageous personality—and mouth—has the tendency to slip out at the wrong time.

Grinning, Myrna says, "Then, perhaps you should watch what you say while in the building. In the privacy of my apartment, fine, but while we're at work..."

Sam huffs. "I didn't *mean* for her to hear me talking about Mr. Daniels like that. And you have to admit, he is scrumptious. What I would give to work on level four with him!"

The Vice President of Ascension Land Management on the fourth floor is one of the most important people in the building, and, yes, he also happens to be "scrumptious." She was just lucky he hadn't heard, and that Cindy had given her the chance to earn back her place.

"You know that won't happen. They don't let interns up on the fourth floor. Or the fifth, sixth, or eighth, for that matter." Myrna pauses as she opens the door to Sam's car. It is what she calls a small SUV. A cute one. The perfect size to transport a dead body—per Sam. "Have you ever noticed anything different about the people on those floors?"

"What do you mean?" Sam asks as she backs out of the spot. They're out of the parking garage before Myrna knows it.

Myrna shrugs. "I don't know. I was just curious if you've noticed anything."

Myrna eases into the seat. She's always found the speed of the car and the way it shifts along the road exhilarating, especially when Sam drives. She's what one calls a "crazy driver." The brake is a myth, and the laws are really just guidelines. So, it's fun to have her behind the wheel.

Sam peels out of the parking spot, barely missing another vehicle. She waves at the other driver before slamming on the gas. Myrna's pressed into her seat with force.

"You mean other than the fact that they're all gorgeous, freakishly well dressed, and like to pretend I don't exist? No, not really." Her head cocks to the side as if realizing something just as she turns right from the left lane, cutting off a bus. "But they all notice you, Myrna Johnson. They either stare at or avoid looking at you, and you're definitely the only receptionist they speak to. It feels intentional, though. Why is that?"

Myrna tightens her fingers on her seat, planting her feet into the floor as they swerve around a slower minivan.

A few weeks and Myrna noticed that pattern, too. Mother and Theia had drilled into her how important it was to notice things like that. For it was often the simplest things that were the most important. They spoke of the darkest secrets and exposed truths meant for those brave enough to uncover them. It was why she'd spotted this one so quickly and had been obsessed with it ever since.

Another of the lessons that had no real explanation behind it.

"They don't." Myrna brushes a piece of hair behind her ear, keeping her eyes locked outside the window. "I mean, sometimes they might, but none of them have ever spoken to me unless they needed something from the Haszwalds team directly."

One more thing that isn't completely true.

Stoplight. Sam taps her thumb on the steering wheel.

What did it mean that they noticed her and ignored Sam and the other interns? Did it have to do with the way she felt about the building itself? And why was she the only one to notice the strange inconsistencies between the people and the floors? It was so odd.

For there are inconsistencies.

"I've seen it, Myr."

"Well, I don't know, then. All I can say is that if I ever catch them looking my way, I just make eye contact and say 'hello.'" Myrna shrugs. "Though I have noticed afterward, a few of them won't look in my direction again. It's like they're scared of me."

"Why would they be scared of you? You're such a peach." Sam reaches over and pinches Myrna's cheek.

Myrna pulls away, batting her friend's hand and causing her to swerve. Sam laughs, then pulls into the parking spot.

"So, you've never noticed anything else? Heard anything?"

The shimmer of silver in someone's eye. Or someone's hair growing overnight and their ears elongating?

"I've told you before. They're just people."

"Right." She nods in response and steps out of the SUV. Her purse loops over her shoulder, her other bags carried as before.

Yeah, just people. There is no way to explain it, and no one she may question. If she did, they'd look at her as though she's mad. Perhaps she is.

Sam and Myrna walk the last block through the high-rise buildings to where the Haszwalds Elite building sits between one of the oldest chapels and a historic library as old as the city itself. Sam is on Myrna's left, her head barely reaching Myrna's shoulder even in the heels. The moment Haszwalds comes into view, Myrna lets out a deep sigh of relief. She glances around to see if anyone else feels the energy pulsing beneath their feet.

No one.

Blinking away the sensation, she looks up at the towering, architectural masterpiece. It stretches endlessly for the sky as if craving the touch of the clouds passing overhead. Tall arches, sharp spires, and unique carvings she wishes she could run her manicured fingers over, each meticulously crafted and standing as a testament to the ingenuity of its creators. Even the gargoyles are beautiful. They're intricate and hold stories within their designs, inviting those who look upon them to ponder the tales they silently narrate, battles and ballads alike. Myrna loves this building. To her, entering it is an experience every single time.

The doorman's there, opening it with a polite, "good morning." The foyer appears before them, the arching ceilings leading the eye high up to the skylight far above their heads. Myrna can't help but gape at its magnificence. Early morning light casts gentle rays across the glittering marble floor. They caress her skin, tingling warmly as though in welcome. Myrna sighs once more. It's as if the building wraps its presence around her.

"Every morning? Seriously, Myrna, it's not that impressive." Sam grabs Myrna's arm and pulls her forward. "We're gonna be late! Let's drop our bags."

"Right, right," she says, quickening her pace. Her gaze stays on the ceiling for as long as she can before she focuses her gaze forward, somehow managing not to trip along the way. They head toward the elevators and to a small, shared workspace reserved for the interns. In this space, they can work on special projects assigned as part of their class, usually with the middle-level business associates stationed in an office across the hall. But before the view of the grand space disappears, Myrna takes one last look over her shoulder. To herself, she says, "But it is impressive."

A woman stands in the center, hands on her hips, glare locked on Samantha.

"You're late," Cindy says.

If Myrna didn't know her better, she'd swear Cindy is about to spit acid at her dear friend. So, without hesitation, she calmly steps in front of Sam to block Cindy's view.

This safe haven from the rest of the building is the one spot they can get a break from the constant questions and watchful eyes. But today, the scent of the Hawaiian air freshener does nothing to block the sharp tang of Cindy's perfume. Myrna breathes through her mouth, hoping it will dilute the bombardment of fragrance hitting her all at once.

Myrna smiles sweetly. "Good morning, Cindy. How are you?"

Taken off guard, the tension releases from Cindy's shoulders at the sight of Myrna's tall, blond figure. She clears her throat. "I'm well. Thank you."

"I'm so glad!" Myrna crosses the room to her locker and opens it up. "Oh, my goodness. You should have seen me this morning. I was a total mess! I fell down the stairs in front of my apartment while on my way out to Sam's car. Sam drove up right when it happened, but I broke a heel. I had to run up and get a new pair. Can you believe it?"

Cindy's eyes soften as she takes in Myrna's story, the fire floating away and disappearing beneath concern. "Oh, no. Are you all right?"

She links her fingers together before her and bites her lip. "Yes, ma'am. I am bruised on my, um...behind"—giggle—"pretty badly and my thigh, but I am fine. Thank you." Myrna gestures high up on her leg.

Sam moves to the desk, and Myrna sees her tug her ear. It's a sign they came up with in year one of college to let Myrna know when she'd reverted to the formal speak she used with Theia and her mother. Otherwise, the other students would pull away, thinking Myrna strange. It didn't happen often as it used to, but in moments like these, it would slip out. Myrna is grateful for her friend's diligence.

With a tilt of her head, Myrna moves to the line of lockers along the far wall opposite the three desks she shares with the other employees. She favors her one side, running a hand up the supposed injury. To the right, an even smaller alcove filled with copy equipment branches off.

"Do you need to take the day to recover?"

From where Sam now stands behind Cindy, Myrna sees her mouth drop open. She holds her hands up in a very clear "what the hell" motion but drops it right before Cindy spins to look in her direction. There's Sam, all-worried expression, placing both their lunch boxes in the small communal fridge.

"I asked her the same question," Sam inserts, stretching to her full height before taking a seat at the desk and starting up the computer. "She insisted on coming in. She knows how important it is that we have someone who the specialty floors trust. I made sure to check her ankle, though."

It takes effort for Myrna not to laugh.

"Good, good." Cindy nods.

With an appreciative smile, Myrna seconds, "Thank you, but it's not that bad. I just feel stupid. You know? Plus, I'm meeting with Mr. Lawson today about the O'Brien Project. I don't want to miss that."

"Well, if you're sure." Cindy sighs. "I'm glad Sam was there to take care of you. She's such a good friend. Now, let's get to work, ladies. We have a busy day ahead of us. You know the schedule, so let's get to it!"

With that, Cindy exits the room, off to her nicer, more luxurious accommodations in the suite with the rest of the mid-level managers on this floor. She's hot stuff ever since she was promoted and has a window.

Giggling comes from the desk in the back. It's then that Sam and Myrna realize their coworker was hiding behind her cubicle through that entire show.

"I love having you two working here." Rhonda leans back in her chair and spins to face them, a squeak filling the air. "You make my mornings so much more entertaining. Can I assume you did not, in fact, fall down the stairs?"

Sam laughs, then stands so she can see Rhonda. She rests her hip against the desk, crossing her feet at the ankle. "Um...no." She looks to Myrna. "Where did that come from? I mean, thanks, but..."

The door to her locker opens smoothly, and Myrna pulls her name tag free, then slips her bag inside. Closing the door with a soft *click*, she turns to her coworker. "Well, Sam was about two seconds from getting written up again, so I figured I'd play distraction."

Rhonda grins at Sam. "She really does hate you."

"Yeah, I should probably stop speaking while in the building. I swear every time I let my guard down, she catches me saying something I shouldn't."

"Maybe stop drooling over the men?" Rhonda says.

Pouting, Sam whines, "But they're all so pretty..."

Rhonda laughs while Myrna shakes her head as she heads over to the desk to pick up her task for the morning. A research project she can work on while manning the front desk and welcoming those entering the building. It was her favorite time of the day to be up front, which was why it was most often assigned to her.

"She's helpless," Myrna says. "I'm going to head up front. Rhonda, keep Sam from doing anything crazy while I'm gone."

"Deal, but I can't promise anything about that one." She points to Sam.

Myrna laughs and exits the office to the sound of Sam's, "Hey!"

Behind her, the door closes slowly and, in a tone so low she's surprised she catches it, Myrna hears one last thing from Rhonda. "You have a good friend there, even if she's so strange. Why does she talk like that sometimes? It's creepy."

Myrna's heart drops, her stomach roiling. She bites her lip, but continues forward, the sound of her heels clicking on the tile floor all she can focus on. Even those nice to her face think something's wrong with her. Her breaths become heavy until the open main room comes into sight and a rush of peace flows through her.

This is where she's supposed to be. But why?

CHAPTER THREE

A Balance Beholden?

THIS IS SUPPOSED TO be just a desk job, a way to pay the bills and get those last few credits for her degree. A degree she had to fight for, and nearly didn't get to enroll for, when Mother deemed it unnecessary. But Theia had stepped in. The ever-calm voice of reason, supporting Myrna and stating that a degree in International Business would be essential, considering their family situation.

Even now, Myrna wonders what that means, but once again, the Qhuinn family secrets are hidden behind a wall Myrna cannot break through. *I miss going by my real name.*

Then the low buzz of conversation ramps up as the rush starts, and happiness hums in Myrna's veins.

But this was unusual, right? Didn't most people hate work?

"Well, you don't." Myrna smiles at her own whispered words.

The reception booth sits off the main doors where the flow of people incoming pass on their way to the elevators or to the businesses located in the back. The skylight overhead provides heat and a gentle glow to her morning as she welcomes anyone new to the building and directs them as necessary. Should they need to be called up to the appropriate office, she contacts the lead secretary of that office prior to sending them up.

Simple. Of course, they are also in charge of maintaining the reception area.

"See, just another desk job," Myrna tries to convince herself as she takes her seat and turns on the computer. With a quick glance around, Myrna removes her heels below the desk to press her bare skin to the tile. An energy vibrates up her legs.

It's heaven. She closes her eyes, allowing a few seconds before slipping the heels back on. *No, it's in your head. Now, pay attention.*

One after another, the businessmen and women enter the line of doors. It's fascinating to watch them, every one so very different from the next. Tall with coal black hair. Sleek pantsuit and heels. Balding with his gut protruding over his belt. Floral dress a little too short. The woman who used to have blue eyes, but now has silver. It is interesting how, after all this time, she can almost tell which floor they work on, even if she has no clue exactly what each company does.

Wait. Myrna scans the crowd again, leaning to the side and trying to find the woman again. Had that been her imagination?

She frowns. Had to be.

"Good morning," she says as they pass.

A few mumbled "hellos" come back her way. Most don't respond, too sucked into their morning routine to acknowledge someone as insignificant as she. Plus, their coffee holds far more of their attention, for which she cannot blame them. She is on her second cup already.

But when Stephan O'Malley walks into Haszwalds, things change.

Stephan is unique. A creature created of the grace and power expected of his station. His back is straight. The suit, an armor he wears of the highest caliber both in this form and his native one. And although he is here to meet with someone who others consider the most important being here, Stephan is more excited to meet with Myrna—a puzzle of a girl who sits at the front, welcoming those to this honored establishment without hesitation or fear. For she is an enigma that challenges the very fabric of their world.

"Myrna, my girl!" Stephan says, stepping into the grand entry-way.

Myrna looks up from her work, her eyes instantly finding her favorite visitor. It's been a few weeks and so the grin blooming across her face is honest and bright.

"Mr. O'Malley, is that you?"

"It is!" he says, stepping up to her podium. "I was hoping you would be in today. I've brought you something."

Myrna freezes, her breath catching in her throat, but not because of his comment. This is not the man she remembers. Her eyes roam over him, scanning him—devouring him. Her heart beats faster, and her head swims.

His shoulders straighten, and his brow furrows. "Are you well?"

Myrna blinks quickly to clear her vision. "Oh, yes. Sorry. I have a headache. It's been a day." She presses her fingers to her head and prays that Stephan believes her. She lowers her voice as if to impart a secret. "Cindy wore the rosy perfume this morn. Bathed in it, in fact."

Stephan grimaces, and Myrna thinks her lie has worked and that her shock at the change in his appearance was missed. For this is not the man she remembers; he is different. The voice and eyes are the same, but the Mr. O'Malley she knows is a man in his late thirties with dark brown hair and an unassuming face. Handsome, but more for his easy smile than anything else.

The person before her, however, has silver hair that falls to his chin, and his mouth looks wrong somehow. Different. She can't place why until he smiles, and two sharp canine teeth peek out.

She has the urge to step back, but she won't. The years of training beaten into her has taught her to never show fear, never retreat.

"Are you not going to ask what it is?" When she doesn't respond, instead continuing to stare, he adds, "Myrna?"

Myrna blinks a few times and, as if it had been an illusion, the abnormal dental ware disappears. Had this been her imagination, too?

No. It can't be. The hair is still there. Myrna breathes slowly and deeply. *What the hell is going on?*

"Oh, yes. I'm sorry," she says, pulling herself out of whatever trance had taken over. She stands so she may meet him eye to eye.

Never allow someone to look down upon you, Mother's words slither through her mind.

Myrna speaks to her friend—yes, her friend—faster this time. "I was a little shocked by your hair. It looks great. But, um, yes. I am interested. What did you bring me? Tell me, is it from your travels?"

Stephan's eyes narrow, and he runs a hand through his hair. He brushes off the comment, then holds out a small, square object to Myrna. "It's something I found while visiting a library back home. I thought you might enjoy it."

The package is heavier than it looks and is about the size of her hand. A book, perhaps? Electricity jolts through her when he places it in her palm. Myrna's eyes widen, and she unwraps the periwinkle cloth with golden stitching which protects the leather sheathed pages. Her fingers gently caress the embossed calligraphy that marks the front cover.

"Oh, my," Myrna breathes, warmth rising in her chest. "Celtic folktales..."

Ever so carefully, she opens the book. No, the relic. Her fingers trace over the pages, the scrollwork along the sides that tell a story in and of itself. Sweet musk wafts from the pages like whispers of the memory held within. She closes her eyes for a long moment, taking it in. There is a power to the scent. It hums in her blood, heavy like the book itself. She turns the page and continues her examination. "It's beautiful, but I-I can't take..."

The room has gone silent. The humans continue to move about, but every entity with power has stopped to stare. For the moment Myrna's fingers run so lovingly along the edge of the tome, a heaviness fills the air. Electricity. Power. Fate.

The book has been without a master for too long. It has sat alone, lost in the shelves, pleading for its match, and it had called out to Stephan that day as he walked the halls of his family manor. And Myrna is its match, Stephan the vessel to connect them. Perhaps here and now is not the best place to introduce them.

Myrna turns the page and traces the ornate illustration. The hair on her arms stands up, and her eyes widen.

Holy knights.

Myrna's in awe. This book was old, filled with beautiful drawings of ancient mythical creatures that have danced in her dreams. She wants to curl up and read each page, then dissect the images with the eye of a scholar. It is as if a piece of her has been missing and here it has returned. But it's a book!

She looks up to find Stephan watching her intently—eyes locked on her, mouth parted. When she meets his gaze, he grins, and she immediately feels the blood rush to her face. More embarrassing are the others dispersed throughout the room, watching the exchange.

The cover of the book makes a soft hushed sound as it closes. *Did it sigh?* And Myrna presses it between her palms.

She holds the book out to him and repeats, "I cannot take this. It is too rare and precious."

He takes a step back, linking his hands before him. He bows his head slightly. "No. That book is destined for you. When I saw it amongst the other bindings of my familial home, I knew it."

Familial home? What? Her heart stops. She can't take this!

Myrna skitters from behind the kiosk of desks which make up the reception area. She approaches the man who has been the most welcoming of all those she's met here. From the very first time he found her fumbling with the intercom, he's been kind and generous with his words. Patient as well. Though he does not work for Ascension Land Management directly, he's a regular visitor to Mr. Kelan Daniels and someone she looks forward to conversing with.

She meets his eyes and reaches out to touch his arm with just the tips of her fingers. It's a serious break in protocol, but Myrna must make him understand. It is necessary for him to see that this is too much! Not only could this be seen as inappropriate for her position here, but it is an old tome pulled from what must be a beloved collection.

A warmth spreads through her and into him, a spark of respect and perhaps a hint of desperation.

Never break, never back down, and never be the last to look away. Mother's words again.

Stephan's eyes blink slowly, but do not stray from hers.

Lowering her voice, she says, "Familial home? Stephan—Mr. O'Malley—sir, you said while on your travels. I—"

"Stephan?" a male voice says from beside them.

The deeply resonating voice is loud in her ears, causing Myrna to jump but then pull away. As if on reflex, she yanks the book to her chest to cradle it.

Stephan shakes his head then steps away, quirking his head like a dog trying to untangle a mystery. A wicked smirk raises the corner of his mouth.

"I knew it. It is meant for you," he whispers, flicking his eyes to the book.

At the same time, the man speaks again. "Stephan. What are you doing here so early? I thought we met at nine." The thick accent is hard to mistake, lyrical and beautiful. Few speak with such directness, command, and sheer power.

It's like the floor drops out from under her when she realizes it is Mr. Daniels himself. If he thinks she has hurt or offended Stephan in any way, he could easily have her removed. Her heart is pounding painfully. She swallows hard but manages to keep her expression perfectly calm.

Myrna wants to reply to Stephan's comment, but he's already turning.

"Kelan, my friend!" Stephan says, clasping Daniels's extended hand in his.

As she watches—and for a blink—Myrna sees Stephan's ears change. One moment normal, then pointed. His suit is flashing from black Armani to some ancient-looking tunic made of forest green with ruby and gold stitching along the hem and down the cravat to wrap along the chest.

"I came by early to speak with a friend of mine. Have you met Myrna Johnson?"

Myrna's eyes go wide, and she skitters back behind the desk. Taking a seat, she makes herself as small as possible. When she looks back, Stephan is himself again, all but for his hair, and Daniels hasn't even glanced in her direction.

"You don't have friends," Daniels jokes, but his expression is serious as he takes in his friend. "Have you been compelled?"

Stephan pats Mr. Daniels on the arm, his other hand waving off the comment. "Unintentionally. Completely unintentionally, but I must speak to you."

Daniels lifts an eyebrow. "Then come, let's head upstairs. We can speak before Sola arrives. There's much to discuss and many developments have occurred since we last spoke."

"I was afraid you were going to say that." As they walk to the elevator, Myrna's gaze stays on his back, ears tracking the conversation. Just as they step inside, she hears Stephan ask oh so quietly, "Do you remember the *Balance Beholden*?"

Daniels starts, his head snapping up, eyes narrowing. "I thought your mother destroyed it."

Myrna glances around, then back, straining for his response.

Stephan shakes his head. No one else dares to enter the small space with two such high-ranking Guardians. "Nay. And it has just responded to the receptionist and the friend I mentioned, Myrna."

Myrna's diaphragm becomes heavy, and her breaths deepen. She squeezes her fingers on the book at the expression passing over Mr. Daniels's face. It's blank. Too blank. It's an expression she recognizes. It whispers of danger.

Her muscles tense at what would come next had her mother been standing before her and the expression been on her face.

Daniels's head turns, gaze locking on hers.

Myrna's been caught in a trap. It isn't until the elevator closes that Myrna takes a breath. Another minute until the world stops spinning, and she peels her fingers from the book.

Myrna's eyes scan the room, taking in the audience who've stopped to watch the exchange. She meets their gazes, holding each until they look away, backing down the judgment they throw in her direction. She may not understand exactly what just happened, but she will not be shunned because of it.

Myrna places the beautiful book on the table, her fingers running along its edges. Excitement tingles through every nerve as they absorb the gentle texture of the fibrous cover. She'll need to find a way to give this back to him, for it belongs to his family, and she doesn't deserve it.

"He'll take offense if you try to give it back to him again. It's an honor to be gifted such. Take it as a compliment and cherish it." A woman stands next to her desk. She has brown hair pulled up in a simple bun. She wears nothing extravagant or brings any attention to herself. In fact, she doesn't even look up from the newspaper she holds. It's as if she isn't speaking to Myrna at all.

"Excuse me?" Myrna asks.

The woman says nothing else. Instead, she glances in Myrna's direction so quickly it could have been by accident, then escapes toward the elevators. But in that flash of eye, Myrna sees one more thing that solidifies her belief that there is more to this place and the people within it.

Silver ringed irises.

CHAPTER FOUR

Secrets All Their Own

CRIMSON SPLASHES AGAINST THE mat as Myrna hits the floor, the droplets bouncing like a rock against the surface of a lake. They shimmer darkly, fuel to the flame deep within her. Jaw aching and the cut on her lip throbbing from where the fist made contact, she pushes to her feet.

That one smarts. For someone so small, Theia hit like a tank.

Wiping a hand across her mouth, she uses the corner pad of the ring to push herself up. While she does, Myrna scans the two opponents smiling wickedly back. Wildly contrasting and yet so similar in the way they stand ready. Myrna can't help but be amused. One is all dark sass, while the other is pale with a kindness that lights the room. They wait for her to find her feet, but Myrna knows they will not hesitate long.

Still, Myrna knows better than to show any form of vulnerability or amusement. It's a lesson drilled into her by Mother. *Feel the emotion, but do not show it.* This sticks with her even while battling with Sam and Theia.

"Come, child," Theia says as a water bottle falls to its side then rolls to a stop against the gym's cold block wall. Perhaps it's trying to escape, not wishing to be a casualty. "That volley was not so excessive. Laoise expects better, as do I. Do not make me inform her you are lacking."

Myrna narrows her eyes at the threat, but after such a strange day at Haszwalds, Myrna had needed such a hard workout. So, she smirks, then jumps to her feet.

"Yeah, well, her mother's nuts," Sam says.

"Sam," Theia warns.

"I thought you said we were working with staffs, and that you, Sam, had a date." Not her favorite weapon, but against two opponents, it leveled the playing field. Plus, she loved the heft of the wood in her palms.

"You needed me here," her uncouth best friend says. "So, shut your trap and stop stalling."

This gets a tiny glance and expulsion of air from Theia. Not quite a laugh, but probably the closest they'd come while in battle from someone as experienced as she.

Sam wanted to be here to support her when she told Theia about the internship even though Myrna hadn't asked her to.

Even so, Myrna has only enough time to lift her hands into a defensive position before Theia moves; quick and graceful like the air itself. Slide right. Dodge Theia's jab. A punch flies toward her cheek once again, faster than should be humanly possible, but Myrna's ready. She blocks it with her forearm, sharp pressure vibrating through the limb.

Myrna returns the hit, Theia stumbling back a step, then she spins on her feet just in time to stop a kick from Sam. She bends her elbow, linking her arm beneath her friend's limb and lifts with all her might.

Sam goes flying, flipping through the air to land on her stomach. She grunts, but Myrna can't stop, for Theia is on the move again, and Myrna's left her right side open. She mouths a silent curse.

Theia's weight shifts, her knee on a path toward Myrna's abdomen.

Like a dancer, Myrna's foot skates along the matted floor in a half-circle and opposite from the prone Sam. It glides away, her body shifting out of range of the blow. Mid-spin, Myrna kicks out and connects with Theia, sending her off balance.

Theia's about to push an attack when Sam says from the floor, "Son of a waffle nut, Myr. That was both awesome and sucky." She groans and gets to her knees.

The comment has both Myrna and Theia stuttering in their next advance. They exchange a glance, then burst out laughing, but not before they both move toward the downed girl.

Sam's already pushing to her feet, rubbing a knot on her chin.

"Oh, darling, are you all right?" Theia asks, lifting Sam's chin to examine it.

Warmth runs through Myrna. It's impossible to count the number of times Theia has tended one of her wounds in just the same manner—love and absolute tenderness in every touch and glance.

"I'm fine," Sam says, eyeballing Myrna. "I've just never been spun like a top and flipped at the same time. That was disorienting."

Myrna bares her teeth in an apologetic wince. "It was the best option open to me, and you've been vicious to me this evening. Perhaps you should've gone home after you canceled your date."

"Myrna," Theia scolds. "That was unkind."

"She doesn't mean it," Sam says as Myrna wraps an arm around her shoulders.

"I don't. She knows I always want her here."

"That's because she can't resist my sense of humor."

Someone claps their hands near the front door to the training room. All three women turn to face the man leaning against the doorframe.

"Ladies! I think it's time for a break," Tomas, the owner of the gym, says.

He's tall with short, black hair and kind eyes. When Myrna first met him, she was intimidated by his wide shoulders and harsh demeanor, but then he'd knelt and grinned. There was humor in his eyes as he'd glanced up at Theia, then back down at her. It had made him less scary somehow. Then, they'd spent time "training." At the age of six, it was more like play—an obstacle course she mastered in mere weeks. Now, he was a staple in her life that she wouldn't know what to do without.

But we must not mention his presence to Laoise. The memory of Theia's request races through Myrna's thoughts. Why, she is not entirely sure, but Myrna had never said a thing, for he is too much fun.

Tomas grins, then gestures toward the hallway. "You've been sparing for almost two hours already. I've got water and some food."

A soft smile lifts Theia's lips. "Thank you, Tomas. I think this is a perfect stopping point. Myrna seems tired, and perhaps we need to go over her steps some more."

Myrna had asked Theia once if she and Tomas were in a relationship. Myrna has never seen Theia laugh so hard. Gracefully, of course.

"I'm not tired." Myrna groans, following Theia and Tomas through the door and into the back room. "You're turning into Mother."

It's a small space with a tiny kitchenette. The counter lines one wall, a simple table surrounded by chairs sits in the center, the food resting along the top. When the scent reaches Myrna, her stomach growls.

Theia snorts. From the noise or her comment? "Well, she did not put me in charge of your training and safety for nothing. And there are lessons you must learn. We've explained this to you. You must be able to protect yourself. You know this," she says, taking a seat.

Assigned to raise her, protect her, and train her, but not to love her. That had been a side effect, part of Theia herself. Though maybe Laoise had hoped for such. She had never said.

Theia doesn't just take a seat in the chair, though. Tomas pulls it out, and Theia lowers herself into it like it's made of the finest quality and not of flimsy red plastic. She crosses her ankles and rests one hand atop the other as she gazes softly back at Myrna.

"Yes, Theia. I understand, but why? From what should I be on guard?" She's returned to the speech only their family shares. It's more lyrical, accented, and, apparently, lacks contractions. Per Sam.

Instantly, heat fills Theia's eyes, and it's as if she's a completely different person. Her chin dips, and Myrna has the urge to push back in her chair.

So rarely does Myrna see *this* side of Theia. There is demand, anger, and perhaps a bit of fear there.

"That is nothing you need to worry about, child." Her tone is stern, her shoulders tight as she leans forward. "All you need to know is that we are here to protect you, and when the time comes that we are not, you must be."

A shiver runs up Myrna's spine. *Because that's not ominous at all.*

"And you, do you not enjoy training?" she continues.

"I do, but…"

"I change my vote," Sam says from her seat. She's taken a relaxed pose, but Myrna can see the tension in her. "I'm voting Russian Mafia."

She starts nodding slowly, a bobblehead sitting on the dash of a moving car, slow and steady.

Theia blinks, and then the tension drains out of her.

Myrna presses her lips together and tries not to smile. She fails, especially when Theia smirks. Myrna meets Sam's eye, and she knows this is the moment to tell her.

"Sam…" Tomas says, handing a plate to her friend. He chuckles. "They're not Mob."

"Do you know?"

"No…their secrets are their own." Tomas shakes his head. "Eat your food."

Myrna bites her lip. She appreciates Sam distracting Theia's frustration, but she needs to stop hesitating. Theia is already angry, and it's important that she knows Myrna is taking her safety seriously. Sam nods, giving her the strength.

Myrna presses her feet to the floor as if to ground herself and says, "Um…actually. I need to tell you something."

Theia's eyes narrow as she reaches to the take the fork Tomas holds out to her. She does not say anything, just sets her fork beside the plate and waits for Myrna to continue.

Sweat beads along Myrna's spine. "You know how I said I was coming from classes today?" Theia nods, and Myrna continues,

"Well...do you remember me mentioning the internship required for my degree? Well, it started. So, I actually came from work."

Theia's back stiffens, and she pushes away her plate. Myrna can't help but miss the way Tomas's jaw twitches at the news, either.

"And where is this internship? How long have you been there?"

"A few weeks? It's just been so busy, and it's a few days—"

"Weeks?" Tomas asks, his eyes stormy.

"It's just been so crazy."

"Then we have trained many times since you started." Her tone drops, and the anger leeches into every word. "We talk daily, my sweetling. So, why have you not told me? I could have verified the security of this place."

Sam shifts uncomfortably in her seat. Even she can sense the tension wafting into the air from Theia. It is a palpable thing. Myrna had always assumed it was in her head.

"I'm sorry, Theia." Myrna bites her lip and pulls on her braid. She will not look away, however. "It's been crazy. I know we've trained, but when we showed up, we just dove right in, and then after, we were always rushing out or you had to start the drive back. We just didn't have the time, and I wanted to talk to you about it in detail, not just tell you because it's super exciting." Her words come so fast she stumbles over them.

Myrna's cheeks flush with embarrassment at her loss of control. She links her fingers together and forces herself to slow her next words while speaking in the only way Theia or her mother ever take her seriously.

"This is a great opportunity. If you remember, there were five potential options with varying focuses and levels of expectation for our final projects. To our delight, Sam and I were placed at the same location, the one with the highest prestige requiring the best of candidates. Though this is not surprising, as Samantha is top of her class. Having this company on my resume will be essential for my future career, and I am thrilled even though I do spend most of my time at the front desk." Sam smirks at her comment. "Theia, this is what I need for my future, and the safety of this place is sound. There are guards on staff daily."

"She's right. Theia, it's an amazing opportunity. Haszwalds Elite—"

"Haszwalds!" Theia shoots to her feet, her napkin falling to the floor and the table knocking a few inches forward. It screeches against the linoleum.

Myrna and Sam jump, straightening in their seats.

"I'm sorry, but you can't go back there." Theia's eyebrows draw down. "Ask for a different placement."

Shock drops her stomach to the floor. "What? Why?"

"Theia," Tomas says. It's one word, said in a tone Myrna cannot quite decipher.

But apparently it is enough.

Theia runs her palms down her stomach. She tugs on her shirt, then lowers herself back into her seat while Sam and Myrna stare with wide eyes. Once she's seated, Theia picks up her downed napkin and hands it to Tomas, who exchanges it for a clean one. It isn't until she lifts her fork that she says in her normal, calm tone, "Have you been assigned your final project yet? What is it? For I am excited to hear what you both will be analyzing. You know I love hearing how your studies are going."

Myrna blinks slow and finally releases her held breath. From the corner of her eye, she sees Sam's eyebrows shoot upward before she looks down at her food and controls her expression. *Even she is learning this skill. Perhaps she spends too much time around my family.*

"We are meeting with our mentors later this week to learn what the project is going to be." Myrna manages to keep the confused hesitation out of her voice, but that doesn't mean it's not tightening her thighs, putting her on edge.

"My first meeting is tomorrow." Sam grins. "The guy I am meeting with is the head of one of the mid-sized companies who work with outreach groups all over the world. I guess there's a new foundation coming on, and I'll get to see the process from the beginning!" She's nearly bouncing in her seat, the plastic legs of her chair flexing.

"That sounds fascinating," Theia says. She takes a bite of her food, places the fork down, then pats her mouth with her napkin.

How can she make that look so graceful?

She asks Sam a few more questions, but Myrna does not hear them. Myrna's too lost in her own thoughts as she eats, the constant review of the last years rushing through her mind. The moving from place to place, the half-truths, the constant vigilance. The training. Though she'd come to love that. More, why they did not trust her with the truth. She is an adult. Well, not in their eyes. They loved her, but this is just one more example where she felt separate from everything and everyone else.

"And you, darling?" Theia says, bringing her attention back to the conversation. "What is your project?"

Myrna clears her throat politely. "I do not know yet. Our manager, Cindy, thought she had found one for me, but she did not like the project. So, she decided to request a different one from another group. I have a meeting with them soon, but I do not know what it is yet."

"It is because she is Cindy's favorite," Sam says in a sing-song voice, and Myrna rolls her eyes.

Theia grins. "Well, whatever you do, I am sure you will be remarkable at it." She glances up at the clock on the wall. "Oh, my, is that the time? I must begin the drive back."

They all stand.

"Myrna? Will you walk me out?"

"Of course," Myrna says.

"I'll clean up and meet you out there, Myr," Sam says.

They walk to the front, Tomas following after. He'll take Theia to her car. He always does, but until then, he stands off to the side as the two women stop near the front door.

There is no hesitation as Theia lifts her hands before Myrna, palms up.

Myrna slips hers into Theia's, palms sliding against her caretaker's smooth skin. The moment contact is made, a warm sensation spreads from the touch. *Home.* It is a gesture of acceptance and goodbye. They always depart from one another this way. Myrna sighs, relaxing and curling her fingers around Theia's wrists.

Theia smiles. "You are nearly an adult, my love. Off to be on your own completely, and there is much Laoise and I need to discuss with you. Be proud of the internship and know that you are the elite. You are the best and deserve the position allotted you. Just remember that you are a Qhuinn even if you work under a different name. Work hard, and should you require anything, inform us immediately."

"Thank you." She smiles, then admits, "I miss you."

"As I you. Perhaps we can increase our training sessions to three weekdays. Do you think your schedule can handle that?"

"Is that with me still coming to you on the weekends?"

"Yes."

Myrna nods. "I am here most nights anyway with Tomas and Sam."

Theia releases her and brushes her fingers down Myrna's cheek. "Perfect. I love you, dear one. Be safe."

"And you."

CHAPTER FIVE

Battle of Wills

THE WAFTING SWEETNESS OF Pretty by Elizabeth Arden precedes Sam's appearance. It's a new perfume and, although she usually applies it lightly, this morning she's drenched in it.

Myrna scrunches her nose and breathes through her mouth. She looks up from the project she's been distracting herself with since Mr. O'Malley walked in and caught her reading the tome he gave her. She hadn't meant to bring it to work, but there it was, and she couldn't resist the urge to flip through its pages. Seeing it, and interacting with her odd friend, made her question not telling Theia more about this place and the strange things that had been happening the last few days.

"Hey, Bitch," Sam says.

"Don't call me that here," Myrna says in a hushed, but firm, tone. "And you wonder why Cindy dislikes you."

Sam snorts, her tone dripping with sarcasm. "Yeah, that's why. So, I am heading upstairs for my meeting with Jim. When are you off the desk? Ten?" When Myrna nods in response, Sam continues, "Cool, then do you want to have lunch around eleven? You meet with your team lead after that, right?"

"Yup. I'll be working on this until then. But I think Cindy said she had a project she wanted my help with, too."

"Of course she did." Sam rolls her eyes.

Myrna leans closer. "Hey, did you hear anything about a security issue, or new guards being brought in?"

"No, why?"

Myrna flicks her eyes to two uniformed men stationed at different places around the vast room. Sam's eyebrow lifts, and her lips press into a line. "I wonder—"

"Excuse me?" a deep voice asks.

Both girls jump, turning toward a tall man about their age. He wears a pair of dark acid-washed jeans and a navy shirt. Black curls fall over his forehead. He brushes them back, tucking a difficult one behind his ear.

Myrna stands and smiles. *He feels warm, kind.* Myrna pushes the thought away and says, "My apologies. I didn't see you. How may I help?"

Blue eyes so deep they could suck her in look back without fear. He bows slightly and asks, "I need to meet with Kelan Daniels. Can you help me?"

"And you are?"

"Whoa..." Sam breathes, and Myrna shoots her a glare.

The man does not react.

"My name is Shay Hughes." A dimple pops out through the scruff that lines his jaw.

Thank the heavens Sam's out of his line of sight, for now she's fanning herself.

"And do you have an appointment?" When he grimaces, Myrna bends to pull up the contact information for Mr. Daniels's secretary. "Well, I cannot allow you up without an invitation, but I will send a message to his office and let them know you're here. I will do everything I can, okay? If you can please take a seat, I'll—"

"What are you doing here, filth?" This voice resonates throughout the entire room. It bounces off the arched ceilings, instantly putting Myrna on guard. Even the hair on the back of her neck stands up and based on the way Shay stiffens, Myrna knows this is a threat to him. *Unacceptable.*

The energy in the hall shifts, bringing Myrna's attention to the woman who's just entered through the main door. Behind her, the doorman's flushed, and Myrna wonders what she could've done to put that look on his face. Mike is a pretty relaxed guy, and he's both offended and scared.

There's a low buzz in the air as her four-inch heels click on the tile in demanding strides like tiny hammers. The statuesque woman's midnight hair is pulled in a severe ponytail, the ends falling to mid-back. She wears a pencil skirt that accentuates those long lengths of her legs.

Myrna doesn't remember seeing her before—not that she recognizes everyone—but this woman is someone one doesn't forget. Still, in less than five seconds, Myrna can say she is not a fan. Especially considering the sneer marring that beautiful face or the hatred she shoots at this young man. More interesting is the way she's taken the air out of a room just by entering it.

"Sam, please show Mr. Hughes to the private seating area. It's quieter there," Myrna says, not taking her gaze off the beast approaching. "Mr. Hughes, I will let you know as soon as I hear back from the fourth floor."

"Thank you, ma'am, but I do not fear her."

"Why would you?"

"Okay…" Sam says. "Come this way, Mr. Hughes." His brows pinch together but he allows Sam to lead him away. Sam's back a moment later. She resumes her place just as the woman in heels goes to pass them.

"Where is that piece of garbage? He should not be here." She's beautiful and terrifying all at once, just like so many.

Sam fights the urge to step away as she says, "Hello, ma'am. Can we help you? We can get you checked in and up to your intended floor."

The woman hesitates, eyes narrowing in Sam's direction. She glances toward the waiting room, the elevators, and then back at the receptionist's desk.

"Excuse me?" Somehow melodic and cold as ice, the harpy's voice rolls through both girls.

Sam steps to the side, almost as if she wishes she could dive for cover. Still, she manages to respond in a shaky, but cheery, tone. "Visitors must check in, but we can help you with that. Please, come over, and we'll get everything taken care of and call the floor you're visiting."

The woman's face morphs from gorgeous to evil. Her lips curl back in a snarl, her eyebrows shooting down in a glare. The light in her eyes darkens into something Myrna does not like. Especially not pointed at her best friend.

"Do you know who I am?" she growls.

That is enough. First the comment to Mr. Hughes, and now the disrespect to Sam? A heat builds in Myrna's stomach, and she tightens her abdominals to keep it in check.

Be steady, my child, Mother's voice runs through her head.

"And never expose your hand," Myrna mouths, finishing her mother's favorite saying as she smoothly and professionally steps from behind the desk. She places her hand on her friend's shoulder and gently guides Sam behind the barrier.

She's shaking. Her feisty, fearless friend is scared. It's odd.

The heat inside shifts to something darker, and Myrna's protective nature tempers into a determination that could scald. Myrna keeps her eyes lowered until she's met Sam's eye. "Stay there."

Then she straightens her shirt and brushes her hands down the front of her skirt. It is a tactic learned from her mother. Show that you're not afraid, which Myrna is not. There are far scarier creatures than this spoiled brat. Her mother, for one.

Shoulders back and professional smile in place, Myrna finally looks up at the woman who has yet to remove her dagger-like glare from Sam. Even though Sam is shrinking with each passing second.

"Good morning," Myrna says, moving to block Sam completely. "And I'm sorry, ma'am. We do not know who you are. That is the problem. If you can step here, we'll check you in and get you up to your meeting as quickly as possible."

The dark-haired woman stalks forward slowly, the *clip-clock* of her heels a warning. Her eyebrow raises, and she scans Myrna from head to foot. Then her eyes lock to Myrna's icy blues as though unable to do anything else. Disgust fills her gaze, but this is quickly replaced with annoyance.

"Do you have an appointment? Can I help you get somewhere?" Myrna asks, voice that of the perfect, helpful receptionist. But her sweet smile holds a hint of bitchy anger learned at the hand of Laoise.

The evil queen's eyes—because that's what Myrna has named her—narrow, burning her with their intensity. Myrna does not look away. If she does, it will show weakness, and then she'll never be seen as an equal. Not that she is now, but still.

Always be the last to look away. You have more strength than you believe. Now it is Theia's voice in her head.

Damn those two women. They've drilled these lessons in long before she'd joined the working community. Second nature or not, it will likely get her in trouble.

Which is why Myrna stands frozen, locked in a battle that feels far more important to the evil queen than to Myrna.

Seconds pass, and soon, the woman's fists clench, her breaths quicken, all the while Myrna stands calmly, waiting for her reply. Sweat beads on the dark-haired harpy's brow. It's as she starts to tremble that she finally drops her gaze.

Myrna barely holds back the sigh of relief. That was uncomfortable. Her legs shake, and her limbs feel heavy. She wants to sit down, drink about a gallon of water, and perhaps eat a stack of candy bars. She can't, though.

With another snarl, the evil queen strides over to the sign-in sheet and scribbles her name. Then she grabs a visitor's pass Sam sets on the counter, turns, and stomps to the elevator like an angry toddler.

"Do you need me to call you up?" Myrna asks cheerfully.

"No!" she snaps.

"Oh, all right, then. I'm sorry, miss. Have a nice day!" she calls to the brunette's retreating back. The glare she shoots Myrna as the door closes has her swallowing hard, but she waves anyway.

Perhaps no dark alleys for a few days. Because...pod people. Myrna quietly chuckles. What has Sam done, introducing her to such an odd cinema that *that* was her reference?

Only then does Myrna realize there is another woman standing just behind the harpy.

"Oh. I'm sorry. Good morning."

Interest gazes back from the taller and somehow more statuesque person than the first woman. Her shimmering auburn hair falls to her thigh, thick with a slight curl. Her high cheek-bones and green eyes add to her beauty.

"Please excuse her. She's had a morning," the woman says before stepping forward and signing her name on the sheet as well. Without another word, she follows the devil toward the elevator.

Myrna shakes the experience off, a heavy exhale loosening her shoulders. It'd been a long time since she'd been in that kind of contest of will. Most people glanced around or dropped their eyes naturally during conversation. Part of the reason she'd never understood her mother's insistence.

"Myrna?" Sam's voice is hesitant, but Myrna turns to face her friend. "What-how...Are you all right?"

"Of course, why?" The words are drawn out.

"I've never seen you act like that. That woman was scary, and you-you just...what did you do to her?"

Myrna scowls. "I didn't do anything. What are you talking about?"

Sam glances at her watch and squeaks.

"We'll talk at lunch." She places a hand on Myrna's arm. "That was badass and all, but don't do anything else while I'm gone. She might jump you in the parking lot or something."

"Who, the evil queen?"

Sam chokes. "Oh my god, I love you." She grabs her stuff, takes a few steps back, then says before running for the stairs, "Lunch!"

Myrna stands there, blinking, for a long moment.

Today is looking to be as weird as yesterday was. Few acknowl-edge her presence most days, let alone multiple, and never has that happened before. She clears her throat and takes a quick scan of the lobby. Perhaps some cleaning's needed. She could use the distraction.

Sadly, there's no mess, but there are about a dozen peo-ple scattered around the room watching her. Again! Including the intriguing Mr. Hughes and the new guards. A few look like they've smelled something bad. Others are statues, lips parted. But Hughes? He watches with curiosity. With a quick smile, he ducks back to his seat, and that is when Myrna finds a couple who stands near the coffee shop at the rear of the space. Their amused smiles and knowing glints make her nervous. The fact that Mr. O'Malley is part of that pair, his longer locks pulled back, increases her concern. He lifts the steaming cup of coffee to his lips.

Myrna blinks, spinning away from his piercing gaze, then sits back, her monitor suddenly far more interesting than usual, even if what's on it is nothing but unreadable muck.

"All I did was check her in," she whispers to herself.

But Myrna knows deep inside that the exchange with the evil queen was more than that. The others watching understand this, too. Myrna glances at the name and floor signed onto the log.

Niandra – Fourth Floor – Meeting: Nozia. And behind it, *Sola – Fourth Floor – Meeting: Kelan Daniels.*

Shit. She should've known. No matter what she did, Myrna found herself drawn to those of the mystery floors.

CHAPTER SIX

Enigma in a Pencil Skirt

KELAN DANIELS SITS, ANKLE resting on his opposite thigh. He leans back in his overstuffed chair and looks out the wall of windows overlooking the forest below. It's lush and green, the moss thick and lumpy along trunks. The canopy's yet to thicken from winter, but the bite of sweetness in the air seeping through the window hints it's coming sooner than later.

Kelan's thoughts stray back to his meeting with Stephan O'Malley. It was a hard one, but not unexpected. The peace between the two courts had been precarious for millennia. The truth of the invasion from King Brennan Murray and the Court of the Indomitable Moon requires an immediate and absolute response or their enemies will think them weak.

As Stephan is the emissary and Guardian for the sector of Faerie expected to be hit hardest, it is up to him to ready the people. It's a travesty that the unsteady peace they'd maintained these last decades is finally coming to an end.

The real debate being the inciting event. Some assume King Brennan is going mad. Others see it as a push for supplies. What Kelan surmises is that the unpredictable ruler is beginning to question the queen's power and her decision-making ability. An offense, but as they are nearly eight decades into the hundred-year law, *The Norsthana Maskia*, it is not surprising.

Never has either court been without an appointed heir for so many years—a queen allowing the threat of no ruler, unprotected magic, to stand for so long. A risk to her people and Faerie herself, should she fall. For she is the conduit between them both. Still, why attack so early?

But saying this theory aloud would be treason, and with Sola, the right-hand attendant and lacky in the room, it would've been suicide. Sola had been playing the game for years, climbing the queen's ladder, hoping that, one day, she'll be appointed heir. With her bloodline, power level, and dedication to the crown, it wasn't an impossibility. Though Kelan didn't trust her.

Did he trust the queen? That is a stupid question.

And yet, with all of this, it is not the thought of Brennan's betrayal on the people of Faerie that held him perplexed. No. It is the story of the fair-haired girl Stephan is so fascinated with—and not in the way Faye men can often become with pretty human women. For Stephan is not like that. He'd formed a friendship and, in doing so, had determined that there is something more to this girl.

"I believe someone has put a block on the poor child. I worry that when she goes through the changing, she'll be caught off guard," Stephan had said.

"The changing?" Kelan had said, voice rising. "You believe her Faye? Well, if she does not have a warden, and a human is caught in the crossfire—"

Stephan had narrowed his eyes and then threatened him. "You will *not* put her down, Kelan. I will not allow it."

He'd never seen anything like it. Stephan is even keel, a Guardian of almost six and a half millennia. This would not be the first youngling he put down for risking exposure.

Kelan lifts his glass to his lips and takes a sip, remembering the fury that had flashed through his veins at the comment. A betrayal to their queen's order and the oath they'd both taken. It could end him. Stephan was powerful—powerful enough that a fight between the two would be well matched, but it might just kill Kelan to end his friend's existence.

"What do you wish to do, then?" Kelan had asked instead.

"Watch over her. Perhaps the favor of you evaluating her and seeing if you sense what I do. You're better with latent magics than I am."

It was curious. Why had his old friend been caught by a receptionist? Not for love or for need of a slave.

Kelan runs a finger along his bottom lip, his gaze tracking a hawk as it cascades over the trees in the distance. The river just to the left of the palace shines blue in the morning light.

And he gave her the artifact...

No, Stephan's obsession is something else. Something he could not yet decipher.

Noise from the hallway has him turning toward the door. There is a bellow of rage and then a flow of quick words. That shrill tone is one he is familiar with, not just because of the times he's been forced to work with her, but for his time in court. Had he not been a trained Guardian, he would've shuddered.

With relaxed ease, he stands and strides to the hallway. Whomever had spun Niandra to such a rage was either a hero or had a death wish.

"How dare that mortal confront me! She should be torn limb from limb! The muscle peeled from her bones and fed to the Dranmik Laron."

Kelan chokes. *Holy Knights.* Talk about a brutal death.

"I will not stand for this!" Niandra's anger is such, a sheen radiates from her like a mirage of light. Should you approach too close, it could burn the skin.

"Madam Niandra," Nozia says placatingly. "Please explain, and we will address the issue straight away." Nozia keeps her eyes lowered, the power coming off Niandra too much for the lesser Faye to handle.

"That human girl at the reception desk!" Niandra shrieks, and Kelan's ears perk up. "She must be fired. That child, that stupid twit, demanded I sign in before coming up and, when I refused, had the gall to force a challenge of will! With me! I'm of the Noble House of—"

"Who was the victor?" Kelan asks and steps from the shadows, making himself visible. The moment he appears, several of the lesser Faye bow their heads in deference.

Niandra goes silent. She turns slowly, her eyes lowered but hopeful. Perhaps she believes he'll go off and kill an unsuspecting human for her.

Internally, he snorts. Hardly. It's surprising that after such a long life, she's not learned the truth of their relationship.

Niandra's jaw tics, and Kelan has to fight to hold back his grin. It speaks to the barely contained fury just beneath the surface.

This girl has to be special if she can do this.

Niandra stays silent.

"Ah, I see," Kelan says with a smirk. Then he spins in his lace-up, knee-high boots and strides for the portal, his elaborate tunic shifting to the perfectly tailored suit the moment he steps inside. The elevator doors close, and he finally allows his lip to lift in a satisfied smirk. It is nice to see Niandra get what's coming. She thinks too much of herself.

When the doors open back in the mortal world, his gaze lands immediately on the female in question.

Her head is down, but her posture is perfect otherwise. She's lost in whatever project she works on, the thoughts unreadable on her face.

Not something he's found in many mortals.

She glances up, gaze bouncing round the grand room, and Kelan realizes she's faking. She may be attempting to work, but it's a struggle. The crowd of—what she doesn't realize—Faye are all watching her.

Even Stephan, as he waits for his meeting with the other lords, though he's more discrete, standing at a table in the far corner of the coffee shop near the back end of the building. As if sensing Kelan, he looks up, then nods toward Myrna. It's as if he says, "I told you."

Slipping his hands into his pockets, Kelan nods and moves forward. Each step allows him a second to examine the youngling. His powers glide forward, and it's like the girl senses them. She looks up and meets his eye.

Youngling.

Power trapped behind skin of porcelain.

Stephan was right. She's not human. She's Faye. But that is one hell of a binding she holds. One so strong she probably has no idea what she is.

Myrna's face pales, but then her chest expands in a deep breath. She stands. It's as if she's readying to meet a firing squad. Is it so bad that he speak to her?

"Good morning, Mr. Daniels," Myrna says jovially.

"Good morning, Myrna," he says. It shocks her that he knows her name. Odd.

She flashes a smile, but it is replaced by worry. He gives her credit for trying. She asks, "Am I in trouble?"

"Why would you be in trouble?"

She licks her top lip. Her gaze flicks away, and then she says, "I fear I may have upset one of your visitors, though I am not sure why."

She is not sure why?

"Ah...Yes, Niandra." Kelan nods, a kind smile spreading his face. He isn't sure if the smile makes her more comfortable or less. "Well, she is a force best not worried about. From the story she told, you did your job as required."

Myrna lets out a breath, a more relaxed smile replacing the professional one. "Thank you, sir. Truly. I did not mean to offend."

Interesting. Is she aware she speaks in the cadence of the court? Kelan could even detect a trace of the accent as well. *It does not seem so.*

"You did not."

With a nod, she continues, clasping her hands before her, "Glad to hear it. So, how can I help you?"

Kelan can sense that while she's playing the perfect example of professional poise, with her straight posture and steady breathing, she's really using the opportunity to get a good look at him. He wonders what she sees.

In his glamoured form, he's shorter than most men, his hair cropped on the sides and longer on the top. The color, however, is the same—a dark chestnut brown. There is less gold scattered throughout, though. Humans don't take to that color quite the same way. He watches her with a calm intensity, his face stoic.

Yet, he cannot hide the curiosity he feels, and, for some reason, he suspects she senses it.

"May I ask you a question?" Kelan slides his hands into his pockets.

"Of course, sir."

"How do you like your position here at Haszwalds Elite?"

Myrna shows no surprise in her expression, but he does notice the slight fidgeting of her fingers. "I am grateful for such an opportunity. My degree means everything to me, and this place"—she scans the grand room, taking her eyes off him—"is one of the first places I have ever felt at home. I traveled a great deal as a child, and it is nice to finally have purpose." Myrna blushes and pushes a stray hair back behind her ear.

A youngling with no knowledge of what she is, or home to center herself or her magic? That is a dangerous thing. He probes the binding then, testing her reaction. Nothing. He becomes more invested. It's so tightly wound it would not only hide her power but could alter her memory and even change the way she reacts to things.

"My apologies," she adds with an embarrassed giggle. It tinkles, sending warmth through him. He startles, but stops, captivated by her next words. "That was a great deal more than you asked. As I said, I'm excited for the opportunity."

Kelan makes the decision on the spot, asks, "Is Cindy McNeil available? I have an important matter to speak with her about."

Her eyebrows draw together for a split second before she regains that perfect professional mask.

"Of course, one moment, please." With a grace of movement, Myrna takes the phone and dials her extension. "Good morning, Cindy. Yes, I'm well, thank you. Mr. Daniels is here. He's requesting a moment of your time."

Before Cindy can speak up, because Kelan knows she'd rather meet him out here, Kelan says, "I would like you to escort me to the office to speak with her, if at all possible."

Through the phone, there is a sharp intake of breath. Kelan can hear it even from where he stands. Then Cindy says, "So...I, uh, heard that. Sure. Myrna, do as he says and please bring him back to the main room. I'll meet you there. I'll send Rhonda out to cover you."

The panic in Cindy's voice makes Kelan want to sigh. She's one of the few humans who knows what they are. An accident of discovery, to be sure. She's been terrified of them ever since, even as she wishes to gain their favor.

"Yes, ma'am." Myrna replaces the phone. She bends, logs out of her computer, then grabs the folder and book resting on her desk.

There is a sharp influx of static the moment her fingers touch the cover, and Kelan's eyebrow raises. *Oh, I must know who you are, youngling.*

With a professional smile, Myrna says, "If you will follow me, please."

They've exchanged but a few words, and Kelan completely understands Stephan's fascination. There's something here; a draw to power, a need to protect. He can't explain it, but it's there. Perhaps it's the need to discover who put the block on her, especially one so strong, but he doubts it. Either way, it's up to him, or the queen will have his head.

Kelan nods and falls into step with Myrna. They pass a small human female, and she shoots the girl a reassuring smile. Once inside the hallway, two men cross their path, one of which scans her from head to toe. He leans to his friend and whispers, "You know, Myrna'd be hot if she wasn't a freakin' robot. She's got a nice rack, though."

The other laughs. "Yeah. She creeps me out sometimes."

Kelan grinds his teeth, but Myrna just blinks down at the floor before glancing at her watch.

Her lips press together before she takes a breath and says, "Hey, Michael. Mrs. Glanis came down looking for you. Your meeting was moved up. If you head there now, you should get there in time."

The guy who'd said those horrible things freezes as if realizing who she stands with. "Oh. Thanks, Myrna." Then he runs off.

She'd clearly heard his words, and yet she helped him. *Kindness, too. She truly is an enigma. Or just weak.*

Myrna meets Kelan's gaze, all the hurt from those words gone from her face. "I hope your meetings have gone well so far this morning."

Shock runs through him when she doesn't look away and instead continues to hold his stare even as they make the turn into the hallway. He feels the probing of his shields. A flicker. Like a child playing with their powers, but her eyes widen nonetheless.

Not weak then, but she's not aware of what she does, Kelan thinks.

"It's been interesting. Not what I expected for the day," he says, maintaining eye contact. He presses his will into his gaze. She does not react, just continues to hold his eyes with no effort. Warmth on his palms. He presses his tongue to the top of his mouth. How has she maintained the lock for so long? Few can.

She smiles sweetly before her attention shifts to the door. Not because she's giving in or due to the strength of his will, but to swipe her ID card and push the door open. They enter the small space to find three desks lining one side and a set of lockers along the far wall.

Cindy stands from one of the desks. He knows this is not her main office, but Kelan doesn't care if it means this conversation can occur. Her throat bobs as she swallows, then holds her hand out to shake.

"Mr. Daniels, how can I help you?" Cindy says.

Myrna bows her head, then starts to step away. The wish for an unnoticed exit? No.

Kelan reaches out and touches Myrna's arm at the elbow. It is a slight touch, a request to keep her from leaving, but in an instant, he realizes his mistake. She gasps. He pulls back as a burst of heat exchanges between them. It's instantaneous and filled with light and sound. His ears buzz, and there are sparks dancing at the corners of his vision.

Oy Verenestra! He sucks in a few deep breaths, raising his eyes to hers slowly.

"Please," is all he says.

There's more expression in those ice blues than he's seen yet—shock, excitement, fear. Eyes that feel familiar somehow...

She recovers quickly, but in that glimpse, it's clear that she's seen through his glamour. All of it. Her eyes are narrowed, her focus sharp. She sees his hair and eyes, the pointed ears. She straightens as if to measure his true height against hers. How she keeps her composure even as her breaths come quicker is astounding. The control she has over herself speaks of some form of training. Full lips mouth "glowing" before she glances at her boss, then nods once.

What did Mrs. McNeil say while he was distracted? Thankfully, Cindy doesn't notice anything is awry. Kelan clears his throat and addresses the older woman. "Mrs. McNeil, I'm here to inform you that Ms. Myrna Johnson has been promoted. She's made a great impression on my staff, and they've offered her a position. She'll be starting immediately."

"What?" Cindy stutters, her mouth dropping open. "Why didn't you tell me you applied..."

"She did not. The decision was made above floors."

Cindy shifts from foot to foot and steps closer to Myrna. "And what if she doesn't want it or doesn't like the position?"

Kelan smiles. Next to him, Myrna's eyes flash down to his mouth.

Yes, she can see straight through my glamour.

And she could. For in that moment, Myrna is transfixed on the way his sharp incisors make his smile more of a snarl. Or the way the florescent light glitters off the gold in his hair. It makes Kelan wonder how much she knows of the mythical creatures of the Faerie. Was it just the fairy tales told, or had her upbring-ing allowed for more, whispering of the true world worshiped long ago? This information often explained why those like Cindy smiled, so transfixed at those like him, for he is otherworldly even to those who did not truly believe in myth.

Kelan presses the tip of his tongue to his canine, gaze flicking to the entrancing Myrna. She shivers, gulps, but it is the sharp intake of breath which causes him to grin.

Addressing Cindy, Kelan says, "Don't worry, that won't be an issue." He turns to Myrna. "We're providing an opportunity for her to learn about an entirely new project; to fill in the gaps, ask questions, and to research topics she's never dreamed of."

Myrna's scanning him, reading into every word he's said, just as he'd intended.

"Please collect your things, and we can get started. There's much to discuss that I must explain to you, and my team is waiting."

At first, Kelan is unsure if she will agree. He hadn't offered this opportunity prior to telling Cindy. Most people don't like being told what to do, and he gets the sense that she's no different. Perhaps more so. This is a gamble, one betting on her need for answers.

"This is an offer like none other. A learning opportunity. The one I think you've been waiting for."

"And I will get answers to my questions?"

He nods. "On my honor."

She seems frozen to the spot, but with those words, she defrosts. It's like she can finally take a full breath.

"Okay," she starts, but catches herself when Cindy sharply whispers her name in chastisement. "I mean, yes, sir."

She moves to the lockers and proceeds to remove a pink backpack, purse, and a small gym bag. She opens the bag and throws everything remaining inside it before closing the locker. Myrna uses the time to get herself together. No longer a panicked mess, she is now a ball of energy he can't fully read.

When she rejoins him, Kelan extends his hand out to her.

She pulls the pink monstrosity closer and says, "No. That's not necessary."

With a kind, but slightly wicked grin, Kelan insists, "I assure you, Ms. Johnson. It is."

"And I assure you, Mr. Daniels, that although I appreciate the gesture and would receive great amusement watching you carry this hot pink and blue bag through the building, I have items for training later, which my instructor would not approve of allowing an untrained person to carry. So, I apologize. I must insist." Her eyes are hard, challenging. This is her first test to Kelan, just as his was the job offer.

Smart, too. For she plays with him as a way to distract from her nervousness.

"Weapons?" Cindy squeaks.

"Untrained?" Kelan asks, and it's time for Myrna's eyebrows to lift teasingly. Her eyes flick down to the sword at his waist.

Oh, she is going to be a challenge. Kelan pushes his will into his shields, totally and completely unsure if it does anything to block her.

Like a pro, Myrna turns to Cindy. "Of course not. They are instruments, Cindy, and they are fragile."

Cindy presses a hand to her chest. "Oh, I must have heard you wrong. Sorry, darling."

Kelan's lips twitch. Myrna purses hers together. She's fighting back a laugh as well.

"Well, I'll need to get her a new badge," Cindy says.

"No need." He taps his chest as if to indicate he has one in the suit pocket. "I have it here."

"You do?" Myrna looks skeptical.

Kelan pulls a badge out and holds it up, a new picture of the girl visible on the front. "Are you ready to proceed?" Myrna nods, swings her purse and bag over her shoulder, then strides for the door. Before they exit, Kelan inclines his head to the worried Cindy. "Thank you for your time."

There's a sigh from the older woman, and then the door *snicks* shut.

CHAPTER SEVEN

Lapse of Control

KELAN'S GUARD RISES AS he takes in the crowd still waiting in the foyer. The poise of this youngling is unconditional, even as they enter the hall, and all fall silent. It's impressive and speaks of the training she's endured. Which causes more questions. He should've guessed they'd stay. Niandra's powerful, and for the youngling to best her, it whispers of unusual happenings. And so many who are on-site today are from the palace, here for the hearings regarding the attacks from the enemy court. Which means they're known for their nosiness.

"Why are they watching me?" she asks in a whisper.

"Because you're different, and they know it."

"I don't know what you mean."

Neither does Kelan respond nor acknowledge the onlookers. Instead, he leads her into the elevator and enters the number "four." He holds out the new ID card.

"Why do I need a new one?" Myrna asks.

"It's required to access the designated floors."

Her hand lifts hesitantly, but there's no missing the hungry gleam peeking through. It changes to shock the moment her fingers brush the plastic. The emblem along the edge brightens to a golden yellow. A shimmer of the deepest purple flashes at the edges, then disappears so fast that Kelan thinks he's imagined it.

Definitely of our ilk then. Even if the flash of violet is worrisome to the base of her power.

Myrna freezes, her mouth dropping open, dumbfounded.

"How did you come by it, anyway? I noticed you didn't have it when you came down."

"Did you?" He cocks an eyebrow.

Myrna nods. "There was no bulge in your breast pocket until you"—she runs a hand through her pale blond hair—"um...changed."

She meets his eyes as if pleading for him to explain. There is so much tension held coiled within the girl.

Thankfully, his words are steady. "Interesting. Now, scan your badge, and we'll be on our way."

She does as he bids, then runs a finger along the now-dark emblem. The elevator moves.

"It will not brighten again. It was to verify you're welcome on our floor."

"What do you mean?"

"Well, only one of us is allowed above. As I suspected, you are."

"One of you..." Myrna shakes her head and steps back. It's as if something stops her, telling her she must not retreat. It's fascinating to watch. The scent of fear in the air disappears. "I need an explanation."

How can she control herself so well? "Then ask a question."

She swallows, thinking, then asks, "Why does your suit keep shifting?" She squints, and he lifts an eyebrow. "Is that a tunic?"

Kelan licks his lip, his eyes narrowing ever so lightly. Her innocence is both sweet and dangerous. But now he has the confirmation he needs. It does not make him feel better. "You can see through my glamour? Tell me, what else do you see?"

"Everything? I can see the gold in your hair and eyes, the sword at your waist. The knives hidden... You're taller, too. And..." She reaches up as if to brush his pointed ears, but he grasps her wrist. She looks away as the sound of her pants fill the quiet space. "I'm sorry."

He releases her wrist. She rubs at the reddened skin. They face forward, the silence deepening. Part of Kelan feels bad for scaring her; the other part does not. No one touches a Guardian without their permission.

Clearing her throat, she exhales long and heavily. "My apologies. I did not mean to offend." After a long moment of silence—the correct amount for deference—she continues, "Mr. Daniels, can you please tell me what's happening?"

He's not angry with her. It is clear she has no understanding of their laws or any control of her power. So, it is hard to be offended by her blatant disregard of their laws.

"You have no idea what we are? What *you* are?"

"I mean, I can guess," she says, facing him again. "There are stories I remember, but to be perfectly honest, I'm not sure I want them to be true. Granted, I don't know what myth and movie is any longer."

Who told you these stories? "I will not hurt you."

Myrna smirks. "Yeah, because I should always trust the word of a stranger. Anyway, I'm not like you."

"Yes, you are. Though, it seems you do not know the rules of what we are. No one has taught you about your powers, how to control them, or the laws which govern our people. They've left you unprotected, and should you offend the wrong creature, you'll be put down."

"What?" Myrna's voice rises in pitch. Her entire demeanor changes, and suddenly she is ready for a fight. But then, it's as if the rest of his words sink in. Her face scrunches cutely. "Powers? I don't have powers."

Kelan leans closer. "Yes, Myrna, you do. They're just locked away." Kelan shifts on his feet. "But don't be afraid. We will uncover it and all will be clear very soon."

Myrna drops all pretenses. She sets the bags on the floor and rolls her eyes, shooting him an exasperated look. "Don't be afraid? Seriously? You realize you just told me I'd be 'put down' if I irritated the wrong person, right after you said you wouldn't hurt me like the most cliché movie villain on the planet. All while you have me locked in a closed space alone. Come on, this is the perfect setting for a horror movie if I've ever heard one."

Kelan can't help it. He bursts out a laugh. It shakes the very air. The girl is afraid, and yet she can control it, push it down, and harness it for her own use. She is a mystery, to be sure.

The youngling's eyes crinkle as she laughs, too. The elevator shifts, and she reaches out to steady herself on his arm. He stiffens but does not pull away. He does, however, block any potential reaction.

"And yet you are not afraid of me." He lifts his opposite hand and runs it along his jaw.

"Should I be? I mean, I just tried to touch your pointed ears. You could've ripped my arm off. You didn't. Perhaps you told me those things, but they were more of a warning than a threat."

Kelan examines the youngling. "Point. Even so, most are. You, however, do not flinch away. Nor do you shrink from my power." His tone has shifted, taking on a more confused lilt. He places his hand over hers and leans in, inhaling slightly. She sucks in a breath but moves toward him in response.

"I'm sorry to disappoint, Mr. Daniels, but you're hardly the scariest creature I've met."

"I'm curious, now. Who is then?" The corner of her lip lifts, and Kelan narrows his gaze. "Who are you, Myrna?"

She pulls away slightly. "I am no one, but I can tell that you're not someone to be feared. You give off more of a protector aura than serial killer."

He chokes. "Some would disagree."

"Yes, well, they haven't met my mother. As she's always said, 'Power is in the choices we make and the person we strive to be.'"

"Your mother?"

His hand flexes against hers. There's heat between them. Even as he blocks her, he longs to open the connections and see what might come of it. She's unique. How had Stephan kept her secret for so long? Hell, how had he not noticed her before today?

You're an idiot, that's how.

As if without conscious thought, their bodies square to one another. Kelan lowers his shields just a bit. He wants to know what will happen. Will it be as instantaneous as before? Will it be as uncontrolled?

He tells himself this is a test to see how much power she holds, but there are other ways he *should* do this. Safer ways. Sanctioned ways. And yet, the urge to test her himself is like nothing he's ever felt. This pull to her doesn't feel romantic or sexual. No, it's visceral as if it were at the center of his very being.

Whatever it is, he must do this slowly. The softness of her palms as they skim against his callused hands causes a shiver to run down his thighs. Lightening crackles, and a weight settles around them. His limbs become heavy, and he can feel how her hands settle in his.

More.

His hands move to grip her wrists. Her graceful fingers clasp his as if she has done this a thousand times before. This time, he drops his shields completely and pushes his energy toward her, testing the limits beginning to emerge within her. Those beautiful blue eyes close, and her head tilts back before sparks flash just above their skin. Their fingers tighten in unison, their breaths syncing, becoming deeper.

Myrna's eyelids open, her gaze heavy as it finds Kelan. One more level is safe.

Just one more.

Kelan's mouth parts as he releases more of himself into the connection between them—testing, tasting her energy. He wants to know how close she is to the changing. What her power is. Which court her bloodline stems from. Some he may glimpse, other pieces are unlikely, but his blood sings to try.

The elevator shakes beneath their feet. The sweet, smoky scent of vanilla lifts his tongue as her aura brushes against his. She's delicious; spicy, with a note of earth that sings through him.

"Do you taste cinnamon?" she asks, her voice husky. Power disturbs the air around them as her fingers dig into his flesh. She licks her lips.

Kelan tracks the movement. He is a male, after all. Almost without thought, his hand moves further up her arm. She's so soft and smooth.

There's a *bing*, and the doors to the elevator slide open. Kelan freezes at the audible gasp from many. Not one or two, but dozens.

Queen save us. Kelan doesn't want to let go. The connection is strong, her very self having pulled him until they're inches apart.

Hundreds of years he's been a Guardian. He will not let *this* affect him.

"It'll be fine," he whispers, pulling every ounce of his power back.

Creating space between them, he looks to the crowd watching them from the doorway. *Shields up, training in place.*

Perhaps coming here was a bad choice. Technically, there is a back way into the executive hallway. One that would've kept him out of this space—the reception area and portal room into Faerie. A large room nearly as grand as the one they'd just left, but this one narrowed down near the back, splitting off into seven separate directions of Faerie. It is also filled with people, many of whom had beaten them from below. And all their gazes are locked on them. Or more specifically, their linked hands.

I'm daft.

Kelan adjusts her hand to rest at the crease of his arm. Her increased heart rate slams against him where they touch. They step from the transport, the door shutting.

One of the lesser Faye who helps in the office stands nearby. He gestures to her bags. "Take them to my office." They nod and do as instructed.

"This place is incredible." Myrna scans the room, the wonder of her expression mesmerizing anyone who sees it. She's, once again, perfectly composed even as he internally freaks out at the idea of the entire room seeing the spectacle of them sharing power. He'd gone too far, let his instincts take over, and now there would be talk. And because of it, Myrna would be even more of a target.

What was wrong with him?

"This cannot be the building we were just in."

Floors of polished white and blue stone pavers shine in the light spilling from massive arched windows, which show forest on the outside.

"Technically, this is still Haszwalds Elite, but in truth, this area… she prefers to be called Faerie." He glances down. "What you're seeing is one of the traversing rooms to our true home. It's both inside the building and not, with pathways to places across Faerie approved by the crown. There are similar traversing rooms on the other floors leading to specified locations necessary for their business. All warded, of course. Only those such as us can enter here." He squeezes her hand. "And please, call me Kelan."

Creatures from Myrna's dreams wander about. They stop to stare. Others have followed. So many people watch as Kelan leads her through the large space and toward the second hallway on the left.

"We're to go to my office and then we will discover who has put this binding on you."

"Binding?"

Kelan stops and faces her. "How old are you, Myrna?"

Her brow furrows. "Twenty-three. Why?"

Kelan leans in and whispers so low she alone may hear. "Nay. For you to be this close to the changing and so strong, you have to be approaching five and seven."

Myrna's feet stop moving, and she pulls Kelan to a stop. Her pupils have dilated, and her pulse races beneath his fingertips. She pulls him close. "That's impossible. Seventy-five?"

"Myrna, you've a binding on you so strong that not only do you not know you're Faye, but your memories must've been altered to keep you from recognizing your true age, your growth patterns, and who knows what else. This is a matter for the queen."

"Wha-what?" Myrna squeaks. "Faye? Kelan..."

The sound of his name on her lips is the most beautiful thing he's ever heard. It fires a warning somewhere deep within him. Moving on. "It's true, and you're strong. You even bested Niandra this morning."

"That beautiful woman from the lobby?" she says in full volume. Several snickers filter back from the crowd remind Kelan they need to get somewhere private. They start toward the hallway once more as Myrna continues, "How did I—"

"You!" the booming feminine voice has Myrna's head snapping up. She's there, in their path, and ready to eat the poor youngling alive. Hell, she might. Niandra's not known for kindness.

"Faye?" Myrna asks Kelan, the word hinting of the pieces being put together. He nods, and she bites her lip, then laughs. "I've read stories of Water Faye, but I never thought them real."

Kelan lifts his hand to touch the bridge of his nose. In reality, it's to hide his grin. She sees through her glamour. *Damn impressive.*

In her natural form, Niandra's just as beautiful, but in a menacing way instead of bitchy. Her delicate teeth are sharpened, making her cheekbones stand out more than before. Her black hair is woven with what looks like seaweed, and she has scales down the left side of her face.

Even looking like this, Myrna doesn't seem afraid. She looks thoughtful. "I expected more of a change with your glamour gone," she says.

Niandra pulls up short.

Kelan glances to the heavens. "Myrna, you should not—"

"How dare you! You should not look at one of my house without glamour. Especially not without permission!" Niandra snarls, then cranks her arm back as if to cut her with claws now visible.

The Guardian within Kelan rises. He steps between them. "She already has, Niandra, and it is clear she does not understand our laws. Her power's active at all times, which is why she does not realize she uses them."

Myrna's brow furrows. Sweat beads along her forehead. "What power? I have no power."

Kelan nods to Myrna. "Yes. You do, and in spades, it seems. You see, our people determine rank in society based on dominance. We are *other*—a species that has a wilder nature, and so it is natural to lead with the stronger beast within."

"Okay." Myrna's brow pinches, her lips pursing before she asks, "Is there some sort of reading I can do on this? An orientation so that I stop offending harpies? Although I think I can take her, I'm pretty sure that would cross a few lines on day one." Her snark gets a few chuckles, though Kelan notices several who back away from the confirmation.

Not Niandra, of course.

"But the scales along the side of your face are beautiful," she muses, as if she cannot help it. Myrna leans closer to Kelan. "Though why are they only on the left?"

The feral scream that escapes Niandra before she lunges, claws extended, is not unexpected. In fact, Kelan is ready. Apparently, so is Myrna, based on the readied stance. Even so, Kelan pulls her behind him, his sword drawn before Niandra has the chance to take more than a step.

"Guardian Kelan? How can you...it is against our laws! And just rude! I demand..."

"*Halt!*" The one word causes the entire hall to rumble. Every faerie in the room spins toward the voice and falls to their knees, the power too much for them to bear. Her Majesty's voice is enraged, the warning clear. "You shall not touch her!"

Kelan doesn't return his sword to its scabbard. He doesn't lower his guard. Negative. If the queen's here, things may get worse before they get better. He pushes up from his knee, glancing to Myrna to verify her wellbeing.

But she's on her feet, seemingly unaffected by the wave of power thrown by the queen. Well, not completely. Her hands press to her ears, and her eyes are wet with pain, but she's standing. *How?*

A question for another time. Right then, it's his duty to protect her, even from the Queen of The Court of the Radiant Sun. Kelan wraps an arm around Myrna's waist and tucks her to his side, then spins her so that his body is between the youngling and the new threat. Myrna sags into him, which means the queen's will takes a toll.

Steady, harsh steps approach from the most guarded gateway. The one which leads to Tara, the capital city for The Court of the Radiant Sun, and the palace at its center.

Shining in her beauty, terrifying in her dominion, the queen approaches, a braid running across one side of her head. Her silvery golden hair falls to the swell of her butt, pink woven through to deepen to red at the tips. It suits her. Adds to the image she maintains—lovingly, obsessively protective of her people while ruling with an iron fist of passion.

A gown of sunflower gold hugs her torso, then flares at the waist. With a dramatic flick of her wrist, she orders Kelan to move.

Show me the child, the gesture says.

Kelan takes a breath, then does as commanded. He shifts so Myrna is visible. Myrna's mouth drops open when she sees the figure. At first Kelan's amused, believing that she is in awe, but then the queen winks, and his stomach makes a trip south.

CHAPTER EIGHT

Okay...Not Mafia

"MOTHER?" THE LAST SYLLABLE squeaks as Myrna tries to come to terms with what she sees. She steps away from Kelan's side, his arm dropping limply away. "What are you doing here? And looking like that?" Myrna holds her hands out, gesturing to the beautiful gown Laoise wears.

"Mother!" Niandra screeches.

She steps forward and runs her fingers over the lush gold fabric.

Myrna hadn't realized how silent the room was until she reached out. Then screams fill the air.

"How dare you touch the queen without permission!"

"Offense!"

"Her Majesty the High Queen allowed it?"

"She should be hanged!"

"Feed her to the Dranmik!"

"Hello, Sweetling." Laoise scans Myrna as if verifying she is in one piece, though it feels more like a judgment, then she pulls Myrna in for a quick hug and to press a kiss to her cheek. This has the desired effect. The entire hall goes silent. Then she says, "I heard you made an impression downstairs and knew my presence would be required."

"That doesn't explain—"

Kelan steps closer to Myrna, a scowl plastered across his face. Myrna can't help but notice the sweat beading on his face as he leans in and asks, "Did you say 'Mother'? You're saying Queen Laoise Qhuinn of Faerie is your... mother?"

Myrna knows the wicked smirk Laoise wears. It's one she's familiar with. She's enjoying Kelan's—and the others'—distress. Myrna's is just a bonus.

Laoise shoots Niandra a vicious glare.

The Water Faye skitters back, her heels clicking against flooring. She stops a few yards away, her head down in subservience, but it's obvious to Myrna that she's still listening.

"I'm sorry, what did you call her?" Myrna asks Kelan. Her stomach sloshes, and she suddenly feels ill.

Laoise takes pity—if that is what one calls it—and chuckles. Dress rustling, she steps forward and places her hand upon Myrna's cheek. "I have missed you."

"As I you."

With a grace even more exaggerated than Myrna is used to, Laoise inclines her head to Kelan, a knowing smile tilting her lip. She must've seen the way he protected her. No doubt she believes more goes on here.

"Is this the boy you spoke of when we last met?"

"What?" Myrna's cheeks go ruddy. "No! And, Mother, this is not the time." She lowers her voice, her eyes narrowing. Through her teeth, she says, "And of all things you're going to say to me right now, it's that? Instead of explaining this?" She motions exaggeratedly between them. "How could you have not told me?"

"My queen." Kelan executes a bow almost as graceful as Laoise's. "Perhaps we should take this elsewhere. We are headed to my office."

Laoise's chest rises, her very being seeming to grow. The room goes perfectly still. Myrna pales, as do many of the surrounding patrons.

Myrna quiets. She understands the rules. Some things are meant to be discussed behind closed doors.

She addresses Kelan. "You are right. It is time to move this conversation to a more private venue. Let us retire to your office. Myrna, you will say nothing until we speak. Do you understand?"

She nods, and then there is a minute flick of her wrist. There will be no other discussion here. She schools her expression, but the emotion roiling within her threatens to escape. Yet the lifetime of training this woman has put her through is too strong. She knows what will happen if even a scowl twitches across her young face. And either way, Myrna refuses to let her mother see how much the last hour has shaken her, so with that breath, she tightens her diaphragm and shoves it deep.

A kind, joyous smile lifts her cheek instead as she faces Kelan. "Shall we?"

Kelan's gaze shifts from mother to daughter. She can almost feel the way his eyes examine every part of her—her long lean frame, her pale blond hair, and fair skin. Though his manner has not changed, she sees his hesitation even through the stoic expression he keeps plastered on his face. The emotion exuded in the elevator is locked up tight, hidden behind walls of thick concrete.

He bows his head to Myrna as she retakes the spot next to him.

It is then that Myrna realizes that in all the time they have stood in the hall filled with people, Laoise has, for the most part, ignored the horde of creatures observing them. It's as if they don't exist. Even the malicious eyes of Niandra have not swayed her.

Speaking of which, the evil harpy—for Myrna realizes she cannot say "queen" any longer—steps forward. There's hatred in her eyes and bitterness in every word. "This cannot be true, Majesty. This *girl* cannot be your child. She is disgusting, weak. She is—"

A hand snakes out so quickly no one sees it coming. Niandra hits the ground hard. She grunts, the stone unforgiving as her shoulder cracks against its hard surface.

Myrna stops the gasp before it becomes audible, but she can't hide the twitch of her hand on Kelan's arm at the brutality.

Laoise looms over the limp form, red droplets falling from sharp nails to contrast the bright white floor. Myrna swears she can almost hear the soft *splash*.

"Hold her," Laoise says to one of the guards Myrna hadn't noticed standing along the walls. They follow her command and grab Niandra. Without taking her eyes from Niandra, Laoise continues, "Take Myrna as ordered. I will be there shortly."

A man of medium height with long legs and blue streaks in his hair clears his throat. "Majesty?" It's one of her high-level advisers. He approaches from Kelan's left side, having entered the hall not long after Laoise had. He keeps his eyes low, and his head bowed when he says, "If what you say is true, we will need a declaration and proof of blood."

Laoise's head swivels in his direction, power radiating off her. It alters the very air around her, the temperature shifting in waves of heat. "You dare question your queen?"

The man does not cower. "I mean no disrespect, but for her safety. Should you claim the youngling as yours..."

Laoise growls, but Myrna recognizes this as one of annoyance instead of anger. Better, but still not a sound anyone should wish to hear. "Call the high court together. Immediately." The queen faces the crowd, her posture perfectly regal, her gown shifting in a breeze Myrna cannot place the source of. Even her skin glows with a radiance that was not there a moment ago.

Myrna leans into Kelan. In his ear, she whispers, "Is she doing something to make herself look like that?"

He shoots her a scornful glare. It's so reminiscent of the one her aunt would give her that Myrna straightens instantly. She focuses all her attention on her mother.

"This girl is under my protection. Should anyone harm her, it will be their end." Laoise turns back to the adviser. "Within the day. No longer. Guardian Kelan, she is your responsibility. I will meet you in your office. Call the attendants to come ready her for presentation."

Laoise shifts toward the Guardians holding the still-cowering Niandra, who bleeds from the slashes the queen's nails left deep in her flesh. That cruel look is back in Laoise's eye, and Myrna doesn't like it, even if it isn't pointed at her.

Myrna stops the Guardian beside her. He, no doubt, wishes to reach out and pull her away.

"Mother? Niandra..." It is said quietly so the three of them alone may hear. "Her insult was not that of your child. It was of an insignificant human who apparently broke several laws and seriously offended her."

It felt weird calling herself a "human." Even if she isn't, in her mind she is. Hell, until Kelan told her otherwise, Myrna never would've thought all this was possible.

Laoise's eyes soften just so, before she says, "It does not matter. She knows better than to speak to me in that tone. As you do." With a gesture to Kelan to get moving, she adds, "You will learn, dearling. We are not in the human world any longer. Here, the rules are not the same and, anyway, I do not like her."

Myrna shoots her an amused look. "We've talked about this. You can't kill everyone you don't like."

That breaks Kelan's perfect composure. He grabs Myrna's elbow, fingers digging in. She doesn't respond to the death glare Laoise sends to her daughter because the soft snort is her real response. She may not show it to everyone, but there's amusement there.

Myrna laughs quietly, unwilling to push any further, and turns to exit the hall.

Kelan makes a gesture she doesn't understand and four similarly dressed guards to Kelan appear from nowhere. Two are blond, one dark-haired, and the last is red, as fiery as a burning ember left to taste the wind as it sweeps over the campsite. They encircle her and Kelan, their steps steady as they move from the reception and into the hall.

Each person they pass is so beautifully unique—a fairy tale come to life, told to Myrna in her caretaker's voice, but foggy as if a memory hidden in time. Was this the block Kelan spoke of? A man, tall and lean with short silver hair and pointed ears. His dark black eyes have a ring of contrasting silver that glows so brightly with hatred. A woman with bark-like skin and hair that resembles moss peels her teeth back in a smile. Or is it a snarl? The youngling is unsure. And then Myrna spots a collection of creatures who are less human—more misshapen and even more fascinating. She would need to ask Kelan about those.

Her chest tightens, and it takes all her effort to keep her breaths even.

The gaze of every creature locked on her puts the weight of their judgment upon her shoulders. Myrna's shields fracture an inch. Her hands tremble. She bites the inside of her lip and presses her palms to her stomach.

The moment Myrna steps into the hallway, it is like a weight lifts from her shoulders. She sighs and whispers, "A place to belong or a place to die..."

The doors close, and Kelan bursts out, "What is wrong with you? How dare you question the queen like that? She could've killed you!"

Myrna looks at the floor, the pattern here darker, made of a black stone with white streaks throughout. Her white kitten heels click along as a sardonic smile lifts to the corner of her mouth.

"I promise you, I've said far worse to her than that. Rarely, but..." She sucks on her bottom lip. She's quiet for a long moment, and Kelan seems at a loss for words. With a shrug, she moves forward once more. When they turn down the hallway that ends at Kelan's office, Myrna says, her tone teasing, "I told you. Much scarier creatures than you."

CHAPTER NINE

Answers Without Answers

As they traverse through the walls of Haszwalds, everything changes. The hall, which holds hints of the office building she adores, transforms, becoming majestic. The ceilings lift; the artwork becomes more intricate. Even the lines in the stone feel richer. Then they enter Kelan's office, and Myrna becomes engrossed in every aspect of the space.

His office is not just an office. Within minutes, Myrna realizes that Kelan Daniels is important, and this is the center of something essential to her mother's realm. For this is a war room. A massive desk immaculately kept and covered in classified reports sits before a gigantic window overlooking a forest, which Myrna gets lost staring at. Mostly because she can't figure out where the hell they are.

When she asks, all he says is, "Faerie."

So helpful.

Bookshelves filled with tomes about war, strategy, and a thousand other topics line the walls. She runs her fingers lovingly over the spines, for Myrna loves reading about all subjects, but especially military strategy. She's been studying it with Theia and Mother for years.

When she tries to remove a tome, he growls and snatches it from her hands to put it back onto the shelf.

"These are not for you, youngling," Kelan says.

Myrna glares, then walks away, moving to the map on the wall. It's the size of her bed, and just like before, when she asks a question, he shuts her down.

"What the hell is your problem? I'm not asking for state secrets here. All I asked, is if this showed all of Faerie and how the sections were separated."

Kelan huffs.

"Where is Mother, anyway?" Myrna asks with more bite than she means to. Her irritation with waiting, being locked in this room with Kelan, and his lack of communication is getting to her.

"The queen does as she pleases."

It's about this time Myrna stops asking questions, realizing that until Mother comes in, she isn't going to get anything out of the brute. Which is annoying as hell and solidifies any question he asks will be shut down as well.

Of course, that doesn't keep her from continuing her exploration of his room. And she finds the coolest thing ever, an old-time table covered with little toy soldiers and ships at sea.

But not like those she'd seen in movies. Yes, it is complete with little toy soldiers and ships showing an advancing army. The small difference is this one is alive and reacts to her presence. Never would she admit how much fun she'd found watching the sands shift beneath the feet of the blue men, nor the air as it fills the sails of the miniature fleet. Though she's pretty sure Kelan knows.

"Will you quit looking at me like that?" Myrna says to Kelan as she strolls once again around the room. "I swear, I can read your thoughts."

They'd been in here long enough for Myrna to circle the room thrice, and she's getting antsy. Soon, she will start asking him questions and, knowing Mother, that wouldn't be good. The fact that he hadn't is a sign of his control, considering they show on his face, begging to come out.

The corner of his lip twitches. "Is that so? And what am I thinking?"

"That I am not acting as I did out there." Myrna goes to the antique armoire standing in the corner. It is gorgeous and clearly from a different age. The ornate carvings adorning its dark oak surface are intricately designed with delicate curves and patterns that seem to come alive in the flickering candlelight.

She yanks the doors open and rummages through it. His perfect calm and silent watchfulness are slowly causing her to go mad.

"Considering you've gone from professionalism to feeling comfortable going through my personal items, I would say so."

Myrna glances at him from behind the door. "And yet you do nothing to stop me."

"Perhaps I am curious as to what you will find important in there. It stores but extra clothing."

"Then you have nothing to be concerned over."

There are several styles of shoes which rest along the bottom and a few changes of clothes hang from a rod which runs the inside length. But Myrna runs her hands along the shelves lined with soft velvet and silk. Each provides storage for his valuable items such as jewelry, ancient scrolls, and clothing. But what she really looks for is something for protection. For while waiting for Mother, she'd come to want something more in her possession. If it is to be anywhere, this is the most likely place.

Look for the divot in the wood at the side, Theia's voice says in her head.

Her finger runs along the side and then she presses just so. The hidden panel pops open and, at the *click,* Kelan's eyes widen. He pushes off the wall where he leans and heads toward her.

Myrna caresses the set of knives so lovingly cared for, then scoops them and the sheath up, heading to his desk. These are perfect.

"You're right. I am not acting like the intern I am at Haszwalds." She sets her foot on his chair.

"How did you? You cannot have those!"

Myrna pushes up her skirt, then secures the harness around her thigh. His eyes follow the movement. "I am in a place I do not know without protection."

His mouth gapes like a fish, and she feels a sense of pride. She stands tall, straightening her skirt over the daggers, then cuts a slit in it for easy access.

"Knights."

"What do you expect, Kelan? You asked me to trust you, and, like an ass, I did. Then you bring me here after finding out who my mother is and shut down. You treat me like an asshole, refuse to answer any of my questions, forgetting the simple promise you made."

Kelan's expression goes perfectly blank.

"Good. You should feel bad, you piece of dung." She has the urge to shove him away.

"Princess..."

"Gah! I am not...Wait, what? I-no!" Myrna's at a loss for words. Okay, yes, she'd understood that Mother was queen, but it had all gone so fast she hadn't really taken it all in. And while in this room fuming, it never clicked what it meant that her mother was the Queen of Faerie. Not really.

The freakin'.

Queen.

Of.

Faerie.

Myrna sinks into Kelan's office chair, her legs suddenly weak.

Kelan moves to stand next to her. He drops so he is at eye level.

"You are the princess. She's confirmed it, called the high court together for your reveal. You may not have known what you were, but if it's true, you're the hope for Faerie."

"No, I'm nothing. I'm..."

He rests his hand on the arm of the chair. "We may not understand your tale, but we will. Soon, you will be confirmed as the heir and—"

"Heir?" Myrna sits upright. Her shoulders hike, and her breaths speed up. "But I don't even know what that means!"

The door swings open, making them both spin toward it. A Guardian with dark black hair and geometric designs near his hairline precedes Laoise, who strides in with powerful presence.

Myrna and Kelan stand, facing the queen. Kelan bows with a quick, "My queen," before taking Myrna's arm and leading her forward.

"Leave us!" Laoise says, so much energy in those two words, the hair on Myrna's arms stands up.

Kelan, the black-haired man, and the others she now notices eying her from the doorway step from the room. Kelan closes the door, worry flashing in his eyes, and Myrna's thighs tighten as he exits. Even if she's frustrated with him, she feels safer with him here. *Why?*

Myrna stands there silently, waiting for Laoise to speak. She is vibrating with the thousand questions itching to escape, but this situation is not a time to lose control. Mother is on edge and should she be pushed too far, Myrna or someone else will pay the price. She will not have that on her conscience.

Laoise's gaze shifts to the wall of maps, the single massive one which had captivated Myrna earlier and the more detailed ones along the adjoining wall. She floats over to them.

"These are of our kingdom," Laoise says, glancing back to Myrna. The girl takes that as an invitation and joins her mother as she continues, "The land our family has ruled over for generations. Our line has kept the people of this realm safe and the magic it holds healthy since the beginning." She runs a finger along the edge of one labeled "Tara." "Even when the Faye were of one court, did our line rule, keeping those of Faerie thriving. It's our honor and duty."

Myrna wets her lips, the confirmation of who and what they are laid out before her. Faye. She could handle this. No problem.

She meets Myrna's gaze. "Our magic connects us to this place. It keeps us healthy, as we, in return, give back. It is one of the reasons you have never felt quite at home in the human world." Laoise focuses off into the distance for a moment. Guilt, perhaps? She reconnects with Myrna. "That will be better now that you are here. But know, we are not quite what humans have written about in their ridiculous stories. We are more. We are—"

"Why didn't you tell me?" The question's out before Myrna can stop it. Inside, she winces, but outwardly, she keeps a calm exterior.

Laoise doesn't move. She doesn't attack or speak right away, and this terrifies Myrna more than her screaming would have. Laoise blinks slowly, her gaze becoming predatory.

"Come on." The exasperated words soften Laoise, so Myrna continues, "How could you not tell me about this? Not just some otherworldly creature, but royalty? Magic? Mother, if I'm so bound to the land, how could you keep me away?"

"It was necessary."

She places her hands on her cheeks. Her chest is tight, and tears burn her eyes. She shakes her head and pushes it all back. "You've said that. That there is some secret putting me in danger. Well, this is a big one. But is there more? I know in front of others I'll need to act a certain way, but right now it's just us, and I know nothing! You've left me at a disadvantage, which is the one thing that you and—"

"Do not mention that name here!" Laoise's power fills the room.

Myrna gasps and slinks back. Her heart stutters as Laoise shoves into her space, heat coming off her body in waves.

Laoise steps closer, flinging the fabric of her gown aside. "The one rule you will abide at all times is that there will be no mention of that person within this land. Do you understand?"

With her gaze lowered, she says, "Yes, ma'am." The power radiating from Laoise stings her skin like acid. Never has she felt this kind of energy from her mother. "But...why?"

Still, she cannot look up at the force which hovers over her. Myrna trembles, afraid by the creature which doesn't resemble the woman who raised her. Waves of power reverberate from her, making Myrna want to cower, ones far stronger than ever before. In her periphery, Laoise's face is pulled up in a vicious snarl, revealing several sharpened teeth. Not like the vampires in the movies Sam showed her, but definitely not human. Her eyes glow as she glares down at the youngling. The power finally becomes too much for the girl. She lowers her head, her shoulders rounding.

There's a sigh, and the energy in the room dissipates some.

It's only when a hand appears in Myrna's vision does the spell break and can she breathe normally. She squeezes her hands together, steadies herself, then she lifts her delicate fingers to take the offered hand. Myrna looks into her mother's face, which is now back to normal.

Perhaps she understands Kelan's hesitation toward Laoise more now.

Myrna allows herself to be led to the window. She holds both hands out to her daughter and, as she'd done a thousand times before, Myrna places her palms on Laoise's and slides them to grip her forearms. Laoise speaks in a low, fervent whisper just as she releases her magic into Myrna, but this time she does not hide it. Instead, she allows the youngling to see it.

Myrna gasps. "Please," she begs, nearly pulling away. "Don't bind me."

"How do you know that word?"

"I was told there's a binding on me. That's why I didn't know what I was. Why I didn't feel the magic coming in, but more that even my memories have been altered. I told them that wasn't possible. No one would change my memories." Laoise's fingers tighten painfully on her wrists, and Myrna knows it's true. "So, I'm not in my twenties?"

Laoise lifts her chin. "It is true, child. You are three and seven. The binding was, mostly, to keep you hidden from those who could track you. The rest was for you to not ask questions. Faye age differently than humans. It was for your safety, and no, I cannot explain why. I will not. But I can begin the removal of it. This will allow your magic to come in naturally from now on and you may, eventually, regain all your memories. Though they have not been altered exactly but consolidated so that the passage of time was less... noticeable."

"That's why we moved so much."

Laoise nods, and a tingling sensation spreads up Myrna's arms. "That, and the occasional tracker who'd come looking."

"I can't believe you did that." Myrna swallows around a lump in her throat. "How else could this have affected me?"

"That does not matter. You will be fine in time," Laoise says, any hurt hidden behind her well-honed mask of indifference. "Now, you listen and listen well. You are forbidden to mention your caretaker by name while in this land, or to anyone from this land, for as far as they are aware, they are dead." At Myrna's shocked expression and parting lips, Laoise narrows her eyes. "It is for their safety and yours."

Heat spreads along Myrna's fingertips the moment she agrees. It travels up her arms, spreading like fire, then around her throat. It stops there, and she coughs.

"You will be unable to speak of your caretaker until I allow it."

Fear shoots through Myrna. "What?"

"So, I deem it, and so you will abide."

The light disappears. Myrna's legs go weak. She throws a hand out to steady herself, focusing on where the burn in her throat settles into a light ache.

CHAPTER TEN

Careful Words with a Binding

A KNOCK ON THE door resonates in the air, and pride fills Laoise as Myrna pushes to an upright position. Another breath later, and the youngling is composed. No sign of the spell she'd just cast, marring Myrna's face. *It must have hurt, too.*

"Come," Laoise says, and the door instantly opens, Kelan leading the way.

His eyes land on Myrna first, examining for injury. Then three women rush in, arms full of supplies requested for Myrna: supplies to do her hair, makeup, and more. A gown hangs over the one in the front's arms, and Laoise grins. It is the one she'd ordered long ago under the guise of another's presentation.

"Kelan, please show the attendants to your chambers so they may ready the princess."

Kelan nods, then heads to the far wall. He sends his arcane magic into the hidden key in the wall and the door shifts, allowing entrance to the room beyond.

Myrna gasps. "A hidden door?"

Laoise nods. "As he is the leader of my forces, he often stays here when the nights are long. It may act as a safe room for those here should Haszwalds be breached. As long as it is not open when the enemy enters the suite, and a spell is activated in time, then no intruder shall enter."

There are more questions in Myrna's eyes, but Laoise is done with this topic. They enter a moderately sized bedroom. It is well furnished with an upholstered bed, a reading nook, and a bathroom. It's filled with items clearly his; a pair of slacks draped on the end of the bed, papers with his neat handwriting, and a novel on the bookstand.

"Lady's maid," Laoise demands, leading Myrna to the oldest of the women. "Please get her ready for presentation."

"Yes, my queen," the servant says, and Myrna follows her to the center of the room.

Myrna looks back, and Laoise sends her a warning look. *Do what I say.*

Myrna swallows and trails behind where the servants immediately get to work.

"Hello," she says hesitantly as one brushes out her hair. Another cleans off her current makeup and starts to apply a new, more appropriate, style.

Frustration hums through her at the sight of the child in this place. She is not supposed to be here. Not yet, but when Theia had called and told her that Myrna had taken an internship at Haszwalds, she'd known it was a matter of time. But *stones*, never had she guessed it would be *this* quick.

How could Theia not know she'd started the internship? How had she not known Myrna's binding was failing so badly? For five minutes in her presence and Laoise had seen it. No wonder someone as strong as Stephan and Kelan had sensed it, too.

And she'd had one day to get guards on her before Niandra had exposed everything. *That bitch.*

Laoise smirks when she notices the knives strapped to her thigh and the slit in her skirt, allowing access to the hilts. *Her training stuck. But where did she find them, for they hadn't been there before?*

It is a few moments later, when they are helping slip off her work clothes down to her undergarments, that Myrna speaks again. "What are your names?"

"You do not need to know their names! They are your servants, not your friends," Laoise hollers, and the servants all cower.

"Of course, my queen," Myrna says, bowing, "but they are being kind to me, helping me as you would, to get ready for a very important moment. Regardless if they are ordered to, they choose to be gentle. I would at least like to know their names. Please, Mother. You have taught me that all people deserve to be respected."

Every eye is on Myrna, shock and awe a tangible thing. But it is when they shift to Laoise that heat rises, building from deep within to heat her skin. She is not wrong, but to speak such here may change how she is seen.

"Bah!" Laoise slashes her hand through the air, and the servants jump away. She stomps, with as much grace as she does anything, to the dress draped on the bed and picks it up. "You, my darling, are a menace."

Myrna grins as Laoise reaches her. To the servants, she says, "You are dismissed. She looks well enough. Close the door behind you."

They stand and hustle from the room, a quick, "Yes, my queen," coming from Alyn.

Just before they disappear, Myrna says, "Thank you!"

Laoise growls, and Myrna shudders. *Good.*

She holds the dress low for Myrna to step into. With all the helpers gone, Laoise says, "The eldest is Alyn. She is your lady's maid. The other two are Giselda and Mora."

Myrna rests a hand on Laoise's shoulder for balance, a small smile on her face, but she releases Laoise quickly as she pulls the gown up. Laoise moves to the back and begins the process of strapping her in.

"Once we are done here, I will leave you with Guardian Kelan. You will stay by his side at all times, do you understand?" Laoise pulls on the strings of the corset, and Myrna grunts.

"Yes, Mother."

"He will take you to the Grand Hall, where I will tell a story." Yank. Gasp. "This is the one you will memorize. It is the one you will use moving forward. When people ask for the names of those who took care of you, you do not know their names. You referred to them as 'madam' or 'mister' as appropriate. I came to visit regularly, but made sure you were not informed of your true heritage to keep you safe. You were unsure of your exact age or your father's identity."

This was the truth, and it reddened Myrna's cheeks with anger.

"Do you understand?"

Myrna nods, even as she presses her hands to her ribs. The girl looks back at Laoise through the mirror with scared eyes, as if she does not know Laoise. Perhaps she does not. This is the first time Laoise has shown her true self to Myrna—her true self.

She better get used to it.

Laoise adds, "You shall never mention the exact locations of your homes in case someone goes looking. That is for her safety."

Myrna swallows, but nods again. Myrna would do anything to keep Theia safe; Laoise is sure. "Of course." Myrna bites her lip. "But you know? Who my father is, I mean?"

Keeping secrets is part of Laoise's life. Never has she known a time where she didn't have a secret to hide. But this one? It weighs down heavily on both Theia and Laoise. It could change the very structure of Faerie.

It might end a war, but it could also start one.

Laoise narrows her eyes, then ties off the dress. "Yes."

That's it. One word for confirmation. Hard and sure and lacking any willingness to elaborate.

"That's it?" Myrna says, turning to Laoise.

Perhaps she needs a reminder of the rules. Laoise snatches Myrna's wrist and digs her nails in deep until red blooms at the connections. "Yes. That is it. You have no right to question me, for I am queen. Do as I say, or I will make sure you remember what happens if you disobey." Myrna pulls away, dragging Laoise's nails along her skin, and Laoise adds, "Must I remind you of your previous lessons?"

Myrna's throat works. "No."

"As well," Laoise snarls, and releases her. Laoise heads toward the door, Myrna on her tail. "Stay beside Kelan at all times. Understood?"

"Yes, Mother."

The door opens as if the person on the other side knows she approaches, and Kelan's face appears. He bows and takes them in.

"Majesty," he says, stepping to the side to let them pass.

Head high, nose turned up, Laoise addresses the handsome man who was once her sister's best friend, as inseparable as Laoise was with her Fianna. A pang of sadness flashes, but Laoise pushes it down almost as quickly as it appears.

It's this knowledge, and his loyalty since, that outlines why he will be trusted with Myrna's safety moving forward. He will protect her if only for how much Myrna resembles the Mareola at that age, her facial features matching more of Laoise's mother than her own. But it is her eyes that speak of her lineage.

"Guardian, I am off to ready myself for the ceremony. Follow once your full guard is here, and head straight there. And, Sweetling?" She glances at Myrna, whose eyes light hopefully at the use of her nickname. "Do not embarrass me." Laoise's tone is biting, a threatening lilt to her voice.

Myrna stares blankly at Laoise. "I know my place. You and"—she chokes and presses a hand to her throat—"you've taught me well."

With a satisfied smile, Laoise quits the room.

CHAPTER ELEVEN

Admiral Younglingsitter

KNIGHTS. SHE'S BESPELLED HER *own daughter.*

This entire exchange has Kelan on edge. Hell, everything about the day has his emotions on edge. Today has not gone the way he'd expected, not in any way, shape, or form. Having the girl Stephan arbitrarily mentioned turn out to be Queen Laoise's daughter? Nope, there was no way to see that coming. But the way the two interact has him thinking that perhaps the old Laoise isn't completely lost to them, but then this.

The door *snicks* closed, and Myrna releases a slow, controlled breath. She blinks, and her entire body relaxes; not back into that of the intern from downstairs, but to that of a different creature. One of power and grace, royal training ingrained even if she had not known that was what it was, for she mirrors Laoise's stance and expression far too well. Or perhaps it's a royal gift, passed down in the Qhuinn family. And yet, Kelan can see through it. Her mother's presence had been too much for the youngling as well.

"Are you all right?" Kelan asks, worry spinning through him faster than he would like to admit.

Myrna presses her palms to her stomach and lifts her eyes to his. "Of course. Why would I not be? Are we ready?"

Kelan scans her face, but apparently Myrna does not appreciate the inspection. She's pissed as she heads for the door.

He uses those moments to take in her transformation: the gown of gold chiffon with black diamonds embellishing one sleeve. There is a contrasting pattern on the opposite ribs. From the fitted waist, the skirt begins to flare and the gold, brilliant in its sparkling glory, slowly changes to vibrant magenta. Near the ends it darkens, the tone shifting to match that of Laoise's hair, a deep penetrating red.

A familiar tang of copper hits his nose, bitter against his senses but with a hint of sweetness that has his blood flaring. His lips fight to curl, his fangs tingling as he takes in the red marks along Myrna's wrist. Between four and six inches long, most are not bad, but a few are deep, red welling where the queen's nails have sliced the skin.

The marks are familiar, made by claws as known to him as his own. Both on his skin and others.

The wounds, the lies, and now this? Kelan presses his tongue to the back of his canines. It does nothing to release the urge to retaliate, but it helps abate the need to dig his teeth into the queen. Still, he doesn't shift his expression from the blank nothingness of a soldier's readiness. He cannot. He will not break his training. Not for some girl he barely knows. But more importantly, he will not break the promise of his oldest friend even if she's no longer here. No matter how much he despises Laoise.

He will, however, help the princess before she enters the Great Hall. It will not help to have her seen as marked by her queen. Not this soon. It is not fair that Laoise would do this to her own daughter.

Kelan rushes forward to reach the door first, but before he checks if the others are ready, he pulls a dark red cloth from his tunic and slips it into her right hand. Her fingers close around the cloth instantly, blinking in surprise. Keeping her face neutral, she moves to clean the blood from her skin. She refuses to make eye contact with him, and his blood heats.

Fine. He could understand that.

So, he changes the topic, understanding how one interaction with Laoise Qhuinn can wipe away every ounce of confidence one has. "Once we leave here, there will be a full contingent of Guardians surrounding you until we get to the palace. We will pass through the main thoroughfare, then past several layers of wards, which protect the portal into the palace. This portal can be activated by either a high-level Royal Guardian or one of the ruling family. Once in the palace, we've been instructed to head straight to the Grand Hall where the ceremony will commence. Do you understand?"

Myrna swallows, then hands the cloth back to Kelan. "I understand."

"Then if you are—"

Myrna lifts her hand and places it on his chest, her eyes locked on the symbol over his heart.

Kelan freezes but doesn't pull away. He really can't without slamming into the door behind him. She's locked on the formal tunic he wears with the symbol on the front—a Hawthorn tree with a snow-white owl perched in its branches. It is as if the insignia enslaves her attention.

"It's like a dream," she whispers, unfocused. "Large eyes staring at me from the trees. Always guarding. The rustle of wings in the darkness of night." Her eyes flash up to his. "But then there'd be tapping at my window and the silhouette of a child, but the soft song of the owl."

"You had a protector?"

Kelan grasps her palm, his thumb along the soft skin. He lowers her hand and releases it.

"Huh?" Myrna clears her throat, blinking away whatever trance she was in. "Apologies, Mr. Daniels. I...I got distracted."

Lines appear between his brows. "It's fine."

"But what is this?" she asks, gesturing to the emblem again.

"It is the symbol of our court. Your court." His gaze locks on her face, so intense as she examines the insignia. With a shake of his head, he shifts his gaze up and says, "By the way, my name is not really Daniels. It's Brynes. Kelan Brynes, but you'll call me Guardian."

This catches Myrna's attention. Guardian.

"What's a Guardian? Mother used that word before."

"Specially trained soldiers of the crown. Sworn to the ruling clan and held to a certain code of honor."

"And why should I call you 'just Guardian?'" When he doesn't respond, she steps just a bit closer, making his heart speed up. Her vanilla scent fills his nose. *Why does this youngling affect me so? I am no adolescent.*

She places her hands on her hips. "Tell me what's going on right now, Kelan. You're acting weird."

Perhaps being honest is the best option for her. "How would you know if I was acting weird?" She glares, and he has to fight the urge to grin. With a sigh, he continues, "You would not address me so informally. People will talk."

"Talk about what? I've been here for like three seconds!"

"I am a servant to the crown, and many witnessed the scene in the elevator." He stares into her eyes, but she isn't getting it. "A servant to you, and it's my duty to protect you. You don't know our ways, but you will. Those not of your class are referred to by their position alone or not at all. If you call me by name, they will think...things."

Myrna snorts. With a pat to his chest, she turns and stalks a few steps away. "Yeah. Sure. Whatever."

"I'm serious, Princess," Kelan snaps.

Myrna rolls her eyes. "Don't worry. I doubt they'll have any reason to believe that you'd debase yourself in such a manner."

To his surprise, that gets a physical reaction from him. He spins her toward him, her gown billowing around her. She gasps as the heat of his rather impressive form seeps into her from where their chests press together.

"You think they or I care about whatever shame of yours"—he grabs her hand and lifts her wrist to eye level—"caused these? You are not the first person to be marked by Queen Laoise, and you will not be the last. All they care about is that you are beautiful and that although I am a high-ranking Guardian, I am still just a Guardian."

Myrna stiffens in his arms. She yanks her hand from his, then shoves at his chest with more force than he'd expect. A wave of power, unexpected and uncontrolled, hits him. Then she yells, "My shame? Screw you, Kelan! You don't know why these are here." Myrna stomps past him toward the door, slamming her shoulder against his along the way. She rips the door open to the shocked faces of eight very surprised Guardians.

"Awesome, more of you." She spins and points a finger in his direction. "And so you know, *Guardian Kelan,* you think far too highly of yourself." Then she strides, without waiting for any of them, back toward Haszwalds.

He thinks too highly of himself? He had meant that she was...that she was better than he.

The Guardians rush to catch up, immediately falling into formation around her as she fumes.

Kelan does too, after speaking with Alyn and sending her and one Guardian on a mission of their own. There may as well be arcane power seeping from her with how much tension she radiates. *Damn his stupid tongue.*

He must make things better, for she cannot enter the ceremony like this. Taking his spot to her left and a very dangerous chance, he says, "So, I hope your meetings have gone well so far this morning."

It's what she said to him earlier, on the way to speak with Cindy.

Myrna stops walking, as if almost against her will. The squad of Guardians remain around them. Her posture stays beautifully perfect, her silhouette pristine for one breath, until she turns her face slowly toward him.

Calmly, she says, "It's been interesting. Not what I expected for the day."

"For me as well." He holds out his arm, a peace offering, which she has every right to refuse. Kelan holds his breath.

Myrna looks down, then smiles frustratedly, but she slips her fingers around his forearm. They continue on, out of his wing, into the traversing rooms where nearly fifty now wait to catch a glimpse of Myrna, through the first ward, past three security checkpoints, down one flight of stairs, through two more sets of wards, up another set, and through a portal protected by even more Guardians.

It takes them a while and, by the end, Myrna's pupils are blown wide as if overwhelmed with all she's seen. Of course, that is more likely the effect of the various wards and her first portal trip.

"Where are we?" she asks once they're through.

"The security wing of the palace," Kelan explains. "We still have a bit of a walk to go, and I know you will want to look around, but we can't. We're already behind on time. Getting you through security took longer than we expected."

She doesn't complain. They make their way, her arm still linked with his, releasing him once when she needs to heft that beast of a dress up to traverse a step. Apparently, it weighs more than she does. *Damn you, Laoise.*

They turn down the last hallway, and Kelan releases a breath when he sees Alyn waiting for them. Thank Faerie. The lady-in-waiting runs forward, a Guardian stopping her.

Kelan waves her forward.

"Guardian, I have what you requested." Alyn holds out the smoothly folded cloth to Kelan, and he takes it. "They are finger-less to allow the pinprick but will cover the rest."

"Thank you, madam." Kelan inclines his head, then turns to Myrna, who examines him with interest. He holds out his hand, asking, "May I?"

Myrna frowns but places her fingers in his. Deftly, he slides a glove over her flesh until it weaves between her fingers, over her wrists, and up to her elbow. The lace is exquisite. Black like the crystal and similar in pattern to the bodice of the dress Myrna wears. She's frozen as Kelan examines her wrist to verify the scratches are appropriately hidden.

The Guardian does the same with the other hand. This time, he cannot help but run a thumb along the red mark, just barely visible. "There. Now no one will misunderstand as I did."

The breathing that had become deep and welcoming suddenly hitches. Her lips part, and she pulls her gloved hand to her chest. She doesn't say a word in response until she turns to the servant.

Myrna's expression softens before she says, "Thank you, Alyn. I appreciate this kindness. It means more than you know."

The servant fidgets, her mouth dropping open. Several others around the hall have glanced her way. They have a right to be surprised. It's been many years since one of the Qhuinn clan treated those of the lower classes so well. Let alone called one by name. It makes him wonder how she knows it.

"You are very welcome, Highness." Alyn bows and scurries backward, disappearing into a darkened alcove.

Totally unaware of the disruption she's caused, Myrna faces forward just as the queen's head attendant, Sola, approaches. The poor female looks as though rotting fish fills her nose.

Without saying anything, she holds out a sealed letter. Kelan takes it and opens it.

Kelan,

Once the ceremony is over, return Myrna to her rooms, where she will remain. She is to learn our ways—our customs, histories, strategies—so that she may be of use to me. There will be no other distractions. As such, you are now assigned as her personal guard. You are responsible to manage her protections and answer questions. Readings will be provided, and I will call on her when it is time for additional lessons.

Myrna, this is what you've been trained for. Do not let me down.

P.S. Should either of you fail me, you will not like the outcome.

– Queen Laoise of Faerie

Kelan grinds his teeth but makes sure to keep his expression clear of all emotion. A *younglingsitter? Is he being demoted?*

If anyone notices any shift within him, it will make it back to Laoise, especially with Sola standing watch. So, he does nothing and leans into the centuries of training to keep himself stable.

Yet he needs to understand. He's the head of the Guardians, the Admiral of the Queen's Army. How is he supposed to do that while acting as the personal babysitter of the princess? This had to be temporary. It had to be...

Kelan shows Myrna the letter, for which the only tell she gives is the slight tremble of her hands. Based on his minimal experience with the girl, he assumes it's anger. She clasps them before her to hide it.

"Thank you, Sola. We will see it done," he says, knowing the message the queen sends by deciding to share this news as they enter the hall. He glances at Myrna. "It is time."

Myrna nods, closing her eyes for one heartbeat.

The doors before them sweep open with burst of wind that smells of moss and fresh blooming wildflowers. Without hesitation, the youngling glides into the room filled with vipers. For that is what they are. The highest class of Faye. Most of which have too much power, land, and influence. They believe themselves better than the rest; sections of Kelan's family among them.

CHAPTER TWELVE

Confirmation in Blood and Court

IT DIDN'T USE TO be this way. When Queen Aoife, Laoise's mother, was in power, the Court of The Radiant Sun was so very different. It was joyful, filled with happiness and the pleasures of life so many took for granted. Then the war started anew, and the universe darkened. The battle was long and hard. So many died—Queen Aoife, the princess, honorable Faye, and his and Laoise's best friends alike. When Laoise was crowned queen, everything changed.

Even the girl with red-tipped locks.

Kelan remains one step behind Myrna, her ever-present guard as they enter the packed room. Those gathered stand in a half circle around the dais, a path between them wide as they watch the girl enter with the grace of a royal. Even as they do, they keep one eye on the queen. Smart, for she is the real threat.

Myrna's a sight to behold in this room, so unlike the rest of the palace. Floors of polished marble shine in moonlight, spilling through six massive windows, three on each side. Above, intricate bracing contrasts the color of the stone, making the room more magnificent. It gives it a sense of ancient glee while bringing it into the modern era. The colors are brighter, less rich, and pull of the cleaner lines of magic. Kelan has always wondered why. Perhaps Laoise was bored, or perhaps she enjoyed throwing people off. Probably the latter.

Either way, as if instantaneously, the room has been transformed to match the dress of the princess and the new gown the queen dons. Which means, instead of wildflowers, there are ones of black and red with darkest green foliage falling from the ceiling and walls. Plus a few the exact color of Myrna's ice-blue eyes. Pops of brilliance against the dark to match the Qhuinn house. And it is magnificent.

Below a cascade of beauty, and upon the dais taking up the back of the room, stands Laoise. Her elegant gown billows out around her, the train expanding backward nearly six feet. The same dark jewels which line the neck of Myrna's gown are on her mother's train. They start at the bottom; dense, but then thin as they reach slowly up her body to reveal more and more of the red fabric beneath. They create a pattern similar to bark that stops near her hips.

Laoise watches Myrna, her face filled with the most emotion he's seen from her in a century. It is pride, and a warning for anyone who would harm her. It shines brighter than anything he's ever seen.

When Myrna reaches the stairs, Kelan steps forward and holds a hand out, which she takes, stepping artfully up to join the queen. He stays below, his hand on his sword and obsidian dagger strapped to his waist. He keeps one eye on the princess, the other on the crowd, for should a threat come, it will be from them.

"Subjects," Laoise says, her stance a perfect mirror to her daughter's. "Today we have had quite a shift. You are confused by this youngling who has entered our world so unexpectedly with a block placed upon her, and whom I have welcomed into my home." Laoise clasps her fingers across her lower abdomen, her eyes scanning the room filled with guests. "Well, the wait for answers is over. This youngling is not just any. She is of my blood, of the Qhuinn womb, and is under the protection of me and the throne I hold."

Myrna lifts her chin and faces the crowd, staring them down exactly as he'd expect her to do. It's impressive. She doesn't give away how nervous she is, which she must be. Hell, there is even a tingle of warning running up the back of his thighs. The judgmental and threatening glares of these particular Faye can do that to a person.

Myrna's gaze flashes to somewhere in the corner.

Kelan follows the path, only to find Niandra glaring. Laser beams based on the hatred she's throwing at the girl. *Okay.* His jaw clenches, his fingers flexing around the hilt of his sword. Kelan steps into Niandra's line of sight and catches her eye. He shakes his head, and she looks down, her shoulders dropping in frustrated resignation.

Laoise takes Myrna's hand, a gesture not meant to be comforting, but Kelan can see the slight softening at the corner of her mouth.

To his relief, another face comes in view. Stephan. Also witnessing the exchange, he shifts to keep watch. *At least she has one friend here.*

The queen guides Myrna toward the crowd and announces, "It is my honor to formally introduce to you, Myrna Mareola Sunrise of the Qhuinn line! In her seventh decade and blessed to mine line by a Guardian of appropriate standing, she will soon complete the changing and ascend to her place as heir."

Her true name. Kelan gulps. *Named for Mareola…*

There is a soft lift to Myrna's lips as she scans the crowd, and Kelan frowns, a jolt hitting him right in the chest. This image is so familiar. Two girls with pale hair, one red-tipped, the other with a pixie nose and ice-blue eyes.

"It is time for the ceremony." Laoise leads Myrna to a male waiting off to the side.

"That's it?" a voice speaks up from the crowd. "That's all you're going to explain? We need to understand her conception, parentage, and why you kept her from us all these years! If she's going to be heir—"

Power fills the room like a heavy blanket. Kelan had readied for it the instant the fool spoke, but still. The queen focuses her attention on the crowd, causing several to drop to their knees at her violent outrage. Kelan, who didn't get the full blast, is sweating.

"You dare question me!" Laoise steps down from the stage. Her voice is dark and threatening. Her eyes narrow, and another burst of heat flows through the room.

"I told you what I wish. Her father was an honorable Guardian, but—" Laoise lowers her gaze and inhales through her nose, a hitch audible to everyone. Kelan frowns. "I will add that he died in the war after she was conceived, in love, during a time of fear and hatred, but for which brought forth light." Laoise blinks as if coming out of a haze. "I hid her for her safety, for there are those inside and outside the court who'd wish her harm. But now, she is of age, close to the changing and not without her own protections. But none of that matters as she is a Qhuinn under *my* protection."

"But we deserve—"

"Isaac of the McGoverns..." The words crackle like wood burning red under the flame's fiery touch.

Those around the male take a step back while he goes pale. His lips part. "M-majesty," he stutters.

Yes, you fool. You have mis-stepped.

His gaze flashes from the floor, but even in his fine tunic, the brocade elaborate in its make, the sign of his tension's there. The tightened shoulders, the badly hidden pants for air, and the trembling hands. At least he is not stupid.

A guard appears—apparently at some unseen signal from Laoise. Isaac swallows before looking straight into the eye of the queen.

Laoise gestures for Isaac to come to her—one long finger beckoning him closer. When he does not move immediately, the guard pushes him forward.

His breathing speeds. "I did not mean to speak out of turn, Majesty. I beg of you."

Laoise takes a step down to where Issac stands. The queen lowers her chin and glares. With lightning quick reflexes, her hand shoots out. Long fingers wrap around Isaac's neck. He gasps but does not struggle. "This is not the first time one of your clan has spoken out of turn. You McGoverns think so highly of yourselves, of your power, but let me remind you..."

Heat fills the room as Laoise releases her arcane power.

Kelan moves closer to Laoise, staying between Myrna and the queen as the princess begins to draw forward. His guess is this is the first time she will see Laoise, Queen of the Faerie Realm.

Laoise's hair blows back from her face, a wind made not from air, but from the power she wields alone. Expression never changing, calm cruelty and determined righteousness, Laoise's hand begins to glow red.

Isaac's eyes go wild, and he tries to back away, but the guard is there to stop him. He cries out, "Please, Majesty. I'm sorry."

Flame seeps from beneath her hand, inching out. It first crawls up her wrist to her arm, then when Laoise deems it, changes its path to encircle the courtier's neck like a vice.

Isaac's screams of agony fill the hall as many look away, but Myrna? She stares, horrified. When she moves to interrupt, moving at an angle and coming down two steps, Kelan rushes to intercept.

He wraps his fingers around her elbow, making sure his body blocks the view of his touch from the crowd. In a low, harsh whisper, he says, "Myrna, stop!"

She fights, saying, "This is cruelty. I need to—"

Kelan tightens his grip just enough that she glances at him. His words are ardent when he says, "This is punishment. You need to understand that this is a lesson as much for him as it is for you. This is Faerie. Go back to your spot, or you will break your word."

Her eyes clear of the panic as if his words finally break through. "What about…"

"He will be fine. Watch." Kelan drops his hold and steps back to give her space but does not go far, should she change her mind or need his support.

Luckily, Laoise is just about done. The male before her is barely standing now, held up by her grip alone, and the fire is receding. When she lets go, he falls to the floor in a heap. "Take him from my sight. Have him watched, then allow tending."

"Yes, my queen," the Guardian says before bending down and hefting the half-conscious male over his shoulder.

The raised red and purple burns where her fire touched make Kelan nauseous. Healing from such wounds hurts. That she demands he sit with them for a while before being treated... Kelan shivers, then looks at Myrna.

Laoise spins and approaches Myrna and Kelan. "Guardian, do you have a cloth?"

Kelan doesn't hesitate. He removes a clean handkerchief from his pocket and hands it to her.

She nods once, then wipes her hands. When she hands it back, she says, "There was skin on my nails." Then, as if that wasn't horrific, she turns to Myrna and smiles. "All right, child, why don't we finish the ceremony? I know today has been a long one, and you need your rest."

Myrna looks like she's about to run. She settles her panting breaths; then, with one last terrified glance to Kelan, says, "Yes, Mother. I am quite tired."

Laoise brushes a hand—the non-skin hand—down Myrna's arm. "We are good here, Guardian. You may return to your post."

Kelan bows. "Yes, Majesty."

He steps from the stage and retakes his position between the princess and the crowd. Slowly, the crowd returns to its previous position.

"Teirnan," Laoise starts, "may we please move forward with the ceremony? I tire of this charade."

The wrinkles on Teirnan's ancient face scrunch at the corner of his eyes as he shakes his head. "My dear, this is important. If she's truly your blood, then she deserves to be cherished." Teirnan has the gall to pat the queen's hand before lifting to press his fingers to Myrna's cheek. "You do have the eyes. Do you not? Come, child."

They shift so both of their clasped hands are visible to the entire room. Teirnan swipes the cape he wears out of the way as he pulls a dagger from his waist. It's short, maybe twelve inches in length, and made of the specialty stone of those from honored classes; Guardians among them. Black obsidian sharpened and treated, but rarely used for the spell to harden it can only be performed by the rarest of the Faye.

A pedestal of glorious white stone stands tall and the three circle it. Sitting atop it is a small black bowl less than three inches in diameter.

Teirnan faces Myrna, the object between them, while Laoise stands next to them facing the crowd. "Princess Myrna, this ceremony would've been performed on the day of your birth, but seeing as this was not an option, we'll do so today. It is a simple ritual, really. I will cut your hand, say a few words while connecting my arcane magic to that of Faerie itself, and she will show us not just that you are of the royal line, but that you are a Qhuinn." He leans in and whispers as if imparting a secret, "I am especially happy that I'm one to be blessed with this task as I performed this ritual for both your mother and aunt."

"Really?" When he nods, Myrna grins and places her hands over the bowl, palms up. It's like she knows what to do. "And how will we know?"

"You will see, child."

Kelan restrains himself as Teirnan lifts the obsidian blade. Teirnan takes her hand in his and presses the tip to the pad of her middle finger. Myrna doesn't even flinch as red wells and blood falls into the bowl below. A stream of droplets, quick and dark. Then Tiernan pulls a cloth from his tunic and wipes the blade.

As he sheaths the black weapon, he hands over the tissue. "Please."

"Thank you," Myrna replies, wrapping it around the wound. Her face never changes from that perfect calm demeanor.

Tiernan places his palms on either side of the bowl, then closes his old eyes. His brows drop low in concentration. Energy fills the room, the power no less for his age, and the air thickens as the particles shift, the water responding as it always had to the old male. His eyes open and the silver which rings the pupils shines.

Myrna smiles, releasing an innocent, joyful sound.

Kelan barely resists the urge to react. Why her reactions affect him so confuses him. Perhaps it's the way she reminds him of his old friend. Or more, it's the innocence she holds. Will this world burn that innocence out?

The crimson droplets lift into the air. They dance, a snake-like trail of grace and beauty.

Tiernan chants an old spell few remember, for the words are spoken in a language long dead. Though they're familiar, they're no longer understood.

Kelan's grandmother once did. She'd sing to him in these words, this tone, but no longer. She's long since found peace in the ground, yet he finds peace in hearing them again.

The old man scans the princess as she watches him.

Unable to resist the pull, Kelan moves forward. He tells himself that it's the need to be between the princess and the crowd, who've all advanced too, the draw of the magic great. But there's more to the truth still. There's the taste of honesty held within this moment. Held within Myrna, herself. He's sensed it since that first moment. Stephan did, too. She tastes like possibility, like everything they've ever wanted.

Let everyone believe it be the spell.

Kelan looks to Laoise and finds her already watching him. Her breathing's faster than before and it's as if she knows what he's thinking. Her eyes flick to Myrna and then back to him. He does not miss the worry. Kelan nods, understanding what she asks.

He will protect her with all he is.

Myrna sighs and closes her eyes. Her head falls back, hands lifting to rest on the pedestal inches from Tiernan's. The instant her hands touch the stone, she begins to glow.

She's radiant, her golden locks lightening to an almost-white hue, and Kelan's heart warms. Her skin's so pale except for the rosy pink at the peaks of her cheekbones.

The high court it too close, and Kelan growls low. He cannot help it. His hand grips the sword, palms itching to remove the weapon from its scabbard. Two more Guardians appear, taking similar positions.

Kelan doesn't see the blood react, but the truth is revealed in the faces of each person in the crowd. Their eyes widen as they drop to one knee. In each face is something that's been missing from Faerie for a very long time.

Hope. Dreams. Joy.

And Kelan realizes that for the first time in forever, he feels it, too.

He felt it the first time his magic attached to Myrna's, and it terrifies him.

"Her line is confirmed," Tiernan calls.

Kelan turns, vision becoming watery at the sight of the shining, silver blood weaving in intricate circles and creating the shape of an owl. Three more breaths and it disappears.

The symbol of the Qhuinn line and the crown.

CHAPTER THIRTEEN

Bite & Boundaries

THE SLAM OF THE massive doors to her suite has Myrna jumping to wakefulness. Her chest heaves as a swarm of attendants buzz into the room, spreading throughout the space like locusts. It's the most people she's seen since Kelan dropped her off here and told her to make herself comfortable.

Three women rush in, their arms full of gowns from another age. Chiffon fabric of the palest pink. Silk in colors of the deepest blue or yellow, pink or purple.

"Um..." Myrna raises a hand. "Hello?"

None acknowledge her. None look her way. They continue on their way into the room beyond. Myrna runs a hand through her hair.

The attendant, Alyn, who'd dressed her for presentation, hurries over to her. She's older than the rest, which means nothing, considering what she's dealing with. Of course, her knowledge of the Faye was limited, confined to the folklore provided in the few books read with Theia and spoken about as though ancient mythology had gotten it all wrong.

"Morning, Mistress." She bows low, her hands clasped before her. "It is time to ready you for the day." The woman's striking dark black curls fall to her chin. Her pointed ears and her rather unassuming face are made remarkable by the vibrancy of her silvery blue eyes. She's uniquely beautiful. But this is seriously diminished in Myrna's opinion when Alyn doesn't wait for Myrna's response and, instead, throws back the covers and grabs the youngling's ankle as if to drag her from the bed.

Myrna yanks free of her grip. Who does she think she is? Is this the way she's seen already? Not from the court—not from this land—and so easily manhandled? A child, a youngling as they say, found in the human world and unaware of the Faye and their customs. Kelan had warned her of that much, at least.

Myrna grits her teeth and, in a voice learned from her mother, she says, "You will not put your hands on me without my permission." It is stern; absolute. Perhaps darker than necessary. But she will not be overrun. Mother's taught her better even if she understands it will separate her further from those she wishes to befriend. Her chest becomes heavy, her heart pierced with a needle no one can see. As the room goes silent, the air becomes bitter to her nose.

Those around her freeze; their eyes lock on Myrna.

Slowly, gracefully, Myrna slips from the bed to stand. She's purposeful and powerful in her movements. *They were readying me all this time because they knew this would happen one day.* Another pin to her heart with realization, but she hides her wince. The two people she could always trust to never lie to her always had. Pushing those thoughts away, she faces the attendant.

"Alyn, I'm more than willing to work with you, but you *will* treat me as an adult and not as some insignificant child. I was raised by Queen Laoise and although it was not here in court, I assure you, I am my mother's daughter."

Several of the girls in the room shrink back, fear filling their eyes. Two steps away. Even Alyn flinches and drops her gaze.

Myrna instantly turns contrite. *But I do not wish them to be afraid of me.*

"I didn't mean to scare you." She sighs and relaxes her shoulders. Running both hands through her hair, she scratches her head and groans. With a glance around the room, she continues, "I just meant that I don't like being manhandled. It's been a long twenty-four hours." With a harsh exhale, her cheeks puff out. "I'm a little on edge."

Two of the younger girls who are hanging up the dresses in the back smile kindly. The one with teal green hair smirks and nods.

"I could, however, use some guidance."

Alyn grins and bows slightly. "That we can understand, Highness. And are more than willing to help, and I'm sorry for crossing a line." She holds her hand out, gesturing toward the bathing room. "Shall we?"

Myrna smiles, and they head into the bathing chamber. Over the next hour, Myrna showers in one of the most elaborate bathrooms she's ever seen. Water flows down from a massive showerhead; one that can be described as heavenly. Whoever created the lie that the Faye were without the luxuries of the human world was wrong. Very wrong. That's not to say the bath isn't ridiculously large. The darn thing can probably fit three people in it. One day, she'll have to try it out. Alone, of course!

Afterward, Alyn and the two other servants do her hair and makeup. She is put in a simple day dress—which is hardly simple—and then she's shown to the main room, where a slew of books wait.

As the three females—which she now understands they prefer to be called—start to leave, she says, "Thank you all. I appreciate your time and what you've done for me today."

Shock flits across each and every face. They're clearly not used to acknowledgement or thanks. The two young ladies bow, then disappear through the door at a near run.

"Did I say something wrong?" Myrna asks.

"No, Highness." Alyn smiles softly. It is her turn to bow. "It was our pleasure. Please call on us if you require anything. If not, I will see you this evening."

Myrna takes a seat, and it is not long before her stomach starts to grumble. She hadn't thought to ask about breakfast. Putting the book she was skimming down, Myrna stands and heads to the door. *Perhaps there's a kitchen or cafeteria nearby.*

She makes it one step out before two males step in her path. Both wear uniforms similar to what Kelan had worn yesterday, but with different markings on the shoulders.

"Return to your rooms, Princess," the taller one with blond hair says. It's longer on the top than the sides, and he has green eyes with red variegations, making them stand out.

They look like leaves. "Excuse me?" She shakes her head. "I just wanted to go get breakfast. Is there a cafeteria or something?"

"We will have food brought to you," the one with short, dark brown curls says. "Return to your room, please."

Myrna stutters, "W-wait, am I not allowed to leave?"

The two Guardians stare down at her in a move she recognizes as pure intimidation.

Her arms cross over her chest before she can think better of it. "Where is Guardian Kelan? I wish to speak with him. Now."

"He is at training, but will return—"

Irritation burns within her. He can go to training, but she can't? Unfair! She thought the message said he was her personal guard. If that were true, why couldn't she go with him?

She tries to move past them, but to her surprise, the Guardians stop her. With force. They pick her up, each taking an arm, and walk her back into her suite.

"Do not touch me!" she screams, kicking out and making contact with one's side. He grunts but does not let go.

They set her down near the couch and the pile of books.

"Sit. Read. Learn," the blond one says. "We will have food brought up."

"What about Kelan or my mother?" she asks, following them.

"They will come in due time."

Then they disappear out into the hallway and shut the door with a resounding *thunk.*

Oh, hell to the fuck no. She will be having a conversation with Kelan. She'd just have to decide if it'll be bloody or not.

CHAPTER FOURTEEN

Bloody Trouble!

KELAN RUNS HIS HANDS through his golden brown locks and tugs. Torchlight flickers in the hallway as he walks toward Myrna's rooms, casting eerie shadows on the ancient tapestries lining the walls. The ceilings arch above in gorgeous sections that draw the eye and remind each visitor of the magnificence of the crown held within these walls. There is a weight to the history and power of this place, as if the very stones whisper of the joy that once graced these hallways, but also the pain, too. Always the pain.

It is a warning.

Reaching the entrance to the princess's chambers sends a wave of reluctance through his warrior heart, but not for reasons he'd reveal to anyone alive. For this room was once another princess's. One who meant a great deal to him, his childhood friend and closest confidant.

Kelan finds it sad that the three days since Myrna's arrival into their world hadn't dampened his reaction to this part of the palace. Perhaps he'd avoided it too long.

Two of his guards stand before the door, swords at their waists.

"Any trouble?" There'd been an emergency and so his return had been delayed, which meant Myrna had been alone in that room for most of the day. The guilt of that sat like an itch at the back of his neck.

Isaiah winces. "She tried to sneak out. Again."

He stills. "Again?" The word comes out slow.

Jaden, the more senior Guardian, takes over the report. "We didn't think anything of it the first night. She didn't try very hard, but last night was…" He rests his palm on the hilt of his sword. "Different."

"You didn't hurt her." It's a statement and a question in one.

Jaden shakes his head, shifting on his feet as if needing the space from the power emanating from Kelan. "But we did have to restrain her and lock the room up tight. You might want to speak to her about the dangers of falling from the third story."

Isaiah nods. "It might be a good idea to have someone in the room with her at all times. She's sneakier than expected."

Goddess help me. Kelan nods. "When your replacements arrive, let them know I'm inside. I'll speak to her."

"Yes, Guardian," they say in unison.

With a breath for patience, for he always seems to need it with Myrna, Kelan knocks. There's no response. It's as if a hand trails along the backs of his legs, up his spine, and across his neck. His eyes flick to Jaden.

"Not again," he whines.

Kelan turns the knob and steps into the suite. The lights are out, the early morning sun not yet high enough to fill the room with its rays. He scans the room, the shadows as well, but Myrna is nowhere to be found.

Not hidden in the rich tapestries adorning the walls, their colors muted by time. They sing of the girl whose room this once was not of the one currently occupying it. Nor by the grand canopy bed whose drapes of a deep lavender fall like water. It stands against one wall, its elegance contrasting with the faint air of melancholy left with her passing. And with it, there is no sign of Myrna. Even though she has been here, the only indication is the books which lay spread across the table in the seating area.

Kelan's careful not to make a sound; for when Myrna gives away her position, he doesn't want to miss it. She can't escape, but also…knowing who her mother is, he won't take chances.

It wouldn't be the first time she punched him. That had been a surprise.

From somewhere deeper in the room, there's a low curse and the sound of broken tile. He moves through the seating room, past the doors which take one to the balcony and into the bedroom. On the right is a wall of windows. They're sectioned, the tops opening for air flow.

She couldn't have.

Another tile falls from the roof just above the window.

"You've got to be kidding me," Isaiah says. "Who is this girl?"

"Is it raining?" Jaden asks, concern lining his voice.

Kelan doesn't respond, but clenches his teeth together and rushes toward the balcony. He unlatches the lock using the key Jaden hands him, then calculates the best route onto the roof.

Blasted hell. It isn't just raining. In the last few minutes, the sky has opened up.

There's a full-fledged feminine curse followed by a much deeper, "Hold on!"

Isaiah and Kelan freeze, exchanging a look.

"Who is that?" Kelan asks, water dripping into his eyes. Using his powers, he clears his face of the offending droplets.

"No one should be up here, let alone up there!" He points to the roof.

Myrna screams and a crushed tile falls. It clatters to the cobblestone stories below. By the sound from above, a body falls upon the tiles, and they clink together.

"I've got you," the male voice says.

Kelan goes for it. Hopping up onto the railing, he takes two large steps, then jumps for the beam sticking from the side of the outside wall. Thank the goddess for his training and the boost he uses from his powers. He swings, placing one leg over the top, and then hauls himself up.

When he finally rights himself, pure and resounding rage heats his blood at the sight of who lies flat upon his belly, touching the princess. His arms are outstretched as the male pulls her back up to a more stable area.

She scrambles to get her wet, slippered feet up the pitched roof. Struggling to find traction against a section which is not just loose and in disrepair, they fight the streams of water flowing between them.

"What are *you* doing here?" Kelan growls. "Get away from her!"

The warning's clear even at this distance and with the cacophony that rattles like millions of tiny hammers ringing around them with each drop of dew.

How the hell did he get up here?

The man looks up, and his eyes roll. "I'll leave once she's safe."

"You're not to be on palace grounds!" Kelan calls over the rain, slipping once as he moves away from the ledge.

"I wasn't," the man calls. "I was walking by when I saw her slip! Now shut up while I save her!" He groans and pulls her up another few inches.

Kelan scans the area, his gaze instantly landing on an ancient tree just outside the palace walls. Its limbs reach just close enough that the boy could have jumped, but...damn, that is a far leap. Plus, he'd had to have moved fast.

Don't be impressed! "You should not touch her!"

Hands still locked around her savior's wrists, Myrna uses his weight to pull herself upright. "Saints! He's already touching me, Kelan. He freaking saved me!"

She doesn't release the boy when they find their feet, but instead, gazes at Shay, the one who shouldn't be here—the one whose family's taint is so egregious he's banned from this place.

"Let's get over there," Shay says, ignoring Kelan completely. "The pitch is less, and you can get your footing. Once the rain slows, then we can get you back to the ground."

"Thank you." Myrna and Shay use each other for balance as they traverse the fifteen or so feet back up the angle to a flatter and safer spot. "I appreciate the assist."

Shay grins, a dimple peeking out. "I'm glad I spotted you. Though this was not how I expected to spend my evening."

"Well, I'm grateful. Especially since my escape didn't go quite as planned." Myrna laughs. They reach the safer spot. They still clutch one another, and each heartbeat they touch infuriates Kelan more. "I remember you. Shay Hughes, right? From Haszwalds?"

His head tilts, and his eyes light. "Yes. How?"

Kelan pushes between them. He breaks their grip, wraps an arm around Myrna's waist to steady her, and swings her behind him.

"I told you to let go of her." Kelan shoves Shay in the chest. The young man barely moves. "How dare you come on palace grounds! That's trespassing."

Shay glares at the Guardian. "If I hadn't, she'd be dead. Perhaps if her Guardians—"

His fist connects with Shay's jaw and the male bends, blood seeping from a cut on his lip.

"Kelan!" Myrna tries to elbow her way between the two men, but Kelan won't allow it.

Heat rolls over her body, her skin becoming hot, and Kelan faces her, livid at her reaction. *One, how is this possible for a youngling and, two, how can she be angry with* him?

"Go back to your room, Myrna. I'll take care of the traitor."

"The traitor?" Myrna says, pushing the stubborn male. "You mean the man who just kept me from falling off the roof?"

He bares his teeth, the water around them starting to vibrate. He needs to get a hold of himself. There's a *thump* indicating one of the other Guardians has pulled himself up, but neither pay it any heed.

"I'm not a traitor and neither was my father. You know this, Kelan." Shay's words have Kelan glaring. "You know him, were there, but you're too much of a coward to—"

In his distraction, Myrna slips her foot behind Kelan's, steps part way around him, and then punches him first in the side, then slams her opposite elbow down onto his chest. He slips, falling to his back upon the flatter side of the roof.

She leans over him and screams, "You're such an asshole!"

Then she stumbles past both men, still on an escape route.

Jaden, who's apparently made it to the roof, chokes while Shay's mouth drops open.

"Hey! Where are you going? Get back here!" Kelan hollers, getting to his feet.

Not slowing, her head turns minutely, the frustration written in every line of her expression.

"Do you really think you'll be able to find your way home?"

"It doesn't matter. At this point, as long as I'm out of that damned room and away from your stupid ass! And anyway, I know how to get back to the portal at Haszwalds, you stupid, overbearing ass!" She wipes back her wet hair. "I'm so over being locked up, controlled, and being around you! Just try stopping me."

"Myrna, wait!" Shay says, and Kelan growls. The sound's so menacing, Shay holds his hands up in surrender.

Kelan passes the younger male. "It's for your protection. We're just following orders. Your mother—"

"Oh! Because she's *totally* acting normal in this place." Myrna throws her arms up in the air, nearly throwing herself off balance. Grumbling, she adds, "I don't know what you've all done to her, but...whatever, you can continue to follow orders. I choose not to. My mother won't kill me for it." She gets her footing and runs along the tiles at a diagonal away from him. She slips once, her breath catching, before she keeps going. Thank Faerie the rain's slowed.

He shakes his head, stands more than comfortable on such an unsteady surface, and follows at a brisk pace. It's not his first time on a roof, and it won't be the last. His steps are sure, much quicker, whereas hers are sloppy.

A grin spreads her pink lips. Perhaps she believes she's doing well. To the untrained, maybe, but it's not long before he's on her, and her expression is darkening once more. With a scream of rage, she strikes out, but he's ready. And he's over it. He will not risk her life over something so stupid. Or anyone else. If she's going to continue this charade, then he'd make it so she'd think twice before performing such physical feats again.

Myrna faces him, her stance that of a warrior and, once again, he wonders how much training the youngling has. For the punch she threw before was well placed. Her footing's good, even while being at such a steep angle. The higher right foot is planted firmly in a crevasse between two tiles, the left along the top of one. Her shoulders are relaxed, the fists she holds ready are both firm and at ease. It's her eyes, however, that are the most telling. She reads him like one who knows what to look for. And even in the dim light of morning, those eyes glow bright.

He can't hurt her. Not really. He'd never forgive himself for it. Doesn't mean he won't drag her ass back.

Which is why Kelan doesn't hesitate. He invades her space, expecting the fist that comes for his side left. He blocks it. Myrna continues her assault on him, swinging high, her left fist aiming for his cheek. He shifts back, then grabs her wrist and attempts to pull her off balance, but she's too quick. She twists her arm, grabs his, and yanks him toward her instead. Her left knee connects with his side, and he grunts.

Not bad.

Myrna smirks. Her eyes hold a dark joy, for battle he understands and respects.

Kelan pushes the advance while pulling his punches but is interested to see how she can really fight. She blocks his first. His second, then tries to kick out when he swings toward her ribs. Predicting the movement, he stops it, grabs her foot, and flips her. She lands on her stomach with a cry, and in the next instant, Kelan has his knee in the small of her back and the tie he's pulled from his pocket wrapped around both her ankles.

"What the fuck, Kelan! Did you just hog-tie me?" Had she a dagger of her own, he had no doubt she'd thrust it into his heart.

"Not okay!" Shay screams as well.

"Do not move from your place, boy," Jaden warns.

"I thought you were supposed to protect me." Myrna's voice is filled with so much anger he is almost afraid to release her.

"This is protecting you. The queen would not find it a hardship to kill one of your guards for the slight of your injury, capture, or death," Kelan says, removing his knee and rolling her over. He leans down to look in her reddened face. "So, you're not to leave the grounds until the queen says otherwise. As for this? It is only your pride that is injured. Now, are you going to return to your room on your own, or do I need to carry you?"

He holds out his hand.

She glares pure hatred in her eye and bats it away. "Screw you."

Kelan releases a harsh breath. "I'm starting to think your time with the humans and this Sam was a bad influence on you. Such language."

"You want to hear my language? Well—"

He bends and sweeps her up, cutting off her words. He throws her over his shoulder like a sack of flour and starts across the roof toward Jaden, whose eyes are wide. He is trying not to laugh. Kelan doesn't react as Myrna screams bloody murder, wriggles, and hits him in the back.

"Stop acting like a child." He smacks her ass.

She goes perfectly still. "Touch me again like that, and I'll neuter you."

Jaden makes a choking noise, and Kelan shoots him a warning glare.

"And how will you do that in this position?"

"She may not be able to, but I am," Shay says threateningly.

"Don't worry. I'm patient." Myrna places her hands on his waist, providing balance, which he appreciates.

"Not from my experience." Kelan pauses. He shoves a finger in the face of the male he can barely look at for how much he resembles his father. "This one time I'll forgive your presence here, Hughes, but only for your saving the princess."

"The princess?" The words are garbled, as if he is choking on cotton.

"If you ever come near her again, I will kill you. Now get off the grounds." Kelan turns away, bouncing Myrna in his grasp.

She yelps.

Kelan heads toward Jaden. He addresses the other Guardian. "I'm going to help her down to you and Isaiah. Be ready." He winks, and Jaden laughs.

"But aren't you worried she'll try to run again?" the man asks.

Kelan tugs on the tie around her feet. Myrna punches him in the side. "No. I think she'll do as I say, or next time I'll verify with her mother what methods I am allowed to use to keep her in her rooms. My guess is, knowing Laoise, she'd have some interesting ideas."

Myrna goes perfectly still in his arms. Instantly, guilt cramps his stomach. *She did this to herself.*

Jaden clears his throat. "Understood."

With that, the man maneuvers over the side and drops back to the balcony below. When he and the other Guardian are in place, they call out.

Kelan sets her on her feet. He glances over the edge to judge the distance, then, without much warning, scoops her up and tosses her over the side before she knows the plan.

Myrna barely has time to suck in a breath and for her eyes to become saucers before she disappears over the edge. Then, she's in the arms of the other Guardians, and Kelan is dropping down next to them all as they set her on her feet. Isaiah releases the tie on her ankles.

Kelan isn't surprised when she hobbles over to him and punches him in the chest before saying, "You're such a dick!" Then she stomps off, back into her suite and where she belongs. "I just want to go home!"

"You are home."

CHAPTER FIFTEEN

Jackwaffle Guardian

THE COLD OF MYRNA'S palms seeps into her eyes. It's comforting as her head rests heavy. Perhaps if she leaves it here, the massive amounts of information she's read won't seep out. Or it'll finally make sense. Maybe...not sound like gibberish...

"How can this be my life?" she whispers to no one. For she's alone except for the lone guard standing by the door, and he's far away, pompous, and frustrating. It annoys her, seeing as he once promised ... *What? What had he promised exactly?*

To answer your questions and fill in the gaps.

She glances at Kelan. But he isn't doing that. Instead, he stands stiff, back straight, his eyes on the wall. A gorgeous sword hangs at his waist and at least three more weapons are hidden on his form. The one she most wants to see, a dagger the length of her forearm, is on his opposite hip. From her reading, she'd learned it was a specialty weapon given to those of a certain class or the Royal Guardians. Even so, it was rare and hard to acquire.

The obsidian blade. The darkest black and infused with an arcane spell few knew to harden it and infuse it with extra characteristics. It is made for battle, allowing the magic of the user to be funneled through it. Not that she understood what that meant.

But after three days in this room with no other interaction—because Mother has yet to show—her stubborn refusal to speak to him after her attempted escape, and the most aggravating books on the planet, it is becoming harder to fight the urge to ask about the blade and...everything else. To see it. Just once.

Then she remembers the way he tied her feet and threw her from the roof. *Jackwaffle.*

Myrna looks away and grinds her teeth, still shocked at his actions. She presses her temples and runs fingers through her hair. She looks down at the pile of books on the table; some pushed aside, others open to pages read over and over. There are images of Faye, stories, and histories of unimaginable people laid out for her to learn from. They're clearly true, based on the detail and consistencies shared from book to book, but what is she supposed to get from them?

Those faces look up at her, and it becomes harder to breathe. She pants, and then the images become too much. Myrna swipes her arms across the table, sending the books tumbling free. They scatter to the floor, a rolling crash of noise filling her chambers as each connects with the tile.

His gaze is judging. She shouldn't care, but she does. It makes her angrier. It's centuries of history he knows, like the back of his hand. Yet he won't answer her questions because they're at a standoff. She tried early on. Then she gave up. He'd stopped answering, saying he'd restart when she apologized. Fuck that. Which means that she has no one and nothing but the blasted books.

Myrna strides to the door leading to the balcony and flings it open. Cold air rushes in, skating along her body like a caress. It flows through the soft fabric of her dress, but she can't care, for she's panting now, panic settling in as she realizes she's in over her head.

Words of the books run through her mind, and the world below becomes foggy as she fights back tears.

Split by power and judged by stability. Taught to control or taught to harness, it is the belief of the courts that determines the placement of the Faye. Upon the rebellion, those with energies based in emotion—fire, water, and radiance—were deemed to stay with the current monarch, the Qhuinn Clan. While structured arcane energies such as wind, earth, and the rare shadows, and those which fall therein, are to be taken to the new court to be ruled by the Brennan Kings.

"Mother, why didn't you come yesterday? I need help." Her fingers tighten on the smooth wooden railing. She rocks back on her feet.

"You need to study," Kelan bites from the doorway, irritation in his tone. It's been there for days.

What's his problem?

"I see that stick's still up your ass." The ache for her friend Sam has started coming out in her phrasing because that was all her. "You don't have to be here. You can send someone else to watch me."

"No, I can't. She assigned me as your guard." Kelan steps onto the balcony.

"Did she assign you to be an jerk?"

His gaze narrows. "No. Did she require you to be one? Why are you acting weird today?"

She leans against the railing. The breeze ruffles her hair, yet even then she does not shiver. Her focus is not on the cold, but on the landscape. It falls to the castle, its massive presence expanding in both directions, watching over the town which sits further down the hill, past the gardens just beneath her window. Even so, she can only see parts of it because it wraps around the mountain and sneaks between the forest where she cannot see. It's unclear how far the town spreads. To the river just over the hill? The mountain range beyond? She doesn't know, but Myrna's mesmerized by the world she glimpses from her window.

"Don't you have better things to do? Based on what I saw in your office, you're dealing with some pretty important stuff; land disputes, training and supply issues, and worse, attacks all over Faerie. Shouldn't you be organizing all of that? Putting all that training to use? Why are you here babysitting me?"

Kelan doesn't respond. She faces him. The tightness in his jaw and shoulders tells her everything she needs to know.

Myrna scoffs. "I knew it! You don't want to be here anymore than I do. This is a waste of time."

"You're learning."

"No! I'm not! How is this learning, Kelan? Yes, I've read book upon book, but half of them speak in code, and I've been stuck in this room for three days. Mother hasn't come to do the lessons like she promised, and the only other person I've seen besides you is Alyn, and she's afraid to talk to me. The books can only tell me so much and half of them I swear speak in riddles!"

"They do not."

She shoots him a vicious look before pacing around the balcony. Twirling her long hair, she pulls it over her shoulder. "Oh, really?" Myrna sucks on her tooth and then says, "'Those shadow marked speak with travel must harness their heart or they will be lost forever.'"

Kelan's mouth drops open. "What?"

"Yeah. That beauty was from the book Stephan gave me." She looks out over the town as if it holds all the answers, her chest expanding to its full width. "Listen, I'm expected to learn about these people, befriend them, but I'm not allowed to meet any of them. I'm supposed to understand the Faye. To know the history and customs and yet I can't even understand the books, or talk to the people they are about. There's no opportunity to help anyone in the castle, the town, to learn about the war, or to help those coming home from it. As far as I'm concerned, I've lost everything. I've lost the degree I've worked so hard for. My independence and the one friend I have isn't here. I have nothing."

Kelan's face goes perfectly blank.

It causes Myrna to get angry all over again. She steps up to him, nearly pressing against his chest.

"And then there's you."

"What about me? I thought you were still angry with me."

Myrna's shrug is resigned. "No. I think you're as stuck as I am, but I also think that we can help one another."

Kelan's eyebrows draw down. "What do you mean, Princess?"

"I asked you not to call me that." Myrna's voice is harsh once more, but there's also a wobble he can't miss. He doesn't respond, just continues to stare down into the ice blue of her eyes until she says, "Neither of us wishes to be locked in this room. This is a prison for us both and doesn't help either of our goals or the people of this realm. You need to protect me. Those are your orders?"

"Yes."

"Well, I need a home. A place where I can finally feel normal." Her traitorous words crack along the edges. "She said I could trust you. Well, if you have additional guards, and I'm at your side at all times, why can't you guard me from Haszwalds? Why can't you also be my tutor? You're ancient and could probably teach me most of what I read about, if not more. Or find me one!"

Kelan stops breathing. He glances out over the town, to a long slow breath, then retakes her gaze.

"There's much I speak about you won't understand or that's irrelevant to your studies."

She scoffs. "From what I read, Mother has to claim an heir within a certain timeframe, or the magic of Faerie will become unstable. I'm surprised they haven't made her yet. But I assume I'm supposed to be that heir, right? So how is any of it irrelevant? I understand strategy and war better than you think. My caretakers and I played such games. But I won't interfere. I just ask that, when you're not in meetings, you help me learn. Allow me to ask questions so that I'm not in this stagnant state any longer."

"It's not safe."

She groans. "Why are you being so difficult? They didn't know I existed before, and you have plenty of guards! Is the risk so much more there versus here?"

"Yes, it is, and the answer is no."

Myrna screams out over the forest when Kelan turns and disappears back into the suite to retake his post along the wall.

Kelan's jaw flexes at the sound of her pain.

CHAPTER SIXTEEN

Then the Bastard Shows He Has a Heart.

KELAN'S KNUCKLES CONNECT WITH the wood, the sound resonating louder than intended, the stress of meeting with the queen still thrumming through his veins.

"I can't believe you went to Laoise. Are you mad?" Briana, his younger sister, says, her expression pinched.

"I had to. Myrna's been trying to escape for days. She's miserable being locked up. She's not learning anything, she constantly grumbles about not being able to train, and I can't do my job as Head Guardian."

"So, you think *this* is a good idea?"

Kelan winces.

"In truth?" he asks, glancing into her intelligent eyes.

"Always."

"It was Myrna's idea, and I refused to take her to the queen. I should not have."

Briana whistles. "I get it now. You feel bad."

"Wouldn't you? Granted, Laoise upped a few of my requests." He exhales and pushes the door open when a soft, "Come in," fills the air.

They enter, Briana a step behind Kelan as he says, "Good morning, Myrna. I need to speak with you, and I'd like to introduce you to my sister, Briana Brynes."

Myrna's eyes sparkle with interest before she takes in his baby sister. "Huh. I knew she looked familiar."

There's no denying the resemblance. They have the same golden streaks in their hair, the same sharp features, but it's the sharp intelligence hidden behind their golden eyes that solidifies it.

"Good morning." Myrna lays the book in her lap to the side.

Balance Beholden. *She reads that a lot.*

"What do you need to speak with me about?" Myrna leans back on the couch.

"I wanted to apologize and let you know I went to the queen this morning to request some revisions to your... stay."

"You did?" Myrna digs her fingers into her seat, and she sits straighter. "What do you mean?"

"Well, you're unhappy and what you said is correct. I need to get back to work, and you need a teacher. So, I've made a deal. One I hope will work for us both." When she stares, Kelan continues, "First, your confinement is revoked, but with certain requirements."

Her breathing picks up. Does she know she leans closer? "And those are?"

"You'll have as many guards as I deem necessary for the situation, but in turn, you will be allowed to explore the castle, grounds, and town. This will allow you to experience our people, customs, and even the politics directly from the source."

A harsh exhale.

"Really?" The single word is filled with excitement. She gets to her feet and moves around the coffee table. "I agree."

"I figured you would." Kelan smirks. "With that, you'll be required to attend training sessions with me at Haszwalds. There—"

"Yes!"

Kelan shuts her down with one look. "There, you'll continue your book studies, as well as observe and learn of strategy and politics. The queen mentioned you've studied some of these prior. We will dive deeper."

"Okay," she says, linking her fingers together. She's beginning to shake, as if she's unable to contain her excitement.

"This may allow"—Kelan runs a hand through his hair—"the opportunity for the finalization of your internship."

She goes still and exhales sharply. "How did you get her to agree with that one?"

"I repeated something you said to me. How you mentioned she taught you to finish what you started."

Myrna's lips part, and her clasped hand moves to her chest. She nods. "Are there any other requirements for this agreement?"

"One."

Myrna's face falls as Kelan stands there and stares at her. He doesn't stay quiet because he's trying to scare her. It's because this one is the rule Laoise added he doesn't like. Everything about it is a bad idea. Briana elbows him in the side, and he jumps.

"Starting tomorrow, you're to begin training with the Guardians. Hand-to-hand, weapons, combat, and more. Your job is to learn everything you can from them as quickly as you can. Even though you'll always have guards, the queen wishes that you also have a complete knowledge of personal protection."

"Oh!" Myrna's face changes from fear to confusion, and back to joy. "Really? That's great! I can't wait. Tomorrow? Are you sure we can't start today? I mean—"

"Tomorrow."

Myrna freezes. "Right. Tomorrow. And...her?"

"Well," Kelan says, remembering his sister's been in the room this whole time. "She's assigned as one of your personal guards moving forward. She's skilled, and I trust her to keep you safe. She'll also act as tutor when I'm unable to fill in." He leads Myrna closer.

"Don't judge me for it," Briana says with a wink, then pats his belly. He glares at her. "This big lug is too serious. But don't worry, I'm not nearly as grumpy as he is. I'm also much closer to your age...technically." One shoulder rises. "He thought we might be able to relate a little more, considering he's ancient."

Kelan wraps his arm around Briana's neck and covers her mouth. "She's willing to help. That's all that matters."

Myrna stifles a giggle when Briana pinches his side and twists.

"You can trust her, too."

Briana gazes up at her big brother with so much love, she can't fight the grin any longer. Only she's kept him sane since Mareola died. A sadness passes over Myrna's face which, after getting to know her these last days, he thinks he understands. *What would it have been like to be away from Faerie and all alone?*

"It's nice to meet you. I appreciate your help. I also appreciate not having to deal with his crap all day, seeing as up until now he has been nothing but a pain in my—"

"Myrna," he scolds.

Briana laughs. "Believe me, I understand. I've been dealing with his overbearing ass for my entire life."

"Ah." She links her arm with the younger Guardian and leads her toward the door. "Then perhaps you can help me find a way to better deal with him."

Kelan's chest rumbles. "This is a bad idea." He passes them, adding, "Come on. Let's go, you two. I've got work to do."

But part of him was happy knowing that she'll have at least one person to connect with. At least he can give that to her.

Chapter Seventeen

For In History Lies the Truth

"I don't understand." Myrna plops her chin into her hand, her elbow pressing into the conference table in Kelan's office. The book beneath rustles, shifting the stack that covers nearly a quarter of the massive tabletop. She eyes Briana, who sits opposite her.

Guardian Briana Brynes, Kelan's little sister and her new tormentor. *Tutor...she meant tutor.*

"Stop whining," Kelan says from his spot across the room, head down, reading some papers. He sits at his desk, shuffling through an endless pile of work, grumbling to himself while the two females have spent the last few hours digging through books.

After being gone so long, he is drowning in work. *Poor guy.*

But Briana's sweet, where Kelan's grumpy. She smiles willingly, is clear in the way she explains things, and loves her people. Myrna's grateful to Kelan for bringing Briana to her. Though she won't admit it to him.

Myrna skims the words on the page. "So, King Brennan Murray the First, arbitrarily determined that earth, wind, and something called shadow were 'stable?'" She shakes her head. "Whatever that means. Then forced anyone with powers that fall into those categories to go with him?"

Briana bites her lip and scrunches her nose. Her head bobbles back and forth as she shrugs. "Yes and no. It wasn't so simple. You see, our abilities ebb and flow. Each person's are different both in level and quality. Some easily fall within one category or another without argument, while others not so much. We also learn differently. These gifts are more structured in the way they function inherently, so he believed that by removing emotion from the casting, it would make the ability stronger."

"So, those of the other court don't feel?"

Briana chuckles. "They feel, but they don't allow emotion to fuel their arcane abilities. Their training, from a very young age, is extremely regimented and suppresses the instinct to push rage, fear, love, et cetera into their spells."

"That seems like it would weaken the fighter. Being steady in battle is important, but there've been times where my emotional reactions have given me an edge."

"Yes, but have you also lost because of one?"

Myrna rubs her ankle but refuses to look in Kelan's direction. *Jerk.*

Briana grins. "Anyway, the divide easily started the way he intended, but even then, some fought because they didn't believe in the decree. Some wanted to stay with the Qhuinn family and in their homes here."

She points to another book spread between them. Colorful images of Faye using power in magnificent ways look back. The intricate designs show them in all states, casting fireballs or ice storms, using siren song, or shifting their shape from human to animal form. Changelings or elementals of all levels, spirits, pixies, and others still. She turns the page, yet more creatures of magnificence appearing.

"The issues began when dealing with people who couldn't be classified or didn't approve of the Murray choice to revolt. The loyalists to the current crown fought and were allowed to stay, protected by the Qhuinn family. For a while. Until those with Murray beliefs started to cause trouble in the streets. Many were killed." Briana's expression sinks. Then she purses her lips.

Myrna plays with the end of her hair. Her brows draw down as she thinks about the destruction such a situation could cause.

The scraping of a chair has Myrna glancing up to find Kelan pushing from his. He walks to a wall of bookshelves and pulls a large tome from the bottom shelf. The binding looks ancient, the edges worn, barely staying together as he nimbly flicks through the pages. He clears his throat.

"Our great-grandfather said it was one of the darkest times in our history. No one was trusted." Kelan stops next to the princess, putting the book upon all the others. Dust puffs into the air, making Myrna sniff. He reads, "'*I cannot justify the lives of so many. There's no trust in the streets. Those who are of the other castes, who are requested to go to the Court of the Indomitable Moon and fall under Murray's rule, are not trusted here. Their lives are at risk. They are seen as other even if they have fought by our sides for centuries. Worse, we've proven some are not to be. They've turned sides and are now the enemy under our own house. It saddens me to find my people a risk, but mine own heart breaks with each life they steal. How do I protect my people when they hide under the guise of loyalty?*'"

Myrna stands and leans in close. His dark cinnamon scent mixes with that of the moldy books, and her racing heart calms even as it hurts as such pain is captured in text. She presses her fingers to the page next to his and the words which sing of regret. "Who wrote this?"

Kelan looks into her eyes. "Your great-grandmother."

Myrna releases a tight breath. She examines the uneven script of a woman long dead. It is shaky, a droplet having damaged a line, the ink torn from its placement without its permission. A *tear, perhaps?*

"I didn't know you were listening," she whispers, then glances up at him.

"You're going to find parts of our past that are dark. You'll learn terrible truths in this room. See death and harsh treatments, for this is not the human world."

Myrna's shoulders are back, books forgotten, when she faces Kelan. "I'm not some innocent child. My life has not been some fairy tale."

"Kelan..." Briana groans.

He does not react, but continues calmly, "But what you will always find are those trying to protect their own, make lives better, and those of your people—your line—doing everything they can to do what's right. Even if you cannot understand the methods."

Myrna blinks. He was not attacking her but honoring her family. Telling her that even though there is darkness, it is always purposeful.

"Thank you for showing me this," she says. Without glancing back at her, he nods once and heads back to his desk. She watches him go.

Briana clears her throat.

"Sorry. So..." Myrna makes a loop around the giant mahogany table. She threads her fingers through her loose hair and looks up at the skylight, which casts light down upon them. "The Murray family rules the abilities which live in the realm of stability, equality, and structure. They believe emotion is a weakness, and it should not be a part of how you harness your power."

"Correct."

"And Brennan thinks that's so easy? Does he have a family? Children?"

Briana flips to another text and shows Myrna what looks to be a family tree. "Aye. The current king was one of five Murray siblings, but from what we understand, the current King Brennan killed his siblings to seize the throne."

"What?"

"Yeah." Briana sighs. "He had four sons; Reese, Pierce, Manthus, and Nordis. From our reports, Reece died in the last siege, Nordis, by internal revolt. Or so they say. We believe that Manthus's son, Colum, killed him, but we don't have confirmation. Pierce stays quiet and away from the castle, so we don't know much of him, though it's believed he has three daughters, for which Brennan ignores. There are rumors that Manthus had two other children. A girl, rarely seen, and another child. But, again, no real proof of the third."

A line is drawn to show this child, but a blank spot where the name should be remains.

"After Colum was appointed heir apparent, Brennan had no obligation to notify Queen Laoise."

"Manthus had two children. That is all," Kelan says, not glancing up.

Briana rolls her eyes in Kelan's direction, making Myrna snicker.

"Ugh, and I thought my brain hurt before." Myrna paces quicker now. She presses fingers to the bridge of her nose. Then she waves them in the air as if to dispel all the information she'd just learned.

"Going backward. So, our court, which includes anyone with fire, water, and... radiance—I have so many questions about that one, by the way—are unstable and emotional? Or are we the emotional ones?" She pinches the bridge of her nose again. She doesn't wait for a response before she rambles, "What in the world is shadow and radiance, and what abilities fall into them? I have a headache."

Briana laughs.

"You're overthinking this." Briana stands and approaches her. "You'll understand more once you've gone through the changing, and your powers come in, but..." She lowers her voice to a whisper and glances at Kelan, who's now on the phone. "I heard there was something that happened between you two in the elevator, a sharing of power that went a little crazy."

Myrna blushes. She can't help it. "How do you know about that?"

That moment had felt so intimate. When all those people saw them embracing, it felt... And now everyone had heard about it and their reactions were so over the top. She isn't used to feeling this sort of embarrassment.

"There were a lot of witnesses, and Kelan doesn't let many touch him, let alone do a power exchange. The stories that are going around about the way your power felt..." Briana fans herself.

Myrna smacks the Guardian's hand, which causes Briana to grin. "Stop that. Your brother is a pain in my side. Please quell those rumors."

"Well, anyway, the point is, that is an emotional moment. You were overwhelmed, and he was trying to understand you. He got carried away—which never happens, by the way." She glances at her brother, who looks up and lifts an eyebrow. Briana waves him away. "The interesting part is you've since shown quite a lot of control, even if you weren't aware of it. Especially considering you haven't gone through the changing. I believe that the training you've received from your mother has allowed you to manage your power so far—control it, even though you haven't manifested your true abilities yet. It's why Laoise is being so protective of you."

Myrna looks down at the floor and kicks some invisible speck of dirt. "She said I should be careful when my power comes in."

"I think that's best. Until you get a handle on it. Kelan taught me about my abilities and, although he is a boorish ass," Briana says, causing Myrna to choke, "he's a good teacher. I'm here, should you need it, too, but you don't know me yet, and Kelan has a vested interest that I don't. But again, we're getting off topic."

"Why would he have a vested interest?" Myrna asks, leaning forward at this very interesting nugget of information.

"Briana," Kelan calls. He puts two stacks together and motions to the door. "You're needed back at the palace. There's an issue in the west wing that requires your help."

She goes pale, but glances toward Myrna. "Are you sure?"

"It'll be fine. I can take a break to finish your discussion before Stephan arrives. Then, we'll head back." He squeezes Briana's arm, focusing then on Myrna. "Did Sam say she'd bring your stuff?"

"Yeah. The three of us were going to meet down at the cafe in"—she looks at her watch—"thirty."

"Perfect. That's about the time Stephan is to arrive. We'll meet him there."

Briana nods, says her goodbyes, then disappears out the door.

Suddenly, the room feels smaller. Or perhaps it's Kelan's attention on her.

He paces to the far end of the table, picks up a large glass of water, and takes a drink. "You two were discussing how emotion is harnessed in our court versus denied in the other, and the importance of it. This can be a hard concept to understand."

"You were listening?"

He frowns and places the cup between the two of them. "Of course."

She leans her hip against the table, and the water splashes over the rim. "I don't know why it confuses me."

"Because of the argument between mastering a skill and weaving emotion into it to push it beyond just talent."

Okay...that might make sense. "Explain."

"Well, our court believes that emotion is important to understand control. This is true, but there's another piece as well. Joy, lust, pain, and anything in between can be an essential tool when used in the right way."

Kelan starts back to the pile of books, and Myrna can't help but to follow. She leans over his shoulder.

"The Murrays teach that nothing but mental control should be used, that pushing one's emotion into the casting is a sin. That it taints the magic and your soul in return. We see it very differently." He runs his hands over the books she'd looked over earlier; the one with the pictures of Faye. "The siren uses love or even vengeance in her call. A shapeshifter of any kind connects to the land, its pack, should it have one, or the very animal side of its nature during its transition. And an elemental calls to the heart of the world itself, allowing his or her very being to connect on a visceral level. Yes, there is a skill to it, but there is also emotion. Always emotion."

"Can you show me?" Myrna crosses her arms over her chest and frowns. "What is your ability?"

Chapter Eighteen

True Emotion Leads to Purest Magic

THE GUARDIAN'S JAW FLEXES, an automatic reaction to her question. He isn't offended since he'd decided to show her days ago. Still, her blunt questions, however innocent they are, need to be curbed or she might offend the wrong person.

Myrna's shoulders droop as if a weight settles upon them. Her expression scrunches. "I apologize. Clearly, it was rude of me to ask."

She is observant. "No. This is not something you should ask outright, but don't worry. With me, you may ask anything, and I'll answer to the best of my ability."

Myrna wraps her arms around her waist. She licks her lips and steps away. "Why?"

"You need to know, and..." He scans her face. It's as if he's hesitant to admit the next part. "You remind me of someone I was once was close with. A friend."

"Who?"

He glances away, the pain like a deep ache that never goes away. "Your Aunt Mareola. She was a childhood friend."

Chills run up Myrna's arms, mesmerizing him. *Why such a reaction?* She opens her mouth, then closes it as if her throat hurts. She glances away.

"Only a friend?"

He frowns. "Yes, why?"

"Everyone talks about her like..." She shrugs. "Never mind."

Curiosity warms his skin at the idea of what she's heard. He rubs his jaw. "In any case, a demonstration would be best. Just remember that people will provide such information should they wish to and in their own time. The good news is soon you'll learn the families and know the lineages. That'll help." He paces the room, the discomfort from the last few seconds still present in the tightness of his back.

"Meaning?"

"In general, gifts are passed down by familial line. Mine has a gift for water manipulation. However, this can manifest in a million different ways, but we'll get to that later."

"Okay."

"We believe that depending on how much emotion you harness affects how your power will manifest. For instance, if I just call water, it may come as I've the talent for it. It may not be controlled or well done, but it'll listen."

The water she'd spilled moves, drawing her attention. Her expression is open and excited as she watches it crawl toward them. Reaching the end, it lifts, dances in the air, then flies toward Kelan. He sends his will into it, moving the particles, demanding they collect, then weave in intricate patterns until they join, becoming a large blob.

"Exciting, isn't it?"

Myrna snorts. "Oh, yes. Quite exciting."

"Would you prefer something more joyful?"

Needing to see her smile, he thinks of a happy memory and pushes the emotion into the arcane he wields. The water splits. It elongates, now two long streams that shape and wrap around one another. The tops flatten, spreading open like a flower—the starlight lily unfurling with magical brilliance. The stalks length-en, leaves growing at unique points on each.

Lips parted, Myrna sighs as she lifts her hands to place them along the backs of Kelan's. She doesn't touch him, just mirrors him. Amazement fills her at the beauty he creates, especially as the lights from above reflect off the glistening petals. "So beautiful."

The corner of Kelan's lip lifts. Pride at what his magic can do fills his heart, and the flower brightens. "I did this for Briana when she was learning her powers."

Or perhaps it becomes more stable, the water no longer shifting.

"Based on my need, I can alter it. But the strength of the emotion determines the strength I'm able to push into the arcane. Should I become determined, angry, or desperate to attack, for instance, it may be stronger than that with love. Either way, water can become ice, but how hard will it be? Even the amount I place can strengthen the casting. Does that make sense?"

"I think so. Is this a spell, then? Like with what humans think witches do?"

He grimaces, lowering his hands but not releasing the control over the water. "No!"

She laughs. "All right, so how is this truly a way of thought versus just becoming skilled at harnessing your ability?"

"In Brennan's Court, they don't harness their power quite the same. They learn to pull and then link their abilities the same as we do, but they're also taught to ignore their emotions. Which, in battle, is a detriment."

"Wouldn't that be better? To not allow your emotions to cloud your judgment?"

"No. Often our quickest responses, our strongest efforts are when we utilize all of ourselves. When we deny them, lock part of ourselves away, this is when we lose."

"I guess I can understand that," Myrna says, her eyes softening.

He's not sure if she's aware she does it, but her hands lift to cup his. Kelan swallows, her touch electric. He doesn't want to pull away. He should scold her, but that is the furthest thing from his thoughts. Her thumb runs along his palm, and he draws her closer. She doesn't resist.

Suddenly, there's a knock at the door and it opens, a familiar face appearing. "Kelan, you didn't answer your phone. Are you—"

Myrna's head turns, a wide grin spreading at the sight of Stephan's kind face. But at the male's double take and bark of laughter, she freezes. Kelan, however, has yet to look from her. She faces him again, and it's like watching her catalog their positioning in one fell swoop. He can almost hear her brain working. But it's when she gets to the flower that her lips part. It shifts magnificently. It's multi-layered, with ruffled petals and long stamens that arch up and over the center stalk, which has now sprouted several more leaves. Sexy and luscious, the color is a surprise. It is a glorious pearled white.

He leans in and whispers in her ear, his cheek brushing sensually against hers. "You're closer to your changing than we thought. I expect within a fortnight."

Secretly, he cherishes her intake of breath and the way her gaze flicks up as he pulls back, her grip reflexively tightening on his.

Stephan coughs. She releases Kelan in embarrassment before moving to Stephan's side. "I thought we were meeting you downstairs."

"I thought so as well, Your Highness, but—"

"Not you too! Stephan, do not call me that! Especially here. Please? Call me 'Myrna.' I need my friend. The one who will just talk to me like a person and not some weirdo."

Stephan laughs, sharing a glance with Kelan. He bows low to Myrna.

He does it with such elegance that she groans. "You're from the court."

He winks. "I am, but I'll do as you ask. When we're here or in private company, I'll address you as only 'Myrna,' but when we're not..."

She waves her hand. "Yes, yes, 'Princess this' and 'Princess that.'" She links her arm through his and leads him to the door.

When she looks back at Kelan, he's dissolved the flower, and his expression is blank once more. But his reaction to her hasn't diminished. *I need to get a grip.*

"We're off to meet Sam to retrieve my things. I don't want to be late, and I fear our lesson has made us so."

Stephan tilts his head. "Lesson? And why are you talking like that?"

Myrna laughs. "Never mind. Kelan and Briana are in charge of my lessons. Guards and teachers in one. What did you think was happening?"

"Nothing." At her glare, Stephan only grins. He looks at Kelan, and he can almost hear the questions. Questions even he can't answer.

Kelan joins them near the door. As he approaches, his glamour shimmers into place and a startled giggle escapes her throat.

"Hey!" She points at Stephan. "Why can I see your glamour so clearly now? It doesn't go up and down like before."

"Probably because you're not fighting it," Kelan explains.

"Huh. What about me, then? I'm wearing this tunic thingy. Not exactly office attire. People will notice."

"You'll have glamour," Stephan says in a singsong voice. She frowns.

"As I could not obtain a suitable outfit prior, there is one option, but you have to agree," Kelan says, a jittery feeling running through him. This is also a bad idea. "It's another reason we have to go with. I'm able to share glamour for short periods of time as long as I stay close. It doesn't change your appearance, but I can alter their perception of you. Moving forward, however, it'd be better if you had your own wardrobe as this is considered improper."

Stephan covers a chuckle with a cough.

"What?" Myrna asks, lifting a hand. She bites her lip and addresses Kelan. "Will you get in trouble?"

Kelan shakes his head. "No, but many consider it...intimate."

She tries to keep a straight face, but he catches her tongue shooting out to lick her lip. "Okay. How do we do this?"

Damn it to hell. With more hesitation than he should have, Kelan grips her arms. She tenses automatically, but then he leans in to press his warm lips to her forehead. Her soothing vanilla scent fills his nose as he sends his magic like a blanket over her.

She closes her eyes, a barely noticeable shiver radiating through his touch. She exhales a shaky breath as he steps back.

To hide her reaction, she says, "That's it? I don't understand what the big deal is. It felt like warm water spreading across my skin."

The magic surrounding her flares. Her mouth parts in a silent sigh, his eyebrow lifts, and he can almost hear the curse she throws in his direction before stomping off.

"He didn't make me look stupid, did he?"

"You look great," Stephan says, giving her a once-over. "Sam will approve."

"Wait. How do you know what Sam will approve?"

"Well, she's been a mess since you've been gone. They've posted her at the front and, since I'm allowed upstairs, and she knows I'm your friend, she sees me as her inside contact. I've been feeding her information."

People watch as the three of them stroll toward the elevator, and he's fascinated by the way she doesn't see them, not really, her interest too sucked into the conversation.

"What have you told her?" The elevators close.

"That you're doing amazing in your position here, and your mother's requiring you to stay with her for a few weeks."

"I'm sure she's loving that." When Kelan perks up at the comment, Myrna explains, "Sam doesn't trust Mother. She thinks her too harsh and isn't telling me everything. She likes to guess what Mother is really into. Her current guess is the Russian Mafia." She lets out an amused laugh at the expression that passes over the males' faces. "If only she knew."

The elevator comes to a stop, the floor jerking minutely. When the door opens, the two males follow the princess at a safe distance. Though not much focus is necessary, he solidifies the connection to Myrna's glamour, the shifting of the clothing and the click of heel against tile. He doesn't want any failures.

"Oh, my gosh!" The squeal has heads turning. There's a rushing clatter, and Sam slams into her.

Myrna wraps her arms around her friend, ignoring how the guards shift from their places. Kelan shoots them a "down" signal, and they return to their places, an unhappy look on each face.

"Bitch, where have you been?" Sam asks.

Myrna covers her face with her palm. "Sam, we've talked about this. Stop using profanity at work!" But Myrna can't help but grin as she releases her friend and leans back to fiddle with the sleeve of Sam's shirt. "This is cute! Where did you get it?"

Myrna mentioned distraction is key with Sam. It doesn't work. Sam slams her hands on her hips, and Myrna holds hers up. "I'm sorry. I know I haven't called, and things are weird."

"Understatement." The harsh tone has several glancing their way.

With one look, Kelan manages to disperse most.

Myrna's relief is palpable. She links her arm to Sam's. "Do you have coverage?"

"Yup. But"—she points to Kelan and Stephan—"do you want to explain why these two are here?"

"Um…Well, you don't mind if Mr. O'Malley and Mr. Daniels join us, do you?" she asks. It's strange, using their human names again.

Sam smacks the youngling. "Have they been standing here long enough to see me acting like an idiot? Myr!"

When Myrna giggles and says, "I've missed you," Sam loops an arm around her friend's waist and addresses the Faye males.

"Of course they're welcome. Good day, Mr. Daniels. Mr. O'Malley."

"Samantha." Stephan laughs. "And you, darling girl, are a delight. The way you treat our dear Myrna means the world."

"Agreed." Kelan looks at the small ball of fire. "But did you bring the things she requested? If so, I can have them taken to my office while we head to the cafe."

Her grip tightens, and her eyes shift back and forth. "They're speaking to me, Myrna. What do I do?" Her grip is like a vice now. She's no longer nervous or acting like a goober. The change has both Stephan and Kelan tensing.

Kelan fights to hold back a smile and says, "Would you prefer we avoid speaking directly to you?"

"Whoa." Sam's lips part as her eyebrows draw down. "They talk like you do."

Slow breath from Myrna. Even she had detected the slight accent now that they were around those who did not speak with one. "They do."

A soft grin lifts her friend's face. Far-too-intelligent eyes move between the three. "Oh, honey... And you're discovering what you've been missing?"

Myrna presses her lips together, swallows back the lump in her throat, and nods.

Tears spring to Sam's eyes.

Complete and utter respect for this human fills Kelan. He slips his hands into his pockets and smiles proudly at the two girls. This human may not know what Myrna has been going through, but they've talked about it. That much is clear. Never could Sam guess how deep it went, but by the look on her face, she knew Myrna.

Sam's soft fingertips lift to Myrna's cheek. "I'm here if you need me. Take your time and find what's lost. But know whatever you discover will not change how I see you. I love you, Myrna. You're my person."

Myrna's lip trembles.

Before Myrna can speak, Sam continues in a whisper. There's a flicker of excitement now. "Let's go eat. I only have so much time to show off that I'm eating with these two gorgeous pieces of man meat. I hope Tiffany sees us. She'll be so jelly." She wiggles her shoulders, then hurries off. With a few words to Rhonda, she is on her way back with Myrna's bag.

"She is something," Stephan says in awe, and Kelan agrees.

Sam stops before Kelan. "Um...who can I give this to?" She smiles shyly. "It feels odd handing it off to the head of an entire company."

"It's fine. Thank you, Samantha." He takes the bag and gives it to one of the Guardians who'd been standing by the wall. He'd approached the moment she'd revealed it. Kelan asks, "Shall we?"

Sam blushes, links her arm with Myrna's, and rushes toward the cafe.

CHAPTER NINETEEN

Leader or Follower.
Protector or Failure.

THERE'S A SPRING IN her step since arriving back in Faerie, and the lightness is a happy change. Time spent out of the castle and back at work was good for the youngling, but it was the time spent with Sam which brightened her the most. The human's joyful exuberance was infectious; even Kelan couldn't argue that. Which is why Myrna is nearly skipping as they traverse the path from the castle and into the town of Tara.

Briana's elbow lifts, indicating her brother. "What climbed up his butt?"

The forest on either side is thick and, even though her companion is talkative, it hasn't gone unnoticed how Briana and her guards watch the trees. This may be the safest part of the forest for all the scouts which patrol it, but that doesn't mean they'll risk the precious cargo in their care. Her.

"Hard day. After having lunch with my friend Sam—whose charms he's not used to—he got some bad news from Stephan." She leans closer. "The threat's increased. The queen and the high court must be notified."

"Charms? Is that what you call them?" Kelan snaps from up ahead. "And don't discuss such matters here. When we return this evening, we'll meet with the court. Until then, keep it quiet." His glare is made more severe by the palm on the hilt of his sword.

"I'm sorry, Guardian," Myrna says, glancing down. His lips thin.

"Well, I hope it's not too bad. Our people don't need more bad news," Briana adds.

He doesn't respond, but his strides lengthen until he's made some space between them.

Myrna plays with the tie at her waist as images of the battle table and the shifting sands representing the encroaching army upon Stephan's territory run through her head. The tiny figurines spread across acres of land, sending cold fear trickling through her veins. Before this moment, she hadn't realized how serious the situation was, or that Stephan, her friend, played such an important role to the protection of their people. He is in danger all because King Brennan is advancing, getting ready to attack for a reason yet unknown.

"Don't mind him. Today's about enjoying your time out." Briana smiles, and the youngling nods in agreement. She's right, of course. There were things she couldn't stop or even help with right now. It sucks. "Just try to learn what you can. Cool?"

They turn onto the main boulevard, and Myrna releases a breath. The mix of ancient beauty and modern glory, a sight she's only dreamed of. This is Faerie, but somehow, it's not what she expected. Streetlamps line the road, the wicks visible from her lower position. Clean stone storefronts of the shops and restaurants hold an old feel while also projecting a modern air. Light fills the windows as customers flow from each, arms burdened with supplies. It's a bustling street filled with Faye of all kinds; tall, short, glamoured and not. High society, soldiers, peasants; they congregate, socialize, and shop for supplies within the massive, centralized area.

The youngling is amazed and amused at her reaction. What had she been expecting? An old decrepit street made of dirt and broken-down horse-drawn carriages? Just because electricity—technology, as humans understood it, didn't work here due to the way magic infused everything—didn't mean they weren't advanced.

Myrna's amazed grin lights her face. "This is remarkable."

"Yeah. I guess." Briana shrugs. "This is Tara. The center to be specific, and where you can find just about anything. In this circle are the best stores, restaurants, and pubs. We can get into trouble here." Briana nudges Myrna's arm with a wink.

She clasps her hands to keep them from grabbing Briana's shirt sleeve and tugging when she spots a store filled with all sorts of weapons: knives, needles, swords. They're beautiful and deadly, just the way she likes them. Next door is a bakery, the scent of pastries divine. She nearly shimmies. "Thank you for coming with me. I know you've been here a bazillion times, but in order for me to understand this place, I must see it."

"Not a problem. Now, what do you want to do? Shop for some dresses, a knickknack, get something tasty to eat"—Briana gestures toward a storefront where the wonderful scent of roasted meat wafts temptingly toward them—"or see the bridge?"

Myrna had heard about the bridge. The second largest in the realm and one of the main accesses to the capital. It runs over the river and out into the forestland. It is supposed to be gorgeous.

"Can we just walk? Being here, experiencing it, is all I want."

Briana smiles sweetly. "Sure."

Left and right, she walks. Street by street with no particular goal. It's a need to see everything while not having focus. It's about taking it all in. The children that run past with giggling laughter. Noting each beautiful face with their unique features and fascinating movements. Blue hair. Scales along their backs or speckles down their limbs. Gills contracting even as their chests expand.

"This place..." Myrna says, her pace slow and steady. She closes her eyes and takes in a long, cleansing breath. "It's like nothing I've ever seen or felt before."

Town center is long behind them, the busy streets and bustle of shoppers from the high society a forgotten memory. It's quieter here; the lanes holding farms cradling ancient-looking homes lovingly cared for tucked within trees. Ivy crawls up the brick façades with chimneys that peek out, smoke curling up into the evening sun.

"Where are we?" Myrna asks, a small collection of buildings ahead.

"We should head back." Kelan's been silent, but his jaw tics now as he glances toward the structures where a group of Guardians surround a man with black hair.

"I'm not ready to go back," Myrna says, continuing past Kelan.

Kelan comes to her, resting his fingers against her skin as if to stop her progression. She looks at the contact, then up into his face. Though he doesn't grip her tightly, she's not happy with the demand in his expression. It reminds her of that night on the roof.

"Release me, Kelan."

His hand wraps around her arm in a real grip. "It is time to return to the palace."

Oh, no. This is not happening. They'd agreed his high-handed approach was over. He's her guard, not her father. "Release me. Now."

Kelan's jaw twitches. "Apologies, Highness, but you're approaching the home of an untrusted familial line. They're disgraced, and it's not safe for you here."

The group ahead is getting noisy, an argument starting. One Guardian pushes the man with the black hair while the other laughs.

Kelan moves between her and the scene when her gaze is drawn to it.

"And that means?"

"It means their family's not of good quality, and someone like you, of royal blood, should never interact with them, be in their presence, or breathe the same air. They do not deserve it." With each word, a snarl curls his lip. "You should be protected from them."

"And what made this family so hated?"

Lips pulled back, teeth clenched, and hostility burning in his gaze, Kelan says, "The father was an honored Guardian. He is no longer."

Myrna swallows hard. This is the most emotion Kelan has ever shown and it's terrifying, but there's something beneath it that could break him open if she isn't careful. A hurt like none other, and yet, it won't relieve the disgust pooling in her gut.

"Wow." Never has an expression affected Myrna so. She shudders, but not due to fear of the family. Those words hold so much hatred. She shakes her head. "I never would've pinned you for a hard-headed bigot. One who would hold grudges and never see past one's nose."

She rips her arm from his grip, shoves past him, and slams her shoulder into his.

This time, he grabs her wrist to pull her to a stop. "You have no idea what you're talking about."

"No, but I do know those Guardians are beating on another Faye, a living being, for just walking through town. And for nothing more." She shoves into his space, so they're nose to nose. She points toward the altercation. "They've taken the things he's purchased from the store, stomped on his produce, and are now beating him while holding him down. For. No. Reason."

He lets go of her wrist, glances toward the fight, then meets her gaze.

"Is this the training you provide? What lessons you teach? Because if it is, I will have a discussion with my mother about your post!" Both Myrna's hands make contact with Kelan's chest when she shoves him.

It's strong, and Kelan stumbles a few feet before he catches himself.

"You got what you deserved, brother," Briana says before she jogs after the princess, who's taken up a complete sprint.

Myrna's fast and soon, she closes the distance, reaching the Guardians and the unarmed man. The Guardian in front pulls back for another punch, but the princess is there. She comes from the side, sliding and swinging her leg out to knock the man's feet out from under him. She moves over him before he is even fully on the ground and lands a punch that knocks him clean out.

The two Guardians holding the man, whose head is bowed, react instantly. They drop him, and he crumples to the dirt.

"How dare you interrupt Guardian business!"

"This is not Guardian business, and I'll have you stripped of your rank," Myrna says before she goes for them.

They attack swiftly, thinking she's but a youngling. It's a good assumption, as she doesn't yet read as Faye in magical signature, but they're wrong. The first one tries to wrap his arms around her.

Dumbass. Myrna ducks, throwing an elbow into his side. She spins, then rams her opposite elbow down across his back. He falls belly to the ground, dust puffing into the air.

The second comes at her, a war cry spewing from his lips. At least he has a proper stance. "Who do you think you are to interfere?"

"You're a coward. Attacking an unarmed man." Myrna spits, her saliva landing on the man's boot. *Maybe not so classy for a royal there, Myrna.*

He roars again and engages with a quick exchange of punches. They're well placed, but weak. She has no trouble stopping the first with her hand and deflecting the second. Then the third Myrna dodges as her left fist connects with his ribs. Just as she thinks another will make contact, Kelan appears, volcanic hate lighting his eyes. He knocks it away.

"You shall not touch the princess!" Kelan bites out.

The Guardian has no time to respond, for Kelan's right fist comes down on his temple. The man staggers, stunned, then hits his knees.

Myrna kicks him in the gut, and he falls to his back.

Cries of the crowd now gathered reach her ears.

Various expressions of shock plaster across the faces of the rest of her guard as Kelan looks down at Myrna.

"I did not need your help."

"Perhaps not, but you have it," he says.

Maybe she hadn't needed their help to take them down, but they could clean it up while she tended the civilian. Myrna looks back at the males sprawled on the ground.

"Lock them up," Myrna orders in her royal tone. "Guardians of the royal army do not act as such. They do not harm innocence for no reason."

"He's a traitor." The Guardian on his back groans.

"I heard the entire exchange. He did nothing wrong. He was here to buy food for his family."

"His traitorous family," the guard mumbles.

Kelan leans forward, hand on his sword. "He's of the line I mentioned."

Myrna's teeth grind together. "And has this man"—she points to the boy, hands in the dirt, head bowed, with his dirty hair masking his features—"committed any crimes?"

The male's blood soaks into the dirt, creating tiny black mud piles.

Myrna stands tall now, and her voice takes on a tone she recognizes. It is loud and strong, meant to project and be heard by all. It is that of a leader, one like her mother. "I want an answer. Has this male been convicted of any crimes?" Her gaze burns into Kelan's.

"Nay. It 'twas his father. Shay has yet to prove his blood is tainted."

"Shay?"

CHAPTER TWENTY

Humbled by Honest Kindness

KELAN'S ARCANE VIBRATES WITHIN him. It hums at his very core, whispering he's not in control. He has not been since the moment she called his ass out for being close-minded. And if what she said was true, he deserved more than what Shay received. Because regardless of the hatred he's held for the boy's father, no one deserved to be treated like that for living one's life—for trying to feed their family.

The boy, who is nearly a man by their standards, kneels, hands in the dirt, head bowed. He spits, crimson mixing to become blackened tar.

Kelan winces at the pain on Myrna's face. Her attention locks on him, and it's as if he can hear her putting the pieces together. The boy in Haszwalds requesting a meeting for help. The man from the other night. A family in ruin. Black hair, dark pants, strong shoulders wrapped in a simple tee.

Yes, Myrna, you know him. Heat tickles up his spine when white fire flashes in her eyes. His imagination?

Her voice squeaks when she asks, "The man who saved my life not two days ago is being abused? By our own guard?"

She's the right to be outraged. Clear-headed, he is too. A heart who'd risk himself to climb upon a roof in a storm to save someone he didn't know didn't deserve to be tortured by those who should protect him.

Shoulders back, head bent low, she snarls, "Take these men to the palace dungeons. I'll deal with them later."

It's the most like Laoise she's ever looked. It doesn't scare him. In some ways, he finds this side of her fascinating. As do others, it seems. A crowd is gathering. Owners and patrons of the shops have come to see the spectacle—the princess fighting her own guard to protect one of their own.

"Rani, Drazi, take them now and do not show them mercy. Put them on Level 3," Kelan adds. He moves closer to the princess. The increasing crowd makes him nervous. These people are innocent, but he will not risk her.

They do as ordered, the three Guardians Myrna took down struggling. They argue, beg apologies and for forgiveness, claiming she doesn't understand.

"He is but a piece of trash!" one calls out.

Myrna steps forward, grabs his collar, and says, "He is worth more than you will ever be. Rank or no, someone who will beat an unarmed innocent does not deserve my leniency." She shoves him to the ground, where he cowers.

Stones.

The crowd perks up. They exchange glances, a mixture of hope and fear filling the air.

Then Myrna regains her composure and poise and rejoins Shay. She takes a knee before him, the black of her pants dusted. She reaches out and runs a gentle hand down his arm.

Shay flinches.

"Do not touch him!" Kelan steps closer.

The hate-filled eyes meet his. The people around him step away or to the side, out of her line of sight.

"Guardian Kelan, you use that tone with me one more time, and we are going to have another conversation. Your job is to listen to my commands and protect me from outside threats. Mr. Hughes is not one. So, go stand over there and shut the hell up. Send Guardian Briana over if you must."

Kelan curls his hands into fists. *This female is a nuisance.* Nearly as bad as Laoise.

Shay's back shakes, and Kelan grinds his teeth. The boy is laughing.

"Are you all right?" Myrna asks softly.

Finally, he looks up, and she seems shocked to find a huge grin splitting his face.

I'm going to kill him. Especially with how much he looks like his father, Declan.

She presses her hand to his cheek. "Well, if you're smiling like that, you aren't dying. But it might indicate brain damage."

Shay laughs again. "No. I'm fine, really. It's just...no one speaks to Kelan Brynes like that." His gaze flicks to Kelan. "It's nice to see."

Myna grunts. "Yes, well. He's annoying. Though Briana tries to convince me he means well, I'm yet to believe her."

Kelan rolls his eyes. He knew getting those two together was a bad idea.

"That's a conversation for a different time, however." Myrna runs a thumb along a particularly large bump on his forehead. Shay winces even as his soft hair tickles the back of her hand. "I repeat, are you okay?"

With a frown, Shay sits back on his heels and runs his fingers through his hair. It exposes the entirety of his face. It's obvious what she sees. It's what they all see—a handsome male with a strong jaw and honest eyes.

She hums deep in her throat. "You're different than I remember. Granted, it was dark and raining that night."

"We've met once before," he says, "at Haszwalds, remember?"

"Oh, yes." She grins and shoves to her feet. When she holds her hand out, he takes it and stands. "Well, that was an odd day."

There's a murmur in the crowd as she helps him up. Exclamations of shock at her willingness to touch a disgraced, and one so filthy, but Myrna doesn't notice, for her focus is entirely on Shay. Kelan gets it. Rare is it one of such a high rank mingle with the lower Faye.

Shay dusts his pants off. The corner of his mouth lifts. "So, what? I save you and now you save me. Is this how it's going to be?"

She shakes her head and lifts one shoulder. "Maybe. Now, come on. Let's get you cleaned up."

Pressing his lips together, he says, "I'm good. Really. I'll just head home. I should've known it was a bad idea to come into town today." He licks at the fresh blood talking causes.

Arms crossed, Myrna steps close. "I don't think you understand. It wasn't a question." She grabs his hand again. He jumps but doesn't pull away as she leads him toward a chair in front of the small store. "You don't have a choice. I'm kinda stubborn like that."

"You're a menace, Princess," Kelan grumbles as she passes. To his surprise, the comment makes her smirk, and part of him feels bad for the kid, considering the terrified look on his face. It's probably been a long time since anyone's been willing to acknowledge his existence, let alone touch him in public without regard. For it to be her? That'd be a completely new level. "And you're making a scene," he says, stopping next to them. Damn, he can't get the annoyance out of his voice.

She pats his chest and talks to him like a child. "Well, then I guess I'm lucky I have your big, strong muscles to protect me."

He groans. When Shay grins again, Kelan bares his teeth. Shay's suddenly very interested in the shop's window and the crowd watching the exchange.

"Guardian Briana?" Myrna calls.

"Highness?"

The princess pulls a small bag from her pocket and hands it to the female. It holds the seal of the queen. "Can you please gather his things and have everything that was damaged replaced?"

"That's unnecessary, Princess," Shay says.

Myrna shoots him an amused, warning glare. "In fact, double anything in there and close any debts he has here."

Shay's mouth drops open.

"Of course," Briana says with a grin, then rushes off to do as ordered.

Kelan stays, Jaden taking a spot opposite him.

"If you two are just going to glare, go stand over there," Myrna mutters. "Otherwise, I'll start thinking I forgot to shower today."

Shay snorts. He leans in. "I promise, it's not that." His gaze darkens. "You smell lovely."

Myrna blushes as those blue eyes assess her.

"Back off, lover boy," Kelan warns.

Myrna rolls her eyes and pushes Shay into a chair. Then she turns to the owner of the shop and bows slightly. "Excuse me, ma'am. I apologize for the disturbance. Is there any way you might have a cloth and some water for which I might clean him up with?"

"You will not be cleaning him up!" Kelan snaps.

The death glare is back. It is so fierce he nearly steps away.

Readdressing the owner, she adds, "I'd appreciate the help and afterward, could you show me around your shop? It is a charming place."

The shopkeeper glows at the request. "It would be my pleasure!"

"How do you do that?" Shay murmurs when she scurries off. He goes to stand, but Myrna stops him with a hand to his shoulder.

"Stay," she warns.

"I wouldn't move if I were you. She will get her way," Briana says, appearing and placing two large bags at his feet. She gestures to the items. "The shop next door is to bring the remaining items shortly."

"Thank you, Guardian."

Shay's eyebrows draw together. It's hard to decide what to think of this unconventional girl; first met at a secretary desk, then on the roof of the palace during an attempted escape. He huffs. A story so many want to know more of, for she is special. Kelan cannot blame him.

Kelan sucks air through his teeth when the bowl of water and cloth arrive for Myrna, and she takes them from the old female. To keep himself from knocking them away from her, he leans against the doorframe, savoring the way it digs into his spine, and watches as she wipes away the blood on his forehead and cheek. She trails the cloth over his wounds with the care of someone who's lived with injury—tended them often. It's pure kindness, something he respects her for and hates that she's lived.

The crowd flows around them, the townsfolk coming to watch the princess tending to a peasant. Kelan keeps his guard up even as a part of his locked-away heart opens when the shock of the moment shifts to respect in their eyes. Soon, a few of the locals approach, bow, and whisper a few words. Most often just her name, or a simple, "Our honor, Highness," but even as she works, she always sends a soft smile and nods.

She has no idea of the significance. Look how tense she is each time they approach.

"I'm sorry this happened," she whispers. "I don't know your story or their reasoning, but it's unacceptable."

The boy shrugs. "I've dealt with this my entire life. You should see what my father has to deal with." Shay glances at Kelan, whose nose twitches. "I can't even get a meeting to discuss essential help my family requires."

"What do you mean?"

He rests his elbows on his knees. "Training, medical care…it's why I was at Haszwalds. I was trying to meet with…" His jaw tics. "Never mind. It's not important."

Myrna laughs once, the sound not humorous but sad. "Considering the stupid things I've heard about today, I can guess."

Done with her ministrations, she places the towel back in the bowl. "Well, I'm going to look at this lovely woman's shop, and then afterward I'll be walking you home, seeing as you have a little more here than you can carry." The heat of her guard's angry stares, Kelan's included, could burn her skin. Myrna comes to Kelan. She pulls him a few feet away. "And no one is going to complain about it. In fact"—Myrna looks at her watch—"it's about shift change. You have to get back to the castle to speak with the high court. It's unavoidable and you know it, but don't worry, Briana and Jaden can stay."

Kelan crosses his arms over his large chest. "They can, but this isn't a good idea. And not because it's his family's land. There aren't enough guards to protect you that far out."

"We have three more on the way," Briana says, joining them.

"Perfect. See, I'll be fine. You know I'm not some wallflower, either." Myrna walks away.

Kelan drops his gaze, his stomach twisting. He screwed up big time today, and he wasn't sure how he would fix this with Myrna, but how could he explain the deep shard digging into his gut at the idea of trusting a Hughes with another Qhuinn royal when the last one failed so miserably?

"I'll keep an eye on her, big brother," Briana says, pulling him out of his thoughts.

Kelan nods as Myrna picks up the supplies she's gathered for the boy.

"Well?" Myrna looks up at Shay through her eyelashes. "Perhaps you can explain a little more about your family as we walk, but only if you're comfortable. I'm trying to learn more about Faerie, and I like hearing things from all points of view."

Shyly, he says, "Well, I can't very well turn you down. Can I?"

With one last glance, Kelan returns to the castle and the meeting that might just start a war.

CHAPTER TWENTY-ONE

New Favorite Place

"THIS PLACE IS BEAUTIFUL." Myrna's mesmerized by the light which trickles through the branches, trellising the road to Shay's land. It's not far from the small cluster of shops they left, and yet, it feels so much more remote. Quieter, too. The new guards are spread out, half in front, half behind, with Briana a few feet from them.

"It is. I love it here. Few people come to visit, for obvious reasons, which means the land is mostly untouched."

"How much land do you guys have?"

"A hundred acres or so, but we back to the river on one side and the forest on the other. So, it feels like more. We moved out of the city after..." He glances away and changes the subject. "The old owner had died in the war, and no one wanted this house, so they shoved us here."

Myrna blinks, sadness filling her at his tone. His family must've lost much.

"It shares a boundary with a particularly prickly neighbor no one else wants."

"Should I ask?"

Shay shakes his head and chuckles. "Not today. But perhaps one day I'll take you to meet them. I think they'll like you." He shoots her a sidelong look. "You have a way with people. I have a feeling you'd treat them with respect regardless, and they'd fall all over you."

"Everyone deserves kindness." Myrna trips on a rock, and Shay steadies her.

"Hmm. In my experience, that's a unique thought process."

"Well, it shouldn't be." She rubs her arm.

They walk in silence after that, but she doesn't mind the quiet. It's actually kind of nice to just stroll, the cool breeze on her skin and an honest person beside her. He feels safe, open. Almost as though she has known him her entire life. *But that is ridiculous.*

He motions to a path on the right. "We're going through here. There's an outcropping with a great view you'll love."

"Really? That sounds great." She follows him, her muscles warming—happy to be used as she climbs the steep hill. Myrna takes his offered hand when she must scale a larger boulder, then steps close, their bodies brushing, when he pulls her up. She pats his chest and moves past. "Thank you."

He blinks fast as he nods.

"Look at that." Myrna's words lengthen with joy. The river, mountains, and cabin look like a painting...or a dream. Over her shoulder, she says, "You get to live here? See this every day?"

He joins her, taking a seat on a rock. "Of all the views in Tara, this is my favorite."

Her knees press to her chest. "I moved around a lot as a child. We lived in a lot of remote areas, but none looked like this. Faerie has a beauty like nothing I've ever seen. The human world's unique. It has so many different types of landscapes, but this place is special." She runs her hands over the stone, through the grass at the base, and over the dirt. There's an energy that vibrates against her skin. "It's like it sings to me."

"You weren't raised in Faerie?" Shay frowns when Myrna shakes her head. His mouth widens in understanding. "You must've felt so out of place. That would've been terrible."

"How do you know?"

His voice drops, becoming kinder, as if he were speaking to an injured creature. *Was she?*

"This place feels different because it is. It speaks to you; it connects with you because our people are a part of it just as it is a part of us."

"Wha-what do you mean?" She trembles, the words from some of the books coming back to her. Ones from the gift given by Stephan, *Balance Beholden*, shining brighter in her memory. Stories she'd read before bed, talking about the connection between the land and beast. She hadn't understood.

"You'll see the longer you're here. Our magics are linked and without that connection, you've been..." He struggles for the word. "Broken. I knew when I saw you at Haszwalds you were struggling, but I never guessed that this was why. Then I heard rumors about a princess being raised in the human world... I'm sorry."

"Ah...rumors." Myrna exhales harshly and lies back. "I'm sure they were fantastic."

"They weren't so bad. Mostly speculation."

"Well, you're right. I never felt settled, never fit in."

Shay extends one leg before him, bending the other to rest his arm upon it. "Do you want to talk about it?"

"Princess," Briana warns.

In an exaggerated movement, Myrna rolls both her eyes and head to look at Briana. "You aren't going to act like your brother, are you?"

"Saints, no! Actually, I wanted to apologize. Shay's right." When the boy beside Myrna twitches at the words, Briana smirks and continues, "I should've thought about how your time in the human world would've made you feel so disconnected. And then they feel so...different from us." She comes to lean against a rock closer to the couple. "To have grown up like that, to never feel the magic. Your comments and reactions to us make so much more sense."

"What do you mean?" Shay asks, looking between the two females.

Myrna shifts in her seat. *What could she mean? Had her actions been pushing the people here away further?* Myrna runs a hand over her face. "Nothing."

"It's like she's afraid she's going to offend us, and we're going to reject her."

"I am not!" Shay raises an eyebrow, and Myrna hides her face with an arm. "You suck, Bri."

Shay lifts her arm and peeks at her. "Well, I've had nothing but interesting interactions with you. It's kinda weird. I feel like I've known you forever."

Myrna shoots to a sitting position, nearly head butting him. "Oh, my god! I was just thinking that! Weird, right?"

Briana laughs. "Maybe. Or your fates were supposed to cross. Either way, it's going to piss off Kelan."

"Good," Myrna grumbles.

Shay laughs as Briana adds, "Myr, with your physical training, we'll also add some grounding work. It'll help you connect with Faerie. Make you feel more at home."

"Sounds like a plan."

"You're welcome to come here anytime you'd like. I know I find it peaceful." Shay's eyes are soft, hopeful.

Myrna smiles. "Will I get to meet those pesky neighbors of yours?"

"I don't know about that," Briana says. "Pixies are trouble."

Excitement has Myrna's chest expanding until a branch snaps somewhere in the forest.

Briana's head twists in that direction, instantly serious. Not an instant later, an arrow slams into her shoulder. She rolls to the ground.

Myrna goes to jump up, but Shay pins her. His body's a shield as he scans the trees and the area from which the arrow appeared.

"Get her out of here!" Briana crouches behind the boulder, her face filled with determination. She breaks off the arrow and pulls out an obsidian blade. "Are you armed?"

Myrna's not sure who she's asking.

In unison, they say, "Yes."

"If you were armed, why didn't you fight back against the Guardians?" Myrna asks.

Through panting breaths, Briana says, "Because he would've been punished more severely had he been."

Needing to get to ground level, Shay helps Myrna slide down the massive boulder they'd climbed. Briana follows, the scrape of her tunic loud in the silence. They move toward the path and peek around the rock to find three men hidden in the trees.

"Isn't that the direction Sable and that new guard were posted?" Myrna asks.

"Aye," Briana says.

"Well, shit."

"We need to get her out of here."

"Follow me." Staying down, Shay leads them through the maze of boulders scattered farther down the embankment. It's an old rockslide long since overgrown. They use the trees, bushes, and rocks as cover. Yet their attackers still manage to keep them in their sights. Arrows bounce off their surroundings. One wedges into a tree. A fight breaks out as Jaden and another Guardian, Zerekule, approach from the other side, notified of the situation by some signal Briana gave.

"I need to learn that call," Myrna says as they climb the hill to the road. There's no sign of the other guards.

"We shouldn't have taken you out without teaching you. Kelan's gonna kill me."

Myrna lets out a curse as four men step into their path. Dressed in all black, hoods up and faces covered, they have no discerning features visible. And with the fading light, it'll become harder to identify them should they run.

Myrna slides two blades from their sheaths in her knee-high boots. Kelan wouldn't let her carry a sword, but that didn't mean she wasn't armed. She takes a fighting stance, Shay on her right, Briana on her left.

CHAPTER TWENTY-TWO

Dude, Your Arms are on Fire

WELL, THIS COULD'VE GONE *better*, Shay thinks before raising his fists and squaring up to the assassins here for the princess. There's no way he'll let them take her. One, she's...well, Laoise's daughter, but more Myrna's also shown to have a beautiful soul, funny and kind.

Watching her stroll through the market and speak to Mrs. Daughtry was like a dream. The girl mesmerized everyone with her easy laughter and natural curiosity. She asked questions about the people around her, the art and jewelry sold, even buying a few pieces when she found out Mrs. Daughtry's daughter made them.

Briana's gaze flashes at his empty fists and screams, "I thought you said you had a weapon!"

"I do. It's just dangerous in tight quarters," he says with a quick glance at the surrounding forest.

"Okay..." Myrna grumbles.

"Queen save us...you better know how to fight, kid," the Guardian says before the invaders attack.

Two go for Myrna, while the others distract her companions. Not surprising really, their goal obviously the princess. But to kill her or to capture?

A sense of satisfaction fills him, watching her battle as the blades become an extension of herself. They slice the air with an ease long practiced. The assassins step away, surprise a quick glint in their eyes.

An attacker approaches Shay, and it's clear he doesn't think much of the boy. There is a low laugh, and he asks, "You really think you can hold your own?"

"I'll do well enough," Shay says, and invades the male's space. Instead of going for the obvious hit first, Shay uses his larger size and knees the male in the thigh, then throws a left cross at the ribs. The assassin stops the hit, but stumbles back, limping and stunned. His eyes narrow under the hood.

Behind his shoulder, Myrna's attackers go for her once again, this time splitting her attention. One swipes low with his knife. She dodges, her gut barely clearing the blade, but as she does, a fist connects with her side. The breath goes out of her. Bending, they use the motion to their advantage and grab her arm. And pride flows through Shay, for Myrna doesn't give in. She swings her blade backward and up until it digs in. The man gasps and stumbles back. Yanking the blade free, he releases her, and she punches him in the face.

He falls, the gasping breath of a punctured lung hitting Shay's ears. Myrna winces, regret flashing on her face for an instant.

Satisfied she's down to one, he focuses on his own combatant. Though he's not as skilled as she, he has been trained by his father. He engages fully, diving into the fray at full speed. The hits are sloppy, and many don't get through, but the ones that do are hard. Shay is strong and, right now, that's what will save him. He can't keep up with a full-fledged Guardian and he knows it, but he can knock one out. He grunts when a fist lands on his side, then stomach in quick succession, but in doing so, it opens up the assassin's face.

A blade slides across the gravel road to disappear into the bush by his feet. Then there's a feminine squeak. Shay's gaze flashes up to find a female hidden in the brush—dark hair and high cheekbones? He cannot tell.

Closer, there's a flash of steel as the male reaches for the knife at his belt, and Shay knows he has no more time. He wraps his hands around the Faye's head and slams his head down as he raises his knee. The male falls flat to the earth.

Shay spins, scanning the street. Briana and her opponent are farther down and locked in battle. He pauses for barely a heartbeat, fascinated by the brilliant skill shown between the two, until Myrna grunts, then cries out, causing him to spin just in time to see her take a hit directly to the ribs. She's thrown off balance, and the male above her grabs ahold of her blond locks.

"Shay!" she screams.

The walls fall on his control. Anger like he's never felt opens the well of arcane within him, and red flashes in his eyes. Determination hardens his features, and the air along the road shifts, a breeze wafting through the trees. He *will* save the person who has treated him with such kindness. This person for whom he's crossed paths with too many times for it to be coincidence and for whom he feels deep within, is meant to be a dear friend.

Arms going straight down to his sides, palms forward, his arms burst to flame.

"Holy shit," Myrna says.

Shay's adversary, who's stirred, gets to his feet and sweeps his arm up and around as if to cast some spell. Which means there is no time. He is not skilled enough for a true arcane battle. One shot—that is his chance.

Shay stomps once, claps his hands, and rolls them as if molding a large ball. Heat radiates from him like a furnace. Then he shoves out, a ball of flame bursting forth toward the male readying an attack upon him. Uncontrolled, unwieldy, it hurdles like a gale force making contact. The body is thrown into the air ablaze in his fire, while screams pierce the quiet of the forest. They sink into the youngling and, just as the memory of the collapsed lung will stay with Myrna forever, so will the sound of this man's screams.

The distraction causes Briana's assassin to stumble, allowing her to overtake him. She knocks him out, then turns toward the commotion. When she sees Shay, she gapes.

"Let her go!" Shay says to the figure who is dragging Myrna by her hair. The color of the flame at his palms deepens even as his eyes brighten with fury.

The hooded figure swoops around, pulls Myrna up, and uses her as a shield.

"Shay, no!" Briana screams. "You're too uncontrolled. You'll kill her."

It's true. The only reason he'd hit his previous target was because they'd been feet away. Shay is a youngling himself, barely through the changing, and without any proper training, he is dangerous.

Just then, the rest of the guards rush from the trees, throwing the bound invaders into the dirt. They take in the scene and are instantly alert. Whether from the sight of him, fire wrapping his arms like barbed wire, or the assassin holding the princess, it doesn't really matter.

Shay's breaths come quicker, his endurance while wielding not as great as it should be. He clenches his fists, trying to hide the way his hands shake.

"Shay..." Myrna whines, but the tone is off. Though a plea, it's also too strong. Then Myrna nods once, holds her palm against her thigh, fingers spread. She drops them one by one, mouthing the numbers, and he understands.

It's a sign to let him know exactly when to act. Either a brilliant idea or a terrible one. Guess he'll find out. She hits three, steps out, and twists around, her hair yanking from its roots, then she rams her knee into the assassin's family jewels.

The male yelps and lets go as if to bend and grab his offended area, but then he realizes his mistake.

Myrna doesn't wait. She rolls out of the way, barely evading the hand trying to grab her again.

Pride fuels this ball as he throws everything he has at the male. Shay lets go of his fireball with a bellow. He closes the distance as he does to minimize surrounding damage. The body goes up in an inferno. Leaves of the bushes nearby curl beneath the extreme heat.

Shay skids to Myrna's side, where she lies on the ground. A few strands of her golden hair are singed, but other than that, there's no visible damage. Still, it wouldn't have been comfortable. Which is why he scoops her up and examines her face. "Myrna! Are you all right? Did I burn you?"

The princess rolls over and presses a hand to a spot on her face where a small scrap tops what looks like the start of a bruise. "I'm fine. I'm just stupid and hit my face on a rock."

Shay chuckles. Without thinking, he does what he would for one of his sisters. He leans in and kisses the spot.

They both freeze. Her eyebrows shoot down.

He grimaces, then clarifies. "I'm sorry if that was weird. I do that for my sisters."

Myrna sits up and looks at him thoughtfully. Then she laughs. "It's okay. Um...I hope you're not offended, but it kinda felt like my brother."

He isn't. Not at all. She's beautiful, but for some reason, his draw to her isn't attraction, but something else. Still, he has to give her a hard time. Shooting her a smoldering glance, he asks, "So, you're telling me you don't find this face alluring?"

She blinks, then shoves his shoulder and pushes to her feet, saying, "Oh my gosh! Shut up." Myrna pulls a chuckling Shay to his feet and gives him a hug. "Thanks for the save... Again."

"What in the queen's army is happening here? And why are you all on my land?" a booming voice echoes down the street. Shay winces. "Hold. Shay, is that you?"

Shay drops his arms from around Myrna, then turns to make eye contact with a man who looks quite a bit like his son. "Yes, Father, it's me. Everything is fine. I'd like you to meet Princess Myrna."

Of all the times to walk up...

Myrna's cheeks are pink as she lifts a hand and waves. "Hello, Mr. Hughes." She steps forward. "I'd like to personally apologize for all the trouble my presence has brought to your beautiful land. I feel so bad breaking such harmony."

"It wasn't your fault, Myr," Shay says, irritated. "I was the one you had to save in town."

"No. If my guards weren't being turdnuggets—"

Shay chokes. "Turdnuggets? That has to be a human term."

"A Sam original, I think."

The two younglings look at one another for a long moment before they break out in uncontrollable giggles. The older Faye watches them, a mix of confusion and awe on all of their faces.

Myrna is the first to get a hold of herself. She approaches the much larger Faye and holds her hand out. Three of the guards rush forward as if to stop the exchange. Myrna points at them. "I swear, you will treat him with respect on his land. Now go make sure there are no more waiting to attack."

They do as she orders, and Shay laughs. Myrna looks up at him, a question in her eye. "He's confused by your actions. Well, probably our actions."

"That's fair," Myrna says, pressing her lips together. "Mr. Hughes, your son had a hard day. There were some issues with some asshole Guardians in town, which I took care of, and then this..." She gestures to the assassins, which lay scattered around the road.

The two he'd burned are smoldering. Their bodies twitch, the last vestiges of their lives seeping from them. Shay's brows draw down, and his gut tightens. These are the first lives he's taken. Whether for an honorable cause or not, they are still souls lost to this world. Myrna notices and tries to comfort him, but in the process brushes the sensitive skin red and raised where the fire left a crisscrossing pattern on his skin.

"You're hurt?" she asks.

"I'm fine. It'll be gone in a few hours." To the sadness in her eyes, he adds, "Promise."

Myrna nods, then readdresses Mr. Hughes. "I'm so sorry to have brought trouble here. I never would've come had I known this could happen and put Shay in jeopardy." Myrna scrunches her nose again.

"You're apologizing to me?" Mr. Hughes looks confused, and Shay can't blame him. He was too, but after the last few hours, he thinks he understands her more.

"Declan." Briana inclines her head to Mr. Hughes as she joins them. "Myrna's different. She doesn't understand our ways, nor does she care about class or past mistakes."

"Briana. It's good to see you in Guardian colors. Congratulations, you deserve it." Declan Hughes's jaw tics. "Though I'd recommend this conversation be short. Should your family find out we conversed, it would not go well for you."

The exchange brings a heaviness to Shay's chest. The Bryneses were once so close. Their loss has been a great one to them all, but none more than his father. Briana was like a little sister to Declan and having to walk away from her broke both their hearts. Which he suspects Myrna reads in them all.

"We must get you back to the palace," Briana says to Myrna. "There might be more of them out here. You're not safe, and I've already sent word to Kelan. He'll be on his way."

Declan's lips curl back. "Guardian *Kelan* Brynes is not welcome on my land."

"I know," Briana says. "Which is why I need her headed back ASAP."

"I can lend you a horse," Declan says. He bows to the princess. "I'm sorry this happened here. My daughters and I were at the house. Had I known, I would've lent you my sword."

"I'm glad you were able to protect them instead. In fact, I wish you to go back and make sure they're okay."

"I am sure they are." He scans the guards warily. "I'll get the horse and have it to you in a few minutes. Will that be acceptable?"

"That'd be perfect. Oh, and…" Myrna smiles and holds her hand out one more time.

It's a very human thing to do, but Declan takes it with an interested air. Perhaps because it means as much to him as it did to Shay.

"Thank you. I'm Myrna Qhuinn, by the way." She lowers her voice and, with a quick flash at Shay, she adds, "Do me a favor. Look after him and let me know he's okay?"

Declan releases her hand. "You worry for him?"

"Of course. He's my friend."

Declan blinks, the corner of his lip lifting, then disappears toward the house. *There are going to be so many questions at home tonight.*

Briana catches Shay's attention. "You did well, considering you've so little control over your arcane. How long have you been practicing?"

He tries not to be embarrassed. Her words were not meant to be a knock, but a compliment, and Shay understands her meaning. He is untrained. That is why he was at Haszwalds to beg Kelan for help. Yes, beg. "A few months. My power is much different than Father's. Far more destructive and so he cannot help much. I've tried to reach out to the Guardians, but..."

Briana looks sad. "Perhaps I may find a proper tutor. Either way, thank you for your assistance. Myrna would've been taken if not for you."

Myrna slams her hands down on her hips like a frustrated toddler. "I would've escaped. Eventually."

They both grin, and Briana says, "We have no doubt."

"Hey, Bri? Can I say goodbye to my friend before you drag me back to the castle, and I'm never allowed out again?"

She nods, then gestures to the group managing the tied-up prisoners. "Yeah. Jaden looks like he needs some help, anyway."

Myrna leads Shay a distance away. Not so far as to make the Guardians nervous or for them to be unsafe, but far enough that perhaps their conversation won't be overheard. She plays with her thumb and says, "Thanks for bringing me here. It was nice to feel normal. To be out with anyone." She glances off into the forest.

"Are they keeping you locked up or something?"

"Not exactly. It's only been a few days since I found out about Faerie and that I'm Faye. Let alone that my mother is queen." She laughs without humor, then presses her hands to her ribs. They slide down her sides, the pressure nice until she hits a sore spot. "It's just been a lot."

Shay's at a loss for words.

"Yeah. Kind of been a busy week. You're the one person I've met who didn't *have* to interact with me, or be nice to me, or serve me. It's..." She exhales. "Part of me misses the human world. And now it's my job to learn everything and become the best heir I can be, and I don't even know where to start. But I did get her to agree to let me explore and see the town. Then this happened." She looks down at the ground and kicks.

Sadness fills him at the confused sorrow he senses swirling within her.

"Just...thank you," she says one last time.

Knowing this will probably get him in trouble with the Guardians and not caring a bit, Shay grabs her shoulder and pulls her into a hug. Myrna stiffens, but then she wraps her arms around his waist.

"You're the first friend I've had in a long time, too," he says into her hair. "I don't think you understand what you've done for me today."

"Does that mean I didn't scare you off?" she says into his shirt. The words are far more vulnerable than he'd expect from such a strong person.

Shay pulls back and looks down at her. "Why the hell would you have scared me off? Myrna, you're a blast to hang out with."

"I don't fit anywhere." Heat rushes to her face. "I'm gonna be super embarrassed by this conversation later, so you know."

He laughs and wraps his arm around her shoulders to lead her back toward the disgruntled Guardians. She links hers around his waist as he says, "I think you fit in better than you realize."

The sound of a horse trotting up the main road has them turning as one. Their arms drop, and Myrna approaches Shay's horse, a beautiful beast of a male. Shiny black coat with white legs, he towers over her. Declan dismounts and grins at the way the horse locks on the princess.

"Well, aren't you gorgeous," she says, holding her hand out. He sniffs her, then butts his head into her chest, demanding she wrap her arms around his big head. Myrna presses her face between his ears.

"I see you've made a friend." Shay chuckles, then asks, "I'm never getting my horse back, am I? His name is Shadowmar, by the way."

Myrna laughs, her nails digging into the hairs of the horse's neck. "As long as I can come to visit him. Maybe."

CHAPTER TWENTY-THREE

Shh, Little One. I Know What You Are

KELAN TRIES TO ABIDE the request made. He truly does, but his patience has been ripped to shreds—his very control scattered to the universe—all because that blond-haired vixen sent him away and then had the gall to get attacked.

Do not enter the Hughes Family Land, brother. Myrna is safe and unharmed. Shay protected her with his life. Do not dishonor that. I will bring her to you.

But as the time passes, his patience wanes. The steed beneath him, usually so steady, senses his unease. The additional seven Guardians surround him, their horses huffing in the fading light.

"No longer," Kelan says.

"Sir, no!" Isaiah calls after. With a curse, his horse pushes forward, following the already speeding Kelan onto Declan's land. "Kelan, this is a bad idea. You were specifically requested to wait. Guardian Briana has the situation in hand."

"I know she does." And yet, he pushes his horse faster until the figures come into view and Myrna's blue gaze swings to his.

She sighs, then turns to Declan with a sad smile. "Sir, help me mount, and I'll get everyone off your property. I do not wish you any additional trouble."

The words pull Kelan up short. He slows his horse, coming to a stop several hundred yards away as Shay helps the princess onto a horse of midnight black.

She slips her foot into the stirrup and Declan secures the straps, verifying they're set for her height. "I promise to return him to you as soon as I am able."

Backing away, both of the Hughes males bow low, clearly making the youngling uncomfortable. Declan addresses Myrna formally. "It has been our honor to have you here. I'm sorry this happened, but I am proud Shay protected you so well."

"You have raised a good male. I am lucky to have him as my friend." With that, she tugs the reins, leading the great beast toward Kelan. Briana and Jaden flank the horse at a jog until they catch up with Kelan far down the road.

Jaw aching, he looks her over, then snaps, "I told you not to come here." He clears his throat. "Are you injured?"

"Not really. We were able to fight them off." Her face is hard with annoyance.

As they exchange words, her Guardians mount the extra horses they brought with them while three additional soldiers run past to help clean the scene.

"We'll talk about this in your rooms."

"Probably better. I don't want them to witness me yelling at you."

Jaden coughs, drawing Kelan's attention. He pounds on his chest. "Sorry. Dust."

Kelan glares at him. *Sure.*

The ride through town and to the castle is quiet. The rhythmic beating of hooves on stone is there to settle his nerves. It helps, but only as long as he doesn't glance at the girl on the horse next to him, settling into the ride like a natural.

Shadowmar is glorious a beast. Among the best and to see her on him... It's beautiful, the horse beneath her steady and strong.

Crossing through the gates, he gives them the signal to close them. Myrna looks surprised.

"You were just attacked, Princess. Less than five miles from the palace. What did you think would happen?" Kelan slides from his horse, his eyes never leaving her. "The palace is on lockdown, and the town and surrounding areas are being searched."

He moves to her side and reaches up, his hands resting at her waist. She hesitates for only a moment before, as if realizing again how huge Shadowmar is. She rests a hand on his forearm, then slides one leg over. The horse shifts. Myrna runs a hand along his neck, and he settles. She places both her palms on Kelan's shoulders and allows him to lower her to the ground.

"Come, I need you to tell me what happened."

"Will you make sure Shadowmar is taken care of and returned with care? He's a good horse." There is concern in her eyes.

Kelan's fingers flex on her waist. Her eyes widen minutely. "Of course. I will make sure he's returned unharmed. You have my word."

Jaden, who's taken the reins, says, "He will be fed and allowed to rest, as should you. Do not worry, Princess."

Kelan releases her, and Myrna brushes her hands down her tunic, flattening the rumpled fabric, dirty from both the battle and the ride. But it isn't until they're in her suite and the door has clicked shut that Kelan speaks. "Are you hurt?"

Myrna lowers herself gingerly into a chair, her movements stiff. *Is she sore from the ride or the battle?* She rubs her side, hip, and then lower back. The movement tells him nothing. He moves closer but doesn't take a seat.

Kelan's heart rate picks up once more, the worry within him spiking like he cannot explain. Never has he reacted to someone like this. "Answer me. Are you hurt?"

Myrna sighs. She unties the sash at her waist and slides the tunic down her shoulders. The undershirt she lifts to expose her ribs. "See? I'm fine. Just a bruise."

Kelan sits, no longer able to resist. "May I?" he asks, and when she nods, he palpates her ribs and belly, checking for any serious injury. She grimaces but doesn't shy away. She's right; they are fine.

"This is their fault." Kelan puts the shirt back down, stands, then stomps from the couch. "That damn family. You shouldn't have gone with him. You shouldn't have touched him. You don't understand; they—"

Heat rises on her cheeks, stopping Kelan's words. Warmth radiates from her, the arcane craving to break free. A spark at the corner of Kelan's vision, just near the tip of her fingers, has him watching her even more carefully.

Her changing must be days away.

"Are you really blaming an attack on my life on an innocent family? A family who welcomed me onto their land for a walk to view my domain, then fought by my side?" Myrna shoves to her feet, then stalks toward Kelan.

Kelan gulps. It's like back on the road before she saved Shay. When he'd known the words coming out of his mouth were stupid, wrong. That they tasted bitter on his tongue, but the hurt within refused to allow him anything but shield his heart and believe the lies he needed to survive. So, he said stupid shit. Like… "You don't understand."

"I don't understand?" Her voice is higher than normal. "I don't understand how you continuously treat people who've been nothing but kind and protected me with derision." She holds her hands up and walks in a circle before returning to him. "You know what's funny? Is even in Haszwalds, I remember watching you and thinking you were so fascinating because you had the power to help so many. But now, looking back, I also remember how you treated those you didn't deem worth your time as lowly pieces of trash. Those like me."

Kelan's lungs seize. "All I do is give myself to protect my people. All of them."

"And yet you don't because you don't respect them. For someone who has so much power, you don't see that all you fight for is the land." She points toward the balcony, to the town far beyond. "But it's just as important to protect their minds and hearts."

He's suddenly in her face, his chest pressed up against hers, grip tight on her wrists, his breathing fast. He's embarrassed by the quick pace of his heart. Yet, he can't stop himself from saying, "You'll judge me by my interaction with one family? Even when you don't know what he's done."

"The way you treat the most vulnerable reveals your true heart," she snarls. "But fine. Explain it to me because right now, all I see is a coward."

That is it. Those words snap something inside Kelan. His power lets loose with a ferocity only one other female has ever wrested from him. All the vases in the room explode, and water shoots out in all directions, droplets dispersing in the air.

Myrna gasps, then her eyes turn white. Her mouth opens in a silent scream as power rises within her. But it's too early. She is not yet ready.

Goddess help me. This is power he's rarely seen.

Kelan attempts to loosen his grip, but it's as if they're glued together.

White flame crawls up her fingertips like water to wrap around his wrists. It curls, weaving between them, like silk ties connecting them more firmly together. It's warm but doesn't burn as it pulls his arcane to the surface.

He moans as his power simmers, connecting with hers. The water which floats around them congeals, beginning to dance to a music no one can hear.

"What's happening to me?" The terrified plea is so familiar, and it pulls him from his euphoria.

A flash of memory snakes through his mind. Mareola sounded like this once after her Radiant Light spiked for the first time. It was a few days before her changing, too.

"Shh. You'll be fine, little one," he says, pulling her to him so he may rest his cheek against hers.

Her skin is hot, so he creates a barrier of water between them. *It's just like before.*

Then, after Mareola's changing, she'd burned a hole through a crop of trees. She didn't remember doing it. But when she'd awoken, her skin was on fire. Kelan found her just before her power had ignited again. The one thing that calmed it was...

Kelan whispers in Myrna's ear, "You must get control. Breathe with me. I'm sorry, Myrna. I did not mean to scare you. In. Out. In. Out."

He closes his eyes, heart aching with the similarities and the differences. He sways with her, in time with their breaths.

"I hate you." Her words are a lie. He tastes it in the sensation of her magic. The way it caresses and protects him even when it's not fully manifested.

She protects him. He shifts their arms so that her hands may press to his chest. Her magic re-orients, the radiance pulsing with his heart, allowing him to wrap his arms around her. It means she's calmed and trusts him to bring her back to normal.

"I know. I hate you a little, too. But I will fight for you, and I do not wish you hurt. So, please, breathe with me, and we'll work to control your light—your white fire."

Through clenched teeth, she asks, "My white fire?"

"Yes, love. Your line holds two of the strongest gifts," he explains, keeping his words rhythmic. Unbeknownst to her, this allows her breathing to match his. "Red fire and white fire, also known as Radiant Light."

"Which do I have?" Her voice is less strained. The light coming from her eyes has dimmed as well.

"You're like your Aunt Mareola. She had Radiant Light, too. It fits you. It's beautiful and strong, just as you are." He tightens his hold. He's said too much. "Now, take a deep breath, feel the energy flowing wildly within, and draw it to one area."

He lays a hand to her chest, just over her breastbone. He counts to ten, each breath deep and powerful. She joins him, and he feels her magic pull back. As it does, she relaxes into him, her head sliding to rest along his neck. "Once it's there, imagine you wrap your hands around it and squeeze. Then take another two breaths. Do you understand?"

She nods, does as he asks, and suddenly, the connection is gone. The water throughout the room falls to the floor in a tinkling spray. Myrna collapses against him, her legs giving out with the energy expenditure.

He scoops her up. "Well done. How do you feel?"

She groans. "Tired."

Kelan carries her to the bed.

She plays with his shirt even as her eyes close. "I still don't like you." Her head lolls, the heat of her breath on his neck. "You're controlling butthead."

He laughs, placing her on the bed. Looking into her sleepy eyes, he says, "And you're stubborn." He slips off her shoes, then covers her with the blanket. By the time he reaches the door, she's already asleep.

Glancing back, he whispers, "But you did well. We need to work on your control, though."

He runs a hand over his face. *Queen save me. Radiant Light.*

He is in for it. There are few who have held this ability and even less who know how to train it. But he has personal experience. Because his best friend was one of them and for her, he'd make sure her niece is safe and proficient at using it.

CHAPTER TWENTY-FOUR

Charcoal Shall Never Dull Radiance.

THE KNOCK COMES LATER than expected. After attempting work and failing, Laoise had sent everyone away and had been doing laps around her room as she waited for someone to come and provide an update on Myrna's return. Though she knew the girl was well, she needed confirmation she was within the walls of the palace and safe.

The handle is smooth as she opens the door to find a very out of sorts and disheveled Kelan waiting. *It has been a long time since I've seen you like this.* His hair's a mess, his tunic mussed, but it's his eyes that have her trying to dissect him for the reason.

"Guardian Kelan." She moves back so he may enter. He does, and she closes them in. "I was expecting you earlier. How is Myrna, and what took you so long?"

He scans the room, taking in the neatly made bed, her desk filled with papers, and the candles lit and filling the rounded alcove where she was sitting. She smirks. *Thought I would be entertaining instead of worrying. Did you, Kelan?*

"The princess is fine. She has some bruised ribs. They're not bad, and she's uninjured otherwise."

"Mmm. Now explain to me how you let this happen."

Kelan does, and Laoise listens quietly for once. He tells her about their day at Haszwalds, their trip to town and stroll through the countryside. Pride laced with annoyance runs through her when she hears Kelan's retelling of Myrna's saving of the Hughes boy. Perhaps it's not annoyance so much as guilt, but that's for another day. Still, Myrna made a good impression on the people and fought off the assassins. Overall, a win for the day.

And yet, they couldn't risk another situation like this, so she says, "You could've just thrown her over your shoulder and dragged her home." Laoise takes the seat at her desk, then leans on the arm and crosses her legs beneath her gown.

"Perhaps, but she's still your daughter, and she's trying to find her place. Should I always control her, her place in this kingdom will never be respected."

"Fair. Is there no reasoning with her?"

Kelan huffs. "She's as stubborn as you and your sister were at that age."

This gets a grin. "I see that as well. So why do you look as though you have bad news? Did the fight not go well?"

"It did. Mostly because of the Hughes boy."

"Explain."

"I've been notified he didn't develop the same level arcane as his parents. His is much more impressive. So much so, I think you'd be interested to witness. But it is also unstable. He requires training, or he could be dangerous."

Laoise steeples her fingers. She presses them to her lips. This is complicated. "They are traitors to the crown. Deemed such for oaths broken."

Kelan's canines appear as he snarls, "Yes, but your daughter does not seem to care." He takes a breath, then looks at the floor for a long moment. "She's befriended the boy and refuses to heed my warning."

"Well, neither does she understand our ways nor, I am sure, did you fully explain Declan's crimes." When Kelan doesn't reply, she continues, "What do you wish to do?"

"I've yet to decide, but he cannot be left as is. His arcane is too great. He could burn down half of Faerie without intent."

"That could be a useful tool, especially if he's become friends with our dear Myrna."

"Speaking of your daughter—" Kelan links his hands behind his back and moves closer.

Laoise watches in interest. This must be the real reason he is so worked up.

Kelan squeezes his fingers together, feeling again the sensation of her light against his skin. "I know what her ability will be."

Laoise shoves to her feet and closes the distance quicker than she can think better of it. "What do you mean?"

Kelan manages not to flinch, but Laoise catches the surprise in his eyes.

"I order you to tell me everything," Laoise says, which does nothing to settle his nerves.

Face neutral, Kelan explains, "Upon returning to her rooms, we got into an argument. After checking her ribs, I said some terrible things about Shay and his family. I scolded her for going to their land and spending time with him. We argued. I'm not completely sure what set it off, but suddenly, her eyes lit from within and my hands, which were on her wrists, locked to her."

Laoise's entire body relaxes; her shoulders deflate and her breathing steadies as she listens to his words.

"Our magic connected. It took me a few minutes to talk her down and for her to get control of her Radiant Light."

Laoise lets out a relieved sigh. Breathlessly, she says, "Radiant Light."

Kelan nods. "Aye. It is just like Mareola's." Laoise presses her lips together, then returns to her seat as Kelan adds, "My queen, she's powerful. If I'd not been there, she would've taken down her entire room. I would like your permission to work with her on control and harnessing her power. I know she's not through the changing yet, but I suspect that'll come in the next few days."

Laoise nods, not making eye contact. She keeps her gaze on other things. "I approve. Please start immediately. And perhaps bring the Hughes boy to the training."

"But, my queen!"

Laoise holds up her hand. "It'll give her a friend. Consider him a trained soldier, not a Guardian, if that makes it better for you.

He'll be a soldier willing to give up his life for the crown if you succeed. We always need more of those."

A rapid flurry of knocks comes from the door just over the queen's shoulder. It's the pathway leading to her personal throne room. Brow lowered, Kelan strides to it and opens the door to find Laoise's head attendant, Sola, standing on the other side.

"Majesty, King Brennan contacts us. He wishes to speak with you." Sola is sweating; her hands are trembling. But from the interaction with the king or from interrupting Laoise's evening, Kelan's unsure. Sola's been working up her chain of command for a while, but it is not easy being in her employ.

"How was the message received?"

"The mirror."

Saints. The Mirror of Connection hadn't been used in decades. Mostly because Brennan was a dick and refused its magic. So, the Qhuinn family had assumed he destroyed it. Apparently not.

The queen and her Head Guardian exchange a look.

"Tell him to wait." She strides over to a hook on the far wall and removes the robe she wears over her nightdress and hangs it up. She replaces it with a gown that wraps around her slim form and ties it around her waist. It's not as formal as the queen would normally prefer, but King Brennan cannot expect much more on such short notice. Then she stops before a mirror and flicks her fingers through the strands framing her face. The red tip of her braid falls across her right shoulder.

"Do you think he's contacting you about the invasion in Arinsthial?" Kelan's reflection asks in the mirror as he examines his uniform. Kelan straightens the cuff and shirt, brushes a few specks of dirt, then runs a hand through his hair.

"Unclear. You'll stand behind me, but you will not speak," Laoise says, striding from the room, Kelan a step behind.

"Yes, my queen."

The Mirror of Connection is just off the personal throne room, guarded and monitored at all times, seeing as it can be used to connect to various points across the realm. At least, to the few who know how to use it, or to the twin held by Brennan.

Laoise is all grace and fiery strength as she enters to find the image of the male Faye and threat to her kingdom arguing with her staff. Disgust pools low in her gut as she takes in the male. Once handsome, his greed and gluttony has shifted his appearance to something slimy, dirty even. His hair is dark, slicked back and shimmering with the oils he overuses, and the weight he carries is odd for a Faye. Yet one would never think him weak. He feels too giant for that, his essence weighing down his room, and even seeping through the glass. Oddly, he's actually no larger than she. It's just the power he exudes is incredible, leaving the bitter scent of charcoal and overcooked meat.

"My darling," King Brennan's voice drawls. Its silky-smooth quality causes the hairs on the back of her neck to stand on end. Never would she allow a daughter of hers alone in a room with this male. "You look well."

Voice devoid of emotion, Laoise asks, "To what do I owe this honor, Brennan?"

His eyes go hard, the smile disappearing. "That's King Brennan."

"I will use your title when you use mine," Laoise says. "You will not address me as 'my darling' or any other such platitude. Now, how can I help you? Are you here to negotiate a ceasefire and stop the fighting before it begins?"

Brennan smirks. "Now, Queen Laoise, why would I want to do that? Your land is healthy, quite profitable, and people consistently sinful. I think they'd benefit from a lesson." He waves both hands in the air. "And who better to teach them than me? Especially considering you don't seem to be doing it."

Laoise holds her cool indifference. His words are nothing she hasn't heard before, except for maybe that little tidbit about her land being healthy. Was the king aware he'd just confirmed the information of his land's illness? For her informants spoke of the plague and the sickness spreading through the Unseelie Court.

Laoise remains stock still, fingers linked and face blessedly calm. "I warn you. My patience is waning when it comes to you, King Brennan. Do not trifle with me."

His smirk darkens, becoming a grin laced with evil. When he speaks next, his voice is silkier, deeper, and filled with threat. "Ah...but I heard a rumor. One deep from within your lands. That you've something you're willing to protect over your own dear people. So much so you kept it a secret for nearly a century and perhaps explains another question we all have held so very long." Brennan leans back on his throne and rests his hands on his extended abdomen. "I think we should address this rumor, so that I may know the truth, for it is tradition for our courts to share such news."

Her breathing hiccups. There's a hesitation. Not long enough for Brennan to notice, but it's too much of a reaction. *You knew this was possible. Now play your cards.*

"It has come to my attention that you have an heir." His head tilts, leg extending, and Laoise is surprised his fancy tunic does not burst. He runs a finger over his cheekbone. "And not only do you have an heir, but she's nearly fully grown. Please, Queen, explain to me how this is so."

"How did you come by this information?" Laoise ignores his questions, and the panic building within her. Things were not in place yet.

"That is of little importance, my dear. What is, is you did not follow protocol, and I am in my rights to demand a meeting with her. It is required to keep peace between our realms. Plus, perhaps she would make a match for my son or grandson and align with our philosophies."

"Like hell!" Kelan snaps.

Laoise's head turns slowly toward the Guardian; the warning glare is clear upon her beautiful face. *Shut your mouth, or I will shut it for you.* Kelan becomes a statue in response.

"Ah... Guardian Kelan, it is always so nice to meet you. I see she's yet to put a leash around your rather thick throat. Were you in my court, such outbursts would've been beaten out of you by now."

Kelan straightens but doesn't respond this time, which is good because Laoise would not have gone lightly on him.

Laoise returns her attention to the king. "You have heard correctly. My heir, Myrna Mareola Qhuinn, has returned to the court. I raised her under protection, considering the unstable situation between the Seelie and Unseelie Courts these years."

"Are you saying you do not trust me?"

"Are you ready to negotiate, step down, and integrate your people into my court? Or are you still hell bent on dominion?"

Laoise's voice holds curiosity. When he stays silent, his face reddening, she continues, "You, King, cannot maintain the health of Faerie or those under your care. You are not made for it. Especially considering you keep killing off your consorts."

For a man who speaks of control and stability—for never allowing emotion to rule—it's amazing how quickly his anger ignites. He jerks closer to the glass. "How dare you say such things to me! I am twice the ruler you are, and I will take everything from you, including your daughter. Understand this. It is law that you allow me to meet her and approve your choice prior to appointment as heir. Which means I'm coming for a visit, and I will find out what you're hiding about this girl, whether you like it or not."

"What *am* I hiding? Paranoid, Brennan? And no, King, I do not require your approval to appoint my heir." She pauses, holding the stare of the venerable, difficult king. "Contact me when you wish to discuss your surrender."

Laoise flicks two fingers, indicating to Sola beside the mirror to end the call. Instantly, she does, sending arcane over the edge in a precise pattern, then slips from the room. The image of the king disappears, and Laoise's shoulders sag.

"I really despise that male." Laoise turns to Kelan. "Does he look heavier than the last time we saw him?"

Kelan smirks. "He does and more...sickly."

"The threat increases, Kelan, and I fear Myrna is at the center of it all." Bile burns the back of Laoise's throat. She shakes her head and heads back toward her room. "Begin her training. Keep her safe."

"Should I tell Myrna about the king's demand to meet her?"

"She is already aware of the *Norsthana Maskia* and the timeline for me to choose an heir. It is in one of the texts I provided." Laoise's heart deflates one ounce further, but she says, "Therefore, his request will not surprise her, but perhaps keep his phrasing between us."

"And the king?"

"I will deal with the king."

CHAPTER TWENTY-FIVE

Swallow One's Pride

BAD IDEA OR NO, this does not deter the Guardian. For his duty and pride tell him there's no one else who can do this task. If not for the fact it is important to Myrna. Yes, the queen had recommended it be him, but it had not been an order. Not exactly. Which was strange from Laoise.

Kelan shifts the reins of the horse, guiding his mount down the dirt road. Shadowmar follows behind. He's nearly to the house when a bolt hits a tree near his head. Kelan pulls the horse to a stop, the large black beast stopping as well, his disgruntled whinny his only show of irritation.

"You aren't welcome here," the gruff voice of Declan Hughes says from somewhere in the trees. "Leave."

"I'm here on the queen's business. I'm here to speak to your son and... to verify the return of Shadowmar as promised by the princess."

"You have no business with my son." Declan steps from the trees, a crossbow armed and ready in his hand. It's an interesting weapon, considering this man was once a Guardian, trained in far more impressive choices and considering his talent. Perhaps this is just one of the protections he's placed around his home. "But do tell the princess thank you."

Kelan lifts his hands. "I mean you no harm, but I must speak with Shay."

Declan's eyes narrow, distrust written in every line of his face.

It's a face Kelan knows well. One he's trusted since the day he was born, a brother, but not of blood. No longer.

Keeping the bow trained on Kelan, he says, "Get down from your mount and disarm, then I will take you to him."

This is fair, Kelan thinks, considering their last one-on-one exchange. So, he dismounts and methodically removes his sword and the knives. Kelan places them on a stump to the side of the road, then walks forward, holding the reins of both horses out toward Declan.

The male's expression shifts to surprise. "You truly wish no harm? You would disarm around me, in order to do as you request?"

Kelan's stare is unwavering as he says, "Aye. I'm here to offer him official training as a thank you for the assistance provided to the princess. Shay has significant arcane power, but it is unwieldy. Dangerous." Kelan drops the hand holding the leads to his side. When it looks like Declan is about to speak, Kelan finishes, "Plus, the princess will be going through the same training. She could use a friend—a sparring partner. In truth, this training has been held from him for far too long, anyway."

Declan's arms cross over his chest, but his face has gone stock white with shock.

"Yes! Please, yes!" Shay trips on a root as he stumbles from an outcropping of bushes opposite the two males, cutting off Declan's words before he has a chance to speak. He face plants, but shoves to his knees to look up at the two warriors.

Declan shakes his head and rubs his forehead, the crossbow now hanging at his side. Kelan lifts an eyebrow.

Shay stands. "I mean... Guardian Kelan, if at all possible, I'd very much like to train with Myrna."

Kelan doesn't laugh, no matter how much he wants to. At this moment, the kid is exactly how he remembers Declan in their teens.

Declan gestures to a tie-up just up the road. "Put the horses there, and we can talk."

He doesn't lead Kelan to the house, but instead takes them to a small shed near the horses. There's a forge and a set of rickety chairs. Not surprising as Declan's arcane lies in weapon creation. After taking a seat, Declan asks, "What does this entail?"

"The queen heard about what Shay did on the road. Someone so strong requires training. It's not safe otherwise."

"We've requested this before and been denied."

Kelan inclines his head. "It's not being denied now. You'll be training with Myrna. Although she's new to magic and you aren't, you're both about the same level."

"But she hasn't come into her arcane yet," Declan says, confused.

Kelan shakes his head slowly. "No, she hasn't, but it's seeping through. What I can tell you is when it does, it'll be something."

Declan's eyes widen, and he looks at his boy. "Then she'll need a friend. Having someone to lean on will make it easier."

The bile in Kelan's stomach turns. Declan had been that person for him.

"Yes," Kelan agrees. "She'll be training daily, both in physical combat and the arcane arts. I'm requesting you attend both as they're essential to harnessing all your potential. Are you willing to do this?" Kelan locks gazes with Shay. "Understand, I will not allow laziness."

"You will be his trainer?" There's a bite in Declan's words.

"Yes, for I am in charge of Myrna's." The two males stare at one another for a very long time. "Declan, regardless of...everything, I give you my word I will not treat him any less than I would another trainee."

"How can I trust that?"

Kelan grins. "Because Myrna won't let me."

Shay snorts and then laughs. "She really won't. Father, she put him in his place in the middle of town yesterday. You should've seen it!"

"She's also not afraid to beat the crap out of me if I need it or...attempt to, anyway."

"Sounds like another Qhuinn we used to know." The words are out before Declan can stop them. Pain flashes across his face, and his eyes drop to the ground.

"The similarities are difficult sometimes." There's a hard silence. How could he admit this to, well, anyone? Then his lip lifts in annoyance. Kelan shoves to his feet and, in a voice much harsher than before, demands, "Are you in agreement or not?"

"Y-yes. When do—should I?" Shay stumbles over the words.

"That's up to you. Myrna's training now, but if it's too soon, you may come tomorrow."

"Father?"

Declan clears his throat. "I agree. Kelan," he says, standing. "Please do not let our past get in the way of his future. He's a good kid."

And although Kelan wants to hate the male before him, he doesn't. Declan was a brother once, and no matter the hurt he carries, that feeling has never truly gone away. Even if it had, he's not the type to put the hatred onto another. Not really.

"I give you my word. I will train Shay with all the fairness I do every other soldier that comes through my door."

Declan places a fist on his heart and bows, for he knows that Kelan takes his job seriously. It's been his life's calling.

Shay joins Kelan, and they ride back to the palace. It doesn't take long before they're entering the gates and dropping the horses at the stables.

"Where do we train?" Shay asks. He's fidgeting, glancing at every tiny piece around him. He's never been inside the castle grounds, and Kelan's sure it's overwhelming. It doesn't help that courtiers watch them with interest, questions about what a commoner is doing with the head of the guard filling the square.

"We have a special wing where the Royal Guard trains. As the princess doesn't train with the soldiers, but with them, so shall you. Understand this is a privilege and, should you break it, it'll be your end."

The muscles in Shay's throat work. "I understand, Guardian. I won't let you down."

Kelan nods. "I know you won't."

"Sir, I did want to tell you one strange thing about yesterday." When Kelan's eyebrow lifts in interest, Shay continues, "Well, during the fight yesterday, I swear I saw someone else in the forest. A female with black hair and some sort of growth on her arm or shoulder. I didn't see her well as I was fighting, but I thought it odd."

That's strange. Especially for it to be out there. "I'm glad you told me. Let me know if you remember anything else—"

A visceral scream fills the air. It sends a shiver down the spines of everyone in the square.

Kelan spins on his heels. He knows that voice. Then light and power blasts the glass from the windows along one side of the building, cries he recognizes following—Briana and Myrna both. The entire side of the building ignites with light. More calls for alarm resonate through the square and castle as cold ice threatens to freeze in Kelan's veins. *Queen save us.*

"What is that?"

Kelan doesn't think. He just breaks into a run.

CHAPTER TWENTY-SIX

Arcane, an Unstable Mistress

IT BURNS LIKE ACID *in my veins. I'm going to explode!* Tears form in her eyes, but she fears they too will become flame.

And they're watching. All of them. The Guardians and approved members of the court who are scattered around the training room sparring or practicing their arcane. The weight of their eyes—their judgment of her lack of control—heightens her panic.

But it wasn't panic. It was a hit to the temple with Briana's staff. Something so small, and she is a threat. Even now, Briana's screams beneath her burrow into her psyche.

Another burst of arcane light and the Guardians around the mat cover their eyes, stepping away from the heat and flame which erupt from the princess.

Myrna dives to the side and curls into the floor. Her back arches as pain lances through her, spreading from the impact point, then seeping in hot tendrils until it escapes from her nail beds. White light manifests as incandescent fire spreading across the mat.

People stumble back while Jaden runs forward and grabs Briana to pull her from reach. Cries of those around are nothing, for all she hears are her own wretched screeches.

Then there're running steps and the sliding scrape of clothing on the mat. A rush of water against her skin, between her and the floor, cool and warm at the same time. The brush of a finger down her cheek, and then she's being cradled against a hard chest. Myrna sinks into the scent of cinnamon even as a sob wracks her. *Kelan.*

Myrna opens her eyes to find a barrier of Kelan's water surrounding them, spinning in a torrent of glittering majesty. It blocks them from the others, and she is grateful. *So bright.*

"Look at me, little one," Kelan demands, rubbing the base of her neck with his thumbs. She moans.

"You must leave. I'll burn you," Myrna whines. "I burned Bri."

"You won't." He tightens his grip on her neck and repeats his demand, "Look at me."

Opening her eyes once again, the light lessens from the pressure he's applied and releases the tension which holds her captive. A tear runs down her cheek, and he wipes it away.

"You're okay. We're going to get you through this, and I'm going to teach you. You've done nothing wrong."

The kindness and understanding in his eyes has more tears falling. He brushes these away too.

"How can I hate you one moment and feel safe with you the next?" Her light drops one more level, allowing the fire dancing along the floor to go out. The tips of her fingers no longer glow. She lifts them and runs them along his jaw.

"We've a complicated relationship."

Myrna snorts.

"Now breathe and tell me what happened."

She lays a hand on his chest and does just as he asks, focusing on matching his breaths. "I was sparring with Briana. I asked to work with staffs because I missed my training with..." she chokes, and the light intensifies for an instant. Kelan rubs the back of her neck once more, and she calms, allowing her to continue, "my caretaker. It was an accident. I dropped my guard."

"Ah," Kelan says, eyes locked on hers. She is nearly back to a normal level, but he does not seem to want to let her go just yet. "Do you feel better?"

She nods, clears her throat, and straightens in his grasp. Their noses kiss. "Thank you. Where did you come from? I thought you were out of the castle." Myrna shivers as the hand resting at the base of her neck trails down her back to rest at her hip.

"I was, but I'd just returned." He brushes stray hair behind her ear.

"How did it go?"

"Are you well enough to stand?"

"Kelan." She places a palm on his chest, irritation rising within her. It feels weird being in this little cocoon while his magic surrounds them, blocking them from the rest of the world. "What happened? You weren't cruel, were you?"

He sighs. "I'm not as terrible a person as you think I am." He sets her on the ground, stands, then pulls her to her feet. "In fact, I've obtained a special permission of sorts and brought you a present." He leans in to whisper in her ear. "So, stop thinking me the villain."

Unable to fight the temptation, she tilts her face so the scruff of his chin rubs against her cheek. Sparks shoot through her.

He exhales sharply. "You're so frustrating."

Kelan steps back and drops the veil of water to reveal Shay standing at the front of thirty very worried Guardians.

CHAPTER TWENTY-SEVEN

Princess, You're Not Alone

"HOLY KNIGHTS! WHAT WAS that?" The Guardian who asks this is tall with blond hair that's a stark contrast to her sun-kissed skin. Guardian Serena.

"Is Briana all right?" Kelan asks, his hand dropping from Myrna's waist when he notices Shay's gaze locked on it.

Jaden and Isaiah stand to the left, part to reveal a very pinkened Bri resting on a bench. Her eyes are bloodshot, and her face is drawn, but other than that, she seems fine. Another Guardian by the name of Nichols has his hand on her shoulder.

"I'm good, Boss," Briana says with a nod. Then she addresses Myrna. "Are you? That looked and sounded like it hurt."

The voice that comes from the princess is like nothing any of them have heard before. It's weak and filled with regret. It has Kelan taking her hand. She squeezes in return. "I'm so sorry. I didn't know that was going to happen." Her voice cracks, and her eyes fill with tears. "I didn't mean to hurt you. I-I'm dangerous."

"You're not dangerous," Isaiah says. He shrugs. "You're powerful and just learning." Each and every person nods in agreement even as he continues, "We've all done something stupid and almost hurt someone when our powers were coming in."

"But Briana."

"I almost burned down my house," Shay says. He scrunches his face. "With all of us in it. Dad made me sleep on a boulder outside for a week."

"I almost drowned my cat," a Guardian in the back says.

One after another, the most outrageous stories were shouted out until soon a smile lifts Myrna's beautiful, drawn face. She looks up at Kelan, his eyes still sad.

Briana leans into the Guardian behind her as she says, "I cut myself with my own ice pick."

Kelan snorts. Rolling his shoulders, he adds his own to the mix. "When I was training with your mother and aunt—we were a few years younger than you are now—we broke a dam that flooded half of a small town. Your grandmother was furious. She didn't let the three of us use our powers for almost a month." For a moment, he allows himself to get lost in the eyes that remind him so much of his past but are so very much Myrna's. "See, you're not alone. And everyone's here to help. Which is why it's time to train." He runs his thumb along the back of her fingers. "Do you feel well enough?"

Myrna lays her hand over his, squaring to him. The others get the hint and wander off as Myrna asks, "Did you really bring Shay so that I could train with him?"

"He has permission to train with you. Full access to the palace. You deserve to have people you're comfortable with surrounding you, and he needs training as much as you do."

To his surprise, Myrna goes up on her tiptoes and kisses his cheek. "Thank you. For everything."

Then she runs off to welcome her friend.

To the crowd as a whole, he says, "For the next few days, I'd like the mats around these two clear, just in case. We can still train, but we need to give them some space."

There's a general murmuring of agreement. With the nearly forty-foot ceilings, his voice carries without much issue. The crowd disperses off to the various spaces broken off for all types of training—sparring, balance, weights, weapons, and even the arcane magics. Kelan goes to Briana to check on her, but she waves him off, instead gesturing to Shay and Myrna. So, he redirects, motioning Jaden over.

"All right, you two." Kelan stops next to the two fidgeting younglings. "We're going to start slow. Myrna, I'm sure you want to start with all the pointy things, considering you've been training with the queen, but right now, your powers are a little unsteady. So, I instead want to focus on grounding, balance, then hand to hand. This will allow me to evaluate where you're at, but help you find focus and teach you some skills for centering the spirit."

"Will this help me keep from losing control?"

"It should, but also Shay will help."

"Really? Not you?" Shay asks. Then at Myrna's strange look, he adds, "I mean...why do you say that?"

"A lot's changed for our Myrna in the last weeks. She needs stability; she needs friends."

Shay's head tilts, and Kelan feels as though he's being dissected. "Aren't you her friend?"

"I'm her Guardian."

Shay's eyebrow raises.

"I mean, I'm assigned as her Guardian. To protect her."

Scratching behind his ear, Shay presses his lips together, clears his throat, and says, "Uh-huh."

Kelan claps as Jaden watches, eyes sparkling. *Damn observant kid.* "You know what? Why don't you take a lap and get warmed up?"

"Yes, sir," Shay says with a chuckle. Then takes off to do his lap.

"I didn't have to run. Should I go?" Myrna points over her shoulder.

Jaden laughs, hand over his mouth. "He just wanted to shut Shay up."

Kelan shoots him a warning glare. "You're fine. You already warmed up. Are you sure you're well?"

"Yeah, I feel fine. I don't want to waste the time we've got. Especially if all we're going to be doing is basic movements and sparring. Trust me, I've fought through much worse injuries."

"Why?" Jaden asks.

Myrna shrugs. Before she heads toward the mat, she touches his arm as if taking strength from him just one more time.

In his mind, he hears her words from before. *You've met my mother, right?*

Kelan leans against a pillar as he watches Jaden work with the younglings. They go through the first series of exercises the Guardians are taught. It's not long before Kelan realizes Myrna already knows them. She anticipates the next lesson, quickly falling into a rhythm that shocks and mesmerizes those watching.

"Laoise's been training her as a Guardian?" Briana asks from his side.

"There's no way Laoise taught her this. She had to have had a Guardian for a trainer. Someone else."

"Why do you say that?"

"Laoise was never taught them. She never trained with the Guardians. It was below her." *But it wasn't below Mareola.*

"So... did she have a Guardian trainer? I don't understand."

Neither did Kelan. There's a lot about this girl that didn't make sense. Hell, the whole story Laoise told didn't. Yes, Laoise had disappeared for nearly a year, but her body had not changed. And although she was cold, he couldn't see Laoise leaving a child behind. Perhaps others could, but not Kelan. He'd grown up with the Qhuinn girls and both had dreamt of families.

And there was no doubt Myrna was a Qhuinn. From the instant she'd walked into his life, this youngling had felt familiar. Like a missing piece of himself had been returned. It annoyed him how much she reminded him of Mareola, but there are also similarities to the queen he could not deny. The way she carries herself is all Laoise, but the kindness and open-minded beauty is Mareola to a T. The way she sees the world and even how she puts him in his place is like a memory come to life.

After warm-ups, Jaden has the two face up to begin sparring. They do, and they revert to laughter. Mostly because he's so much larger than she. But soon, it's made clear she has more training.

"It's a good thing you're doing for them. You know that, right?" Briana says.

Kelan releases a long breath. She's right. "They could both use a friend, I think."

"How did you know what to do? I've never seen anything like that."

The change in subject doesn't surprise Kelan. He'd expected it from his sibling. He takes a moment to answer, too caught up in Myrna's mesmerizing movements. They tickle something in his memory. She's graceful, her feet quick and sure, gliding across the floor while her fists connect in quick, precise strikes. She dives, spinning out of the way in a familiar move.

Kelan rubs the back of his neck, reorienting to Briana's question. "Few have. I knew someone once that manifested just like that." He meets Briana's eyes. "Exactly like that."

"Oh, Kelan..."

"I'm fine, Bri." His gaze returns to the girl beating the crap out of a boy twice her size.

There's something off about Myrna. *I can't put my finger on it, but...*

"You like her."

Kelan's head jerks up. "What? That's not what I—"

Shay cries out as he hits the floor.

"Oh my gosh, Shay!" Myrna rushes over. "I'm so sorry! Are you all right?"

He moans. "Damn, now I know how you took down those Guardians in less than ten seconds."

She laughs as she looks down at him, hands on hips, and nudges him with her boot. "I barely touched you."

Kelan disappears into the past memories of dead friends haunting him as they haven't in decades.

CHAPTER TWENTY-EIGHT

Welcome to Court

TODAY SURE HAS BEEN *interesting*. Nails scrape against the wooden bench. A high-pitched complaint hits Niandra's ears as the varnish peels away. She rests in a far-off corner, out of sight of the gathered crowd. It's where she prefers to be. Because here, the Guardians don't bother her, nor do they notice her skill, the viciousness for which she fights. It's better that way.

And although the queen allows her access to the exercise area, she doubts Laoise would be happy knowing someone as dangerous as she was within these walls. Especially when they were not so trustworthy. Granted, Laoise did not seem to fear Niandra. Why would she? The queen is a force to be reckoned with.

Focus. It is the child who holds the key now.

The blond-haired brat who currently practices with the tainted one. It's a disgrace that boy is within these walls. Kelan stands nearby watching, Jaden having performed the initial instruction and drills. In truth, there wasn't much to see.

Niandra kicked herself for not being here when that bitch Briana and the princess had sparred. Upon hearing of it, she'd rushed over, but it was too late. The drama had already resolved. The day has not been a complete loss, however. In observing the session, she'd been able to evaluate their young princess.

A body slides onto the bench next to hers, legs a mile long extending before her. Niandra takes in the female with auburn hair falling to her waist even while tied. She is the sexiest thing Niandra has ever seen.

"You should not be near me. If they see us together—"

"They will believe I am here to scold you for how you acted today at counsel," Sola says. She rolls her shoulders, then glares at Niandra as if she is doing exactly that, but her next words are anything but cruel. "That outfit is sinful."

Niandra's lip lifts. She crosses her legs, making the leather pants she wears stretch and creak. "I'm glad you approve. You may help me remove it tonight."

Sola hums deep in her throat. She faces the room once more. "Learned anything hiding over here in the dark?"

"The girl's well trained. You can see it in the way she moves, but the moves are odd. I see the queen in her technique, but there's more, too." Niandra bites down on a sharpened thumbnail.

"Such as?"

Niandra shakes her head. "I am not sure. Not trained by a human, but not only influenced by Laoise."

"Interesting."

They're silent for a long moment, and then Niandra says, "Either way, I do not like her. She poses a threat to your place here. You've spent these last years in that bitch's employ, doing whatever the queen requires of you, and then one day this brat is going to come in and take your chance as heir? No."

The tightness in her jaw is both a welcome and a discomfort.

"My love, she is not confirmed yet." Sola crosses her legs and leans back against the stone wall, her much more subdued but no less form-fitting outfit accentuating that voluptuous body. "My family holds much sway."

"Yes, yes, you are like royalty. I'm aware."

Sola snorts and knocks her shoulder against Niandra's. "Well, perhaps we are looking at this incorrectly."

Niandra caresses a leather-clad thigh for the briefest of moments. "How so?"

"Well, I see two options. Either I am selected as heir, or she's our ticket out of this hellhole."

"You think our friend would be interested in information?"

"Based on the conversation I overheard?" Sola says so low Niandra must strain to make out the words. "Very much so."

A slow smile spreads, and Niandra licks the tip of her sharpened canine. "Hmm. Yes. With her here, Laoise would be too busy to notice our leaving." Niandra's voice becomes introspective, taking on a singsong quality. It snakes into the air, capturing her lover's attention. Sola cannot resist Niandra's call and runs a palm down her back.

"Perhaps it is time we see what information they might be interested in," Sola says.

Niandra glances at her lover from beneath an amused eyebrow. "And what he might trade for such in return."

On the other side of the room, training wraps up. Kelan pats Shay on the back, speaking to him quietly as they walk from the gym. Before he disappears, he says, "Myrna, I'll be right back."

The other Guardians file toward the door as well, while Myrna tells them she'll be right behind. They try to wait, but she says she needs a minute.

As there looks to be no one else remaining in the space, Niandra and Sola so well hidden in the shadows, Jaden agrees, "All right, but we're just right outside."

Myrna nods. The youngling looks up at the ceiling, a satisfied grin on her face. Apparently, time and quiet are all she craves.

"This does not mean you cannot play with her first," Sola offers, grinning. "You, of course, have issue to settle with the child."

"Sounds like fun," Niandra croons. She glides to her feet, Sola following, lip lifting in an anticipatory smile. Though her shoes hardly make noise, Myrna hears her approach and looks up.

Sola keeps her face blank, but as they reach the princess, she shoots a glare toward Niandra. "Do not forget the queen's warning. Behave next time, or you will feel her wrath."

Niandra's act of obedient subjugation is honorable. "Yes, Lady Sola."

She watches the attendant to the queen leave, then refocuses all her attention on Myrna Qhuinn. "Well, well, well. Look who they finally let out of her cage. And they're actually letting you train? Aren't they afraid you're going to break a nail?"

Myrna shifts to rest her elbows on her knees. She keeps her expression neutral. *Impressive.*

"It's not like they're actually letting you train, though." Niandra strolls around the bench between them and onto the mat. "Probably because you're so inept and not because you're new."

"Is that so?" Myrna asks. "And you have so much experience, do you, Niandra? Because every time I've ever seen you, you've just been cowering—in the corner, on the floor."

How dare she! Luckily, Niandra's mastered her control and doesn't show it outwardly, for she has to physically restrain the urge to lunge. "Child, if you think you can beat me, why don't we spar? Just a quick one between friends to loosen up the muscles?"

"I can't. Sorry. I've a meeting I must attend."

"You can't, or you're scared?"

Myrna doesn't respond, only brushes her hands together. She moves toward the exit.

Niandra shrugs. "It's fine. I understand you're tired and fearful." She goes to turn away, but stops, a thrill of triumph rocking her when Myrna says, "All right. Let's go, you crazy bitch."

Fangs tingling, hands flexing, Niandra backs onto the mat. The urge to sink her teeth into the princess's throat is visceral. Myrna joins her and, the instant she finds her stance, Niandra attacks. She slides forward and spins, landing a blow to the ribs, for which she knows are already sore. She does not slow her speed but uses all her power.

There's a sharp intake of breath, but no sound leaves the youngling.

I'll have to try harder. Without giving Myrna a chance to recover, Niandra throws another blow, connecting with her chin. Myrna's head flies back. Then she slams her knee into the youngling's. Myrna's leg gives out, but she does not fall fully. Niandra uses her higher position to her advantage. Her elbow comes down on the side of the princess's head, causing her to stumble. Myrna tries to get her stance back and return the volley, but before she can, Niandra's landed two more into her side, grabbed the youngling's tunic, and rammed her knee into the girl's stomach.

Myrna crumples to the floor, gasping.

Never will I bow to you. Niandra leans over the panting princess. "Consider this payment for our first meeting. Do not embarrass me again. And remember, you'll never be welcomed here. We all sense your difference. You weren't born here, raised here. I know the truth of who and what you are. You can't hide forever." Niandra's lip pulls back to reveal her canines, then she spits in Myrna's face. "There are others far better suited for the throne than you."

She throws Myrna down, and the girl grunts in pain. Then she digs the heel of her boot into the girl's hand.

Myrna cries out, and satisfaction fills Niandra as tears slip from the princess's eye.

With an unconcerned air, Niandra strolls away.

When she exits, Niandra's evil smirk has Briana running for the door.

Chapter Twenty-Nine

Love Heals. Hate Doesn't.

THE QUICK, RESONANT THUD of boots running has Kelan's heart picking up. They sound ominous. Why? He isn't sure, but something within them speaks of warning.

Isaiah slides around the corner, face stricken.

Kelan doesn't wait—he breaks into a run, meeting him halfway. "What happened?"

He'd already been on his way back, but now the path seems so far.

"Niandra." The single word says more than it should. Filled with anger, worry, fear. "Apparently, she was watching the session and when we filed out, she confronted Myrna. She's bad."

His legs burn, chest constricting as the blood within them turns to ice with the idea of Niandra being alone with Myrna and what she could've done to her. They take the last turn, and it feels like before, Kelan bursting his way into the gym, Guardians scattering from his path. When they part, his gaze lands on the curled figure, and he curses. Blood drips from her temple, a bruise darkening her porcelain cheek. Briana cradles her head, a steady hand caressing that beautiful hair which is now tinted crimson. Kelan freezes.

"I'm going to kill that bitch," Briana says.

Kelan says nothing, just closes the distance and slides his hand against her cheek.

"The doctor's on his way," Zerekule says. "She's not responding though and, based on the blood, the way she's curled around her ribs, and that rattle in her chest, we're worried about internal damage. A punctured lung in particular."

And with her healing still being human speed...

"Find Niandra and take her to the brig." The order is a growl. Considering the way his fangs are out, he's not surprised at the fear on all the Guardians' faces.

"Myrna," he says. "Come on, honey, I need you to open your eyes." He doesn't care that everyone can hear the desperation in his tone or that his hard-won mask has slipped. Somehow, this girl has broken through, shattering every wall he's ever erected.

Someone near the door says, "Oh, we'll find her."

"Where's the doctor?" he snaps incensed. "Why aren't they here?"

A Guardian in the back, Matthews maybe, says, "He was out on a call. We're trying to get him. His assistant is on his way."

"Can you do anything for her?" Jaden squats next to them, his eyes boring into Kelan. "You have the most medical training of any soldier I've ever known."

Sadness crosses over Briana's face when Zerekule says, "He doesn't heal anymore."

It's true. Not since he couldn't save Fianna, Laoise's bonded friend, and Mareola died while guarded by another. They both lost that day, the two closest friends either of them ever had. He doesn't know if he still can, but as he stares down at the female who questions everything he is, his stomach clenches and every muscle within him seizes like a vice. She is the only one who's caused such feelings to rise within him.

What if I can't?

Then Briana's concerned-filled gaze meets his. "Brother, you have a connection with her. Please, try."

His breath catches. The fear that he might've lost this skill doesn't matter. If there's anyone he's going to relearn it for, it's her.

Kelan slides his arms around Myrna without shifting her too much to cup the back of her head and neck. Briana moves away as Kelan places his cheek against hers and reaches deep within himself. Then, he finds the emotion he locked away so long ago. It's been seeping free, drawn by the unconscious girl in his arms, one infuriatingly aching moment at a time. The air around them cools as water collects on his forearms, warming with his will.

"I'm going to help you, Myrna."

Shimmering streams of warm, calming water that glitters a soft gold flows from his skin and across the wound at her forehead. She cannot be a willing participant in the healing, so he must push his will and force their magics to react. He does not like it, but it's a small allowance done in an emergency. With it, the cut heals before their eyes. Fingers move to her jaw and the arcane probes the injury. There's a break in the bone. He snarls, causing Briana to scurry away.

"Her jaw's broken. When I find her—"

"Fix Myrna. Should you focus on revenge, you'll not be able to heal her. Focus, brother. You know as well as I do that hate does not heal. Love does."

Kelan's heart constricts as he looks to Briana. "I do not love her."

Briana crosses her arms and stares. There's no time to argue. And yet her words hit home. The golden glow brightens. How she knows exactly what to say astounds him. *So much like Mother.*

He refocuses, caressing the bruise with his arcane. When Myrna winces, he says, "I'm so sorry I wasn't here."

Closing his eyes, he shoves as much energy as he can into knitting the bone back together. Pain shoots like a needle into the back of his eye. *Too long. Too long since I've practiced.* He never should've let these skills wane.

He moves to her ribs, knowing the worst of her injuries are there. He hadn't started there for fear he'd forgotten the craft, but he can't hesitate any longer. Her breathing's worsened, becoming labored, a rasp deep and gurgling. It terrifies him to his bones, and when Kelan barely brushes her side, she screams, her eyes flying open.

Briana and Jaden are there to hold her down.

"Shh. I've got you. Stay still," Kelan says, his voice somehow both soft and stern. "Don't move!"

"Kelan…" His name's a prayer on her lips. "I can't breathe." She snakes her fingers around his arm.

"Look at me!" Her gaze flashes to his at his demand. "I can help you, but you have to open to me. This wound's bad, and I need you…" He caresses her cheek.

"I'm always open to you," she whispers.

Those words must be a delusion—a slip of the tongue said because of the pain. And yet, they blast something wide within him. Hope he refuses to acknowledge expands his chest thrice fold.

Myrna's eyes close, her lips part, and she sighs. Then her power opens. From one breath to the next, light pours from her. It seeps from beneath her closed eyelids and shines from her palms. Exhaustedly, she runs hands up both of his arms, which currently wrap the sides of her rib cage. It leaves a trail of white fire in their path.

Kelan doesn't waste time. He takes the energy running along his skin and absorbs it, mixing it with his own arcane. It feels like heaven having a part of her inside him, but he won't be distracted. Kelan shoves his will into the healing.

There's a loud *crack* when the broken rib snaps back into place. Myrna presses her face into Briana's leg and cries out. The punctured lung within knits together, her breathing becoming less shallow and raspy. It is not over yet.

"We need to get the fluid out. Cough." Kelan helps to redirect the fluid so she can breathe even as she does as he says. Pink spittle lands on the mat. Then Myrna is lifting, her arm snaking around his shoulder. She rests her head on his chest as the rest of the fluid is absorbed back into her body, thanks to the mixing of their arcane. Her breathing returns to normal.

Then Myrna drops every shield.

Briana and Jaden scoot back as Myrna's skin begins to glow.

Kelan gasps as Myrna's light circles him, and an image wrapped in violet appears in his mind. It's of a teenage Myrna. Her hair is short, arms scrawny. She's training with Laoise on small swords, and the queen looks so happy. But there's another figure, cloaked in darkness, standing off to the side, laughing in lyrical tones that sing to his heart.

"Do you smell that?" Jaden asks, bringing Kelan back to the here and now. Especially as Jaden's eyes dilate.

"What?" Then Briana curses. "Knights. Jaden, get the hell back, or Kelan's going to kill you."

Almost in the same heartbeat, Kelan pulls Myrna fully into an embrace, her body encased in his arms as her legs splay out behind him. He moans at the sensation of her in his arms, the smell of her on his skin. So enticing, so sweet...

Bloody hell. Fangs flash, and he spins to put himself between her and the other males. "Get back!" he orders.

Every male in the room stands, noses flaring, gazes locked on the princess. They cannot help it, and he knows this. Yet he hates them for it. Females release specific pheromones that are irresistible at certain times in their lives, one being during the changing.

"Get her out of here!" Briana says.

Without another word, Kelan scoops up the princess and runs for the door. They're at her suite moments later, three female guards flanking them.

When he goes to take her inside, one asks, "Sir, do you think that's a good idea?"

"On my honor, Guardian Serena, nothing will happen. But I *need* to watch over her." Kelan swallows hard. "You may all come in and attend her, verify her safety, but I will not be leaving her side. Plus, we'll need someone to help control the white fire."

Serena's tight smile is kind. "Okay. But this is your one warning."

Kelan nods in total agreement. "You have full authority to throw me out. You are in charge today." Shock flashes in Serena's gaze, but he ignores it. This is what he'd require had this situation happen with his sister or Theia. It's what every female deserved. Respect and honor. "Can you get Lady Alyn, please? She will feel more comfortable with her here."

"Of course."

The other guard, Nora, who's watched the exchange with confused awe, nods once, then rushes away. Then Kelan bursts into

Myrna's suite, all the while pushing down the urge to rub himself all over her because damn, she smells wonderful.

CHAPTER THIRTY

Drool... Awesome.

"IT'S INAPPROPRIATE FOR YOU to be in bed with her." This is not the first time Alyn's said this, nor will it be the last. And at this point, Kelan couldn't care less.

Myrna's changing had been a rough one. There were bursts of power that threw her attendants to the ground. Ones that would've lit the entire room on fire had it not been for him. She'd cried and screamed, her tears glowing like that of a goddess brought from heaven. And the one thing that calmed her was him. He didn't understand it, nor had he cared, but the moment he'd pulled off his shoes and climbed onto the massive bed to allow her to rest on his chest, she'd fallen asleep. They may fight, and he may irritate her, but she trusted him to keep her safe.

"I understand your concern, but we're fully clothed and there's nothing untoward happening," Kelan says.

"She's lying on your chest!" Alyn exclaims.

Myrna twitches, so Kelan runs a comforting hand down her hair and along her back. She settles instantly. Her skin's still hot, the fever of the changing not yet broken.

Alyn narrows her eyes at where his palm rests at the small of her back, just above her shorts.

Kelan blushes and moves it up to between her shoulder blades. He does not want to move it. He wishes to lower it, pull her close, and bury his face in her neck. *Stop that right now!*

Verifying his voice is steady, he says, "I'm one of the few friends she has here. As are you, dear Alyn." The servant blushes. "As is Shay. They've known each other for two days. I could bring him here, should you prefer."

"Saints, no!"

Serena and Nora laugh.

"Or I can stay and make sure our princess is content and stable. I've made no advances, nor do I intend to. I'm not some fledgling, and there are guards with full authority to geld me should I try." When Alyn huffs, stomping toward the bathing room, he looks to the other females. "I've been a gentleman, haven't I?"

They both laugh again. Serena nods. "Yes, but your affection for the girl is obvious. Your eyes nearly rolled back into your head just now."

"Ugh." Kelan *bonks* his head on the headboard. "I shouldn't have asked."

They chuckle.

He looks down at the sleeping girl, now through the changing. She is the same and yet not. Her hair has lightened, pearlescent white strands mixing with her soft blond hair. Cheekbones are more defined and her ears...they lift to soft points that accentuate the graceful curve of her neck.

Good lord, I want to trace that neck with my...

Stop!

Nora chokes. "Kelan, if Alyn sees you looking at her like that, she will drag you from that bed. So, get a grip."

"I wasn't!" he says. *I totally was.*

The two Guardians exchange an amused glance as he takes a deep breath.

Myrna moans, grips his side, then uses his chest to push up. She looks down at him, rubbing the drool from her lip. "Was I sleeping on you?" When Kelan nods, red flushes her cheeks. Apparently, it's going around this morn. "Well, that's embarrassing."

"No, it's not. It's what you needed. How are you feeling?"

She looks away. "Stupid. My skin is vibrating. Plus, I'm…" She clears her throat and sits up. "Never mind."

He breathes in deep, tightening his fingers in the blanket when the scent of her arousal blossoms in the air. He's been a gentleman, yes, but that's been difficult. Hair a mess, indent of his shirt on her cheek? She's absolutely beautiful. He looks away, then moves to the edge of the bed as his pants become…never mind. Kelan runs a hand through his hair. "What happened, anyway?"

Myrna scoots to the headboard, then pulls her knees to her chest.

"I was stupid." She licks her lip. "Niandra was in the gym. She waited until everyone left, then decided to taunt me. I was going to leave, but…" She shakes her head, and Kelan knows what happened. Niandra's words got to her, then Myrna's pride was too stubborn. "I wasn't even on the mat before she attacked. I should've been ready, should've known what she was going to do."

"That's complete and utter bullshit!" Serena says. The Guardian walks to the end of the bed. "That's against the rules, which she knows, and sure as hell isn't how you spar with the trainee. Let alone the princess!" She looks at Kelan. "Do you think this is enough to get her rights revoked? We've been trying for a while."

He nods.

"She's going to face justice for more than that, I think." Kelan gestures to Myrna, who shifts over without hesitation. To Serena, he says, "Can you two please notify the queen that Myrna's awake, and"—he tests her forehead—"her fever's waning. She's officially through the changing. I am sure she will want to come check on you again."

"Again?"

"Yes. Once we realized Jaden and the others weren't of the right mind enough to do so, Nora informed her. She stopped by and left you in our care."

"Why were Jaden and the others not able?" Myrna asks.

Nora presses her lips together. "Honey, you were giving off some serious pheromones. I'm pretty sure all the boys in your general vicinity were off to… spend some time alone…or not."

Myrna steps away, shooting Kelan some serious side-eye. Passing the two women, she says, "I guess I understand why you two are inside the room, then."

They crack up, and when Nora finally calms, she says, "It was his request. Don't worry, he was a perfect gentleman—his words."

Kelan grabs his boots and moves to a chair. "You needed my help. Your power was out of control, and I'm old enough to control my... reactions."

"That had to have been hell of painful, though," Serena mumbles.

"Oh! Princess! Wonderful, I've drawn you a bath," Alyn says, bustling from the room beyond, the scent of oils on her skin. "I thought it might soothe you after such a night."

Myrna smiles at the lady's maid. "That would be great. Thank you, Serena and Nora, for watching over us. And Kelan..." The floor is suddenly very interesting.

"I'll wait out there." He points to the seating area near the door. "I still need to speak to you about the Niandra thing and..."

There's a beat of silence of them just staring at one another.

"Well, before I die of embarrassment, I'm gonna go." Myrna scans him, her eyes going soft. Then she follows Alyn into the bathing chamber.

Kelan walks the female Guardians out, taking the time to straighten his uniform, then he sits in the seating area where Myrna spends much of her time. A book on the table catches his eye. It's the one Stephan gave her and regularly sees her scanning. From his understanding, it presents itself as a set of old Celtic tales to most, but to whom it chooses holds secrets of unbeknownst power. Kelan picks up the tome, wondering if *Balance Beholden* had chosen Myrna and revealed anything special.

He opens the cover and brilliant, colorful images fill the page. Script beautifully transcribed outlines tales of creatures which haven't existed in a millennium. He gets lost in the images, the minute details of the forest, bringing the image to life. Never has he seen such a gorgeous display of history.

"Hey," Myrna says softly, coming around the chair. "Are you all right?" She takes a seat next to him, hair wet and skin flushed.

Kelan closes the book and returns it to the pile. "Yeah. Are you feeling better?"

"Definitely. Have a few bruises, but I feel like I should've been way worse off."

"You were. I healed you." He's not surprised she doesn't remember. She'd been pretty out of it. "Or, the worst of your injuries, before the changing kicked in."

Myrna threads her fingers in her lap. "And became a sex magnet, apparently."

Kelan chuckles. "Not quite, but you were definitely"—he inhales sharply—"vulnerable."

"Well, thank you for keeping me safe."

"Always." Leaning in the corner of the couch, he says, "Actually, it's been a long time since I've used that particular ability, but you punctured a lung and couldn't breathe. I couldn't leave you."

A bitter smile lifts her lip. "She caught me off guard, Kelan, but that won't happen a second time." Myrna turns to face him on the couch, her knee bent, arm along the back. "I'm sorry. I won't let anyone—"

Kelan grabs her hand. "You did nothing wrong."

Myrna's breath stops.

Just then, Alyn rushes from the room, and Kelan pulls his hand away. With a quick goodbye, the dirty uniform from yesterday in her arms, she leaves.

They're silent for a few moments as Myrna chews on her lip. Then she says, "I look different."

Kelan shakes his head. Unable to resist, he brushes the hair back from her face. *It's so beautiful.* "You look like you. And don't worry, personal glamour back to your youngling form is easy. If that's how you see yourself, hold it in your mind that way, then that's how you will be seen. Most don't have to think about it."

"Then how come I see through yours?"

"Because I allow it. I want you to see who I am."

The words have more meaning than first glance. Myrna's lips part, and his eyes are drawn down to the motion. *It's only the changing.*

Myrna clears her throat. "Enough of that. I have a few questions."

Head reeling, he asks, "And they would be?"

"Why am I humming?"

The leather of his boot crinkles as he rests it on his knee. "Your powers are becoming active, and you've a great deal of energy coursing through your veins. More than I've seen in a very long time, but they'll settle down as you get a handle on them."

"Will I explode again? Like before?"

"Not necessarily. Moments of high emotion or tension may cause your power to amplify, but it shouldn't be like before. And over the next few weeks, we'll really work on your control. The good news is, even though you weren't raised here, it seems like your mother made sure you were taught significant control over your mind. Very few have had the control you've shown prior to and during changing."

The question is in her eye as she plays with the golden fringe on the pillow.

"When you were injured, I asked you to open to me so I could heal you. You did, even in your injured state. I think our complete, unhindered connection was what sent you into alteration."

He knew it. There was no barrier between them in that moment. It had been exhilarating, but he couldn't tell her that.

"How did you heal me?"

Kelan exhales slowly, his gaze locking on where her fingers shift through the fringe. The light bounces off the glimmering thread. "Do you know why your mother assigned me to you? I thought it odd at first, but I think I get it now."

Myrna shifts in her seat, pulling the pillow onto her lap to hug it to her chest.

"I grew up in the palace. My father was one of the most trusted Guardians to Queen Aoife, your grandmother. There were few children. The two I played with the most were Laoise and your aunt Mareola."

Myrna fidgets, catching Kelan's notice. "What is it?"

She sucks on her bottom lip. "Um... It might be silly, but I have to ask."

He waits, interest piqued at what makes her so uncomfortable.

"Is the reason Alyn has such an issue with you being here because you're so much older than I am?"

Kelan's body heats, knowing what she's really asking. He can still feel the imprint of her body on his chest, the tension constantly between them. The smile demanding escape is barely held in. With a shake of his head, Kelan says, "No. We can live thousands of years, Myrna. Tens of thousands." Surprise flashes in her eyes, but he continues. "She was concerned for propriety's sake alone. Your honor specifically. In general, once we are of age, it is up to the individual persons to determine how they feel."

"Oh." Myrna looks down, the pink of her cheeks brightening her beautiful face. "That makes sense."

Perhaps he should say more but, if he did, she might very well disappear into the couch.

"Anyway, Mareola was more than just any friend to me. She was my most trusted confidant. Closer in age than Laoise and I, we did everything together."

Her embarrassment suddenly forgotten, replaced with the need for answers, Myrna leans forward. These are the pieces she's been craving, the possibility of truths she hadn't realized were missing.

A flash of panic in her eyes.

"Were you in love with her?" She covers her mouth. "Sorry. I shouldn't have asked that."

"No. Never. She was my best friend, and that's it." His eyes stare off into nothing. "Near the end, I think she fell for someone—true love—but I don't know who it was. That's a story for another time, though. The point is, I know how to help you because of her."

"How so?"

"When we were kids, her Radiant Light tried to engulf everything, but she was my Theia, and there was no way I would let her fail." Myrna goes perfectly still, but Kelan is too lost in the memory, the story, to notice. "We figured out how to control it and, with my help, we somehow learned how to. And she mastered it. She was so powerful. Beyond anything we imagined. That's why it was such a shock when she died." The last word wavers, and the muscle in his jaw tics.

"Mareola, is this...what did you call her?"

Confusion tingles down his back. *Why does her nickname throw the princess?* "Theia. I called her Theia after the goddess of light. It was the nickname only I could use."

Myrna goes stark white, and she blinks slowly as if her thoughts are too much for her. "And she's dead?"

"What? Theia?" Kelan rubs his jaw, a soft scratching sound reaching his ears. He needed to shave. "Yes. You know this."

"What happened to her? Exactly."

"She was killed in the last great battle. They were on the way back to the palace from the front line. Their party had some prisoners with them. They were attacked, and she was injured. So, they stopped to tend to her when another contingent found them. Mareola fought back, but Her Majesty saw her fall. Laoise reported the enemy took her body." His lip curls. "A crime against our kind. It was the end of any politeness between our realms."

Myrna jumps to her feet. She's shaking, her breaths coming quick. She shoves her hands through her hair as she paces to the far wall, then back.

Kelan stands, concerned. He wants to grab her shoulders and shake her, but with his luck, Myrna would punch him. "Lady, what's wrong?"

"I need to tell you, but..." she tries again, "I need you to not say no right now, but to trust me. Can you do that?"

"Myrna, what—"

"Please! We need to go somewhere. I can't explain or tell you"—she caresses her throat, then steps into his space and presses her hands to his chest—"but I can promise you it'll explain so much. But it can only be you who comes with. Only you. Please."

He stares into her pleading eyes. The need. The desperation. Kelan nods once.

CHAPTER THIRTY-ONE

On My Honor

"WHY ARE WE AT Haszwalds?" Kelan asks as Myrna pushes him into his office and shuts the door.

As she wasn't allowed to take her cell phone with her into the other realm—or more, it didn't work in Faerie—they'd had to come here before they could go to their final destination, for she needed outside help.

"You promised me you'd trust me."

Brow furrowed, Kelan scans her face. "Why can't you just tell me?"

"Because I can't." If there was a way to send the truth to him through the bond she feels growing between them.

Kelan does not like it, this is clear, but as the seconds go by, Myrna sees him fall back into his promise to trust her. "This is a bad idea."

"It's important. I swear." Somehow, Kelan manages to frown deeper, and Myrna lifts her thumb to rub at the wrinkles between his eyebrows. When he grabs her wrist, she asks, "Do you have my phone?"

Releasing her, he nods and moves to his desk.

Myrna pulls up Sam's number. When everything happened, Laoise weirdly deleted Theia's information so anyone looking wouldn't become suspicious. Myrna now understood why, but that meant she didn't have another way to get a hold of her. Luckily, Sam had Theia's number, too.

Sam picks up on the second ring. "Hey, beautiful. Where have you been? It's Saturday. Are you in town?"

It is Saturday? Saints, she really needs to pay attention to the days of the week.

"Yeah. Actually, I was wondering if there's any way you could do me a huge favor?"

"Name it."

"Can you set up a training session for me? In like an hour. Just the gym owner and my partner? Though I'd love you there, I need to work on something particular." Myrna looks away from Kelan's penetrating gaze.

"Yeah, of course. I've got a date at noon, anyway. Do you need me to drive you?"

"Oh my gosh, yes. I love you so much."

There's a smile in Sam's voice. "Love you, too."

"And um…I'm at Haszwalds. Also, I expect you to tell me about this guy."

"Oh, I will." Sam giggles evilly. "But later. Give me like ten minutes to get all the plans set. I'll call you back. Cool? Then I'll come pick you up at work." The last word has far too much emphasis, telling Myrna she'll be required to explain why she's there on a Saturday.

"Thanks. Sorry for being weird."

"No problem. And stop worrying. You'll tell me everything when you can. Kisses!" With that, Sam hangs up.

Kelan leans against his desk, watching her as though she's got three heads. It's an interesting expression for him. Perhaps the idea of taking her away from Haszwalds, without security, and with no additional information was catching up to him. She needed to be careful. If he thought too much, he'd change his mind, and they'd never leave.

Myrna needed him to see—needed him to understand what she'd just figured out. Because this was one hell of a revelation she felt stupid for not realizing before. There'd been slips over the years, comments made by her mother and Theia, but she'd just thought it was because of their close relationship. But no…it was more.

Almost on cue, Kelan says, "You're asking me to take you away from Haszwalds? Without additional security? I can't do that. Especially after what you just went through."

Myrna gets in his path as he stalks toward the door. He shudders when she threads her fingers in the hair at the back of his neck. "We'll be okay. We'll sneak out, be quick, and get back before anyone notices."

"Myrna, there have been multiple attempts on your life, and your power, it's…"

Something has changed between them over the last twenty-four hours. Perhaps it's been growing all along, but Myrna has seen it in the way he constantly frets over her safety. But waking on his chest had been a new level of intimacy. He'd taken care of her. He always took care of her even as he drove her to insanity. Just the fact he was allowing her to touch him this way was different. Made her feel powerful—special.

She guides his head down so their foreheads touch. "Just this once, stop being a brute and trust me."

He exhales slowly, then nods once.

She runs a thumb over his lip, desperately wanting to lean in and—

"Stop, Myrna."

Her gazes flashes up to him, embarrassment and shock causing her stomach to drop to the floor. She steps back and turns away.

"Myrna, it's fine. We just… shouldn't—"

She holds her hand up and rubs the bridge of her nose. Just as she's about to speak, her phone goes off.

"Hey, I'm downstairs," Sam says. "They can meet you right away. Apparently, they were already there."

"That's perfect. We'll be right down."

"We?"

After that awkward moment in the office, Myrna's unsure if she's angry or lost. The last few days have been crazy, so perhaps Kelan has a point. Their relationship had the tendency to fluctuate from hatred to uncontrolled attraction, protection to heated battle in a heartbeat. And now, her body doesn't quite feel like her own. Energy crackles through her veins like she's never felt before, heat riding her in ways that feels both magical and sexual. She doesn't know where to begin with that one.

He's such a tasty specimen, too, Myrna thinks.

Good gods, Sam. What have you done to me? It's official. Myrna can finally see how Sam, and probably Laoise, were bad influences.

Which is why Myrna is taking so much joy at seeing Kelan as uncomfortable as he is. In her confused state, it is also *his* fault. Emotions are weird that way.

Granted, the white-knuckled grip of the warrior scrunched into the backseat of the mini-SUV is the best thing she's ever witnessed. Especially as his jaw tightens, and he shoots her a menacing glare as Sam takes a turn at full speed. The car crosses three lanes of traffic, cutting off a city bus. Myrna's never wanted to laugh so hard in her entire life.

"Isn't this such a nice car, Mr. Daniels?" Myrna asks sweetly. "So roomy."

His eyes narrow further, her skin tingling with the threat of power seeping from his being. With a forced smile, he replies, "Yes. It is."

She grins. Myrna could've warned him about Sam's driving, but after his snub, this felt a little like revenge, however innocent it was.

His words give Sam the go ahead. She dives into the tale of how she acquired the car, used, from an old man who'd taken excellent care of it. She's so proud of her negotiating skills.

Sam breaks hard, causing Myrna to throw her hand out to brace on the dashboard. Not a second later, her foot is back on the gas, and Myrna is plastered against the seat once again. Sam speeds around a car going the speed limit, then she takes a right turn at nearly full speed.

"Samantha, do you always drive like this?" Kelan asks.

"Like what?" Sam asks, her brow drawing down in confusion.

Myrna hides her smile, her eyes flicking to Kelan. He may be surprised, but she's caught the terrified glee on his face. Each time it has her giggling, and Sam questioning why. At least his unwilling enjoyment is better than the constant questions of where they're going. It's beginning to hurt—the need to tell him, but the binding Mother put on her keeping her from it.

"Like a getaway driver for some heist," Kelan mumbles so low Sam can't hear. Myrna bites back a laugh.

"Okay, so next question," Sam says, and Myrna sighs.

"Sam, you've peppered him with questions since the poor man has entered the car." And she had. "You've also threatened him—my new boss, no less—that if he didn't treat me well—"

"Don't think I don't see how you two look at and act around each other." The girl scrunches one side of her face in what Myrna has learned is her "duh" expression. "I'm not stupid. It's my job to threaten him, even if he's only a close friend. But I am going to need the story of how *that* happened because I know better." She winks.

Myrna covers her face, shakes her head, then returns her stare to her friend. "Leave him alone."

Sam meets her gaze. "One more question?"

Myrna exchanges a glance with Kelan, and he shrugs. The youngling finally relents. "Fine."

"How do you keep yourself in such great shape?" Sam asks.

Myrna slaps her friend's arm. "Appropriate! Really?"

"What?" Sam huffs. "I didn't ask him what I *really* wanted to. Do you want me to rephrase, Myrna? Do you? Because I will!"

Sam's on another level.

Myrna feels her cheeks heat just imagining the things that could come out of Sam's mouth. "Oh, dear lords. Please, no." She presses a hand to her head. When she glances at Kelan, his eyes are lit with interest and amusement. She faces forward. "Hey! Look, we're here! Take a right, remember?"

"Yeah!" Sam hollers. The car fishtails into the parking lot of the gym.

Kelan grunts, and Myrna laughs. He shoots her a glare that only makes her grin widen as the seatbelt tightens against her chest. The car comes to a stop, and Myrna leans over to give Sam a quick hug.

"I'll be back around two. If you need more time, text me. Or, if you've already headed back, just let me know," Sam says. "Have fun!"

"Thanks. I will." Myrna slinks out of the car and joins Kelan—who jumped from the vehicle as quickly as possible—on the sidewalk.

Sam waves, then speeds away. The car she cuts off slams on the brakes and lays into the horn. Myrna winces.

"That's one terrifying human," Kelan says.

Myrna chortles, a feminine snort slipping out before she can stop it. Her hand flies up to cover her face. "That she is, and I love her to pieces."

"I can see why. She seems very protective of you. Quite colorful the way she outlined the ways she'd harm me." Kelan laughs low. It's deep and warm; unexpectedly comforting.

A sweet smile passes over Myrna's beautiful face.

"Now, are you going to tell me why we're here?"

Myrna takes his hand, turns to head inside, and says, "Just don't hurt anyone, and promise me this stays here. That you do not repeat this to anyone. Ever. Give me your word."

"On my honor."

The gym is quiet as they enter, the owner probably having closed early so Theia could train. It's peaceful like this; the mats bare, gloves resting on their shelves. But Myrna's favorite is the punching bags hanging from the ceiling like quiet guards ready to act at a moment's notice. Myrna closes her eyes and takes in a calming breath.

Tomas, the owner, steps in from the back. "Myrna, my girl, is that you—Kelan..." His question turns to a growl.

Kelan grabs Myrna and shoves her behind him. She stumbles but catches herself.

"What the holy hell are you doing here, deserter?" Kelan snarls.

"Deserter? That's rich." Tomas rolls his shoulders, taking a fighting stance Myrna recognizes. At the same time, she sees a flicker at the corner of her eye.

Wait. She squints, focusing on him again. He's different from the last time she saw him.

Kelan's removed his sword and is ready to fight.

She shoves forward. "You're Faye!"

"Stay back, Princess," Kelan says.

"Oh, shit, you know?" Tomas grimaces.

Kelan starts, his sword dropping an inch. "You know?"

Myrna shoves Kelan's arm down, then pushes between the two stupid males. She throws her arms out as they both scream her name in protest.

A sweet, calm voice fills the room, coming from the doorway which leads to the back.

Princess Mareola of the Faerie Realm says, "Of course he knows."

Kelan's gaze snaps to her, his sword falling to his side. Myrna watches in awe as Kelan's face morphs. Her Guardian, normally so stoic and hard to read to most, is open and raw. He's a book, pages revealed. His throat works, his eyes fill, and his lips part on the breath of her name. "Theia."

Then he strides, each step slow as if afraid she will disappear. Once before her, he lowers to his knees. His chin meets his chest, and Myrna swears she sees a tear fall to the fabric of his tunic.

"Hello, old friend. It's been too long," Theia says, reaching out and placing a hand on his shoulder.

His eyes squeeze closed before he looks into the face he grew up with. A childhood friend, lost in a war and thought gone forever.

"You're supposed to be dead."

A sad smile lifts Theia's lips as she nods. Her eyes flick to where Myrna stands, then back to him. "That's the lie we told, yes."

Kelan glances to Myrna, then back. His voice is strained when he asks, "But why?"

"Someone needed to protect Myrna, and I volunteered for the task. Laoise and I realized it would be safer to keep her hidden until she was old enough to protect herself. Until she could be integrated. As you know, I was done with war and the Brennan politics."

"You should've told me," Kelan says, voice cracking. He pushes to his feet. "I would've gone with you."

"I needed you to protect Laoise. She does not hold allies well, and I knew you would protect her for my memory alone." When Kelan narrows his eyes at her, Theia laughs. "I was right. Was I not?"

His lip lifts in distaste. "She's still as when we were children."

Theia snorts, the sound so similar to the one Myrna made earlier. "A beast, you mean?"

Kelan rolls his eyes. "Yes."

"Yes, well." Theia sighs. "And Tomas came with me at the risk of everything he holds dear. Please keep that to yourself. Sister does not know. She thinks him a deserter as you do."

Myrna can almost feel the way Kelan's response to her aunt affects Tomas. It's in the lowering of tension in the air, the way he shifts, and the change in his breathing. They speak of relief and gratitude. Tomas was afraid of how Kelan would take Theia being here, but it is the look of apology which comes after that has Tomas swallowing hard and crossing his arms protectively. Myrna gets it. Years, who knows how many, of hatred learned were for nothing.

Emotions roil through Myrna so fast she's unsure where the floor is. Happiness and joy for her Guardian, relief for Tomas, but anger and hurt at the confirmation she was lied to by the women she loves most.

Theia's gaze lifts to Myrna's, and Myrna asks, "How could you lie to me? Never tell me who you really were? Never say you were my family, my aunt, no less."

"We were always family, my love. That's the truest statement of this life."

The world becomes shimmery, and Myrna blinks away the tears.

With a knowing smile, Theia says, "Why don't we head to the back, and you, darling, can tell me what happened to call on me when you know Laoise would not approve."

"Of course, Theia," Myrna says, trapped next by the emotion leaking from Kelan in waves. It's an emotion she doesn't totally understand.

"That's what the binding was. You weren't able to speak of her." When Myrna nods, Kelan lunges forward, wrapping her in a hug.

Myrna closes her eyes and returns the hug, her ribs aching at the pressure. "This was the only way I could tell you. But it's dangerous. I'm trusting you with a secret that's close to my heart. The person who raised..." Myrna chokes and pulls back to find Kelan frowning. "The person who's more than a caretaker. Do you understand?"

"Aye. She's as important to me as she is to you, for Theia is family."

Myrna squeezes his bicep before stepping back and going to her aunt. Just the sight of her, the fact she's here, it means everything. All the emotions she's been holding in burst free. "I miss you. Why didn't you tell me?"

Myrna falls into Theia's outstretched arms. "I'm sorry, my darling," Theia says as graceful hands caress down the child's back. "I wish I could've been there these last weeks."

"You should've been." Myrna wraps an arm around Theia's waist, and they move down the hall, the males following. "It's been crazy. I found out I've made an enemy, got promoted to princess, punched Kelan, met some weird guy named Tiernan, almost fell off the roof of the palace, made a new friend, and discovered I'm developing Radiant Light."

"Damn," Tomas laughs.

Theia licks her top lip. "That does sound exciting. I'm impressed. Where'd you punch Kelan?"

"The first time or the others?"

"First time?" Theia chuckles, then looks back at Kelan with a shit-eating grin. "I taught her that."

"I thought it felt familiar," Kelan says with a glare, but there is humor in his eyes.

They find a small table set off in the back and take a seat. Theia claps her hands, then says, "Now, in all seriousness, why are you here? You shouldn't have called on me. And you, Kelan, shouldn't have risked bringing her here."

"It was my idea," Myrna explains. "Kelan has been by my side, even helped me through the changing—"

"How so?" Tomas growls, gaze and rather aggressive stance locked on Kelan.

Myrna pushes Tomas back. "By controlling my Radiant Light and verifying there were always three females in the room to protect me from any males who might find me a tempting specimen as I apparently released so many pheromones the entire castle went on high alert."

Theia squeaks a giggle and covers her mouth as Tomas looks to Kelan and says, "Apologies."

Myrna sighs. To Theia, she says, "I just couldn't let him go on believing you were dead."

Her aunt cups the youngling's face and presses a kiss to her forehead. "You are a gift to us all."

Myrna's chest expands slow and wide, her shoulders rising with breath.

"You said Radiant Light?" Theia paces away, then turns to glance between the two of them. When they both nod, she exhales. "And it manifests like mine?"

Kelan shrugs. "Mostly."

"How is it different?" She comes the few feet back and presses her lips together.

"I can't explain it. It...feels different. Like a shimmer at the corner of my awareness."

"Knights." Theia licks her lips, squeezing the back of her arm.

She's not acting like herself. Kelan and Myrna exchange glances.

"It's probably just because she's so new to the power," Theia says, refusing to make eye contact with any of them. "Kelan, you remember how unsteady mine was when I first started? Just take it slow and listen to Kelan."

"Why are you acting strange?" Myrna asks.

Tomas and Kelan are also watching Theia as if she's been replaced by a changeling.

"I'm not, child. It is just concerning being so far away from you. Not being able to protect you when I know Brennan will want to get his hands on you."

Kelan's gaze bounces between the two females.

Theia's eyes shift to the shell-shocked face of her old friend. Her eyelids flutter as the two exchange an entire lifetime of words in that moment, and yet Kelan remains as confused as she. A spark of jealousy hits Myrna before she can stop it.

"I will watch over her, Theia. Train her, and if I notice..." Kelan trails off.

Unable to take any more, Theia pulls Myrna to her feet. "You must go. You've been gone too long. It is not safe here." She holds out her hands, and Myrna instantly accepts. Light erupts from between them, and Myrna's mouth drops open as Radiant Light—both their Radiant Light—fills the room.

"It's warm," Myrna says with a sigh. "I can feel you."

"And I you." Princess Mareola grins. "Stay safe. Trust Kelan. He may be a pain, but he will protect you." She brushes the hair back behind Myrna's ear. "Don't let your guard down and continue to train hard. Stand up for yourself, but do not lose yourself. Remember, kindness is always more powerful than hate." Theia kisses her cheek and whispers in her ear, "And be patient with Kelan. You do not understand what my lies did to him."

Myrna frowns. "I don't..."

"Just be patient." Theia turns to Kelan. "I'm dead. Remember?"

"But why?" Kelan's menacing with his arms crossed over his chest.

"Because. That's an order from your princess and friend." It's a tone Myrna has never heard from Theia. One oddly similar to Laoise and it sends cold ice down her spine.

Kelan narrows his eyes, then bows low. "Yes, Highness."

She meets Myrna's eyes. "I love you."

Myrna's eyes water. She hates this tale. It wipes away a history that's bright and beautiful; a woman who is kind and loving. As always, though, Myrna will do anything for this woman. So, she presses her lips together, then with a long exhale, says, "I love you, Auntie."

CHAPTER THIRTY-TWO

Increased Pressure

MYRNA WATCHES THE SWEAT drip to the floor. It falls in slow motion, and the princess blinks, mesmerized with the way it reflects the light. It's been two weeks since she left Theia and Sam in the human world, and although she's come to love the way Faerie speaks to her very soul, and she's thankful for her friendship with Shay and even Briana, Myrna's lonely. Part of her still wonders if what she's created here's real.

Perhaps it's because what she has with Theia was so absolute. Never wavering, a constant connection of respect and love. Then there's Sam. She'd been by her side, seen her darkest parts, and loved her for the secrets she couldn't disclose. That's a rare gift. So, only seeing her at the occasional lunch just hasn't been enough.

"Hey," Shay says, sliding onto the bench next to her. He bumps her shoulder, then wipes his face. "You okay? You've been off the last few days."

"Have not."

Shay shoots her an unbelieving look. "Don't lie to me, Myr. We agreed."

It is true. For the hours they'd spent together, beat the crap out of one another, and tormented the others in the castle, they'd developed a bond of friendship that was hard to deny. The guards hadn't understood the friendship at first, but it didn't take long before they'd seen the connection. He'd earned their respect for how he saw Myrna as nothing more than she was, his friend and never the princess. Their humor was an even match to their compassion. He made her laugh, pushed her, and never let her doubt herself. Shay'd become a staple in days.

Myrna shrugs. "Tired? The schedule's been crazy, and I've added more lessons with Mother." Myrna lowers her voice. "There've been more advancements by Brennan too, but no actual attacks, which is weird. Add on the three more assassination attempts this week and..." Shay winces, and Myrna continues, "Yeah. The Guardians are on edge. We're up to eight total."

Shay throws his arm over her shoulders. He lays his cheek to her head. "What can I do? I hate that I'm not nearby when you need me."

"What?" Myrna's jaw drops. "You have been! At least for a few of the attacks and that's too many!"

Shay rolls his eyes and pushes to his feet. The towel hangs at his side. "Consider those real-life practice."

Myrna gets to her feet and shoves him, making him step back. "You're an idiot."

The dumbass's rolling laugh has Zerekule heading over. "Hey, guys, breakfast time? Princess, Kelan's gonna meet us at Haszwalds."

"Oh." Myrna frowns. "He's not here yet?"

"No. He's in with the queen after the escape..." He looks away. "So, he's gonna meet us there."

"Escape?" The word comes out slowly as a spark of warning tickles the back of her neck. When Zerekule doesn't respond, it only increases. He isn't the one to normally withhold information.

"Zerekule?" Myrna's tone has Briana and Jaden joining them.

Zerekule releases a long sigh that has Myrna shifting on her feet. "Niandra's cell was found empty this morning. Her guards were incapacitated."

"What?" Shay exclaims, the outrage Myrna feels in his words even as she keeps her composure. She must, for she is princess and Laoise's daughter, but inside? "How could she escape? How could the Guardians let this happen? She nearly killed Myrna!"

Jaden flinches, but lowers his voice when he answers, "We don't know. That's what Kelan went to go figure out. As of right now, though, it will not affect you...much."

"Much?" Myrna asks.

"We will be adding a few extra guards to your contingent until we can verify she is not in the castle and the risk to you is minimal."

Myrna nods and, keeping her voice flat, says, "Completely understand. Please let me know what I may do to be of assistance."

Briana lays a hand on the princess's shoulder. "We have no reason to believe she's coming for you. Not really. From everything she said and what your mother got out during her...ministrations, Niandra wishes to leave our court."

Except Niandra made it perfectly clear she wished to hurt me.

Myrna swallows hard at the memory, then heads for the door. "Come. I am hungry."

Dammit. She'd flipped to formal speak in her discomfort, which is why her friends watch her with terrified, sympathetic eyes.

They hurry to catch up, Shay at her side and the Guardians taking their formation around her. Several new guards join the group. Myrna hates how she breathes easier with their presence.

"So," Myrna says, distracting herself, "we need to make this quick. I've a meeting with Stephan and the lords this morning to talk strategy. Afterward, we're planning to meet with Mother and debrief her before our abilities training. It's gonna be a long day."

"How does it feel taking all of this on?" Shay asks as they reach the entryway. He looks impressed.

The dining hall is packed with people today. Tables along the back wall are piled with china, covered with the finest silks. Fruit of every kind, whole and sliced, are laid out for those to choose from. Meats, cheeses, and salads rest on platters next to other mounds of foods Myrna can't even identify. It's the most glorious display she's ever seen. Of course, she always thinks that when she enters here, and this room is meant for the guards, staff, and court. It's always available for those who are hungry, and it never ceases to amaze her. The few meals she's had with her mother? Those have been a dream.

She feels like an intruder as she passes the groups enjoying their meals, still afraid they'll ask her to leave. To Shay, she says, "There's so much I need to learn. I've done war games and strategy, but never to this scale, and never with real people at stake. It's scary. The staff and lords are getting used to me, but they don't *know* me or trust me yet. It all still feels so...unstable."

"You just have to prove yourself," Shay says, "and you will."

Myrna's eyes are drawn to a set of Guardians she doesn't know. They jump from their table, looking down at a drink knocked over by one of the males. They yell at a passing servant and demand she drop what she's doing and clean it up. He towers over the poor girl as he snaps insults about her intelligence and speed.

Myrna shakes her head. *This happens too often. Wherever this entitled arrogance came from, it needs to stop.*

"It was not always like this," Jaden says from the back of their group. He must've seen where her attention lies. His tone is solemn, quiet. So it will not carry. "It's only been since your aunt and grandmother died that the tone of this land has changed."

"And it's been as if the land has been dying ever since, a plague spreading this hatred ever so slowly..." Briana mutters, gaze also locked on the exchange.

They approach the table of goodies, and Myrna huffs. "Well, perhaps it's time for it to revert back."

Then she strides forward, ignoring the wide-eyed stares of her companions. She stops just as she reaches the table.

"Be careful what you say," Briana says, "for even what Jaden said could be considered treason as it goes against the queen."

"If it's my mother who allows this, then she's not the person who raised me." The sharpness of her words has heads turning in her direction.

The three males turn at her voice and the poor girl, now done with her task, disappears off into the back. At least she was able to provide an escape route.

Myrna ignores them all, stomach grumbling. *The food looks fantastic.*

"Princess Myrna." An attendant rushes to her side. He shifts uncomfortably, casting glances at the display as if worried it is not perfect. "Is everything to your liking? Come. Come, take a seat and we will put together a special plate for you."

"No, that's unnecessary." Myrna smiles. "What you have here is beautiful. Please tell the staff that you have done a remarkable job. I'm excited to be allowed to partake in this. It makes me hungry just looking at it."

"But we could have something more—"

She glances at the others. "Isn't it magnificent? The cured meats smell divine and those candied dates!"

The attendant's shoulders rise. His chest puffs. "Thank you, my lady. We do our best. If you will not allow me to make something special, may I help make your plate?"

"Hmm. Well…" She leans in as if to impart a secret. Her volume does not change, however. "Only if you show me your favorites."

He beams. "It would be my honor."

Passing through the line, they all interact with the attendant. They ask his name, compliment the presentation, food and quality, as well as the room at large. There are jokes about Myrna's likes and dislikes, her love of chocolate and strawberries, and her aversion to sauerkraut. The attendant takes mental notes, and, in the end, they hold the entire room's attention as they walk to their table with plates filled high.

"I am grateful to have met you." Myrna thanks the male, bowing before she takes a seat. He goes to leave, and Myrna touches his forearm.

The male nearly jumps from his skin.

"Will you do me one more favor?" When he nods, she says, "Please ask the girl who had to deal with those three males to come here."

The attendant frowns but disappears and returns with a gorgeous young woman a few years younger than Myrna.

The girl curtsies but keeps her head down, eyes on the floor as if she is about to be scolded. "Highness."

Making sure her voice can be heard by all of those in the hall, Myrna says, "I want to apologize for the deplorable treatment you received from three of the Royal Guard." Myrna's gaze locks on the males for a moment, and they pale. "They should know better. I want to assure you they will be... re-educated on how to treat those of our kind with respect. I give you my word."

"Madam, I—" The girl trembles. From fear, sadness, embarrassment?

Unable to resist any longer, Myrna slides from her seat and pulls the shaking girl into her arms. Shocked gasps fill the hall, and Myrna closes her eyes.

How can a place so connected to one's arcane—one's soul—not see how the heart means everything?

Myrna places her hands on the girl's shoulders. "No one deserves to be treated like that. I do not care whether you are of the court, the guard, forest, or the staff. We're all part of Faerie and this court." Myrna's heart blooms as she takes in the joy looking back at her. "Now, do you feel well enough to continue with your duties, or do you need time?"

With more light than she'd seen in this girl before, she says, "I'd very much like to return to my duties. I'm almost done with a special dessert. I heard you say you liked them. May I bring one out to you?"

"Do you have enough for me to share?" Myrna's eyebrow raises.

"I should, yes."

Myrna rubs her hands together and smiles widely. "Yes, please!"

With an excited curtsy, she runs off, the attendant following. Her face shines, a beautiful grin plastered upon her face.

"Myrna." Shay's fork is halfway to his mouth as she returns to her seat. A piece of roasted meat dangles precariously. "That was amazing. You say these people don't know you, that you fear you don't fit in, but every time you interact, you show the truth of your heart. You may not see it, but you, Myrna, are winning this land one heart at a time. By your honesty, your kindness, and your fierceness."

Heat rushes to Myrna's cheeks.

"He's right," Zerekule agrees.

"Yup." Briana nods before shoving food into her mouth. "I can't wait to get those three the 'training' you mentioned. They're dicks."

"Bri!" Myrna laughs. Then the words of the others sink in. "But I didn't do anything. Not really. Just treated them like…"

"You learned about him, and you treated her like she was special," Shay explains.

"She is."

They all smile.

"You showed them both honor and respect—as an equal and not a servant." It's Serena who's decided to add to the conversation this time. "Princess, you spread love, kindness, and you feel…"

"Like home," Jaden adds. His eyes are focused on his plate. "Like Faerie."

"That makes no sense," Myrna says.

Shay shakes his head. "It doesn't have to. You're changing things whether you mean to or not. You've changed my life."

Myrna goes silent.

Was what they said true? If so, it's huge. She'd been thrown into this world and was trying to survive. Maybe figure out if this could be the home she'd always dreamed of. If it was right for *her*. She'd never considered her effect on them. She'd been in survival mode, trying to find her feet and not drown, while never losing the lessons Theia taught her.

Be kind. See other's hearts through their actions. Fight for what you believe in. Protect the weak.

Was she being selfish for not considering them? Probably. Especially if she was on a path to be heir. For any choice she made would change the course of their lives, too. Hurt them in return. Her existence, her role, affected an entire species. Shape an entire culture for good or bad. That is a heavy thought. But did she want that kind of responsibility?

Myrna stares at her food for a long moment.

"Hey." Briana bumps her shoulder. "What's up?"

Myrna shakes out of it and takes a bite. "Nothing. I'm good."

But shit. I need to do better. Over the last few weeks, she'd been going through the motions. That isn't enough. If she has even a chance of being heir, she needs to put every molecule of herself into it. Because they deserve that from her at the very least, and how else would she know if she can do it?

Food forgotten and energy focused solely on her new goal, Myrna jumps from her seat. "I've got to see Kelan. I—We have a meeting."

"But your food," Shay says.

Myrna scoops the pastries and muffins from her plate and shoves them into her tunic. Then grabs the bacon and says, "I can eat on the way. I need to be there."

Giving him a one-armed hug—while he looks at her as though she has three heads—she adds, "See you this afternoon?" He nods. "Great! And can you tell the girl I'm sorry I left before the dessert? Ask her to send a few to my suite and I will make sure we all try them. I know we're excited."

"You're scaring me, Myr."

She waves him off, already out the door, her assigned guard right behind.

CHAPTER THIRTY-THREE

Game of Chess

Could this be going *any worse*? Kelan breathes the tension-thick-ened air, his chest expanding in slow methodical movements. If he didn't focus on this, he too would look like the others; sleeves rolled, hair a mess, or their knuckles white as they grip the edge of the simulator with frustration.

He cannot blame Stephan nor the other lords. King Brennan's movements make no logistical sense. The areas he engages are of no value, and there's no focused target.

"Why now?" Lord Merkin says, eyes locked on the image of the army moving toward the town nearest his lands. "After so many years. Why now?"

"Has Brennan communicated any demands or reasons?" Lord Ardian has been doing circles around the table. "For as far as the queen has told us, he's been nothing but cordial. That's unless she isn't telling us something. Kelan?"

"As far as I'm aware, no. Brennan's provided no reason for this recent incursion." However, Kelan doesn't mention Brennan's offense at not being told of Myrna's existence.

Stephan rests a hand on his hip. "If he pushes any closer, I will have to respond. I'll not let that town fall. There're too many innocents there. I will protect them."

Slapping his friend on the back, Kelan agrees. "We'll back you. In fact, we'll be sending reinforcements. The queen has already approved it. It—"

The door slams open, and all heads spin toward the noise.

Myrna's face reddens with embarrassment. She stumbles to a stop.

"My lords, my apologies." She curtsies. "I didn't realize you were already in session. I would've been here sooner and not have made such a terrible entrance."

Her quickened speech and the way she glances away nearly makes him laugh. If only he didn't sense her underlying tension. Something's bothering her.

"Give me a moment," Kelan says to the group. He leads Myrna to the far corner. "What's going on? You never barge in like that unless you're upset."

Myrna tugs on her braid. "I just..."

Kelan shoots her a "spit it out" glare when she doesn't continue.

"Did Niandra really escape?"

He exhales slowly and shoots a glance to the group. "Yes, but we have it handled. I promise. Now, what else is bothering you?"

"How do you know—"

He closes the distance between them. Her hand lifts on reflex to rest on his stomach. "Because I know you."

She presses her lips together, then shrugs. "I just had a realization at breakfast, and it kinda threw me through a loop. Made me realize that if you were here, I needed to be here, too."

His eyebrows draw down in question.

"I've been selfish—"

"Hey, guys, everything all right?" Stephan calls.

They step apart. *Why can't he keep his distance?*

"Yeah. We're coming." Kelan nods and slides a hand to rest at her lower back. To her, he says, "We're going to finish this conversation eventually because you, Myrna, are anything but selfish."

Myrna grunts.

"Everything is great, but perhaps not for you guys. I assume things have gotten worse?" Myrna asks, and Kelan nods. "Can I see the maps?"

Kelan leads her to the edge of the table and looks down at the advancing army, which has doubled in the last twenty-four hours. The attacks have spread from a few locations to nearly two dozen.

Myrna's jaw drops. "Holy shit is right! Kelan, this is bad!" She grips the jacket at his waist. "He's attacking my people. But there's a…"

Myrna's focus narrows and her eyes glaze as she analyzes the moving pieces on the table. The moving men shifting along the map show not only where they came from, but the expected path. Her breath catches, and all eyes fly to her.

"Princess, if you know something, tell us." Lord Merkin's the first to speak up, but they all wish to.

"It's there," she says in a haze of a voice.

"What do you see, Myrna?" Stephan asks.

Then her head snaps to look at him, and she says, "We need Mother. Now!"

Kelan does not hesitate. With the hand not around Myrna's waist, he jots a note on some parchment and gives it to Jaden, who waits outside. The rest of her guard are released for a break while here. "To the queen. Immediately."

A swift agreement, and the Guardian disappears down the hall.

With that done, Myrna returns her gaze to the board, pointing out what none of them had seen before. It is as if she is in some sort of trance. He's watched her do this while observing a game of chess.

"Look at how he advances. He's going to hit there and there, taking out those two towns and the smallest of our forces. Then he'll force his way through to Tara." She faces him once more. "Kelan, you told me what he said to Mother. He doesn't want land. He's coming for me."

"Myrna, he's angry he's not provided rights to meet you, but—"

"He wants to stop the *Norsthana Maskia*, the hundred-year law. If he does so, our court is weakened, and he has a chance. Just look!"

Every member of the group leans forward. *Knights. That is not a strategy they'd seen.*

Myrna continues, "I bet you they'd even attack Haszwalds if they could. Come in from the human world."

A boom rocks the hall on the other side of the door. There's a scream. And another.

"By the wild. Why was she not here from the start?" Guardian Snormai says, removing his blade from its sheath with a *snick*. He jogs for the door. "Get her out of here, Brynes. I don't know what Brennan wants with her, and I don't care."

Kelan grips her waist hard now. "Come. Into the back room. To the emergency portal."

"But the others..."

"They'll be fine once you're out. You're a beacon now that they're in the building."

"Meaning?" she asks, rushing to follow.

"This close, your power gives off a very distinctive taste." He glances at her. "We need to work harder on your shielding."

"He's right," Stephan says. "If they're here for you, Brennan's people will leave once you're gone."

"We should've been working on this the entire time!"

"We have been." Kelan opens the hidden door in the wall and shoves her into his private chamber.

Myrna growls. She understands that the smartest thing is to run, but she hates it, nonetheless. "I can fight! I've been learning to use my Radiant Light, or I can just kick some ass."

Kelan pulls back a large tapestry, flinging it to hang over the top of a bookcase. He sends his arcane into some markings etched in the stone wall. They're almost too tiny to see, but the moment his will touches them, an archway lights up.

"Neat."

The sound of clashing metal, grunts, minor explosions from blasts of arcane power and hollered insults sing through the air. The door behind them blows apart, shards scattering across the floor, sliding to their feet. Wind whips Myrna's hair as the battle outside enters the small chamber, and a male somehow familiar steps into the room.

Kelan's arcane activates the spell created specifically for emergency situations, and a doorway appears. Then he swings Myrna between him and the portal just as it comes to life. Not waiting another second, he dives for it, sending his will into the magic with both the location and the instruction to close once they're through. As they fall, Kelan meets the eye of King Brennan's nephew and right-hand male, Colum, just as he takes aim.

Too quick. Colum's bow is drawn taut, an obsidian-tipped arrow glimmering in the candlelight.

Myrna presses closer into Kelan as the light of the portal shimmers at the corners of her vision, and Colum Murray's cry of fury fills her ears. He releases the arrow even as Kelan spins to block Myrna from the shot.

The arrow slams into Kelan's back, and he grunts.

Myrna cries out, her hand going to the arrowhead now sticking from his shoulder. "Kelan!"

The portal closes, and their new location materializes around them. Kelan glances around.

Fuck. This isn't where we're supposed to go.

CHAPTER THIRTY-FOUR

Hard Landing

"FATHER, CAN YOU HAND me an apple?" Shay sits down in the modest living room of their home and bends to remove his boots. The living, dining, and kitchen area isn't over eighteen feet square, but it's clean and filled with signs of a happy home. Remnants of the dessert he brought home to his sisters, made by the servant girl Myrna helped, are scattered in the sink.

Declan grabs a perfectly ripe green apple from the basket on the windowsill, then tosses it over. "How was practice?"

"Not bad. But breakfast was a pain."

"Why?" Declan leans against the tiny table.

"I told you about the issue with the Guardians and the servant girl, but then"—he sighs and unties his other boot—"we found out Niandra escaped."

"What!"

"Yeah."

Suddenly, the room becomes noise and light. The sound of battle fills the space, wind blasts f

rom the fireplace, and then there is a crashing as two bodies stumble, then fall. It takes a second to realize what he's seeing is Myrna hitting her knees on the back of the couch, and then flipping over it.

He, his father, and even his sisters who sit in the far corner cry out in surprise even as they push back to get out of the way.

The flash of the portal—he now realizes—closing helps them settle.

Impressively, Kelan rolls them, limiting his weight down upon Myrna, until she's half atop his chest. Even so, she moans, and Shay's not surprised. That looked like it hurt.

"Gods be damned!" Myrna curses. After a quick scan of her surroundings, and apparently deeming them safe, she slips from beneath him, crawls to her knees, and breaks the back of the arrow off. "Hold still."

Kelan grinds his teeth as his gaze flashes up to Shay's siblings.

"Stop worrying about them and look at me." He does, and she continues, "Are you ready?"

Before he really has time to recognize what she's going to do, she yanks the arrow from his flesh.

"Holy knights," Shay whispers.

Kelan cries out, the sound turning into a moan.

Declan shakes his head, then calls to the girls to grab some clean cloths. He throws one clean one to Myrna, who immediately presses it to the oozing wound. Then Myrna yanks off the tie of her tunic and wraps it around the whole thing to staunch the bleeding. It's impressive how quickly she works.

"Are you good?" Only when Kelan nods does she help him to a seated position and acknowledge Shay and his family.

"Declan, Shay, and who would have to be his sisters. How are you?" she says.

Shay laughs and scans their now-destroyed living room. His sisters have varying expressions of shock, but Declan looks more pissed than anything.

"I'm sorry, Mr. Hughes," Myrna says, her voice hurried through panting breath. "I don't know how we ended up here, and I'm so sorry about destroying your house. I—"

Declan steps forward. "Child, calm." He looks at Kelan, whose face is pale. His gaze returns to Myrna's. "What happened?"

"Yeah. I just saw you," Shay says.

Myrna jumps to her feet and then pulls Kelan up. "We were at Haszwalds for a meeting. I figured out Brennan's attack plan and then we were...well, attacked."

Kelan and Myrna step to the side as Shay and Declan right the couch.

"But I don't understand why we're here," Myrna mumbles.

Kelan speaks to Declan. He holds his arm close to his side, gently rolling his shoulder to test its mobility. "Colum Murray was there. He came himself. We barely made it through the portal."

"And you came here?" Declan asks.

"I'm sorry," Kelan says with a shake of his head. "I was intending to go somewhere else, but my concentration dropped when the arrow hit me. Myrna must've been thinking of Shay."

Declan's eyebrows raise. "Her will's so great as to overtake yours?"

"Myrna's a force to be reckoned with. Much like her mother." Kelan scowls.

Shay ushers the girls to another room. Before they disappear, he orders, "Get some towels and water. Then get an overnight bag ready."

"I don't understand. What're you guys talking about?" Myrna says.

"We weren't supposed to come here, Myrna. The portal was supposed to take us to a safehouse apartment in town close to the castle."

Declan laughs, then throws a cloth to Kelan. "But apparently, you're stronger than our boy, and you brought him here."

When Kelan tries to wipe the blood seeping from the wound, Myrna bares her teeth and tears the cloth from his grip. She carefully maneuvers it beneath the wrapping she'd already placed. The adjustment helps. He squeezes her hand.

"We must go. Declan, Shay—" he pauses, staring at the two men. "I shouldn't ask...We're far from the castle and under attack, but we can't stay here. She's too exposed, already been attacked here once, and if they got into Haszwalds, they could have assassins in town. I need to get Myrna back to the palace, and I've no Guardians to protect her."

Shay crosses his arms over his chest and steps forward. "You're kidding, right?"

"Yeah," Myrna agrees. "If you weren't hurt, I'd smack you upside the head. I can take care of myself."

Declan snorts.

Shay sighs. "I didn't mean it that way, Myr. I meant you're my best friend. He doesn't have to ask. I'm going to fight by your side, whether or not he likes it."

Kelan looks to Declan. "And you?"

"Does she remind you of anyone else?" Declan asks, humor in his eyes as Myrna continues to tend to Kelan, then proceeds to tell him to "stop being a baby" when he makes a noise.

"More than you know."

The two men share a look full of meaning. It's one full of history and friendship, something Shay hasn't seen his father have in a long while. It holds a secret, hurt, and also regret. Yet, Shay hopes this might not be the last time he witnesses it.

"She is my princess. One day to be my queen. I will protect her with my life. It's the vow I took, and regardless of my current status in the eyes of the crown, my heart has never changed."

As Kelan and Myrna face him, Declan drops to one knee, his hand over his heart. Shay's breath catches, and the back of his eyes burn.

Letting go of Kelan, Myrna moves to Declan. She places her hand on his bowed head. "And this, I will be forever grateful for—the heart of a true Guardian. Perhaps one day, you will trust me to share the truth of your past."

He winces. "It's a crime you will never forgive. And you should not. I am just grateful you do not hate my son for it."

A sad, resigned voice speaks up from behind them both. Kelan's voice is the rawest Shay has ever heard it. "His crimes... are a lie. You, my dear Myrna, proved that to me just days ago. If not for you, my belief of his innocence would still be tainted black."

Declan's head snaps up, Myrna's hand falling away.

The breath in Shay's lungs seizes. His face flushes, and the world tilts. "What do you mean?"

"It was my fault. I let her—"

"Nay. And when I can prove it"—Kelan approaches the man who was once a brother to him—"When Myrna and I can prove it to you, we will remove the mark on your family name. I give you my word as a Guardian."

Chills spread over Shay's entire body as Declan's eyes meet his.

Chapter Thirty-Five

Who Betrays Whom?

As the scent of spoiled bodies and desperation is swept away and replaced by that of pine, sun, and earth, Niandra breathes deep. Laoise would've kept her there forever, hidden beneath the palace and left to rot for what she had done to the princess had Sola not come for her. If not for nearly taking the youngling's life; that and the other smaller crimes placed at her feet.

Stupid bitch.

She hums. Perhaps Niandra had been less careful with her schemes than she'd realized. As seen by the wounds covering her body.

But the truth of their contact in the Unseelie Court? This is yet undiscovered.

The last arch of the underground passageway passes overhead, leaving the smell of death behind them as they enter the forest. A male lies prone beneath a nearby tree—the scout for this area left unconscious. By Sola, no doubt.

"Hurry," Sola says. The cloak which covers her face falls in thin sheets, distorting her form so she does not look like herself. It is the same for the one Niandra dons, too. "The next guard will be coming around shortly."

"You risk too much," Niandra snarls at the female she adores. "Should the queen find—"

Sola grabs Niandra's arm and drags her forward, through a thicket of trees. "A necessary risk. One you would have taken too. And I have a way for us to leave this place forever."

This stops Niandra's tirade. She stumbles a step, and pain lances up her side—remainders from Laoise's ministrations. Ignoring it, Niandra rushes to catch her lover as they climb the embankment, which leads to the river and around to the far side of Tara.

"And that is?" Niandra asks, a clear bite in her tone. They move through the trees, hiding from a hunter and his wife as they check their traps, the castle and the guards long behind them. Niandra's legs burn, the cuts down her arms and across her ribs tear with each long stride, but she refuses to show it.

"I've made a deal with the king." Sola glances behind her before weaving toward a place Niandra knows well. The bathhouse they often visited and run by her cousin.

Dranmik spare us. It had been their hope, but still. They reach the back of a row of buildings and skate along them.

"Given the intel we've provided these years—" Sola glances down the alleyway, then motions her forward before stepping in line with her and murmuring, "he agreed to make a deal. Should we help him with his task of capturing Myrna so he may verify her lineage and attachment to Laoise by opening a portal, he will allow us entrance to his court."

"He does not believe she is Laoise's?"

Sola shrugs. "Not our concern. Only that he's willing."

Fair. "Did he accept the offer I sent, or was it another request?" Niandra holds her breath. She'd consider another option if it did not put Sola at risk.

Either way, a portal is a simple task, impossible inside the castle due to the wards and difficult for most arcane magics, but simple.

Niandra stops Sola, pressing into her space until they're huddled against the back wall of the bathhouse. She uses the moment to catch her breath. Her entire right side burns, yet she keeps her breaths steady. "Brennan does nothing without payment, so what was it?"

Sola turns, her distress a small tightening at the corner of her eye. Her voice is that of the perfectly professional attendant. Niandra hates it. "He accepted your deal. Your hand for our entrance to his court, but should you not produce a male heir within two turns, then your life is forfeit."

Niandra stills. The air becomes lead in her lungs. *And you?*

"Don't worry. I'm allowed entrance and full honor as your mistress," Sola finishes, gaze tracing across Niandra's face. No doubt searching for a reaction.

"And you're okay with this?"

"I'm tired of the power play," Sola says simply.

She's played Laoise's game so long, Niandra thinks.

Sola brushes Niandra's face. "If this is our opportunity to leave and provides a way to get back at Laoise and this court, then we should take it."

Teeth aching, Niandra presses further into Sola's space, making the wood dig into her shoulder blades. Niandra wraps her hand around the female's neck and slams her lips down upon Sola's gorgeous mouth. The kiss is hard and deep. Possessive. Sola digs her fingers into Niandra's hips and, although the bruises beneath the cloak scream in protest, Niandra revels in the embrace. She pulls away and looks into those eyes, her hand still gripping the auburn locks of silk.

"You are mine." The words are spoken against her lover's lips.

Sola's eyes narrow as if challenging Niandra's comment. Though they are lovers, both are also dominant, wild creatures. "That will never change."

"Good." Niandra's lip pulls back in disgust. "Perhaps it is worth it, then."

Sola's sinister smile sends fire through Niandra. She wants to pull her back in for another kiss, but there is a warning in the eyes glaring back. "Then we must get inside and create the portal. I want out of here and away from Laoise's reach."

Niandra releases Sola harshly, and the female sucks in a breath as she rights herself. Bumping her shoulder, Sola shoves past her and to the back door of the building.

They enter, her cousin stepping from the back room.

"Sola, what are you... No, she cannot be here!" her cousin says, eyes wide as she takes in Niandra's hooded figure.

"Go," Sola orders. "You did not see us. If you betray me, I will find you."

The girl pales and nods. "There are five others working today."

Niandra and Sola stay silent. They would deal with them.

Dismissed, the female rushes toward the exit, passing Niandra. Before she can escape, Niandra pulls the knife from the folds of her cloak and swipes it across the throat of the young Faye. Deep. Sola releases a quiet, surprised cry even as Niandra covers the mouth of the dying female and lowers her to the floor. As this girl has little magic, her death is quick, her healing not strong enough to stop the bleeding.

Sola stalks forward. "Why did you do that?"

Face blank, she wipes the blade clean on the cloak and pushes Sola toward the empty bathing chamber. "She was a risk we could not afford."

"She was family," Sola snaps.

"She is Seelie, and we will not be, come end of day."

Sola blinks, and the truth of those words wash over her. Her shoulders soften, and her chin lifts. "True. Then perhaps we should get started."

Sola pulls a satchel from beneath her cloak. From within, she removes a broken piece of a mirror and a handful of other ingredients.

Niandra's eyes go wide. "Where did you get that?"

"Mother. Apparently, the family has several pieces. I stole this last year." Sola smirks as she sets it on a side table.

Incredible. Mirrors of Connection are rare. Even a broken one is powerful if the operator knows the right spell. Most don't, and to try usually causes death. The fact that her family has found one and kept it instead of destroying it...

"And you know how to use it? Safely?"

The smile that spreads across Sola's lips is filled with promise, but it is the darkness in her gaze as she lifts her eyes to meet Niandra's that has tingles running across her skin in anticipation. "With your reflections and my arcane to power it, we'll be fine."

Sola doesn't explain the spell to Niandra. After decades together, she trusts Sola and does as she's told. Only for her does she make this allowance. The mirror is prepped with some runes Niandra does not recognize, and Niandra is asked to extend her arcane across it to create a reflection extending the surface of the mirror large enough for someone to pass through. It shimmers with blue light, glints of a soft green like that of an oyster shell radiating across its surface.

"It's time," Sola says, looking up from her crouched position. She's been bent over, chanting in a language Niandra doesn't know. She stands and pushes one last burst of arcane through the shimmering mirror on the table.

The reflection solidifies.

Almost instantly, the image of a forest with a contingent of Unseelie soldiers standing ready appears. Niandra will need to ask Sola later how she so easily connected to them. Another secret she's been keeping?

The assassins dress in black, the single defining factor a small sliver of blue at their chests.

The one in front smirks, then steps through.

Niandra swallows the mix of regret and excitement his presence brings. This is true treachery. She is betraying innocence. Younglings. She knows this, and yet it thrills her, for her hatred of this court has grown for centuries—a prison to her true nature run by a clan who deserves nothing but despair.

"Welcome," Sola says, "to The Court of the Radiant Sun."

"Lady Sola. Lady Niandra." The Unseelie soldier grins, stepping out of the way of nearly twenty more black-clad soldiers. He bows slightly. "I've been asked to thank you. The king sends his gratitude. This is a much more advantageous way for us to capture the princess."

As they speak, the soldiers slip through the back and side doors of the bathhouse like wraiths. They're silent, sliding into the streets of town and looking for who they know is there, for the fight at Haszwalds has gone exactly as the king had predicted. So many possible outcomes, but this? The princess, out in Tara with too few guards as protection. Perfection.

Niandra pushes her shoulders back, resting her hand on the blade Sola gave her. "And what is your interest in the princess?"

The soldier's gaze moves slowly to her. It's creepy. Niandra's impressed. She could like this one.

"That is none of your concern," the Unseelie says.

"But if we are to be part of your court, then..."

"You are not yet." The words are short. Simple. He walks to the windows, which line the side of the room. With no concern of being seen, he props one open so he may see the street beyond. It overlooks the main thoroughfare, and the scent of the food markets wafts in.

Sola follows. Her posture is perfect, defiant. "We are ready to see the king. Take us to him."

The male scoffs. "Nay."

Niandra grinds her teeth. *Of course.*

"Why?" Niandra asks. She can almost feel the panic seeping from Sola.

"The agreement was you open the portal and help capture the princess. You are in the optimum position for this." The male turns, facing Sola with hard, black eyes. There is no empathy as he rips apart their plans. "Should this infiltration not work, then you will need to return to the palace and bring Princess Myrna to us in order to fulfill the agreement."

"This is not what we agreed!" Sola hollers, her tone harsh but steady. "Take us to Brennan now!"

"What if we just went through now?" Niandra asks.

"Then the soldiers on the other side would kill you. Or you'd be lost in the dark wood, as the portal point was not at the palace." He lifts a brow. "Do you think us stupid?"

Bile creeps up Niandra's throat, and her claws tingle with the urge to rip out the man's throat. She knew this would happen. Damn the Unseelie.

"This is unacceptable! We agreed..." Sola trails off as the noise of a fight draws their attention to the window once more.

Several of the male's brethren approach a group of cloaked figures. They're too far for them to hear the exchange of words, but as the battle begins, excitement rises in Niandra's chest.

Perhaps Myrna will die, and Sola can take her place here as originally planned. Then, all would be fine, and they would not have to deal with Brennan at all. They could finally kill Laoise from inside the palace once Sola is appointed heir.

Magic comes into the battle and everything changes. It's clear who the princess is. If not by her head of pearl-white hair and long, thin frame, then by the bright light which bursts from her fingertips. Screams pierce the air as the Unseelie soldiers go down one by one.

Yet this is not what has both Niandra and the male spinning. It is the gasp and curse of triumph from Sola. The female runs to her bag, falls to her knees, and pulls a piece of parchment from it.

"That lying piece of dung!" Sola mumbles. "I knew there was more to that girl! I knew it."

She writes something upon it in tight, quick strokes, then folds it as if her life depends on the words within. Perhaps it does. Before she jumps to her feet, she seals it with a whispered spell coded for Brennan.

"Sola? What's happening?" Niandra asks, having been unable to read the scribbled words.

Before the male has a chance to recover, she grabs his arm and yanks him toward the still portal. Too surprised, he does not resist. That, and Sola is stronger than she looks.

"Your men will have to find another way if they still live. This is more important."

"Wha—?"

Before the word is fully out of his mouth, she shoves the letter to his chest, then kicks him through the portal. "Take it to the king. Now!"

Then she closes the portal.

Niandra's mouth drops open. "What was that?"

Sola's shocked eyes meet hers. She shakes with energy. "He needs to get that letter to Brennan. There is no other option. That letter will solidify our place."

"How do you know he'll take it to him?" she screams.

Sola swipes all the items into her bag. "He will. He will."

As her lover rushes to the door, an electric energy still pouring from her, Niandra races after her. "How do you know, and how will we get there?" She grabs Sola's arm and swings her around. "Tell me what it was about!"

Her eyes are about to bug out of her head. "Laoise's been lying. About it all." She inhales slowly. "Do you remember the stories of the final battle when Mareola went missing?"

Niandra stills. "There were a lot of rumors surrounding her death. Why?"

"What were they?" she asks, breaths coming quicker.

"Um..." Niandra thinks back, her head pounding with confusion. "That she took the Marista Blade through the heart and is now lost to time. That Mareola was seen with an Unseelie courtier who swept her away. Another said he died for her." She shakes her head. "Um...The most believed is she used the last of her powers to burn away an entire contingent, then her arcane engulfed her. All stories end with the Guardian who was her ward and in charge of her protection being stripped of his rank and marked a traitor for not stopping it."

"Yes," Sola says, "but all end with her body being irretrievable." Sola's breath comes in heaving gulps. "We have another part to play here, and it requires making sure Myrna's exposed."

CHAPTER THIRTY-SIX

Desperation in Battle Leads to Control

THE DEPTH OF HOPE brewing in Shay's chest is almost embarrassing, and the same light grows in Father. But Kelan would not elaborate on his father's innocence or the removal of the mark. At least not right then, but his promise is everything.

"We need to get back before Mother loses her shit," Myrna says.

Kelan grumbles about Sam being a bad influence—a common thing between the two and further solidifying Shay's need to meet this feisty human officially. Luckily, it was right when the girls came back with their stash of weapons from the workshop.

"Time to head to the forest, girls," Declan says, kissing them each on the forehead. "You know where to go. Don't leave until I or Shay come for you."

"Yes, Father," they chorus. With a quick hug for both him and Shay, they disappear from the door, a bag of clothes over their shoulders.

"They'll be fine, Father. Don't worry. They're not as helpless as you pretend." Shay pats Declan on the back before digging through the bag of goodies. At fifteen and twenty, they were still children, barely having started training. Still, they were strong.

"I just wish your mother was here to protect them."

Shay's heart constricts, his hand freezing on the way to a set of knives. He flexes his fingers and moves forward.

"They'll be fine," he repeats.

They leave Shay's land not from the main road, but through a private path through the woods leading into the back alley of town. The high stone walls are clean, rising several floors on either side. Doors allow entrance to shops at regular intervals while windows litter the upper levels. Every few inches, pillars peek from the structure like tiny fingers waving to say hello.

Reaching the end of the alleyway, Kelan says, "Stay together. Myrna, don't leave my side for anything."

They keep to the shadows, zigzagging through the street filled with people. Which is hard as it's midday, the sun high and markets buzzing with life. Yet even so, they don't stand out with the simple hooded cloaks they wear, covering defining features.

Even more shocking, however, was how, before they left, Myrna allowed Kelan to cover her in his glamour, distorting her features even more. This was why she needed to "stay close." Neither Shay nor Declan had liked it.

"This thing is hot," Myrna complains about the cloak.

"Two more miles," Shay says.

"Why did today have to be so busy?"

"Hush," Kelan scolds. "Stop bringing attention to yourselves. Do you want—"

A knife flies toward Kelan, but Myrna spots it first. Their movements become a dance as she hauls him from its path. Trusting her without question, he steps in front of her, and they spin together.

"Run!" Declan calls, and the four of them break into a sprint.

They make it less than two hundred yards before four Faye dressed in all black jump to block them. Their faces are covered just like the time on Shay's land.

"Their clothes are glamoured. These are Brennan's people!" Myrna says.

"Are you sure?" Declan asks.

Myrna's eyebrows shoot down, then she throws her hands, palms up and out, and blasts them with a shot of Radiant Light. But the color's off, tinted with a violet hue. The four shy away, blinded, and then they scream, patting out the tiny flames burning across their clothes.

Knights, her spell is consuming the glamour. Tunics of cornflower blue and pale lemon mark them for what they truly are.

A shopper cries out, "The Court of the Indomitable Moon!"

Myrna pats at her own hair, her hood dropping back. "Knights. I burned away my own glamour!"

Shay doesn't have time to register the words, for civilians run. Doors slam, the echoing warnings continuing through the streets for all to hear. He raises the crossbow, holding it on the attackers and waiting for a signal.

"Whatever," Myrna says, refocusing. "You're not welcome here. Leave now!" Several pick up children who scurry away, while a few of the old Faye move forward to flank Myrna and her group as if preparing to fight.

Damn right. Their people are strong.

"Give us the princess," the one in front says.

Three more civilians join their ranks, their clothes covered with flour. One stalks up, a pickax pulled from the cart in his hand. They place themselves between her and the assailants.

"Get the princess out of here," the female says as she removes her apron. She takes a fighting stance. "We've got these."

The baker's fingertips begin to glow as Kelan says, "Thanks, Maggie."

Kelan grabs Myrna's arm and pulls her away. Shay and Declan follow. It takes everything to ignore the sounds of fighting behind them, but they will not take their help for granted.

"Don't worry. Maggie knows what she's doing," Kelan says, noting Myrna's pinched brow.

"As do the others," Declan seconds.

Two streets, then they take a left. They're almost to the next turn when another assassin cuts them off. He engages Declan. Blade on blade, the clash of steel sends sparks through the air. Worry turns Shay's gut, but he pushes it down, knowing his father was once one of the best Guardians there ever was. And, even now, he fights with a skill like none other. Not lost for time.

"Shay, come. He'll catch up!" Kelan ushers them past, leading them both through a small shop. The owners don't hesitate to help. "There are a few horses out front. Myrna will be on the horse with me. Shay, you get the other."

"What about Father?"

"He'll follow. Don't worry. He knows what to do."

"You trust him?"

Kelan meets Shay's eyes. "In a fight? With my life."

Shay blinks quickly, and Myrna squeezes his hand. "On the count of three."

When she hits three, they make their move toward the horses. Not surprisingly, two more black-clad attackers appear. Myrna and Kelan engage while Shay goes to unhook the horses.

I should be the one fighting, Shay thinks as he unties the leads. *Damn stubborn female.*

Myrna hits the smaller of the two in the side, her fist amplified with the power Kelan's taught her to harness. She's faster than she was, and the female assassin's emerald eyes go wide. Her combatant grunts, spins, then returns the punch, for which Myrna blocks. The second jab, she does not. Myrna takes the blow to the cheekbone, and her eyes go hazy. She stumbles back a step.

"I'm coming!" Shay says and swings up on the horse, ready for them to mount. A new attacker appears from around the corner. Shay pauses, lifts the crossbow, and releases two quick shots. The first one hits home, but the second, the assassin manages to knock away by throwing a rock between them. Still, Shay moves for a better angle and to provide a barrier for Kelan and the princess. He releases another bolt and hears a startled, "oomph!"

A body falls to the dirt a moment later.

"Your weapon, Myrna!" Kelan cries, bringing Shay's attention back around. He grunts when an arcane power makes contact before the fist. "Shay, get the horses!"

"Idiot!" Myrna mutters, then unsheathes the two needles hidden beneath the sleeves of her tunic.

The horses free, he leads them forward, gaze caught by the glint of such a beautiful weapon. Myrna had told him Laoise had given them to her, but he hadn't seen them yet.

Sharp at the tip and filed on one side, the needles are carved with intricate patterns of flame along the handle. But the important piece is these are cored, filled with obsidian and capable of harnessing arcane when mastered.

The smaller fighter throws a gust of wind at Myrna, causing the youngling to fall hard against the wall of the shop. She comes closer, not using her power for another attack. Her power must be limited.

Myrna must recognize the same thing, for she slides sideways, avoiding the assassin's blade and raises her needle to stop the blow. Sparks fly as metal connects.

Shay gasps. White fire, Myrna's Radiant Light, is seeping from her fingernails and across her blade. *She's funneling it. That's impossible.* That's a skill she hasn't been taught yet.

The assassin sees the spell, too, and says, "He was right. You are one of us!"

Shay blinks, then notices what she did—a tint of violet so dark it's almost black. It's like a shadow hovering between the fire and metal blade. Bees flutter in his stomach, their sting jolting him as he screams, "Myrna!"

He breaks Myrna from whatever panic has frozen her at the sight of the change in her arcane. Myrna swipes upward with her opposite arm, flipping the needle mid-movement. The female tries to block, but she's not fast enough. It drives in at the seam of her armpit; the fire burning through the garment as if it were butter. Myrna's opponent screams, then falls to the ground.

No hesitation, Myrna runs for the horse Shay holds and swings her way up. He throws her the reins.

With Myrna safe-ish, Shay scans the area, crossbow at the ready. He provides cover, but the street's empty except for a few he recognizes watching the alleyways and their backs for attack. A sense of grateful pride fills him. Myrna has made an impression.

"Get her home," Kelan orders, sending a blast of arcane at his attacker.

The assassin slides beneath it, using his own wind to redirect the hit and reengaging with speed and steel.

"I'm not leaving you," she says. "So, end this and get your butt on this horse."

Kelan groans. His opponent's fast, stepping back from the obsidian blade and returning with a swipe of his own. It misses

Kelan's stomach by inches, the armored tunic untouched. Even so, Shay knows such a weapon could do damage. As the assailant steps forward to invade Kelan's space, Kelan hooks his left foot around the male's ankle and, at the same time, swoops his elbow around in an arc. The man in black falls, Kelan's blade plummeting with him to sink into his neck just above his collarbone. Kelan's lip pulls back as he lowers the male to the ground.

Even from the horse, Myrna sees the man's eyes. They're narrowed in pain as the obsidian slides free. Blood spills to the stone walkway in a flood, but Kelan's already turning. He gets a running stride, grabs Myrna's hand, then swings onto the horse behind her. Not a second later, the two animals are racing toward the gates.

CHAPTER THIRTY-SEVEN

Shadows Can't Hide Forever

TODAY HAS GONE TO the drogues. Laoise exits the palace and over-looks the outside grounds, her very blood aflame with wrath at the gall of the Murray clan.

How dare they enter neutral ground. Moreover, how dare they attack my heir!

Thundering hooves are the precursor for the horses coming around the bend at a breakneck speed. As *well, they should.*

Myrna and Kelan sit astride one, and the rather gifted, tainted one's son, on the other. Kelan is paler than normal, his shoulder coated red and a bandage wrapping it. Yet, his powerful arms still wrap Myrna protectively. They're barely through the gates when the huge metal monstrosities are slamming behind them.

Laoise descends the steps in seconds.

"Are you well?" The words, though calm, hold a hint of panic. This is her darling, after all. Only then does Laoise notice the blood seeping from a deep cut along Myrna's right bicep. The child is also favoring her left side. Laoise's lips peel back. "Minor wounds. Still…"

"I am not wounded, Mother. However, Kelan was struck by an arrow. Additionally, we've another man who's behind us. He's been essential to our safety and arrival here." She turns to the guards at the gate and, without even blinking at the idea that Laoise might disagree, she orders, "Guards, when Declan Hughes arrives, let him inside. I wish to speak with him."

"Ah... but he's not allowed on these grounds," Laoise says.

Myrna raises an eyebrow as she looks down upon Laoise. Strong, defiant...beautiful.

Kelan slips from behind her, then reaches for her. Myrna takes the proffered hand. Then she says, "But, Mother, he defended me when our guards were unavailable, risking his life to verify I made it home safely."

Laoise's fingers twitch as if this is not important. "This did not matter with your aunt. It's his fault she is not here."

Even as Shay drops his head and steps back, Kelan steps into Laoise's space, Myrna joining him. She presses a hand against his chest as he says in a voice so quiet and threatening, it sends chills up Laoise's spine, "You know that is a lie. You've let him live as a traitor for decades and all this time to hide your deceit."

The mix of relief of his knowing and rage at his audacity has the muscles along Laoise's back tightening. The air becomes heavy, and anger flares in her eyes as red flame threatens to break free.

Lightning quick, she grabs Myrna's chin and hisses, just as silently, "What did you say? You should not have been able." Laoise examines the binding she placed on Myrna.

The entire square goes still. They can feel the power radiating from Laoise, but do not know the reason. The boy looks between the three like they hold answers to the universe. Perhaps to him, they do.

Through clenched teeth, but not without a certain amount of attitude, Myrna says, "I said nothing."

"Then how?"

"Perhaps you are so deep in lies, Mother, you can no longer see when you slip." Laoise shoves Myrna away. She stumbles, but Kelan catches her.

"Let Declan Hughes in and send him to me," Laoise commands, irritation in each word. She points to Myrna and her companions. "Come!"

They're nearly to the throne room when Finch, another of her attendants, appears, a note in hand.

"Where's Sola?" Laoise asks.

Finch flinches. "In town, I believe. My apologies, my queen." He holds out the note once more, cornflower blue paper with a ribbon of lemon yellow.

The color has Laoise slowing her hurried pace. Without a word, she extends her palm. The hallway's silent as she reads.

My Dear Queen Laoise,

Your lies astound me. Did you think I would not find out? Such subterfuge cannot stay hidden forever, and younglings are fickle. They cannot resist breaking promises and divulging secrets. Such as the fact a particular princess is still alive?

And isn't that interesting? For should our dear Mareola indeed be alive, it would put into question the real reason you hid Myrna from me. That, perhaps, she is the true mother of the princess. For we both know what happened that day. Those weeks. Do not fret, I will discover the truth.

Though I recommend you provide an answer to all my questions, or my siege will not end. Either way, I've sent many to help persuade you.

— King Brennan Murray

An inhuman screech echoes through the castle as Laoise crumples the letter in her hand. She bolts forward and slams Myrna against the wall, fingers wrapping around her throat.

"You! This is your fault! You went to her, didn't you?" Laoise snarls.

Myrna does not flinch. Perhaps she'd expected this. "I think this conversation would be better held in private. Or would you prefer an audience?"

The youngling indicates the growing crowd of courtiers and staff who've come at her loss of temper. Some even peek around items; they're listening. *Damn Myrna and her calm. I have taught her too well.*

She will be an excellent queen.

"In. Now!" Laoise drops Myrna and points to her study.

As graceful and unworried as she's ever been, Myrna strolls inside. The two males flank the princess. It's sweet how they believe they can protect her. Also, stupid.

"How could you let this happen?" Laoise waves the letter in the air. "It was not time yet. You were not ready yet for all to be revealed! I hadn't..."

Laoise kicks out, and the leg of an innocent table topped with flowers crumples, the limb buckling. Glass shatters and tinkles across the floor, water spreading in a wave between them all.

"You hadn't what? What happened?" Myrna asks as the door closes, Laoise's guards forced to remain outside.

"He knows." Her canines sharpen with her rage.

"He knows what?"

Laoise looks to Kelan, then back to Myrna. *Has he figured it out?*

She curls her fingers and screams once more, then says, "That you are not of my womb!"

The very air in the room stills, the energy afraid to move in fear it will anger the princess and set her on a path of collapse. And perhaps this is not too far off, for Myrna frowns, blinks, then holds out her hand.

As she takes the letter from Laoise, she examines the faces of her friends. Shay is a mixture of surprise and acceptance. As if he is both shocked and not. Laoise wonders why. Then Kelan, who's inhaled and now looks as though every piece of the puzzle has fallen into place. This is the one which will test the child.

Myrna opens the letter and reads. She frowns, unable to understand everything. Her breath hitches. She glances from Laoise to Kelan. Pain flashes across her face as she sees what Laoise does. To him, she asks, "You knew?"

He clears his throat. "I... suspected."

"That's what the conversation in a glance you two had before we left was." Myrna covers her mouth, attention snapping to Laoise.

Laoise's shoulders rise. "You drew them to her, and if he finds her—"

"Me? You're going to yell at me?" Myrna closes the distance between Laoise and herself. "After not telling me that my *real* mother—the person you've allowed me to believe is only my care-taker—is actually my mother?" Myrna's voice cracks, and tears sparkle at the corner of her eyes. "You've allowed me to call *you* 'mother' in front of her!"

"I-we never confirmed you were from my body." Laoise's voice mirrors Myrna's, the pain in Myrna's voice too much, for she knows how much this has hurt Theia, too. "You were the one who labeled us as such!"

The youngling's face becomes introspective as she thinks back, as if replaying all the times and questioning, *Had Laoise called me 'daughter'? Did they confirm what Theia was to me, or did I ask?* Myrna's eyes clear.

"How could you?" Myrna asks Laoise, then she turns to Kelan. "And you? How could you not tell me when you figured it out?"

The room drops in temperature with Kelan's aching heart. "I was not a hundred percent sure. And if Theia wanted it hidden, then it was for your own safety. For a reason."

The reminder of how this all came to be heats Laoise's blood all over again. "And it is because of your stupid choice to go see her that this secret is out at all!"

"No!" Myrna snaps, and Laoise's impressed by how Myrna's power matches Laoise's own. With this level of ability, she likely burned through the bindings ages ago. Not that the child would be aware of it unless she broke and spoke of Theia. *Which proves Myrna tells the truth.*

The princess waves Brennan's letter in the air. "It wasn't us going to see Theia that did it. We were careful! You know me. You know Kelan. We took every precaution, had Sam drive us, and we met at the gym which is, apparently, warded. It had to be something else!"

"Ah...the gym. Yes, Mareola does believe I don't know of the Guardian, but Tomas would have it warded."

Myrna freezes. "You will not hurt Tomas."

Laoise frowns. "Of course not. He is her protector."

"Then how has Brennan discovered this?" Shay asks. Unaware he should not bring her attention again while Laoise's so blood-thirsty, Shay says, "And even then, so Myrna's Mareola's and not Laoise's, this doesn't change her status as heir, right?"

The crunch of glass beneath her feet as she walks toward Shay mimics the sound of broken bone. It makes her giddy as she says, "No."

"So, then, what's the problem? Why's Brennan so obsessed with Myrna?"

Laoise runs a clawed finger down Shay's muscular chest. He thinks his question so innocent, but it balances on a truth too painful...

It's impressive the boy does not flinch. Stupidity or bravery, she cannot tell.

"Do not hurt him. He's my best friend." Myrna rests a palm on his shoulder.

Laoise meets the youngling's eyes, and the betrayal that looks back digs deep. Today has hit Myrna hard. It is expected. Laoise drops her hand, then turns to continue up to her desk. Instead of digging the nail into the flesh as she wishes to, she does so with the wood. Not as satisfying, but it keeps her from carving into the closest male.

So instead, she answers his first question. "The only thought I have on how Brennan found out, or even suspects, is that he had Myrna watched. She is much like our Theia. In her mannerisms, her fighting, and, especially, her heart. Someone inside the court must have suspected—"

A hurried knock, and Kelan rushing to the door has Laoise flashing back to a few weeks ago when Brennan had just found out of Myrna's existence. How had that been mere weeks ago? Knife in his uninjured hand, Kelan opens it a crack. It is Finch again. Apparently, Sola has yet to return to the palace.

Another letter; a mirror to the last. Finch's quick words filter to them all. "This came with an urgent warning."

The wax seal splits with a pop, and the words sway before Laoise's eyes.

I've found her. Now I will discover the truth. Mareola will be mine, and soon, so will that sweet Myrna Qhuinn, for shadows cannot hide forever.

— Yours, King Brennan Murray

Her body is suddenly stiff, even as the letter threatens to fall to the stone floor. It hangs in her grip, the shaking making the parchment flutter.

"What does the letter say?" Myrna asks. When Laoise does not speak, for she cannot, Myrna adds, "Tell us. We can help."

"My queen." Kelan moves closer, reaching out. "What does it say?"

Laoise snarls as she folds it in half and slips it into her bodice. "You are to go back to your room and get medical attention. I will deal with it."

"Deal with what?"

"This! All of this!" The tension Laoise has been holding for what feels like years bursts forth. Arcane power explodes from her in a wave of energy. She yells, a low tone so guttural it vibrates in the bones of even those in the hall. Myrna leans into the torrent while the others fall to their knees.

"This was not supposed to come out. You were supposed to be protected! Mareola wanted you safe, I wanted you safe, for you are the best hope for all of Faerie." Laoise shoves her hands into her hair and pulls on the strands. She takes comfort in the pain. Tears she's held within for decades leak from her eyes, burning her pale skin with their cold emotion.

They watch her as though she has lost her mind. Perhaps she has, but Laoise knows more of the story than the rest. If she could, she would tell them everything, but Myrna's not ready. She fears she may lose the girl forever. It is a risk she will not take.

Kelan drags Shay backward by his shirt as Myrna moves closer. She takes slow, hard steps as if pushing against a great wind.

"My dearest queen"—Myrna reaches out—"I know not what you speak, but I see that the secrets you've carried have hurt you."

Myrna stumbles a step. She falls to one knee, then struggles back to her feet. A hot wind of Laoise's arcane whips around the room, for Laoise has lost control. Papers fly, and furniture squeaks against the floor as it tries to escape her wrath. Myrna's eyes glow as she harnesses her power—her love, worry, and hurt, too—to straighten her spine. She looks as though she's swimming through sand.

Then Myrna lifts her shoulders and glares at Laoise. "You've hurt me, but you've also protected me. These lies changed you. I've seen it in our kingdom and the stories I've heard from those closest to you—from our people." Myrna gulps. "This land used to be filled with joy, love, loyalty, but now it's nothing but bitterness and hate. Our Guardians attack their own subjects. Those of the higher classes mistreat the lower tiers, and you can no longer see the truth of it. But I know it's not how you want it. It's not the truth of your heart, of the legacy you wish to leave. Not really."

"And how do you know this?" Laoise shakes all over, the images of her sister as a youngling flashing through her mind's eye.

"Because you raised me. And even though you were strict, you always made sure there was love and laughter. You made me who I am."

Laoise's teeth snap together.

"It was Mareola."

"No. It was as much you."

Light appears across Myrna's skin, and Laoise gasps. It's kind and gentle. Warm. Then white fire slithers across her palms and wraps around her wrists like the intricate braids of hawthorn vine. Small flowers bloom across the bracelets.

"Our people are afraid of you, but I am not. And I get it now. The lies tainted who you once were. That's what started it." Myrna's eyes are glazed, her voice strange. "I didn't get it at first, but I see it now." Myrna steps forward, and Laoise's eyes widen. "Without us with you, and while keeping such a secret, you lost sight of who you were, of the lessons taught to you by Grandmother, and the meaning of our place."

"I don't know what you mean," Laoise says. But she does. It's there deep inside, niggling at her core.

The stares of the two males are hot as Myrna reaches Laoise. The queen's power is waning, or perhaps Myrna's words are getting through.

"The lessons were harder for you to maintain alone. You were lonely. So, you took a harsher rule." Myrna slides her hands over Laoise's until she grips the female's forearms. Laoise doesn't fight. Why would she? "That injured you deeply, like a glamour you've held for too long, and it's now stuck, unable to break free."

The princess's voice has become rhythmic, and Laoise cannot look away. She's mesmerizing.

The hawthorn vine unravels from her wrist and extends to encapsulate Laoise's as well. The flowers grow. They become brighter, the Radiant Light they exude washing over the queen as she drops her will. The males sink to the floor with an exhale as Laoise allows the girl she sees as a daughter to cleanse what's broken. No one else would Laoise trust to wield such power over her. It is interesting Laoise allows this at all.

Though really, Myrna is not asking. *Her spell is strong.*

"I've heard the reports of how the people see you, Myrna. They adore you as they adored my mother. They think you are kind, funny, and generous. But also stern and perhaps a bit cruel." Laoise smirks at the youngling. "I am proud."

The air around them blows a small cyclone as Myrna's power wraps them in light. Brighter and brighter until it is hard to make out the figures within. Then the world within the bubble becomes violet and dark stars shimmer, reflecting like a kaleidoscope. The violet shadows sink into Laoise's skin. They find the tainted magic; the parts twisted and damaged, then dissolve it as if it were always meant for this task.

Both females cry out as Myrna's power consumes them, burning away the fake glamour, the illness Laoise's been carrying for all these years.

"Shadow..." Laoise whispers.

"*Stones.*" Kelan's single word of understanding hits her ear before voices from the hall. The door slams open, and Delcan, Briana, and a few other Guardians burst in.

Briana grabs Declan, and they come to a halting stop, their mussed forms hinting at the difficult battles both had seen in the last hour. "Holy knights."

The light dissipates. Laoise pulls back from the child. She sways, blinks, then stronger, says, "Confine Princess Myrna to her rooms. Do not allow her off the palace grounds!"

"What?"

"Brennan's after Theia," Laoise says. "He claims to know where she is and has a head start. I will not let them get you, too."

"What? No!" Myrna spins and runs as if to escape before they can catch her, but her legs give out.

Kelan catches her before she can hit the floor, but Shay's the one who sweeps her up when Kelan curses the pain in his shoulder too much to lift her.

"Kelan, please…" Myrna begs. "Theia."

"We'll figure something out." Shay adjusts her higher in his arms, moving closer to the door and farther behind Kelan.

"You need to do something," Kelan pleads. But there was no way she'd meant that, right? "After everything… you're just going to leave her on her own?"

"How dare you question me! How dare you assume…" One hand on the table for support, Laoise says, "When Haszwalds was attacked, I sent a message. She's in hiding. Moved to the house most loved. He won't find her and, as you already know, she's not alone. My sister has made sure of it *against* my order. So, no. No official mission is authorized under the crown."

"But…" Shay says with a passing glance at Myrna.

"Kelan, you shall not move forward with a rescue mission. Do you understand?"

"Shay, set me down." He does. Myrna doesn't collapse immediately.

Kelan curls his fists. "Understood."

"Good. Now, Guardian, protect Myrna, visit the infirmary, and do not break my orders. We cannot afford to lose you now, too."

To Laoise's surprise, it's Myrna who responds.

"I will see to it, my queen." Myrna grabs Kelan's arm and tugs. With her other, she holds Shay for balance.

It sends a warning through Laoise, and her lip twitches. *Sneaky child. What is she up to?*

"Yes, Your Majesty," Kelan agrees, pressing his lips together to keep himself from saying anything further.

When the thick hardwood separates her from all the rest, Laoise collapses into the deckchair. *Sister, be safe. And please don't let Myrna do anything stupid.*

CHAPTER THIRTY-EIGHT

Unauthorized

WHAT IN THE EVER-LOVING *chaos has he gotten himself into? How was this his life?* Shay half carries Myrna through the hallway toward her rooms. Technically, she is walking on her own, but the spell for which she performed on Laoise drained her, and she leans on him more with each step.

Kelan's on her other side, his bald-faced lie still ringing in Shay's ears. How they'll get around a direct order from the crown is the question.

The entire experience has them holding their breath, the walk heavy with silence. Even Father is quiet, a tension radiating from him that is almost tangible. Perhaps his battle here did not go well. He'll have to ask.

They enter her suite, and Shay lowers Myrna onto the couch, Kelan beside her. She releases a grateful sigh before he steps back.

With a nod to him, Briana comes to examine Kelan's shoulder.

As she does, Shay asks, "Are you well after that spell?"

"Yes. It… caught me off guard. I didn't see it coming, but Mother…" She trails off. "Not Mother, aunt." Myrna pinches the webbing of her hand. "Laoise lost it. She needed help. It was eating away at her."

The lost look in Myrna's eyes has him patting her knee. "I'm sorry, Myr."

"What did you do to Laoise?" Kelan asks.

"I don't really know. I cleansed the sickness?" Myrna shrugs. "But that's not important right now. Are you okay?" Myrna asks Kelan. The soldier looks like hell.

"Shot through with an arrow..." Briana grumbles.

Shay stands, goes to the door, and asks for a doctor while Briana begins to clean the wound.

All the while, Kelan's gaze hasn't left Myrna's. "I'm fine. I'm worried like you. But the good news is Laoise got a warning out. She's gone into hiding. She'll be fine. For now."

"We can't leave her alone!" Myrna says. "She needs our help. She needs to be here!"

Kelan takes Myrna's hand. "I know. We'll make a plan to—"

A fist slams down on a table along the wall, bringing all their attention to Declan near the door. His expression is locked on something far in the distance as if a truth is just out of reach. Tension vibrates off him. He clears his throat, then one word chokes from his throat in a painful rasp. "Sister? Laoise said 'sister.'"

Shay hadn't realized he'd been in the room for that. His heart hits the floor as bile threatens to escape.

Both Myrna and Kelan freeze. The others in the room—Briana and Jaden—all seem to shrink into themselves.

Kelan drops Myrna's hand, then rubs it as if he misses the support of Myrna's touch. But after everything Shay's learned today, he's not sure Kelan deserves it. He sure as hell knows Laoise doesn't.

That's not fair. Laoise lied to Kelan, too. Perhaps, but that didn't mean he had to be such a dick.

Which was true. For years, Kelan has treated Declan as a traitor, as if he had completed the worst of crimes. He'd sat back as his wife and children were abused, mistreated as outcast.

Kelan braces his elbow with his opposite hand and says sadly, "We were lied to that day. The stories they told, the memories of Mareola's disappearance? They were false." Kelan's voice is rough.

"A few days ago, Myrna showed me how wrong I've been but I was sworn to secrecy. I'm so sorry, my brother."

Declan steps back, his eyes jumping from person to person. Shay would move closer, but he already resembles a caged animal. Probably better to let Kelan handle it.

"What do you mean?" Declan asks.

Unblinkingly, and with as clear a voice as he can manage, Kelan says, "Princess Mareola, our Theia, is alive. Laoise lied, then had the only other witness killed. When you and the princess were discovered, it was not by Brennan's people. It was by Laoise's. She helped the princess escape and go into hiding. They used you as a distraction while Theia was whisked to the human world to...to protect her pregnancy."

"Her pregnancy?"

Myrna smiles softly, the expression sadder than anything as she plays with a stray thread of the pillow.

"She's alive?" Declan's gaze flicks to Myrna before he plops into the chair next to her. He leans forward and stares at the floor. "It can't be true. They said the ambush...I failed her. The Unseelie got past me. I tried but there were too many. I can still hear her screams. She died, I swear it."

Limbs becoming heavy, Shay finally takes a chance. He moves forward and places a hand on his father's shoulder. His father can't lift his head for the grief which weighs him down.

"I've seen her, Declan," Kelan says, and Shay swears tears glisten in his eyes. "Myrna took me to her. I thought she was a ghost, but I swear she lives."

"For truth?" With Kelan's nod, Declan slumps. "I was beaten for my weakness, stripped of my rank. I lost my friends, my brothers, my culture."

"Had I known..."

Myrna stands, legs shaky. *Can she tell how close both males are to breaking?* She goes to Declan and kneels before him. "I don't know your battles, or the horrors you've suffered because of the lies my family's spread because of me. I do know it's not right. I'm sorry, and I hope that one day you will forgive me."

A tear tracks down Myrna's cheek.

Shay jumps, shocked, when Kelan nearly bursts up from the floor. "Myrna, this is not you. I should've known! Grew up with Laoise. I was closest to them both and Declan. I should've seen this plot!" Kelan knocks a book off the table. "The things I have said to you, Declan—the way I've treated you! I should've trusted the man you are; known you never would've turned over her position!"

Kelan throws a fist out, connecting with a poor, innocent cabinet. The wood crunches beneath his knuckles. Kelan shakes the pain away, but it does nothing to help the rest of them from gaping.

A small figure appears at his side. She takes his hand in both of hers. "Stop."

He settles instantly, but more for the way she watches him, calmly and without fear. She is a steady presence that has all of them watching her. Even Shay calms at the tone she uses on Kelan.

"None of us can change the past or the decisions made for us, but we can decide how we move forward. My real mother"—her voice cracks—"is out there, without protection, and Brennan's hunting her for the sole purpose of discovering the truth about me. Though what more there is..."

"We can't move to save her." Kelan's sigh holds the weight of all his regrets.

"Not yet, but if I've learned anything about Theia, it's that she can take care of herself. So, I've two questions." Myrna turns to Declan. "First, after hearing what you have, and understanding my family's taken so much from you, Declan Hughes, will you help me? Or would you prefer to go back to your home and to safety understanding that, when this is done, I'll restore your name?"

"Even if I don't help, you'd do that?"

"Of course. On my honor."

"She would," Shay says. No doubt in his tone.

Declan presses a fist to his heart. "I am at your command. And the second request?"

"Will you take Kelan to the infirmary and deal with his boorish ass while he gets medical attention? If we're to do anything, we'll need him healthy."

This gets a chuckle from Declan and an outright laugh from Briana. Shay smirks, fascinated at how she's wrangled them all. Myrna's playing a game. She's being too sweet—too charming.

What are you doing, my friend?

Kelan crosses his arms, then winces, dropping them back to his sides. "We need to make a plan."

"See," Myrna points at Kelan.

"I'll go too," Briana says. She stands from her perch on the arm of the chair. "Declan should get checked out too. They'll both be good as new in a few hours. I'll be back once I know they're settled. Don't start anything. I have so many questions."

"We won't. I'm tired and hungry. I'll have Alyn bring some food. And, hey, Jaden, can you see if you can get any information on Brennan's advancements or Colum's whereabouts? It might come in handy." She scrunches her nose, and Shay narrows his eyes at her.

Shay leans against the wall and crosses his arms.

"That's, of course, if you're in on this. It's dangerous. I don't—"

"We're in," Jaden says, ushering the others out with them.

"Awesome. Thanks." Myrna shoves Kelan toward the door. When he resists, she says, "Get fixed up. I hated ripping that arrow out of you. I need you better."

"They'll have me fixed up in no time."

Briana grunts. "I'm gonna make them take him to the healing waters of the temple."

Shay watches the fake interaction between Myrna and the others as she asks what those are, then loses interest, claiming they can explain later. *How can they not see she's trying to get rid of them?*

When Myrna closes the door, then leans her back against the dark wood, Shay shoves up from his spot along the wall. It's as if she counts to twenty. Fists on hips, Shay looks down at her.

"What in the world was that?" Her eyes widen. "You tell me right now, Myrna Qhuinn, what evil plan you've schemed up and how much I'm going to regret being your partner in crime."

A slow grin spreads across her delicate face, then she bounces toward her closet. "Follow me! We have little time!"

Shay blinks but does what he's told. They go through the main room, passing her bedchamber, and into a space as large as his bedroom. It's filled with clothing, shoes, and accessories.

"Holy closet, girl."

"I know, right? Sam would die if I brought her in here. It's ridiculous. Why would I need all this?" Myrna heads to a drawer along the back. She yanks it open, then proceeds to busy herself around the room. She pulls items from hidden compartments, drawers, and shelves alike, piling them on a center table and next to the bag.

"What are you doing?"

"We're leaving."

"What?" It's more an exclamation than a question. She steps forward, examining the pile of items she's chosen. "Where did you get all these weapons?"

Myrna removes two black cloaks from the farthest corner of the closet and an electronic device he's seen others who work in the human world use. A cellphone? "Some were here—Theia's from when she lived in this room, I assume—others, well...the Guardians don't count their weapons. Not very smart, really."

"What do you think you're doing, Myr? The queen said we couldn't go on a mission. She ordered the Guardians to keep you confined to your room."

Myrna stops and looks him deep in the eyes. It's as if she wants to make sure he understands the details of what she's about to say. "No. Technically, the order was only for the Guardians. She stated I was to be confined to my room, and that there was to be 'no *official* mission authorized by the crown.'" Myrna gestures between the two of them. "We're not official in any sense of the word."

Shay's lips part, and he looks up to the ceiling. He ruffles through the items she's chosen. *Not bad.* "That's why you had them leave, sent them to the infirmary. They can't go."

Myrna removes her jacket carrying the royal seal and slides a plain tunic on. She bought it a few weeks ago from one of the markets. It's not as thoroughly shielded, but it would do. "They'd stop us, or if they agreed to come, they'd be stripped like your father was. I'll not risk them."

Shay stops Myrna from shoving some supplies into the bag. "We don't even know where Theia is."

"Yes, we do. Laoise said that Theia was in the 'house most loved.'" Myrna rubs her chest. "I know where that is."

Shay perks up. "You do?"

Myrna smiles. "Yes, but we're gonna need some help. I can get it, but it's not safe for me to go alone."

"We're untrained, Myr. This is stupid. Even I know better than to risk you. And how would we get out, anyway?"

Myrna moves around the center island separating them. She stops to hold out a short sword of obsidian. A weapon neither of them should hold. Well, except for the needles she carries. "First, I'm going with or without you. As for the escape, we'll be leaving the same way we met...officially. The roof. It'll allow us to get to a portal not far from here."

"There are no portals nearby. None not controlled, anyway," Shay says, her story becoming crazier by the moment. "If there was a portal within fifty clicks of the castle, the queen would know, and she'd have disabled it."

From the pile, Myrna slides a book free. "Have you ever heard of some of the really old, weird relics? The ones that speak to you?"

Shay's breath stops as he looks down at the ancient pages of a book he's only ever heard legends about. Balance Beholden. *Where did she get that?*

She runs her fingers over it, and the pages shimmer, altering to allow him to see the true nature of what they read. *It's allowing me to see the truth. Holy knights.* "How do you have that?"

"It's showing you, isn't it?" Myrna grins and runs a loving hand over the cover. "Well, Stephan O'Malley gave it to me. It was his mother's, and inside are many lost truths."

CHAPTER THIRTY-NINE

It's an Easy Jump

Cloak flowing over their forms, Myrna leads Shay to the balcony. Bags filled with food, water, her cell phone, and *Balance Beholden* are strapped over their traveling tunics. Weapons cover their forms in various sheaths, ready to be used at a moment's notice.

Myrna ties her hair into a bun as Shay hoists himself upon the roof. Lifting the hood of the cloak to cover her blond hair, she stands upon the railing.

He leans over and says, "Give me your hand."

She shushes him and glares. Seriously? Then she jumps and flings herself over the edge and up onto the roof. As she straightens, the weight of the satchel settles at her back like an old friend. Memories of all the times she and Theia ran away tighten her chest.

Shay smirks, lifting his hands in surrender.

The two friends traverse the peaked tiles of the roof, running quietly along the leveled top edge and keeping low to stay out of sight of any guards. Which, from their position, are twice as many as usual.

"This is a stupid idea," Shay whispers. They press close to a wall, out of sight of a passing patrol.

"You can turn around, but I'm going."

"I'm not backing out, Myr." The guard passes. Shay continues, "The tree I jumped from was removed. Kelan was pissed there was one so large and close enough to both the outer wall and the palace roof line, but there is another option."

"And that is?"

"Follow me." Shay jumps, sliding sideways down the angled peak of an adjacent building. Reaching the leveled section once more, they hurry across it, bending beneath a block arch. Glancing both ways, he freezes. A few heartbeats pass before Shay walks out onto what looks like a stone gutter with a gargoyle on the end. He points to something down below them. "It's not far. We can make it."

"Are you nuts?" Myrna's question is harsh even as it is quiet. "You think I can make it that far to land in that tree?"

"Because it's downhill, yes. It looks far, but it's really not. The distance is down more so than out." Shay calculates the descent again.

Myrna groans as she, too, calculates the distance. "And it's outside the wall."

"Exactly. No one can get in here, but we can definitely get out."

Myrna covers her face. "I don't like this. I don't like this."

"We don't have to go."

Myrna shoots him a droll look. "The patrols outside the walls have been changed, but usually they pass every fifteen minutes. I'd guess after today, they're half that." She scans, then gestures to a figure passing about a hundred yards from the tree they're aiming for. "There's no way they won't hear our fall."

Shay swallows, his slow nod filled with tension. "Which is why we need to make it to that knoll right over there." He points to a small mound of rock covered in vine. The downed trees crisscross over the top. "On the far side, there's a hole where I think both of us can fit."

"Okay... Fall, don't break yourself, and then run for the small hole where we shove ourselves in and hide from Guardians that will kill us on sight or turn us in to the queen. Awesome." Myrna squeezes her fists together, and they shake. "Sounds like a great plan!"

Shay chuckles, the sound lined with nervousness. Before he can say anything else, Myrna takes a step back and launches herself off the side of the castle.

She sucks in a breath but doesn't scream. Her stomach lifts into her throat, which is good because the branches slam into her gut, threatening its contents. They whip her face and arms. The leaves rattle, vocalizing their unhappy appreciation of her presence. She feels like a cartoon character covered in welts of bright red. Myrna slides from the branch she balances upon and falls the remaining ten feet to the ground. Her knees take the impact easily, though she must fight to inhale. Not waiting, she makes for the hiding space even as Shay's landing disturbs the branches above, but this time with a deep grunt in sequence.

There's no way the patrol didn't hear that. Damn.

Shay required much less time than her to recover, it seems, as his footsteps follow instantly.

Doing everything she can to leave no tracks, Myrna skitters toward the hiding place. At first, she cannot see it, but then she slides down the rocky hillside, approaching from the opposite direction and finds what looks like a cliff—a hard edge of rock and dirt. The trees arch above her approximately twenty feet from the ground. Vines and long strands fall from them, seeming to climb along the cliff face, but the more she looks, the more Myrna realizes they're not attached. There's space behind them. Carefully, she sweeps them aside to find a tiny cave the width of a standard bathtub, but shorter.

"Knights. You said it was small..." Myrna mumbles to herself. She slides inside and holds the curtain of green open.

A male barks an order, and Myrna's breath catches. There's the sound of gravel and sliding boots. Shay appears, but the relief is short lived, for he runs in the opposite direction. The urge to call out is so strong. But should she do so, it will give away her position and diminish his sacrifice. Heart aching, she lets the vine fall, and Shay disappears into the forest.

Myrna shoves against the hard rock as another set of footsteps precedes a Guardian she doesn't know. She doesn't have to. If he finds her, he'll drag her back. The Guardian slows, then glances around as if sensing another presence—hers.

Shit. I need to hide. Hearing Kelan's teaching words in her head, she focuses on how to mask her power. He says she's not great yet, but perhaps desperation is key. Or more, the Guardians' distraction will be enough. Slow the heartbeat and press her magic down until her energy no longer radiates outward.

The Guardian frowns, shakes his head, then continues after Shay.

Myrna sighs. *Can this mission succeed without Shay?*

It has to. Theia needs backup.

Myrna sinks into a crouch. She waits until enough time has passed that Shay has either taken them far enough away that they will not hear her, or they've given up and moved on to their normal schedule. Myrna slips from her hiding place, saddened she's alone now. Then she stalks through the woods toward the hidden portal *Balance Beholden* has imparted to her.

She travels silently, alone, for nearly an hour, careful to avoid the patrols, which seemed to have resumed. Myrna worries for her friend, afraid they've taken him to prison, or worse, to her aunt. What would Laoise do to find the truth?

"Took you long enough."

Myrna flings a knife at the voice.

Shay dodges it with little difficulty, laughs, then pulls the blade from the trunk of the tree it embedded into.

"Oh, my Gods!" Myrna runs and wraps her arms around Shay's neck. "You got away?"

Shay returns the hug, lifting her feet from the ground. "I've grown up in these woods. I know all the hiding spots. Don't worry. I wanted to get them off your trail. Figured I'd just catch up."

She smacks his arm, then pushes him away. "Not cool. You don't wanna know the terrible images I had in my head."

"Sorry. I knew I could lose them and catch up." He squeezes her shoulders. "Are you okay? Ready to get going? We're near the portal."

"Yeah, let's go."

It took less than an hour for them to traverse the forest, sneaking around two more patrols and a group of pixies far too interested in what the friends were doing. They are deep in the dark wood, a place even the eldest Faye did not come, where it was dangerous and filled with creatures wild and unpredictable, when they came upon a cropping of trees oddly spaced. To the naked eye, they might be considered natural, but as Myrna was looking for it, she couldn't miss the far too-perfect rows or the pattern, which from above would look like several squares, each slightly turned and overlapping the other.

Myrna removes *Balance Beholden* from her satchel. The book hums beneath her fingertips. She opens to the page with the map previously shown to Shay. His warmth appears at her back as he looks over her shoulder, and she examines it for more detail.

"There were two portals mentioned. One that moves and is open for anyone, but in very specific situations. And then the one that is always present but hidden to those who do not know of it. We're going for the second." Myrna lifts her gaze to the two largest hazel trees she's ever seen, thick with wide leaves and budding flowers. They stand at the top of the hill directly at the center of the patterned growths. "There."

"What are you seeing that I am not?"

"With the sky being overcast, the first is not an option for"—she reads from the text—"'the moon's reflection upon undisturbed waters will allow the entrance of those who seek transport to the land of Faerie.' See, not possible."

Her tone becomes rhythmic and laced with magic. Myrna caresses the map hidden in the image of a Celtic goddess balanced on a boulder covered in moss and vine. She glances up to the hill before them. Had she not read this tome, she would've missed it, but now, she can see the specifics of this place. The care for which the original owners of this land took to make this place holy.

Myrna steps forward, and a jolt of energy flitters through her. "This land was once protected—held by those who loved it. Cherished by the ancient ones and honored for its power. *Balance Beholden* indicated there are multiple of such places." Her words are in time with her steps, the calming voice of someone who's in touch with the land and the spirits within. "And should one know of them, they may travel freely through Faerie. All they must do is ask and they shall find the shimmering gate between the two hazel trees which speak the truth of the world."

"Wha—"

Myrna takes his hand and guides him forward, up the hill, until they round a small embankment. The air shimmers in time with Myrna's happy giggle.

Shay's jaw drops.

"Are you ready?" Myrna asks.

"I've never been in the human world. Other than Haszwalds...so, not really."

CHAPTER FORTY

Or...Maybe, Desperation in Battle Leads to Lack of Control

"SHIT, MYRNA!" SAM, IN all her fiery glory, stands, fists on her hips before her SUV along the side of the tree-lined road. The sky's dark, the moon high. "You call me in the middle of the night, beg me to come pick you up along some random highway an hour outside the middle of fucking nowhere, and you expect me to do it with no answers?"

The glare Sam hits Myrna with has her shifting. Are her clothes too tight? If she didn't know Sam was human, Myrna would think she was forcing her will on her.

She points at the princess. "You tell me what the fuck is going on, or I'm going to beat it out of the pretty boy before I leave you both here and go back to bed."

A startled laugh bursts from Shay.

Myrna smirks, stepping forward to hug her friend. "I missed you, too."

She pushes Myrna away. "That won't work this time. I love you, Myr, but no. Tell me what's happening and understand that no matter what, I'm staying by your side this time."

"It's not safe where we're going. We have people after us."

"Even more reason." She crosses her arms, and Myrna swears she catches Shay glance at her ample chest. Myrna smacks his shoulder.

"What?" he asks.

Sam doesn't acknowledge the exchange. "I'm capable, and you know it. I may spend my days in heels, but I've been training with you for the past three years, and you know the way my dad and I camped as a kid. If you're in danger, then I'm by your side. No matter what!"

"I like her," Shay says. Sam thrusts her hand out and introduces herself. Surprised, Shay hesitates, then shakes. "I'm Shay. Nice to meet you."

"Nah," Sam refuses his name. "You're 'Pretty Boy.'" She returns her attention to Myrna. "Now, tell me what's going on."

Myrna sighs. Her stomach clenches with hesitation as that same fear of her friend turning away from her in terror or disgust lifts its head once more. *It doesn't matter. We need her help and...you know Sam. You trust her.*

"You can trust me," Sam says, reading her mind.

So, Myrna explains everything. She explains it all; the truth of her being Faye, her royal lineage, the magic, King Brennan Murray, Laoise not being her mother, Theia, Shay, Kelan, all of it. The explanation's quick and stilted, but it's enough.

As she speaks, Sam's eyebrows rise, her lips part, and then she leans against the hood of her car. Once Myrna's story slows, Sam licks her lips and steps forward to wrap her arms around her friend. Myrna doesn't miss the wetness in her eyes.

"So, you can see why you can't come all the way. We just need you to drop us off and then I'll come find you later."

Squeezing her so tight, Sam says, "I always knew you were special. I'm sorry I couldn't be by your side during this, but I'm so glad you had Shay and Kelan. I'll owe them for all of my life."

Myrna's shoulders sag, the weight she's carried falling with the caress of her friend's hand as it runs down her spine. Her breath hitches. "I thought you would hate me."

"The day we met, what did I tell you?" Sam asks, pulling back and glaring into her eyes.

"That we were destined. Sisters intended for a purpose."

"That's right. That hasn't changed, and now you need me. I may not be Faye, but I can help."

"These are not humans," Shay says.

"Maybe not, but I'm not helpless. If I'm going to die for anything, I'd rather die for someone I love." Sam's expression is hard, filled with the stubbornness Myrna's all too familiar with.

She won't back down.

"So get in the damn car because, based on what you told me, we need to find Theia and get to her before Brennan's people do, right?"

Myrna nods.

"Well, then, let's get moving. How far are we?"

Shay slides into the back, Myrna taking the front. She shows him how to use the seatbelt, and they get moving. "We need to head about two hundred miles south. Once there, there's an unmarked road we'll take for another ten miles. After that, we hike."

Shay leans between the front seats. "How long will it take for us to get there?"

"With the way Sam drives?"

Sam giggles and slams on the gas. Shay's thrown against the seat with a grunt.

They tucked the car beneath a thicket of trees and between two boulders nearly an hour back. Shay and Myrna are impressed with the way Sam's kept up with their harsh pace. In general, once through the changing, Faye are faster, stronger, and have more endurance than most humans.

"I don't know how you stood it, Myr," Shay says as they crest another hill. His voice shows no sign of strain following the hour of running. He releases Sam's hand after helping her over a large drop.

"What?"

"This place feels odd. I didn't understand. Not completely." He brushes a tree. "Living here, growing up, and not having that connection? No wonder you felt so disjointed. The land feels dead."

"Really? Weird." Sam's eyes are lit with curiosity. "But are you better since being in Faerie?"

Myrna smiles kindly. "Yes. I finally feel whole. There's a connection we have to everything there. It's so different."

"And the people?" She tilts her head.

"For the most part, people are welcoming, but they act weird toward me. Like I'm some"—she thinks of how to phrase it—"oddity."

Shay laughs, his eyes scanning the forest. "That's because you're so open. You break the rules from the way Laoise's run Faerie for so long."

"Laoise does seem to be a little different. She's special."

Shay is swept off his feet and thrown through the air. He hits a tree hard. The trunk groans in protest as he slides down to the ground.

Myrna spins toward the gust of wind. A Faye, clad in black, a thin stripe of blue running down his chest, peeks out from an embankment. Brennan's.

There must be more. "Sam, be ready."

Her friend is, for another approaches from the front, their face covered but eyes glowing with power. Sam is unfazed. She takes a fighting stance, placing herself between Shay and the approaching enemy.

Pride and fear wells in Myrna's chest. Because how can a mere human fight against magic and win?

The Faye lifts his arms, sweeping his hands through the air. Rocks lift, then fling toward them. Sam dives, rolling behind an outcropping of rocks a few feet high.

Leaving Sam to deal with that, Myrna engages with her own attacker.

"Really?" Sam says. "Throwing rocks? That's what you're gonna do?" With sass apparently.

Sam grabs a handful of rocks from the ground and chucks them in the direction of her attacker.

His jaw drops as two hit their mark—one into his gut, the other hitting his knee.

Myrna's unable to hold back a grin. Her friend warned her. In a past life, she'd played something called softball. Saying a quick prayer that Sam can hold her own, Myrna closes the distance, moving in an uneven path, dodging the gusts of wind thrown at her from the combatant. Close now, she uses a low branch to swing from and kicks the fighter in the chest. He falls to his back.

The male rolls, then jumps to his feet before Myrna can get to him. He pulls a dagger free from its sheath and slices the princess. He's skilled, far more so than those who infiltrated the capital. Brennan must've sent a better squad this time. *Doesn't matter either way.*

Myrna doesn't stumble or alter in her attack even though fear taints it. She returns his with the same ferocity, pushing him back down the hill they just climbed. As she does, Myrna feels a darkness welling, moving to the surface like a snake and mixing with her blood. It's a shadow of her power but tastes different than the Radiant Light she's honed these last weeks. It holds the bite of aged citrus, luxuriously dark. In a way, it whispers of long-held secrets.

Myrna pushes it down, deep into her soul and locks it away for protection, for she cannot be distracted. Not right now. Especially with at least ten dark-clad soldiers slipping from the forest. *Queen save us!*

"Shay! Wake up! We need you!" Myrna screams. He's on the ground behind Sam, her friend still sending a flurry of projectiles at the Faye, too shocked at the human with great aim.

An elbow connects with Myrna's cheek, and she hits the packed earth. Stones dig into her palms. With a roll, Myrna barely evades the next strike. She jumps to her feet and skitters back, irritated to find a large rock stopping her progress. Myrna tries to clear her head. She shouldn't have gotten distracted.

The Faye's on top of her in an instant, his knife pressed to her throat. He knocks away one of her needles.

Myrna cannot believe she's let herself be backed into a corner. Her mother would be so disappointed. As would Kelan. Though, it's his disappointment which would burn the most.

Myrna lifts her hands as if to throw light or a well-placed fireball, but the male is ready. Another blade presses against her ribs just as the knife at her throat digs in deep. Her chin lifts, a whine slipping free. The sharp sting of the blade prickles her skin.

"I may not be able to kill you, Princess, but there were no rules saying you had to come back in one piece. Now drop it." The cruel rasp of his voice has her hair sticking up. "Do not test me."

Myrna lets go of her last needle. It falls to the forest floor. Now it was time to find a way free. For she'd backed herself into a corner and can no longer see Sam or Shay. At least Shay's cries indicate he'd rejoined the fight. There is a roar of fire, and Myrna says a prayer of gratitude.

"You're disgusting," Myrna says. "You come out here and attack me for no reason at all. You'd harm an innocent person, injure them, and drag them back for what?"

The Faye ignores her words. He leans in and runs his nose along the side of her jaw. "You don't smell like one of them. Your power tastes... different." He shifts back. "And to answer your question, my king ordered your return so that's what I'll do, but perhaps I'll have a little fun before I—"

A sword cuts through the male's body. The blade appears between them, next to Myrna's breast, then slices upward, catching on the man's ribs. He chokes, blood spewing from his lips, splattering on her face. His grip fails, the knife at both her neck and ribs falling to the dirt, and then Kelan yanks the male free.

As if tossing a bag of wheat to the floor, he drops the body. Then, as if in slow motion, Kelan's blade slips free, and the male falls.

Kelan's eyes meet Myrna's. "I know. You had it in hand."

Myrna laughs. He pulls her up, and before he can move away, she wraps her arms around his neck. His tighten around her. Myrna presses her cheek to his, breathlessly saying, "Thank you."

It scares Myrna how much he feels like home. Still, she takes it in and accepts it for the bolster it is. Myrna swallows hard, unable to miss the barely disguised fury in his gaze. How could she when he glances away from her face so fast after catching him looking at her?

"You weren't supposed to come. Mother..." Myrna makes a sound of frustration. "Laoise will be angry. You'll be punished."

He cups her cheek. "If you don't understand how important—"

"Kelan, this is my trouble, not yours. You shouldn't be here. You don't even like me. You-I was just trying to—"

The Guardian exhales harshly as if frustrated. Then, in one motion, pulls her to him and presses his lips to hers. It's soft and hard at the same time—passion and desperation written in every stroke.

Holy...Gods damned. Myrna melts into him, her hands tangling into the front of his tunic. She goes to deepen the kiss, but he pulls back. Myrna whimpers.

He presses one last gentle peck to her lips.

"I came for you. For as long as you allow it, I will always be by your side. Do you understand?" Kelan runs a thumb over her cheek, and Myrna nods. "Good. Now we need to go save our friends and then find Theia."

Myrna nods again, a little more fuzzily this time, but picks up her weapons. She gets herself together as they head up the hill where Briana, Declan, Sam, and Shay battle twelve Unseelie. Two more are unconscious on the ground. One is the male Sam had been throwing rocks at.

"We're so outnumbered..." Myrna whispers.

"Remember, not all Faye are magically gifted. They may have physical prowess—increased strength and agility—but that doesn't mean they'd be able to battle with arcane. Powers like yours, mine, and Shay's are rare. We are outnumbered, but *are* we outnumbered?"

Myrna frowns, exchanges a glance with him, and, without another thought, bounds up the hill to dive into the fight.

With reinforcements there, the fight is very different. Myrna and Shay fall into their expected roles learned during training, placing themselves between two of the higher-ranked soldiers and providing help where needed. Sam, as the weakest link, is pushed into the center of the circle, until soon she's throwing curses at them for treating her like a child.

Still, the fight is unevenly matched. Brennan's team is strong.

Kelan and Myrna hold the west side of the small valley they reach. Two of the combatants have ability, but the others do not. One can throw someone off their feet or send an attack off course.

"We need to take her out first," Kelan says, gesturing to the Wind Faye. "She's too powerful."

"If we can get within a few feet, her attacks won't be so effective."

"Agreed. Distract them, and I'll go around the side. I think I can take out two of them." Kelan starts forward, but Myrna stops him.

"No. You're more powerful. They know it. You and Sam distract them. Then I'll slip around."

Grinding his teeth, he nods. "Fine. But you will not go too far."

She rolls her eyes. "Yes, Dad."

He narrows his eyes. "Never call me that."

Sam joins the fight, and they both engage with the ungifted Faye. To say Sam and her opponent are evenly matched isn't fair. Sam's a great fighter, but she's not nearly as strong. She's far slower and, quickly, the fight shifts focus from her being an active participant to straight defensiveness. From where Myrna scurries through the bushes to come around the back, she watches the change, and worry has her quickening her pace.

Sam grunts as the fist hits her forearm. She blocks it, but it's clearly felt throughout the limb. The male kicks her in the thigh, and Sam crumples, a cry filling the air. Still, Sam swipes the small blade toward her attacker.

Not willing to let her friend down, Myrna rushes her target, her dagger ready this time and the needles once again sheathed. Appearing not three feet from the gifted female, she extends her hand, Radiant Light pouring from her and directly into the eyes of Brennan's guard. The Wind Faye screams and covers her eyes as Myrna closes the distance. The dagger digs into the soft skin at her jugular.

"I don't want to kill you," Myrna says.

"You'll have to. We won't stop, Highness," the female spits, eyes blinking—still blinded.

A scream and crunching bone—Sam's. Myrna turns.

The Wind Faye takes the advantage. She lifts her hand and says, "Shut up, you stupid human."

Sam goes silent, her face filled with shock. She cups her throat, and the male above her kicks her again.

Myrna's gaze locks on the extended fingers of the gifted Faye at her feet, the wicked gleam in her eyes. *She's cutting off Sam's air!* Bile rises in her throat, bringing with it a hatred she's never felt before. It starts at her toes, swims across her skin, up her neck and over her lips, then down her arms to her fingertips. Myrna drives the dagger into the neck of the female and twists.

Somewhere through her anger, she takes in the sound of Sam's desperate breath, but Myrna's lost within the shadows burning across her skin, the dark citrusy scent filling her up. She pulls the needle from her boot and flings it at Sam's attacker.

It wedges in the man's throat. He bends, his hands going to the offending object, but what he doesn't realize is that brings him within Sam's reach. She kicks up, her boot landing on the end of the needle. It drives up into his skull, and he falls backward.

Sam collapses back and coughs. Blood stains her lips.

Myrna can't breathe. Her chest is tight, and that citrus scent burns her nose. She scans the valley.

Kelan's fighting and winning, but Declan and Bri...They're being overrun.

Shay screams as the fire burning his arms goes out, for a spear peeks through Shay's side from behind.

White fire shadowed by violet explodes from Myrna. It pours from her mouth and eyes. It wraps around her arms like vine, then travels down her torso. It encapsulates her legs, and it hurts.

"Myr! I'm coming!" Kelan calls, desperation making him more violent as he disarms his opponent.

The shadows leak. Words from *Balance Beholden.* Or another book, but who cares? They spread, following the Radiant Light to overlap and mix, shimmering like midnight stars. The white has all but been devoured. Myrna throws her head back, and a wail fills the night air.

Kelan overpowers his opponent and knocks him unconscious. He skitters to a stop a few feet away, his eyes wide with terror. "Myrna!"

The darkness covers her face. She thinks of Kelan and her sense of home, but the fear in his eyes at seeing her like this breaks her heart. Her next breath rattles as she thinks of Sam, broken on the ground. She may be human, but she is family—accepting and loyal, and loving. Shay who came with her. His friendship filled with humor and joy. He loves her for existing. Then there's Theia—her real mother. These are her family.

Family...

The forest beyond the shadow fire disappears. There's darkness.

Nothingness.

Two breaths pass, and then she stands somewhere else.

The shadows recede, and where the trees once stood are walls of white marble. Where there was once Kelan's worried face is now a girl, shocked but livid. Or perhaps that's interest.

She looks familiar.

CHAPTER FORTY-ONE

Unexpected Detour

THE GIRL COLLAPSES BEFORE Imogen. The Shadowspire wrapped in white light which encapsulates her goes out with the *thwap* of her body against the floor.

Like a flame being snuffed out.

Yet the girl shoves upright, yanks a weapon from her boot, a long metal spike nearly the length of Imogen's forearm, and points it at her. Red streaks the shimmering surface, proving that she has indeed come from battle. Something Imogen is familiar with even if it's been a while.

Like, you hadn't caught that, Im. Especially considering the blood splattered across her face, chest, and arms. Which is why Imogen raises her arms as if to say, "I surrender" or "I'm not here to hurt you."

Can Imogen hold her own? Yes. Is this the right opportunity to? No. Not without more information and not when *that* just happened.

The blond beauty steadies herself and manages to find her feet with great effort. Impressive considering the energy expenditure a transfer like that must've taken. And to a place unknown.

"I'm unarmed." Imogen steps back, giving the girl a few more feet. The squeak of the mattress beneath her slippered feet catches the girl's eye.

"Is that a mattress on the floor?"

Knights. She would know that accent anywhere. It's lyrical—smooth and delicate. It's also that of the Seelie court.

"You're in my home. I have no weapons here, but I can help you. Please."

"Where am I?"

"You portaled into my room, but don't worry. No one comes here. Or they rarely do." She presses a hand to her chest and bows her head, never taking her eyes from the scared creature in her rooms. "My name is Imogen. Just put the weapon down, and I can get you cleaned up. Then we can figure out what happened."

The girl scans the suite, and Imogen knows the instant she recognizes the surprising difference between the grandiose make of the space and the lackluster furnishings. "Are you a prisoner?"

"Of sorts."

Take away the fine dress and linens, and she is not far off.

Tall ceilings arch above, huge wooden beams of dark mahogany contrast the perfectly white stone in almost shocking relief. Pins where tapestries of the finest silks once hung protrude from the walls, lonely against the smooth marble. No other decorations fill the space. It's as if everything was removed. Except for the mattress on the floor, one chair, a bookshelf, and Imogen herself. Because it was. There's no table, and the bookshelf is bolted to the wall, filled with the tattered tomes for her studies. They are the singular kindness her grandfather provides.

"What is this place?"

"Will you put the weapon down?" Imogen asks again.

The girl's eyes widen, and she blinks as if realizing she's still in a fighting stance. "Oh, sorry." Dropping her hands, she straightens, though the needle does not get put away. Imogen doesn't blame her. Keeping herself ready is smart. "Do you have any idea how I got here? Also, why do you look like me?"

Imogen grins, though she isn't sure if she's amused or not.

"There are definite similarities." Imogen steps off the mattress, stopping before the girl. She holds her hand out. "You look about to fall over. How about this? Why don't we go into the bathing room, and we can get you washed up? Then you can tell me who you are, and we'll figure out how you got here. Plus, you'll be out of sight of the door. Just in case."

She bites her lip, as if considering. As if readying herself, she says, "I'm Myrna Qhuinn of The Court of the Radiant Sun."

"Oh…" Imogen's stomach drops. Every cell in her body becomes heavier, pulled downward as if gravity itself has increased upon her alone. She sucks in a breath, then grabs Myrna's hand. The princess jerks away, but Imogen refuses to let go as she yanks her toward the bathing chamber. In a forceful whisper, she says, "We need to hide you. Now!"

Imogen glances toward the door, urgency and fear heating her blood. This time, Myrna doesn't fight. Whether it's Imogen's tone or the willingness to risk her life by Myrna's hand, she couldn't care less. But then Myrna stumbles, so Imogen wraps her arm around the princess's waist. She half drags her to the stool next to the sink.

"Imogen, you said? We must talk."

In a hushed whisper, Imogen says, "You need to keep your voice down. Few people enter here, but if they hear conversation, they will investigate. They cannot find you." Imogen grabs a cloth from one of the drawers. "If there are signs of entry, you hide in there, okay? I will get rid of them."

She points to the dresses bursting from the closet.

"Why?"

"You portaled to Brennan's Castle. You're in the Unseelie Court, and I'm Imogen Murray." She lets that sink in for a moment. "Technically, I'm part of the family hunting you, but I won't hurt you."

To say the girl's face goes pale would be an understatement. She has maybe two more shades before disappearing into the wall behind her. To be fair, it's for good reason. Imogen doubted any Unseelie Myrna's met has been friendly.

Wetting the cloth, Imogen hands it over. Never has the cloth felt so rough. "I guess the rumor is true, then. You're from our court as well."

"I'm sorry, what?" Myrna pauses, the cloth halfway to her face.

Imogen hasn't noticed, instead continuing, "Not just that, your… wow."

She sucks on her teeth. The words stick in her throat, forming an idea that seems so impossible it's hard to speak, let along speak aloud. *But there's no other explanation.*

"I'm what?" Myrna asks, her breaths quicker. She is shaking, but just so. It could be the adrenaline from the portaling. "What did you say?"

She dries her hands on the skirt of her dress and stares. *She has no idea.*

Striding away, Imogen runs her hands over the sides of her braided hair until she hits a bruise left over from her last encounter with the king. It was a particularly bad one. With a wince, she moves on, grasping the end instead and smoothing her thumb over it. A habit she can't seem to get rid of. *I must protect her from him.*

"You portaled here," Imogen says, coming back and taking the cloth. Hesitantly, she swipes the cloth across Myrna's cheek. The red smears with the first stripe but disappears with the second. "The guards told me you had Radiant Light. Is this not true?"

"I do." She grabs Imogen's wrist, who winces. Myrna releases her instantly, and Imogen tugs at her sleeve to hide the fading black and blue marks marring her skin. "What do you mean I am 'from your court'?"

Imogen's lips lift in a sardonic smile. "Myrna, you're even more special than Brennan ever expected. No wonder you've stirred Faerie so. We all felt the change when you came back, but none of us understood why. It makes sense now."

The glare the princess shoots Imogen says her patience is running thin, and she feels bad for the pain this will cause. It is a lot to learn.

Imogen opens her mouth to explain when her attention's drawn to the main room. A knock booms through the room like a gong.

Her hand slips on the counter, and Imogen's breath speeds. She moves, grabbing Myrna's hand and yanking her toward the closet and to the single wrack of dresses.

"Hide and be quiet." The words are low, a bitter whisper and filled with grave intent. Imogen takes it as a good sign that Myrna slinks farther into the wardrobe without complaint.

Heart pounding, she rushes for the door, her slippered feet sliding in her haste. When she reaches her designated spot, she lowers her head and says, "Enter."

Imogen is the picture of demure obedience when the door pushes open.

Although most would not require this submission, she cannot risk it be Grandfather himself, or her brother, Colum. Not after her stubborn mouth got away from her, and Grandfather left her with his favorite masochist, Fletcher.

Her shoulders relax minutely when Braedon appears, carrying a tray of food. His face is lined with worry.

"It's just me, Imogen. You may relax. Brennan and your brother are out."

She does as he says, for he's the one she trusts most. "Are they still hunting the princess?"

"Aye. They have her and her friends trapped. They're also closing in on Mareola." Setting the tray on the ground next to the door, he scans her and shrugs. "I don't think it will be long, considering the information they received from the source on the inside is so definitive."

"The source?"

He nods. "Yes. Your grandfather promised some female and her bitch a place here if she spied." He snorts. "Like he'll keep his word. I don't get what the big deal is, anyway. Mareola's been gone for nearly a century, and this Myrna is nothing but a bratty Seelie. What do we want of her?"

Imogen chuckles, lifting her voice to cover the rustling coming from the bathroom. "True, but you know as well as I do Grandfather keeps his secrets. He has plots none of us sees until he moves his pieces."

Braedon steps close. Gentle hands encircle Imogen's wrist and elbow. He runs a finger below the fabric, sending shivers along her skin even as she winces. "How bad was the last session? It was too soon following the lashes. I was worried."

Imogen spins away, yanking her arm from his grasp. As she does, she notices a pair of blue eyes watching from the bathroom. She shoots them a warning glare, and they disappear. "If I stopped pushing back, it wouldn't be so bad."

"Then you wouldn't be you."

The corner of her lip lifts. "Any confirmation of the girl's arcane, or other rumors going around?"

Braedon sighs. "Confirmation of Radiant Light. Then today we heard she sparked something from our court." He shakes his head. "We put little stock in it. You will not answer my question, will you?"

"No, but I'm fine. Tired." She rests a hand on Braedon's arm. "I'm going to take a nap. I'm sure I'll be pulled out once the king returns." Braedon's eyes go hard. "Did you bring me anything to read?"

The title of the book pulled from his tunic is written in ancient script. Imogen squeals.

"Thank you!" Going up on her tiptoes, she kisses his cheek and then pushes him toward the door. "You better leave before someone gets suspicious. I don't want to lose another friend as a guard."

He looks down at her with sad eyes. "I won't be able to come back for a while, so I brought you extra food. Hide it. I'm sorry, Im."

They say a quick goodbye, making sure she's in the correct position as he leaves. Then she half collapses against the door, her head looking toward the ceiling, the hardwood cold against her back as she takes a few breaths to slow her heart. That was close.

So close. Had he found her...

But she'd learned a lot, and the book he'd brought her was exactly what they needed.

"Holy crap!" Imogen says.

Myrna slips into the room. "I have so many freaking questions."

She almost laughs. Whether because of the girl's phrasing, the look of confusion, or the fact Myrna Qhuinn is in her room.

"I can't believe this is happening." She leads the princess away from the door and back into the bathroom. She needs to have this conversation, and quick. It will not be easy or nice, but that is what they were left with. "Myrna, it is rare indeed to have one take on the arcane of both parents, and that is what you've done."

"I don't understand." Inside the bathroom once more, she faces Imogen.

"You have Radiant Light?" Myrna nods, and Imogen licks her lips. "Okay. And you've manifested Shadowspire."

It's a statement.

Myrna's eyebrows draw down. Her lips part as if to speak, but Imogen continues, "You have. That's how you're here."

The girl's shoulders droop; her hands fall to her sides. "Are you talking about the violet...the violet that sparkles beneath my fire?"

Imogen laughs. "It doesn't just sparkle anymore, honey, and it means something, for Shadowspire has been all but snuffed out by King Brennan." *That is, except for...*

So many lies, especially within Imogen's family. Perhaps she shouldn't be surprised. There is really only one possibility. Her favorite uncle—the man who believed peace was possible between the Seelie and Unseelie. He could've pulled it off. Would have been willing.

His disappearance makes sense now.

For something to do, if nothing else, Imogen picks up the cloth and rinses it. Placing it on the side of the sink, she says, "But you should know, there's only one line that holds this ability anymore. To manifest as you have...that's even more rare. I've known but one who could do so, a male of great arcane and honor, and I have a feeling he's the one we can thank for your being here. I can't believe you got his gift."

Myrna takes a step back, her throat moving.

Imogen squeezes the edge of the sink, then spins to face Myrna. Extending her hand out once more, she says, "I'd like to introduce myself again. I'm Imogen Murray, granddaughter to the king, and your cousin."

"I'm sorry. What did you say?" Myrna asks.

There is no denying it. Though she is dark where Myrna is light, her raven hair falling just below her shoulders and eyes so dark they would fade to the pupil if not for the starlight burst of gold at the center, the resemblance is clear. It's in the shape of their chins and noses. The tilt at the corners of their lips. The biggest difference is in the deeper coloring; a tanned olive to Myrna's porcelain.

"The last clan to hold Shadowspire are the Murrays, and it all lines up. Uncle Reece disappeared during the last great battle; around the time you would've been conceived. Myrna, he too held Transportational Shadowspire."

CHAPTER FORTY-TWO

Balance Bound by Rival

DISAPPEARED DURING THE LAST *great battle. He too held Transporta-tional Shadowspire.*

Myrna collapses onto the settee in the corner of the bathing chamber. Her chest rises as quickly as it had when she first entered the suite. She's just as confused.

So, not only is Mareola my mother, but my father is of the enemy court. And *the prince. The first born heir.*

Myrna sways.

Imogen, dressed in fine silks that are tattered and wrinkled, bites her lips as she drops her hand.

"It's nice to meet you," Imogen says, her shoulder rising slowly and nose scrunching adorably. "Although I'm sure you can't say the same."

Myrna takes in the barren room, filled with necessities and a few books. Her cousin is a prisoner in her own home. Yet, she takes a seat next to Myrna and presses a hand to Myrna's leather-clad thigh, eyes kind and filled with worry. Myrna chuckles. "I don't know. I've always wanted a cousin and, so far, you've been the nicest of my extended family."

"To be fair, they don't know." Imogen's lips pull back, baring her teeth. "Although, if they did, I don't think they'd treat you better. Sorry. Which is why we need to get you out of here."

Myrna turns to the mirror, which covers much of the wall.

Imogen does the same. For a long moment, they stare, comparing one another's reflection.

Myrna's the first to look away. She pinches the bridge of her nose. "How is this possible? I can't"—Myrna swallows the lump in her throat—"there's no way this is possible, too."

"Honestly, I just don't get how Laoise and Uncle Reece got together. They aren't exactly compatible. Grandfather's gonna lose his mind." Imogen pauses, then it's as if Myrna's words sink in. "What do you mean, 'too'?"

Myrna grips her neck with both hands as she stares over at Imogen. Then, unable to sit still any longer, Myrna goes to the sink and splashes water on her face. She takes a deep breath and decides to trust someone she knows she shouldn't, a Murray.

She's protected you so far.

"It's a lie." Meeting her cousin's eyes through the mirror, Myrna says, "I found out a few hours ago that Laoise's not my mother. Mareola is. She raised me and, looking back, I should've known. I was raised by her but thought her a caretaker. She never claimed me and, really, neither did Laoise. I was the one who labeled them. I'm a fool." Her vision becomes cloudy before the rogue tears fall without her approval.

Imogen stands and places her hand on her cousin's arm. "Oh..."

"Princess Mareola didn't die in The Great War. She raised me in the human world and right now, your grandfather..." Myrna's voice cracks, "our grandfather is trying to get to her. I need to find her first, so I may protect her."

"Knights save us." Imogen's head bobs up and down in quick succession.

"I guess the lies make sense now. Princess to both courts and a scandal to rule them all."

Imogen whistles low. "No kidding. Oh, and let's throw in some new Shadowspire manifestation. So, yeah... You're having a hell of a day."

The two girls fall silent, then in sync, burst out laughing.

"Okay. Okay. Shit, we can do this." Imogen turns and bolts toward the front room. Mumbling to herself, she says, "Go

Uncle Reece. This makes so much more sense. Mareola... so bright...yeah, we can't let him get her."

At a half sprint, Imogen stumbles back into the room, fingers already thumbing through the pages of the book Braedon brought.

"I can't believe he brought me this today of all days! It's fate." She takes a seat on the settee, opening the book on her lap.

Myrna finds a spot next to her. "What is it?"

"A book called *Unbound Rival* that's supposed to be the history of Shadowspire. I asked him to steal it from the library archives. It has some great information about portals and how they function. It also goes into the science behind it. Grandfather doesn't like us reading it, but it's the best way for us to harness the magic we have."

"Can I ask what you can do?"

"I can pull shadow, wrap it around myself and others." Imogen looks away and sighs. "Which he finds threatening, but that isn't important right now. Ah! Here it is!"

Looking down at the page Imogen holds out to her, Myrna gasps. "I know these symbols."

"That's impossible. No one knows these symbols."

Myrna swivels the satchel resting at the base of her spine around to the front. She's nearly forgotten it was there. The instant her fingers brush *Balance Beholden*, power radiates up her arms. She removes it from the bag and holds it out.

"Where did you get that?" Imogen asks, eyes wide.

Myrna doesn't respond, just opens to the page she remembers seeing symbols matching the ones in Imogen's book. "May I?"

Hesitantly, Imogen extends the book along her knees so that both tomes are inches apart.

"Look, they're the same. What do they mean?"

"I-I don't know. I've been studying Shadowspire most of my life, training to use it as much as Grandfather will allow, but this book is special. Old. It's why I wanted to study it." Imogen tugs at her sleeves. "And this language is ancient."

"So, I'm stuck here?"

"No!" Imogen shakes her head. "I can teach you the basics—how to harness shadow and make it listen to you. But it's hard. Shadowspire feels and acts differently than most arcane. At least, that's what we're told." Worry laces her next words. "It's worse for you because Radiant Light and Shadowspire are on opposite ends of the spectrum. Light lives in everything, but shadow hides. It slithers between things. Sneaks. So sometimes, it's hard to harness. I'm not surprised you didn't know you had it, and then it took you by surprise the first time."

"It sure did. But how did I get here? Why here?"

"I remember asking Uncle Reece how he chose where he was transporting. He always told me he went where he needed to be. Where his heart took him. What were you thinking about when you portaled?"

Myrna shifts in her seat, her heart clenching. *Was everyone okay? Still alive?*

She needed to hurry.

"We were in battle. My best friend, Sam—she's human—was fighting one of your soldiers. She was losing. I managed to kill him, but she was badly hurt. Then my friend, Shay, was stabbed. I don't know if they're okay." Myrna bounces her knee. "All I could think about was how these people were my family. The first in my life besides my aunt and mother who'd welcomed and protected me. I just wanted to do the same."

"You were thinking of family." Imogen huffs out a laugh. "Well, I guess you got what you asked for. Not quite what you were expecting, but perhaps what we both needed. Here's the deal. In this book is the information you need to learn how to transport. You're going to need this skill. And although this may have been a really terrifying way to find out who your father was, I can tell you from personal experience he was a great man. I miss him so much, and I can see him in you."

Imogen's soft, introspective smile sends a sharp pain through Myrna's heart. *I want to know more.*

Before she can ask, Imogen continues, "So, we need to figure this out now. Your friends need you. It's time for a crash course." She rubs her hands together. "When I was young, Uncle Reece and I read this together."

"You did?"

Imogen nods and flips to a few pages before. "I remember him explaining how shadows are always connected. They may not be visible at all times, hidden by the light of day, but they're always there because they're living memories of sorts, never leaving, but growing with time."

Myrna blinks in confusion.

"Those within your court have taught you to use your ability to pull the energy from around you and harness it for your white fire. That works for most arcane, but Shadowspire's different. It's already connected to you, attached to you and everything around you. But it's deeper than that. Which means you don't pull it, you coax it."

"I don't understand."

"Draw your Radiant Light."

Myrna does, and Imogen grins. "Wow. That's beautiful." Imogen glances toward the exit. "Don't tell Grandfather I said that."

It's Myrna's turn to laugh. "I won't."

"When you did that, where did you pull the energy from?"

"Um...from inside me and everything around me."

"Good. Now look for the shadows."

Myrna closes her eyes. "I don't feel them. How?"

Imogen grins. "When you use your light, you start at your core arcane, right? With Shadowspire, you start from the external memory of time. You find the imprint it's had on everything around you. Reach outward with your arcane, then use the connection you have to find the hiding spots and coax the shadows into the light. They'll come for you."

"You know you don't make any sense, right?"

"You're welcome. Now try it. And remember, this isn't about emotion, it's about connection."

Myrna does. She closes her eyes and truly thinks about Imogen's words. The idea that time and memory leave an imprint on everything, and this is what leaves the shadow—an echo of what once was. At the corner of her mind, there's an itch of... awareness. Always there, connected at all times, and holding power, but always disregarded. It makes sense.

"Humans have a story of a boy whose shadow ran away. I never cared for it," Myrna says, eyes opening slowly. She looks down to her palms where white fire still burns, wrapping around her fingers. She's mesmerized by the way it dances and focuses, finally understanding Imogen's words. Not fully, but as if they're sinking in with each passing moment. A flicker in and underneath starts as violet shadows sneak out from beneath the flame. *It wants to be seen.*

Myrna lifts the fingers of her right hand and kisses the flame. It deepens, then jiggles as if excited. Then she runs them along the palm of her other hand, tracing the path of her Radiant Light where it curls across her wrist. As she does, she asks the shadow to come forth.

It does. It slithers out, wrapping around and encasing the Radiant Light in its starlight glow.

"How did you do that so fast?"

"I think I've been calling it for a while, but I didn't know." Myrna meets Imogen's amazed gaze. She chuckles. "I've seen it a few times. It always stayed underneath until today. But will it portal me like this?"

"No. That's a specific spell few can harness. There are a lot of shared skills Shadow wielders have, but portals are extremely rare. As are skills like mine. With your control, my guess is you'll pick up the easy ones quickly. No wonder everyone's so scared of you."

The fire on Myrna's hands goes out instantly. "They shouldn't be afraid of me! I'm nothing!"

She goes to stand up, *Balance Beholden* nearly falling to the floor, but Imogen grabs her hands and pulls her back down.

"Shh. Quiet!" Imogen snaps, glancing toward the front room. "You are hardly nothing. You portaled across Faerie with no training. You're a child of both courts created out of love."

"You don't know that," she snaps, voice back to normal.

Imogen nods. "I do. Because there's no way Reece would've given himself to a Seelie, or died for one, if it wasn't true."

"How do you know he died for her?"

"I knew him."

The words shoot straight through Myrna. She barely stops the sob those words threaten to release.

"And your arcane is strong enough to heal the plague killing this land and our people. I can feel it." Imogen's hands tighten on Myrna's so hard, she wants to pull away. "There's so much you can do."

"I have no idea what you're talking about. I was human a month ago and now I'm Faye, magical, a princess of two courts, hunted, and now expected to save everything?"

"No." Imogen shifts her grip to Myrna's shoulders. The desperate understanding in the way she leans closer speaks of how clearly Imogen sees Myrna's hurt, her teetering emotions. "You're a girl with a lot on her plate. And the only thing you need to worry about right now is creating a portal and saving those you love. The rest can be figured out later. But know I am on your side. Because I see something in you, as I assume your friends do, too."

Myrna swallows back the emotion threatening to escape. She licks her upper lip.

"Now, let's figure out how to portal, since apparently, I don't have to teach you the basics."

With matching nods, the girls slide closer, lining up the books. They compare the general text, which outlines basically what Imogen already said, but in more detail. Then they get to the page with the odd symbols. Imogen manages to decipher the first line based off some notes scribbled in the front—Myrna's father's writing, she says.

For worthy kin with matching hearts, speak to thy tome and find connection like none before.

"Everything in this place speaks in riddles," Myrna grumbles, making Imogen giggle.

The Unseelie leans closer, hand resting on the symbol of the book she holds. Her knee bumps Myrna's book. "These symbols have to mean something."

Myrna caresses *Balanced Beholden*, then reaches over and touches the matching one on the book Imogen holds.

The scent of ozone fills the room, and electricity crackles in the air. Light sparks at Myrna's fingertips, disappearing into the pages. Shadow responds, sliding back up, through, and from

Imogen, and along the connection, creating a complete circuit between the two girls and the two ancient, sentient tomes.

Myrna and Imogen gasp as images of past Shadowspire wielders flow through their minds. Secrets of each other's histories replay, both good and bad. Hearts connect, then ancient spells long since forgotten download into them both. Their backs arch. Silent screams yank the muscles tight even as they try to pull away. It is not possible. Not until the symbols disappear, dissolving into the pages.

The two cousins who were never supposed to meet are now bound forever by fate. Pain erupts on Myrna's wrist. She glances down to see the sigil, faint and opalescent silver, matching the one that disappeared from the page. They collapse back onto the settee.

Imogen winces as it squeaks against the floor.

They're quiet as they stare into each other's eyes, shock and awe in every cell of their being.

"I saw..." Myrna says.

Imogen's eyes water, remembering the beauty and darkness in Myrna's past. "Me, too."

Myrna's the first to move. She reaches for Imogen's fingers. Her cousin squeezes them ever so gently. Then she turns her arm over to show a matching mark on her skin.

"Well, that's unexpected and potentially concerning," Imogen says, "but I think you can get home now."

Myrna chuckles. "Yeah. Did you hear the initial knowledge spell won't last?"

Imogen swallows and nods once. "But it might be enough to get you home and give you a starting point for your Shadowspire."

Myrna chuckles. "But what about when it disappears?"

Imogen holds her hands out. "I have no idea."

"You should come with me. If they find out I was here, or if they find the mark..."

The couch groans as her cousin sits upright. She pulls down the sleeves of her dress. "They won't."

"Please." Myrna can see her waver.

"I am more unwelcome in your court than I am here. But know, I'm here and on your side. What I saw in you, your heart?" The same respect mirrors back to Imogen as she stands. "Now, you need to get going. You've been here too long already. The others need you."

"Im, I will keep you safe. We will keep you safe." Myrna stands. The dark-haired girl comes easily into her arms; the cousin she never expected to have and who is more like her than she'd ever guess. Her hug is ever so tight. In less than an hour, Myrna created a bond she could never have expected. She pulls back. "Please!"

"Do you think I need saving?"

Myrna takes Imogen's wrists and pulls up her sleeves to reveal bruises. Then she yanks back the collar of her dress to expose a wound that could be made by one thing alone, a barbed whip. "I understand torture. I may have been raised in the human world, but I'm not naïve."

Imogen sighs, wanting to turn away at the shame those words cause. She whispers, "Okay. Yes."

"Good." Myrna slides *Balance Beholden* back into her bag. "Then, let's...Imogen!"

Imogen spins. Mid-motion, she freezes. There's a man in the doorway, his sword out.

Braedon.

Imogen steps between them and spreads her arms as if to use herself as a shield, which seems to darken the Guardian's expression. "Myrna, go!"

Terrified for having to leave Imogen at the hands of an Unseelie guard, Myrna retreats and digs into the knowledge *Balance Beholden* gifted. It flows across her skin like a piece of armor.

"Guardian Braedon, you hurt her, and I will not forgive you for it. And, one day, I'll pay you thricefold for any harm she comes to by your doing."

His eyebrows raise.

She glances to Imogen. "Keep that book safe. I'll come back for you, Im. As soon as I'm able."

Myrna calls upon the Shadowspire like an old friend, for that is what it is, an ancient being gifted to this world to protect it and to provide balance. It is one of the secrets the books have kept within their pages. She will cherish it with the rest of the knowledge they have revealed, as long as it's hers.

Radiant Light mixes with her Shadowspire, wrapping around her like a cocoon of violet-shimmering fire.

Pressing her palms together, she focuses it into a ball. Then with her will alone, she flattens the slimy dark substance and draws it out like taffy until it is the size of a mirror. With one last glance of goodbye to Imogen, Myrna steps into the darkness and away from the Court of the Indomitable Moon.

Chapter Forty-Three

Knowledge, even if Momentary, is Control

SHAY IS A DEAD weight across Kelan's shoulder as he kicks backward, the door to the small cottage slamming open. Careful not to wrack Shay's head against the frame, he steps through. Declan and Sam are already inside, clearing the house.

"Bri, get your arse in here. They'll be coming around any minute. We must solidify defenses."

"I don't like this"—his sister slips inside, then locks the door—"if we go in, we might never come out."

"Maybe, but I need to heal Shay. I can't be dragging his lumbering arse all the way back to court. We need him walking."

She waves away the comment, scanning the forest beyond with the point of her crossbow. "We should have a few minutes. I don't know if they retreated or left."

"They didn't leave." Kelan carefully lowers Shay to the ground.

"Clear!" Declan calls from deeper in the house.

A moment later, Declan and Sam step into the room. They're worse for wear, covered in dirt and grime, but alive. Sam favors her left side, where a few fractured ribs remain after Kelan's healing, but at least the internal bleeding's stopped. That had been touch and go. Humans are more complicated than Faye.

Plus, Sam made him stop, worried he wouldn't be able to heal Shay had he continued with her. Kelan never respected a human more.

"We're secure. For now," Declan says, coming to his son. "But someone was here. The house has been ransacked; the back room is all but destroyed."

Kelan opens his mouth to respond, but nothing comes out. He's too distracted with prodding the wound, where a spear of rock protrudes from Shay's side. He'll need to remove it before he can finish the healing. *I'll need to move quick.*

"Declan, you'll need to hold him. I—" Kelan's words are cut off by a loud fizzing sound. A pinpoint of darkness appears in the corner of the room. "Get back!"

Briana and Sam run behind Declan and Kelan, who place themselves before the growing black spot.

Larger and larger it becomes—first the size of a daisy, then an orange. Soon, it's as big as a shield. The scent of ozone and citrus fills the air, and the hair on Kelan's arms stands up. He knows that scent. Too soon, it's solidifying into something nearly the size of a small door.

"Shadowspire..." Kelan whispers. Bile churns in his gut, for this ability is rarely seen. It's a myth to their people, the truth of it kept to those of the highest rank. Even his knowledge is limited, but he knows the Murray clan are the ones who possess it.

The Shadowspire's texture changes from one blink to the next, then someone steps through. It's as if the world shrinks and the air is sucked from it. Kelan's lungs seize with relief, making his limbs heavy.

Myrna...Shadowspire...

"Myrna!" Sam screams and bolts for her friend. Forgetting her wounded ribs, she throws her arms around Myrna's neck and squeezes hard. The tears are in Sam's words, if not upon her face. "We thought we lost you."

Myrna closes her eyes as she accepts the hug. With a flick of her finger, the portal closes behind her. "I'm sorry. I didn't mean to scare anyone. I didn't mean to leave. Is everyone all right?"

"Yes and no."

Kelan's glued to the floor as Briana and Declan hug the princess. They give her a quick rundown of the last hour—Sam and Shay getting hurt, Kelan healing her during the fight, then them fighting their way through the forest and almost losing Shay. Her face scrunches as she glances in his direction. Even more when they outline the reinforcements, their trip down the cliff, and finding the house. Kelan watches the entire exchange, but for some reason, he can't move.

Myrna comes to him. "I'm sorry I left again, but I met someone important and learned more than I ever expected."

He scans her beautiful face. "Looks like it."

Hurt passes over her expression, and she glances away. It reminds him of the last expression she held before she disappeared—terror that he hated her for what she was. She turns from him.

Never.

Grabbing her waist with one hand and sliding his other around the back of her neck, he pulls her close and presses his forehead against hers. "I told you before. I'll be by your side for as long as you allow it. Nothing you've learned will change that. I know you, Myrna."

She squeezes his arms even as her sad voice says, "Even if I'm part Unseelie?"

The others freeze. Declan had likely pieced it together with her control over the shadow portal, but to hear the words aloud…

"It does not change the person you are." He runs a thumb along her cheek. "In fact, it explains much. Though I do have questions, but not right now. Shay needs attention."

She nods, fingers skating along his arm before she turns, and they both drop beside the injured boy, Myrna across from Kelan.

"Oh, Shay," Myrna says, taking in the blade-like spear of rock protruding from her friend.

"He's in bad shape. I need to remove it, but I'm not sure if I can stop the bleeding. I don't know if—"

Myrna's eyes glaze for a moment. "I've something that can help." The mischievous smile that lifts her lip sends a thrill through him. "I've learned a few things while I was gone. Portaling's exhausted me, but I can do this. Let me show you. Declan, can you please sit behind him? We're going to pull this out, and I'm going to need you to… well, hold him still. It's going to hurt."

To his surprise, she removes *Balance Beholden* from her satchel and places it on Shay's lap. She finds a page, reads it, then says, "That's not the one I was thinking; isn't there one that…"

Kelan shares a glance with Declan. *Her interactions with the book have definitely changed. What happened while you were gone, Myr?*

"Yes, thank you!" She runs a gentle finger down the page. *It's as if the book is part of her. As if she knows every page by heart.*

"Sam, can you go into that closet and pull out three towels?"

"How do you know where things are?" Kelan asks.

"This is my childhood home. Where I grew up. 'A place most loved,' remember?" Myrna mumbles, reading a passage from the book. While she does, she itches at something on her wrist. It's an opalescent mark he's never seen before that flickers in markings matching that of those in the book.

Knights.

"Where did that mark come from, Princess?" Declan asks.

Myrna looks up at them, then down to where she's scratching. "*Balance Beholden* gave it to me. It won't last though, so we need to hurry."

"Did you say this was your house?" Sam says, coming back with the towels.

There is so much happening right now.

"Yeah. That's why I came here. Why I thought you were here. Is Theia downstairs? That's where she'd be."

"Downstairs?" Declan and Kelan ask in unison. Declan shoves to his feet, then he and Briana rush toward the hidden basement door Myrna indicates. He hesitates before disappearing down it to meet Kelan's eye. "Heal him, my brother."

Myrna doesn't notice the chaos she's caused in the thirty seconds of conversation. She's too focused on the book and the unconscious Shay. She takes Kelan's hand. "This will be weird, but I need you to trust me. Can you do that?"

There's no way Kelan cannot trust this female. It isn't in him. He squeezes her fingers, and she places their hands to the page.

"Let's heal him." And with no warning, she rips the spike from Shay's flesh.

Shay screams, conscious with pain.

Kelan's so shocked it takes him a second to catch up. As Sam jumps into action, pressing a towel to the front and back of the wound, while also trying to hold him, Kelan accesses his healing arcane. Diving deep, he calls the power forward, then connects to Shay. Kelan begins to knit the torn flesh and damaged blood vessels, for which there is so much. His head pounds, his breaths become heavy, and his teeth clench as he wills the arcane to bless Shay's life. But the wound's so bad, and he's already drained.

Suddenly, there's a burst of heat from the connection where Myrna and he touch. He opens his eyes. Shadowspire crawls from the world around them, up Myrna, onto the book where it deepens in shade, then pours across his skin.

Kelan wants to pull away, the century of myth telling him it's evil and unhealthy, but then Myrna's gaze meets his.

"There's a balance. Light and dark. It's all energy. You're drained, and I can draw from both. *Balance Beholden* is not touching your power, but it's allowing me to learn how you heal and help, for this one time. Will you allow me to? I want to help because you're tired and this wound is dire."

Kelan swallows the lump in his throat.

"Follow me." That's all he says before he opens his arcane to the girl who's become more to him than anyone has ever been. She connects so seamlessly, and he feels her deep within his soul.

Myrna bows her head and activates her Radiant Light, drawing arcane from Faerie herself. Kelan gasps, the energy boost a boon as they work together to knit the wound closed.

Shay pants through it all.

"The bleeding's stopped." A few more minutes pass, and Sam says, "Holy shit. The skin's closing before my eyes." Then, eventually, "Okay, guys, you can stop. He's good."

And he is. Kelan can feel it. Inside to outside, the damage was repaired by his power and by hers. He doesn't know how Shadowspire healed, but it did. Yes, her Radiant Light provided an energy boost, but it was the shadows which melded so seamlessly to his arcane. And that citrus taste, the way it felt next to his...wonderful and different.

A hand grips Kelan's wrist.

"Thanks," Shay pants, complexion pale. No doubt, he'll feel like shit for a while still, but he'd live.

Kelan pats the boy's uninjured shoulder. "My pleasure."

Getting to his feet isn't as hard as he expects, the energy not as drained is it would've been had he done it all alone. Fingers still linked with Myrna's, he pulls her up with him. "We need to have a conversation when we get back."

They move away as Declan reappears and helps Shay to his feet. He wraps his son in a massive hug.

"You have no idea," Myrna says. She turns to Briana. "Where's Theia?"

Briana stands near the kitchen door, weapon hanging by her side. At the question, her face falls. "I'm sorry, Myrna. We didn't realize this was your home. King Brennan was here. He captured her." She wipes her brow with the back of her hand. "The battle was confined to the back room and... downstairs..."

"Downstairs what?" Myrna bolts toward the kitchen.

Briana attempts to stop her, but Myrna shoves her out of the way with a blast of arcane. "Myrna, you don't need to see!"

"Shit!" Kelan sprints after, taking the stairs at a dangerous speed. He comes to a halting stop at the bottom when he finds a frozen Myrna at the base.

What was once a living room to one side and a workout space to the other has now been completely destroyed. Chairs are broken in half, pictures destroyed and strewn across the room, weights embedded in walls. Nothing is where it should be. The battle that had happened here must've gone on for a while.

What's worse is the sight of the once-proud warrior lying prone and motionless on the floor. Blood pools beneath him, slash marks cross his abdomen and neck so deep no creature could survive. And the burn marks.

"Tomas," Myrna cries. She jerks forward, but Kelan grabs her by the waist and pulls her to him. She struggles, but Kelan refuses to let this be the last memory of the man she respected so dearly.

A man who served them well in the human world, who acted as a father figure. She curls into his shoulder.

"We will come back for him. I promise. He will have an honored goodbye," Kelan says and leads her up the stairs.

"They left a note," Declan says, his face grim. He hands it to Kelan. The parchment is thick, a rich cornflower blue. "They have Theia."

Myrna's jaw tics as she glares at the note. Her expression shifts from devastation to determination before his eyes. It's a look that terrifies and thrills him, for it is one of the Qhuinn line, one of power. One he will die for.

"Give me the note." She holds her hand out, palm flat.

Declan glances to Kelan, but does he's asked.

"Sam, Bri, Shay! Get in here. It's time to go home!" Myrna hollers and, without reading it, she folds the letter and tucks it into her tunic. Proof for Laoise and fuel for revenge.

Were he not so terrified of the female before him, he'd kiss her.

Moving to the center of the dining space, Myrna calls forth her Radiant Light, but this time there's something more to it. A violet shadow slithering beneath. It snakes free to collect into her palm just as the others enter the room. She squishes it between her hands and extends it out, opening a portal as if it were nothing at all. The marking on her wrist glows bright, though to Kelan, it looks incomplete. Not as it had when she first arrived.

"Queen save us," Briana whispers.

"No. She has things to answer for. Now come, I want to go home and have a conversation with my aunt."

Travel through Shadowspire takes but an instant, but it's like the universe flips on its head. Time, one's very existence, weighing upon them as the air is sucked from their lungs. But then they're through.

Myrna steps free first, Sam's hand tight in hers, the chain of companions right behind. When the last is through, the portal flickers, then goes out. Her legs go weak, and Myrna crumples.

Sam catches her, crying out.

Declan and Briana are the closest, and they help lower Myrna to the ground.

"You do know that you're still injured, right?" Briana asks Sam.

"Are you telling me you wouldn't have caught her?" Sam asks. Her eyebrows are pinched in pain.

Briana assists Sam into a chair. "Fair."

"I'm fine," Myrna says. She rubs her pocket as if the letter burns her through her clothing. Kelan understands, for it is not some poison or spell, it is the truth that they'd failed. Once again, unable to save Mareola from the evil out to get her. He feels it, too.

Only this time, Brennan has her.

"How do you feel, Princess?" Declan asks.

"Fine." Ignoring the complaints from the others, Myrna stands, verifies she's steady, and heads for the door. "Come on, we've a meeting to attend."

"You should rest," Kelan says. "Approaching Laoise now is unwise. The power you've used…"

Myrna spins on her heels. "You don't understand all the lies! The secrets!"

"Then tell us!" Briana says.

It's as if she doesn't hear the words, for Myrna continues to address Kelan. "I'm going to the throne room, and I need you by my side as I speak to the queen. I can do this alone, but I don't want to. Theia's life may depend on what we do now."

"You are such a frustrating female." Without even looking at his friend, he calls, "Declan?"

From the side, Declan tosses Kelan a bottle of water and an energy bar. Kelan catches it and holds it out.

Myrna narrows her eyes. "Fine, but I'm eating it on the way."

Briana hums as she falls in behind them. "Always nice to meet the queen with food in one's teeth."

"And you say I'm the frustrating one." Myrna takes the snack and water. She gulps them down as she exits the suite. The others flank her as they hurry through the hallways of the palace.

"Sam, you should stay here."

"I'm not leaving her. I don't care if Laoise freaks out. I will not leave."

"Then stay between Declan and I," Briana says.

Sam murmurs her agreement, quickly coming to understand their concern as the bustling palace hallways fill with spectators, servants, courtiers, and peasants. Why they are all out, waiting in the halls, Kelan cannot guess. They stare as they pass, murmurs of surprise at seeing their state, and Myrna's presence especially proves that her offense is well known.

When they reach the doors of the throne room, Guardians flank either side.

Isaiah rushes forward at their approach. "Where have you been? We've been trying to track you, but nothing. The queen is in a state. She's called council and—"

Myrna gives him no heed. She walks past him, slamming the massive doors open with a burst of arcane. They bang against the walls in a resonating an eruption of noise. The entire room shifts, all attention landing on their party. Still, Myrna doesn't slow. She strides to where Laoise stands on the dais. The forty or so high court step against the wall, making way for their party.

Instantly, the tone in the room changes. Laoise's power resonates in a wave aimed directly at them, but it seems Myrna's ready. She ignites her Radiant Light just enough to shield those behind her. It's a trick learned from memory of those long dead.

Courtiers all submit to Laoise's arcane while Myrna and her clan stand firm. Again, unconsciously, Myrna rubs at her wrist.

"My queen," Myrna says with a bow. She manages to keep the sarcasm out of the movement, yet Kelan can sense that her aunt picks up on it, regardless. "We have some things to discuss."

"Do you, now? Well, perhaps you should've been here when we called for you instead of disobeying my order." Laoise's tone is hard, deadly even.

"I did not break your order," Myrna says with a wicked gleam, "for you only stated that there would be no officially sanctioned mission from the Guardians."

There is a shove of Myrna's arcane toward the room at large.

"I am not a Guardian, nor do I currently hold an official title, as none has yet to be bestowed upon me."

Laoise freezes. Her fingers curl into fists. The room holds its breath, then slowly, those claws unclench one millimeter at a time. It's as if she finally sees Myrna is no longer willing to sit back and watch the game Laoise plays. Instead, she wishes to be an active participant.

"So, you see, dearest, I did not break any order, and neither did the others, as they came searching for me. They are my personal guard, after all."

Holy shit. She'd just cleared us of all wrongdoing. Making it seem like they'd actually followed Laoise's orders. *Brilliant.*

"But I do have word as we learned much on this venture." Myrna's voice drops, her chin dipping so she watches Laoise through her eyelashes. "Things which must be dealt with, you must answer for, and plans that cannot be disregarded."

Laoise scans the determined group around the youngling princess. "Perhaps we should speak in private."

"No, Auntie. I think it's time the high court understand that I am not from your womb, just as they must accept there is a spy in their midst."

For the first time in Myrna's life, Laoise looks scared.

Gasps echo through the throne room. Myrna takes a step forward as Laoise steps backward, her hand going to her stomach.

The youngling scans the crowd. "It is true. I was notified this very day that my true mother, Princess Mareola Qhuinn, who raised me, was being hunted by none other than King Brennan himself."

Laoise's lip twitches. The warning in her stare burns.

Myrna continues, "All in an attempt to goad me out so they may capture me and prove my true lineage. What he doesn't understand, however, is that I'm not afraid. For my mother taught me to stand against all threats, and my aunt"—she inclines her head to Laoise—"taught me to never back down."

The courtier Myrna'd spoken to during her introduction calls out from the back, "Princess Mareola's alive?"

"Yes, but today, King Brennan sent a contingent of soldiers to capture her. Queen Laoise, under the guise of hiding the truth of my birth, refused to send backup. I snuck out of the palace and, with the help of my two friends, Shay and Samantha, we attempted to get to her."

"Queen," one of her highest advisers and supporters says, "how could you do this?"

"To protect them both!" Laoise is no longer scared; she is angry. "To protect Faerie and all that live here, for Myrna is our greatest hope."

"What—" the adviser starts, but Isaac pushes forward, cutting him off.

"What happened today, Princess? Where is Mareola?"

Myrna has never looked so fierce. Perhaps it is the way her power amplifies her presence, but Kelan does not believe so. She stands, chin up, feet shoulder width apart. Her entire body looks ready for battle while also being perfectly relaxed. She commands attention, respect.

"My mother"—solidifying the truth of her parentage, for sure—"was captured by King Brennan."

Power explodes from the queen in a wave. She jumps from the stage and is in front of Myrna in an instant. The room's exclamations fall silent as they submit once more.

"Had you not gone after her, they wouldn't have found her!"

Through clenched teeth, Myrna snarls, "She was gone when we got there. And because of you, all the protection she had was Guardian Tomas. A loyal friend and protector who has now fallen." Her voice cracks.

"He was a traitor, not a Guardian."

"He stayed by our side all these years. He was family, and he is a Guardian! His death, her capture, our injuries. These are on your hands for not disclosing my lineage!"

White flame tinted violet at the base bursts across her palms in a brilliant display. Never before has Myrna created such, but her anger, sadness, and fear mix. She sways, then drops the arcane, closing her fist quickly as if suddenly unwilling to let her second secret out.

Kelan steps closer in case she requires assistance.

"My queen," Finch says in a loud voice, interrupting the two females. He steps in from the far door and bows low. "I'm sorry to interrupt, but the king calls. He is..." Finch's lip raises in disgust, "especially improper today."

Chapter Forty-Four

Bastard King Said What?

This is worse than Laoise could've expected. That child barges in and announces she's not only lied to the court, but that it's led to the capture of Mareola. How this will play out will determine the punishment for the child. For there is no way she can let this go. Even if Myrna is meant to rule one day.

Of course, the changes within Laoise since Myrna's spell speaks of another response. Acceptance and pride for Myrna's actions. So, which will she choose? For Myrna's presence in Faerie has started something—a shift back to the light her court is known for. And Myrna is the key to their success in the future. Truth. Honesty. Joy.

She's even captured the loyalty of Kelan and Declan. Two of the most hard-headed Faye Laoise's ever had the displeasure to know. Never would she say it aloud, but she respects them both.

Laoise's eye twitches. Breaking the staring match with Myrna, she heads for Finch and the call, which may change even more in their world.

With no hesitation, Myrna takes her place by Laoise's side. *Damn you, child.*

Laoise takes in Myrna's blood-splattered clothes, the disheveled hair, the darkening bruise on the youngling's collarbone. Then the group which follows so loyally behind, regardless of her obvious distaste. Though she's sure the others expect a biting response to Myrna's disobedience, it is something entirely different which comes from Laoise's lips. "Are you well?"

Yes, the words come out harsh, but they do not taste bitter on her tongue. In fact, they sound more right than anything that she has spoken in years.

"I am fine, Auntie. In need of food and rest and a check-up for us all, but we made it back in one piece. Are you angry I left?" Myrna asks as they exit and slip through the hall leading to the Mirror Room.

"Furious, but not surprised. I would've done the same had I noted the same misstep." Laoise flicks a glance at her niece. "I did enjoy seeing you soar over the west wall, though. Far more graceful than the Hughes boy."

A laugh bubbles from Myrna, and she covers her mouth. Myrna sends an amused glance to Shay.

"If you knew, then why didn't you send…"

Laoise sighs and meets Myrna's eyes. "I'd already made my ruling."

Myrna purses her lips and assesses her with those far-too-intelligent eyes. "But you did not stop my guard."

"No." Simple.

"My queen," Myrna says in a much more formal tone than before. She pulls her to a stop just outside the Mirror Room and speaks in a soft tone. "I apologize for my rash movements, but I could not leave her alone. She's my—" Her throat closes, and she cannot continue. Myrna clears her throat. "I couldn't."

"I know, dearest. It is hard for me as well." She runs a comforting hand down Myrna's arm. "We will speak more on the subject, but first it's time to show a united front. Regardless of your disheveled state, I need you by my side, for it's time to get our Theia back."

Laoise stands taller, royal in her elegance. Myrna's shoulders straighten, her reaction nearly the same. And, as if there is no other way this is to occur, Myrna links her arm with Laoise's and says, "Let's go find out where our missing family member is, shall we?"

There's something in the youngling's tone, which has Laoise's lip curling with wicked glee. Perhaps it's how much it sounds like Theia, so powerful and sure, or maybe it is how the tone hints of the ruler she will one day become.

Laoise takes a steadying breath, shallow enough no one will notice, but inside, it helps settle the emotion boiling within. For this man has her sister and would end her people if given the chance. What he does not seem to understand is Laoise will burn the world down to protect them all.

"Be steady, my child," Laoise says.

Myrna inclines her head. "And never expose your hand. Stand firm."

"Strike when all your pieces are in place," Laoise purrs. "That's right."

Only Myrna, Kelan, and Laoise enter the Mirror Room—Myrna to Laoise's right, Kelan to her left. The others stay beyond, outside the visibility of The Mirror of Connection. Their expressions are grim as they watch.

The male in question reclines upon his throne. He's screaming at Leaf, demanding the queen's presence immediately—the boorish ass—and it's only when they appear that Brennan calms. He smirks, his gaze traveling across the females.

Laoise's stomach turns, bees rummaging in her gut, for this is the first time Brennan has seen Myrna. She does not care for the way he examines her so closely. Will he see what others have missed?

The air becomes heavy with Myrna's unease. Laoise places her hand over the child's upon her arm, and the tension lifts.

"Brennan," Laoise snaps, "that is no way to speak to my staff." Almost as quick as the slash of her hand, Leaf disappears from the mirror's view. "Additionally, I have received some unhappy news, for which you must explain yourself."

The low, menacing chuckle comes from not just Brennan, but his nephew and appointed heir, Prince Colum. He stands over his left shoulder, the tilt of his head throwing shadows over his face and making him look deranged. To the right stands his niece and Marshal to the Throne, Princess Imogen.

Interesting. She never appears. Her military role and title are nothing but lies. A title used to cover the likely mistreatment of a power-hungry king.

Myrna's fingers flex at the sight of her.

"We have much to discuss, my queen." He steeples his fingers. "For it seems you have been keeping a secret. One no one would've guessed." His gaze moves to Myrna.

Baring her teeth in what one might believe is a smile, Laoise asks, "Where is she? Return her to me unharmed or—"

"Who?" Brennan asks with a false sweetness. "All we found was a ghost."

"You step too far, Brennan. Kidnapping a member of the Qhuinn line is a declaration of war. Is that what you're after?" Laoise glares at him through her eyelashes.

Brennan lays his hand to his breastbone. "War? But how could I have such a person?"

"Stop the charade," Myrna speaks up. Laoise tightens her hold on the child, but she continues anyway. "We know you received information from someone within our court. Information that Princess Mareola was alive and had gone into hiding to raise a child. Me."

The massive man leans to the right, resting on the arm of his throne. "I may have heard such, but it is the more concerning part that you, child, are in fact hers and not our dear queen's that interests me."

"And why does this matter, King? Either way I am heir, same as Colum is to you."

Laoise's grip loosens as she looks at Myrna. The youngling's expression is calm, unperturbed at speaking with such a powerful being. It is both impressive and stupid.

"So, it is true?"

"I did not say that. I simply point out that your argument for attacking the Seelie Court is invalid. Yes, I was raised in the human world by Princess Mareola, but her withdrawal from society was due to an injury and"—Myrna glances at Laoise—"my mother's wish to raise me in a quieter, safer environment. This information was already given to you."

"You lie," Brennan growls. "You are Mareola's, and your father was of our court, which means you are required to spend time here as well! That is why they hid you from us."

Without hesitation, Myrna responds, "My father, the male who raised me, was killed this very day by your own people. My guess by your nephew." Her chin lifts to indicate Colum. When she speaks again, there is pain. "Guardian Tomas died protecting her, in my childhood home, at the hands of your people."

Laoise cannot decide if she hurts for the girl or wishes to smile. This is brilliant, for there is truth in these words. Tomas is the closest thing to a father Myrna had. Always, there is a protector and confidant, trainer and role model.

Laoise allows Myrna to pull away even as she takes a step forward. She's done well so far; weaving this believable lie. "King Brennan, you may claim offense that my queen lies, but you are the one who has lied. You are the one who is broken the accords—the law set forth by our people for peace. Over and over, you claim peace, but in truth, all you crave is dominion."

A breeze ruffles the skirts of Laoise's gown.

"I will prove you are one of us. Then I will show you what true dominion is."

A deep menacing reverberation rattles Laoise's chest. A second echoes from Kelan.

Myrna grins, but there's too much snark for it to be kind. "I am of the Qhuinn line."

Power fills the room. It reaches toward the mirror. It smells of her warm vanilla, but now, there's a new scent—baked citrus.

The perspective of the image shifts as Brennan stands. His head tilts as he approaches the mirror.

Behind him, Imogen, normally so statuesque, crosses her arms, flashing her wrist. A mark shimmers on her skin. It's a symbol of the old language, which sends a tendril of warning through Laoise.

Almost instantly, Myrna links her hands before her, and it's as if they share a thought, for mirrored expressions flash across their faces.

What is happening here? She's unsure, but Laoise does catch the faint glimmer of the same sheen through Myrna's fingers at her wrist. *What have you been up to, dearest?*

Either way, the way Brennan's nose flickers does not sit well. Laoise captures Myrna's hand and tugs her back.

"Whatever information you received," Laoise says, taking over, "you were misinformed. Now return my sister."

"There's something different about this youngling. I can sense it even from here, Laoise. I am going to find out what it is." This sounds more like a threat. Brennan rubs his hands together, beginning to pace back and forth in front of his throne. "And the best place to discover it is from the person who raised her. But don't worry, she's safe and secure. No one can get to her."

It's as if a thousand redcaps are draining the blood from her all at once. The long extinct creatures are back to pull her to hell as she waits for the anvil to fall.

"Return Mareola, Brennan. I warn you."

"I cannot. Not yet. It's all right, though. She's secure in Merizalmek, and soon, we'll all know the truth. And when I'm done, I'll return what's left."

A blast of pure arcane explodes from Laoise like a bomb.

Myrna steadies herself, but barely. Other items in the room are not so lucky. A table blows apart, tapestries yank from the walls, and onlookers fall to their backsides, skidding along the floor.

"A member of the Royal House of Qhuinn does not belong in Merizalmek!" Teeth bared, red fire lighting her palms, she snarls, "How dare you!"

Laoise stalks forward. Perhaps she's angry enough to activate the mirror as a portal and kill the king once and for all.

"Release her or I swear you will have all of my court bearing down on you within a fortnight. And should she be harmed, we will take down every brick until there is nothing left."

The slow maniacal grin tells Laoise that she reacted exactly how he'd hoped. That this has been the game the entire time. *Knights.*

"Agree to the terms of the heir exchange and allow Princess Myrna to come learn our ways as is our custom, and I'll return Mareola unharmed. I just wish to verify Faerie is in the best hands, that your court is in the best of hands. Myrna would be perfectly safe."

Lies! Brennan destroys his own family. Tortures them. Kills them, for anyone he sees as a threat has an "accident." He killed Prince Reece for loving Mareola. It had nearly killed her sister in return. And should Myrna go to his court, there would be no way to hide the truth of what Myrna is.

Someone pulls Laoise back from the brink with one gentle hand.

Myrna's calm voice says, "You go about this the wrong way. You've kidnapped one of ours, expecting me to willingly come to you. How can we believe that my safety would be protected? This is not how this is done. You, Brennan, have lost your touch." Myrna bows, a sweet smile on her face, firm against his curious glare. "But do not worry, I will teach you."

Myrna reaches out and sends a burst of her arcane through the Mirror of Connection. The image of King Brennan and the others disappears.

Laoise's mouth drops open, her fury suddenly gone. She laughs. It feels like the first time she's laughed in forever. "Darling child, did you just tell King Brennan you were going to teach him?"

"It's been a long day. And I'm pretty sure that is not the only stupid thing I've said today."

"Well, you definitely have him confused. Gave us more time, at least."

"That's my hope." Myrna stares off for a moment, her eyes glazing over. Laoise is about to shake her from it, then she shakes her head. "Sorry. Which leads me to my next question. Do you approve a rescue mission?"

The world spins, and Laoise applies pressure to her stomach. The motion does two things—it settles the universe and hides the trembling of her hands. Laoise takes in the stubborn child and braces herself for the backlash the next words will cause. "The Merizalmek prison is one of Legend. There is no getting into it."

The response is slow. Heat raising from the floor, spiraling up to blow back her hair and pushing her already burning eyes over the edge. Tears glitter and fall.

"You're giving up?" The words are a menacing howl filled with power.

"No, but you need rest, and there is much to research. Tomorrow we'll discuss everything, including this." Laoise grabs Myrna's forearm and holds it up to the light. She curses when the barely there shimmer of a long-dead language sparkles in the light. *Foolish child.* "Until then, there will be no rescue. We cannot attempt one without all the information. Now, go to your room. I'll have a healer sent to you."

CHAPTER FORTY-FIVE

Collapse is Sometimes Needed to Build Again

"WE'LL FIGURE THIS OUT," Kelan whispers against Myrna's ear.

The comforting caress of his hand on her back does nothing to make the news they just received better. Nor does the room full of her friends and confidants. Though, it surprises her how many have stayed. Shay and Sam sit on the couch, sharing the plate of fruit. Jaden and Briana are at the table playing a game of tiles. Declan's reading a book while Isaiah leans against a windowsill. Never has she felt so supported and so alone at the same time.

A lump forms in her throat, and it pisses Myrna off. *Get a grip and stop being a baby.*

But how can she?

All attentions shift and their knowing stares are too much. She lowers herself into the closest chair, a ragged breath turning into a sob.

"Laoise was very detailed in her orders this time," Kelan says, his gentle hand caressing her shoulder now. "Due to the complexity of the Merizalmek prison, there is to be no attack on it. Therefore, no rescue mission is to be attempted by our court and, should *anyone* attempt it, it will be grounds for immediate and severe punishment."

Myrna covers her face, unable to contain her reaction. "There are no loopholes. She didn't just order Kelan or the guards. She ordered me as well." Myrna hiccups before continuing, "'No one shall attempt to break into Merizalmek, as it's impenetrable by all knowledge and reports, and the magic inside this is as alive as Faerie itself.'"

Sam kneels at Myrna's knee. "Honey, I'm so sorry. Then what's her plan?"

Kelan answers. "The queen indicates she's waiting on responses from some other allies. She's also meeting with the king again, but I doubt much will change in that regard. We know what he wants."

"He can't have Myrna," Shay says, his arms crossed over his large chest.

"No, he can't," Kelan seconds.

The conversation continues, but to Myrna, it fades away. With each word, she sinks further into the chair, her heart squeezing as if the king's hands are the ones tightening around it. *What's happening to Theia while they wait?*

Myrna's skin prickles as images of her childhood, them together, filter through her mind. Theia's hugs each night as she tucked Myrna in so tight. Her obsessive protectiveness that never felt confining. Not the way Laoise's did. Snuggles on the couch, painting flowers on the porch, laughter as they trained for battle. Each memory is filled with joy and love. *Always love.*

Knocking Kelan away, Myrna rises to her feet so fast Sam falls to her butt. Myrna rubs her eye as she says, "I should have known!"

Rushing to her bedchamber, she buries her face in the covers to hide the tears flowing down her cheeks. It is improper for the others to see her like this—breaking down and no longer in control. Or that's what Laoise would say.

"Myr?" Sam and Shay say.

Steps follow, and she winces when Kelan says, "Give us a minute."

Technically, there is no door between the main room and the bedchamber. She won't ask them to leave. She's too lost in her grief. And anyway, it's fine. They don't judge, understanding she needs a moment of space, for these days have been a lot.

The truth of my family. The rescue attempt. Negotiations with the queen. Hell, your time as the princess in general!

A weight settles next to Myrna. She doesn't acknowledge it, just lets him remain. Then, when he reaches out and rubs her back, she takes the comfort he offers. Always.

"You didn't fail."

She winces. *How does he always know?*

He tugs her shoulder, a gentle request to turn over.

With reluctance, she does. His calm expression helps settle her. She squeezes Kelan's forearm as if it will hold her steady.

The tear-soaked hair fights as he peels it from her cheek. "You've been alone a long time. When you came here, you were so afraid you wouldn't fit in. That we'd—what did you say?—realize you were a fraud."

The tears slow, but it takes the muscles in her chest longer to respond to the cadence of his voice.

"Do you not see that room? The people dedicated to you? You've done more in your short time here than I ever expected. You've started to change whether you're aware of it or not. And when we get Theia back, I know you'll continue to surprise me."

"When we get Theia back?"

He pulls her to a seated position, bringing them closer. Inches separate them. "Do you know why Laoise refuses the mission?"

Hard right turn, but Myrna'd go with it.

"You know I knew both Laoise and Theia when we were children, and, although I was closer to Mareola, I was friends with Laoise, too."

Myrna stays perfectly still.

"She's always been strong willed, but I think that's more because so many, like you, rejected her. She was to be queen, and so, she was to be respected—feared. They treated her differently than her sister, refusing to get to know the real her. So, when Theia died, she mourned not just the loss of her sister, but...in my eyes, a loss of her freedom as well."

Myrna thought about those words. Their meaning reached deeper than expected. Crossing her ankles, she tucks her feet beneath her. It brings their faces even closer.

"You coming here? It opened her back up. Which is why she refuses the mission, not because the odds are stacked against us, but because she doesn't want to lose you like she lost her sister. Should she lose you both? I think it would break her."

Myrna's shoulders sag. "Oh...but how can she just sit by and leave Theia to that fate?"

"I doubt she is. Laoise's clever. I suspect she's planning as we speak."

Heat rises against her will all over again. "But she refused, Kelan. She ordered us to stay behind! She said—"

"She said we couldn't break in."

Myrna freezes. She scowls as she rolls over the inflections used in that single sentence. There's meaning there. *What am I missing? What piece can't I see?*

"Luckily, we don't have to," Kelan says, the corner of his mouth lifting.

Words swirl in her mind, but they don't fit together.

Then, the emotion of the last few days mix, and it's like they form a picture. She lets out a soft, "Oh."

Myrna throws her arms around Kelan's neck. They tilt back, but he steadies them. "How did I not...I can't believe I didn't..."

Kelan smirks. "I figured that's why you didn't tell the queen about the Shadowspire. That you saw the loophole and were going to use it."

"No. I-I was just mad. She was so decisive right when we entered. 'You will not go'...blah blah blah." Myrna rolls her eyes. His lips turn up at her antics; how quickly her mood shifts. "I started arguing and so when she asked what happened yesterday, I didn't want to tell her. She didn't deserve to know."

Never has she felt something so wonderful as his hand on her cheek. "Well, then, we aren't out of options. But Myr, never give up hope. Ever."

Sam appears in the archway. "How's it going in here?"

The small drop in her stomach when his touch disappears is a little too telling.

"Yeah." Slipping out of bed, Myrna grabs Kelan's hand and drags him to the door. "Actually, Kelan realized we aren't out of this yet."

The three of them join the group, where she apologizes for her outburst.

"That was nothing compared to Briana's fits on the regular," Jaden says, expression flat. Without a glance in Briana's direction, he dodges the figurine she chucks at him.

Still, Myrna can't help but carry the embarrassment.

Kelan explains what really happened in the meeting with the queen. How when they entered, Myrna didn't even have a chance to say "good morning" before Laoise nixed the mission and any hope of going after Mareola.

"Wait, so you didn't tell her you could create portals?" Declan asks.

"No, not intentionally. I was so mad. By the time she asked, I wasn't willing to speak about anything, let alone the new things I learned. I'm supposed to debrief on everything later."

"What exactly did you learn?" Shay asks. "We haven't really had time to talk about it."

That's a fair question. Perhaps it's time to tell the whole story.

Myrna eyes those in attendance, stopping on those who hadn't been on the mission. "Jaden. Isaiah. I'm not sure you should be here for this. The less you know, the better."

"Princess, we wanted to be on that battlefield with you." Jaden moves to the back of the couch and leans on it. His muscles flex. "The reason we didn't join is because someone had to stay behind to keep your departure quiet for as long as possible."

Myrna accepts their choice. She looks to Kelan, who scans the group; then, after a moment, meets her eyes and nods. It's as if he says, *"These are the ones we can trust."*

So, Myrna recounts the story, starting with her near death during the fight, only thwarted by Kelan's appearance. Then, she moves to the odd change in her arcane amplified when she witnessed Sam's fight and Shay's injury.

"Something happened. My white fire was taken over, mixed with something else. Violet and citrus, and starry nights. I was transported to an all-white room with a girl in it."

The group is enthralled, leaning into the story of a girl in a marble room and willing to help the enemy. She leaves out she's a captive herself. When she admits it was Imogen Murray, there's a generalized gasp. The confirmation that Myrna indeed has Shadowspire has lips parting.

"Per Imogen, there's really one person who could be my father, Prince Reece Murray. He had Transportational Shadowspire, too. The other princes were either dead or useless." Myrna's clothes become too tight, their shock locking their gazes to her, but Myrna continues anyway. She must get it all out, or she'll lock up forever.

When *Balance Beholden* and the connection is explained, the reaction to both their magics, the air itself doesn't dare move, for how could Imogen and Myrna not be connected by blood, but now by fate?

"When I touched it, it was like I downloaded hundreds of years of information," Myrna explains, "but each time I use the information—my Shadowspire—I feel some of it disappear. Now, many of the spells are like a memory just out of reach. Like a dream right after you wake, they're about to dissolve into the light of day."

Myrna shows them the emblem on her skin. It's faded, but definitely proof enough for them.

"Transporting all of you was harder. It took so much energy. I think that's why the power of the book's spell started to wane so quickly. When we got back, that's when that feeling of the memories disappearing started. It wasn't as easy the first time, but...I worry..."

"What?" Kelan asks from his seat beside her.

Myrna inhales, calm and slow. She closes her eyes and calls the arcane within her. Thinking of the words Imogen used about coaxing shadows forth instead of drawing the magic to her, she asks for the ancient power to appear. It does, strong and true, its violet light seeping free. But it's hard, and she pants as it collects in her palm. The weight of the others' eyes on her doesn't help.

Trying to remember the steps of creating the portal, Myrna squishes her palms together, the shadow connecting and molding. But the textures and taste against her skin feels different. It vibrates, tingling. As she starts to pull it apart, it fights, not as malleable as before.

"Something's wrong. I can't reach it like before," Myrna whispers. And then it snaps, and Myrna gasps, the strands of darkness whipping her skin and leaving burn marks across her biceps.

"You found the loophole, but I can't do it." Watery eyes meet Kelan's. "The only reason I was able to do it the first time was because of the book. I'm of no use."

Her wrist burns and a pinpoint needle of pain shoots into her ear just at the connection of her jaw. Myrna rubs at the spot. She groans as a voice fills her ear.

Myrna? What's going on? I can sense your distress. It's Imogen's voice.

"Holy shit," Myrna says aloud. The others frown, but Myrna's too focused on the literal voice in her head. Both aloud and in her head, Myrna says, "*Imogen? Is that you?*"

Acceptance and acknowledgment comes back as the others' expressions darken further. Myrna holds her hand up when Shay opens his mouth.

"Are. You. Okay?"

"*Yeah... freaking out a little. Laoise won't sanction a rescue mission, and I can't make a portal. The memories are fading, and I don't have enough practice to know what I'm doing. I'm useless.*"

Myrna refocuses on the people she can see. Kelan leans in, staring at her intently, but Shay doesn't get the hint. He's trying to make her feel better.

Meeting Kelan's eyes, she points to her wrist, then her head. Again, both aloud and to Imogen, she says, "*I don't know what to do. In order to get inside Merizalmek, I need to portal in, but when I try, it feels wrong. Tacky.*"

"*That's because you're pushing too hard. I can help with that, but Myrna, the bigger issue is, how do you portal into a place you haven't seen? That's not safe.*"

"Oh." Myrna blinks and straightens.

"What did she say?" Kelan says, and the others glance at him. They've gone silent, realizing something crazy's happening, but clearly not catching up as quickly as he has.

"She makes a good point. How do I portal into a place I haven't seen?"

"Imogen, have you been there? Do you have any pictures of it?"

A hard *"no"* comes through the connection from Imogen. *"Oh! And you should know Merizalmek doesn't allow arcane usage. It sets off the alarms, for obvious reasons—the prisoners could get out—but Grandfather made sure Shadowspire's okay."*

"You can speak to Imogen? From here?" Briana asks.

"Apparently." Myrna shrugs.

"Hey, Myr, if you need help training, let me know. I'll sneak out. Just send word. If I don't answer, let Braedon know."

"What? Why?" The panic in her voice has the others shifting.

"I got to go. Brennan's here, and he's angry."

"Imogen!" The connection cuts off. It is a hard snap, like she'd flipped a switch.

Myrna flinches, then meets Kelan's eye. The back of her eyes burn, her fists clenching, but Myrna knows there is nothing they can do for the young princess. Her chest rises faster than normal, and damn Kelan for seeing it all.

"What happened?" Sam asks.

Imogen deserves her privacy. "She says she's willing to set up a training session to help. We just need to send word of a time. If I can't get a hold of her through this"—she taps her temple—"then we send word to Braedon."

"Braedon?" Declan says. His tone is not kind. "That guy's an arse."

Kelan ignores him, though no one misses his agreement. "We'll need a place of neutral ground to practice. Somewhere we can guarantee safety for you both. I might have a place. Let me see if I can beef up the wards. Jaden, I'll need your help."

"Not a problem, Boss." Jaden nods from his position against the wall.

"Question," Shay asks, breaking the stand-off. "If the book beefed up her powers before, could it do it again?"

"I don't know." Myrna pops up, then runs to her room. She returns with the book in her hands, already opening it. "I don't think so. The symbol that was in here isn't there anymore. Perhaps it was a one-time use type spell?"

"What do we know of the book?" Briana asks.

Kelan leans back and crosses his leg. He rubs his cheek, and she can hear a soft scratching from the stubble. It makes her want to reach out and touch it. "It once belonged to Stephan's mother. She was terrifyingly powerful, but there was something off about the magic, too. I think we should summon him to see if he can give us more information."

"Jaden, can you do that while we solidify the story we're going to tell the queen about yesterday?" Kelan asks. With the way he looks at his old friend, Myrna can tell he's relieved Jaden is on their side. "It'll take him at least a day to get here, and we'll need him to cover while we're gone, anyway. Then you and I can set up the meeting place."

"Of course," Jaden says, and then exits the room.

"So, what's next?" Sam asks.

Declan leans heavily on the arm of the chair, one leg extended out before him. "We verify a story to tell the queen about yesterday. One we all use in the meeting with her tonight. Then, we find out as much information about this prison as we can because"—he looks Myrna dead in her eyes—"I assume you still want to rescue Mareola, right?"

"Absolutely." No hesitation from the princess.

"And everyone in here is dedicated to help Myrna in this task? Understanding this may lead to your death or exile." Declan scans the group.

One by one, they each confirm with a simple, "Yes."

"Then we make a plan. Who goes? Who stays? How we're proceeding. Then we collect supplies and get moving," Declan says, the venerable soldier coming out in his voice. It is the first real glimpse of the man he once was. It's remarkable.

The room stays silent as the entire group sits in the weight of all he outlined. The importance of all Declan proclaims. Then, it's as if they all wake up at once, and they move.

Papers for notes. Plans for the collection of supplies. Volunteering for runs, raids, or research. Ideas discussed of where information might be of the horrific prison that is Merizalmek.

CHAPTER FORTY-SIX

Shadowspire at Its Base

"ARE THE TREES REAL?" Myrna asks. She paces across the clearing filled with trees the color of fall. Orange and red, yellow and brown, they shift in color like some of the most remarkable places she's seen in the human world. But more, this room, hidden inside this strange section of Faerie, is massive in scale. Its sides and end not visible, but the roof and arches evenly spaced every hundred feet.

Kelan looks at her like she has three heads. "Of course they're real."

"Is the room, then?"

"Myrna..." Her name is a scold more than anything else, and it has the youngling rolling her eyes.

Perhaps it is an illusion caused by the shimmering fog which encircles them. A line of arcades a hundred feet high mark each side and rise so high the tips of the arches disappear into the low-hanging clouds. Occasionally, she gets a peek of the brocade covering the walls. It is happy, the fabric a bright, summery pattern.

Neutral ground, it seems, is meant to be a joyous place. A place where both parties can feel at rest. Though, from what Kelan says, it's rarely used. Owned by Haszwalds and linked through the thoroughfare on one of the many floors the Faye uses, this quiet place guaranties no harm will come to the other—where competing groups meet and discuss business without fear of retaliation from any outside political influence.

"What if our messages didn't get through? Or..." Myrna rubs the back of her arms.

"Or what?"

She couldn't hold it in any longer. "Imogen said Brennan was there and angry. What if he hurt her?"

Kelan goes still. Then, ever so slowly, he thaws once more. "She'll be fine. You've sent messages through your arcane before, plus you sent a message through your new link. Don't worry."

Myrna captures his words and holds them to her heart. She must, for the idea of Imogen hurt...

"It seems dangerous to have fog surrounding the clearing," Myrna says. "Wouldn't people be able to spy on you?"

"No." Kelan leans against the closest tree. His nonchalance is almost irritating. "It's enchanted. It inhibits such things. You're unable to see into the clearing until you've stepped within."

"Exactly!" a familiar voice says from the far end.

Myrna spins on her heel, a wide grin appearing at the sight of her cousin. When she goes to step forward, Kelan stops her.

Braedon appears, his expression sour and hand convulsing near the blade at his waist.

"He knows the rules. Wait until we can see all of whom is with her. Do not approach her until she's past the stone line."

"Did you have any problems getting out of the palace? What happened yesterday? Did they find out I was there?" The questions tumble out so fast the words flow into one another.

Kelan shoots her an amused look, then leads her toward a set of high-backed armchairs strategically placed in the very center of the clearing.

Imogen laughs and joins Myrna, Braedon at her side. "I'm fine. They didn't find out and getting out of the palace was...complicated, but we did it. It's nice to use my arcane again."

When Imogen's finally close enough, Myrna rushes forward and wraps her arms around her cousin.

Both Guardians startle, then exchange a shocked glance, especially when Imogen returns the hug with the same amount of enthusiasm.

"I was so worried. When I saw you on the screen behind Brennan, I thought he dragged you out to taunt me. And then yesterday...you scared me."

Imogen smiles so sweetly Myrna knows her concern means much. "Yesterday was nothing. I was able to defuse His Majesty. Do not worry."

Myrna looks to Braedon. "Does she lie?"

Braedon blinks. "Um...no. She speaks truth."

Then Myrna lets go of Imogen enough to lay a gentle hand on Braedon's arm. He jerks but doesn't pull away.

Kelan's at her back in a second but does nothing. He's there for support only. Yet, he's sucked in, watching as yet another person becomes trapped by the magic that is Myrna Qhuinn.

"Thank you, Guardian Braedon," Myrna says honestly. "I know you could've called the guards...done so much more"—she looks away—"but you didn't. You protected her. I'm so grateful because it wasn't her fault, and then today you helped."

Braedon scowls. His mouth drops open. It closes. Then, to Myrna's surprise, he bows. "Highness, first I say, it is Guardian Mac. We are not so informal as the Seelie."

"Oh! I'm sorry."

"No, don't be. It is only meant to inform should you come across one of us in the future. That said, you are welcome to refer to me as Imogen does. As Braedon." He glances at his princess. "Which is when I add, thank you for caring for my princess as I do. Few see her for the jewel she is."

Myrna hides her surprise and squeezes his arm before letting go. Then her attention is back on Imogen.

"Are you ready to get to work?" Imogen asks, her smile grateful.

"Yes, for the knowledge is gone."

"Aye." Imogen presses her lips together. "For me, too."

Her heart sinks. "How am I supposed to portal as I did before? Imogen, I'm not a skilled arcane user."

"Myrna," Kelan interrupts, "you are far more skilled than you give yourself credit for. Even before your connection to the book, you harnessed your arcane faster than ninety percent of the students I train."

Really? That is a compliment. But could she believe it?

"Seriously?" Braedon asks, and Kelan nods even as he glares.

No. Myrna plops down on the chair.

Braedon's eyebrow lifts at the unladylike gesture. "She's…"

"Like nothing you're ready for." It's not just Braedon who hears the truth and warning in the words. Myrna rolls her eyes.

"This is such a bad idea," Braedon mumbles under his breath as Kelan activates a spell which will lock the room to any intruders from either side. Should anyone approach, it will notify him.

"You know what I mean, Kelan." She looks at him like Briana once did in her teen years, an annoyed, petulant young woman. But where it made his sister look younger, this is the glare of a grown woman. There's challenge there. "I can't portal like I did. It was so easy, I could grasp it like I'd been doing it for centuries and now"—she rubs at her eyes—"it's like everything's gone, like the shadows disappeared."

"Then we start at the beginning. We get you calling your arcane again, have you mold it, and see if that triggers anything in you." Imogen lowers into the chair opposite Myrna. "Gentlemen, give us some space, if you please."

They do, spreading to opposite ends of the clearing.

Imogen smiles. "So, we know the book's spell connected us."

Myrna responds, "*In unexpected ways.*"

Imogen grins. "That's so cool."

Braedon glances between them as if he's, once again, out of the loop.

"Agreed, and it doesn't seem to be fading. But I wonder if there's some other part of the book's link we haven't discovered yet."

Imogen runs a hand over her bound hair. "There probably is. We'll figure it out, eventually. Until then, I think we start at the beginning of how Shadowspire works, then move up from there."

"Perfect."

Oh, so gracefully, Imogen half stands, grabs the underside of the chair, and crabwalks while dragging the chair forward until the two girls are a foot apart. Dust puffs into the air, and a track is left in the mud and moss from where the feet scrape into the earth.

She sits down again to the disgusted stares of both males, and says, "What?"

"We could've done that for you!" they say in unison.

She waves them off and faces Myrna, taking her hand. Myrna wants to laugh, but she holds it in. *Oh gods, I love her already.*

For the next hour, Imogen takes Myrna through the basics of Shadowspire. Drill after drill, she tests Myrna's control and her ability to coax the shadows within herself. Then, they move on to those which live in the world around them. This drains Myrna far more than any practice with the Radiant Light ever has. Why? No idea. Perhaps it's the way the shadow sits like tar against its host, unwilling to release. So, when it's called, it resists like glue nearly bonded.

"You've nearly got it. Now, I want to show you something more advanced," Imogen says. She stands and walks to the edge of the forest where shadows darken the space the farther one goes. "I told you my specialty is veils. That I can mask myself and others. It's both similar and different to yours, but I think seeing it may help you."

Imogen closes her eyes, then clasps her hands before her. Power fills the air, the shadows around the Unseelie Princess deepening as she calls them to her. Then, Imogen peels her hands apart, slides them up her body, over her face and head, then down her hair like a cape. As she does, the shadows cascade over her like silk flowing through a soft breeze. Then, from one second to the next, she just disappears, fading into the background.

Myrna shoots to her feet. "Holy crap! That's amazing!"

"The shadows alter their shape, drawing old magic held within their very makeup to hide me. They do so at my request, not my demand." There is nobody to go with the voice. Not until Imogen reappears.

"Your turn."

Myrna gulps. She tries to use the helpfully confusing tips Imogen gives her. *Don't use emotion, call with confidence and sternness, but don't be cruel. These are ancient creatures...but not creatures. This is not like Radiant Light, it is structured. Old.*

Nothing happens. She can't even get the shadow to collect. She attempts it a second time. They come, but they won't spread apart. It's like they don't want to listen, and the knowledge of how to keep them together and spread them apart has disappeared completely.

Myrna wipes at the sweat on her brow, frustration in her movements. She walks toward the table filled with water and snacks they brought, her legs a bit shaky. She grabs two of everything. "It's sealed, but should you wish me to taste it first, I will."

A low chuckle causes butterflies to appear in Myrna's stomach. She turns to Kelan, whose gaze is on Braedon. The man in question closes his mouth. *Ah, he's about to stop Imogen from eating. Understandable.*

"It's so much harder without *Balance Beholden.* I don't know if it's the knowledge or a spell I linked to, but it's like I can't connect at all."

Imogen shrugs, examining the packaging of the rather tasty travel bar the Faye has created, then takes a bite. Who said only humans saw the importance of portable food? "I'm sorry. Maybe if we reviewed the book?"

Myrna reaches under her chair and removes the book in question. As if able to sense the book just as Myrna can, Imogen's head tilts and her eyes glaze over. The two females smile in unison.

Suddenly, there's a loud buzzing. Myrna and Imogen cover their ears.

Braedon unsheathes his weapon—a crime here.

"Put that away!" Kelan orders the other Guardian. Then Kelan's eyes glaze over for a moment, and he grins. "That's the warning system. Your Highnesses, someone's just arrived who can help understand more about your special situation. But only if you approve."

It takes a minute for Myrna to catch on, but then she jumps to her feet with a squeal.

CHAPTER FORTY-SEVEN

Blood with an Arcane of Mirrored Core

"STEPHAN'S HERE? I THOUGHT it would take another day for him to arrive!" Myrna nearly trips on a rock on her way toward the fog, and Kelan can't help but find it endearing. Why she's befriended Stephan so wholeheartedly he can't guess, but he enjoys it immensely. But the feeling goes away when she freezes after Braedon speaks up.

"We agreed no one else would be here." His tone is dark with warning.

Holding her hands up, she grabs the book and waves it before saying, "You're right. Mostly because we didn't know he would be here, but Stephan was the one who gave me this. When I was human and *before* he knew who I was. When he found the book, he was compelled to bring it to me. His mother was the previous owner and since then, there's been no one for whom the book has spoken to. Until me and, apparently, Imogen."

Imogen's eyebrows nearly meet her hairline. She turns to Kelan. "Go get him. Now."

"But, Highness..."

"It'll be fine, Braedon. They mean us no harm. And we'll not be here much longer anyway."

"Yes, ma'am."

With a respectful bow to the three, Kelan disappears into the fog. His friend is in a joyous mood as they exit the mist, his laugh proceeding him into the room, but when he spots Myrna, his grin widens. Instantly—and to annoy her, Kelan is sure—Stephan pauses his stride and bows low.

"Highness," he says, waving his hand exaggeratedly.

Yup. Just to annoy her.

"Don't call me that," Myrna warns, a weak threat behind her words, especially as she runs to greet him, wrapping him in a hug.

"You're okay! We were so worried after the battle but heard that you got out unscathed after fighting Colum. Put on an impressive show of skill from what I heard"—Stephan elbows her in the side—"but I feel better seeing your smiling face."

Myrna ignores his compliments and instead continues to tug him forward. "Well, I'm awesome. Anyway, I have someone I want you to meet."

Stephan doesn't stumble or hesitate when he spots the princess of the Unseelie Court in their midst. In fact, he does the opposite. He drops Myrna's hand, executes a deep, respectful bow, then says, "Princess Murray, it is my unexpected honor. I am Lord Stephan O'Malley."

Nicely done, Stephan.

Imogen worries her lip, but she nods once.

Myrna moves forward and takes Imogen's arm. Kelan nearly laughs at Stephan's affronted expression.

"Myrna," Stephan scolds. "You should not be so informal. It's not like that in the other court, and you do not know her. Kelan, tell her!"

Both girls burst into laughter. They share a look, and Myrna says, "Stephan, Imogen is my cousin, she saved my life, got me back to Kelan, and um...*Balance Beholden* likes her."

Stephan's face goes blank, a dark emotion brewing within him that has both Guardians stepping closer.

Myrna's shoulder lifts. "Us, actually. Which is why we need your help."

"Oops." Imogen shrugs.

"I know I wasn't supposed to share the book with anyone. I'm sorry." Then, Myrna explains everything, even going so far as handing *Balance Beholden* back. By the time it's all done, every ounce of threatening energy has left his body. He takes a knee before Imogen.

"Thank you for helping my princess."

"She's family. The one of whom I like." Imogen smiles.

"She has that effect on people. Now, how can I help?"

"We're hoping you can give us more information about the book—its history, magics, anything. The tome from our court, the twin to this one, I was not able to sneak from the palace."

Kelan and Braedon move back to their spots, listening intently as Stephan replies. He goes into the basic history of how his mother got a hold of the book, how long she had it, what she used it for, et cetera. He talks for a long while, but the information is pretty basic. Almost nine hundred years. Found it discarded in a cave, as though someone had tried to dispose or hide it. To gain power of influence within Faerie. She tried to keep it hidden, he said, so that no one knew she had it in her possession. But the longer she kept it, the more she couldn't refuse its companionship.

Stephan presses his lips together, then reaches for Imogen's hand. "May I see the mark?"

Shifting uncomfortably, Imogen allows the contact.

He runs a gentle thumb over the opalescent mark and says, "I've seen these markings before, but never quite like this. When Mother performed spells from the book, they'd stain her skin red for a time. The more she used them, the worse it got. As she started to crave more power, they smelled of sulfur. They were never this color, nor did they feel this...pure."

He leans down and sniffs the princess's wrist. Myrna doesn't miss the shudder that runs through the girl. When he straightens, he glances curiously at Myrna. "It hints of your signature."

"You're kidding."

He takes Myrna's wrist, and Kelan has the urge to rip off his hand.

Whoa, Kelan.

"And yours does hers." Stephan releases her instantly and steps away.

"I guess that makes sense," Myrna says. "What did the page say? 'For worthy kin with matching hearts, speak thy tome to find connection like none before.'"

"Do you have the same draw as Myrna does to the book?"

Imogen's gaze locks on the worn cover. "There's so much knowledge in there. Endless chances to categorize the world. Could you imagine what that information could do to help our people?" There's a deadpan quality to her voice. As if this isn't an emotional thing, but just truth as one of a royal lineage. A duty.

"And you, Myrna?"

Myrna rubs her hands together. "I've read every page of that book. There's so much to decipher. Spells and histories that could teach us how to live to our fullest lives. I want to understand it all, for this information is an opportunity. A way to help others connect to Faerie again."

Kelan's eyebrow lifts as he makes eye contact with Stephan. He notices it, too. This gives him an idea.

Kelan steps forward and says, "Ladies, please stand across from one another."

They do, curiosity lighting their gazes. It's strange how even with her darker coloring, he recognizes the similarities between the two girls and not just in their appearances. Their personalities mirror each other, even if their demeanors are different. Almost as though they were raised together. Myrna is outwardly vibrant and exuberant, learned from her mother and aunt. She jokes openly with the sweet but stoic Imogen. Their mannerisms occasionally match. It's odd.

"Highness..."

"Please, Guardian Kelan, call me 'Imogen.'"

Kelan smiles gently. "Then I am 'Kelan,' in return." She smiles, and he continues, "You've trained for much longer than Myrna. As such, I can sense the way your power functions much better, even though I am closer to her. That said, I think there's something deeper we can learn here. Stephan, Braedon, watch and see if you can see the difference as well."

"Ladies, one at a time, will you please call your shadows?"

"Okay…" Myrna says, and she faces Imogen. Both girls draw in a breath and focus their arcane within them.

The difference is noticeable in an instant.

With a blank face, Imogen calls the shadows, and they listen, crawling across the floor, slithering until they sink into her skin. Soon, they appear on her palms and collect.

"Wow," Stephan says. "She's meticulous. Can you feel the cold beneath?"

"Yes," Kelan says.

Braedon shakes his head. "It feels like Imogen."

"Huh?" Imogen scowls.

Kelan nods. "It would, but now compare her arcane to Myrna."

Nervousness shows in the pinched corners of Myrna's eyes as she does the same, calling on the darkness of the room. As with Imogen, the shadows come willingly this time.

"Oh…" Braedon's eyebrows lift, and he steps closer. "That's incredible."

"What?" Myrna spins toward the Unseelie guard.

"There's a temperature to your magic, my friend," Stephan says. "I'm not sure if it's the way that you've been taught or something about you inherently, but—"

"Imogen's not cold!" Myrna snaps.

Stephan holds his hands up. "I meant no offense. In the time I've spent with her, there's nothing cold about her. What I mean is underneath. There's a scent—a signature—of cold. Darkness maybe. It makes sense."

"He's right," Braedon says. "You two read differently. Fire and ice."

Kelan shifts his weight. "Which is why, though her teachings help, they don't work as well. It also explains why the book connected you. You're two sides of the same coin."

"It's why the book chose them," Stephan says.

Imogen shakes her head. "I don't understand. Ice is of your court."

Lips pursed, Myrna says, "I think I do. Here, call the shadows again." Myrna holds her palms toward Imogen. She does the same, skin inches apart.

The darkness collects, traveling across the skin to their hands, then it reaches out. Myrna closes her eyes as the power lifts her heart. For something that used to scare her, it now feels warm and comforting. Though what changed it, she's not completely sure.

"It wants you…" Imogen says in a hazy voice.

Myrna bites her cheek, thinking about all the times she shared power with her mother and aunt, then presses her shadow to Imogen's. Both girls groan. They close their eyes as a burst of energy shoots through the room.

Kelan and Braedon stumble back as Stephan falls from his perch on the log. They rush to pull them apart but stop when they see both are smiling.

They need to leave here quickly. Someone might've felt that.

"Look at their wrists." Stephan jumps to his feet.

Where the sigil once glowed an opalescent white, now, the shadows from both collect and seep into it. Slowly, the color shifts, becoming a dark violet as it settles beneath the skin. Air rushes from between Myrna's teeth as Imogen grinds hers.

Light appears behind Imogen's golden irises. "Oh, Kelan's wrong."

"He usually is," Myrna whispers, and Stephan snickers.

Kelan moves to give them more room but stays ready to step in if they need it.

"He is also right," Imogen says. "We aren't opposites, but we are from different courts and train differently. So, the book connects to us in unique ways through the shadows and creates a circuit of connection between us. Time, memory, life, all have both stability and emotion in them. They require one to balance the other.

"And the way we've learned has shaped our signatures. You are a summer's fire—white fire." Imogen grins. "Yours expands, shifting with emotion and heat."

Myrna takes up the explanation. "And yours is the darkest winter. It's still, unmoving like the coldest night, pulling the heat from everything around it."

Imogen draws her shadows over her skin. They thin and stretch, covering her entire body. At first, Myrna doesn't believe there's enough to cover her, but they continue to move until every piece of Imogen's body's hidden beneath the darkness. "This step is similar to when you say you stretch the shadows like taffy. But my next step is different."

She lifts her chin, and through the bond, Myrna senses her cousin's will to solidify it. Imogen tells the shadow to hide her. *Hide her?* And before her eyes, they move across Imogen's skin and shimmer, allowing the girl before her to disappear from sight.

"I can feel it. Amazing." She holds her hands, but even that doesn't help her brain see the princess. "How are you a prisoner in your own home? How have you not escaped or—"

Kelan's thighs clench, Myrna's hand flies to her mouth, and Imogen flickers back into existence. Her eyes are downcast, and her cheeks flame red. "I *will kill Brennan for all he does.*"

"I'm so sorry. I shouldn't have..."

Imogen clears her throat, dropping Myrna's hands. "Were you able to feel the difference?"

"Im, I'm sorry." Myrna shoots a quick glance to Kelan and Stephan, who both stand stock still, their expressions neutral. The sadness in her eyes causes a twinge in his stomach that it shouldn't. She knew she's made a grave mistake. It was her fault, not his.

Imogen looks up at Myrna. "They already knew, Myrna. They're not stupid." She reaches up and brushes the tear Myrna hadn't realized she'd let fall. "Now, are you ready to try?"

Myrna shrugs, still sad.

"You burn hot with emotion and flow more openly than I do. I was trying to hold you in a box. I think your Shadowspire needs to be less contained. Instead of trying to do what you think you should, feel it."

Myrna blinks. "You said Father always went where he needed to go. That sounds more emotion based than structure based."

"He never believed that the arcane was meant to be held by one ideology. Any of them."

A sudden ache in her chest has Myrna rubbing her breastbone. "I don't think so, either."

"Then stop trying to fit into what others want you to be. Listen to their advice, and love them for it, but find your own path."

Imogen squeezes Myrna's arm. "Now, stop being afraid of your power and create a damn portal."

Myrna's afraid of her power? Is she?

With a deep breath to steady herself, Myrna shakes out her hands. "Find my own path."

She calls the shadows together one last time. Fascinatingly, they trail behind her as she walks a circle around the room, then collect up her legs and into her hands. It's the largest collection Kelan has ever seen. Slowly, a ball grows between her fingers. Then, she claps her hands together and pulls her hands apart like two paddles drawing sugared candy in a store.

With each pass, the strands became softer, longer.

Back at Kelan's side, Myrna makes a circle with her hands and creates a portal as if it is nothing. The image of her bedroom inside the palace appears, Sam and Shay playing a card game on the other side.

Knights.

"Is that a human?" Imogen asks.

"Yeah." Myrna laughs without humor. "She's my best friend. Both of them are, actually. She is the one who got hurt when I activated my Shadowspire."

"That's Sam?"

"Yup. And I don't want to send her back unprotected while injured. She's not really safe here though, either."

"She's lucky to have you."

Sam looks up, her eyes narrowing in on Myrna. She opens her mouth as if to say something. Before she has the chance, Myrna closes the portal.

Kelan joins them. "I knew you'd get it. But we still need to unravel the book, especially considering the mark solidified."

Imogen rubs at the mark, which is about the size of a silver dollar. Her throat moves, and she shares a long look with Braedon.

"Yours is different than mine," Myrna says. "Yours has one line swooped upward where mine's straight."

Stephan opens *Balance Beholden.*

Not caring about personal space, Imogen flips to the page where the mark had been. Myrna and Imogen reach out to touch the page at the exact same time.

Words appear where the symbol had once been.

With respect comes connection. Connection creates a bond. With a bond comes knowledge. But with knowledge comes a weight to bear. Together, it becomes easier.

Imogen and Myrna's eyes meet, then they glance down at their wrists once more.

"The knowledge is to come back..."

Myrna's head moves up and down slowly.

"And it's going to be hard?"

"That's how I read it too," Myrna whispers.

"Okay... Well, at least we don't have anything else going on."

Myrna laughs, turns, and gives Imogen a hug. "We need to get you back to the palace. You've been gone way too long."

"Yeah."

"Are you sure you can't come live with me?" Braedon growls, so Myrna holds her hands up before adding, "Okay, okay, big guy. You can have her back."

His lip twitches, but he doesn't smile.

They say their goodbyes, but Imogen refuses a portal, saying she can't guarantee someone won't be waiting for her. And, as Myrna doesn't know the palace, she can't send her anywhere else. It kills Myrna to send her back to the castle, especially with that mark on her wrist so visible and nearly identical to hers.

Chapter Forty-Eight

No Time to Waste

"Hey, Myrna."

Myrna rubs her eyes and pushes up from the bed, Imogen's voice waking her. After returning to the castle from training with Imogen, she'd been exhausted. So, Kelan and Sam bullied her into resting, seeing as they needed her in top form.

"Yeah, Im. I'm up. What's going on?"

"I've been called into a meeting with the king. He's going over the attack with Colum and me." Imogen does not sound happy. *"He brings us in when he considers it a "learning opportunity," or we'll be needed to provide strategic support. He may hate me, but I'm still technically royal."*

As she speaks, Myrna rolls to the edge of the bed and stretches. The others notice her, and Kelan heads her way.

"You provide strategic support?"

"In the past? Of course. You're the enemy."

Myrna wants to laugh at the lack of intonation in her voice because Myrna can also hear a sense of distaste in the admission. Imogen hadn't liked the task.

"Thanks. Keep me updated."

Then, surprise flickers on her and an image flashes through her mind. A picture of a book. No...a map.

"What the hell was that?" she asks Imogen. *"Are you reading a book? Wait, did you just send me an image?"*

"You look like you've seen a ghost," Kelan says.

Myrna's mouth is agape as she meets his eye. "No…"

"I think I just found an old map to Merizalmek. It's the receiving room or something. The—"

Just then, Shay and Isaiah rush back into the room. The door slams as they shut it, making Myrna jump. Kelan makes a face as they nearly trip in excitement.

"We found something," Shay says, pulling a book from his pocket. "It's not much, granted, but it's something."

Shay sits on the bed, and Kelan smacks him on the back of the head. The boy jumps up immediately. "Perhaps we look at it at the table?"

Myrna rolls her eyes, grabs Kelan's arm, and pulls him along.

The binding's falling apart, the pages burnt at the edges. "This bad boy outlines a ton about the prison. A lot of it we already knew from some of the other archives; the shifting layout, the poison gas, arcane sets off all the alarms, and a crazy list of creatures roaming the halls. Though none state any actual detail of the creatures or the threat they cause."

"Probably because there are no survivors that make it out," Declan says, joining them.

"Probably," Isaiah agrees. "But this book has one additional thing."

"And that is?" Myrna asks.

Going back to the tattered book, Shay flips through the pages, then opens to an image of a room so beautifully drawn it's hard to believe it's a sketch. The detail is remarkable. It looks real. Devastatingly, creepily real—a nightmare come to life. It's the image of the inside of the prison.

"I thought you said no one's ever made it out," Myrna says.

"Based on this, someone did." Kelan leans on the table to get a closer look. "And they documented it."

"Turn the page," Imogen says.

She must've sent what she's seeing by accident. Myrna flips it, but there's a page missing.

"There are apparently two copies, for I have the other, but mine has the opposite page missing."

"How do you know it's the same?"

"The page before and after is identical," Imogen says.

"Knights." All eyes turn to Myrna. She runs a finger along the torn section. "Guys, we have what we need. Imogen has the same book, but with the first part of the map to Merizalmek."

No one moves. It's too shocking. How can this be?

"This is the reference image." Myrna scans the group, then says, "It's time. We need to complete the plan."

Her friends look at her with determined eyes, loyalty and trust shining as they outline all the preparations they've made.

"We've collected supplies; food, weapons, medical kits, all under the nose of the queen and her people," Briana says.

"They've been separated and are ready at a moment's notice. Clean, unmarked armored tunics are ready for each of us going," Declan adds. "We'll get changed whenever you're ready."

"Stephan took Sam back to Haszwalds and will keep her safe until we know Brennan's no longer a threat." Isaiah shifts back and scowls. "I'll join him. On the way, I'll spread news that you've all returned to your homes."

"Which leaves me, Briana, my father, Kelan, and Jaden with you on the mission." Shay marks the page and closes the book. "If you've got the layout, then we have what we need."

"I still wish you'd stay and watch your sisters," Declan mutters, to which Shay groans.

Kelan mumbles under his breath, "As I wish Myrna would stay."

Myrna's brain stutters, unsure she really heard those words.

"I'm sorry, what?" Myrna bolts upright.

Kelan looks anywhere but at her as the room heats with arcane power.

Myrna barely hears someone say, "Did he just?"

"Yup." Shay nods slowly.

Myrna grabs Kelan's arm, forcing him to look at her. "What did you say?"

"I didn't mean—"

"Yes, you did! Kelan, what the hell? You just think you're going to walk in there and magically poof back out when you find Theia?"

"No." Kelan clicks his tongue. He walks away, then stomps back until all there is, is the heat radiating off her. "But Brennan must have a portal there. Maybe we could use it and not have such a liability with us."

"Whoa... Seriously, Kelan?" Briana says from somewhere off in the distance.

Myrna's power rises, her face a mask of hurt and anger. "I can't believe what I'm hearing. Do you think I can't do it? Is that it?"

"What? No!" Kelan yells. His arms flail before he digs them deep into his hair. "You need your rest. You need to be protected."

"Wrong thing to say..." Shay says. The boy yelps as Declan smacks the back of his head. "Ow, twice. Really?"

"Stop saying that! I can protect myself. You just don't believe in me." She's yelling now, too. "I thought we were over this."

Kelan shoves in so close their faces nearly touch. "Myrna, you're remarkable. I know you can create a portal and hold your own. Why can't you see I have every faith in you?"

All the arcane in the room disappears. Myrna freezes, her face scrunched in confusion. "Then what is it?"

"You're everything your mother and aunt have made you. You're more." He closes his eyes, glances away, then refocuses on her. Myrna waits in bated silence. "You're too important, and I can't imagine losing you."

Kelan's let his guard down in front of everyone. He's shown her everything—even his heart.

She's aware of the room going silent. Her heart beats so very hard for him. But could she allow this? Their relationship is so complicated, and yet, he is...everything.

"Ugh!" Myrna screams, making everyone jump. "You're so frustrating!"

Myrna grabs the back of his neck and pulls his lips to hers. He drags her to him; one hand finding her lower back, the other cupping her cheek. When Kelan moans deep in his throat, a full body shiver has her pressing closer. His lips are heaven as they master hers. Never has anyone kissed her like she's the most precious thing in the universe. She could get lost in this.

Home.

Getting ahold of herself, she pulls away, then lifts her thumb to rub it over his bottom lip. It's his turn to shudder. To Myrna's appreciation, the group has all dispersed to the front sitting area. So, she doesn't hesitate to continue the intimate exchange.

"I'm going. You may not like it, but I'll not leave you with no way out. I will be as safe as possible"—she brushes his hair back—"if you agree to do the same."

He leans in to whisper in her ear. "I do. And I vow to keep both you and the boy safe."

She sighs and lays one last peck on his lips. "Do not make promises you cannot keep."

Closing her eyes, she rests her forehead against his for one steadying breath. They part, the loss of his heat harder than she can admit. She picks up her black tunic and her weapons, then heads to the bathing chamber while he moves to join the others. Perhaps the real reason she retreats is for the minute break to gather herself after that kiss. Because damn. Myrna licks her lips.

While she's there, she reaches back out to Imogen and gets the image one more time just to make sure she has it memorized. When she joins the others, the bags with supplies and weapons are spread between them. They speak softly, already in their battle wear.

Upon her appearance, they go silent. It's Briana who says, "Everything all right, my princess?"

It's the sly smirk that has Kelan shaking his head. "Let it lie, sister."

The others chuckle, but don't speak up.

Myrna's face heats. "Um...So, are we ready to go?"

They all nod, and Isaiah says, "I'll head out once you're gone."

"Then, let's do this." And with no warning, she draws on her arcane and summons the portal. She's about halfway there when banging starts at the door. Panic tightens her shoulders and the violet in her hands flickers.

"Keep going," Kelan demands. "We've got it bolted!"

Damn her for losing her temper! Her energy use probably set off Laoise's warning bells. Then, when Laoise sensed the Shadowspire, she came right over.

Myrna refocuses, doubling down on what she's doing as Declan, Briana, Kelan, Shay, and Jaden skate closer.

"Open this door, Myrna." It's Laoise's irate voice this time. Deadly even. "I do not know how you've managed it as these rooms are warded against them, but I can sense the portal magic. You will not go through! That is an order! I will not lose you too!"

It's enough to rattle the hardest forged soldier. Yet, it does the opposite. Myrna stands taller, her jaw hardens, and she snarls; the hurt at Laoise's choice evolving into determination. The portal opens to show the room from the book. Myrna puts one foot through to hold it. Then she gestures for them to move.

The doors fly off the hinges, slamming into the ground and shoving her seating area into the walls. The coffee table crunches, and Briana has to jump out of the way.

"Go!" Kelan shoves Declan and then Shay through the doorway. Kelan steps through, Briana right on his tail, but a stream of red fire slams into her side, knocking her to the floor.

Briana screams, sliding, her body curled as she falls feet away. She cradles her side.

Jaden, too, is hit by one of Laoise's attacks. He slams against the wall, falling to the floor in a lump. His chin hits his chest.

"You'd rather attack us than let us save our own?" *Who is this female?* Myrna sweeps her arms in a circle, keeping the arcane strong and in place.

"You have no idea what you're doing, child."

"Yes. I do." She narrows her gaze on the woman she once loved as a mother. No longer. For this creature is not the same person. "I'm going to meet Grandfather dearest, save my *mother*, and then I'm going to end him."

Myrna steps through.

She snaps her fingers together, and the portal closes on the terrified expression of Queen Laoise of the Court of the Radiant Sun.

CHAPTER FORTY-NINE

Merizalmek

KELAN'S GRIP DIGS PAINFULLY into Myrna's shoulders. "Did you just say you plan to kill the king?"

"What?" Myrna says, amused. He's surprised.

"You've no idea what that'd do, what repercussions it will have on Faerie. Let alone the fact that you aren't strong enough!"

"Are you telling me he doesn't deserve it, or you wouldn't do it if given the opportunity? King Brennan's a plague."

Kelan's hands drop, and his face stills.

"That's what I thought. So don't give me that shit." She steps away, the hairs on her arms standing up as she takes in the room.

It's as scary as she thought it'd be. Walls made of bone, but none that match. Or perhaps they do. Only the person who'd put the puzzle together didn't know themselves which pieces fit together. More concerning is the flesh which still graces the occasional piece. Flesh or leather, the scent permeates regardless.

Shay and Declan wave them over. They crouch behind an ancient stone sarcophagus, Declan tapping his ear.

A soft scraping echoes from around the corner.

Scraaape. Thunk. Tink. Scraaape. Thunk. Tink. It's an uneven gait of metal scraping against stone.

Over and over, it repeats until the oddest creature Myrna's ever seen passes the door. Short and thick, with prominent teeth and wrinkles that make its face look as though he's melting. The long nose and large, fiery red eyes are barely visible through the grisly hair, which streams down to his shoulders. Skinny fingers, which sharpen like an eagle's talons, hold a pikestaff.

Myrna squeaks and before she realizes what's happening, Declan's thrown a hand over her mouth. He presses a finger to his lips. He's breathing hard, and he's gone pale. That alone has her blood stopping in her veins. Never has she seen either of these men scared. Not like this. Her head jerks in quick acknowledgment, and he releases her.

"What are they?" she mouths.

"Redcap." Not even the air moves with the word.

The redcap stops at the door, and the four of them hold their breath. He looks around, raises his head into the air, and sniffs.

In the past, Myrna was the one who gave them away, the control over her arcane not yet absolute. It's worse when she's nervous. Kelan's concerned stare confirms it, so she takes a shaky breath, slowing the inhale to focus within herself.

Myrna, the best way to remove the excess power is to imagine a piece of cheesecloth passing through the body, the memory of Kelan says. It made little sense at first, but after working with Imogen, the pieces fell into place. It's about understanding oneself, not being afraid of the power within. Seeing it as a part of her and not a separate entity.

Myrna traps the excess arcane in her imaginary cheesecloth until every rogue molecule is bound at her center. Then, she mentally wraps the ends around the ball she's created, a second layer of protection to shield her signature.

When she opens her eyes, Kelan looks at her with pride. Whereas Declan's spun to see if she is still there.

Over the edge of the sarcophagus, the creature grunts, confused, shakes his head, and moves on. The lumbering gait of his iron shoes sends that same warning through her because, regardless of his ancient stature, that thing is deadly.

They wait until his steps have faded before Declan says, "Well done. Your signature's disappeared completely. That takes centuries for most to master."

"Yes, well. We don't have centuries. Now, what is that thing?"

"Something that's supposed to be extinct." Kelan moves to the door. He pops his head out into the hall. "As far as we were aware, they died off a millennium ago."

"This is worse than we thought. We're not ready for redcaps." Declan shifts his short sword from hand to hand. From the moment the redcap had appeared, so had his weapon.

"It doesn't matter. We're here now," Shay says, adjusting the bow on his back. A short sword hangs at his waist. "Which way?"

Kelan checks the hallway one more time, making sure the redcap is nowhere in sight. "Well, it's the receiving room, as you suspected, and, from the information we have, it's likely he's holding her in the West Wing. Which means we take a left. Do you know which hallway that is?"

Myrna peeks out and nods. It matches the image from the book. "The second from the left. Which means we'll have to cross the one the redcap went down. It's kind of an open area, but once we're through, it should be..."

Myrna rubs at her wrist. She's been doing it for a while, for as the others have talked, images have been flowing through her mind. It's an extension of the map. "*Whoa, Im, slow down.*" "Wait! We need to go right. The farthest right."

All three men spin to her, various expressions of shock, interest, and confusion looking back.

"Princess, that makes no sense." Declan's arm drops limply to his side. "Our information—"

"—is invalid."

Kelan is the first to understand. His gaze goes to where her thumb caresses her skin. "What's she telling you?"

"She's in a meeting with a bragging Brennan, and she has a full view of the map. He has a special room here—an experimental room. A torture room." Myrna gags, the sensations she's getting from Imogen too much. "But Imogen can see the whole thing, including where Theia is." Her eyes glaze over. They move from side to side as if memorizing some table they cannot see. Then she blinks, a wicked smile exposing her sharp canines. "I know where we need to go."

An evil glint lights Declan's eye. "Then a right it is."

"I don't suppose she's able to tell you what crazy obstacles are on the way, too, huh?" Shay asks.

Myrna elbows him. "Not so much. Let's just hope we don't find any more redcaps."

She doesn't miss the nervous glance the warriors share.

Yeah, definitely hope to avoid those.

They dive into the hallway, feet silent on the stone floor, but as this is their first real mission, Myrna can't help but be concerned she'll forget her training and all the intricacies of battle. If she does, it could cost a life. So, she follows the older Guardian's instructions to a T.

"I thought you said there was a turn here?" Kelan asks.

"There is!" Myrna scans the passageway. "That's what the map says! We should be able to turn here." She runs her hands along the wall, looking for a hidden latch or door. "I don't understand."

"Perhaps you don't remember the image correctly." Declan's back is to her, watching the way they'd come so he doesn't see her glare.

"I can still see the image. There is a door!"

Shay runs his hands over a different part of the wall. "Didn't the book say Merizalmek was alive? That the walls move?"

All three of them look at him. If that were true, how are they supposed to get where they needed to go?

When Myrna asks such, he shrugs. "You know the direction we're going. You can sense it, right?" Myrna nods, and he says, "Then keep us on track. We knew this wasn't going to be easy."

"Queen save us. All right." Myrna follows the hallway in the opposite direction, but keeps her bearings, knowing that soon there *will* be a door they can take which will lead them right and into a cellblock filled with prisoners. Or hopefully.

She speedwalks, unfocused, concentrating too hard on the map within her mind. It's a rookie mistake.

"Myrna, stop!" Declan cries.

Too late. She walks face-first into a web of invisible filaments. Myrna screams as the silk-like strands send shocks of electricity through her body, sucking at the arcane she's locked away. It's as if they shoot harpoons into the ball she's created and yanks pieces free. With them, chunks of her very self come with.

"Let's hope the redcaps didn't hear that." Screams to a minimum. Got it. She bites her tongue as another wave of electricity shocks through her.

Off to the side, something half-spider and half-beetle shimmers into existence up on the far wall. The fact it's several webs away and along the intricate maze of threads this creature's laid out does nothing to stop the terror racing through Myrna's heart. It overpowers the pain as she begins to thrash. It's a trap for any of those unknowing of its existence. Its long, hairy limbs creep forward, hundreds of eyes locked on its prey.

"Don't look at it!" Shay says, unable to hide his own fear.

But how can she not? It is a thing of myth and nightmare.

Hands grip the back of her tunic and haul her backward. The webs stretch, but don't give way. She screams again. Little hooks have dug into her skin and clothing like the cholla cactus in the human world, never willing to release once they get hold. Lessons in pain were well earned during the years lived in the desert, and Laoise was a fan of training where she would not forget.

The spider-beetle thing spits webbing over her shoulder, and the person pulling at her releases their grip with a curse. Myrna springs back with a resounding bounce that causes the hooks in her skin to dive deeper. Yet for some reason, Myrna's able to move her wrist and the obsidian blade she holds twists just right, and she's able to cut the thread running across her forearm. The pain lessens, and she's able to take a breath.

Hope springs in her chest.

"Obsidian cuts the threads," she croaks. Not an instant later, two more threads release, and they fall away from her skin to hang limply. *Thank the queen.* She hangs at an angle, unable to do much more than wait for help.

"The webs are a pattern. They don't cover the entire hallway." Kelan's voice is hard as he moves to put himself between her and the spider. "Shay, get her free. Now!"

But of course, the creature takes notice. It bends its too-long limbs then jumps, flying through the air, to land a web away.

Declan joins Kelan, and they spread as far as they can and draw the spider-beetle's attention as wide as possible. Granted, now with them as measure, it's clear this thing is nearly seven feet tall.

Its abdomen alone is the size of a couch and from where she's held, the thick hide glimmers like armor.

"I'm gonna get you out of here." Shay swings his obsidian dagger, borrowed from one of the Guardians, and cuts her free.

"Gah!" Myrna collapses, relief and agony causing her legs to give out, but Shay catches her.

"Feet under you. Come on, Myr. We need you in this."

Kelan engages the creature, swiping at its leg with his sword. It kicks out. Kelan dodges just as Declan goes in for an attack. The angry *click-click-click* of the spider's front pinchers has Shay glancing over his shoulder just in time to see his father get his feet knocked out from under him.

Digging deep, Myrna finds her feet, whimpering as her muscles spasm. She grinds her teeth and rips the translucent web hooked into her skin away. It may not be electrified anymore, but as it tears free, the crimson prickles make her look like a bloody pin cushion.

The creature scuttles toward Declan, lifting its second appendage high as if planning to dive it down into Declan's prone form, but Kelan's already moving. He runs, drops to his knees, and skids beneath the spider. He thrusts his blade up into the belly of the beast.

The screech that fills the air as it pulls back has them all dreaming of throwing their hands over their ears.

Declan crawls backward as blood coats Kelan's blade. More sprays across the Guardian's shoulder, and Kelan cries out as the fabric of his tunic begins to smoke.

"Get out of there!" Myrna says. For the spider is still over them both. She removes one of her needles from its holder and flings it at the creature.

It digs into the center eye and screams again. This, though, has it scuttling backward along the web.

They don't wait. Shay and Myrna grab Kelan and pull him to safety as Declan joins them. Bile rises when the effect of the spider's blood becomes clear. For Kelan's burned-away clothing is nothing compared to the smell.

The spider continues its retreat. As crimson pours from it, the creature slips off the filament and tumbles to the floor. It lands on its face, sending the needle farther into its eye. The cries become weaker. Then the view of it flickers as if it wishes to hide itself.

They take it as the gift it is and pull Kelan to his feet.

He cradles his arm and sways. "It's fine. Let's get distance from this thing."

Myrna rests a hand on his back. Not to hold him, but there if he needs it. "Lead us through, Declan. You spotted them first. I don't want to cross paths with another one. I got him."

Declan dips his chin and moves.

It takes them longer to get through the maze of web than Myrna likes and, when they do, Kelan's leaning on her. The hallway opens into a larger space with several offshoots of rooms, pathways, and what Myrna believes is a kitchen. Prisons need kitchens, right? They find a small space where they can hide and set Kelan down to tend his wound.

Myrna cleans it, and it's exactly as bad and worse than she expected. The blood was like acid. It had eaten through his tunic and the armor woven through it. More importantly, it had begun to eat away at his skin and muscle. His left shoulder and deltoid muscle were a pocketed mess of flesh.

He bites down and groans deeply as she rinses it again. "Hand me the medic kit in my bag."

"Hurry up," Declan says, keeping watch. "I think there are a couple redcaps out there. We're too exposed."

"We're in a separate room." An office of all things. Who knew prisons had offices? "Deal with it, Declan."

Myrna misses Declan's affronted glance.

"I'm fine. I've had worse." Kelan tries to stand, but he can barely lift his arm. Luckily, she has some pretty potent magical treatments in her bag, stolen by Briana from medical. *Probably should apologize for that later.*

"Sit down; this shouldn't a minute. Shay?" He's already there. He helps her apply an antibiotic, healing, and pain-relieving ointment before wrapping it as best she can. "That's all we can do for now, but like you said, you've probably had worse. Can you move it?"

His complexion's already improving. *Nice.* This is the strongest she had. She doesn't know what was in that paste, but she'd have to thank the doctor.

"Yeah. It's countering the acid."

"Good. And I've got news. That right turn? It's right outside."

"Well, shit," Declan says.

"What?"

"We've got two redcaps about to bear down on us."

They move.

The redcaps hadn't quite come around the corner yet, but their slurred, old form of Faerie is clear enough. Myrna can understand one out of every four words, but she isn't sure if that's because of the way they speak or the language itself.

"They must've smelt the blood," Declan says. Kelan's, Myrna's, or the spider's—it didn't matter.

The chatter picks up, and so does their gait. Where before it was slow and almost lazy, now it's disturbingly fast, sending a shiver down Myrna's spine. She tries the door, and it's locked.

The redcaps come around the corner. Sounds of delight, which resemble something closer to the smacking of lips, overpower that of their boots.

"Get the door open! Shay, remember, no arcane."

Myrna dives for the lock as the males sink down into their thighs, weapons ready. Myrna picks the lock as metal hits metal. The urge to help is great, but her focus must be on the deadbolt.

Kelan engages the redcap. The creature is smaller than he, but the Guardian is not so vain as to believe he's faster. Redcaps are some of the strongest warriors of all Faerie. The pike swings toward him, and Kelan jumps, but the tip twists, catching his boot. Yet, he's able to stay his fall and instead jumps with his other leg off the wall, sending his momentum in a spin. His obsidian blade comes down.

The redcap's pike is there, stopping Kelan's blade inches from the blood-soaked cap. It's close enough that the pressure causes new streams of crimson to drip down the wrinkled, leathery face. He snarls. With one shove, Kelan is thrown back.

His feet slide on the floor, but he's balanced and instantly attacks again.

Declan and Shay trade blows with their redcap. Sparks fly as obsidian reacts to this one's scythe, the second most favorite weapon of the redcaps. Shay's quick as he slides beneath the scythe, his blade finally making it through its defenses.

Blood of an unnatural brown weeps from the gash above the creature's knee. It keeps its feet until Declan sneaks behind it and dives his own sword into the back of the same knee. The beast falls with a roar. Still, the redcap fights, its scythe marking the obsidian as no other creature can. He tries to get to his feet, but as it swings the long weapon around once more, Declan takes a chance. He leaps onto its back. It falls to all fours, and Declan rams his small obsidian knife into the redcap's neck, right at the base of his skull.

The scythe falls. There's a *thump* as the redcap hits the ground, and Declan rolls from its corpse.

The lock clicks nearly in time with the first redcap's demise. Myrna jumps to her feet, pulls her short sword, and braces for a fight. One redcap to go.

Kelan's made progress, but with one and a half arms, he's having a hard time. Had he not been who he was, this would be a very different situation.

The four spread out, surrounding the frenzied creature. Then, one after another, they trade blows, the sounds of battle bouncing off the raised roof.

"We need to end this before more hear us," Myrna says.

Kelan takes a hit to his shoulder, and he falls to one knee, his hand on the wrapping. Never has she seen such agony on someone's face. She shoves him to the door.

The redcap focuses on Shay. It's backing him into a corner.

Declan tries to draw his attention, but the redcap knocks him away with one swipe of his pike. The Guardian flies backward and hits the wall. He slides down and lies limply.

Myrna runs forward.

Shay's sword arm falls as if he's tired. Not surprising considering the strength these creatures hold. The pike comes down and Shay stops the blow, both hands on the hilt of his sword, but still, it brings him to his knees. He cries out.

The princess is within the redcap's range, but he hasn't seen her yet. His armor is too great from this position, but she can provide distraction. Myrna swipes her short sword, as hard as she can, along the edge of the redcap's armor at his belly. His flesh is thick and hard, but her blade is sharp.

The redcap yowls. He lifts his pike, lets go of it with one hand, and moves to swat her away, but before he gets the chance, Shay is up and thrusting the dagger he'd pulled from his boot into the hollow of its throat.

Myrna stumbles back. Shay grabs her by the shoulders, and they run to the door where Declan and Kelan wait.

"Holy shit," Myrna gasps.

"I agree," Shay says.

By the time the redcap hits the stone floor, they're through the door and standing inside Cellblock One.

Chapter Fifty

Cellblock One

Cellblock One, the sign says.

It's probably filled with the worst of the criminals here. Who else would be in Cellblock One? Shay thinks.

"Myr, why did you have to take us through this block specifically?" he whispers in case anyone's here. The cells are all shut, no windows present to allow them to see in. But they can't see anyone. Not the prisoners or guards. Which seems strange.

"It's the quickest path," Myrna says. "It's where the king said the guards didn't go."

"Why not?" Declan asks.

"She didn't know."

"Well, that's good news," Shay says and steps forward just as Declan and Kelan reach out to try to stop him.

"Wait! There could be traps triggered by—"

They're too late. The softest *click* has their words cutting off.

Shay's chin hits his chest. "That's why there doesn't need to be guards for the prisoners."

Booby traps. Awesome.

A sickly yellow slime seeps from between the seams of the tile he stands upon. It reaches for Shay's boot before he has the chance to jump away, attempting to latch on like some toddler in need of affection. Or perhaps a hungry one.

Shay squeaks—a rather unmanly noise—and tugs his foot back. A wet suction sound comes from it before the ooze reaches for him once more, more agitated than before. Thank the Goddess it hadn't gotten a real grip.

"Ozekan..." Kelan mumbles. "Run!"

It does not take more than that. After their last encounter, both younglings are weary.

As he runs, Shay takes in his surroundings. Twenty-foot ceilings with lanterns that hang from the roof. And the doors which line both sides, as far as he can tell, are the cells. Bars occasionally break up the space. To allow the area to be cordoned off? Maybe. Either way, the corridor wasn't that wide—maybe twenty feet—which meant the ooze, or ozekan, was appearing through a good portion of the crevasses of the floor, and the path remaining wasn't great.

Kelan pushes in front of him. "Follow the open path and don't touch it if you can help it."

"What the hell is this stuff?" Shay jumps over a tendril that lunges out to grab him. When his foot comes down, the tile he lands on depresses. He stumbles, then curses when arrows begin shooting at them from chambers which have opened high up in the walls.

"Damn it, Shay. Stop stepping on the stones with the divots at the corners! They're the ones with the triggers!" Declan grabs Shay's neck and spins, ducking his head low just in time for an arrow to pass overhead. He knocks away three more arrows with his sword, then he shoves Shay forward.

The ooze has collected into pools and is moving toward the protected path. It grows with every second, shifting forward far faster than anything like it should. Then, the larger puddles become one, and they snake out to grab the intruders. Shay's breathing hard, his feeling of idiocy not helping his stamina.

Kelan jolts to the left, barely missing the arm of one, but in the end, another grabs hold of his leg. The tendril's small, so his blade is able to cut it, but had it been any thicker, his sword would've lodged within. That's the problem with this type of entity.

"Shay, to answer your question, this is an ozekan, a mix of Faye—both water and shifter." Kelan's panting breaths are a surprise. The pain from his shoulder must be bothering him more than he thought. "Extremely rare and dangerous because once they get a hold of you, it's nearly impossible to get out, which is why we need to find a way out of this room. Now!"

The floor shifts. *Did I just imagine that?*

Myrna, ahead of him, yelps. "Is the floor moving?"

Nope, not in his head.

The stone pavers lift like a wave, making it nearly impossible to stay upright. "Myrna, are you having flashbacks to the palace roof in the rain?"

"Little bit, yeah," she says, then falls to her knees. Kelan pulls her to her feet, and they speed up.

The ooze has grown around them, and arrows still fly at their heads. Myrna knocks one away, then rolls. That one nearly landed in her shoulder.

Shay grunts, and searing pain lances through his thigh. He falls to one knee as he looks down to see his own stupid arrow sticking out from his flesh. *Knights! I'm really tired of getting shot.*

Should've been paying attention.

His teeth grind, and his jaw twitches. This will slow him down.

"You all right?" Declan says.

"We'll deal with it later," Shay says, pressing a hand around the arrow he swears is the size of a damn tree. *It's not that big, but Gods damn, that hurts.* And putting weight on it is worse.

"How do we fight this thing?" Myrna asks as she knocks away a tendril. Her blade gets stuck in its glue-like body. She yanks it free and almost loses her balance.

"The way to fight it is with water and ice," Kelan says, meeting her eyes for a split second. "But if we do that, we give away our position. That'll bring everything in this place down on us."

"Yes," Kelan says.

Screw it. Shay jerks the arrow from his flesh and throws it to the ground. At least it is easier to run.

"We're almost to the door."

It is true. They pass through two of the gates and, although one tries to close on them, they can see the end of the hallway. If only the floor would stop moving.

"This reminds me of that mat thing Theia and I walked on at the ocean," Myrna says.

"What?" Shay asks.

"In the human…You know what, never mind!"

He guessed it made sense. This reminds him of Faerie's oceans too, but why would someone put a mat on it?

The ooze gets angrier…if ooze can get angrier. It grabs ahold of Myrna's arm, and she yelps.

Between her and Kelan, they pull her free, but a bright red welt is left behind.

"Careful." Kelan's voice raises over the cacophony of moving stones and roaring water. Kelan continues, "If you stay too long inside it, the ozekan will dissolve you."

Stomach crashing to the ground, Shay says, "Run. Definitely run."

Kelan chuckles at Myrna's disgusted expression, and together they speed up, fighting their way over the shifting tide of stone. With each other's help, they fend off the slime, occasionally getting caught in its grip. Luckily, it's never so much that they can't get free.

"The slime's collecting! How far?" Declan asks through panting breaths. The sickly yellow bastard's become huge and is advancing. Any larger and they won't be able to fend it off.

"I'm here!" Myrna curses. Quite colorfully. "It's locked!"

Declan throws Shay down next to Myrna. There's a massive, intricate mechanism securing the heavy iron monstrosity to the frame as well as the wall.

"I know these markings. They're from Imogen's book." Myrna runs her fingers over them. "Shay, these are the markings for Shadowspire."

"Seriously? Are you telling me you have to use your power to open it?"

Myrna scans the door, her lips parted in horror. "I think I do."

"That's why Theia's in here. Only the king and his minions can go in there." *Queen save us.* "Kelan, kill that thing! Myrna's got to use Shadowspire, anyway!"

"What?" Kelan asks as he dives away from a tentacle, then dodges a stone it throws at him.

"Do it!"

For the first time in his life, Shay is shocked silent, for Kelan trusts him. The temperature dips as Kelan takes hold of every molecule of water in the air. Then a spear of ice appears in his fist a foot long. He throws it at the creature now nearly as tall as the ceiling. One after another, the spears embed in the blob, digging deep and acting to Kelan as grounding points. He sends his will into them. Ice crystals shoot from the spears outward, growing through the ozekan, moving faster and faster the more it spreads through the water-like substance.

The creature tries one last attack, but the crystals are too many now. It shakes, a high-pitched harmonic filling the room.

Myrna's speaking to herself as she says, "This is Brennan's play area—Theia's prison. The image says she's two rooms that way. His playroom's on the other side, and then there's Theia's cell. All you have to do, Myrna, is open it."

Shay places his hand on her shoulder. He avoids her array of wounds. "You've got this. Remember what Imogen taught you and breathe."

"What would Sam say?" Kelan screams over the harmonic noise, which has reached a peak.

Shay winces. Then it deepens and, for two heartbeats, there's silence. Then the creature explodes. The males dive to cover Myrna as pieces burst over them. *Ew...shards of booger-colored ice crystals.*

Myrna laughs. "Ice boogers?"

"Did I say that out loud?"

Myrna smirks at Kelan, takes a big breath, and holds out her hands. "Fuck it. Let's do this shit."

Kelan cracks up. "Make Sam proud."

Myrna coaxes her arcane to life, unwinding the binding she placed upon her power. It bursts wide, happy to be free. Myrna draws the Shadowspire open. She sends it into the world, coaxing the shadows both within and without, asking them for help. They answer, joyous in the response. Then, following the spell-like markings on the door, she sends them into the locking mechanism. It's intricate and complicated, but soon it is as if the shadow she's called allows her to understand.

There's one thud, a second, and then a third. Her hands move to the turning mechanism.

The door at the far end of Cellblock One crashes open and redcaps flow in. Not just one, but many. Their iron shoes against the stone are as loud as their angry, slurred voices. But it's the contrast of their blood red caps against the stone and their glowing eyes that terrifies Shay the most.

"Please tell me you got the door open," Declan says.

"Let's get the hell out of here." Myrna turns the handle and shoves it open, grabbing her weapon off the floor as she goes.

They practically fall through the door and into Brennan's personal study in a rush to slam the door and lock it. The redcaps roar in frustration.

Myrna's the first to turn, the weight of someone's gaze too much to ignore. She squeezes Kelan's shoulder and that's enough for him to know something's wrong. He, too, straightens, pulling the blade from his belt once more.

"That was close," Shay says, pressing his head to the door, but he doesn't have any time to rest, for his father slaps him on the shoulder. He favors his good leg as he faces a darkened room, only the center illuminated. The room must be much larger than it appears, for the thirty-foot ceilings disappear into the shadows and the sounds move farther.

Overhead lights allow them to see the center while the sides are darkened, pitch black.

"Well, well, well," a voice says from the shadows.

They all sink into fighting stances.

"What an entrance you make, Princess Myrna Mareola Qhuinn."

There's a squeak from somewhere in the blackened shadows of the room. *He is keeping it dark on purpose. A mental game to mess with them.*

King Brennan Murray, tall with black hair speckled with silver, steps into the light. His nose is rather bird-like, and eyes creepily bulged. "It's interesting to finally meet you and here of all places. I take it you've come for something specific. Or are you wishing to learn our practices?"

He waves his hands, and the lights come up.

They'd expected to find Theia confined. But restrained and between two guards with blood smattering her clothes and bruises covering her arms and legs? That is less expected. Perhaps the others had thought it a possibility, but he had not. With the way Myrna refuses to look in her direction, he suspects she assumed it an inevitability.

Myrna tilts her head and examines the man before her. She takes two steps forward, Kelan mirroring her.

"Well, Grandfather. I expected more." She sniffs in disgust. "I'd like to say it's nice to finally meet you, but I'd be lying. In truth, I'm less than impressed."

Well, shit.

CHAPTER FIFTY-ONE

Predestined Encounter

MYRNA'S NOT SURPRISED BY this play, but she won't let it distract her. She won't look at Theia, for she knows what she'll see. So, right now, the swelling on her face doesn't exist, nor does the torn clothing. All that matters is the king.

The only way to do that is to kill the man before her.

The room is a torture chamber; a personal playground hidden away where no one else can see. The racks bolted to the wall hold tools of all sorts: spikes, scissors, forks, saws, screws, swords, mallets, poles, rocks. On and on they go, shifting in style, then growing in size from the smallest to largest. It's a vast collection of toys. *Impressive. Almost as nice as Laoise's.*

There are tables with varying restraints, a desk littered with papers, and bookshelves filled with journals, but it's the drain at the center of the room and the hole in the sidewall for disposal that turns her stomach. What did the king really use this space for and why?

With the meticulous nature everything is kept and the protective, irrational gleam in his eye, there is no way to truly know.

Myrna smiles slow. She'd thrown him off by calling him "Grandfather." Her cousin Colum and their guard, too.

Colum stands near Theia, a hand resting on the hilt of his sword. That cocky smirk makes her want to smack it right off his handsome face. She may not know him, but she doesn't need to. He's like Brennan.

"What did you call me, child?" the king asks, redness making the pores along his nose stand out more against his pale face.

"Do you need to sit down? You're looking a little winded." Myrna pats her belly. "I know it can be hard walking around with such a big head. Throw in all that extra weight and…" She grimaces. "But really, you don't look so good."

Colum's lips part as the other guards look to their king, who's charging forward. If it were possible, steam would be spewing from his ears.

"Myrna," Kelan warns.

"What's wrong, Grandfather? I thought you wanted the truth, to spread it to your people, and to hear what I thought about you and your court. That you'd be excited to meet me." Myrna begins a slow path to the right—at a diagonal toward his desk and away from where Theia is confined. This allows the others to spread out as the king's gaze tracks her.

He, too, shifts closer as if they orbit one another. "Why do you call me this—'Grandfather'?"

"You know why." Her boots click on the stone. "Or you suspected. Yes, you wanted to get back at Laoise for not playing your game, but the real reason, the one you don't want anyone knowing and the reason you went after my mother, is because she is the last witness of your crime."

"You have no idea what you speak! He's committed no crime!" Colum hollers. "You're the one who's broken the treaty by coming here!"

Myrna scoffs. "You entered Tara, you dimwit. You've been invading our lands for months. Shut your dumbass mouth and stand there and look pretty." *Okay…perhaps put Sam back in the box.*

Several of the guards choke, covering up their laughter with a cough. Colum goes to retort, but Myrna's already moved on. She focuses her attention back on the king. "Isn't that right, Brennan? Mareola was there. She knows what you did, and that's why you're willing to bring down the entire Unseelie Court for little ole me." Myrna's voice rises. "Because you know it would cost your throne."

All eyes are on the king. Exactly how Myrna wants it.

"He deserved it." His upper lip twists. Brennan spits on the floor. The darkest evil looks back at her when he says, "He fornicated, no, fell in love with a Seelie! A Qhuinn of all things! My son didn't deserve the throne."

"Grandfather?" Colum says, but no one hears him.

"Scared. Interesting," Myrna muses. She continues her trek to the right. The guards shift away, staying with their king. "But that changes nothing. You killed my father, Prince Reece Murray, first born to The Court of the Indomitable Moon and defender of the Seelie people. *Balance Beholden* showed it to me, and you will pay for your crimes."

"*Balance Beholden...*" His eyes spark, and his fingers flex.

Myrna dips her chin and shoots him an evil grin. She flicks her eyes to her companions, but they are already braced for whatever she's going to do next. *Excellent.*

"And I can prove it," Myrna calls. "Easily, as you've made it clear who is of our clan."

Releasing the ball of energy at the core of her, disintegrating the tightened cloth around her power, Myrna throws her hands down to her sides, palms out. Radiant Light fills the room, blinding the guards as it shoots from her palms and encases her forearms. They throw their hands up to shield their eyes, and Shay and Declan move to engage.

"This proves nothing! Radiant Light is a disgusting power, and that of your filthy mother!" In response, Brennan lifts his arms and darkness descends, pushing against her fire. It suffocates her flame with ice-cold nothingness like sharp spears of pain digging into it as he rips away the energy with each of his devastating swipes.

She swirls her arms in a giant circle, then slams her palms together, pulling them away and extending her white fire until she's created a shield of light. She sends streams of it at him, for which he barely evades. Over the roaring crackle created by both their gifts, she says, "Ah, but Grandfather, you're right, this is my mother's gift, but that is not what I wish to show you. This is!"

Myrna blasts the will connected to her Radiant Light outward, pushing back against Brennan's influence.

He grunts, his feet scraping across the floor. The light goes out, and all which remains is the shadow beneath. Everywhere that was once her Radiant Light is now violet Shadowspire. Tongue pressed to the top of her mouth, she shoots him a wicked grin and motions to something behind her.

"You see, I wasn't trying to show off. Just trying to distract you," Myrna says.

Kelan and Theia step from the portal behind her. Theia leans heavily on the Guardian, but they've made it through the tunnel from the other side of the room. It isn't home—there's something about this room which stops her from portaling from the space itself—but at least Theia is within their care now.

Whatever that's worth.

Brennan freezes.

Confused, Colum glances behind him. The guards which had flanked the now-empty rack lie motionless, crimson staining their clothing. The great warrior that is her cousin hadn't even noticed Kelan sneaking behind him and breaking Theia free. With Declan and Shay fighting the guards, and her distracting the king, no one had. That was the plan. *Dumbass.*

Brennan roars, "You cannot be my granddaughter!" He curls his fists into Os and violet tube-like protrusions grow.

Ancient images from mythology learned in human schools flash through Myrna's mind—ones of Zeus as he conjures lightning to throw. Myrna shifts her weight to her toes as the long, spiked tips shimmer with ice.

He pulls back and throws.

A shield of ice appears between them. Kelan. It stops the first spear of the king's Shadowspire, but shatters with the second. Myrna flashes her arm upward, knocking away the spike of violet with white light. Hardening her light, she pushes energy into it. It crackles and returns his volley. One lands on the door they entered from. It opens, and redcaps flow in.

Stones. We're never getting out of here.

"We've got this. Take care of Brennan!" Kelan says, planting his back to Theia's. Instantly, the sound of battle shifts as the redcaps attack.

"Oh, but I am your kin! More, I'm proof love between our courts can happen. That not only is it possible, it's best for this land. And you know it. You've sensed it, haven't you?"

For such a heavy man, he moves quite well. He spins, circling back around. He removes a sword from his belt. The obsidian blade glistens in the low light, especially as her fire glances off it with her next attack.

"Careful, Theia!" Kelan calls.

Light flashes, and a cold wind blows her hair back, but Myrna stays focused. She has to.

"I've got her." Declan slides past her view to join the fight with the redcaps and knocks one off of her mother. Declan hands her an extra dagger, and they go after the downed creature.

"You've known it's what is best," Myrna says, refusing to look back. The grunts and growls of the redcaps are as terrifying as her friends' responding noises. "That's why you killed my father and why you captured my mother. You've been hiding that you betrayed Faerie and your own people."

Myrna holds her sword before her and closes the distance. Perhaps it isn't the best idea as he's had centuries of battle behind him, but what other options does she have? It's time to avenge her father and prove she's the true heir.

"But don't worry, the rightful ruler of the Unseelie Court is here. And without you, I'll fix the plague you've spread through this land!"

"Ruler? I am heir!" Colum screams. He dives forward. The path takes him into battling guards. Colum doesn't stop. Instead, he takes the direct path, knocking Shay into his opponent and taking the opportunity to swipe his sword across the young Faye's thigh.

It's so close to his other wound.

"Ah!" Shay falls to one knee. He raises his sword just in time to clash with Colum's. Sparks fly, and Shay uses them. He exhales, amplifying the embers, then sends fire in a stream across the chest of the man above him. It's enough. Colum retreats, and Shay gets his feet back under him. Barely.

Blood pours down his pants from the slice, but Myrna's too far to help. And with Brennan closing in, her friend is on his own. *Damn, Colum.* She calls out, "Use your fire where you can. I'll be there soon!"

Wait, she can do one thing. It's something Imogen taught her. Myrna curls her finger and requests the help of shadows nearby. They wrap around her cousin's ankle and dig into his skin, sharpening, then heating with her will.

Colum snarls, then throws his hands out, shoving away the offending shadow with his own arcane. His gaze snaps to her.

Distraction enough to get him coming toward her again.

"Rightful ruler?" Brennan scoffs as if unaware of what has just occurred. The fool. "You've been Faye for weeks, and you believe you have the right, the skill, to take on such responsibility? It takes effort. Study. Respect for one's people."

"Fear, you mean," Kelan says from behind Myrna. The words are between clangs of metal, but they fall with no less weight. He continues between exchanged blows with a skilled redcap, the shorter creature slicing with a claw between swings of his pikestaff. "All you've gained is fear, King. You've taught your people emotion outside of fear is a weakness, but that is wrong. Honor, respect, trust, kindness, love; these are"—grunt—"most important. They're what keeps this world whole. What feeds Faerie, and Myrna has shown more in her short time here than you ever have."

As Kelan speaks, Brennan's shadows collect around his sword, but she's ready and no longer afraid.

The words must hit too close to home for, in a flash, Brennan strikes. His sword swings upward.

She brings her blade to the side, stepping from the strike. Then she pools her arcane within and readies her muscles for their next encounter, knowing strength is needed to fight the Shadowspire he's shoved within his weapon. She advances with a returning blow to his shoulder. The reverberation as they collide aches through her entire side. *Holy knights.* She blinks as, instead of sparks, globs of a tar-like substance drip to the floor. It sizzles and smokes, the scent of burning rock hitting her nose.

"Focus your radiance into the blade," Kelan calls. Blood splashes across his face as a blade cuts his shoulder open. He cries out before he drives his blade into the redcap's jugular. It gurgles, then falls. "Do it!"

Myrna trusts Kelan's advice. Her blade erupts in a kaleidoscope of color as a white light shines from within. The obsidian stone glimmers, lighting the room with the miraculous color of the sun as her power shines through its crystalline structure. The next time their blades meet, a blast of sound has all combatants throwing their hands over their ears.

He swings at her flank, and she shifts out of the way. Myrna lunges for a side blow, catching his rib with the tip of her blade. The light there dims as crimson coats the tip like the paint of an artist's brush.

Brennan roars, slicing her on the calf as he slams his elbow across her spine. She stumbles, then rolls, coming to a stop on her back, Colum hovering over her. The blade she once held is now dark where it lays a few inches from his boot. Her cousin grins, and a shiver runs up her spine. Never has she felt such hatred thrown in her direction.

"She is mine!" Brennan says, but Colum ignores him. He raises his weapon and brings it down as if to cut off her head.

"No!" Shay screams, knocking the last guard to the ground and diving in her direction.

Myrna kicks up, connecting with his knee just as a blast of power comes from Brennan. Her cousin is thrown off balance, and the killing blow swings wide. Myrna reaches for her sword, but Colum kicks it. The blade clatters against the stone, then slams against an iron table only to break in half. Her stomach drops, and her mind goes blank.

Declan takes a pikestaff tip to the side. It buries into his stomach. He bends. "Myrna!"

His cry distracts the redcap enough that Declan's able to swing his obsidian blade backward. Just before it makes contact, the stone flares red with Declan's flame, a far weaker arcane than his son's. Still, the redcap's head thumps to the floor.

Desperately, Myrna crawls backward, swallowing hard as her cousin follows.

Relief rushes through her when a hand grips her under the arm and yanks her upright. But that disintegrates the instant she sees who it is...

Brennan.

Terror freezes her. She tries to pull away, crawl toward Kelan, but his grip is too tight. She's so stupid. Cold seeps into her, and it feels as though her skin is going to shatter beneath the Shadowspire digging into her soul. Never had she thought Shadowspire could be used like this.

His acrid breath heats her face when he says, "You're just a child. You don't deserve my throne and neither did your father."

"Protect her, Kelan!" Theia bellows.

Those words—that sound—shatters something within the princess. The world goes silent for three whole breaths, her mind empty even as Brennan shakes her. He screams something else in her face, but Myrna doesn't hear. Kelan too says something, but it's unimportant.

For until that point, she'd refused to see... to acknowledge the cruelty done to her mother, because she'd worried it would break her. That if Myrna saw the damage, it would make her too weak to fight, but that wasn't the truth. Instead, it was everything Myrna needed. It was right there in Theia's voice.

The pain.

The betrayal. The sadness.

The love.

The truth...These men had tried to break the brightest light in this world. They'd tried to dim it, taint it... They'd tried to snuff it out. To kill her mother. The woman who'd raised her, protected her, and loved her more than any creature. A truth which had never been in question. It had always been Mareola.

"Shut up, you stupid whore!" Colum hollers at Theia. "This is your fault! Reece was such an optimist, a sentimental fool! He deserved to die. I'm proud Grandfather killed him. Had he not, I would have."

Brennan leans in and whispers in her ear, "And when I'm done with you, I'll kill my son's whore of a mate, and it will be all cleared away. There will be no proof. No memory of this."

Her blood is like flame. It coils within her, spreading, heating with those words and filling her with the determination to protect all she loved. Hotter it becomes as it approaches her core and the ball of arcane at the center of her being. Where the Radiant Light and Shadowspire connect. Speak. Interact. Are one.

A memory *Balance Beholden* showed her flashes through her mind. A handsome man, her father, protecting Theia from this man. The hope for a new world filled his eyes.

The fire in her blood connects with the arcane within, and Myrna screams as a wave of raw emotion erupts from her core. It burns of the combined nature of both her Radiance and her Shadowspire.

Everyone but the king is thrown to the ground. The redcaps cry out as violet flames engulf them. The few guards who are still alive writhe as shadows curl around them and squeeze.

That's new.

Her team sits up and watches, mouths agape. Shock and awe keep them frozen as Myrna punches the king in the jaw.

He laughs. "I'll give you credit. You're definitely stubborn like your father, but I'll never accept a mutt like you." His fist compresses her side, and the air rushes from her lungs.

Her light flickers, but it doesn't dwindle, the hatred and determination too strong, the love she feels from both her father and mother never faltering. She will never let them down.

"Good thing I don't need your permission," Myrna snarls in his face, scenting the smoke and lemon that is specific to his arcane.

She grabs his tunic and, with one hand, slides her last needle from her belt, the mix of Radiance and Shadowspire instantly filling the obsidian center. Twisting, as if to snake away from his next blow, she uses the motion to slam the needle up under his ribs. Then she focuses her arcane and shoves all of it through the center of her spindle and into his very core.

Brennan's eyes widen, a hand flying to where it punctures his flesh. His mouth opens, and he sucks in a breath. "You'd kill your grandfather?"

"As you've done, my father and tried with my mother."

"Then you are my blood!" From out of nowhere, Brennan produces another knife. He plunges it into her stomach just above her hip.

"No!" Theia screams.

But there's no Shadowspire on his blade. Myrna's burned it all away.

They stare into each other's eyes. Myrna, shoving more of herself into the power burning him. Brennan as he turns the blade to tear at the flesh of her body.

They don't see what the others do. Colum grasps the back of his grandfather and pulls. Brennan falls into his grandson's arms, skin pale and body limp.

Kelan catches Myrna as she, too, falls, the whimper as the dagger slides free echoing through the chamber. Declan's there, sliding additional hands beneath her. Together they move through the burning bodies and away from the screaming Murray heir as he jerks Myrna's blackened needle from the king.

They don't look back, but shift through the door and back into the room of horrors, the shattered ooze sparkling in the torchlight.

Theia closes the door and locks it, praying neither Colum nor Brennan have enough will left for a chase.

"Baby girl," Theia says when they lay her on the stone floor just outside Brennan's torture room.

"Is he dead?" Myrna groans.

Kelan grimaces. "I don't know, but you gave it your best effort." He presses his palm to her face. "Love, I need you to open a portal before you pass out. Can you do that?"

Myrna nods. She tries to sit up and screams. Blood pours from the hole in her side.

Kelan curses and presses his hand to the wound. He sends his healing magic into her, aiming to stop the blood. It's all he can do.

The noise that escapes Myrna's lips is one of agony and not healing. "It's not working. It feels wrong." She groans. "It's fine. I can do it."

Closing her eyes, she says a prayer to the universe, and reaches for the shadows in every crack, cell, and corner, for the power is draining out of her with each heartbeat. They come, but their voices are far off.

"I can barely grasp them. I'm out..." she pants, swallows, then groans as Kelan shifts her against his lap. "Don't have enough."

"Yes, you do. You're the future queen and the hope of all Faerie. You're the daughter of Mareola Qhuinn and Reece Murray, and they've set this world on a path which we will see through to the end."

Declan and Shay watch on. Shay leans against the door. All his weight is off his injured leg as Theia sways next to him. Declan stands, his hand on her shoulder, the other pressed to the bloody mess of his side.

"Look at me." Kelan places a hand on Myrna's cheek. "I've got you. Always. Now, take what you need." Kelan opens his power to Myrna, and in the next instant, she throws her head back as arcane magic spreads between them.

Theia jerks forward, but Declan stops her. "He won't listen. They're bonded. Don't interfere. It'll hurt them."

Theia's eyebrows draw together as she glances to Declan and then back to the couple.

None can blame her shock. Rare is it that a Faye will allow power to be shared as such, and not in battle. When mortally injured? Never.

Myrna touches her cheek to Kelan's on instinct. A tear slides between them, and confusion fills her, for she does not understand their concern. Kelan and she have connected magics before. On smaller scales and while she lost control, but still... He's mentioned it's looked down upon, but not why. This, though, how is it different?

Kelan opens himself completely, and she gasps. He releases everything he has to her. *Oh... this is trust.*

His water. Her fire.

His ice. Her Shadowspire and light.

They combine and spin, creating a sphere which extends to encompass them all until Myrna controls it and focuses it. In small movements, she creates a portal and throws it against the closest wall. Through it, Laoise in full military armor appears, sitting on her throne. Her eyebrows raise, and she jumps to her feet. A hell of a reaction.

"Go!" Myrna whispers, and the others do as told. To Kelan, she adds, "We must hurry. I don't feel well."

"I've got you, love," Kelan says as Declan throws Shay's arm over his shoulder. He grabs Theia's arm to steady her and leads them both through the portal. Once through, Shay's leg gives out. Then Theia faints. Declan barely slows her fall.

Kelan lifts Myrna with a groan. His own injuries tear, blood trickling down his uniform. Kelan falls to his knees just as the portal collapses, leaving Merizalmek quiet in their wake.

The noise in the hall is far different from in the prison. Cries of "What?" "Where did they come from?" "A portal!" "How!" fill the air.

The newcomers ignore it all, totally focused on themselves and the chaos they've brought with them.

Shit. Others.

"Healers now, or the princess dies!" Kelan orders. He lays her flat and cups her face. "Myr, stay with me. You've made it this far. Don't leave me."

The queen rushes to her side even as her stride is threatening. Several others do as well, but one retreats, their hand over their mouth.

"Guardian. Explain her injuries," Laoise demands.

Kelan looks up before applying pressure to the wound at her hip. He does not shy from her glare. "She took on the king."

"And?"

CHAPTER FIFTY-TWO

Warm Welcome Home

WHERE ARE THE DAMN *healers? Has time stopped?* Why wouldn't it with Myrna gasping for breath and her lifeblood staining her lips? The dirt and grime which cover them may be an issue, but not as much as the speed for which the fluid tries to escape.

"Declan, lift her legs!"

He does so as Shay takes her hand. "Myr, you made it this far. You can't die now." The boy doesn't look much better. His pallor is sheer white, and the legs of his pants are soaked.

The voices of the others in the room are frantic, questions of the mission, what happened to them, the king's well being thrown around and making his head pound. He sways but refuses to remove his gaze from her. All he knows is this is not the entire high court, but a small contingent. It seems the queen had reconsidered her opinion of a rescue upon Myrna's rash decision. Or that's his guess based on her dress.

Maybe she just knows he will retaliate. Also possible.

"The king is dead?" Laoise asks. She lays a hand on the scabbard at her waist, hope and fear lighting her strangely expressive face. It's been decades since so much has shown there.

"Unsure." Kelan shakes his head. "Myrna stabbed him in the chest with a Radiant and Shadowspire-infused needle. When

Colum pulled him away, he looked closer to death than Myrna does."

Someone far off says, "Shadowspire?"

Another voice asks, "What do you mean, 'she infused it with Shadowspire'?"

Declan meets the queen's eye. "We had an opportunity to escape, and we took it. We had Theia. Myrna had incinerated the redcaps—"

"Redcaps!" one of the council members exclaims. "Not possible. They're extinct!"

Kelan closes his eyes. *Shut up!*

"And there were more on the way," Declan continues. "I'm injured. Shay, too. Kelan's burned. We were able to retrieve Myrna, so we took it."

"This is ridiculous," one courtier says. Kelan looks up, but his face is fuzzy. Not a good sign. "You're all talking crazy. What do you mean the princess has Shadowspire? Did she—"

Kelan snaps. "Be quiet!" Everyone freezes and looks at him. "Myrna is the child of Princess Mareola and Prince Reece, okay? She's manifested both their abilities, but the only thing that matters right now is that Myrna gets the help she needs! So, where are the fecking healers?"

Myrna laughs. She caresses his cheek. "Looks like Sam's been a bad influence on you, too."

"She's entertaining." Kelan smiles down at her.

Shay snorts.

Healers rush through the door. Two attend Myrna, pushing Kelan and Declan away. Their magic flares to life, causing Myrna to writhe. They attempt to heal the stab wound in her hip, but there's something wrong. The healers wince.

"It fights," one of them mumbles, confused.

The female healer turns to the queen. "Majesty, the blade was enchanted. The bleeding won't stop. We'll need to cut away the taint. We'll need to take her to the Rasinka."

The waters of healing. Below the palace. *Goddess above.*

"Do as you must. Save her life or it will be yours," Laoise warns.

The two bow, unsurprised by the threat. Perhaps they knew what was to come the moment they'd seen the patient. They place her on a litter. With the help of two Guardians. they carry a worried, struggling Myrna toward the door.

Kelan's hand falls from Myrna's. He tries to follow. Theia does too, but Laoise's voice rings out.

"Restrain him!" Laoise commands. She ignores his low "please," instead continuing, "Take these three to the dungeons. Healers, treat their wounds, then make sure they find cells all but clean enough that they do not perish."

"You can't be serious!" Theia steps between Laoise and Kelan. Where her time with Brennan shows in the grime, blood, and bruises, it does not show in her stance or her voice. "You will arrest them for rescuing me? So, it's true. You really were going to leave me there and allow the king to continue his torture."

Laoise's eyes glisten.

"How could you, sister?" Theia pleads. "After everything we've been through. You would've allowed Brennan—"

"I would not have allowed him to take her!" Even Kelan can hear the pain in her voice, and yet, the queen stands tall. She purses her lips. "Merizalmek is impenetrable. There was no way we could guarantee a successful rescue mission. I love you, sister, but I promised you on the day she was born that I would love her as a daughter. That I would protect her and keep her alive. But she is like you, and she is like me. But more, she is like her father."

Theia laughs at the frustrated respect in the queen's tone.

"And she did not provide me all the information. They went against my ruling. Therefore, she and those who stand by her must be punished. Regardless of their success or their well-meaning intent, they chose to disobey a direct order from their ruler." The arcane seeping from Laoise causes the hairs on Kelan's arms to stand on end. "And it is my duty as queen to make sure their crimes are punished by the full extent of the law."

Kelan's heart dips until it sits in his stomach. "Please, my queen, let me stay with her. Or let Mareola go to her. Myrna should not be alone. Please, I beg of you."

"You should have thought of that before you kept her powers from me and dove through that portal."

But there's something in her tone. Regret maybe?

Guardian Sable approaches him, his expression blank. He takes Kelan's good arm and meets his eye. There's approval there.

"Yes, my queen," Kelan says on shaky legs. He bows. It's neither low nor respectful. If she is going to play this game, fine.

The wounds of his arm and shoulder make him nauseous; the cuts to his side and thigh, which are severe enough on their own, are a dull ache in comparison, and the broken ribs and various other scrapes... they are a reminder of his betrayal of his queen. But they are all worth it if Theia is here and Myrna lives. If the king is dead? Bonus.

Kelan steadies himself before trudging to Theia and linking his arm with hers. They leave the room behind, the healers carrying Shay.

"Shay? Talk to me, boy."

"He's lost consciousness, Guardian. His wound is severe. We are also taking him to Rasinka," the healer says.

Kelan's heart stops, and his promise to Myrna runs through his head. Looking at Declan, who stares at his son, he says, "I'm sorry. I didn't know he was so bad. I would've tried to heal him."

Declan leans toward Kelan. "When? This is not on you, my friend."

My friend. Kelan exhales harshly.

Theia lasts until the door is closed before she throws a hand out and grips the Guardian next to her. He startles but sweeps her up as she slumps.

"Apologies for the forwardness, Princess." The Guardian adjusts her against his chest.

She pats his arm. "Thank you, Guardian Ranier. I'm going to sleep now."

"You remember me?"

"Of course. Kind. Courageous..." she slurs and falls asleep.

The closest healer places a hand on her stomach. "We need to get you all to the infirmary!" He glances between Theia, Shay, then Kelan. "I don't care what the queen says. Let's go."

Their guards glare but do not fight the healers as they quicken their pace and lead them to the infirmary.

Kelan rests on his cot as they work on his oldest friend. Bruises cover her entire body. Cuts and abrasions that prove she did not break. He rests his head against the wall, the pain making his head foggy. The adrenaline's wearing off, and the mangled flesh is speaking of its unhappiness. The spider's blood had eaten away his flesh like acid.

"What happened?" Ranier appears with a small kit. He lifts his chin, indicating the source of his torture.

"Big spider-beetle."

Ranier's eyebrow lifts. "Well, that's...something. They wish me to clean it while they're working on the others."

Kelan nods. He unties his tunic, and Ranier and another Guardian help slide it off his shoulders. He groans as they pour an antiseptic potion over it. It sizzles, a pungent scent filling the air. Darkness flickers at the corners of his vision.

"How's Mareola?"

The healer comes to Kelan's side, the Guardian moving out of the way. "She has internal injuries but is well. Sleep and rest are the best for her now. Let's get you checked over."

Kelan zones out as he's examined. The treatment for his shoulder is painful, taking a healing and a salve that will need to be applied multiple times a day. The pain is such that he blanks out most of it, a skill he learned long ago in battle. *Thank the knights for that.*

They've moved on to a stab wound in his side when an explosion rocks the castle. The walls shake, and fire shoots from the doorway from which they'd taken Shay.

Healers duck, hands flying to cover their heads. "Rasinka!"

Kelan exchanges a look with Declan, and then they're both moving, all injuries and healing forgotten.

CHAPTER FIFTY-THREE

Healing Crimson Waters

"You ruin everything!"

Myrna's ears ring. *Holy harpy.*

Claws wrap around Myrna's throat. A weight settles on her chest. Legs encase her ribs and squeeze, pressing her to the hard rock. A ridge of stone digs into her shoulder, and Myrna winces. Her abdomen hurts. There's so much pressure, but she no longer feels like dying. Which means some healing has occurred. But how much? As she's not fully recovered, she assumes little time has passed.

Gasping, Myrna's lids lift to find Niandra sitting astride her. Water laps at Niandra's thighs, Myrna's waist. It's warm and sings to the injuries within Myrna even as the female atop her attempts to take her life.

How can I find her scales beautiful right now? Shimmering blue green with hints of gold at the tips, they're more striking with drops of water glistening along their shining surface. The same covers her exposed limbs, but in wrapping strips which start at her hip and move toward her inner ankle. *Focus!*

Desperate for breath, Myrna grips Niandra's wrists and attempts to tug them away. The female's grip is too tight. Myrna tries to roll, but all that does is slosh water into her mouth. Soggy tendrils of golden hair stick to her face. She chokes on them, fighting to spit them out before they are what takes her and not the bitch holding her down.

Niandra leans down, spittle spraying with each word. "You! It's your fault! You took away our one chance here, and now you stand in our way to leave this hellish place and go where we'd be cherished and seen for what we are—royalty!"

"What are you talking about? Who's 'we'?" Myrna croaks. She slips a finger beneath Niandra's grip and breaks the hold enough to suck in some air. With her opposite hand, she punches the harpy in the ribs. Niandra grunts but doesn't let go.

"Sola was to be heir. It would be so easy. Then you came along!" Niandra snaps.

Water rushes in, choking Myrna when she's submerged for an instant. She comes up coughing. Niandra's hand slips, and Myrna gets a peek of the room as she bats her attacker away. But before Myrna can get free, Niandra shoves Myrna back to the stone by the shoulders.

Luckily, it's enough for Myrna to get stock of her surroundings, because the last thing she remembers is the healers taking her away from the others. Cots line the far wall, a few holding severely injured Faye with bandages wrapping large portions of their bodies. Another Faye floats in the water with her. The hair is familiar, but from her angle she can't see who it is. Near the edges of the pool, several other lumps lie in heaps, crimson seeping from cuts at their throats and into the water. *This must be a special part of the hospital, and those are healers.*

Her heart aches. Still confused, she asks, "You and Sola?"

What she does understand is, Niandra killed the healers. Here of all places. A sacred place of healing and within the palace, no less. Her sadness for those who'd dedicated their lives to helping others and died because of this selfish, bitter female, shifts to rage. Myrna's skin goes hot.

Niandra screams, her claws digging into the flesh at Myrna's shoulders. "And then I was to be Brennan's bride. If I brought him you, I would be his! You ruined it again! We were finally going to live a better life away from this wretched place!" She spits in Myrna's face.

Sola's her companion. No, accomplice. Myrna grins evilly. "But I killed the king."

Wrong thing to say. Niandra yowls.

Now!

Myrna clenches her abdominal muscles, braces for the pain, then initiates a move learned from Laoise. The water helps, making Niandra's place on the slippery rock less sure. As quickly as she can, Myrna curls her bottom half and swings her leg up and around the bitch's neck. Then she yanks down and to the side. As they roll, sparks of agony shoot through Myrna's unhealed wound all the way to her very soul. Myrna ends in a crouched position while Niandra splashes into the deeper water.

When Niandra resurfaces, standing in the waist-level water, they lock gazes. Niandra's out for blood. "Which means I no longer need you alive."

Myrna tightens her belt, moving deeper as well. Her shirt's torn to shreds. The healers cut it to treat the wound, but that didn't really matter. She'd fought in less. Yet through the torn threads, Myrna sees the nearly healed injury. *How had they made such progress?* She would never get used to healing magics. Even those who moved at rates slower than Kelan's.

Myrna readies herself for attack as the air crackles. Then Niandra lunges, swiping her claws down the front of Myrna's collarbone. Blood drips into the pool, spreading—watercolors on a puddle.

Myrna narrows her eyes and returns Niandra's attack with a lightning-fast jab. The bitch expertly parries it, their bodies moving in fluid synchronization as they exchange a relentless flurry of blows and blocks. A sharp left hook sails toward her, water droplets dancing in the air, catching the moonlight like liquid diamonds as it lands on Myrna's torn shoulder. Niandra laughs as Myrna falls back. The princess gets to her feet, returning the blow nearly as quickly. Their fists meet with a resounding clash, sending a ripple of pain up both females' arms. The pool's surface trembles beneath the power released from the blow.

"Which means we're back to plan one. You're not strong enough, Princess. Definitely not worthy of being queen."

The combatants circle each other. Myrna pants. Her chest burns, and her side aches. If she doesn't finish this soon, she's going to pass out.

"I think the king would disagree." Carefully, she takes the ramp to shallower water, away from the sleeping figure. Niandra follows. "Especially as I ran my weapon through his heart. He didn't think me weak then."

Myrna steps onto dry land. Niandra, too.

Niandra's fists clench, and her knuckles whiten. Arcane blasts from Niandra—the most Myrna has ever felt from her. It's slimy and wet, slithering along her like kelp in the water. Then Niandra dives for the princess, claws out. Fists blur in the firelight, and claws flash like lightning in the darkened chamber. Their battle reverberates off the ancient stone walls, creating an otherworldly cadence. Myrna's surprised it doesn't draw attention, but perhaps they're farther away from the main castle than she knows. She wishes it were different, for she could use the help. Niandra's wild, uncontrolled, and the instability in the female's eye scares Myrna. Still, she never loses focus and waits for the right moment. If she goes too soon, it will be her downfall—Myrna's death.

There. Niandra steps wrong, shifting back after Myrna presses an advantage. There's just enough room. Myrna shoves extra energy into a spinning kick and, with balletic precision, she connects with Niandra's breastbone.

Niandra flies backward, landing in the water with a splash. She disappears beneath the water with a cry, and it gives hope that perhaps Myrna finally has the upper hand.

Myrna inhales slowly but doesn't drop her guard. Not until she knows Niandra's down. She steps to the edge. The waves settle. The bubbles dissipate.

But there's nobody.

Frantically, Myrna scans the water.

"This is all your fault, all those who entered that prison." Niandra appears next to the body floating in the water. "If you hadn't gone, we'd be at the Unseelie Court now, and the power would be mine."

The identity of the injured man sinks in.

Niandra digs only the tips of her claws into Shay's neck, ready and willing to rip out his throat. He lies there unconscious, completely unaware of the surrounding battle.

Myrna's heart stops. She drops her fists to her sides. "Please don't."

Shay... her best friend. The person who makes her laugh, who accepts her and all her oddness, who doesn't expect her to be anything else than herself.

"Why? He's disgraced. Not worthy. The fact that he's in these waters is disgusting! And you, the princess, beg for him!" Niandra's expression morphs, darkening into something inhuman. Her scent changes, becoming bitter. Almost rotten.

"Niandra, something's wrong with you. Please let me help!" Myrna shifts closer, the warm water licking her toes.

These are the wrong words. Niandra thrusts her nails deep into Shay's neck.

"No!" Myrna screams as blood spurts over Niandra's fingers and down his skin.

Myrna's ready. Or nearly.

Too far away for a physical attack, Myrna takes the panic of seeing those sharpened claws at her friend's neck, the fear of them spearing his flesh, and the love she holds for him to fuel one of strong arcane magic. Radiant Light and Shadowspire build so fast she almost can't control it. Her core explodes outward with her scream as she releases it toward Niandra. It's similar to the blast during the fight with the king, but more focused.

The room ignites into white light, blinding even the caster.

Niandra wails, her sharp screech piercing Myrna's eardrums. There's a splash. Another.

Myrna blinks to clear her vision. Then she's rushing through the water, desperate to get to the sinking form of her friend. Grabbing hold of his shoulders, she pulls him through the darkening water and to the ramped section. She lays him across her lap and compresses the wounds in an attempt to staunch the blood. Choking tears trail down her face.

"Please, Shay. Don't die," she sobs, but the sound of his breaths is too shallow for her to hear, and the blood just keeps coming. "You have to be okay."

She peeks beneath her hands for an instant, then redoubles her efforts. Niandra didn't rip out his throat, but her fingers did a hell of a lot of damage. She presses her forehead to his. *Maybe there's hope.* "Please...you have to."

Thundering footsteps. A flurry of shocked cries.

"Queen save us," someone says. The words are half prayer, half expulsion of breath.

"Open the sluice gate!" another voice echoes, bouncing off the walls.

Water splashes over Myrna as someone jumps into the water and drops to their knees. She blinks and looks up to find Kelan. Declan and another Guardian follow. Ranier, she thinks.

Kelan's stark white, his brow furrowed and hands hesitant as he reaches out.

Something touches Myrna's left shoulder. She jumps when she finds the bottom half of Niandra's body floating, her foot bumping Myrna. The female's been torn in half, Myrna's blast having burned straight through her. Her scales are blackened closer to the wound and the upper half is nowhere to be seen. Yet Myrna somehow knows its location. Bile rises in her throat. She moans and leans away, unwilling to remove her hands from Shay's neck.

Kelan pushes the body away just as the current picks up. Whomever is with them has opened the gate and now the underground river flows freely, clearing the blood staining the sacred place. For there is more to Rasinka than the singular pool they'd lain in. It is one piece of the magic held by this cavern.

"Kelan, she dug her claws into his throat," Myrna cries. Her whole body shakes. "I couldn't stop her. He made it home, and then she killed him."

"He's still breathing, love. Give him to us."

"But the healers."

A man in an all-white robe steps into the water. He nods to Kelan, then removes Myrna's hands by force. "His lifeblood! Kelan, you have to heal him."

But she relents and relinquishes her hold when she realizes who the healer is. The three move the boy farther to the fresh, clean water. Light appears beneath the healer's palms, and Myrna sags.

"What happened? Who attacked you?" Kelan examines the bruises around her neck, the cuts across her collarbone, and the knife wound from the king. He drags her back a few feet, placing himself between her and those working on Shay.

Rasinka will help. It will help, but they need Kelan!

"It doesn't matter. You need to go help. Please. Use your power. Save him! You promised!"

He wraps his arm around her and splashes water on the weeping wounds. She winces. The clean water burns like salt water in a cut.

Kelan swallows hard, looks down, and shakes his head. "I can't. I'm burnt out. I gave everything to you to get home. I'm sorry, Myr. He's got healers and—"

"No!" The word comes from her very soul. She fights to get to the males attempting to save Shay, who's yet to open his eyes or even twitch. "Why won't you help Shay? You hate him, that's it. You're jealous of him!"

Kelan reels back. He grabs her shoulders and forces her to face him. "Are you kidding? No. He's my friend! Myrna, he's going to be okay. The healers are doing all they can—"

If she'd only look, she'd see the truth, but the terror riding her holds her hostage. Never has she felt so out of control. She struggles, body flailing, needing to break away from his grip, but unable. Her ability to fight is gone. She feels human. Finally, she knocks his hand away and slaps him across the face. "You hate him! You wish he was dead!"

Declan meets Kelan's gaze over his son. He looks to the exit, which leads up to the main hospital. More guards are coming from it, Jaden and Serena included. Kelan calls out to them, but Myrna can't understand the words. Seeing the thrashing princess, they run to help. They get her out of the pool, give Kelan a hand up just as another healer slips into the space. The healer's eyes go sad when she sees her comrades dead on the floor, but then she spots the princess. She walks over and lays a hand on her head.

"Sleep."

Myrna goes limp.

Chapter Fifty-Four

Broken

"What are you going to do, sister?"

It is like a dream for Laoise, seeing Mareola standing here, dressed in the courtly finery. It's been so long since her uniform has been shorts and a simple tee. She made even that perfection.

"You know she is not a traitor. None of them are and should you mark them as such, I will not forgive you," Theia adds.

And it would kill me to do so. Yet how could she solidify her dominion when such disrespect was paid?

Laoise rustles the skirt of her gown. It's a dark midnight blue, the stars added-in jewels. When she moves, it is as if they blink out beneath the shifting folds. She squeezes the bodice, facing her sister. "Our Myrna has chosen to disobey her queen. Her insubordination must be punished; otherwise, how am I to keep the people's respect? Hold my power?"

Theia sighs. "What did Mother always say? Change the narrative."

Laoise flicks her fingers at the annoying beast that is Theia. "Go wait in my personal throne room. You shouldn't be down here, anyway."

"Neither should my daughter." But Theia curtsies and gracefully heads back the way they came.

Laoise glares at her retreating form. *Snarky female. I'm not sure I'm ready for her to be home.*

The queen nods to Guardian Sable, then enters the cell for which Myrna has been kept the last day. It's clean; the cot she sleeps on is well kept. It is not dungy like the others of the levels below. She gave the girl that much, at least.

Upon entry, the healer bows and says, "She is soon to wake."

Laoise inclines her head, and the male leaves. She stays right where she is, hands clasped against her stomach. It does not take long for Myrna to come to.

She groans and stretches but sits up quickly as if sensing someone is with her. A rainbow of emotion crosses the poor girl's face when she spots Laoise. Love, fear, pain, worry, excitement, terror. So many pieces to decipher.

"Auntie. I mean, my queen." Myrna swallows. Shifting her legs off the bed, Myrna places her slippered feet on the floor. She stands, legs shaking.

No doubt she is sore and tired. The youngling has been through much, but her injuries are all but healed. The memory, her body will carry for a while still. That fact is not something anyone can help.

Laoise stays silent, watching the girl and waits. For she knows the first question—the most painful—and it must be dealt with before the rest.

"Shay?" She presses her fingers to her forehead. "He was in the water with me. Niandra attacked, dug her fingers into his neck—" her voice cracks, and she chokes before continuing, "Kelan pulled him away. Auntie, what happened to Shay? Please."

Laoise squeezes her fingers together and says what she wishes was not true, for the response is clear. "Shay passed. He rejoined Faerie in the beyond."

Myrna's chest constricts, a sob wrenching from her throat. Her legs give out, and she falls back onto the cot. Laoise's love breaks before her as she learns one of her best friends in the entire world has died, passed from this life.

It is an emotion she knows well. The same she felt when Fianna died.

Laoise floats forward. She kneels before the girl whose sobs wrack her body so hard her shoulders hunch upon themselves. Tears trail down her cheeks to fall to the floor. Laoise rests her hands on the girl's knees. When she flinches, it breaks her heart. So, she puts them on the bed on either side of her.

"I am so sorry," Laoise says, even though she knows in her core Myrna does not want her there. In fact, she blames her for his loss. "Losing someone you care for is never easy, but someone who connects to your soul is harder."

Myrna looks up, confusion and interest in her eyes. She wipes her nose with her sleeve. *Ew.*

"I have watched you these weeks. You were bonded friends. Rare. And your Shay Hughes proved in his young life that he was a male of worth. He did not deserve this end, but we cannot always fight our fate."

"It wasn't fate." Myrna hiccups. "What am I going to do?"

"You're going to honor him." Laoise stands and pulls her niece to her feet. "I've already approved he be given a Guardian's burial."

"What?" Myrna's eyes fill with a fresh wave of tears.

"Do you disagree with the choice?" Laoise lifts a brow.

"No. Thank you." She sniffs. "Will I be able to attend it?"

That is the correct question.

Laoise strides away, toward the door. "Come."

Myrna follows, and as they step into the hallway, six of the queen's guard join them. They're the best of the best, save Kelan. The youngling does nothing to hide the proof of her sorrow. As Laoise leads her to the queen's private throne room, she does not wipe her face or straighten her expression. She uses the time to slow her breathing. Then, when she stands before the door, she inhales slowly and straightens her spine even as her nervousness shows in other ways.

This room is smaller, but still able to hold a crowd of people. Myrna nearly trips over her slippers as she enters, for not only is the high court there—who had witnessed their arrival from Merizalmek—but Theia, Teirnan, and her friends are. Of course, they are chained.

Pride for Myrna rushes through Laoise as she holds her composure. Barely recovered, and in a simple gown, Myrna is strong against the world, regardless of knowing not what is to come. And much of this is Laoise's fault. She'd kept secrets too long. Allowed them to taint her throne, her heart. Now it is up to her to set things right.

Laoise latches onto Myrna's arm. She drags her to a spot before the dais, then, leaving the princess there, Laoise steps to her throne so she may sit regally, presiding down upon her people.

Her gown billows before her, the fabric expanding in all directions, spreading across the floor to nearly touch the steps. Laoise lays her arms on the rests and scans her subjects.

"You told her?" Theia says, concern upon her beautiful face. She stands to the side, gazing at her daughter with pain. As do many of the others. Laoise cannot blame them. For as healthy as she may be, she looks a fright—broken.

Laoise shoots Theia a warning glare before addressing the room, "Princess Myrna Mareola Qhuinn, did you or did you not go against the order of the crown, attack the prison Merizalmek, with the sole mission to save your mother, Princess Mareola?"

Eyes forward, Myrna says, "Yes and no, Majesty."

The queen's lips part. She blinks.

"Forgive me, my queen, but your order, even your description just now, stated an 'attack upon Merizalmek was not approved.'" Her tone is flatter than the flooring. "You are correct that our mission was technically against the order of the crown. We did fight the creatures, which reside *within* the prison, and our goal was to retrieve Princess Mareola, but at no time did we attack the prison itself. This is because I was able to use my blood born gift to portal inside."

Oh, smart girl. "When did you discover your Shadowspire ability? Your true lineage?"

Myrna blinks slowly and glances toward the crowd once as if considering how much they know. Something within Myrna decides she no longer cares what they think. Laoise guesses losing her friend has caused this. The queen can relate.

"The day before. During the battle, to find Princess Mareola at my childhood home, I accidentally triggered my Shadowspire and portaled myself into Brennan's palace."

Laoise's jaw drops. She snaps it closed, but finds herself leaning forward as Myrna continues, "I made a...friend who protected me."

The crowd is getting restless. Yet they watch the tennis match conversation with interest.

"And so, you went on your mission"—her hands clench on the armrests—"got Mareola back, and came back in pieces. But there is still the question of what happened down in Rasinka."

Myrna flinches. A tear trails down her porcelain skin.

"Myrna..." Kelan whispers.

"Quiet!"

With a lift of her chin, she says, "The mole I warned you was in your court decided to reveal themselves."

"Ah..." Laoise stands. She strides forward, glaring down at her darling child. "But you did not leave enough to be identified."

"Oh, but I did." Before anyone may stop her, Myrna dives into her core, pulls upon her Shadowspire, and sweeps her arms in a circle. In the next instant, there's a portal to her right. A dark room she remembers shimmers beyond it, the basement training room of the house in the forest.

Holy shit. Laoise really did like Sam.

Myrna steps into it, and the Guardians rush forward. Her chained friends pull on their bindings as if they, too, wish to follow. Even Laoise steps down.

Guardian Sable reaches it first. "Princess! Come back! You're on trial, you—"

Something flies through the portal to flop onto the floor with a squishy *thump*. It slides, leaving a trail of brownish red. It stops at the feet of two of the courtiers, who jump back with shouts of surprise.

Myrna steps through the portal as if nothing just happened, and she pats Sable on the chest with an ash-covered palm.

"Hey, big guy, can you get Sola for me?" Then she walks over and picks up the hunk of meat. She bows to the horrified crowd. "Sorry. The door was small."

Laoise has to bite her cheek to keep from laughing when Theia looks at her and says, "She gets this crap from you."

Myrna walks right up to Laoise and holds up what's left of Niandra so that it's eye level with the queen. Her fingers grip her hair, but it's the skin and sinew dangling from the cut which makes the scene so disgusting.

"Well," Laoise says with as little humor as she can manage. "There is no denying that. Now, pray tell, what do you need with my adviser?"

"Laoise," Theia says, her tone exasperated. Apparently, it wasn't as unamused as she intended.

Guardian Sable appears with a struggling Sola. She takes one look at Niandra and screams bloody murder. Sola lunges for Myrna, fingers extended, but Sable catches her. "You stupid bitch! First you take my throne, then my chance at Brennan's, and now you kill my love! I will destroy you!" She dives for Myrna again, and Sable grunts. The hall goes silent except for Sola's continued admissions.

"That." Myrna glances to another Guardian, who instantly comes and takes the decaying corpse from the princess's grasp. Myrna casually meets Laoise's stare. The two watch each other heatedly.

So much power. So much potential.

"I would've gotten everything I've ever wanted!" Sola says.

"What do you mean, Sola?" Myrna asks, her expression calm. "'You'd get what *you* want?"

Sola stills. Her focus sharpens, and her weight shifts into her hips. Her voice deepens to a tone none of them have ever heard. "I've given so much to this court, and for what? To have some little brat come in and take the power I'd been working so hard for. Nay. If I can't have it here, I will get it elsewhere."

"And you were willing to use Niandra to do it?"

"Brennan doesn't want someone so lowborn as she was, but me? He'd consider my bloodline. So yes, I would." Her lips peel back as Guardian Sable tightens his hold. "I was to be queen, his bride, but you've ruined everything."

"And Niandra?"

Sola snorts. "She would've gotten over it."

Without looking away from Myrna, Laoise says, "Take Sola to the dungeons."

The queen does not need to confirm the order. Every Guardian and civilian in the room can agree the order is warranted. Another guard appears and drags the traitor away, kicking and screaming. Her threats and warnings do nothing but solidify her fate.

"Well, my child." Laoise grasps the sides of Myrna's head and kisses her forehead. "You have done brilliantly, my love. Not only have you confirmed all that has occurred, but you have verified the logic behind the actions you and your people took. You've shown your loyalty to the crown."

The princess's lips part. "Of course I am loyal to the crown, my queen. You are my family. One of the few who has shown me true love. Seen me for who I am, even when you think I am mad."

"I still think Brussels sprouts on pizza is blasphemous," Laoise says.

Myrna chuckles. "You've taught me to fight for what is right. This was right."

Laoise's head tilts to the side. "Teirnan, it is time."

"Yes, Majesty," the old man says. He stands from the spot way off in the corner and grabs the royal orb. The hoodless cloak he wears is elegant, ornately decorated, and covered in finely polished gems. "Princess, if you may." He holds a folded piece of fabric as finely made as his own.

Laoise takes the girl's arm and leads her toward Teirnan. To the Guardians holding Myrna's friends and team, she says, "Release the prisoners."

Instantly, they do as ordered, moving to Jaden and Kelan's shackles first.

"What?" Myrna says, coming to a staggering stop.

"What?" they all second.

Laoise grins. "How else are they to be your personal guard if they are handcuffed? With Teirnan performing the ritual to confirm you as official heir, you will have an even larger target on your head." Laoise pretends to frown. "Do you wish for another option, for them to remain disgraced?"

"What? I mean, no!" Myrna says. She holds up her hands. "But I have harpy ash on my hands. How can I..."

Tiernan laughs deep and loud. "Considering the circumstances, I think it warranted."

Chapter Fifty-Five

By Your Side

T HE VIEW OVERLOOKING S HAY'S land is just as it was before, and yet it feels emptier somehow. The beauty hasn't changed. The river off to the right is just as magnificent. The mountains fill the horizon in layers, providing mesmerizing depth, which disappears into the distance, and the forest of trees below the outlook creates a carpet of colorful foliage. Faerie is a dream.

But it is the cottage just down the hill, so simple and beautiful, which makes her heart spasm painfully, for she knows the walls within will never be graced with the one person for whom made it brightest.

"Myrna?"

She flinches at Declan's voice. She does not mean to, but she's been purposefully avoiding him since Shay's death. Never again will she not feel guilt looking into his face. Nor will she see Shay in his structure. She doesn't look up, but remains knees to her chest, arms wrapped around them, and chin resting on her wrists.

Heavy steps approach, and then his big body slides into the spot next to hers upon the rock. In the same position his son sat that very first day here. How had he gotten through the contingent of guard encircling her? She'd asked to be left alone.

He is silent for a long while, and when he does speak, it is not what she expects. "When Shay was a child, maybe five, he snuck out of the house and went into the forest. He was too young to go wandering off on his own, and his mother was furious with him." Declan puffs a laugh. "She was even more angry when she found out he'd made it all the way down to the pixie forest."

"No, he didn't," Myrna says, turning her face to him.

"Oh, yes, and they were not happy, for they are not friendly to us since we pushed them from Tara. But there he was, this loud little creature, playing in their pools—the sacred ones, no less. Naked."

"What?" Myrna screeches.

"Yeah." Declan grins. "At some point, he'd decided it was best to strip down, for 'it was never nice to get clothes dirty and wet.'" The last part seemed like a quote. "He also said he didn't want the paint he'd had on his shirt to get in the water. You see, we'd been in the workshop earlier that day.

"So, there he was, this black-haired demon child thinking of wanting to play with the pixies, but never wanting to harm them in return. He was a jewel to the world that day, for most consider pixies lesser Faye." Declan stares off into the distance, toward the river and where the story must have taken place. "They fell in love with him right then and there. When we found him, he had a slew of them around him, playing and taking care of him. They demanded we all stay for dinner, both that night and many after."

Myrna shifts so that she can rest on Declan's shoulder.

"The only thing that ever brought him as much light as opening friendships with the pixies and other lower Faye..." He goes silent for a few long breaths, "was you."

Myrna chokes, tears burning the back of her eyes.

"I'm sorry, Declan. I'm sorry I couldn't—"

"Myrna, stop." Declan grabs her shoulders and runs his hands up and down her arms as Theia used to when she cried. It is a parental gesture she understood. "This is not your fault. He was mortally injured when we came through the portal. He knew it then. Hell, several of us were, and we knew the risks of what going into that prison were. We were willing to die for our cause. There were no guarantees the healers could save him. You need to understand that. Really accept it."

"But..." Her words cut off as a sob racks her.

Declan pulls her in for a hug. "Honey, Shay was young, but he lived brightly. And these last weeks meant everything to all of us. He was lucky to have had you for as long as he did. He said so himself."

"Me, too."

Declan holds her as she cries, and it feels right, for she knows he misses Shay as much, if not more, than she. The sun lowers, the clouds glowing red and orange.

"Has everyone left?"

"Not everyone." With that, he kisses her head and gets to his feet. "Know you're welcome here anytime. I expect you, even."

She smiles sadly.

Declan glances over his shoulder, and Myrna follows the movement. Her gut sinks when she sees who it is. She gets to her feet and steps toward the forest. Kelan's eyes twitch.

"I don't want to speak with him."

"Myrna, it's been a week. You must."

"But he didn't heal—"

"He couldn't!" Declan shakes her. It's light, but enough of a shock to make her listen. "Myrna, when we escaped that room after you fought Brennan, you couldn't even call the shadows. You were burnt out. Kelan gave you every ounce of the magic he had left. He performed something we're not allowed to do in battle because it's forbidden. Do you know why?"

Tears well again in Myrna's eyes. He lets her go, but stays close and speaks fervently, "Because when you merge arcane during battle—open yourself that freely while mortally injured as you both were—should one injured party give too much and die, so shall the other. With you two, the connection is unique. It's more. He could've given you his entire life force in order to keep you alive. His life *for* yours. Hell, had the healers not shown up when they did, he might have."

Myrna is speechless. Does her heart beat any longer? "Why would he do that?"

"You know why, Princess."

A ragged breath rattles her frame. Myrna walks to the edge, crossing her arms. The view and the sense of Shay's presence warms her, helping to settle.

Declan strolls toward Kelan. He pats his friend on the shoulder, links his arm with Theia, who stands just up the hill, and leads her through the ring of guards to wait for Myrna.

When Kelan's steps approach, Myrna closes her eyes and takes a hard breath. Then she turns toward him, refusing to hide this time.

The usually stoic Guardian is anything but these last days. Although she's been avoiding him—okay, everyone—she hasn't missed his sullenness or how he's been hesitant and a bit snappy. He glances away before he reaches her. The guilt in his gaze saddens her, especially after hearing what Declan just revealed. *Did he know?*

As always, Kelan rests his hand on the hilt of his sword. "Stephan reports they've pushed back the Unseelie. Minimal casualties." He runs a hand through his hair. "They're still pretending the king's fine, alive. Though all communication is coming through Colum." He scans the forest, then clears his throat when she says nothing. "Have you heard anything from Imogen?"

Myrna rubs her wrist, then instantly stops the nervous gesture. The fact she hasn't spoken to her cousin is another source of her distress. Is she injured, been found out, or has the connection been cut because of something they did? The overuse of power, maybe?

"No." Myrna's silent for a moment. "But...is this why you wanted to speak with me?"

Kelan exhales and kicks at the ground. "No. I wanted...I wanted..."

His face crumples, and Myrna's heart breaks.

"I failed you, Princess. I gave you my word, and I wasn't strong enough. Shay...he was such a good male. Your friend, and I—" There's so much pain in his voice, and Myrna doesn't know what to do other than to throw herself against his chest. His arms wrap around her. "I would've done anything had I been able."

She knows that. She does. She closes her eyes and tries, *tries* to take in the warmth he offers. To give what he also needs, but the hurt is too fresh, and the feeling of betrayal in that moment... she can't get rid of it. It's burrowed deeper and deeper into her as the memory of those moments in the temple replays in her nightmares.

"I hate you, Kelan," she says into his chest, and he presses his cheek to her head. Even she doesn't believe the words. Her fist curls next to her face. "You're every frustration and everything I've ever..." The words trail off, her heart unable to fully let go of the questions floating between them.

She pries herself from his warmth; it breaks her in two.

"Myrna, please." Kelan reaches out for her.

She steps back, staring down at his outstretched hand as a voice—so familiar tears instantly spring into her eyes—fills her head. *Are you really not going to forgive him, Myr? You know this wasn't his fault.*

Shay? Myrna thinks. Goosebumps cover her skin.

You and I both know he would've died to save me.

Myrna rubs her temples and glances around the forest. The shadows of the trees shift with the setting sun. Dizzy, Myrna sucks in a pained breath, then meets Kelan's eye. "I can't. I'm sorry."

Unable to look at him any longer, she moves toward the road.

His voice cracks when he asks, "Is there a chance you'll ever forgive me?"

"I-I don't know. I need time."

Myrna shoves down the wave of emotions rushing through her. A new one, confusion, added to the mix. She curls them into a ball, thinking of the container she once made for her arcane and shoves them into it to turn them off. One day, they'll make an escape, but not now.

Because there is so much to do. Too much to deal with. Since Merizalmek, things have worsened. The battles have increased. There are now signs of the blight Laoise spoke about, and it's spreading. How this was not a more urgent issue, Myrna is unsure.

She jumps down from a boulder and savors the pain that radiates up her legs. Then she starts the final upward climb to the road, nodding to Guardian Jaden as she passes, the steps behind her comforting in their consistency.

Then, of course, she must also prove Brennan's dead and verify Imogen is safe. Even rescue her. Myrna also guesses it's time to take this heir job seriously, for there is an entire realm depending on her. Good thing she isn't alone. Not completely, at least.

Myrna straightens the tiny tiara pinned in her hair before she mounts Shay's horse, Shadowmar. No, her horse. And begins her ride back through Faerie to the palace, Kelan and her guard by her side.

The End

Thank you!

Dear Reader,

Thank you so much for reading the first book of the Shadow Faye Series! This book was a very different undertaking for me. Written in a new style and point of view, it was a challenge! Which is why it took so much longer for me to write. It's also why I spent extra time verifying I'd done it and the characters justice. The multiple rounds of edits, betas, editors, and help from my critique group meant a lot of hours spent at the computer.

Which is why I am grateful for all of those who helped make this book what it is. First, to my son, Tristan, for our brainstorming sessions in the car. Aenea for being my constant cheerleader and helping me work through issues when I'm stuck. You are my biggest fan. Thank you to my developmental editor, B. Stedman, for allowing me to see the pieces that were keeping this piece from shining. Working with you allowed such growth and in a fun way. To my alpha and beta readers; including, but not limited to, Vanna Campion, Cori Kuehn Holt, Shannon Takawaki, and Autumn Painter. And, as always, thank you for my speculative fiction group, who are always willing to review and critique my work. Marc DeGeorge, E. Marie Robertson, Michelle Darnell, J. Logan Rice, and Joe Creech, I've grown so much because of your help.

As you can see, it takes a village of fantastic individuals willing to take time out of their lives to read and provide feedback. It is because of them we have Unbound by Shadowspire! So, thank you. A future thank you to them for their work on book 2 because it's even bigger! :)

If you enjoyed **Unbound by Shadowspire,** please consider leaving a review. Reviews help authors more than you know by letting other readers know how you feel about the book. I enjoy reading them, too!

To leave a review with this vendor, please visit the vendor website and click on the "Leave Review" button. You may also leave one on Tracey's GoodReads Page at **https://www.goodre ads.com/traceycanoleauthor**and find the book listed. Of course, this is never required, but always appreciated. You can also review Tracey's other works here, too!

Exciting News! This is only the first installment of the Shadow Faye Series. Currently the series is planned to run for three, maybe four, books with the second to come out later this year! If you'd like to stay up to date on any of her new releases and giveaways, then please head over to her website at TraceyCano le.com to join her mailing list. Thank you again!

About Tracey Canole

Tracey Canole is a Science Fiction and Urban Fantasy author. Her stories take you on an adventure, drawing you into characters and their experiences as they navigate their extraordinary lives. Tracey loves stories based in reality and those that bend our understanding of the universe. Her favorites are those that have a fantastical element, allowing the reader to go somewhere they never expected.

When not writing, she enjoys reading and dabbling in many different art forms. You can often find her painting, crafting, and or playing with clay. But her absolute joy is found in exploring the world with her husband and two children. She's recently even had the opportunity to live overseas, experiencing the wonderful cultures the world has to offer.

This is Tracey's first true fantasy novel, but it won't be her last. Not only with this series continue, but there are more in the works! Let's just say fantasy and science fiction are in her blood. Check out her other works on her website TraceyCanole.com. There you can sign up for her newsletter to keep up with new releases, giveaways, and all things going on.

Interested in other works by Tracey Canole? Check out her adult science fiction, **The Secrets of Eronis 8**, then get access to a FREE short story!

<u>The Secrets of Eronis 8</u>

Leaving the homeworld was easy. Time becoming their enemy is the hard part.

The spacecraft, *The Aspire*, has one mission: reach the new world so its 3,500 passengers can start a new life. When Captain Mitchel Remian awakens from hypersleep to find life support down and the crew maintaining it missing, it's up to him to save what's left.

That Herculean task becomes even more urgent when a hostile alien presence is discovered. Crew are dying, their timelines seized and bled dry with an unnatural violence.

They must find a way to treat the ship and stop this malevolence before they get to their target destination or it will spread. The answers hide outside *The Aspire's* walls, but in the race against time with a life-sucking enemy and a deteriorating spaceship, it will take every bit of cunnin the crew can muster to reclaim their timelines and survive landing on their new homeworld.

The Secrets of Eronis 8 is a thrilling adventure, exploring planet colonization and first contact science fiction. It is an odyssey across our galaxy to start a new life in a new colony, but first they must defeat a parasitic time-altering menace.

Haven't captured your interest yet? What if I offered a **FREE SHORT STORY**! Meet The Aspire's crew from before they stepped onto the ship and see who almost didn't make it on. From **The Secrets of Eronis 8,** *I introduce you to....****Designating the Future***. **S**ign up for his monthly email by following the QR code below and get this **Free Story**!

<u>Designating the Future:</u>

The newest colony, Merocius, represents hope for a brighter future, away from the overpopulated Homeworld. But landing a spot on The Aspire is difficult, though.

They need the best of the best on this mission because there's no room for mistakes. The ship is the largest, the distance the farthest, and the solar system the most unexplored. Nothing can go wrong.

To say they're being highly selective would be an understatement.

Click or Scan Here!

www.ingramcontent.com/pod-product-compliance
Lightning Source LLC
Chambersburg PA
CBHW062110290726
48975CB00001B/181

FREAK SCHOOL

For The Ladies

FAYE JOSEPH

Freak School for the Ladies
by Faye Joseph

1. Freak School for the Ladies
2. Freak School for the Fellas
3. Freak School: Bride on the Run

ISBN (paperback): 979-8-88636-065-3
ISBN (ebook): 979-8-88636-064-6

FIC049030 FICTION / African American & Black / Erotica
FICTION / Romance / African American & Black
FIC027010 FICTION / Romance / Erotic

Printed in the United States of America

SHErotica Books

For all the ladies who need to get their freak on
and remember who they really are,
this series is for you.

Orientation Ain't Just What You Think

Summer Sinclair didn't know what to expect when the black Escalade pulled up to the gated hotel property just outside Charlotte, NC. The wrought-iron sign above the driveway read, "The Fordham Hotel." But nothing about this felt like a yoga and green juice retreat.

She clutched the handle of her Louis Vuitton roller bag like it was a lifeline. Her fiancé, Marcus, had called this "an investment in their future." He said Freak School was "a sexy little crash course to prepare for marriage." But all she could think about was the fine print she'd signed:

Six weeks. No safe word unless in physical distress. Complete sexual submission required.

She hadn't even met her instructor, and already she was wet.

Summer had been to spas, wellness retreats, and a tantric couples workshop in Tulum once. Still, none of them started with a nondisclosure agreement, a safety waiver, and an acknowledgment of the silence policy inside the orientation chamber.

The hotel was stunning. White stone walls, towering hedges, and staff dressed in black who moved like shadows. Her heels clicked against the marble as she entered the building through a hallway so pristine it felt sacred.

A woman approached her wearing a black wrap dress; she had milk chocolate skin, flawless auburn-red silk press down her back, and medium-length French tips shaped like claws with a 2.5-carat pear-shaped diamond on her ring finger with an infinity band. Her stomach is flat. She had a rockin' fat ass, ample breasts, and hips like heaven. I would place her at size 16, she thought. She wore a 20-inch gold chain with a charm that said "Mrs. Collins," and she strutted with the confidence of a woman whose life is completely fulfilled.

"Summer Sinclair?" she asked.

"Yes." Her voice sounded tight, unsure.

"I'm Natasha Collins. Headmistress of Freak School. Please, follow me."

As she turned, Natasha's smile curved into a wicked smirk because she knew this chick had no idea what was about to happen.

"First time?" Natasha walked and talked, not bothering to turn around.

Summer clutched the handle of her roller bag, trying to keep up. "Is it that obvious?"

She peered back. "Yes, darling. Freak School students have a look, and you've got it."

Summer exhaled, unsure if she felt flattered or exposed. Maybe both.

Summer gulped. She had on a white jumpsuit with a linen blazer and conservative French tips. Nothing in her Ivy League education had prepared her for this.

They walked silently down a curved marble hallway. At the end stood a pair of double doors, black lacquer with gold handles shaped like dicks.

Summer blinked hard and thought to herself, *"No. That can't be..."*

The doors opened. They walked into a sleekly decorated room that looked like a holding area or green room.

Natasha instructed her, "Leave your luggage here. It's time to get started. This is orientation, baby. And you'll be naked in about ten minutes."

"Wait—like, fully naked?" Summer said.

Natasha stopped, turned, and looked her over. "Sweetheart, this is *Freak* School, not a Catholic boarding school. We train women how to suck dick until a man cries. How to ride a man like it's an Olympic sport. How to tie a cherry with your tongue and own your pleasure like a CEO."

At the far end of the room, the other four women in the program stood in silence, with shocked and worried looks on their faces.

Emily had no words.

Mel said to herself, "Lawd, what did I sign up for?"

Teri said to herself, "My body is what it is. I hope the room is dark."

Bianca started taking deep breaths, terrified.

These ladies all have their own baggage and reasons to be here.

Emily Jackson, Richmond, VA, age 24

She was an elementary school teacher.

A virgin. Engaged to be married.

But no ring could mute the insecurity in her eyes.

"I want to serve my future NFL husband in all the ways he needs so that I can keep the hoes off him."

Bianca Bennett-Douglass, Charleston, SC, age 42

A walking brand of elegance and broken trust.

Her dream life was shattered. Her husband left her for his 27-year-old assistant. She showed up like she belonged in Hollywood, with designer heels and signed divorce papers still warm in her bag.

"My husband quit on me, and I have a rage that needs to be rewritten as power."

Mel Diebert, Rochester, NY, age 52

A widow with grace and grit.

She hadn't been touched in two years, at least not the way she wanted.

She came to Freak School with one goal:

"I don't want to remember who I used to be. I want to discover who I've never dared to become."

Teri Worthington, Charlotte, NC, age 43

The mother of two suffered a viral heartbreak.

Her fiancé left her for a man and then posted about it online.

The group chats and blog mentions of the scandal. She had a lot of shame.

But now? Teri was here with a fresh weave, a tight jaw, and something to prove.

"I'm not here to cry. I'm here to make somebody else scream for once."

Summer Sinclair, Atlanta, GA, age 31
A radiant Atlanta beauty engaged to Marcus Delacroix, heir to the Renald fortune. She enrolled at her fiancé's suggestion to up her skills before their pending wedding, even though she thought it was his skills that needed improving. She wants to use the opportunity to discover her own pleasure, power, and voice.

"I'm not here just to please my man; I'm here to figure out what I really want and finally say it out loud without shame."

Natasha gathered them together and started giving them the inside scoop.

"Ladies," she said, her voice smooth and commanding, "this is the last day you'll show up for anyone but yourselves. I'm about to tell you something that might sting before it sets you free: some men are sophisticated thinkers, but as women, we are more advanced thinkers. Most men's #1 goal is to tear women down to assert control. They make us vulnerable and insecure, so we are easier to manage.

Most of them don't understand their assignment. We are valuable. But ladies, you must internalize your value first. If you aren't thoroughly enjoying yourself and climaxing during sex, then you've got a serious damn problem. And it's not your fault, but it is your responsibility to fix it.

Here at Freak School, we don't just teach you how to give pleasure. We teach you how to own it. Control it. Command it. Because a screaming, back-arching orgasm isn't just a reward, it's a requirement," the ladies snickered.

"And you can start mastering it in just three steps. Let me break 'em down for you real quick:

Step 1: Handle Your Stress or It'll Handle Your Pussy

I'm serious. You can't cum consistently if your mind is overwhelmed, your jaw is clenched, and you're mentally running down your grocery list during missionary.

Stress is the ultimate orgasm blocker. Science backs this up, but think about it. That anxiety you're carrying? That tension in your shoulders? It travels right to your clit and slams the brakes on pleasure.

As she walked the room, she continued, "So while you're here, focus on your breath, stretch, and meditate. And unclench your ass," she said, looking right at Summer.

Take Back Your Power, Ladies. Before you lie down, let go.

Step 2: Know What Turns YOU On, Then Demand It.

Most of you have been trying to moan your way through mediocre sex without ever stopping to figure out what you actually like. That ends today.

Your job while you are here is to figure out what turns you on, what gets you wet, and what sends your toes curling, and then communicate that without shame.

Your man is not a mind reader. And if he's going to make you cum on command, he's gonna need instructions, guidance, and a few do-overs. Until you get him trained.

Step 3: Me Before We

Repeat after me: 'I must know how to make myself cum before I ever expect someone else to.' Say it!

If you don't know how to take yourself to the mountaintop solo, you'll struggle to get there with a partner. Here at Freak School, we teach solo pleasure as a foundation. Once you master your own body, once you know what feels good without pressure, you bring that wisdom into every bedroom you enter. In your rooms, you'll find a self-pleasure care package. Use these tools to explore your own body.

Stop chasing climax, start chasing pleasure, and climax will follow. And don't be cute with it; be curious. This week, your only job is to explore your own body and learn how to become a headmaster. Play, touch, test, ask questions, and moan freely.

Because when you leave here, your man's gonna need a prayer, a towel, and a neck brace.

With that, ladies, welcome to Freak School."

After Natasha left the room, the ladies stood in a loose circle, each trying not to be the first to speak.

Bianca was the first to break.

Arms folded. Brows raised. "Well. That was no TED Talk."

Her voice had bite and silk in equal parts.

Teri blew out a slow breath. "Did she really say 'tie knots with your tongue'?"

Mel, warm but watchful, responded softly. "And suck a man until he cries. Can't say she didn't warn us."

Emily still hadn't spoken. She stood near the back, hands clasped in front of her, eyes wide like she'd just walked into the wrong kind of church.

Bianca clocked her immediately. "Let me guess. You thought this was a bridal bootcamp? Signed up thinking you were gonna learn how to twerk in heels?"

Emily swallowed. "I—I-I'm getting married in six months. My cousin Trina... signed me up. She said, "My husband wanted a freak in the bed, and I needed skills to keep the hoes away.""

Bianca blinked. "Oh, baby. Becoming a freak all begins on your knees. Then, she burst out laughing like a hyena.

Mel intervened, her tone firm but gentle. We don't have to come for one another, ladies. Not today.

"Look, I'm here to figure out who the hell I am when I'm not trying to be wife material," Summer blurted out, annoyed by the conversation.

Teri snorted. "You speak for yourself. I came here to collect my dignity and get my groove back."

Mel straightened her spine. "My ex left me for a man. Then, posted about it. With emojis."

Bianca burst out laughing. "Girl. Please say it was the peach."

Teri grimaced. "He used the peach, eggplant, and two pink hearts."

They all laughed; it broke the ice.

Mel looked around at all of them and thought to herself, "What a crew: widowed, engaged virgin, divorced, dumped, and engaged but reconsidering."

Bianca raised her invisible glass. "Here's to the broken pieces. Let's make them sharp enough to carve out the women we were always meant to be. Freaks!"

Two

The Orientation Chamber

The butler, Ron, came and escorted the ladies to the Orientation Chamber. He reminded them that this was a place of silence.

The room glowed red, like desire had a color, and this was it. It smelled faintly of jasmine and sweat. Along one mirrored wall stood ten shirtless masked men, each wearing a different-colored mask: black, silver, red, green, orange, bronze, white, yellow, blue, and lavender.

They stood still as stone, but the man with the black mask. He drew Summer's attention.

He stood like he owned the air. Quiet. Watchful. His body was made for sin. And Summer felt it instantly.

He didn't make a sound, but his presence was loud. His broad shoulders glistened. He stood firm with his gloved hands clasped behind his back. His full lips were the only thing visible beneath the mask. And when he caught her checking him out, his lips curved into a smirk like he already knew what her moan would sound like.

Her stomach tightened.

Natasha said, "Let's not waste time, ladies. We train your bodies here, but more importantly, we untrain your shame."

She walked the line slowly. "You came here to please a partner. That's sweet. Noble, even. But what you don't know is that this place will teach you to please yourself. First, ladies, this is your new reality, and we only have a few rules here.

"#1 You don't say no. It's all for your pleasure and training.

"#2 You don't kiss your instructors on the lips. You can kiss anywhere else, however.

"#3 You are never, ever allowed to see your instructor's face. Masks must be worn at all times, including during shower training.

"#4 There are no timeouts here; we believe in corporal punishment. If you misbehave or whine to your instructor, you could be spanked. Now, some of y'all might start whining on purpose, trying to get spanked. But this is very serious here.

"Oh, and there is a safe word; it's 'Sugar Daddy,' and if you use it, you'll be sent to the Adult Playroom. You'll all be trained on the tools in our sex dungeon during your stay here, but do you want all of our instructors to have a turn? That is what happens in the playroom. So use this word with extreme caution. "Our process is designed to turn you into a CEO of your own pleasure. A woman who loves sex and is willing to do anything is a woman your husband or partner rushes home to love on every night."

The women were silent. Some were nervous—some curious.

Summer? She swallowed hard. She couldn't stop staring at Mr. Black, secretly hoping he was her instructor.

Natasha called each student one by one and the mask color. Each woman approached an instructor with the color mask that she was assigned. Then, the instructors, without clients, left the room.

When Summer's name was called, her heart slammed. You're assigned to Mr. Black.

She stepped forward, heels clicking like gunshots on the marble, until she stood before Mr. Black. He towered over her. The air between them pulsed.

"Remove your clothes, all but your panties," he said.

His voice was deep. Summer froze for a second.

Their eyes locked.

He didn't repeat himself. Then, she slowly removed the jacket and unzipped her jumpsuit. Her lace bra was next.

She stood there in only a pair of lace panties and heels. The room spun just slightly.

He circled her once. Then again. Not touching, just observing. And yet, her skin burned under his gaze.

"You're holding tension," he said quietly, stepping in closer.

Summer blinked. "Where?"

He didn't answer. Then, he knelt, put his right hand on

her waist, and gently pulled her panties down with his teeth. She stepped out of the panties and caught her breath. He whispered to her, "The heels stay on."

She stood bare. Exposed. Her nipples tightened under his gaze.

He circled her once. Then again. Like she was prey, and he was deciding how he'd eat her.

Finally, he slid a gloved hand between her thighs.

She gasped.

Wet.

He didn't smile. Didn't smirk. He just pulled back, satisfied. Then he spoke again.

"On the table. Now."

Summer climbed onto the table, the leather cool against her bare skin. Her legs trembled slightly as she lay back, her heart pounding like a bassline in a strip club.

"Raise your arms above your head," he whispered.

Click.

Straps secured her arms above her head.

Then he moved to her feet.

Click.

Ankles too.

She was fully restrained now. Arms above her head, wide. Legs open. Her pussy was already throbbing.

"This is your initial evaluation," Natasha's voice rang out from somewhere behind the red lights. "Each of you will be assessed on responsiveness, obedience, and orgasm potential."

Mr. Black leaned over her, his mouth just beside her ear.

"I'm going to make you come in under five minutes," he murmured. "If you do, you pass. If you don't..." His fingers grazed the inside of her thigh. "Then my techniques will get more extreme. No release. No mercy."

Summer whimpered.

He reached beside the table and retrieved something—a feather? A tool? She couldn't see.

Then, she felt it: the lightest touch at her knee. A gliding sensation, up her thigh. Barely there. Her muscles tensed, then softened.

Another stroke. This one down her side. Her arms. Her collarbone.

Her body became hypersensitive. Aroused but not invaded. It was maddening and magnetic all at once.

"Focus on your breath," he whispered.

So she did.

The strokes continued. Teasing. Measuring. Every inch of her skin was aroused. Her pussy was very wet by the time Mr. Black finally placed his tongue on the center of her clit, so warm and soft; she felt like she could cry from his touch.

"Let go," he said.

She didn't know what he meant. But she did.

Her body bucked when the sensation between her legs exploded—he was still applying light pressure, a warm breath against her clit.

She was floating.

The room disappeared.

She moaned, arching her back.

He slapped her right cheek lightly, controlled, and possessive.

"Don't move," he warned.

Natasha's voice broke through the haze. "Excellent, Mr. Black. She's already in phase one surrender."

Summer moaned, half in pleasure, half in embarrassment.

Then, two fingers slid inside her.

Curling. Pumping. Finding the spot. Like he had a blueprint to her body.

He licked her clit in time with his finger stimulation, slow and deliberate. He moved like he had all night to break her down.

Her eyes rolled back.

Her thighs quaked.

"Oh my God..." she whispered.

But he didn't stop.

Didn't *need* her permission.

"You're close," he growled. "Come for me. Now."

Summer shattered.

Her body snapped into climax so hard her breath was

caught in her throat. Legs shaking. Nipples tight. Vision blurred.

Her orgasm rolled through her like thunder.

She moaned so loudly, even the walls blushed.

She collapsed into the table like she'd been exorcised. Her legs trembled. Her arms ached in the cuffs. Her nipples were so sensitive that it felt like air could make her come again.

Mr. Black stood over her, silent, powerful, and unreadable.

"You pass," he said coolly, undoing her restraints.

She blinked, dazed. Her body was still lightly convulsing.

"That..." she whispered. "That was..."

He leaned down, his lips brushing her ear. "That was five percent of what I can do to you."

She lost her breath again.

"Once all the ladies were successful whimpering, Natasha's voice echoed, smooth and sharp like a blade dipped in honey. Excellent, ladies." Now we know that you guys can cum.

She stepped into view, arms folded. "Congratulations, ladies, you've just completed orientation. And let me be very clear, this was the warm-up."

A few of the women gasped. One laughed nervously. Summer didn't speak.

Mr. Black helped her off the table. Her knees nearly buckled.

"Next time," he said, brushing a hand over her lower back, "you'll scream louder than you did just now."

Behind the tables was a row of red mid-length silk robes. Summer found her robe and wrapped it around her shaking frame. Her brain screamed at her to remember why she was here: Marcus, her fiancé. This training was supposed to be for him—a gift.

But all she could think about was the man behind the black mask.

The way he owned her body without apology.

The way her soul leaned toward his voice as if it had known him before.

She wasn't sure what she came here looking for, but now she was more excited than ever to get schooled.

THREE

Luxury Accommodations

Each of the five ladies was given a sleek waterproof bracelet to wear at all times. It wasn't just a fashion statement; it was their key. With a simple wave of the wrist, their doors opened like magic. No locks, no knobs, just a quiet click and the soft swish of luxury welcoming them inside. It was also a tracking device, so security could keep them safe on the property.

Summer's room, like the others, had a five-star feel. The front area featured a plush cream couch, a glass coffee table, a mini fridge, and a sleek flat screen mounted above a long console. A modern desk sat off to the side, equipped with a Freak School-branded journal, pen, and a note that read:

> *"Your body is the* canvas. *Your pleasure is the point. Use this journal to capture your thoughts on this journey."*
>
> – Natasha

But it was the bedroom that made her clutch her imaginary pearls.

A sprawling king-size bed dominated the space, draped in purple silk sheets and a velvet comforter that practically whispered, "You won't sleep alone in here."

The vanity setup was high-end, with soft lights, a magnifying mirror, a drawer full of high-end toiletries, and a basket of sex toys. To the left, a walk-in closet with costumes, heels, thigh-high boots, and lingerie in every shade of bold. It even had bondage wear. To the right, a spa bathroom was so stunning, it looked like it belonged in a billionaire's penthouse.

There was a private toilet area, a clawfoot soaking tub, and a massive walk-in shower with a built-in bathroom that had an oversized showerhead, a handheld wand, and six wall jets.

Summer also spotted a small stool nestled in the corner of the bathroom.

Smirking to herself, she whispered, "I guess I'll find out what that's for soon enough."

Just then, there was a knock. Her door slid open as Ron, whom she had met earlier, came into the room.

He wore a sleek, black uniform; he was a small-framed man, 5'8" and a smidge, about 170 pounds, and with deep brown and butter-smooth skin. He clearly worked out; he had muscles on muscles and smelled nice, and his smile was all charm and mischief.

"Miss Summer," he said with a slight bow, "I'm Ron. I'll be your personal butler during your stay."

"Nice to meet you formally," she said.

Ron walked her through the features of her room. "TV has all the usual channels, plus access to a few X-rated channels if you are into that."

Her brows shot up. "Whatever you are into, we can provide it here," he winked.

He opened the nightstand drawers, revealing sex shop treasures. "Here we have a full selection of flavored oral aids, lubes, and condoms."

Then he set down a pair of fuzzy pink handcuffs and a personalized paddle. "For when you earn your first reward... or punishment," he teased. Summer's name was gold-stamped on it. "It's yours to take home when you graduate. But, uh, don't wait till then to break it in."

Summer raised an eyebrow. "Should I be concerned?"

Ron grinned. "Let's just say... Everything is here for your pleasure. You will have sessions in your training area, but some of your training will take place in your room."

She moved to unpack her own bag, pulling out the items listed on her intake form: multiple sets of heels, red lipstick, waterproof eyeliner, a journal, and a small bottle of her signature perfume. As she reached for the drawer to put her things away, she stopped.

"Wait... these aren't mine."

Ron turned. "Ah, yes. That's the Freak School starter wardrobe." The drawer was filled with thongs, crotchless panties, garter belts, matching bras, and lingerie in black, red, purple, and emerald, and matching satin robes. Sizes have been pre-fitted based on the information provided in your intake forms. You'll also get additional pieces based on your training regime."

Summer looked into the drawer and shook her head. "Damn. Y'all don't play."

Ron walked her over to a sleek black hamper beside the vanity. "Laundry gets picked up every two days. Washed, sanitized, and returned with a little surprise if you've earned one."

He paused, then added, "Speaking of maintenance, you'll need to go to the eighth floor today to see Willie, the grooming specialist."

"Wille?"

"Mmm-hmm," Ron said, leaning on the doorframe. "He handles all client and staff grooming. Coochie, booty, legs, pits. Full smooth realness. Natasha and Warren require it for everyone. Clean skin, clean experience. You'll have an initial evaluation today and go back every two weeks for maintenance."

Summer blinked. "Booty too?"

"Especially the booty. William's motto is *"No hair, no hesitation."*

She burst out laughing. "I'm dead."

"You'll love him. He's gentle and fast, and he hums Luther Vandross while he works. You'll feel like you're getting prepped for a music video."

Summer sat on the edge of the bed, looking around her suite. It was sensual, luxurious, and designed for a journey she couldn't fully see yet, but her body already knew it wanted.

"Thanks, Ron."

"My pleasure." He winked again, then paused at the door. "Oh, and just a heads up... Tomorrow evening is your first private training session. It starts at 10 pm.”

"With who?”

His grin widened. "Mr. Black.”

As the door slid closed behind him, Summer’s heart skipped.

She looked at the paddle on the nightstand, then thought about orientation again. Lord, what does Mr. Black have in store for me?, she thought.

Then, she whispered to herself, "Freak School really ain’t for beginners.”

FOUR

The Wax Inspection

Location: *11:00 AM | Freak School Spa*

Summer stepped off the elevator onto the eighth floor and immediately caught the scent of eucalyptus and coconut oil. The floor was different up here: white tile, gold trim, and soft jazz playing low from hidden speakers. It felt like a spa crossed with a secret club.

A sign on the wall read:

"Smooth skin, smooth ride. Welcome to your wax awakening."

She smirked. Freak School really had their branding on lock.

A statuesque woman with platinum hair and a tight bodysuit checked her in with a tablet. "Room three. Wild Willie, I mean Willie, is waiting for you."

Wild Willie? She thought, "Oh hell."

Summer took a breath and followed the white marble path to a black curtain. She pulled it back slowly. Inside, it looked like a high-end wax studio had met a very naughty dentist's office, with an adjustable table, dim lighting, and a rolling tray of shiny instruments.

And there he was.

Willie, or as she was apparently supposed to call him, Wild Willie, stood at the far end of the room, organizing wax sticks and smiling like he knew all her secrets. He was in his early forties, with caramel skin, dreadlocks tied up neatly, and a body that said he lifted more than wax pots in his free time.

"Summer Sinclair," he said, voice like molasses. "Right on time. Strip from the waist down and get comfortable on the table. A towel is optional, but trust me, honey, I've seen it all."

She raised a brow. "Are you always this forward?"

He grinned. "Only when I'm about to spread hot wax on your labia."

She laughed. Nervous, but excited.

The first few minutes were standard. He looked at what she was working with. He asked her how often she got waxed or sugared. He noticed she was pretty clean, but there was a landing strip that needed to be snatched.

And what about that booty hole? Does she get waxed, too? She shook her head no. Then he said, "Well, she will be waxed here. You're about to be as hairless as a Barbie doll, honey."

He adjusted the table for her knees, pulled on latex gloves, and used a warm cloth to clean her. She relaxed under his touch. He was methodical, not too clinical, and not too familiar. Just right.

"I like to take my time with new clients," he said, warming the wax in a pot. "Everybody's body is different. Everybody's pain threshold is different. And sometimes, pain brings up other things."

Summer raised an eyebrow. "Like what?"

"Old shame. Unspoken fantasies. Or just plain arousal. This table sees it all."

She swallowed hard.

First, he trimmed her hair with clippers to ¼ inch.

Then came the first strip.

Hot wax, firm pressure, then R-I-P.

"Whew!" she yelped.

He chuckled. "Yeah, baby. That first one always hits."

He pressed a gloved hand gently against the freshly waxed skin. It was oddly comforting.

"You okay?"

"Yeah," she said breathlessly. "Just wasn't ready."

"You're doing great," he said, dipping more wax. "And we're halfway done. The front, anyway."

She nodded, relaxing a bit.

But then he paused.

"Now...I do offer a little relief service. Optional, of course."

Summer looked at him sideways. "Excuse me?"

He didn't flinch. "Look, this shit hurts. Some clients find

it easier to endure when there's a little release at the end. It's discreet. Respectful. You control it. But it helps."

She blinked. "You give... happy endings?"

He nodded slowly. "Especially if it really hurts."

Her thighs clenched.

"Let's finish the front. And then you can tell me if you want the full experience."

He waxed her inner thighs, outer lips, and even the tiny strip she didn't realize she had near her hip crease. He was *thorough*.

When it came time for her to flip, he raised the table slightly.

"Okay, let's do the back."

She positioned herself on her hands and knees, face in the cradle, ass in the air.

"You're gonna feel a stretch," he warned. "And then some pressure."

She felt the warm wax between her booty cheeks, then his hand on her lower back. He was firm but gentle. There was nothing overtly sexual about it.

Until he spoke.

"You're taking this like a champ. You'd be surprised how many women flinch when I get back here. But not you. You're brave, and your body responds well."

Summer didn't know what to say. She just breathed.

R-I-P. She gasped. Then his hand. Rubbing slowly, low on her back, not quite her ass, but close. Calming. Warm.

She moaned—just a little.

"You want the tension gone?" he asked. She hesitated. "Yes."

He opened a drawer. Pulled out a small bottle. Something with a natural scent, like coconut and eucalyptus. "This is a CBD recovery oil. You'll feel a cool tingle. And then some magic."

She closed her eyes.

His hands massaged the oil in. Over the waxed skin. Over the tension. Over her curves. It wasn't fast or groping; it was care. She whimpered when he hit the right spot.

"Shhh, breathe." His fingers moved with intention. Not deep. Not vulgar. Just right. When her legs began to shake, he slowed down. "Let go, Summer." And she did.

A soft, shuddering orgasm rolled through her; it wasn't explosive. Just a release. Pure, unexpected pleasure in the most unexpected place.

He held her hips gently until the tremors passed.

Then he wiped her clean with a warm cloth. "See?" he said with a smile. "Wild Willie makes it all better." She got dressed slowly, her body light.

As she left, he handed her a card.

WILLIAM T. KELLEY
Licensed Esthetician
Waxing & Recovery Specialist
"Smooth is best for the groove."

She looked up at him. "You do this for everyone?"

He winked. "Only the ones who need it."

She floated down the hallway, no longer worried about her first training session tomorrow evening.

Summer was officially ready.

She ordered room service for dinner, wrote a little bit in her journal before bed, and got a good night's sleep.

Five

Dick Suck Prep

Location: *10:00 AM | Orchid Room*

As the morning sun hit, all the ladies were delivered room service and a note from Natasha.

> *"Enjoy your breakfast. Meet in the Orchid Room at 10 a.m. sharp—wear your Freak School robe and no panties. Today, we are learning about blow jobs."*
> – Natasha

Summer grinned as she read her note. "Whew, she wastes no time."

The Orchid Room was fragrant and opulent. Velvet drapes in deep purple. A mirrored ceiling. Plush chaise lounges are arranged in a semicircle around a small stage. Five chairs were set up, each with a tray.

Summer took her seat and peered down at the contents: three bananas (thick and curved), two dildos (one slim and one realistic), and a small container of flavored lube labeled *Freak Juice*, no doubt their private label brand.

Natasha entered the room like a dominatrix queen. She wore a red latex corset, booty shorts, thigh-high red boots, and a gold chain around her neck that read "MRS. COLLINS."

After she walked in, she introduced her husband, Dr. Warren Collins. He was tall, with broad shoulders and a chiseled chest, and fine enough to make a nun slide off her pew. He had slight grey in his beard. He was in his early 50s and definitely didn't need any Viagra to handle his business. He wore a silk robe and a knowing smile.

Natasha grinned. "Ladies, welcome to your first official oral mastery class. Let me be clear: this is not just about sucking dick. This is about power. Control. Influence. And pleasure, yours and his."

She turned to Warren. "Let me introduce you all to my husband. Dr. Warren Collins, the president of Freak School, and my Dickdaddy."

The ladies gasped and giggled.

He smirked and dropped his robe. It hit the floor like thunder. And yes, every inch of him looked like God took his time.

"Watch closely," Natasha said, kneeling on a square pad she had laid on the floor.

Then, she proceeded to put on a damn clinic.

She teased the head with her tongue, kissed the shaft from base to tip, then sucked one ball into her mouth, slow like a jawbreaker. Warren groaned. She moaned around him.

Summer's eyes widened as Natasha deep-throated that man like a pro, then pulled back to spit on it, and took that shaft double-fisted, and rocked him back and forth with purpose.

The room was dead silent except for wet sounds and soft moans.

For the finale, she locked eyes with the ladies as she sucked the life out of him, then swallowed all of it, with a dramatic "Ahhh."

Applause? Yes.

Warren pulled her up and tongue-kissed her like we weren't even watching. After her man finished slobbing her down, the girls felt like they wanted to applaud again.

Natasha winked and said, "He loves tasting his cum in my mouth."

I'm a Dick Sucking Queen. Like Cardi says, "I don't cook and I don't clean... but let me tell you how I got this ring."

The ladies hollered.

Warren put back on his robe with a satisfied smirk and walked out like he had just been prayed over and paid in full.

The ladies just stared.

Emily's jaw was on the floor. Summer was biting her lip.

Bianca whispered, "Goddamn." Teri whispered loud enough for all to hear, "That was the most amazing thing I've ever seen."

Natasha stood and dabbed her lips with a silk cloth, as if she'd just done something as casual as folding laundry.

She turned to the room with a slow, sly smile. "Now that's the technique you all need to master."

The ladies looked at each other nervously.

"I know that was a lot," Natasha said, pacing the room like a professor. "But let me be clear, this is a skill you can and must learn.

Ladies, this isn't just about dick worship. It's about power. You get your mouth right. You can get a ring, a Benz, and peace in your damn household."

She paused. Let it land.

"Now, let's talk about one of the most important things you'll ever learn here."

She turned and wrote on the whiteboard: "CONTROL YOUR GAG REFLEX."

"Some of y'all were already thinking, 'How the hell am I supposed to get that whole thing in my mouth without dying?'" She said.

"That's fair. But it's not impossible." She leaned on the desk like your favorite bad teacher.

"About 37% of women don't have a gag reflex at all, bless them. But for the rest of us, we've got to train our throats like we train anything else. And yes, baby, it takes practice."

She handed each woman a clean toothbrush handle, a small dildo, and a guide sheet titled 'Throat Training: Level 1.'

"This is how you desensitize your gag reflex over time so you can deep-throat like a grown-ass woman who runs shit."

Natasha's 7-Step Throat Training Guide:

1. Choose your tool.

Finger, toothbrush handle, clean dildo—whatever feels safe and firm.

2. Ease it in.

Place it into your mouth slowly, heading toward the back of your throat.

3. Trigger it on purpose.

Eventually, you'll hit your gag zone. That's okay. You're training it.

4. Hold & Breathe.

When your reflex kicks in, try to suppress it. Focus on breathing through your nose. Relax your jaw and throat.

5. Time it.

Hold the item steady at the back of your throat for up to 10 seconds. Do not move it.

6. Repeat daily.

Practice this 2–3 times a day. By the end of the first week, you'll already notice improvement.

7. Add movement.

Once you're stable with pressure, start slowly moving it in and out, like simulating the real thing. Your reflex will scream at first. Ignore it. Stay calm. You're a queen in training.

When she finished the lesson, Teri said, "I'm going to learn this." Summer was nodding with purpose. Bianca was already testing her throat. Emily held her banana like it was holy.

Natasha closed her lecture with a smirk. "Once you get this down? You'll make him forget every other mouth that's ever touched him. And you'll never be afraid of the words 'deep throat' again."

The ladies got to work. Natasha walked between them, giving tips like a naughty coach.

"Spit is your ally, ladies. Don't be stingy; use it like lube straight from heaven."

"Emily, you can't approach this dick like you are afraid. Charm it like you'd charm a snake: steady, confident, and entrancing. And watch the teeth. Pretend it's a blessing, not a carrot stick."

"Mel, you must breathe out your nose or you'll pass out.

"Teri, that dick is a sensitive instrument; seduce it like you're playing the flute.

"Let's do a little exercise, ladies. I want you to grab your dildos, the realistic ones; let's put a little peanut butter on them, and then lick and suck them off.

"Another tip: if you close your eyes to focus, that's good

technique."

Mel was imagining that it was her late husband's dick, so she was good once she relaxed.

"Summer, you don't seem to be struggling too much with this one. I'm pleasantly surprised."

Summer was focused. She tested angles, speed, and pressure. The banana was quickly slick with lube, and her lipstick smeared halfway to her chin.

"This isn't about porn, ladies," Natasha reminded. "This is about how you want him to feel. Worship the dick. Respect it. Command it. That is your dick, your pleasure stick. No one should be able to service that dick better than you."

Ok, use the toy cleaner to clean any extra peanut butter off, and let me show you something else. She picked up the lifelike dildo and showed the stroke-while-suck combo.

Then, she added one last thing that will blow his mind. "If you are on your knees, and he is standing while you deep-throat him, extend your hand and start licking his testicles. The key is keeping him deep in your throat as you do this. Suck the dick and lick the balls underneath. This will make him go crazy."

The women mirrored her moves. Some gagged. Some giggled. Some found a rhythm.

Summer looked around and grinned. This wasn't a class. This was a sisterhood of future headmistresses.

And she was ready to earn her crown.

Six

Mrs. Natasha Collins

Before she was Headmistress of Freak School, wearing red lace corsets and thigh-high latex boots, Natasha Daniels was a brilliant, bold, plus-size marketing executive with a taste for erotica and no time for boring men. She never married or had kids. She once wanted that, but when she turned 40, after severe medical complications from fibroids, her dream changed. But she never stopped being open to the right life partner.

Natasha was a thick, elegant Black woman with honey-brown skin and long red hair. She was 5'6" with a voluptuous size 16, with a flat stomach, 42 Double D breasts, and a booty that could make an ass man a person with an addiction. Her curves were like poetry, and she had gorgeous, thick legs that could make traffic stop.

She was always a big girl, wickedly smart with a healthy sense of herself. We can all thank her daddy for that. Her father told her every day she could do anything and that she was beautiful. By the time she landed in a top-five business school to get her MBA, she took great pleasure in besting her classmates. She viewed her body as a gift. But it took time for her to learn how to harness her sexual power.

After grad school, she dated Jonah, a man 17 years her elder, who taught her about her body and made her his freak. After their three-year relationship ended, she realized that if her potential partners couldn't match her sexual appetite or skill level, it wouldn't work.

She began her professional career selling high-end accessory lines and luxury beauty brands before realizing she was working nonstop and promoting the upscale lifestyle rather than living it. After attending a few exclusive retreats for Black women executives, she recognized how unhappy so many women are with their sex lives. She wanted to become a sex therapist to help women capture sexual power. She went to school online and earned a master's in counseling and worked two years under a clinical psychologist to become a licensed sex therapist.

Her life changed in the erotic section at a bookstore in D.C.

On a rare day off, she was crouched low, flipping through *The Sexual Life of Catherine M.*, when a shadow fell across the shelf.

"You've got good taste," a deep voice said.

She looked up and saw him.

He was a tall, handsome, mocha-colored man with a close fade, glasses, a mustache, and a tapered beard. His broad shoulders fit his navy blazer perfectly.

It was Dr. Warren C. Collins. She smiled and thought to herself, "This man's voice is sexy. He's buttoned up, educated, and fine enough to make your thighs applaud and your ass clap. Good Lawd."

Then she blinked and said, "You read this stuff?"

He smirked. "It's research."

She furrowed her brow. "Really? For what?"

He leaned in and lowered his voice. "I reference these books in my private practice."

"Do tell," she quipped.

"I'm a clinical psychologist and sex therapist. I help individuals and couples reconnect with their desire. I do intimacy coaching. I also teach clinical psychology courses to Ph.D. students at Whitmore University in Charlotte, North Carolina.

Natasha stood slowly, book still in hand, and said, "I was just recently licensed as a sex therapist here in D.C. I have my master's in counseling. You should give me your card."

He handed it over without hesitation.

Warren C. Collins, Ph.D.,
Clinical Psychologist/Relationship Therapist
Private Coaching & Couples Therapy

wcollins@whitmore.edu
704-394-7245 (c)
704-521-1108 (o)

That night, she emailed him.

He was in town for a few more days, so they made the most of his time in DC. Their first date lasted four hours. Clothes stayed on, but their minds got naked.

By the third date, they were lovers. She blew his mind the way she sucked him, and she quickly craved his stroke game and how he ate her like his favorite gourmet meal.

Mostly, they loved just lying in bed naked, talking about life, their needs, and their dreams.

The night before he left D.C., he invited Natasha to dinner at his hotel. They barely got through drinks before Warren led Natasha to his hotel room. Once inside, he pushed her back to the wall with a soft thud, his mouth already on hers, hungry and precise. Warren kissed like he thought about it all day—how he would devour her. His hands were warm and steady, roaming up and down her body like a man tracing his future.

"Can you handle all of this?" he asked between kisses, voice low, breath uneven.

Natasha smirked and pulled him closer. "Of course, tell me what you want."

That was all it took. Warren reached down and touched her wetness, brought his finger to his lips, and said, "I want this pussy to be mine!" in his raw, guttural voice.

Their clothes fell in a blur, and soon she was straddling the edge of the bed, nude, slick, and electric. He knelt and spread her legs. "You're gorgeous," he murmured, running his fingers along her thighs. "And dangerous."

He kissed the back of her left thigh, slow and deliberate. He murmured. "I've been waiting all day to taste this pussy, and I'm going to take my time."

Natasha grabbed the sheets; his thumb rubbed her clit as he buried his face between her legs. She gasped sharply but didn't move. His tongue traced her slit, slow, luxurious, and deliberate.

"My favorite thing is feasting on the part of a woman most men pretend not to crave."

Then, he went back to work, slowly, thoroughly, like a man on a mission to make her forget any man who had come before him. Warren took great pride in pleasuring her. He licked her like he had all night and intended to use every second of it. He loved edging her and not letting her climax. She begged him to let her cum, but Daddy wasn't having it. He wasn't stopping until his mustache and beard were soaked with her juices.

She reached down and palmed his head, not to guide but to stay connected. Warren hummed in response, a sound so low and satisfied it reverberated through her. He undid every ounce of power she thought she had, just to give it back, worshipped and dripping.

After 44 minutes of complete oral pleasure, Natasha's orgasm exploded. He got off too and stayed hard. Natasha wanted to taste him, but he waved her off. "There'll be time for that later; right now, you need to feel these 10 inches I got for you." She slid back on the bed so he could finally get in it with her. His lips crashed into hers as he kissed her deeply, then he rolled her and slid into her. It felt so good; he groaned like he was transported to an out-of-body experience. "Damn, this pussy is so wet and tight."

His rhythm started slow as he railed her, but she threw it back on him, daring him to go deeper. She squeezed him from inside. His pace stuttered as her grip tightened. A slow, wicked smile curved his lips. "Oh, you're getting it now," he said. "Give it to me, Daddy," she whimpered.

He slammed his hips with the kind of stroke that rewired her nervous system. That night, they didn't just sleep together; they collided, claimed, and memorized each other.

And by dawn, neither of them had any doubts. She wanted to be his, and he had already emotionally made her his queen.

When he went back home, they talked every day. His was the first and last voice Natasha heard every night. A month later, when she visited him in Charlotte, he told her that he could barely stand to be apart from her. When Warren started talking about the future and her moving to Charlotte, she felt like she needed to say something. "Now, Warren, I don't really believe in living together, and you're asking me to consider giving up my friends and community I've built over the last 15 years and moved here to the South to be with you. I am not asking you to do anything yet; I'm just letting you know my intention. I want us to be partners, in and out of bed.

From the moment he laid eyes on Natasha, something inside him quieted. He wanted to be with her because she didn't just look at him; she understood him. The healer. The visionary. The man who carried desire not as shame, but as sacred power. With her, he could be all of himself, a gentle guide by day, a ravenous lover by night. She saw his soul first and his hunger second. And that was the moment he knew: she was the one he longed to have by his side.

Warren thought her most endearing traits were that she was unapologetically sexy and a marketing genius who was brilliant in business. She had already been building a side business as a sex therapist and working on her book, *Freak in the Bed*, when they met. She loved helping women of all sizes get their freak on and own their pleasure. When she pitched the idea of Freak School to Warren, he didn't flinch.

Within a few months, they got engaged, Natasha put her DC condo on the market, and moved to Charlotte with Warren. He had a three-story townhouse, and he made one of the guest bedrooms into her office. He had an office on the first floor of the house and one at the university. He served private clients from a suite in a medical office building not far from his home.

She still had a few consulting clients in the luxury retail space. However, her priority was completing their business plan for Fordham Enterprises, a 5-star sex education and training company. She developed the business model and marketing plan. They would have a hotel, which would include a training/retreat space, a luxury spa, and Freak School training programs serving married couples and single women targeting an A-list of clients. Natasha called her college roommate, Cinda Lewis, an IP lawyer in Atlanta, to trademark their logos and business brands.

The other key to their plan was purchasing a hotel or

warehouse property that would be their corporate offices and a functional hotel. Warren worked with his best friend and former college teammate, Eric Lyons, to secure the SBA loan to purchase an old warehouse that they transformed into the Fordham Hotel. Eric came on board to manage the construction/renovation project with plans for him to run the hotel as general manager upon its opening.

A month after she arrived in Charlotte for good, Warren and Natasha went to the courthouse on a Thursday afternoon and got married. Eric and Cinda came as witnesses. Natasha's ivory wedding dress was elegant and fitted her like a second skin. The silk crepe hugged her curves from the bodice down to the mid-thigh before blooming into a subtle fishtail hem that swept just past her ankles, revealing her sharp red bottom stilettos. She wore a pillbox fascinator in her hair, with a mini veil.

They took an SBA loan, the budget they were going to use for the wedding, and the proceeds from the sale of Natasha's DC condo, and a significant portion of Warren's savings to renovate the 10-story warehouse into a luxury boutique hotel with a state-of-the-art luxury spa, restaurant, and training facility. They also decided to build a penthouse suite for them to live in, with a private rooftop terrace, and a second one for their most exclusive celebrity clientele. The project took 18 months to complete.

After the opening, they moved into the penthouse and kept Warren's townhouse in case they had family or out-of-town guests that they didn't want in their business. They built executive offices, counseling areas, meeting rooms, a recovery suite, a workout center, and a meal/food prep area. Thirty hotel rooms were set aside for residential staff/Freak School students, and two floors were their training center and a private spa/grooming salon. They also built a separate VIP entrance and elevator system for the Freak School clients to protect their privacy.

Together, they built a public and secret empire.

By day, he operated in academic excellence and conducted research and taught graduate students, and by night, they built curriculum for Freak School. Natasha built the instructor team and developed their intensive training program, and she also built their brand in elite circles. Warren continued seeing patients and teaching. Natasha did podcast interviews, keynote speeches, posted blogs, and video reels for women who needed to spice things up and stop tolerating mediocre sex.

Just as they were opening the hotel, Natasha released her book, *Freak in the Bed: How to Own Your Sexual Power, Mouths, and Moans to Get Anything You Want*. She recruited the first cohort of ladies for Freak School from her workshops to promote the book.

Warren focused on teaching men how to please their partners and worship them as a way to train them to be the sexual vixens they needed.

It's been five years since they opened The Fordham Hotel. Now, they run quarterly retreats for power couples and churches, host black-tie masquerade kink weekends in secluded mansions, and partner with luxury brands. Their husband-and-wife podcast, *Naked Ambition*, has 1.2 million monthly listeners. Warren and Natasha teach that a sex life doesn't end at the altar; it should begin there.

The women always asked Natasha how she pulled a man like Warren.

Her answer, "Warren is so brilliant and handsome that he could've had anyone. But when we met, his vibe met my vibe, and it was electric. He's the only one who could hold all of me. He doesn't just love me; he builds with me. Warren makes my mind tingle and my body melt, and our purpose is our legacy. He encourages my bright light and never tries to dim it. He is my soulmate."

Natasha swore she was allergic to the South and had no intentions of ever moving below the Mason-Dixon Line, but Warren got her to leave DC and marry him within months of knowing him.

Natasha smiles every time she thinks about her hubby and the dream life they've built.

She's Mrs. Natasha Collins, Headmistress of Freak School, and loves every minute of it.

Seven

Dr. Warren C. Collins

By day, Dr. Warren C. Collins is the picture of Black excellence, fit, tall, handsome, and brilliant. Perfection in a tailored suit. A Ph.D. in Clinical Psychology and a Harvard Fellow and tenured faculty at the prestigious Whitmore University, one of the A-list Historically Black Colleges and Universities in North Carolina. He carries himself with calm authority, the consummate professional, always in control of his emotions. But by night? Warren peels off the suit and steps into his whole truth, a freak with a vision, driven by purpose and pleasure.

He's known he had a kinky two-sided personality since undergrad.

While his peers were getting off to dorm hookups and Greek life parties, Warren was always about business. You could find him in the library reading publications from the Kinsey Institute for Sex Research, *The Joy of Sex*, and Dr. Ruth's Guide to Erotic and Sensuous Pleasures. His undergraduate thesis was on the intersection of sexual pleasure and emotional intimacy. By the time he finished his Ph.D., his research was focused on one specific demographic: happily married couples who have consistent, explosive sex.

He wanted to crack the code. Why do some couples keep the fire, while most lose it by year three? He interviewed more than 100 couples. Unfortunately, his personal life didn't reflect his academic genius.

He married his college sweetheart, Maxine Kelly. A good woman. Church girl. She held a Ph.D. in library science and worked as the chief librarian at a local community college. She was a fantastic researcher. Perfect on paper. But their sex life was bland and predictable. Twice a month, if he was lucky.

And never with the lights on.

Warren hid his kinks. His toys. His thirst. For six years, he played the role and never cheated on his wife. But deep down, he wanted to; he was starving to scratch his freaky itch.

Finally, he left. They had no kids, so there was no drama. When he made his silent exit, he vowed never to suppress himself again. Love wasn't enough; all of his needs had to be met.

After Maxine came Renee. Wild, gorgeous, and deep in the swinger lifestyle. For a while, Warren loved it—the parties, the group scenes, and the no-judgment freedom. But eventually, the novelty wore off. What he really craved wasn't more options. He wanted one woman, his own personal freak. A partner. A queen. A woman who wouldn't just tolerate his desires but match them. He stayed single for more than a decade after his divorce.

One day, he wandered into a local Black-owned bookstore while on a business trip to D.C.

He was in the nation's capital for a conference and wandered into the Romance Erotica section, which he often did when he was travelling. Natasha was crouched low, flipping through *"The Sexual Life of Catherine M.,"* a raw, controversial memoir that Warren knew well. Warren noticed her thick thighs and red hair and was totally intrigued. She was a masterpiece in black yoga pants. Confident, unbothered, immovable.

He was standing three feet from her, pretending to read something by bell hooks, but he was watching her and studying her. Not in the creepy way, more like a man witnessing a glitch in the Matrix. Then he finally asked her what she was reading. She smiled, stood up, shook out her long red hair, turned, and looked directly at him.

"You read this stuff?" she asked, lifting her chin toward the title in her hand.

He grinned. "It's research."

She was 5'6" and had a beautiful face, full lips, curvy hips, and a flat stomach. Her executive presence made the air around her heavier.

He'd seen beautiful women and slept with more than a few. But this one? Natasha Daniels made both his dick and his brain wake up at the same time. She was the kind of woman who didn't ask for permission to be seen. And she saw him.

She eyed the book in his hand, then his shoes, then his mouth.

She smirked, trying to decide whether or not she wanted to devour him. Then, she said, "Clinical research or personal enrichment?"

Warren chuckled. "Hopefully both."

That's how it started, with banter and books and glances that lingered just a second too long.

The rest moved fast.

Coffee the next morning turned into dinner the same night. He had only three days left in town, and he spent as much time as possible with her before leaving. Within weeks, he was the first and last voice she heard each day. He knew her laugh and playlists, and he studied her body like scripture. She asked hard questions and didn't back down. She challenged his emotional intelligence and then fed him crab cakes she'd made from scratch when she visited him in Charlotte. After that, he didn't let three weeks pass before he saw her again.

He told himself to slow down, but Natasha was always on his mind. He wanted to be with her all the time. When she left, he would smell her pillow on his bed. She didn't just excite him; she made him better.

His friends were stunned when he proposed after only four months. Some thought Natasha was too bold, but Warren didn't care what anyone thought. As far as he was concerned, she was his rib. "She's the perfect business partner and lover," he told his closest friends. "And the only woman who can match my intellect and my appetite."

She had the mind of a CEO, the mouth of a porn star, and the body of his wildest fantasies. Warren was an ass man, and Natasha was a whole buffet. More importantly, she saw him. The therapist. The freak. The visionary. The man who wanted to teach the world how to stay sexually satisfied.

Together, they built Freak School, their pleasure empire.

Warren used his clinical expertise to design male and female course curriculum, everything from anatomy education to orgasm mapping to emotional resilience. Natasha created the instructor training. She also handled all marketing and branding, and the look and feel of the training areas and the hotel property. Velvet luxury was all her idea. She oversees the Freak School staff, trains the instructors, and manages the student selection process.

Warren is sexually evolved, emotionally intelligent, and spiritually grounded. He believes erotic mastery is just as important as emotional maturity, and he trains men to embody both.

Some men play golf. Warren co-hosts curated luxury intimacy retreats with his wife across the globe.

Moguls. Doctors. Athletes. CEOs. Singles and couples fly in, undress, and trust them with their deepest desires. They lead people through sexual transformation.

So when people ask how Dr. Warren Collins, the tenured professor in custom Tom Ford suits, ended up married to a red-haired siren who trains women how to ride like CEOs and squirt on command, he doesn't flinch. He leans back, smiles like a man who knows he hit the jackpot, and says:

"Because she didn't just turn me on, she turned me out. She saw all of me: the academic and the animal, the healer and the hedonist. And she didn't run. She invited me deeper. Natasha didn't just match my freakiness; she met my purpose. Together, we made pleasure a profession and intimacy an empire. She is the reason I get to live in full alignment every single day. Loving her is the freest I've ever felt, and building this life together? That's the real climax."

EIGHT

Sexy Core & Twerking with Keisha

Location: *8:00 AM | Fitness Studio*

Keisha came to class wearing a sheer black bodysuit with long sleeves that hooked around her thumbs. It was accented with a super short red satin skirt and black suede lace-up peep-toe thigh-high boots. She looked amazing. Afrobeats were coming through the speakers.

Class began with a demonstration.

She bent down and got her Eagle on, and you could see her red thong as her knees fanned open and closed. Then, she turned to the side and rolled her body up and down a few times. She had complete control and balance.

Then, she stopped midway down, shaking her booty while fanning her hand. She went up and down a couple more times, put her hands on her hips, and twerked her booty with wild abandon for almost a minute. She looked like a woman fully posed. She could make a man scream before he ever touched her.

Next, she started turning toward the class with one hand in front and one hand behind and showed us standing hip tilts.

The class didn't begin with a stretch. She put them in front of mirrors.

She had each woman look at herself and say out loud, "My body is not a problem. My body is a promise."

Emily choked on hers. Mel raised an eyebrow. Teri rolled her eyes, but she said it. Quietly.

Keisha clapped her hands.

"Good. Now let's get into these hips."

She took them through squats, hip rolls, and twerking techniques, but then, she paused and turned to Emily.

"Emily, baby, your booty's moving like it's writing in

cursive, but the pen ran out of ink. Come here.”

Emily blushed but stepped forward.

Keisha stood behind her, hands lightly on her waist.

“This isn’t about being sexy for him. This is about you knowing you can move like a woman who knows her worth.”

She guided her hips. Showed her how to tilt, pop, and reset.

Emily started to sweat a little, but her hips slowly began to sway.

Twerk. Bounce. Shimmy. The whole room erupted when she finally got it.

Meanwhile, Mel was sweating like she hadn’t in years. “Jesus, these squats are disrespectful.”

“You used to dance, right?” Keisha called out. Mel nodded. “In a past life.”

“Then dig that woman out! She’s still in there under all that bank manager energy. Let her grind!”

Mel let out a laugh, arched her back, and gave the mirror a look that said, “Yeah, bitch, I still got it.”

She bounced once. Twice. On the third, she caught the rhythm.

Keisha screamed, “That’s it! Move them hips like a mortgage, locked in!” Teri?

Teri had forgotten how much she loved to shake that ass.

Keisha walked by her mat, leaned down, and whispered, “Sis, if your man were behind you right now, you’d own his life.”

Teri gasped. Then, pushed her ass higher.

She smirked.

And said to herself, “Let me stop playing; I could still take a man’s soul in this position.”

Keisha closed class with wall squats and pussy pulses.

“Every time I say squeeze, I want you to contract that pretty little kegel muscle like your man’s dick just hit the right spot.”

“Squeeze, release, squeeze. Hold that shit.............5-4-3-2-1 Release!”

Summer was squeezing, bouncing on tiptoes.

Bianca held hers so long that she got dizzy.

Mel started giggling uncontrollably.

Emily whispered, "This feels… powerful."
Teri squeezed it so hard and thought, "I will own him."
Keisha walked to the front, smiling widely.
"This is the warm-up. This is the foundation. You move like a goddess before you let anyone worship at your temple."

NINE

Summer & Mr. Black

Location: *10:02 PM | Training Suite 2*

Summer stood in front of the black door with her name on the gold plate.

She hadn't stopped thinking about Mr. Black since orientation. That first orgasm had cracked her open like a peach—sweet, dripping, needy. And now she wanted more.

The note on her bed this morning had said:

> *Come to Training Suite 2 at 10:00 PM.*
> *Come in your robe. Bring your mouth. Leave*
> *everything else.*

When she arrived, the door opened. The room smelled like leather, citrus, and anticipation.

Red velvet curtains lined the walls. A black leather lounge sat in the corner. The lights were low but warm. In the center of the room was a padded mat with pillows on the floor. One stool. And Mr. Black, standing shirtless and barefoot, in baggy black linen pants that showcased his muscular physique. His mask covered everything but those sinful lips.

"Take off your robe; let me look at you," he said.

Summer obeyed, shrugging off her robe slowly.

She was ready.

She just didn't know for what.

Mr. Black's voice was calm, deep, and firm.

"This week is about mouthwork. Before you can ride or dominate or beg to be filled, you have to understand how to *honor the dick.* You think you know, but most of y'all have just been spitting and praying."

~ 43 ~

Summer bit her lip.

"I don't want performers," he continued. "I want worshippers."

He circled her like a lion. "And I think you've got something special in you, Summer. I saw it on day one. You just need refinement. A little practice, and a lot of praise."

Then, he sat on the stool and spread his legs.

"Let's begin."

But instead of pulling his dick out, he pointed at the plush, fluffy rug on the floor and said, "Lie down."

Summer blinked. "I thought we were starting with…"

"I said, lie down."

She moved quickly.

And then, without a word, he dropped to his knees and buried his face between her thighs.

He started with her right inner thigh and licked her slowly, then he started sucking on it.

She gasped. "Oh my God…"

Then, he blew on her kitty lightly, and it started getting really wet, but he wasn't ready to go there yet.

He had to tease her. He raised her arms, placed one of his hands on each of hers, and held them down.

Next, he ventured down to those titties he was dying to taste. He started on the right, then moved to the left. He sucked and licked her, and then he gently bit on her nipples. All Summer could do was moan in pleasure.

He gently whispered, "Do you like that?" She moaned, "Yesss." Then he quipped. "I know what you need." He moved down to her belly button and licked and sucked on it, licking his way to her inner thigh on the left. Then he groaned a little as he licked and sucked on that side.

All of this was mind-fucking the shit out of Summer.

When he heard the right kind of whimper, he leaned in and got really close to her ear, saying, "Are you ready for Daddy to eat that kitty now?"

All Summer could do was moan a weak response, "Please, Daddy, I need it."

Then, he pulled her legs up and held them at a 45-degree

angle and just barely licked her clit with the slightest tongue pressure, and that made her arch off the mat.

He moaned into her pussy and rubbed his smooth face all in it. He gripped her thighs with firm hands and sucked on her clit like he was gently drinking a Slurpee that was almost gone. She was trembling in minutes.

"See," he said, lifting his head just long enough to speak, "a good mouth starts with generosity. I give first. So when I ask, you'll crawl to give it to me."

Then, he dove back in.

Light tongue strokes. Then suction, blowing, licking, and sucking more. She was breathless.

She had never experienced anything like this. She sobbed in ecstasy. She wasn't even trying to be sexy; her body was just unraveling.

He brought her to the edge three times. Denied her twice. Each time, he would come up for air and talk smack to her. "I know you ain't had it like this."

The third time, he sat on his face and licked and sucked it so she came in his mouth. He sucked the organism right out of her.

Her legs were shaking like never before. Pussy pulsing. Voice broken.

Then, he held her there, still lightly licking it and blowing on it. Summer was begging, "Please stop, Mr. Black." I can't take it anymore.

He smacked her ass, as if to say, "I'll stop sucking when I'm done." He licked that clit for one more minute before he finally stopped.

When she calmed down and slid off his face, he stood. Yeah, that kitty's going to be throbbing for a minute. I like giving you head. I love your moans, and I like the way you taste. Get yourself together, and then crawl over here and show me what you can do with this dick.

She was still panting as he dropped his pants.

He didn't even have any underwear on. He was rolling free Willie style.

His big black dick was hard now; it was thick, dark, and

curved slightly up.

The sight of the dick made her heart tremble. Her first thought was to go push him down and ride the dick, but then she remembered her assignment.

Then, she looked at his dick like it was a final exam.

Summer rose to her knees slowly. Her legs still felt like rubber from the orgasm he'd just gifted her, but she had a job to do. Her eyes locked on his dick. Up close, it looked even more intimidating, thick, veiny, and mouthwatering.

"You're not here to be cute," he said, voice low and deliberate. "You're here to learn how to use that mouth like it's magic."

Summer licked her lips, heat pulsing between her legs all over again.

"I want to see your grip," he continued. "No teeth. No hesitation. And don't you dare break eye contact."

She leaned in, inhaling his scent, clean and masculine, with a hint of leather and power. Then, she wrapped her hand around the base of his dick and kissed the tip gently.

"Good," he murmured. "Now take it slow. Use your tongue."

She circled the head with her tongue, teasing the slit, then licked down the shaft and back up, her hands stroking in rhythm.

He grunted.

"That's it. Show me you want to control this dick."

She opened her mouth and took the tip in, just the tip at first, sucking softly, keeping her eyes on him the whole time.

His breath hitched. Summer knew she was breaking him down. His fingers tangled in her curls. He pushed down slightly to keep her on his dick.

"Now double-hand that shit," he growled. "Get messy."

She moaned around his dick and did as she was told, both hands working in tandem, her spit dripping down to coat him.

He hissed. "You're a natural, Summer."

She went deeper, slowly pushing her limits, taking more of him, and gagging just slightly.

He pulled back. "Don't choke. Control it. Relax your throat."

She nodded, eyes glassy with effort and arousal. She took it back in slowly, and this time she was deep-throating him. After a couple of minutes, he said, "Now, fondle the balls while you deep throat it," he commanded.

She felt like an oral gymnast, but she did as she was told. When things became really tough, she removed her mouth from his dick and began gently cupping his balls with one hand while jerking him with the other. She sucked one into her mouth like a lollipop after kissing them. She then completed the other one.

"Fuck," he let out. "That's it. Just like that."

She pinched the one she had just licked with her tongue and started feverishly sucking the head while double-fisting his big black cock, lapping that dick like a good girl gone bad.

Then, he started to holla. When he finally came, she caught most of it, but she couldn't swallow.

She pulled back and spit it out. She was dripping with spit, eyes dazed, mouth swollen, and glowing.

He was impressed. "That was damn good, I can't lie. You definitely put your all into it." She responded, "Let's say I was inspired to pleasure you.

"Yes, I think you were. Next time," he said, "you're gonna swallow it."

She looked up at him, breathing hard, flushed and high off the praise.

"Yes, Sir."

He leaned down, hugged her, and whispered, "Class dismissed, Headmistress-in-training."

Summer and Mr. Black's Reflections

Journal Entry: *1:32 AM | "I Impressed Myself"*

Summer laid across her bed, savoring her afterglow, her skin still warm, her breath still shallow, and her body humming like a slow jam that wouldn't fade out. Her thighs were damp. Her lips tingled. Her jaw ached, in the *best* way.

She'd just given the most intense blowjob of her life. And for the first time, it wasn't about performance. It wasn't about being good at it. It wasn't about the man she was supposed to impress. It was about her.

It was about the way she felt when Mr. Black looked at her like she was the only woman in the world who'd ever made him exhale like that.

It was about the way her body came alive just hearing the words, "Good girl."

She pulled the sheets over her breasts, still naked, still basking.

Her hand drifted over her inner thigh. She wasn't trying to cum again.

She just wanted to feel herself.

When she was on her knees, his dick in her hands, mouth, and throat, she forgot everything else.

She forgot about Marcus.

Forgot about the wedding planner's timeline.

Forgot about her mother's warning that "respectable women don't do all that."

Because it wasn't performative, it felt earned.

She felt proud. Like every moan he let slip was her reward.

The taste of him was still on her tongue—clean, salty, and masculine—and she wasn't disgusted. She was turned *on*.

She remembered the moment his hand slid into her

hair. He let her pace herself and then took control once she surrendered. The tension between domination and trust was electric.

And that first time, she gagged just slightly, and he growled? She almost came on the spot. What surprised her most wasn't that she enjoyed sucking him; it was that she wanted the power it gave her.

She grabbed her Freak School Journal off the nightstand and flipped to a fresh page. Natasha had instructed every student to "write your body's truth." No editing. No apologies.

> *Tonight I felt powerful. I felt seen. I felt hungry.*
> *Every twitch of his hips, every hiss from his lips,*
> *energized me.*
> *My decision to serve and seduce. I'd never felt that*
> *kind of control before.*
> *I never knew submission could be so gratifying.*
> *His dick felt like a reward. But so did his praise.*
> *Is it possible to fall for someone who hasn't even taken*
> *their mask off?*
>
> *- Summer*

She shook her head and thought, "Don't get ahead of yourself. That's not what you are here for."

Mr. Black's Reflection
Instructor's Journal: *1:13 AM | Subject: Summer*

Mr. Black sat in the instructor's lounge, robe open, chest bare, a glass of bourbon in his grip. He couldn't get her off his mind. Still half-hard. Still hearing her breath hitch when his tongue hit that spot—still tasting her on his lips. He opened his instructor journal to write his thoughts.

> *I had my first training session with Summer tonight.*
> *She is special. And that is dangerous.*
> *I wasn't supposed to like touching her as much as this.*

Not really.

My job is to instruct. Train. Deliver orgasms and discipline and spank a little, then walk away like a professional.

But Summer followed every command like she was trying to get a good grade.

She wants to learn everything.

And that kind of submission? That kind of hunger?

It wasn't just her mouth skills; it was her intention.

I could feel it in the way she looked up at me as she sucked me, not with fear or neediness, but purpose.

She has impressive dick-handling skills. She sucked me like she wanted to map every vein of my dick with her tongue and take mental notes. New students typically don't possess those kinds of skills.

She didn't flinch.

Didn't perform.

She was focused.

I loved that. Too much.

And when she moaned while sucking me? Fuck.

I could barely keep myself under control.

There was a moment, just before I came, when he almost screamed her name.

But I bit my tongue. Held back. Because if he spoke her name, if I had kissed her

She'd earned my attention. And if I'm not careful, my heart too.

As he closed his journal, Mr. Blue was walking into the lounge. "You good, Black?" he asked as he passed through the lounge.

"Yeah, I'm okay," Mr. Black said quickly and quietly.

But his mind whispered, "No, you're not okay."

Because he was thinking only of her.

Ten

Emily Jackson

Location: *1:00 PM | Natasha's Executive Office*

Emily Jackson hasn't had intercourse, but she has orgasmed twice from oral with her fiancé. During orientation, when Mr. Green was eating her, she faked it.

At twenty-four years old, she was a virgin by conviction and fear. The only one-eyed snake she had ever handled was the few times that she attempted to suck off her then-boyfriend, back in college.

But here she was. Sitting in a velvet chair at Freak School and wearing nothing but a silk robe, lip gloss, and a look of confusion.

If her mama, the first lady, knew what she was doing, she would die, but she wants to keep her man, so she is here to learn.

Emily was the only daughter of a Southern AME preacher and a mother who was an accounting professor at a small college in Richmond, VA, and a first lady admired by all. Her household was holy, orderly, and quietly repressed. There was no talk of sexuality, other than how fornication was a sin.

She pledged her virginity at 16 at a revival. Wore a ring and signed a purity contract. But then came Kenny.

Kenny Leftwich, the star running back at Librea College, a Christian school nestled in the foothills of the Blue Ridge Mountains in Radford, Virginia. He was a walking muscle with dimples and ambition. He led the Fellowship of Christian Athletes and carried a Bible in his bookbag.

They met in their first year when she was running track. He prayed before every meal when they went on dates, even if it was ice cream. To her, Kenny was a good guy and believed in God with all his heart. Kenny was no saint. He messed around on Emily with girls he didn't really care about, but he did love her and wanted her to be the mother of his children.

When she graduated a year ago, they got engaged. Kenny had one more year in school since he started as a redshirt freshman. She went home to Richmond and started a job as an elementary school teacher.

After he graduated, he got drafted in the second round of the NFL by the Tennessee Vipers.

And the closer she gets to her wedding date, people, namely her ratchet cousin Trina, who was a celebrity hair stylist, pull her aside with warnings about groupies trying to get her man.

"Baby, I know what you were taught, but if Beyoncé can get cheated on, Chile, anyone can," Trina said over brunch one Sunday after service. "You need to make sure you can compete. Your man is in locker rooms with half-naked groupies willing to do anything. God may have your heart, but you need to learn some skills to keep your man's attention."

"Trina!" Emily shouted, embarrassed by this conversation.

"Hush and listen. I'm paying for you to go to the Freak School, the place you told me you saw that online ad about. I'm going to CashApp you. Don't tell anybody. Consider this an early wedding present. And don't waste my money. Go learn some tricks to keep your man at home and make your parents some grandbabies."

Emily nearly fainted in her shrimp and grits.

She took the money and registered. That was a month ago, and now she was sitting here waiting to be deflowered.

She watched Natasha perform oral sex on her husband the day before and had nearly gone into cardiac arrest from shock, awe, and curiosity.

The other girls, Summer, Bianca, Teri, and Mel, seemed so much more confident. They twirled dildos like batons and swallowed bananas whole like they were trained at the circus.

Emily was so scared of choking that she mostly stared at her banana.

She wasn't sure if she could command a penis. She knew her dick-sucking skills were not stellar. Kenny had shut her down before, and she never forgot it.

But somewhere, beneath the fear, was curiosity.

She wanted to feel sexy.

She wanted to stop being afraid of her own sexuality.

She wanted Kenny to want her, not the girls he used to run through back on campus.

So, when Natasha scheduled a 1-on-1 with her, she knew why.

Natasha wanted to help Emily with her sexual mindset. Shame is a significant issue for people, especially church girls who've been taught to keep their dress down and their legs closed.

Now, when she and Kenny were in college, she had gotten naked for him a couple of times and tried to give him blow jobs. He had eaten her and fingered her, but beyond that, they hadn't really had sexual contact in years.

Emily was nervous before her private session with Natasha, but she was ready. The appointment note said, "Come to my private office in only your freak school bathrobe."

Emily's hands were slightly trembling as she knocked.

The room was soft-lit, warm, and private. Candles flickered along the windowsill, and soft jazz played low in the background. Natasha smiled at her like a big sister, not a dominatrix.

"Sit," she said gently. "We're going to start slow. We're going to start with you."

Emily blinked. "What do you mean?"

"I mean, your pleasure. Your power. Your confidence. Before you can suck a dick like a queen, you have to feel like one. Lay back. Let's talk."

For the next hour, Natasha asked her questions that no one ever had:

What is your favorite thing about your body?

What did her body like to feel?

Had she ever looked at herself in the mirror naked and said, "Damn, I'm beautiful"?

What fantasies did she have when she was alone?

The answers to Natasha's questions had been hesitant. But they came. And with every truth, Emily felt the chains of shame breaking.

Then, Natasha handed her a mirror and gently instructed her to look between her legs.

"You should name her," Natasha said, smiling. "Try Susie." Emily laughed nervously, eyes still wide. "Susie?"

"Yes. So when you leave Freak School, I want you to have so much sexual confidence that you call Kenny on the phone and tell him that Susie needs to speak to him. So that he knows what time it is when he gets home."

Emily laughed so hard she thought she'd combust. Natasha pulled out a sleek red lipstick vibrator from her drawer and placed it in Emily's palm.

"After this session, go use this. Just to explore. You don't have to finish; just get familiar."

By the end of the session, Emily was smiling. Natasha handed her a banana. "For now? Get comfortable. Own it."

Emily held the banana gently, eyes wide.

She whispered, "I can do this."

Natasha replied. "You will, honey."

"Your instructor, Mr. Green, is gentle, sweet, and just a tad awkward—perfect for you. He'll approach you with empathy, understanding what it's like to feel uncertain. That's why I trust him to guide you in discovering your power."

Emily felt a flutter in her chest as hope began to bloom where fear once resided. She nodded slowly, a smile starting to form on her lips.

After Emily left, Natasha recalled the first day Donny Sims, aka Mr. Green, walked into Freak School looking for a job. Just a shy, quiet guy, he stepped through the door with his light skin and striking green eyes, standing at only 5'8" and barely 170 pounds, lacking in confidence. We could have placed him in the hotel, but she decided to take him under her wing. She built his confidence, introduced him to a strength training routine, and equipped him with skills that made women weak in the knees. Now? He's a force to be reckoned with in the bedroom. But the best part? He remains humble.

Unlike the other instructors, who flaunt their egos, Mr. Green stays grounded. He's gentle, intuitive, and, above all, empathetic.

Natasha knew he was the right choice for Emily; he's firm enough to stretch her boundaries, yet soft enough not to break her.

She whispered to herself, "He's exactly what Emily and Susie need."

Eleven

Bianca Bennett-Douglass

Location: *11:00 AM | Freak School Spa*

Bianca was a loyal, ride-or-die wife for nearly 17 years. When her husband quit his job to start his own business, she stood by him, covering all the bills for years to help him get his venture off the ground. An excellent mother to their two boys, she maintained a spotless home while working full-time as a director and later a VP at a local bank.

But when he found success, he began an affair with his twenty-something assistant. Bianca discovered the betrayal one day after accidentally switching cellphones with him. A glance at his text messages revealed plans for the weekend with her. Heart racing, she logged into their family app, pulled his texts from the past thirty days, and browsed the pictures in his cloud. That's when she knew he had betrayed her.

Confronting him, she demanded the truth, and he admitted to everything. But he didn't ask to stay married to her. Without hesitation, she filed for divorce and allowed her teenage boys, ages 16 and 14, to live with their father.

After so many years of prioritizing everyone else's needs over her own, she finally felt free. But beneath that newfound freedom lay a heart deeply wounded.

That chapter of her story was closed, filed under **Never Again**.

It was her therapist who suggested she attend Freak School.

"You need more than closure," Dr. Judith Thomason said. "You need some time away to reconnect. With your body. With your desire. With yourself."

Bianca rolled her eyes. "So... you want me to go to Freak camp?"

Dr. Thomason just smiled. "I want you to go where you're

seen."

That line stuck.

Now, here she was. Day 2. In a silk robe, freshly waxed, sipping cucumber water in a five-star spa at Freak School, waiting on her deep tissue massage appointment.

Her back ached from years of tension.

The first day at Freak School was a blur of orientation, lectures, watching Natasha show out on Warren, and being handed a custom paddle with her name on it.

At first, she felt ridiculous. But something in her was changing.

When she was a full-time wife and mother, she did the most. She hosted harvest parties for the kids, organized the church bake sale, was a super soccer mom, and always looked fabulous doing it; her face card never declined.

She thought she and her husband were happy.

Now, she's divorced, and it was a hard decision for her to let the boys go with him, but she thought they needed their dad more at this stage.

She thought back on what Natasha said during orientation, "You've given everything to everyone else. It's time to demand pleasure on your own terms." Bianca blinked like she'd been slapped with truth.

Now, she lay on her stomach in the private massage suite, the warmth of a heated bed enveloping her naked body under the sheet. The door creaked open, but she didn't look up.

"Hello, Bianca," a warm, deep voice said, smooth and confident, sending a shiver down her spine.

She turned her head slightly, curiosity piqued. The man stood before her, wearing a silver mask, loose black linen pants, and nothing else. His skin was a golden brown, radiant and soft-looking, as if he had moisturized his very soul. His hands were large, promising both strength and care.

He wheeled over a cart filled with oils and tools. "Remember me? Mr. Silver," he said with a hint of playfulness. "In addition to being your instructor, I'm also a licensed massage therapist. When I heard you made an appointment, I knew I had to work on you. May I begin?"

Bianca nodded, her throat dry with anticipation. He approached the table, pressing his hands firmly into her shoulders, gradually working his way down to her lower back. He kneaded her glutes gently, then moved to her thighs and calves, expertly easing the tension from her body before pulling back the sheet to her waist.

"Would you like some lavender aromatherapy?" he asked. He poured lavender oil into his hands, then instructed Bianca to breathe in deeply three times. As she exhaled, the release startled her, a wave of tension melting away.

He rubbed his hands together to warm them, then began his work on her shoulders, slow and intentional, each movement designed to coax her into a state of complete relaxation.

"You carry everything here on your left side," he said, digging gently under her left shoulder blades. "Tension. Frustration. Disappointment."

She closed her eyes. "I'm sure I do." He quickly checked her. "No, you're here to create a new normal for yourself."

"I'm going to do some deep tissue work on you. Is that okay?"

"Yes, please." Bianca was so excited. She couldn't remember the last time she had made time to do something for herself.

He took his time with her neck and shoulders, working on those knots to release them. He took one arm, slid it behind her back, and reached the top of her shoulder blade, then did the other side.

Then he worked down to her lower back with gentle stroking movements using palms to relax muscles. He was working her over. Then he started kneading her back in a circular motion. He kept squeezing and kneading her muscles to release tension.

He began working long, gliding strokes along her arms, each movement making her limbs feel as if they were floating. Then, he knelt beside her, gently lifting her arm over his shoulder to help her stretch, his touch both firm and reassuring. He massaged her hand, carefully attending to each finger, sending waves of relaxation through her body.

Next, he draped her shoulders and back with hot towels

from the steamer, the warmth enveloping her in a cocoon of comfort. Then he turned his attention to her glutes, kneading her butt with a focused intensity. He dug in with determination, knowing that was where much of her tension lay. He squeezed and kneaded until her muscles felt like butter under his skilled hands.

The next sixty minutes delivered the best touch she had felt in years. It wasn't sexual; it was deeply sensual. With each stroke, he expressed admiration for her, reminding her that she had a beautiful, curvy body that deserved attention. "You deserve to be adored," he said simply.

He worked meticulously on her thighs, moving with care, alternating between firm kneading and gentle strokes, feeling every contour of her legs.

Next, he focused on her calves, his hands gliding down the length of her legs. He kneaded and rolled the muscles, releasing any knots that had formed, and she could feel the heaviness of her limbs begin to loosen.

Finally, he dedicated time to her feet, cradling them in his hands as he massaged each arch and toe. He used his thumbs to apply pressure to the balls of her feet. The sensation was blissful, awakening every nerve ending, leaving her feeling both weightless and deeply cared for.

The experience was overwhelming. Tears slipped out of her eyes.

When he reached for a warm towel to cover her, she stopped him.

"Wait..." Her voice shook. "Do you think I'm still beautiful?"

Mr. Silver stepped close. His voice dropped.

"I think you're divine. I think any man who left this, as he traced a line down her thigh, was blind."

And I can remind you exactly how worthy you still are."

Her breath caught. She nodded.

He bent down and kissed her ankle. Then, the inside of her knee.

Then, with her permission, he kissed her stomach.

And at that moment, Bianca didn't feel like a cast-off wife.

She felt like a damn goddess.

By the end of the session, she was glowing. No orgasm. No penetration. Just intimacy.

Real intimacy. The kind she forgot existed.

As she got dressed, she caught a glimpse of herself in the mirror. And for the first time in a long time, she genuinely smiled.

Mr. Silver knocked and ran back in to remind her, "Don't forget our other session at 10 PM tonight. Can't wait to spend more time with you."

Twelve

Emily & Mr. Green

Location: *9:05 PM I Training Suite 3*

Emily's hands trembled as she knocked on the door to Training Room 3.

She was wearing her silk Freak School robe, no bra, hair wrapped in a satin scarf, and nothing but hope and nerves underneath.

In her right hand. Her practice banana. In her left? Her courage.

The door opened, and there he was.

Mr. Green.

About 5'8". Compact. Cut. Beautiful, warm brown skin. His mask was green velvet with black trim. His arms were lean but strong; his energy was different. He was calmer and gentler.

Emily exhaled.

"Miss Jackson," he said, smiling behind the mask. "Come in."

The room was softly lit. There was a padded stool in the middle and a table filled with tools: flavored lubes, a variety of dildos, a water bottle, towels, and a small mirror.

Emily's heart thumped against her ribs.

Mr. Green gestured for her to sit.

"Before we begin," he said, "how are you feeling?"

She tried to smile. "Nervous."

He pulled a chair beside her instead of standing above her. "That's okay. Nerves mean you care."

She bit her lip. "I've never done anything like this."

"I know," he said gently. "And you're not here to impress me. You're here to learn."

Emily nodded, swallowing hard.

"Good," he said. "Then let's start with breathwork."

For the first fifteen minutes, all they did was breathe.

Inhale through the nose. Out through the mouth. Eyes closed. Shoulders relaxed.

Every few breaths, he reminded her, "You are in control."

"You are safe here."

"Your body knows how to give pleasure; your mind just needs to stop fighting it."

She felt her body settle.

Then, he handed her a small silicone dildo.

"Your first tool," he said. "It's clean, soft, and won't complain. Let's practice on this before we try the real thing."

Emily giggled. "Should I name her, too?"

He grinned. "Only if it helps."

He guided her through hand placement, lubrication, and how to open her mouth without clenching her jaw.

"Give it a kiss first," he whispered. "Start with intention. Then, explore."

She followed his lead, kissing the tip softly, running her tongue along the sides, and letting her hands find a rhythm.

He watched, silently.

"Good. Breathe through your nose. That's it."

Her tongue circled the head again, then she took the tip inside.

"No teeth," he reminded her gently. "Just lips. Let your mouth become soft and welcoming."

She gagged slightly.

He reached forward, not to scold, but to steady her shoulder.

"Don't panic. Pull back. Breathe. Relax."

She took a break, and went back in.

This time, she got a little further. Still shallow, but with more confidence.

"Now look up," he said. "That eye contact? That's power."

Emily's whole body flushed. But she looked up, dildo in her mouth, eyes wide.

Mr. Green's breathing shifted, just a little.

She was getting it.

"Let's add your hands," he said. "Grip the base. Start to twist, gently."

She did.

"Now suck while you stroke."

She obeyed. Lips tight, hands working.

"That's it," he murmured. "You're doing beautifully."

After twenty minutes, he set the dildo aside.

"How are you feeling?"

Emily blinked. "Empowered. Wet. And a little hungry."

He smiled.

"Are you ready to try with me?" he asked. "Only if you want."

She hesitated. Then nodded.

Emily watched as Mr. Green stood, his green velvet mask still on, and unfastened his pants. He moved slowly, deliberately, as if waiting for her to change her mind.

She didn't.

When he slid his briefs down, she blinked.

It wasn't too big.

But it was beautiful.

Smooth. Brown. Just enough curve. Enough to scare her a little, but not enough to make her run. "Start like you did with the toy," he said, sitting down. "No rush. No pressure. Just you and me."

She dropped to her knees between his legs. And exhaled.

She kissed the tip first.

Then ran her tongue along the underside.

He hissed through his teeth.

"That's it. Let your mouth tell me you want this."

She opened her lips and took him in, just the head, softly, carefully.

She looked up and saw his eyes were closed behind the mask, his head tilted slightly back, and his hands gripping the armrests.

She swirled her tongue again. Then pulled off with a soft pop.

"How was that?" she asked, eyes wide.

He groaned. "Dangerous."

She grinned.

She went back down—this time with hands.

One hand twisting gently at the base, the other cupping his balls like Natasha had demonstrated.

She took more. When she gagged a little, she didn't panic.

He whispered, "Good girl. Control it. Breathe."

She did. She wanted to.

She sucked him slowly, letting spit run down her chin. She got messy. She wanted to feel it.

And when he groaned, she smiled without losing her grip on his dick.

Then, he stopped her. "Look at me." She did.

"You're doing so well. But I want to finish this lesson right."

He stood. Helped her up.

"Lie back," he said. "You earned your reward."

Emily blinked. "Reward?"

"Lesson two," he said, climbing between her thighs. "It is about receiving."

Then, he kissed her inner thigh. And lower.

And when his tongue met her pussy, she arched so hard, she almost levitated.

Emily wasn't sure if she was breathing anymore.

Her back arched, legs trembling, as Mr. Green's tongue moved like a prayer between her thighs. Gentle, rhythmic, reverent. He took his time, with no rush and no pressure, just presence.

She'd never been touched like this. Not in college. Not by Kenny. Not ever.

She felt seen. Worshipped. His hands held her hips, thumbs stroking slow circles into her curves while his mouth lavished her like she was the last meal before a fast.

"Mr. Green..." she whispered, her voice barely there.

He didn't respond with words. Just a deep, low hum against Emily's clit that made her cry out.

She gasped. "I think I—I'm..." Her whole body seized. Shook. Then melted.

Her first orgasm hit like a tidal wave—fast, hot, and absolutely undeniable.

She was panting. Disoriented. Floating.

He crawled up beside her, stayed masked, but whispered in

her ear:

"You're amazing." She turned her head to face him.

Tears slipped from the corners of her eyes, not from pain, but from release.

Finally feeling what it meant to be wanted. Held. Respected. She didn't say anything. She just curled into his chest.

He held her. Let her feel it. Let her own it.

At that moment, Emily Jackson stopped being scared and started becoming a freak.

Emily's Reflection
Journal Entry: *1:27 AM I "I Think I Like This!"*

Emily lay on her bed, silk robe barely covering her damp thighs, the scent of her release still clinging to her fingers and the air.

She hadn't moved since returning from her session with Mr. Green.

She didn't want to. She needed to feel this.

Her body was buzzing gently. Like an echo of the orgasm was still humming through her bones. Her mouth was sore from practicing. Her throat was a little raw.

But she was smiling.

She reached for her journal. Natasha had said to write after every breakthrough.

At first, she thought that was corny.

Now?

She clicked her pen and wrote her first reflection:

> *I had my first orgasm with another person today. He wasn't my fiancé. He wasn't my boyfriend. He was my instructor, and he made me feel safe.*
>
> *I wasn't scared. I wasn't ashamed. I didn't flinch or fake it.*
>
> *I felt worthy. Like someone finally saw me. He touched me because I wanted him to, not because I earned it by being "good" or "pure."*

Now, this sucking dick thing. I think I like this.

-Emily

Her eyes went wide. Then she giggled. *Out loud.*

She covered her mouth, as if someone would barge in and take it back.

But no one did.

She lay back on the pillows, her legs parted, her robe open. For the first time, she looked at her own body without judgment.

Her breasts.

Her soft stomach.

Her bare, smooth pussy.

She whispered, "You deserve to be touched like that. And again. And again."

Then, she said it louder.

"You deserve to cum."

For the first time in her life, Emily Jackson didn't feel like a virgin waiting for permission.

She felt like a woman learning how to ask, no, *demand*, what she needed.

She closed the journal, kissed the cover, and whispered to herself

"Susie's just getting started."

Thirteen

Teri & Mr. Red

Location: *10:04 PM | Training Suite 1*

Teri Whittington had never cried over a man.

But when her fiancé posted a picture of himself kissing another man, four months before their wedding date, she had to excuse herself from a PTA meeting to sob in the parking lot.

She hadn't seen it coming.

Not the affair.

Not the betrayal.

Not the fact that the man she had given five years to had left her for a personal trainer named Malik, who wore waist beads and eyeliner.

And now, here she is: 43, a successful school leader, exhausted, and painfully aware that her vibrator had been her most reliable partner for three years in a row.

When her cousin sent her the link to Freak School, she rolled her eyes.

But then she clicked.

And saw the words:

> *"Confidence isn't about being chosen; it's about remembering you're the one who gets to choose."*

She registered the next day.

Now, standing in front of Training Suite 1, wearing a wine-colored robe that clung to her curves, Teri felt something she hadn't felt in a long time: *curious.*

Her session card said, *"Instructor: Mr. Red."*

She had imagined someone older. Gentle. Maybe quiet.

Who did she get?

A 33-year-old walking sex symbol with abs carved by God, with caramel skin, a low fade, and a voice like melted honey.

"Miss Whittington?" he said, grinning behind his red mask.

"Just Teri," she replied, folding her arms across her chest, feigning composure.

He opened the door and gestured for her to come in. "Then just Teri, come on in."

The room was warm and smelled like amber and spice. There was a black velvet chaise and a mirrored wall.

"Today's about body appreciation," he said, closing the door behind them. "Touch. Confidence. Control."

She raised a brow. "You're younger than me."

He nodded. "And well trained to make you forget that."

She smirked. "Cocky."

"Only if I earn it."

He handed her a silk scarf. "Tonight, I want you blindfolded. Just for the first part. Let your body respond without your mind interfering."

She hesitated. Then tied it around her eyes.

Soft darkness.

Then, his fingertips.

Slow. Featherlight. Over her arms. Her collarbone. Her thighs.

She gasped.

Mr. Red electrified her skin.

She expected eagerness.

She didn't expect reverence.

Mr. Red wasn't rushing. He wasn't touching her like she was an assignment.

He was touching her like he meant it.

Fingers skimming along her stomach. His breath was close but not touching. Every time he exhaled near her inner thigh, she shivered.

"You feel that?" he whispered.

Teri nodded under the blindfold.

"That's anticipation. Not fear. Not shame. Just want."

Her chest rose and fell with each slow, teasing stroke of his hands. He massaged her calves like they deserved it. Traced the stretch marks on her hips like they were love letters written in flesh.

"I know what you're thinking," he said softly. "That you're too much. Too old. Too tired. Too something."

She didn't speak. She didn't have to.

He whispered, "You are perfect. You've just never had a man young enough to match your fire and mature enough to handle your storm."

Teri let out a breath she didn't know she'd been holding. He untied her blindfold slowly.

When her eyes opened, she saw him, still masked, still clothed, but watching her like she was art.

"Stand," he said. She stood.

He walked behind her. Gently untied her robe.

It fell. She didn't flinch.

Didn't cover herself. Not this time.

Mr. Red stepped closer, leaned down, and kissed the center of her back.

"I'm not here to fuck you tonight," he said. "I'm here to remind you that you are desired. And when the time comes? I'll give you all the pleasure you want. But tonight?"

He turned her to face the mirror.

"You're gonna watch me make love to your body with my mouth."

He dropped to his knees.

And for the next forty-five minutes, he kissed, licked, sucked, and adored every inch of Teri's thighs, belly, and breasts until she forgot all about Malik and those goddamn waist beads.

When he finally moved between her legs, he didn't ask.

He just looked up, eyes blazing behind the mask.

She nodded once.

And then, she saw stars.

When she came, loud, shaking, and undone, her hand gripped his dreads, and her knees nearly buckled.

He caught her.

Held her.

Smiled.

And whispered, "You still got it, Teri. You just needed the right man to show you."

Teri's Reflection
Journal Entry: *2:07 AM | "I Chose Myself"*

I wasn't supposed to come here.

I was supposed to take a solo trip to Aruba, drink rum punch by the pool, and pretend my ex didn't dump me for a man named Malik with an ab tattoo and a skincare routine better than mine.

But here I am at Freak School.

And tonight? I saw myself again.

Not Principal Whittington.

Not the "pillar of the community."

Not the woman people whisper about in church because her man left her, and she never had kids.

Tonight, I saw a woman.

A whole, luscious, deserving, divine woman.

Mr. Red didn't fuck me. He didn't strip me like a conquest.

He kissed me like it was sacred.

He held my thighs like they were silk.

He touched me like he had all night, and nothing else mattered.

I didn't feel used.

I didn't feel like I had to perform.

I felt wanted.

Do you know how long it's been since I felt that?

Since someone looked at me and didn't see my résumé or the scandal?

I cried a little after he left. Not because I was sad. Because I forgot I was that bitch.

Now, I remember. The next time he touches me? I won't flinch.

Because this time, I'm not asking anyone to choose me.
I choose myself.

-Teri

Fourteen

Mel and Mr. Bronze

Location: *9:57 PM | Mel's Suite*

Mel Dibert had sold software contracts bigger than most people's mortgages.

She could close a $2 million deal over a steak lunch, read a man's intentions in under five minutes, and run a strategy meeting in Louboutins without breaking a sweat.

But here?

At Freak School?

She felt like a freshman again.

Mel Dibert had everything except someone who touched her like she mattered.

At 52, she retired early from a two-decade-long career at IBM, lived in a beautifully restored brownstone in Rochester, NY, and enjoyed the sweet chaos of being "Honey" to her three-year-old granddaughter.

She had money, freedom, and peace, but she hadn't been touched in two years.

Not since Ronnie.

They'd been married 26 years and raised two good kids. Took anniversary trips to Bermuda, Fiji, and Ghana; paid off the mortgage early; had a vacation home in Myrtle Beach; and loved each other faithfully until the night he died in his sleep of a widow-maker heart attack.

One moment, she was booking their trip to Napa. Next, she was burying him with all the grace she could muster.

She'd worn a black dress and said the prayers. Received the casseroles from everyone.

She did what women like her were taught to do:

Keep going.
Keep showing up.
Keep smiling.

But inside? She was sad. She missed being wanted.
It was her daughter, Candace, who pulled her aside one afternoon and placed the Freak School brochure in her hand.
"Mom," she said gently, "you've done everything for everyone else. Maybe it's time you did something for yourself."
Mel raised a brow. "You want me to go to sex school?"
"I want you to stop pretending you don't want love again. And I want you to stop waiting for permission to get it."
That line stuck.
Now, she stood in her private Freak School suite, wearing a silk robe over skin she'd started moisturizing again. Her makeup was soft. Her confidence is still warming up. She finally admitted what she hadn't said out loud in two years: I miss being touched.
On the bed: a journal, a box of toys, and a paddle with Mel D. Her suite was warm. Soft jazz played overhead. There were oils arranged like perfumes on a gold tray. A handwritten note rested on the bed.
She picked it up.

> *Ms. Dibert,*
>
> *You don't need to be fixed. You need to be felt.*
>
> *I'll come to pick you up at 10 p.m. tonight. There will be dancing.*
>
> *-Mr. Bronze*

She read it twice.
Something in her chest cracked.
Her lips curved.
When Mr. Bronze entered her suite, she inhaled sharply.
He was tall and clean-cut, with a salt-and-pepper beard cut close. He had smooth, glistening melanin skin.
He moved like a jazz solo: slow, confident, and with no need

to show off.

He didn't flirt. He didn't leer.

He bowed his head respectfully. "May I join you?"

She nodded, her body tense but curious.

He sat beside her on the velvet chaise.

"I'm here to help you remember what you already know."

"And what's that?" she asked softly.

"That you are worthy of touch," as he kissed her shoulder.

His session wasn't about sex. It was about surrender.

Mr. Bronze didn't take her to a massage table.

He took her to the rooftop.

Freak School's Rooftop Garden. Elevated, secluded, wrapped in sheer white drapes and low golden light. The city twinkled below. A vintage record player spun John Coltrane in the corner.

Mel had expected oil. A firm touch. Maybe a compliment.

She didn't expect a spread like this.

He poured her a glass of red wine, Malbec, rich and dark, and said, "No instructions tonight. Just let your body speak. If you want to be touched, lean in."

She sat across from him, robe still tied.

He said nothing more.

He just sipped. Watching her untie her robe on her timeline.

Mel sipped too. Let her legs part slightly. The air kissed her inner thighs.

She leaned in.

He stood. Then he held out his hand.

She took it. They began to dance. Not fast. Not close at first. Just a sway.

His hands were on her hips. Hers on his chest.

She felt his strength through his linen shirt. She inhaled his skin, sandalwood, clean linen, and grown man.

"I haven't danced like this in years," she murmured. "Then you haven't been touched right in years," he said. His hands slid lower. He pulled her closer.

And when their hips met, she felt it. He was hard. She gasped, her eyes searching his behind the mask. "I want you to feel beautiful," he whispered. "Not because you performed. Just because you *are*."

Her robe slipped open. He didn't stare. He groaned softly like he'd been waiting to see a woman like her all his life. "You're breathtaking." She hadn't been naked in front of anyone since Ronnie. Not sexually. Not emotionally.

And now?

She untied her robe in front of a man whose voice sounded like midnight and whose presence filled the space before he ever spoke.

Mel swallowed hard. His voice made her thighs clench. He held out his hand. "You set the pace." She hesitated. Then placed her palm in his. His fingers traced her collarbone. Then lower.

When he finally kissed her, just below her breast, she moaned, deep and involuntarily.

He pulled back. "Too much?" he asked, voice husky. "Not enough," she whispered.

He dropped to his knees.

On the rooftop. Under the stars. Then slowly kissed and licked his way up the inside of her thighs. No rush. No pressure. Just worship. She let out a soft whimper.

It startled her. He didn't flinch. "You okay?" he asked.

She nodded, eyes glassy. "I didn't realize how much I missed this."

Then, he continued to enjoy her thighs.

Every stroke said, "I see you." You are still desirable. You deserve this.

And when his tongue finally met her pussy, she melted.

Not just because of the heat. Because it had been so long since someone touched her like she was a gift.

He didn't stop when she cried.

He didn't flinch when she moaned, loud and shameless.

He licked her *through it (to stretch the orgasm).*

And when she came, deep, guttural, thighs locked around his head—she didn't say thank you.

She said, "Again." And he smiled because he planned to.

After he made her purr like a kitty for the second time, he

looked up at her and said, "Oh, next time you're really gonna get it."

She quipped back, "I sure hope so, Mr. Bronze."

He told her, "You carry yourself like music."

And somehow, that hit deeper than a thousand "damn you fines."

Then he helped her sit up. Her robe was still open. She didn't bother closing it.

She looked at him thoroughly for the first time.

And said, "You didn't ask me for anything."

"I never will," he replied.

Mel smiled. Then reached up and cupped his cheek, still masked, still mysterious.

Then, she ran off, and he leaned back and started thinking about this remarkable woman with whom he had spent the evening.

That night, Mel wrote her first journal entry.

Mel & Mr. Bronze's Reflections

Journal Entry: *1:31 AM | "Feel Alive Again"*

*I am writing in my journal under the light of the
moon. I feel alive again, as if I've awakened from a
long slumber."*

*I just came under the moonlight to a jazz record,
and that sensation is still coursing through my body.
There's a warmth blooming in my chest, a reminder of
what it feels like to be desired, to be seen, to be whole
again.*

*Tonight, Mr. Bronze instinctively knew what I
needed. He didn't just touch my body; he touched my
soul. In his arms, I remembered how much I loved
to dance. The way we swayed together felt like a
beautiful reunion with a part of myself that had been
buried beneath the weight of grief. It was as if he had
unlocked a door to a room in my heart that I thought
was closed forever.*

*Mr. Bronze helped me remember that I am a woman
deserving of love, passion, and adventure. He made
me feel beautiful, not just because of the way he looked
at me or how he held me, but because I finally allowed
myself to be vulnerable again. His voice, warm and
reassuring, wrapped around me as he whispered,
"You carry yourself like music." Those words hit
deeper than any compliment I had heard before and
ignited a spark within me. I want to hold onto this
feeling and build a new story for myself. I want to
embrace the woman I can become.*

Tonight was a reminder that my spirit can soar higher than doubt and fear. I want to be open to new experiences, new connections, and maybe one day a new love. The thought of Mr. Bronze and our next encounter fills me with excitement. I can't wait to see where this journey takes me."

Mr. Bronze's Reflection

Warren and Natasha had been trying to convince Dr. Samuel Boggs to join Freak School for years. Their discussions were often punctuated by the clinking of whiskey glasses. One evening, the three of them gathered in a dimly lit bar, not far from campus, the air thick with the smoky scent of an old-fashioned, his favorite drink.

"You're already doing this work on campus, Sam," Warren said, leaning forward. "In your feminism classes, you're making a difference. The girls in your seminar are leaving their boyfriends because you've taught them what it really means to feel seen and valued."

Sam, nursing his drink, shook his head. He respected Warren's clinical work with women to create sexual awakening, but he didn't want to be thought of as some high-paid gigolo. To him, Freak School was a lot. He didn't do gimmicks or theater. He didn't want his name whispered in locker rooms or splashed across anonymous group chats. He was a man of subtle seduction, not spectacle.

But then Natasha, ever the provocateur, pulled out a piece of paper and slid it across the table, her eyes sparkling with mischief. "Look at this," she urged.

He glanced down at the paper and saw her name and picture. "Melissa "Mel" Dibert, 52. Widowed. Executive-level. Daughter enrolled her."

He didn't read the rest. Something shifted within him—a visceral reaction that he felt in his gut upon seeing her picture. This woman was remarkable, an undeniable truth that resonated through him like a low hum. "Tell me more," he responded. She's a widow; her husband of 26 years died suddenly two years ago. She was a career woman in IT sales, a sapiosexual who loves jazz from New York, who took early retirement a year ago. Two grown children, and she's a grandma. The description was compelling. As their conversation continued, he couldn't shake the image of Mel from his mind. He pictured her graceful presence and quiet strength. She wasn't just any client; she was someone whose longing for connection mirrored his own.

After their first evening together at Freak School, he found himself in his condo, cradling a warm cup of ginger tea. The steam curled as his mind drifted back to the memory of being with Mel, her laughter, the way her eyes sparkled as they danced, and the intoxicating energy between them. He could still feel the heat of her body and the way she leaned in, inviting him to explore the depths of her soul. He decided to capture his thoughts in his private journal.

Journal Entry: *2:02 AM (private & unpublished) | "Jazz and Honey"*

> *When I saw her tonight, she was everything Warren and Natasha said she would be. Mel wasn't performing. She wasn't trying to be sexy. She just was. The moment her robe slipped open, and she didn't cover herself, I had to compose myself. That was the real climax. She's like Jazz and Honey. Her orgasm was dessert. She didn't just receive touch. She metabolized it. It was like her skin had been starving and forgotten how to ask permission. And when she said "again," she wasn't talking about the orgasm. She was talking about being chosen. I'm not falling for her yet. But I'm invested in her happiness. Mel is not meant to be touched. She's meant to be held. And I plan to do both.*
>
> *-Sam*

Fifteen

Bianca & Mr. Silver

Location: *9:59 PM | Bianca's Suite*

Bianca opened her door right at 9:59 PM.

She was ready.

Silk robe. Hair pinned. Freshly waxed. Lips glossed.

And a slow-burning ache between her thighs that had built for 24 hours straight.

Because last night, after Mr. Silver massaged every ounce of grief from her body and kissed her skin like it was scripture. He even circled back to remind her of tonight's session:

> *"Don't forget our other session tomorrow at 10 p.m. I can't wait to spend more time with you."*

She hadn't forgotten.

She'd replayed his hand touching all over her in her mind all day.

He stepped into her suite tonight with quiet command.

Silver mask. Chest bare. Slacks hugging all the right places. Barefoot, again.

No games. No music. Just them.

"I've been thinking about your moan," he said calmly. "The way your legs twitched when I kissed your ankle."

Bianca swallowed hard.

"I want to feel more of you," he continued. "From both sides."

He reached for her robe's sash and tugged it loose. "You up for a little choreography?" he asked. She raised her chin. "Only if you plan to follow the rhythm.

They started on the bed.

She was on her back. He was kneeling above her head. His man muscle, long, thick, and heavy, was right in front of her face. It twitched when she licked her lips. "You start," he said, his voice smooth and deep. "Take your time."

Bianca reached up slowly, wrapping one hand around his shaft, marveling at the warmth of his skin. Leaning forward, she pressed a soft kiss to the tip, teasingly gentle. The moment was electric. He groaned, deep and low, a sound that sent a thrill coursing through her.

Emboldened, she opened her mouth wider, teasing the head and exploring its contours with soft, deliberate strokes. "God, yes," he murmured, his voice thick with pleasure. She wrapped both hands around him now, one stroking the base while her mouth sucked with more pressure. Picking up the pace, she took him in deeper, allowing herself to get lost in the rhythm. Bianca gagged slightly, pulled off, and then dove back down, wet and messy. Taking him deeper than before, she could feel the tension building in his body. "Please don't stop," he gasped, and she felt exhilarated by his urgency.

Her fingers explored the base, gently squeezing and rolling his balls as she lavished attention on him. Encouraged, she took one into her mouth, then the other, sucking gently while continuing to work him with her hands. The taste of him was intoxicating; the way his breath quickened and his hips bucked slightly, she could feel him on the brink, and she returned her focus to the shaft, taking him deep again, her throat constricting around him as she pushed herself further. The sensations were overwhelming. As she continued sucking him, she could sense him nearing the edge. She accelerated her rhythm, the sounds of her mouth working him filling the air. "That's it, just like that," he urged, his voice barely a whisper, and she felt a surge of satisfaction at his praise.

With one final push, she took him as deep as she could, her lips wrapped around him, swirling her tongue in a frenzy of pleasure. Finally, with a deep, guttural moan, he released, filling her mouth with warmth. She savored every wave of his release, her own pleasure building as she felt him quiver above her. When the last tremors subsided, she pulled back, breathless and dazed, a satisfied smile playing on her lips as their eyes locked. He immediately reached down and kissed her. He wanted to taste his fluids on her lips. The connection between them felt electric, and then he said, "Now let me please you, Queen."

Mr. Silver lowered himself slowly, his mouth hovering above her pussy, the anticipation thick in the air. She could feel her heart racing, the warmth pooling in her core as he teased her, hovering just out of reach. But then, he began licking and sucking on her inner thighs, his mouth exploring the sensitive skin with deliberate slowness. Each flick of his tongue sent shivers down her spine, a tantalizing promise that made her breath hitch. Just when she thought she couldn't take it any longer, he finally leaned in, his mouth capturing her clit with a soft, eager suck. She squirmed beneath him, desperate for that next rush of sensation. Mr. Silver's rhythm was relentless, his tongue working her with expert precision, alternating between sucking and flicking as if he knew exactly how to drive her wild. She could feel the heat rising within her, the tension coiling tighter and tighter, each flick of his tongue sending her closer to the edge.

Her hands found their way to his head, holding him in place, her body instinctively arching. He responded to her movements, diving deeper, his mouth a masterful instrument of pleasure, pushing her to new heights. With each passing moment, she felt herself teetering on the brink, the world around her fading away until only the sensations remained, his mouth on her. She was consumed by pleasure until she finally let go, surrendering to the waves of ecstasy that crashed over her.

As she rode the waves of her climax, she could feel the intensity of it all pulling her under, and she cried out, the sound muffled around him as the pleasure enveloped her completely.

When the waves finally receded, she drew back, breathless and dazed, a satisfied smile playing on her lips. Mr. Silver looked up at her, his eyes dark with desire, and she knew that this was only the beginning of their exploration together.

Mr. Silver murmured to her, "This pussy tastes so good." She moaned. Loud. He pulled back and *spanked* her clit, just one more time with his tongue. She screamed. And came.

She tried to stop him to catch her breath. But he said, "Nah, baby, you got one more." Then he licked her more; she convulsed, thighs shaking, bedsheets soaked.

Then, he kissed her thigh. Then her ankle. "You don't know what you're doing to me," she growled. "You're not leaving this bed until your legs forget your name," he whispered.

Her body trembled as his tongue found a rhythm on her clit—soft circles, light flicks, then deep suction that made her thighs close around his head like a vice.

He didn't stop. He slid two fingers inside her as he licked.

"Oh fuuuuck..." she moaned around his cock.

Her whole body went tense. Her hands clenched. She felt the wave before it hit.

She came.

Hard. Full body. Twitching.

They laid there for a moment—both of them panting. His face was resting on her lower stomach.

"I forgot what that felt like," she said softly.

He leaned over. Kissed her cheek. Then said, "You just remembered. I'm here to make sure you never forget again."

She turned her head slowly, grinning. "You think you can handle me?"

He licked his lips. "You bet."

Bianca & Mr. Silver's Reflections

Journal Entry: *1:26 AM | "I Did That."*

I was just with a man who whispered my name like a prayer and licked me into oblivion twice.

A full-grown, masked God with a tongue like a love letter and a dick I deep-throated without apology. I did that.

I saw stars. I saw spit. I saw my own power.

He held my hips like they were holy and fed me his thickness like he trusted me to honor it. I didn't fake it. I didn't shrink. I slayed.

That man ate me from the soul out.

And when he buried his face between my legs, he held my ass like it was art.

I came. I conquered. I collapsed.

And I want more.

Saturday, 10 p.m. Round two. With mirrors.

I'm ready to watch myself win.

- Bianca

Mr. Silver's Reflection
Instructor's Audio Log: *1:37 AM | "The way she sucked me"*

She sucked me like a competitive sport.

Bianca didn't just learn from her first session; she claimed her place.

She was wild. Honest. Loud. And still graceful.

And I let her dominate me. Gladly. This one made me forget the mask.

The way she sucked me... That shit rewired my damn nervous system.

I'm gonna hear those moans in my sleep.

Her face when she swallowed my juice? Undeniable.

I should keep it professional, but I'm not sure I want to.

Can't wait for Saturday at 10 p.m. Mirrors. Mouths. More.

Sixteen

Sensual Movement with Yolanda

Location: *7:00 AM I Fitness Studios*

The ladies showed up looking tired. The air was thick with a strong bassline and the scent of jasmine oil. There were six purple yoga mats aligned on the floor.

The music was slow, throbbing, and dangerous. "Today, we focus on choreographed surrender."

Yolanda, barefoot and radiant, had on a skin-tight tigerprint backless bodysuit that showed her perfect phat booty.

She stood in the front, her arms crossed, her body still, her eyes sharp as glass.

"Take off your shoes and socks," she said. "I want to hear you connect to the floor."

The students obeyed, nervous and eager. "Welcome to the only room at Freak School where you'll learn how to hold tension without begging to be released."

We'll start with Goddess Waistline Circles.

She squatted down on her mat and showed the ladies what to do.

She rocked her hips with in/out waistline circles and then twerked better than any belly dancer or stripper they ever saw. She has such control over her waist that she could make a man scream just watching her.

She said, "This work releases tension from your thighs and loosens those hips. It also gives you the leg strength to ride nicely." She smirked.

"Your turn, ladies. Get on your knees, ladies, then sit on your feet and widen your knees. Put your hands behind you for support. And keep your spines straight."

They watched her wind her waist. Then, she turned around so that they could see her booty pop as she did the move.

Then, she slowed it down for them.

She started with in-and-out pelvic tilts. "Keep your hands behind you for your balance. Inhale on the 'out,' exhale on the 'in.' Then she moved to squats: up, down, up, down, up, down. We are going to do two sets of 20, ladies."

Then, she showed them diagonal pelvic tilts, right cheek, left cheek. She called it out, "Right cheek, left cheek. Right cheek, left cheek."

"Yes, Summer, do it.... Bianca, I see you, girl, or Miss Emily, put your ass into it, girl. Pop that booty!"

Ok, let's put it all together—the hips, waist, and chest in a full body rotation. Werk it, ladies.

She walked through the room as they moved, lifting their hips and fixing their posture. She grabbed wedge pillows for Teri and Mel; they were struggling a bit.

She kept cueing their breath, posture, and control.

"Ladies, this is the foundation to riding him and one of the best ways to make yourself cum during intercourse."

Every movement was designed to tease the edge of pleasure and power.

"Clench your core. Contract your thighs. Don't just bounce; grind those hips. I want to see the way you carry heat. Don't run from it. Channel it."

Then, she had them put their legs in front of them and shake their legs out.

Next, she had them do a series of stretching exercises.

Then, she has them do 25 lady push-ups. One woman whimpered from effort.

The ladies thought they were coming to tone their core, but Yolanda had other plans.

"Ladies," she said, stretching her long caramel arms overhead. "This isn't Pilates. This is pleasure prep."

They dropped to the floor.

High plank. Low plank. Hip dips. But then the real work began.

"Hold the plank," Yolanda instructed. "Now, rock forward... and back. Just like you're riding."

Groans. Giggles. Gasps.

"Stay in it. This isn't just about abs; it's about core strength, which is essential for building stamina. Build the rhythm and drive your orgasm."

Then, she moved through them, adjusting her hips, tightening her form.

"Now, add the whisper," she said, as they pulsed their hips in time. "Say what you want. Say how you want it."

Women moaned into their mats, some laughing, some letting go.

"This is how you train to ride a man's mind, not just his body."

When they collapsed, sweaty and breathless, she instructed them to get into child's pose, smiling.

"That's how we build queens who ride like warriors."

Yolanda leaned down beside Bianca, whispering, "You think your instructor makes you scream? Try holding a plank for ninety seconds with intention. Gurlies, they're going to be scared of you."

The class moaned in pain and revelation.

This wasn't about sweat. This was about building strength and stamina.

Every set ended with breathwork. Every circuit closed with a question:

"Where do you hold your shame?"
"Who taught you to shrink when you take up space?"
"What part of your body haven't you forgiven yet?"

They didn't leave, just dripped. They left stripped. Lighter.

And for Yolanda, class didn't end when the music stopped. It ended when the women finally walked out with their heads held high, reclaiming more of their power.

Seventeen

Natasha's PTSD Masterclass

Location: *10:30 AM | Orchid Room*

The ballroom lights dimmed to a low, honeyed hue. The bass rumbled from beneath the floor like a warning. And then, click...click...click...

Natasha Collins entered the room like a damn storm in heels.

She wasn't in a robe. She wasn't in workout gear. No. The headmistress wore a black lace corset with garters and high-cut black lace panties. It clung to her body like it had been molded just for her. Her boots were thigh-high. Her choker sparkled under the lights.

The room fell utterly silent. She didn't speak right away. She strutted.

All the way to the center of the room, where a velvet chair and a full-length gold mirror waited behind a low platform. Natasha turned. One hand on her hip. Her voice was calm. Dangerous.

> *"Ladies, today's lesson is about handling the dick and not catching feelings from it. Not losing your damn mind behind it. And absolutely not forgetting who the fuck you are because a man hit your spot like he invented it."*

Someone gasped. Emily choked on her water. Teri whispered, "Oh shit," under her breath.

Natasha smiled, just a little. "You may think this is about technique. And it is. But it's also about discipline. You can't be in your power if you're addicted to his dick."

She pulled up a PowerPoint slide: "The 5 Stages of Dickmatization."

1. He blew your back out
2. You start cooking for him
3. You start compromising for him
4. You ignore red flags
5. You let him hit raw without a title

The class screamed.
Natasha snapped her fingers.
"Okay, ladies, raise your hand if you've ever loaned money to a man who couldn't even give you a consistent nut." Hands went up like a gospel revival. "Exactly. And that's why today's session is about discipline."
She gave them tools:

- "The 3-Day Post-Dick Rule"—no decisions or texts for 72 hours
- "Nut Notes"—journaling what you learned after every orgasm
- "The Pleasure Essentials"—a checklist of emotional AND physical skills a man must meet before you invest. Anyone can get a copy at www.freakschoolbooks.com, so share that resource with your girlfriends.

Then, she made them repeat her mantra:

"I will ride him, bless him, and release him if necessary."

And just like that? Dickmatization canceled.
She walked to the mirror, turned, and ran her fingers down her own curves.

"Now, let's talk about skills and technique. It's all about the grip. Not your hands. Your pussy."

A soft ripple of shocked laughter echoed through the air.

"Your walls are muscles. Have you trained them? Can you squeeze him at the top of his stroke and make his toes curl? Do you know how to milk him in slow motion until his voice cracks?"

You might think these workout classes are about fitness. No, ladies, I'm trying to build up your core strength, leg squats, and Kegel skills to handle these dicks.

Mel muttered, "Jesus," and crossed her legs.

"Because that's how you become unforgettable. You don't ask for a title, and you don't whine for a ring either. You ride him into submission, and he'll give you the title for fear that you'll stop turning him out."

Natasha moved to the velvet chair and sat, legs wide.

She pulled a dildo from a silk bag. "Some of y'all think riding is just up and down. That's cardio. I'm here to teach you control." She placed her hands on the armrests and began to roll her hips in slow, lazy figure eights. Deep. Grounded.

"Use your knees. Use your core. Maintain eye contact while riding and, whenever possible, refrain from blinking. And if he grabs your hips to speed it up? Slap his hands. You set the rhythm."

Mel was literally sweating.

Bianca whispered, "This bitch is the truth." Natasha stood again, never breaking her flow.

She walked to the mirror and placed one palm against it.

"The best orgasms don't come from chaos. They come from precision. Know your positions."

Natasha paced the floor in those thigh-high boots like a preacher delivering a soul-snatching sermon.

She paused, turned, and locked eyes with the class.

"Some of y'all think a position is just about his angle. But real freaks know it's about your pleasure first."

She strolled toward the velvet chaise, then turned to face the crowd again.

"Let's start with missionary, but not the 'look up and fake a moan' kind."

Try this next time. "Put a pillow under your hips. Legs up

on his shoulders. Tighten that grip and watch how deep he gets. If his stroke is right, he'll hit your G-spot so perfectly your eyes will cross, and your soul will levitate. I call that the Pillow Princess."

The girls howled.

Natasha smiled and leaned on the back of the chaise.

"Now let me explain the cowgirl." She pulled out the dildo from earlier. "This is where you run the show. You grind, not bounce. You want to apply pressure to the pubic bone. That's your cheat code to the clit. And if you ride him like you've got somewhere to go and all day to get there…" She demonstrated by rolling her hips in a lazy, delicious circle. "…you can cum on his dick without him even moving."

Bianca whispered, "That's a sermon."

"Figure eights, slow drag, squat grind. If you do it right, you'll leave him with PTSD—Post That Stroke Disorder. Give him pleasure trauma so he doesn't ever forget stroking your pussy. You will become a core memory."

Emily fanned herself. Natasha adjusted her corset.

"Spooning. Side-saddling. Don't sleep on it. One leg hooked over his, and boom, you've got deep penetration and access to your clit."

She smirked. "Perfect for slow mornings or freaky brunch sessions."

The ladies laughed, breathless. "Then, there's doggy style, with elevation."

Natasha leaned forward on the chaise, arching her back with surgical precision.

"A pillow or two under your stomach to get that booty up. Chest down. If you relax, he'll hit your G-spot like new money, honey."

She added, "Bonus points if he reaches around and plays with your clit while he's hitting from the back."

Teri muttered, "Damn…"

Natasha glanced back. "And for those of you more experienced, try a flat doggy. You are lying flat, legs together. He slides in and grinds like he's pressing his soul into yours. It's called The Spinal Tap. Now, that shit right there? It'll make you grab the sheets like a demon is entering your body."

She stood again, slowly, like she knew she'd already set their souls on fire.

"Now, if you've got a partner who loves to be close, you can do the Lotus on him. You straddle him face-to-face, chest-to-chest, wrap your legs around his waist, and grind your clit against his pelvis while you kiss the life outta him."

Emily's eyes were glassy.

"If he's soft, you use your mouth to perk him up. If he's tired, you ride his face. If you're tired? Use your toys. But don't ever just lie there and wait to be pleased."

She took a breath. Let the silence stretch.

"Do you want consistent orgasms? Master these positions. Know which angles get you off. Control the pressure. And breathe through the buildup like you're riding waves in the ocean, not dodging pain in a dark room."

She walked slowly across the stage, chin lifted. "You aren't a passenger in sex. You are the damn pilot. Ride. Grip. Grind. Squeeze. And speak up and direct the action if you need to! The orgasm isn't the finish line; it's the confirmation that you remembered who the fuck you are."

She turned and faced them all, grabbing a small bottle of lube. "Use silicone lube for a slick glide when you're on round 2 and beyond, or if he's not going to eat it first. Always use water-based lubricant for toys, and please clean them weekly. Grab the CBD lube when you want his soul to leave his body.

"And if the dick goes soft? You don't panic. You revive it. Stroke it slowly. Kiss the tip. Lick under the head like you're tracing a secret. Then, whisper something filthy to your partner. Something like, *"You gonna let me sit on your face till this shit's hard again or what?* That's how you reset the game."

Emily gasped. Again.

Bianca was nodding like a church usher.

Summer was thinking of how to use these techniques in her subsequent encounter with Mr. Black.

Natasha looked out across her class of hungry, wide-eyed freaks-in-training.

"You are not here to be chosen. You are here to choose. Ride him. Ruin him. But do not lose yourself in the dick. Make him lose himself in you."

Then, she smiled and said, "Class dismissed."

There was thunderous applause. Some stood. Emily sat in stunned silence. But every single one of them left with one undeniable truth: they learned how to fuck well and own their own orgasm.

Eighteen

Summer & Mr. Black

Location: *10:03 PM | Velvet Room*

Fresh off Natasha's master class, Summer hatched a plan to bring Mr. Black to his knees. She adjusted her lip gloss and stepped into the Velvet Room with an attitude that said, "Tonight, I'm not here to learn. I'm here to leave a core memory."

She wasn't nervous anymore.

She wasn't wondering if she could keep up. No. She had her hair pinned up, a barely there robe hanging open over her cocoa butter skin, with confidence coiled in her spine like a loaded weapon.

Mr. Black was already waiting, shirtless, barefoot, with sweatpants sitting low. He leaned on the bed like a fantasy, with arms crossed, with a dark, dangerous grin stretched across his face.

He didn't speak. He looked at her like a hungry lion. Slow. Lustful. Hungry.

He finally said, voice low. "You come to play or perform?"

Summer closed the door behind her. "Neither," she purred. "I came to ruin you."

He laughed deeply. He was surprised by her confidence.

But Summer didn't crack a smile. She walked toward him with a saunter, her eyes never leaving his.

"Tonight," she whispered, pressing a single finger to his chest, "you're gonna learn about a condition called

PTSD."

He raised an eyebrow, a grin still playing on his lips. "Oh yeah? What's that stand for?"

She leaned in so close that her lips brushed his ear.

> "Post. That. Stroke. Disorder. I'm gonna fuck you so good you'll twitch every time someone says my name. You'll never forget stroking this pussy."

> "I will become..." she whispered, gripping his waistband, "...a core memory."

And just like that, Mr. Black forgot how to speak.

Summer shoved him gently onto the bed, threw off her robe, and straddled his face like a queen taking her throne. She ground her wetness onto his cheeks, slow and steady.

"You feel that?" she asked. She dragged her clit over his face and chin, teasing him with nothing but slick heat and intention.

"You need to make me good and wet for what I'm about to do to you. He grabbed her hips to make her sit still so that he could gain back some control. Summer's breath hitched as Mr. Black's hands gripped her hips, anchoring her as he pulled her down closer. The warmth of his breath sent shivers through her, igniting a fire within. She could feel his hunger for her, and it only intensified her desire to take control.

"Good and wet," she repeated, her voice a sultry whisper, "but I need you to work for it."

Mr. Black's eyes darkened with a mix of challenge and eagerness. He pushed his face into her, his tongue darting out to tease her slick folds. The sensation was electric, causing her to gasp and arch her back, feeling the weight of his mouth on her. He licked and sucked, his tongue dancing over her clit with expert precision, coaxing out the pleasure that built within her.

Summer bit her lip, trying to maintain her composure. She wanted to stay dominant, to keep the upper hand, but the way he was working her sent waves of heat coursing through her body. Her fingers held the sides of his face as she grinded on him, losing herself in the moment.

"Yes, just like that," she encouraged. "You're doing so well. Keep going."

With each flick of his tongue, he drove her higher, sending her spiraling toward the edge. The heat pooled in her belly, tightening, and she could feel her climax creeping closer. She wanted to hold on, to savor the moment, but the way he devoured her made it impossible to resist. "Don't stop," she gasped, "I'm so close."

He responded by intensifying his efforts, sucking the juice off her clit while thrusting his tongue deep into her. The combination was overwhelming, and she felt her body responding instinctively, tightening around him as pleasure coursed through her veins.

"Mr. Black," she cried out, the name slipping from her lips as the tension finally snapped. She came hard, waves of pleasure crashing over her as she ground against his face, the world around her fading into bliss.

As the waves of ecstasy subsided, she pulled back, breathless and flushed. Mr. Black looked up at her, his face glistening with her essence, a satisfied grin on his lips.

"Thank you so much. Now," she said, her voice low and sultry, "it's your turn."

Without waiting for a response, she slid down his body, her lips trailing kisses along his chest. She could feel his anticipation building as she reached his waistband, her fingers untied his black linen pants, and she teasingly reached beneath the fabric, feeling the heat radiate from him.

"Let's see if you can keep up," she teased, pulling his pants down just enough to free him, her eyes widening with delight at the sight.

He sat up so he could remove his pants, so the party could really start.

She kissed him deeply first when he got back on the bed.

She stroked him to make sure he was hard. One stroke. Two. Then she straddled him again, guiding him into her slowly.

They both moaned when he got all the way up in there.

Her hips began to move. Not fast. Not desperate. Just focused. She squeezed him with every rotation. Kegels trained. Walls tight. Pussy pulsing like a metronome.

He gasped. "F-fuck... Summer..."

"That's right," she said, "Say my name."

She leaned back, hands behind her, grinding deep while clenching him in rhythmic waves. "You feel that grip? That's my signature. I sign every dick I ride."

Her words made his pulse quicken. The audacity of her claim sent a rush of heat through him, igniting a fierce lust that had him teetering on the edge of losing control. He had always prided himself on being the one in charge, the one leading the dance, but Summer was turning the tables in a way he had never anticipated.

The way she moved, the way she owned her pleasure, sent shockwaves of arousal coursing through him. He was entranced, watching her expertly control the rhythm, her body undulating with confidence and power. Each clench of her muscles drew him deeper into a whirlwind of ecstasy, and he found himself lost in the sensation and completely at her mercy.

"God, you're incredible," he breathed. The sight of her dominating him was intoxicating, and he felt his own desires rising to meet her boldness. He wanted to give in, to let her take him on this journey.

As she continued to move, he felt himself slipping further under her spell, ready to surrender to the wild ride she had initiated.

At one point, he tried to buck up. Tried to meet her stroke for stroke.

She pinned his wrists. "Nah, baby," she whispered. "You don't get to lead. Tonight, I'm the one you'll see in your dreams."

He came hard, hips shaking, jaw clenched, and eyes rolled back.

And Summer? She kept riding. She wasn't done yet. Mr. Black tried to recover.

He was still inside her, twitching. Overstimulated. Breathless.

But Summer didn't move. She just stared down at him with a delicious smirk that said, "You thought it was over? I'm just getting started." She said softly, rotating her hips like a slow spell was cast.

"This pussy got phases, baby," she whispered. "You just survived the first one."

He groaned. His hands gripped her thighs.

She clenched again, tight. Measured. Intentional. She leaned forward, her breasts brushing his chest, her lips at his ear. "Round 2... is for discipline."

With a sultry grin, she lifted herself off Mr. Black, savoring the way he twitched inside her. "Hold on," she teased, turning around to face away from him. She positioned herself above him, lowering her hips for the reverse cowgirl. Then, she leaned forward, resting her hands on his thighs for support.

"Let's try something different," she purred, guiding him deeper as she tilted her hips back, bringing him into a new angle that sent shockwaves through her body.

In this position, she had complete control. With her back arched and her thighs burning, she began to ride him again, this time with a more intense tempo, her body moving in a circular motion that sent waves of pleasure coursing through both of them.

Mr. Black was mesmerized, his eyes glued to the way she moved and the way her body enveloped him and drove him wild. He tried to buck up, to meet her stroke for stroke, but she was having none of it. "Nah, baby," she whispered, pinning his wrists to the bed again, reminding him. "Tonight, I decide the pace."

With each thrust, she felt the pleasure building within her, and she leaned back further, allowing him to penetrate her even deeper. The sensation was intoxicating, and she could feel herself getting closer to the edge again.

"This is your reward for being so good," she teased, her voice breathy yet commanding. "But don't think I'm done with you."

With a determined focus, she shifted her weight, bringing one leg up and resting it on the edge of the bed, allowing for an even deeper connection. As she rocked her hips, she clenched around him, each movement designed to drive him wild while keeping her dominance intact. "God, you feel amazing," he gasped, his voice thick with desire.

"Just wait," she replied, her breath quickening as the pressure built inside her. "I'm almost there." She leaned back even further, arching her back, and rode him with fervor, her body pulsing in rhythm with his. Every clench of her walls, every intentional movement, brought her closer to the edge.

Finally, as she felt the wave of pleasure cresting, surrendering to the sensation, she moaned, "I'm cumming!" Her body convulsed around him as she reached her climax, the pleasure washing over her like a tidal wave.

She rode out her orgasm, her hips moving in small circles as she felt the bliss consume her, the world around her fading away. Mr. Black groaned beneath her, in awe as he witnessed her pleasure. He thought to himself, "She had full control of her walls, squeezing me like she'd built choreography into her damn vagina."

As her ecstasy subsided, she collapsed onto him, breathless and satisfied. "That was just Round Two," she whispered, teasing him. "You good?" she said, licking and sucking his neck while she took a little breather. "I'm about to ruin you for everybody else."

For Round Three, Summer decided to switch it up again, wanting to keep Mr. Black on his toes. She turned to her side, gesturing for him to spoon her from behind. "Let's get cozy," she said.

Mr. Black eagerly shifted his body, aligning himself with her as she nestled her back against his chest. As he slid inside her again, she felt the warmth of his body enveloping her, a delicious contrast to the heat building within.

"Just like this," she whispered, her voice sultry as she rolled her hips back against him, coaxing him deeper. "I want you to feel every inch."

In this position, Mr. Black had the pleasure of holding her

close, his arms wrapping around her waist as she took control of the rhythm. She pushed her hips back against him, setting a slow, enticing pace that allowed her to savor the feeling of him inside her.

He grunted, feeling the way her body moved against him, every thrust sending waves of pleasure coursing through them both. Summer could feel the tension building again, her body responding instinctively to the way he filled her.

"Just relax and enjoy," she instructed. She increased the intensity, her movements becoming more passionate, and she could feel his breath quickening behind her.

As she continued to rock her hips, she leaned back slightly. He kissed her shoulder, gave her a light bite, and sucked her neck. She whispered sweet nothings that drove him wild. The intimacy of the spooning position heightened their connection, each thrust echoing with the promise of pleasure.

"Oh my goodness, Summer," he gasped, his hands gripping her hips tighter as he tried to match her rhythm.

"Just let go," she said, as she edged him closer. "I want you to enjoy this."

With her body enveloping him, she felt the pleasure building to a peak once more. "I'm getting close," she moaned. "Are you ready?"

In response, he thrust deeper, the sensation driving her to climax. "I'm cumming!" she cried out, the pleasure washing over her like a wave, sending tremors through her body.

As she rode out her orgasm, Mr. Black followed close behind, overwhelmed by the intensity of it all. He held her tight, feeling her body contract around him, and the connection between them felt electric.

Finally, as the waves of ecstasy subsided, Summer turned to face him, a satisfied smile gracing her lips. "That was incredible; thank you for a funky time."

When she finally let him go, he was a mess.

Eyes glazed. Chest soaked in sweat. Dick still twitching and completely mentally fried.

She leaned down and whispered in his ear:

"Now every time you stroke… you'll remember this night. That's PTSD, baby. I warned you."

She kissed his cheek, slipped on her robe, and walked out as if it were the scene of a crime.

Mr. Black's Reflection

Instructor's Audio Recording:
2:21 AM "That Woman Rode My Soul"

Deep exhale. *Man—I got fucked tonight. That woman rode my soul.*

Pause.

Not laid. Not smashed. Fucked. Proper. By a woman who came in like she had a vendetta and left like she needed a trophy. Summer ain't a student. She's a goddamn problem—a storm in a silk robe with a Ph.D. in pressure and a black belt in grip control.

Another pause. He sips water. Chokes slightly.

The shit she did to me on that bed? That wasn't technique. That was possession. She didn't ride me; she wrote her name inside my soul. At one point, I swear to God, I came, and she kept going. Looked me dead in the face and said, 'This pussy got phases.'"

Phases, WTF? I've been at Freak School for a long time. Watched these girls come in nervous and leave confident. But this one? She skipped confidence and went straight to creating a chest-thumping core memory."

He deeply exhales through his nose. Still not recovered.

She hit me with that PTSD line—Post That Stroke Disorder—and I laughed at first. I thought it was cute. But now? I can't close my eyes without feeling that grip. I swear, I walked past the training mirror on my way out and almost flinched. My dick was hard and scarred.

I shouldn't be this emotionally invested in a single session, but damn. Summer didn't just master the assignment. She rewrote the syllabus.

And the worst part? I want more.

She said she came to ruin me. And she did it in the best possible way. Summer won this round.

But I'm coming back for revenge.

Just know that.

NINETEEN

Emily & Mr. Green

Location: *9:30 PM | Emily's Suite*

Emily felt calm and nervous at the same time. She decided to give her virginity to Mr. Green tonight.

She stood barefoot in her room, a robe tied in a knot at her waist, her hair tucked back in soft curls. The air was warm, laced with lavender oil and vanilla.

Then came the knock.

Soft. Intentional. She opened the door, and there he was. Mr. Green.

His mask was on. He looked good to her. His shirt was unbuttoned just enough to reveal a smooth chest and a thin gold chain glinting at his collarbone. He didn't smile, but his eyes did. Gentle. Grounded.

"Hi," she said, her voice barely above a whisper. "You look beautiful," he replied. "Are you still sure you want to do this tonight?"

She nodded. "Yes, I want... to give this to you. Not because I feel like I have to. But because I trust you to handle me with care."

Mr. Green stepped inside. He didn't touch her, not yet. He just stood with her for a moment in silence. Then, he extended his hand. When she took it, her body relaxed like it had been waiting for this exact moment.

He undid the knot of her robe like it was sacred and helped her onto the bed. She was shaking slightly, but not from fear. More from the emotion of everything, every inch of skin was suddenly aware of what was happening.

Mr. Green's fingers brushed her shoulders as he pulled away to undress. When he was fully unclothed, he slid into bed beside her.

"We'll go slow," he murmured. "If you want to stop, say the word. I'm here to guide, not take." Emily nodded, eyes shining. "I don't want to stop."

He kissed her first. It was soft like a promise wrapped in heat. His fingers danced down her sides, tracing the delicate lines of her body, pausing at her waist before moving down to her thighs. She felt alive, every nerve ending tingling as he explored her with the utmost care. By the time he brushed his fingers against her inner thighs, she was trembling with excitement.

"Are you sure?" he asked, his voice tender. "Yes," she breathed, her heart pounding. "Please."

What followed wasn't fireworks; it was something quieter and more profound, like music that can only truly be heard with your eyes closed. Mr. Green adjusted to every sound she made. His hands were teasing her gently, coaxing soft gasps from her lips.

He slowly lowered himself between her legs, his breath hot against her skin as he began to eat her out, his tongue exploring her gently. He took his time, savoring the moment, listening intently to her reactions, and gauging her pleasure and comfort.

Emily's body responded instinctively, arching towards him as waves of sensation began to build. "Oh... that feels amazing," she gasped, her fingers rubbing his head, urging him closer.

"Just relax and let me take care of you," he murmured against her, the vibrations of his voice sending shivers through her body. It fueled his desire to give her everything she needed.

With every flick and swirl, he drew out her pleasure, teasing her to the brink, then easing back to let her ride the waves of sensation. She felt herself getting lost in the experience, every touch igniting a fire within her.

"Mr. Green," she gasped, her voice breathy and filled with need. "I'm so close..."

"Let go," he encouraged, his eyes locked onto hers as he continued to gently suck on her clit."

Then, she felt a euphoric release that made her body

tremble. "I'm cumming!" she cried, feeling the world around her dissolve into pure bliss. As the waves of pleasure subsided, Mr. Green gently eased back, allowing her to catch her breath. He watched her, a satisfied smile on his lips. "Are you ready for the next step?" he asked softly, his voice filled with tenderness. "We can take as much time as you need."

Emily nodded. "Yes, I really want to do this."

He smiled at her reassurance, then positioned himself between her legs. He took a moment to admire her, the way she glowed with anticipation and vulnerability.

"Just remember, I'll be right here with you." He moved closer and pressed a gentle kiss on her lips. Then, with careful precision, he lined himself up at her entrance, pausing to give her a moment to adjust.

At first, it was just the tip, a gentle intrusion that made her gasp. He paused, allowing her body to adjust to the sensation. "Breathe," he instructed softly, his voice soothing as he watched her closely.

With every inch he entered, Emily felt a mix of sensations— excitement, slight discomfort, but also a growing sense of fullness that felt strangely right. "You're doing so well," he encouraged, inching deeper. "Just relax."

As he pushed in more, Emily felt a brief sting, but Mr. Green's gentle touch and calming words made her feel safe. "Just a little more," he said, his voice low and reassuring. "You're almost there."

With a final thrust, he was fully seated within her, their bodies connected in a way that felt both intimate and profound. He didn't move right away, allowing her to adjust to him completely. "How does it feel?" he asked. "It feels... different," she admitted, a smile creeping onto her face. "But good."

"Okay, good," he replied, a sense of relief washing over him. He wanted to make this experience memorable for her, something she would cherish.

After a moment, he began to move, pulling back slowly before pushing in again, taking his time to find a rhythm that felt right for both of them. Each thrust was deliberate and gentle, and he focused on her reactions, adjusting his movements to ensure she was comfortable and enjoying the sensation.

Emily's body responded instinctively, her hips meeting his with every thrust, the initial discomfort fading into waves of pleasure. "Oh, Mr. Green," she breathed, feeling herself getting lost in the moment. "This feels amazing."

He smiled at her encouragement, feeling a rush of pride at being able to give her joy. "You're incredible," he murmured, increasing the pace slightly but still keeping it slow and intimate.

As they moved together, the world around them faded away, leaving only the two of them in their own bubble. He could feel the tension building between them again, a shared energy that pulsed with every thrust.

"You good?" he asked, his concern evident as he watched her closely. "Yes," she breathed, a smile lighting up her face. Her words emboldened him, and he began to move more confidently, his thrusts becoming deeper and more passionate.

The sounds of their bodies meeting filled the room. As the pleasure intensified, Emily could feel herself approaching another climax, her body responding to his every movement. "I'm so close again," she gasped, her fingers digging into his arms as she held on tightly.

"Let go, Emily," he urged, his voice a low murmur as he quickened his pace slightly. With one final thrust, she felt the waves of pleasure crash over her. "I'm cumming!" she exclaimed, her voice ringing with pure joy. She had never felt that much of everything in her life.

Mr. Green followed closely behind her; after feeling her body contract around him, as he felt the overwhelming sensation, he quickly pulled out of her. Then he held her close in his arms. They lay there, breathless, basking in the afterglow. "Thank you," Emily whispered, her voice soft and filled with gratitude. "That was... beyond anything I imagined."

Mr. Green smiled, brushing her face. "You were amazing. I'm so glad we shared this."

A few moments later, she surprised him.

She leaned down to his ear and whispered, "I want to ride you." Mr. Green felt a rush of exhilaration at her words. "Yes," he replied, his voice low and encouraging. "Whenever you're ready."

As she climbed atop his lap, he could see something shift in her, an awakening confidence that made his heart race. She settled into position, her hands resting gently on his stomach for support, her eyes locked onto his as she took a moment to find her balance.

"Just like before," he reminded her softly, wanting her to feel safe and in control. "Go at your own pace. I'm here."

She nodded, a spark of excitement shining in her eyes. Slowly, she began to lower herself onto him, taking him in with a measured, deliberate movement. The sensation was electric, and she felt every inch as she sank down, her body trembling with anticipation.

Once fully seated, she paused, her breath hitching slightly as she adjusted to the fullness. "You feel amazing," she said, a shy smile spreading across her face.

He rested his hands on her hips, ready to guide her if she needed it. "Whenever you're ready, you can start moving."

After a moment's hesitation, Emily took a deep breath and began to rise, her body responding instinctively as she lifted herself, then lowered back down, finding a rhythm that felt right. She could feel the sensations building within her, the warmth of Mr. Green beneath her fueling her confidence.

"That's it," he encouraged, his voice deep and soothing. "Just like that."

As she started to move with more fluidity, she could feel the power of her body, the way her muscles worked in harmony with her movements. With each rise and fall, waves of pleasure coursed through her, and she felt herself getting lost in the moment.

"Am I doing okay?" she asked. "You're doing amazing," he praised, his eyes filled with admiration. "You're beautiful."

With his words of encouragement, her confidence blossomed. She began to move faster, her hips rolling in a rhythm that felt exhilarating. "Let go, Emily," he urged, as he watched her with hungry eyes.

The pleasure intensified when he started pumping lightly under her. "I'm so close," she gasped, her breath quickening as she moved with abandon, losing herself in the sensations. "Let it happen; I'm right here with you."

With one final thrust of her hips, she felt a wave of pleasure crash over her once again, her body trembling as she cried out in ecstasy. "I'm cumming!" she exclaimed, her voice ringing with pure joy.

Her pussy was so tight, it didn't take much for Mr. Green to cum closely behind her, feeling her body contract around him, pulsing with warmth and pleasure. He groaned, "You feel so good, Emily," as he quickly pulled out of her.

He collapsed, pulling her close into his arms, giving her sweet kisses all over her face and neck. They lay there, breathless and entwined, basking in the afterglow.

"Thank you," Emily whispered, her voice soft and filled with gratitude. "That was... beyond anything I imagined."

Mr. Green smiled. "You were amazing. I'm so glad we shared this."

In that moment, they both knew they had created a memory that would linger long after the night had ended, a beautiful beginning to what could be a cherished connection.

Emily & Mr. Green's Reflections

Journal Entry: *1:44 AM | "I Finally Let Go"*

Tonight, I gave away something I'd been guarding for so long that I almost forgot why I kept it locked up in the first place.

It wasn't perfect. It didn't need to be. It was real. It was warm. It was safe. And it was my choice.

I didn't expect to feel so powerful in the moment; I was supposed to be at my most vulnerable. But that's what Mr. Green gave me; he didn't take my virginity. I gave it to him freely. He gave me control, space, and safety.

Everything about this night was amazing. He ate me so good; he looked at me like I was a woman. Not a fragile thing to protect. But a force. A flame. A body worth honoring.

And when I flipped him over and asked if I could ride him, I saw his surprise, his trust, and his surrender. That changed everything.

I came into Freak School wondering if I could ever compete. If I could ever make love like a woman who wasn't ashamed of wanting to have sex. Now, I know I can. And I will.

Tonight, I didn't lose anything. I found myself.

And maybe... I found something in him, too.

-Emily

Mr. Green's Reflection
Instructor's Journal Entry: *1:57 AM* | *"She Changed the Tempo"*

"I've helped a lot of women cross that bridge the first time. It's beautiful to feel them letting go."

"But Emily was different. She changed the tempo."

"She didn't just open her body; she opened her soul to me. And somewhere in between her first tear and the second orgasm, I realized I wasn't guiding her anymore. I was following."

"She asked me not just to take something but to help her remember it."

"And I will."

"Her voice when she said 'please'? It wasn't scary. She was ready. And when she looked at me after she came, all soft and proud, something shifted in me."

"This job isn't about the climax. It's about the moment a woman sees her own power reflected in her. And Emily? She looked in that mirror and stood tall."

"I came into her room tonight to be her first."

"She left me feeling like it was mine too."

-Green

Twenty

Mel & Mr. Bronze

Location: *10:00 PM | The Music Suite*

The invitation arrived for Mel at 8:47 PM
Handwritten on a linen card, sealed with a bronze wax stamp that smelled faintly of tobacco and sandalwood.

Mel,

You set the tempo last time.
May I take the lead tonight?
Meet me in the music suite at 10 p.m.
                              -B.

Mel smiled to herself as she stood before the full-length mirror.
No robe tonight.
She wore a fitted black slip dress with a thigh-high slit, no bra, no panties, and her signature red lip. Her curves glowed. Her eyes? Curious. Ready.
She picked up the key, slipped on her heels, and made her way upstairs.
The music suite wasn't like the other training rooms. It was low-lit, warm, and masculine.
Velvet curtains. A turntable spinning Coltrane in the corner. Fresh flowers. A tray with bourbon and chocolate-covered figs. And Mr. Bronze, waiting by the window in a fitted black shirt, sleeves rolled up, no mask tonight.
Mel froze. She was shocked to see his face. "He is beautiful

with his salt-and-pepper beard trimmed close," she thought. His chestnut skin glowed in the candlelight—eyes soft but focused, like she was his favorite sheet of music.

"Hi," she said, voice catching. "Hey, Mel."

Just that. Soft. Familiar. Like they'd done this a hundred times already.

He didn't undress her. Not right away.

He took her hand, leading her to the center of the room, where the soft glow of moonlight bathed them in soft golden light.

As he placed his palm on the small of her back, the warmth of his touch sent a shiver of anticipation through her. Then, they danced.

No words were exchanged, just the low hum of the saxophone wrapping around them like a warm embrace. Their bodies moved in perfect harmony, swaying as if they had all the time in the world.

"You always lead?" She whispered in his ear, her breath warm against his skin.

"Only when the woman lets me," he replied, his voice a low, teasing murmur.

He spun her gracefully, catching her effortlessly as she twirled. Time seemed to stand still as he let his hands linger on her waist, savoring the moment.

"I've been thinking about your moan," he confessed, his gaze intense and full of desire. "And?" she prompted, wanting to draw out his thoughts. "I want to hear it again. But this time? I want to earn it."

With a gentle tug, he asked her to remove her slip dress. She didn't hesitate and complied willingly, letting the fabric fall like a whisper to the floor.

She stood bare before him, radiating confidence and vulnerability. Not ashamed. Not performing. Just present.

He knelt before her, eyes locked onto hers, and kissed her thighs softly. His lips trailed a tantalizing path, licking the inside of her knee before ascending, teasingly slow, until she gasped in anticipation.

"You remember how to ask for what you want?" He

murmured, his fingers resting gently above where she throbbed with need.

"I do," she replied, her voice steady. "Then tell me," he demanded, a smile playing on his lips.

She met his gaze and said, "Put your mouth on me. Slow. Don't stop until I beg you to."

He exhaled through a smile. "Yes, ma'am."

What followed wasn't rushed; it was a masterpiece. His tongue painted pleasure in slow, deliberate strokes, each movement a brush of artistry as he paused to listen to her breath before diving back into the depths of her desire.

He held her thighs like they were fragile, his tongue flicking, lips sucking, humming softly against her heat, creating a symphony of sensation. Each caress ignited a spark within her, and the world outside faded, leaving only the intoxicating rhythm of their bodies.

When she finally fell apart, she threw her head back, legs trembling, hand gripping his head, while he just kept going. He didn't rush; he savored every moment, like her pleasure was his language.

Later, when he lifted her onto the bed, his movements were deliberate, and as he entered her with a slow, deep stroke, Mel didn't just moan; she sang out. Their hips met in a dance of intimacy that was both passionate and tender.

Their climax? Mutual. When she came, it was a sweet note that resonated deep within him. As he reached his peak, he kissed her shoulder, whispering, "You're unforgettable."

They lay in silence, wrapped around each other like a warm blanket. Mel turned her head on the pillow and smiled, her heart full. "I think you just became my favorite song."

At that moment, she felt like her body had been unlocked note by note. He didn't treat her like something to be conquered; he treated her like she was already whole, and tonight was about rediscovering every room inside her. Every breath, every favorite stroke, that secret place on her neck that drove her wild. He explored her with one perfectly timed kiss at a time.

When they were ready for another round, he didn't rush in.

He held himself at her entrance, teasing her folds with just the tip, his gaze never leaving hers as he watched the desire grow in her eyes. She moaned in that low, rich way he remembered from their first encounter, and he felt his heart race.

"You sure?" he asked, with longing and care. "Don't ask me that again," she said, as she wrapped her legs around his back, pulling him in.

His hips rolled into her like a slow tide, and her heels dug into his back as she matched him stroke for stroke, each thrust filled with desire and understanding.

He paused when her breath caught, adjusted, and continued more deeply. When she came, it didn't sneak up on her. It climbed, circled, and demanded to be released. He held her face while it happened, watched the way her eyes fluttered shut, and kissed her cheek when her voice cracked in ecstasy.

And when he came, he buried his face in her neck and groaned, low and long, like the final note in a jazz solo that left the audience stunned in silence.

Afterwards, he kissed her shoulder, her hand, and her left hip. She rested her head on his chest and let the afterglow settle in. There was no awkward fidgeting—just the sound of two bodies breathing in harmony.

"What now?" she asked softly. "Now," he said, brushing his fingers through her hair, "we see if this encore has another set."

The sheets were still tangled around her thighs when she turned her body, slow and deliciously sore, to face him again. Mr. Bronze was lying back, one arm behind his head, chest rising and falling in a steady rhythm, like the night had settled into him.

Mel traced a lazy finger across his chest. The candles still flickered. And her pulse was still singing.

"Are you awake?" she asked. "I'm listening," he said, without opening his eyes. She smiled. That made her heart squeeze in a way she wasn't prepared for.

She sat up, one leg tucked under, her bare skin brushed by the silk sheets. She could still taste him on her lips. But something lingered deeper than the afterglow.

"I know what your hands feel like," she said softly. "I know the way your mouth finds my rhythm. But… I don't even know your name."

He opened his eyes. Looked at her. Not startled. Not amused. Then, he sat up, too.

"It's Samuel," he said. "But the people who really know me… call me Sam."

Mel nodded, rolling his name around in her mind. Sam. Mr. Bronze has a name.

"Well, Sam," she said, leaning in close, lips brushing his. "I think I'm ready for more. His smile returned. "For you? Always."

This round was different. Not because it was slower. But because it was deeper.

Mel climbed up on top of him. She didn't ride him like she had something to prove. She moved like she had nothing to hide.

She straddled him and let her body find the rhythm. His hands stayed on her waist, thumbs circling, guiding but not controlling.

Their eyes never broke. "You're beautiful," he whispered. "You are quite handsome yourself, sir," she answered, breath catching.

Mel climbed up on top of him, feeling a rush of excitement and empowerment as she straddled him. Each gentle sway of her hips was an expression of freedom, an exploration of her own pleasure.

His hands rested firmly on her waist, thumbs circling her skin in soothing patterns, guiding but never controlling. The warmth of his touch sent shivers down her spine, every caress igniting a fire within her. Their eyes never broke. "You're beautiful," he whispered, his voice thick with admiration, his breath warm against her skin. "You are quite handsome yourself, sir," she answered, her breath catching in her throat, heart racing under the weight of his loving gaze.

With slow, deliberate movements, Mel's body savored the sensation of him filling her. A breathy sigh accompanied each rise and fall, her body responding instinctively to the pleasure coursing through her. "Just like that," he encouraged, his voice low and gravelly.

As she found her rhythm, she felt the tension building within her. His thumbs continued to circle her waist. "You feel incredible," he murmured. Mel smiled, exhilarated by his praise. "Oh, I'm just getting started," she teased. Then she picked up the pace, her hips rolling in a way that felt both powerful and freeing. The sensations were intoxicating, and she let herself get lost in the pleasure. "Don't hold back," he urged, his voice thick with desire. With his encouragement, she embraced her body and the pleasure it could bring. She arched her back, allowing him to see the beautiful curve of her form. Mel closed her eyes and let out a soft moan; it was like their bodies were communicating in their own language.

As she moved faster, he rocked her from underneath. She could feel herself nearing the edge of a blissful release. "Sam," she gasped, his name a plea that hung in the air between them. With one final thrust, she felt the waves of pleasure crash over her, her body trembling as she cried out. "I'm cumming!" she exclaimed. He kept thrusting through her orgasm and soon released right behind her.

As she fell apart, he was captivated by the beauty of her pleasure. When she finally regained her breath, he pulled her close, their foreheads touching as they both caught their breath, a smile breaking across her face. "That was incredible," she whispered, her heart racing with exhilaration. "You are incredible," he replied, his voice filled with warmth and sincerity.

She laid on his chest, lips at his collarbone. "Thank you, Sam." "No," he whispered, kissing her temple. "Thank you, Mel." They stayed intertwined, basking in the afterglow, knowing that this moment was just the beginning of a beautiful symphony they were creating together, possibly for a lifetime.

Mr. Bronze's Reflection

Instructor's Audio Log:
2:17 AM | "The Night I Gave Her My Name"

A deep exhale. A pause.

I've been dealing with women for a long time. Long enough to know the difference between a woman who just wants to cum and one who wants to feel. Mel wanted both. Deserved both. And I gave her everything.

The faint sound of his hand stroking the edge of the bedsheet.

She asked for my name tonight. She didn't ask because she needed to label me. She asked because she wanted to see me.

So I told her. And for the first time in years, I remembered what it felt like to be touched by someone who wasn't trying to take anything; she just wanted to be with me. He chuckles softly.

She climbed on top and started riding me like she was claiming her spot, not that bed in my core memory. Mel moved like she knew herself, and she chose to share that side of herself with me. That's a rare kind of power.

And when she called my name right before she came, I nearly lost it. He exhales again, slower now. I'm grinning now, still thinking about it.

She wasn't loud. She wasn't theatrical. She was free. And that's the part that wrecked me. Watching a woman who's held it together for everybody else finally let herself be truly happy.

She let me love on her for a few hours. Not perform. Not fix. Not please, just be with her. And I don't care how many women I've had, Mel Dibert is the one I'll be humming about when I'm old and gray. She didn't just ask for my name; she asked for my name. She made me want to say it.

If she asks again? I'll tell her more. And if she doesn't? I'll be fine just watching her walk back into the room.

Still glowing. Still soft. Still dangerous, still Mel.

Twenty-One

Teri & Mr. Red

Location: *10:07 PM | Training Room 4*

Teri came to Freak School on assignment from her therapist to help her rebuild her pride and confidence. She needed to recover from the part of herself that still flinched when someone mentioned her ex-fiancé's name. But she didn't plan on knocking boots with a young instructor.

"He left you for a man." She'd heard it whispered. Hell, she'd screamed it into a pillow more than once. It wasn't the betrayal that hurt the most; it was the fear that maybe she hadn't been enough to make him stay.

Now, she needed a reminder that she was still a force. A curvy, class-act, thick-thighs-save-lives kinda *force.*

When she entered the dimly lit studio, Mr. Red was already there. He wore sweatpants, a black tee, and a quiet confidence that matched her fire. What she didn't know was that he was a freak for older BBWs. She was just his type.

He walked over to her and cunningly said, "You came to sweat?" She raised a brow and asked. "You gonna make me?" He stepped closer, his voice low. "I plan to help you remember how." He grabbed her neck, pulled her close, and kissed her fast, hungry, and deep enough to make her knees tremble. It was like a flashback to her twenties.

He tugged at her robe until it hit the floor and lifted her onto the bed like she weighed nothing.

"How do you want it?" he asked. "Don't be gentle unless I ask," she replied.

No further instructions were needed. He took his clothes off and stared at her luscious body for a minute, then he knelt and spread her legs as she fell back.

Mr. Red knelt before Teri, the air thick with anticipation as he looked up at her with a predatory glint in his eyes. She felt heat pooling in her core, the excitement of what was to come making her pulse race.

He pulled her closer, spreading her legs slightly, his hands resting gently on her thighs. "You ready for this?" he asked, his voice low and sultry.

"More than ready," she replied, her breath hitching in her throat.

With that, he leaned in, kissing the inside of her thigh with soft, deliberate kisses that sent shivers through her body. Teri gasped, her back arching in response as he slowly made his way closer to her core. The anticipation was electric, and she could feel the warmth of his breath against her skin.

When his mouth finally met her moist folds, a moan escaped her lips. He started with soft, teasing kisses, exploring her with a gentleness that made her body hum with excitement. His tongue flicked and swirled in a way that made her crave more.

"God, you taste amazing," he murmured against her, the vibrations sending waves of pleasure through her.

Teri gripped the edge of the bed. He worked his mouth on her, taking his time, teasing her with a mix of slow licks and flicks and gentle sucking that had her gasping for breath. Her body responded to his every touch. "Don't stop," she begged, her voice thick with need. "Please." He obliged, diving deeper into her, his fingers now joining his mouth as he slipped two inside her. The combination of his fingers and tongue drove her wild, her hips bucking against his face as she lost herself in the pleasure.

"I'm so close," she gasped, her body trembling as he found her sweet spot. He picked up the pace, his mouth working relentlessly, fingers thrusting in and out, pushing her to the edge of ecstasy. He reveled in the way her body reacted to him.

"Let go for me, Teri," he urged. With a final flick of his tongue and a deep thrust of his fingers, she felt the wave of pleasure crash over her. "Oh my God!" she cried out, her body arching as she came undone.

He continued to work her through her orgasm, his mouth

and fingers relentless, wanting to draw out every last bit of pleasure. Teri gasped and moaned, the intensity of her release washing over her like a tidal wave.

Finally, as she came down from the high, he pulled back slightly, his mouth gleaming with her essence, a satisfied smile on his lips. Teri looked down at him, breathless and exhilarated, feeling alive in a way she hadn't in a long time. "Now, it's your turn," she said, her voice sultry and inviting.

With a grin, he rose to his feet, his eyes dark, and he promised. "Oh, I plan to fuck the shit out of you." He positioned himself between her legs, leaned down to kiss her deeply, the taste of her still lingering on his lips.

Then with a swift, powerful thrust, he filled her, and she gasped. The sensation was overwhelming in the best way. He began to move, each thrust deep and deliberate, driving her wild as they found their rhythm together.

Teri wrapped her legs around him, pulling him closer, urging him on as he pushed her to new heights of pleasure. The intensity of their connection was electric, and she knew this night would be one she would never forget.

This wasn't just sex. This was a reset.

His hands gripped her hips.

His teeth grazed her shoulder.

And when he moved? He gave her strokes and eye contact like a man trying to write his name on her spine.

"Say it," he murmured. "Say what?" she panted. "Say you missed being wanted like this."

She didn't answer. Not with words. She grabbed his face and kissed him with the aggression of a thirsty man in the desert who finally got a drink of water.

She hadn't been fucked like this in years.

After the second orgasm, after her moans softened into hums, Teri didn't pull away. She laid on her stomach, his body resting half over hers, their breathing in sync, skin slick with sweat and something more sacred: safety.

He ran his fingers slowly down her spine. Not to arouse, but to soothe. "You okay?" he whispered, mouth close to her ear.

Teri nodded, her cheek against the pillow. "I didn't know how much I needed that. Not just the sex, but the space to feel free."

He kissed the back of her shoulder. "You held it all together for too long, huh?"

Her throat tightened. The words stuck, like they'd been waiting for permission.

"I've been running on empty since he left. I thought maybe I wasn't enough. Too old. Too busy. Too much."

He lifted himself just enough to look down at her. "You're more than enough. And you don't owe anyone an apology for being the full meal. It's time you stop serving snack-sized love to men who can't handle the whole damn entree."

She laughed then, soft and surprised. It shook something loose. "You talk like someone who's been through some things.

"I listen," he said. "Especially to women who forget how powerful they are."

He rolled onto his back, pulling her gently with him until she rested on his chest.

The silence was thick but comforting. His hands never stopped moving and tracing her spine, rubbing her lower back. Squeezing her booty, then back up again. She felt like she was melting into him. "What's your real name?" she asked suddenly.

He smiled. "It's Aaron." "Mr. Red is sexier," she teased. "You call me whatever you want, darling," he said, kissing her nose.

As they laid there, Teri started thinking about how she had forgotten what softness felt like. How, for years, intimacy had been about proving she was worthy instead of being received and worshipped without condition. Mr. Red was in heaven holding her in his arms.

She sat up slowly, wrapping the sheet around herself, the afterglow still humming through her muscles. "Thank you," she said. "For not treating me like a warm-up act." "Teri," he said, turning back to her. "You're the headliner, lady."

And with that, he slipped out of bed and got dressed. He kissed her deeply one last time and disappeared from the room, leaving her with the memory of how it felt to be fully claimed.

Teri & Mr. Red's Reflections

Journal Entry: *12:53 AM | "Mr. Red did not disappoint."*

I walked in thinking I was too broken, too old, too stiff, and too far gone ever to feel soft again. But last night, I didn't just feel wanted; I felt chosen.

He didn't ask me to shrink. He didn't rush. He saw me. Not the principal. Not the woman left behind—just me.

I came. Twice. But that wasn't magic. The magic was hearing him say my name like he cherished being with me. He focused on me; my breath mattered. I melted in his arms.

Aaron told me his name. He shared it like a secret.

And when I walked in, he was a little cocky. He was talking big. But he didn't make any claims that he couldn't keep.

I don't know what will happen next. But I do know this: my ex didn't leave me because I wasn't enough.

He left because he didn't love himself enough to live in his truth.

But last night? I was more than held. I was worshipped. And I think I'm finally ready to stop apologizing for taking up space.

Mr. Red's Reflection
Instructor's Audio Log: *1:42 AM | "Teri is Unforgettable"*

Teri Whittington is not a woman you fuck and forget.
She's the kind of woman who looks into your eyes and

makes you wonder if you can handle her and if you're doing enough with your life, like a naughty teacher.

She walked in guarded. Tight. Carrying years of neglect from a partner who had ignored her. Years of pretending to be satisfied and not prioritizing her needs enough.

That woman rides pain like it owes her something. I didn't need her to open up for me. I just needed her to remember her power. And when she did? Damn. I loved savoring her and making her cum over and over. She gave me more than her body. She gave me trust.

The kind of trust you can't fake. The kind that sits in your hands and makes you handle it like glass.

And when she asked my name? I almost choked. No one asks that, not like that. Not in mid-afterglow, her voice was still hoarse from how I had put it on her. But she did.

She wanted to remember me with intention. And that means something.

I gladly serve her. I'm just grateful that I got to be the man who reminded her that she still had it.

Teri is a force of nature. She's powerful, stunning, and full of intensity. And that soul-snatching thing between her thighs? That's the icing on the cake.

TWENTY-TWO

Bianca & Mr. Silver

Location: *9:03 PM | Mirror Training Room*

Mr. Silver scheduled a mirror session for Bianca.

Bianca stood before the mirror, barefoot on a shaggy rug, her silk robe clinging to her curves like a second skin. The room was lit entirely by candlelight, soft, golden, and endless, reflecting off every angle in the mirrored walls around her. Low R&B music played through the speakers.

She'd never seen herself like this before.

She was looking at a woman who had survived heartbreak.

A woman who had buried disappointment in work.

A woman who had forgotten what it meant to be worshipped.

"Don't move," Mr. Silver said softly, stepping behind her. "You deserve to see what I see." His voice was deep and calm but electric, like a warm current sliding down her spine.

He was close, but not touching her. She could feel the heat radiating off of him and smell the scent of his cologne, cypress, and smoke.

"Drop your robe and look at yourself," he continued, glancing at the mirror as he spoke to her. "When was the last time you really looked at the woman you are?" Bianca's breath hitched. He hadn't touched her yet, but somehow, she was already unraveling.

She turned her head slightly to look at him. He wore slate-gray linen pants and a black long-sleeved button-down shirt, which was open with the sleeves rolled to his forearms. His mask, a gleaming silver half-plate, covered only his eyes, which were focused but kind.

"What do you see?" he asked her reflection. "A woman who's tired of hiding," she whispered. "A woman who's ready to feel again."

"Let me help you remember," he responded. His fingertips brushed her collarbone, slow and deliberate. She exhaled slowly. Mr. Silver stepped forward, closing the small space between them. His hands gently cupped her hips. "Watch," he said, his lips brushing her ear. "I want you to see how beautiful you are when you are worshipped."

Bianca blinked. He leaned forward and kissed her shoulder. Then, the base of her neck. He trailed kisses down her back, and after kissing her right hip, he looked up and said, "Keep watching." Then he slowly moved in front of her, placing four light kisses across her bikini line. Each kiss sent waves of heat radiating through her, igniting a fire within her core. Bianca felt herself dying with anticipation; she was already good and wet, making it hard to think straight.

"What are you doing to me?" she breathed, her voice trembling slightly. "You are radiant. Let yourself feel everything," he whispered.

His hands traced the curves of her thighs, slowly parting them with tenderness.

Bianca's heart raced as she witnessed the transformation unfolding before her. The way he worshiped her skin was intoxicating. And for the first time in a long while, she felt truly seen.

He grabbed her hand and guided her in front of the largest mirror. Their eyes met in the reflection. "You don't have to perform for me, Bianca," he said, "just feel." Mr. Silver's hands, voice, and breath against her skin became instruments of awakening.

"Own your pleasure," he whispered. A tear slid down her cheek, and she didn't brush it away. When watching herself, she saw something she hadn't seen in years: a woman owning her power.

When it was over, she slumped against the chaise lounge with a full heart.

Mr. Silver kissed her hand and sat beside her.

They didn't speak for a long time. And they didn't need to. The mirror said it all.

Bianca rested her head in Mr. Silver's lap. She turned her head up at him and smiled.

"That was powerful," she said.

"You're beautiful," he answered.

She sat up slowly and crossed her legs at the ankles. "I didn't just see a woman seeking pleasure; I saw a woman ready to take her pleasure back."

He caught his breath. Then, Bianca stood up, turned to look at him, and, like a switch, she became a general. "Take off your shirt," she ordered. Mr. Silver blinked, then obeyed.

Bianca kissed her way down his body. Each touch ignited a fire within her, and she felt Mr. Red's body responding to her as her lips explored his skin. "God, you're incredible," he breathed, his voice thick with anticipation.

"Just wait," she replied, with a playful smirk dancing on her lips. She continued her descent of kisses, trailing down to his abdomen. With a flick of her tongue, she traced the defined lines of his muscles. She glanced up at him, catching the look of desire in his eyes. Then, she reached the waistband of his pants, pausing for a moment, her fingers grazing the fabric. "Are you ready to take these off for me?" she asked, her voice sultry. He nodded, "More than ever."

With a swift motion, he pulled his pants off, exposing himself completely. She could feel delicious anticipation coursing through her veins.

She looked down at him, a sense of authority washing over her. "Lie back, please. You gave me mirror work. Let me give you a core memory," she said.

She lowered herself slowly to mount him. As she felt him fill her, a gasp escaped her lips. The sensation was electrifying.

As Bianca began to move her hips, he met her rhythm. She could see the pleasure etched on his face. "I love you like this; use me, baby," he murmured. "I think I will," she replied, as she increased her pace.

With each thrust, she felt herself growing bolder, and they moved in perfect harmony. She leaned forward and kissed him deeply, the taste of desire lingering between them.

He groaned beneath her, his hands gripping her hips, as she

took control. "You're taking me to another level," he gasped, his breath ragged.

Bianca smiled as she rode him with increasing intensity. She felt herself teetering on the edge. She could feel the wave of pleasure building, ready to crash over her.

"Don't hold back," she urged, her voice a breathless plea. "I want all of it."

Mr. Red started thrusting like a bronco rider. With a final thrust, she found her release, sending her spiraling into pure bliss. "Oh my God!" she cried out, the sound echoing in the room as pleasure consumed her.

His climax was close behind, his body tensing as he let go. They held onto each other tightly, their breaths mingling as they came down from the high; a sense of satisfaction enveloped them.

As they lay entwined, Bianca felt a sense of empowerment wash over her, knowing she had taken control of her pleasure and embraced her desires fully.

She leaned down and kissed his forehead. "Thank you for reminding me that I'm a bad girl," she said softly. "And thank you for showing me who you've always been," he replied, his smile breaking across his face.

She climbed off, picked up her robe, and tied it slowly. Then, she walked to the mirror once more and looked at herself. This time, there was no doubt who she was looking at.

Summer & Mr. Black

Location: *10:05 PM | Adult Playroom*

Mr. Black planned his revenge on Summer. The adult playroom had velvet-lined walls, restraints in satin and leather, a throne in the corner, mirrors on the ceiling, swings, and a dim crimson light that made everything feel like sin.

Summer had wrecked him last time. She rode him into a fog, took the crown, and walked out like she ran the school.

Tonight, he was going to take all her confidence back, he thought, as he adjusted the cuffs on the restraint bed.

He wasn't angry. No. He was focused. This wasn't punishment. It was going to be an education for his most challenging client.

Summer entered the room already smiling. Black robe. No bra or panties. She thought they were just here to play.

Until she saw him. Standing in front of the throne. Shirtless. Serious. Silent.

She paused. "You good?" "Oh, I'm better than good," he said, circling her slowly. "I've been waiting for this for days."

Last time, you made me remember you every time I touched myself." He stopped behind her. "Tonight, I will make you forget your name."

The next thing she knew, her robe was off and her wrists were cuffed above her head on a velvet post. Then, he blindfolded her.

He worshipped her with his mouth first, his tongue trailing her skin, commanding her breath.

Feathers brushed against her skin, sending shivers of delight coursing through her.

He alternated between cool ice and heated oil, his touch a tantalizing contrast that ignited her senses. He explored her neck, her breasts, the sensitive skin along her bikini line, and the soft flesh of her inner thighs, lingering behind her knees, but never where she craved him the most.

"You don't get what you want tonight," he murmured, his voice low and sultry as it sent a thrill down her spine. "You get what you need."

Her legs shook, and her mouth parted in silent desperation. Her body betrayed her, responding to his every movement, begging for more before her pride could catch up. "Mr. Black, please," she gasped, the words escaping her lips in a breathless plea.

"Please, what?" he whispered, his mouth brushing against her ear, his warm breath igniting a fire within her. "I want to be yours. Tonight," she admitted, feeling vulnerable yet exhilarated. That was all he needed.

With a swift motion, he unhooked the handcuffs, guiding her towards the padded table. "This time, it's about submission," he said firmly, bending her forward over the table.

His presence enveloped her, his breath warm and tantalizing against her exposed skin. The air was thick with anticipation, the heat between them rising to a simmer. It wasn't just about sex anymore; it was about reclaiming the respect he had lost the last time they were together.

"Are you ready?" he asked, his voice deep and commanding.

She nodded, her heart racing as he picked up the paddle as a reminder of the power dynamic between them. He rubbed warm oil over her cheeks and then delivered a spank. "Say, 'Yes, Daddy,' after each strike," he ordered. Smack, "Yes, Daddy," she gasped, her words a mix of surrender and exhilaration. Another spank landed, and she bit her lip, feeling the heat blossom in her cheeks. "Yes, Daddy," she repeated, her voice trembling but filled with a newfound strength. With each strike, a thrill coursed through her. Then, he delivered another strike, and she cried out, a mix of pain and pleasure flooding her senses."

Yes, Daddy!" She shouted, her body arching instinctively, her craving for more intensifying. "Good girl," he praised, his voice dripping with satisfaction. With the final spank, she felt a rush of exhilaration wash over her. She was his, body and soul. In that electric moment, she felt a sense of freedom, a release of everything she had held back, and she was ready to embrace whatever came next.

"Remember this," he said, "you are mine tonight." Then, he sank to his knees, his eyes filled with desire as he began to rub, lick, and kiss her ass, savoring every inch of her soft skin. His mouth explored her curves, leaving a trail of warmth and sensation wherever he touched. Every strike of his tongue ignited a fire within her, heightening her anticipation.

Once he had her breathless, he eased up behind her, gently spreading her legs apart. The moment was charged with electricity as he began to stroke her, each movement deliberate and tantalizing. Each stroke drew her closer to the edge, only to pull back just before she could fully surrender. It wasn't just sex; he was marking her soul.

"You belong to yourself," he said, "but tonight? You will give me your surrender."

And when she finally let go, the release washed over her like a euphoric tidal wave.

Summer thought the hardest part was over, but in that instant, she realized he had only just begun to explore the depths of her pleasure.

Her voice trembled. Not from fear, but from knowing she wanted what came next.

Mr. Black was a man possessed. To him, she didn't need to be broken. She needed to be reminded.

"You took Daddy bending you over well," he whispered in her ear. "But can you kneel better?" he continued. "It's time for you to suck Daddy." She felt her heart race, a mix of excitement as she processed his request. The way he spoke made her heart race.

Slowly, she sank to her knees, the coolness of the floor contrasting sharply with the warmth radiating from her body. The position felt both vulnerable and empowering. A rush of anticipation coursed through her as she looked up at him and reached for his fully erect love muscle. She leaned forward, took him into her mouth, and demonstrated her dick-sucking expertise.

When he groaned as his body released, she sucked him through every spasm. "Jesus!" he cried out, his hands holding her steady as he rode the waves of pleasure.

As she finally pulled back, her lips glistening, she took a moment to catch her breath, a satisfied smile playing on her lips. He looked down at her in awe. Desire was reflected in his gaze in a way neither of them would forget.

Summer felt a rush of pride swell within her, but she wasn't done. "I want more," she said, her voice sultry and inviting, ready for whatever came next.

Once he caught his breath, he guided her down on all fours, flat palms on the mat, her back arched, and he slid onto his back, a mischievous glint in his eyes as he lowered her down onto his face. The moment she felt his warm breath against her skin, she could already sense the hunger in him. As she settled onto him, he began to eat her out with an intensity that took her breath away. His tongue worked its magic, swirling and teasing, exploring every inch of her as if she were his last meal. Her body responded eagerly to his every movement. She leaned into him, feeling the heat build from within, the tension coiling tightly as he devoured her.

"Oh my God," she moaned, as he licked and sucked with a fervor that made her remember just how good it felt to be worshipped like this. Each flick of his tongue sent waves of ecstasy radiating through her, building towards a peak that felt just within reach.

When she finally came, it was like fireworks exploding in her mind. She gasped as she released herself into his mouth. Although she was cumming, he didn't stop. He started playing with her peach ring with his thumb and kept licking and sucking her clit. He stretched her orgasm ten more minutes and sent another rush of pleasure coursing through her.

"God, that felt amazing," she gasped, but he was already shifting beneath her. He reached behind her, grabbed a bottle of lube, and began stroking her anus, alternating teasing flutters with his fingers and rimming her entry with his thumb. When her moans of pleasure became too much of a temptation, he released her, slicked lube on his thick shaft and more on her, and spread her cheeks apart. The anticipation made her heart race as he positioned himself behind her, the moment charged with electricity. With gentle pressure, he pressed the tip of his dick against her tightness.

She gasped, shock coursing through her as she embraced the sensation. It was new and exhilarating, pushing her boundaries in the best way possible. As she relaxed, she took in an inch more, the fullness stretching her in ways she had never experienced before.

"Good girl," he praised, his voice low and sultry. "Take it. Take this dick."

A moan escaped her lips as she felt both pleasure and pain, but she welcomed it, leaning into the sensation. But when she reached back to touch him, he grabbed her wrist gently, pinning it to the mat. "You don't reach. You receive," he commanded, his tone firm.

With a swift motion, he guided her to go face down, ass up, which is lying flat on her stomach and popping her ass up. "I want to work that ass from this angle to hit your A-spot," he said, his voice thick with desire.

Still blindfolded, she positioned herself as he wanted, and he continued to work his way into her booty hole. This was new territory, but she felt her body responding to his every thrust. Once she relaxed and surrendered fully, it was more pleasurable for her.

He rocked her, each thrust driving her closer to the edge until her climax hit her like an electric shock, so intense that she temporarily forgot her own name. For a brief moment, everything else faded away, and he stopped allowing her to bask in the aftershocks. In that ache, she surrendered completely.

"Please..." she breathed, her voice trembling with urgency.

"Please, what?" He teased, "Please... don't stop again," she begged.

He didn't need to be told twice. With a swift movement, he reached down for a warm towel, cleaning himself and her before grabbing a bottle of silicone-based lube. He slicked it onto his shaft and inside her pussy. Facing her missionary style, he mounted her, slipped back into her pussy, and got aggressive with his strokes. His movements were precise and powerful, using the hook of his shaft to target her G-spot perfectly. He had studied her body, learning her rhythms, and he knew just how to tap into her pleasure.

He played with her, lifted her legs over his shoulder, thrusting his hips and rolling his body, sending waves of ecstasy crashing over her.

"I know you like this," he whispered, his voice low and sultry, and she could only whine and moan in reply. She had never felt this damn good before; it was as if every nerve ending in her body was alive with pleasure.

He grinned as he tore that pussy up. He was painting her pleasure with each stroke, and he reveled in the way she responded to him.

When they finally came together, it wasn't frantic or rushed; it was a culmination of everything that had led up to this final release. Her submission was voluntary and messy, creating a bond that felt unbreakable in that moment.

When he removed the blindfold and pulled her against him, she didn't speak.

She exhaled long and deep.

"You didn't just take my body," she said, her voice filled with awe. "I know," he replied softly. "In your submission, I helped you release your fears and feel ultimate pleasure."

Summer's Reflection

Journal Entry: *2:06 AM | "When My Power Went Quiet"*

I thought being in control made me powerful. That if I rode a man hard enough, made him beg, I'd never feel small again.

But tonight? Mr. Black didn't just touch my body. He slowed me down until I had no choice but to feel everything I'd been dodging. Every unspoken need. All my fears of letting go.

I thought surrender meant weakness. And somehow he made that surrender feel like the most powerful thing I've ever done. My power went quiet.

He didn't shout. He didn't rush. He applied pressure, like a man tuning an instrument that he already knew how to play.

He spanked me, then kissed me where he struck me, held me when I shook, and kept making me feel pleasure.

And when he stopped, right when I was ready to come apart, he waited.

Made me beg for it.

Not for pleasure. But for release.

I didn't know I could cry from being seen. But here I am.

Not because I was broken. Because I was safe.

And damn, that hit harder than any slap.

Tomorrow, I'll be training a more confident woman.

But tonight? I'm just a girl with her jaw and peach

ring still sore, but my soul is a little quieter now. And a whole lot lighter.

-Summer

Twenty-Four

Emily & Mr. Green

Location: *11:01 PM | Video Center*

Emily used to flinch when someone said the word "sex."

Now, she waited for it, wanted it, with breathless anticipation.

Every other day, like clockwork, she stepped into the small studio suite with the muted gray walls and the velvet filming couch, where Mr. Green was always waiting.

Tripod already set up. Two lights are on in the filming area.

The camera is pointed at the center of the room. He never rushed her. He always asked first.

"Are you still okay with this?" "Do you feel safe with me?"

"Would you like to lead, or would you like to be guided?"

And each time, she said yes, not out of habit. But it was her idea to do these extra sessions.

Today was different. Now she wanted to tape them. "I want to see what you see," she said.

Emily wore a pink silk robe. No bra. No panties. Just lip gloss and curiosity.

When Mr. Green reached for the remote and pressed record, Emily didn't look away.

She met the lens with her eyes open, heart steady, and legs slightly trembling, but this time, from excitement, not fear. Barefoot. Her curls falling over her shoulders. Wrapped in nothing but her Freak School silk robe and blooming self-confidence.

For Mr. Green, every moment with her was like watching a flower bloom in real time.

She had been so shy at first. So guarded. Now, she wanted to try new sex positions all the time.

He didn't pose her. He placed her. Like a favorite portrait, arms gently back, robe slipping just off her shoulder, eyes focused on the mirrored wall behind him.

He always started by kissing her gently. Her lips, then her collarbone, then the space just below her ear, where her breath always caught.

And when he finally undressed her fully, he let the camera keep rolling. But not for him.

"This is for you," he whispered. "So you never forget how far you've come." Emily was learning and adjusting fast. She knew how to guide him to her pulse points.

How to arch when he hovered too long. How to whisper his name, not in surrender, but in invitation. She was no longer waiting to be chosen. She had chosen herself. And when she came, she savored the moments.

Mr. Green did anything she wanted; he was completely in love with her, and he always carried the pressure of a man entrusted with something sacred.

Mr. Green didn't touch her right away. He sat on the couch and let her walk toward him. She wasn't shy. She was intentional.

"You ready?" he asked softly. Emily nodded and leaned in, whispering just loud enough for the mic to catch: I want to remember how I sound when I take my time getting to climax.

"Get down on all fours. Today, I want to enter you from the back," Mr. Green said

This time, she complied. But first, he wanted to eat her to make it smoother for him to enter her. She didn't flinch when he asked her to sit on his face. When she came, she reached down and sucked him to get him hard enough to enter her. Then, he moved behind her and started stroking her deeply. She moaned without apology. She knew what her body needed.

She no longer hid from her own pleasure. Instead, she owned it.

In round two, Mr. Green wanted to show her how to throw it back on him as he stroked her from behind. She was excited to learn more.

The camera caught it all, not as evidence of conquest, but as a keepsake of liberation.

Later, when they collapsed into the cushions together, she asked, "Will you watch these videos?" He smiled. "Only with your permission."

"One day, I want to watch this one. I want to see what I look like when I finally feel free."

Mr. Green brushed her hair from her face and whispered, "You don't need a screen to see that. You lived it."

Mel & Mr. Bronze

Location: *9:38 PM | Rooftop Garden Suite*

Mr. Bronze invited Mel to have a session of rooftop realness.

Mel arrived with no makeup, her hair was in an updo, and she wore a floor-length cardigan over her slip dress.

She didn't want to be sexy tonight. She just wanted to be seen.

Sam was already on the rooftop, barefoot, with the red wine uncorked. Billie Holiday hummed on the vintage record player; he insisted vinyl sounded better than anything modern.

No candles. No setup. Just him. And two wine glasses.

"You came," he said. "You asked," she replied.

They sat in silence at first, sipping Cabernet as the city sparkled beneath them. Mel had always loved rooftop views. They reminded her how small her worries really were.

Sam finally spoke. "You know, you are the first Freak School client I ever agreed to see."

"So why did you agree this time?" she asked. "Natasha showed me your picture, and something in my gut pulled me to say yes. When I learned more, I thought that you would be amazing."

Mel looked at him. "Really? So, have I met your expectations?" she quipped.

He smiled and said, "You are beyond my wildest dreams." Sam was a quiet fire, always simmering, never boastful. And when he touched her, he didn't just explore her body. He read it perfectly.

Tonight, though? His eyes weren't reading. They were waiting.

"So why the mysterious invitation tonight?" she asked softly.

Sam turned his glass in his hand. "I feel like I might want to see you after the curriculum ends."

Mel didn't answer right away. Her heart thudded once. Hard. Not from excitement, but from that cautious thrill only a widow knows: the feeling of something awakening when you weren't sure you were ready or could feel again.

"Sam," she began. "I haven't been with anyone since Ronnie. This school was supposed to be my reset. My release."

"And has it been?" He asked. "Yes," she whispered. "More than I ever expected."

"Then let it be that. And let this be whatever we want it to be." He didn't ask for commitment; he just wanted her to know what he was thinking.

Didn't pressure her with fantasy. He just showed up. Fully. Consistently.

They talked for another hour.

About jazz. About their childhoods. About their favorite books and the people they'd lost.

And when he walked her back to her suite, he didn't come inside.

He just held her hand and said, "Let's keep talking."

And she knew then it wasn't just her body he wanted access to. It was her life.

Mel's Reflection
Journal Entry: *11:52 PM | "When the Music Doesn't Fade"*

I didn't expect to feel this soft again.

Not this soon. And certainly not with my instructor at Freak School.

But Sam is far from ordinary; he's extraordinary, and the way he makes me feel surpasses anything I've ever experienced.

He isn't flashy. He's not running game. He's not even asking me to imagine a future.

He's just here. Like breath. Like rhythm. Like a second glass of wine you didn't know you wanted until he poured it.

Tonight, he didn't try to kiss me. He didn't touch me the way he does during sessions.

But somehow? That rooftop conversation made me feel more naked than anything we've done in bed.

He saw me. But part of me still worries about finding love again.

He didn't ask me to change. But am I getting ahead of myself? He didn't ask me to stay.

Just offered to keep talking.

And God, how long has it been since someone listened without undressing me with their eyes? Ronnie was a good man. But even he didn't look at me like that.

Not to be played, but understood. Maybe nothing. Maybe everything. But for the first time in years, I'm not afraid to find out.

Because when Sam said, "Let's keep talking," What I heard was:

"You don't have to be alone anymore. Not unless you choose to be."

And tonight? I think I might choose something different.

The Reckoning

The video played in silence, and Natasha's lips tightened with every frame.

Kissing. Face-to-face eye contact. No masks

Moaning into each other's mouths like they were filming for OnlyFans. "Is that Bianca?" Warren asked, remote still in hand.

"Yes. That's Mr. Silver without a mask with Bianca in the mirror suite. That's not training; that's a goddamn honeymoon reel. Oh, there's more." She tapped her iPad to change the content on the screen.

The footage starts in the studio with soft moaning.

"Is that Emily and Mr. Green?" He asked. "Oh yeah, again. And again," she replied.

"Wait a minute, Mr. Green filmed all these sessions off-book. These are just personal tapes. How many videos are there???" Warren asked.

"I found eight videos," she said, her voice filled with complete fury. "Jesus," Warren shouted.

Natasha rubbed her forehead. "That's the preacher's daughter. That's the one who was a virgin when she arrived." "Is she being exploited?" Warren asked. "Oh no." Natasha snorted, "She was a willing participant; she actually directed half of the videos."

"Now she's got one terabyte of sin on video!" Warren muttered.

The silence that followed was worse than shouting.

"And then there's Summer and Mr. Black?" Natasha added.

"Mr. Black's gone full alpha dog. He took Summer into the Adult Playroom. He handcuffed her, spanked her, and commanded her to suck him like a damn BDSM master. And he did anal on her in the session too. There's footage of him kissing her back, licking, kissing, and sucking her peach ring, too. He's very personally and emotionally invested. Now he did log it in as his training session, but we hadn't authorized playroom training for any of the ladies yet."

"Wow, this is crazy and dangerous. These guys have clearly caught feelings. This could destroy our reputation." Warren shouted.

Natasha stood abruptly, the hem of her silk robe grazing her calves. She walked to the side table, poured herself a full glass of whiskey, no ice, and tossed it back like it owed her something. "This is out of hand, Ren."

"Now, we asked Sam to work with Mel because we thought they could be a love match, and I have footage of him with no mask, too. All these other folks who've been instructors for a long time, catching feelings, are strictly out of bounds. It's not what we teach here," Natasha added.

Warren walked over and stared out the penthouse window of their bedroom, arms folded.

"This place was designed to help people explore intimacy, not fall into chaos. We have rules. And we trained them to respect our process and maintain their ability to keep their feelings in check. These women need to be able to return to their lives, elevated, not pining for their instructors. And we don't need our instructors to be strung out either."

She turned to him. "Maybe they got too comfortable. Did we take our eyes off the operations too much? Am I slipping?" Natasha asked.

Warren met her eyes. "No. If anything, we both got too lax. But we must fix this as soon as possible; our entire program is at stake," he concluded.

48 Hours Later
Mandatory Staff Meeting – *10:00 AM | Executive Training Center*

All male instructors, except Mr. Bronze, were present. He wasn't available due to his teaching schedule.

Natasha stood at the front in a black tailored pantsuit with a silver blouse and no smile.

Warren flanked her, in a black blazer, white T-shirt, and black tailored trousers, his eyes scanning the room like he was reading everyone's secrets.

"Welcome to the reckoning, gentlemen," Natasha said, voice cool and calm. "Let's be clear: Freak School exists because of discipline, not desire. Everyone of you agreed to the rules when you signed the contract to join our staff."

Warren followed, "You know the rules: no off-book sessions, no sessions in the adult playrooms without authorization. No names. No engaging without your masks. And no unsanctioned filming of sessions."

Natasha stepped forward.

"We have watched hours of footage over the last few days. We have read clients' journals with your real names. We've also listened to some of the audio journals, too. We've observed reckless behavior that could destroy everything we've built and expose all of you. Secrecy is the main reason why people come here."

Throughout the room, there were gasps, heads shaking, and guilty eyes dropping.

Someone in the back whispered, "Damn."

"Over the next day, each of you will answer for your actions. Your honesty will decide if you still get to work here," she said

There was silence until one voice broke through. "I didn't mean to fall in love with her," Mr. Green said quietly. He sounded so sad, they almost felt sorry for him.

Mr. Black, you're awfully quiet. We saw the playroom footage. Did you have a good time playing BDSM master?

After sitting there looking horrified, Mr. Black spoke up, "Warren and Natasha, you are right; I let my ego get involved, and my competitive spirit led me."

Natasha then turned to Mr. Silver. "Your antics have also been exposed."

Warren chimed back in, "Listen, those of you who think you are in love, ask yourself this: Are you trying to leave here and build a life with the woman you are coaching? Look, Mr. Green, that girl you think you're in love with is engaged to an

NFL ball player. Can you compete with that?"

"We got caught up," Mr. Silver said. "I think we care too much."

"That's the problem," Natasha snapped. "Care without control is chaos. And chaos will burn this place to the ground."

"You guys have become obsessed with these women. We created the guardrails for a reason."

Warren lifted a sheet of paper and gave a stern warning.

"Every instructor will be interviewed and asked to re-sign the code of conduct today. Every client will meet with Natasha. As of now, all training sessions are under review. If it breaks protocol after today, you'll be deleted."

Twenty-Seven

Who's Still Fit to Teach?

Location: *8:45 PM | Dr. Collins' Executive Office*

Dr. Warren Collins was in his business office. He was a mix of fury and intense curiosity. In the seven years since he and Natasha started Freak School, they'd never had this level of anarchy before.

He muttered to himself, "Instructors catching feelings. What the fuck? It's just sex, skill development, sexual awakenings, and an ego boost after a heartbreak; that's what we do here. Men know how to have sex without getting attached. We train these women to go home and keep their man happy, while also keeping themselves satisfied. We teach people how to enjoy their partners more with kink, spice, toys, and good positions. We keep people together, not wreck homes."

He poured himself two fingers of bourbon. No ice. On the table in front of him was one folder for every instructor. The code of conduct was printed, waiting for signatures. Warren didn't want to lose anyone; they spent too much time training them, but he'd shut down the entire school before letting it rot from the inside.

He hit the intercom to the assistant in his outer office. "Send in Mr. Silver," he barked.

Interview 1: Mr. Silver

Mr. Silver entered cool as ever, in slate gray slacks. White shirt, rolled sleeves. His silver half-mask was resting in his palm instead of on his face.

"Hi, Dr. Collins."

"Sit down." He complied, "Do you know why you're here?" Warren asked.

"Yes, I broke the instructor's code." Mr. Silver responded.

"Which part?" Warren asked.

"No masks. No distance. I was with Bianca after hours." Warren nodded, appreciating the fact that he told the truth. "

Why did you do it?" Warren asked. "I just got caught up and stopped treating her like a student," he replied.

Silence. "I started feeling like I was hers."

Warren stared at him, unreadable. "Do you want to stay?"

"Yes. I can be trusted. I won't cross that line again." Mr. Silver pleaded.

"Good. Because if it happens again, you will be gone the same day."

Warren slid the code of conduct across the table. Mr. Silver signed it without hesitation.

"You're on probation. I've reassigned Bianca to Mr. Yellow. He'll be banging her tonight. Understood."

"Yes, sir," said Mr. Silver.

"Good, you can leave my office," Warren ordered.

Interview 2: Mr. Green

Mr. Green entered Warren's office looking like a heartsick man whose nose was wide open.

No mask. No bluster. Just sadness and honesty in his hazel eyes.

"Mr. Green." Warren addressed him coldly. "Tell me why I shouldn't remove you right now."

"Please don't fire me, sir; I'm good at what I do. Emily came here scared. And I helped her find herself. But I let it go too far." He replied.

"What do you mean by too far? Explain yourself," Warren barked.

"Once I introduced her to sex, she liked it, and she wanted it all the time, and so did I. She is so special but very sexually repressed. She wanted to take on a new sexual identity. She asked me to teach her more stuff and film the sessions to reinforce what she was learning. She even directed me in some of the scenes. I know it got out of hand, and I didn't stop. I adore her, and I couldn't say no." Mr. Green said sheepishly.

"Do you love her?" Warren asked.

Mr. Green hesitated. Then, just above a whisper, he said, "I don't know. But I want to protect her."

Warren sighed. "Son, you forgot your role. But I haven't. You two need distance—no more contact. I'm giving her a new instructor, Mr. Blue. Can you handle that?"

He pushed the code of conduct forward. "Yes." He nodded quickly, just grateful he wasn't fired.

"Prove it. Sign this code of conduct and stay away from her! Now, take your pussywhipped ass to the gym, work out hard, and try to think about something else. No more late-night creeps with Emily."

"Thank you, sir," he said.

"Be gone, Green."

Interview 3: Mr. Black

He entered like a storm on two legs. He was calm on the surface, but his eyes were all fire.

"Have a seat, Mr. Black."

"Thank you, Professor."

"You've always had an edge. You were the second instructor hired here, one of the most successful coaches here. But with Summer, you've become arrogant and possessive. I heard about how she left Natasha's masterclass, came to the session, and turned you out."

"She used me like a tool, Warren, and got under my skin. That has never happened to me."

Warren grimaced, "You were supposed to get her to open up to you; you were never supposed to stay there. This got way too personal. You thought you would enact your revenge sex with her in the playroom."

Silence.

Warren watched him. "You are normally cold and surgical with your dick skills. Did you fall for her, Black?"

Mr. Black looked him straight in the eye. "No. I just finally found someone who could handle me."

"That's not the job, Black! You are supposed to upskill her bedroom acumen so she can go home and turn out her man, her fiancé waiting back in Atlanta to marry her."

A long pause.

"I'm taking you off Summer's case and reassigning her."
"Warren, you must put her with someone who respects what she's become."

Warren nodded. "She's been reassigned to Mr. White. You'll report directly to me and Mr. Blue until further notice."

He pushed the code forward. "Sign this, and you watch yourself from now on."

"It won't happen again, sir," Mr. Black responded.

Now, get out of my office. Warren barked.

Warren thinks to himself. "That fire for Summer still burns in him. Let's see if he can actually stay away from her."

Interview 4: Mr. Bronze

Sam entered the suite without fanfare, in a black tee and joggers. The same steady, confident presence he always brought to a room.

Warren didn't stand.

Didn't smile.

Just gestured to the chair. "Sit down, Sam." He complied

Silence fell for a few beats. Warren let it stretch. Sam didn't flinch. "I need an update on you and Mel Dibert." Sam nodded once. "Okay."

"Is it personal now?" he asked. "Yes. It's quite personal."
She is as amazing as Natasha said she would be.

Warren leaned forward, lacing his fingers. "So are you training her, or are you just sleeping with one of my clients?"

"I'm still training her. But it's not just physical anymore."

"You think that's a good thing?" Warren asked.

Sam looked Warren dead in the face and spoke his truth. "I think she's the most amazing woman I've ever met in my life. And I thank you for allowing me to get to know her. "

Warren smiled slightly and exhaled slowly.

Sam continued, "She came here for healing from grief, to feel her repressed emotions, and to be appreciated as a sexual creature again. And she's been doing the work."

"She didn't have as much to do as the other women here.

I'm sure." Warren.

"I'm just enjoying her. Where do things stand between you two?" Warren asked.

Sam was completely clear. "Honestly, I can see myself with Mel for the rest of my life. Either way, Mel is my first and last client, Warren."

"For what it's worth… Natasha and I thought you two might be a love match.

I appreciate you guys, and I'll keep you posted on my progress.

Sam stood to leave and reached for Warren's hand.

Then, he left.

Interview 5: Mr. Red
The knock was casual—the entrance, slower.

Mr. Red wore black slacks, a mesh shirt, and his signature gold chain. He was still wet from the steam room.

Warren didn't offer a chair. He pointed to it. "Sit." Mr. Red complied.

"Do you know why you're here?"

"You're doing a check-in thing because a few instructors have been inappropriately taking liberties."

Mr. Red raised a brow. "Did I do something wrong?"

Warren leaned back. "Let's talk about boundaries. You've had two private complaints from students over the last two months. One said you made her feel like she had to perform for you. The other said you touched her too long after the session ended."

Mr. Red's smile faded. He sat up straighter.

"I follow the script." He snorted.

"You follow your instincts. Not the protocol, but you are aware that you are kinda young for some of our clients, which means you have to work a little harder to earn and keep trust with them." Warren lectured.

Silence.

Have you had any complaints from my current client, Teri?

Warren's voice dropped lower, colder.

"No, but Freak School is not a place for you to play with

broken women.”

“I wasn’t—” Mr. Red tried to jump in, but Warren wasn’t having it.

“Don’t interrupt me, son.”

Mr. Red shut his mouth.

“You are a phenomenal physical instructor. But if I hear one more story about women walking out of your training room more confused than empowered, you’re gone.”

“Understood.” Mr. Red replied.

Warren slid the agreement across the table.

“You want to stay on the roster? Learn more self-control. Stop flirting so much. No more long touches. No lingering looks. Keep it clinical. You train. You leave. Got it?”

“Yes, I can handle that,” responded Mr. Red.

Warren ordered, “Good. Then, sign this.” After he did, Warren stood and walked him to the door with a parting message.

“Listen, I’ve given you the best job in the world; you get to have sex with willing women almost every day. You teach women how to please themselves and their lovers. You slay our clients with all your young energy and fiery dick skills, but don’t confuse attention for connection.”

Mr. Red nodded. “Won’t happen again, sir.”

“Good. Because fire with no boundaries burns the whole damn house down.” Warren reminded him.

Twenty-Eight

Client Check-ins

Location: *10:00 AM | Natasha's Executive Office*

Natasha called all the ladies in for what were being called "20-minute check-in sessions." Her main problem child was called first.

Interview 1: Emily

Emily came in wearing workout gear, guilt wrapped around her like perfume.

"Please sit," Natasha didn't smile. Emily obeyed, eyes wide but lips pressed together.

"Do you know why you're here?" Natasha asked.

"Yes, ma'am. Because… Mr. Green and I have been doing a lot of extra late-night sessions, and there are recordings, lots of them."

"Yes, you're correct. You've had seven unauthorized sessions with him that you requested, I understand, and you taped them. Why, Emily? Do you realize that you are about to marry someone famous? How could you allow yourself to be videotaped? Make this make sense for me?"

Emily started shedding tears. "I feel safe with him, and once I got over my fear of sex, I wanted to keep exploring all the things I could feel."

"Freak School is about structure and boundaries. You are a preacher's daughter and one video leak away from a damn blackmail scandal that could hurt a lot more people than you."

Emily blinked, but the tears kept coming. "I wasn't trying to be messy."

"Yet, you were." Natasha leaned forward. "I have had all the videos deleted, but let me ask you a question. Are you here to grow? Or are you addicted to being adored?"

Emily sat in silence. "Do you still want to get married, Emily?"

Emily blinked hard. "Of course I do."

"Then, why are you filming a softcore porn series with one of my instructors?" Emily flinched.

"You got a man headed to the NFL, with a seven-figure contract and a whole PR team ready to brand you as the first lady of his franchise; your wedding could make national news, and you're risking it all for a man who doesn't even have a dental plan."

Natasha leaned in, voice low and lethal. "Are you in love? Or are you just dickmatized?"

Emily opened her mouth to speak, then thought better and closed it.

"That silence tells me everything I need to know. You might think this is love," Natasha continued, "but it's addiction dressed up as seeking attention. Mr. Green is being suspended from working with you. Do not have any further contact with him."

Then Natasha handed her a piece of paper with details about her new instructor. "You've been reassigned to Mr. White. There will be no filming. No extra sessions. He's a white guy who loves chocolate girls. He's emotionally disciplined and exactly what you need."

Emily nodded slowly. "I understand."

"Good. Because you don't want to mess up your life for someone you can't build a life with, Mr. Green has nothing to offer you but dick."

"I'll send Mr. White to meet you this evening." Go to the spa, hit the steam room, and relax so you can get your mind right.

Interview 2: Summer

Summer strolled into her office like she was still riding a high from her off-the-chain session with Mr. Black. Natasha saw right through the glow.

"Summer."

"Yes, Headmistress."

"Let's not waste time. Have you fallen for Mr. Black?"

Summer didn't flinch, but she wasn't quick to respond. "I wouldn't call it that."

"So then what would you call it?" she asked.

"I let him in," Summer replied.

Natasha nodded slowly. "Are you ready to ditch your fiancé, Marcus?"

"No." Summer's answer came quicker.

Natasha looked at her with a full bitch face now.

"Really? Let me ask you again, do you still want to be a rich man's wife? Or are you ready to blow up your whole dream because you got bent over in the Adult Playroom?"

Summer's mouth parted, but no sound came out.

Natasha went on, "You spent years fantasizing about being in the elite circles in Atlanta, always drinking from champagne flutes, a house with servants, lunches and brunches, living in a gated community, driving your Range Rover, and never working again. Are you ready to trade all that in for a man who leads with ego and talks in growls?"

Summer tried to interrupt, "Nat—" Natasha put her hand up. "Don't speak. Think!" She shouted. "Are you just addicted to how he makes you feel when he dominates you?"

Natasha leaned forward. "Are you about to let one man's mouth make you forget who the hell you are? You're talented. Lethal, even. But I don't care how good his mouth is. If you forget your purpose here again, I will revoke your access and send you home."

Summer nodded and straightened her posture. "Understood."

"Mr. Black is benched. Effective immediately, your new instructor is Mr. Blue. He's our master trainer. He's hung, disciplined, and perfect for you. And don't get emotionally attached."

Summer's brow lifted. "Are you serious?" she whined.

"Deadly. Your fantasy with Mr. Black is over. My job is to train you how to be a freak to please your man and yourself, not fall in love with the help."

"Now, get your tail to twerk class, and put your back into it.

I'll send Mr. Blue to meet you this evening. Goodbye."

Feeling thoroughly embarrassed, Summer couldn't get out of Natasha's office fast enough.

Interview 3: Teri

Teri came in with her chin up, but Natasha could see the cracks.

"Teri. So tell me, how are things going here at Freak School for you?"

Are you enjoying your young instructor?

Teri blinked hard. "He's very talented. I lost myself for a second."

Natasha leaned back in her chair and nodded. "I get it; he knows how to rub you the right way."

Her tone was low, but not without empathy.

"You're a woman with needs, and Mr. Red's job is to serve you, but this place is about structure through discipline, not chaos."

She narrowed her eyes just slightly.

"So here's the deal: He broke protocol with you, but I'm going to let you keep him as your instructor, for now. I think he's good for you. But no more late-night creep sessions. If I start letting instructors blur the lines, the whole system falls apart.

Teri gave a short nod. "I get it. Understood."

As Teri stood to go, Natasha added one more thing.

"Teri, just because we crave intimacy doesn't mean we get to ignore our own standards. Don't let anyone make you forget that. Now, get yourself back to Twerk class."

Teri smiled faintly, grateful the meeting was quick, and walked out.

Interview 4: Bianca

Bianca strutted into the room like she owned stock in the building. Hair laid, nails flawless, cute workout clothes.

Natasha didn't even look up at first.

"Take a seat, Bianca."

Bianca arched her brow. "Is this about the mirror session?"

Natasha looked up sharply.

"You mean the unsanctioned, no-mask, emotionally entangled, borderline-OnlyFans-style session you had with Mr. Silver?"

Bianca blinked. "It was... powerful."

"It was unprofessional." Natasha retorted.

Natasha leaned forward, voice quiet but cutting. "You came here to reclaim your power, not to surrender it just because a man shattered your soul in a mirrored room."

Bianca shifted in her seat, lips tight.

"I'm a grown woman, Natasha."

"Yes, you are. My job is to make sure you don't ruin your life by falling in love with a man whose job was to help you remember your worth, not replace your ex. You are going through a big transition right now; you need to be careful with your heart."

Natasha let it breathe.

Then she continued, "Do you want to date Mr. Silver when this is over? That is your business, but while you're a student, I decide whose job it is to pleasure you. Effective immediately, you've been reassigned to Mr. Yellow. I'll send him to meet you this evening. He's well endowed; enjoy that.

Bianca exhaled quietly and said, "I understand."

"Now get your fine ass back to twerk class," barked Natasha. She smiled and left.

Interview 5: Mel

Mel entered the office like a soft exhale. She was entirely composed and calm, wearing a pink workout suit. She looked more like a Fortune 500 exec on vacation than a Freak School student.

"Mel," she said, gesturing to the seat across from her. "You look lovely."

"So do you, Natasha," Mel replied with a smile.

Natasha said. "So, tell me how things are going with you and Mr. Bronze."

Mel didn't blink. "Sam and I, we talk. We're deeply connected. We're good for each other, and we're taking things slowly."

"You go by first names," she inquired. "Yes, for a while now," Mel replied.

"We have amazing emotional, physical, and intellectual intimacy. And we've begun to discuss a real relationship outside of this place. He told me I'm his last client either way."

Natasha sat back, studying her.

"I've watched you. You're not reckless. You're not chasing approval. You've been a grown woman since day one—but we can all get caught off guard when a man unlocks the right part of you."

Mel's expression softened.

"I didn't come here looking for romance, Natasha. You know that. I came here because I wanted to feel again."

"And now?"

"Now, I'm remembering how good it feels to be desired. Sam sees me, and his heart is pure. He doesn't see me as a client. We talk for hours, and when he leaves, I can't wait to see him again. He looks at me in a way my Ronnie never did."

Natasha exhaled with controlled excitement. "So here's what I'll say: Warren and I thought you and Sam might fall for each other, so I'm glad to hear I was right about that."

Natasha gave her a rare smile. "Just be careful."

Mel laughed. "Don't worry, we're taking it very slow, but I do love his vibe."

Keep me posted, and enjoy your Pilates class this afternoon.

Twenty-Nine

New Assignments, Ground Rules

Location: *9:30 AM | Executive Conference Room*

Dr. Collins gathered together the newly assigned instructors in the executive conference room.

Mr. Blue—Damien Wells, 44, lead instructor at Freak School. His focus is on emotional intimacy, steady breath, and sensual touch. He specializes in erotic psychology, tantric massage, and embodied sensuality. We give him to advanced students who need to be eaten out and spanked.

Mr. White—Victor Kelsey, 38, a charming white boy who has always dated Black girls. He's very well-endowed, super strong, and sensual enough to be dangerous. Clients often underestimate him at first glance, but they end up clinging to him in the end.

Mr. Yellow—Sunny Fleming, 32, a fresh-faced, nerdy type, focused on emotional intelligence. He's deceptively thin and quiet, but he's a beast who comes on like lightning. They don't even see him coming; he operates like a smooth criminal.

Warren didn't sit. He paced.

"This isn't a welcome. You're here because Natasha and I believe you can hold power without abusing it. Some of your fellow instructors have gotten caught up emotionally with our current clients, and it's created a problem. You need to level set these ladies."

He turned to Mr. White.

"You're assigned to Emily. She's just been reassigned from Mr. Green, and she's fragile, despite the newfound sexual confidence she's been performing. She needs grounding. But listen, 24-year-old pussy is tight; don't lose your mind. Remember, boundaries and clarity protect everyone. She likes to suck dick, so enjoy that."

His instructions to Mr. Blue.

"You've got Summer. She and Mr. Black turned each other out, so don't underestimate her. She's bold, mouthy, seductive, and clever. Don't get cocky. She'll test you. She doesn't need you to flirt. She needs to be reminded that attention is not connection."

Then, finally, he addressed Mr. Yellow.

"You're taking Bianca. She is recovering from a major heartbreak. She's loud, sharp, and emotional. As a corporate VP, she thinks she's too grown to be trained. Your job is to prove her wrong without ever raising your voice. She doesn't need a dominant trainer. She needs a man who doesn't blink. You blink? She'll run you."

He looked at all three instructors. "Fellas, build trust, not intimacy—no unscheduled sessions. No video. Make them feel, but don't let them fall."

"Tonight at 9 PM, you'll each meet your new students. I suggest you wear their asses out and make them forget the other cats and beg for more. Oh, and if any of you confuse their pleasure with your power, you'll be out like the other instructors who forgot their role."

Mr. Blue nodded. "Understood."

Mr. White smirked. "Let me get to work."

Mr. Yellow? He simply said, "Noted."

Warren knew these men were up to the job. "Don't fumble this, fellas."

Thirty

Bianca & Mr. Yellow

Location: *10:01 PM | Training Room 3*

Bianca was used to applause, compliments, and attention.

She walked into every room like a woman born under spotlights, a bright, bold, demanding presence. And Freak School hadn't shaken her yet. Not even the mirror session, not even Natasha's cutting words.

But this was different.

Mr. Yellow didn't speak when she entered.

He didn't smile.

Didn't stand.

He just sat in the middle of the training suite, one ankle crossed over his knee, his long fingers draped across the armrest as if he were carved from stone.

And the quiet?

Ate her alive.

"So, you're my new trainer?" she asked, voice laced with attitude.

He tilted his head slightly. Said nothing.

"You don't talk?"

Still nothing.

She narrowed her eyes.

"Oh, you're one of those mysterious types. That's cute."

His voice, when it finally came, was so soft it felt like it brushed the inside of her chest.

"Take off the robe."

No demand. No emotion. Just a simple instruction.

She hesitated, lips parting in surprise.

"Excuse me?"

His eyes didn't waver.

"You came here to be seen. I won't touch you. Not until you

feel yourself first."

She wasn't expecting that. But somehow, her hands moved.
Robe off. Breath held.

She stood there, exposed, but not because of showing her skin. Because he hadn't moved a muscle, and she was already unraveling.

Mr. Yellow had been briefed on Bianca.

Difficult. Beautiful. Resistant to control. Loves to be the center of attention.

But what Bianca didn't know? He didn't control through pressure. He controlled through presence.

He never raised his voice. He didn't need to.

Bianca thought she wanted a man to dominate her.

What she really needed was one who would watch her, really watch her, until she couldn't hide from herself.

She was pacing now—one hand on her hip. Already fidgeting under the silence.

Good. "Sit down," he said quietly, gesturing to the floor cushion in front of the mirror.

"I don't kneel," she snapped. "Good. I didn't ask you to."

That stopped her.

She sat, her legs crossed, her body tense, her eyes locked on his reflection.

"I want you to look at yourself," he said. "Not for me. For you."

"I know what I look like."

"Do you?"

He stood finally, and the energy shifted.

Not loud. Not violent. Things just got heavy.

He walked behind her slowly, deliberately, his hands never touching, but his presence surrounding her like heat.

"You're beautiful," he said softly. "But that's not what makes you powerful."

"What does?" she asked.

He leaned closer. "Your ability to let go of performance. And feel. For once."

Bianca blinked hard, as if the glass might soften if she stared long enough. The woman looking back at her, with her arched brow, perfect pout, and flawless cocoa-brown skin, was the same one she had always seen. But suddenly, she felt counterfeit. It was as if her reflection was wearing her, not the other way around.

"I am feeling," she snapped, the edge in her voice thinner now, fraying. "You think I don't feel?"

"I think you perform feelings," Mr. Yellow said, calm as dusk. "But I don't think you let them take root."

She looked away. "That's bullshit."

"It's survival," he said. "But you're here now. The act isn't necessary."

She scoffed. "You think you're different from the others? You think this therapist's energy is gonna fix me?"

"I'm not here to fix you," he said, walking back to his chair. "I'm here to give you space to see you."

She folded her arms tightly across her chest, as if that could hold her together. She hated this. Hated that his stillness felt like a spotlight. Hated how the silence felt louder than any praise.

And yet, she didn't move. Didn't run. Didn't seduce. Didn't deflect.

She just sat.

"You don't have to be Bianca the Bombshell in here," he added, voice low, eyes steady. "That woman's exhausted. Let the real one out. I'll wait."

Bianca swallowed hard. And for the first time at Freak School... she felt naked.

Not in body. In her soul.

And she didn't know whether she wanted to slap him or cry. Maybe both.

But she didn't look away from the mirror. Bianca sat still, breathing unevenly, staring into the mirror as if it might offer answers she wasn't ready to ask for.

Mr. Yellow didn't push. He didn't move closer. He just stayed seated, watching her come undone without saying a word.

That restraint. It unnerved her more than if he had pounced.

"I don't get you," she finally said, her voice cracking at the edges. "Every other trainer wants to touch, tease, and take control. You just sit there."

"That's because I don't want your body," he said calmly. "Not until your soul walks in the room with it."

That hit her like a slap. She looked away. "You act like you're so above it all."

"I'm not," he replied, his voice steady. "But I've learned, if you don't respect the storm in a woman like you, she'll drown you in it."

Bianca looked back at the mirror. Her eyes, usually cold, flirty, and sharp, were glassy now. Uncertain.

"Why me?" she whispered. "Because you're so hurt, you fight love like it's a threat," he said, standing again, walking to her this time. "But it's not. It's your freedom."

He knelt in front of her, finally. Not to overpower, but to meet her where she was.

His fingers ghosted over her cheek but never settled.

"I'm going to ask you something," he said, his voice now barely more than a breath. "Do you want this? Or do you just want to feel wanted?"

Bianca's eyes widened. And then the tears came, fast, furious, and unexpected. She covered her face, shaking her head as her whole body trembled.

He didn't touch her. Not yet. He waited until her hands dropped, and she looked up at him, raw.

"I want this," she said. "But I want you to want it too. Not the version of me I pretend to be. But just me."

Mr. Yellow finally moved closer, his forehead resting against hers. "I've been waiting on that woman," he whispered. And then he kissed her. Not a tease. Not a test.

A deep, consuming kiss, like the end of a war. Her hands clawed into his shirt, and he finally touched her. He traced every inch of her skin as if it were scripture.

He didn't rush. He devoured and worshiped her. And when he finally slid into her, it wasn't a fuck session; it was a reckoning.

No games. No poses. Just two people stripped down to their

truths.

Bianca didn't scream. She sobbed into his shoulder, into his mouth, into the moment, because it wasn't pleasure that overwhelmed her.

It was being seen.

When it was over, she didn't say a word. She just laid there in the aftermath, finally quiet and finally whole.

THIRTY-ONE

Bianca and Mr. Yellow's Reflection

Journal Entry: *2:47 AM* | *"Mr. Yellow Shocked Me"*

I wasn't ready.

Not for him. Not for the silence. Not for myself.

I thought I was going in there to prove something, to make another man fall, to stay in control. But Mr. Yellow didn't play the game. He watched me like I was art and ruin at the same time.

No flattery. No hunger. Just presence.

He made me feel myself. And I hated it until I didn't.

He said, "I won't touch you until you feel yourself first."

And when he finally did?

I didn't climax; I collapsed.

It wasn't about the sex. It was about surrender.

And I didn't even know I had that kind of vulnerability left.

He didn't take me apart.

He unwrapped me. Like a gift I forgot I was.

What scares me isn't that I let go.

It's that... I didn't want the moment to end.

God help me, I think I want more.

Not just of him.

Of me.

-Bianca

Mr. Yellow's Reflection
Instructor Audio Log: *4:12 AM | Subject: Bianca*

Control is not about dominance. It's about restraint.

Bianca came in swinging, eyes sharp, voice sharp, and energy on edge. But it was all armor. The kind you wear when you've forgotten you have skin underneath.

She expected to be chased. I stayed seated.

She expected seduction. I gave her silence.

She cracked faster than I anticipated.

Not because I broke her. Because I refused to.

She looked in the mirror and saw the echo of herself, the version she's spent years rehearsing. And for one hour, maybe less, she let the real one speak.

That's progress.

I touched her eventually. Not to conquer. To anchor.

When she cried, she apologized. I didn't let her.

That was the real climax, not orgasm. Permission.

She's not ready for love. But she's prepared for truth.

I'll keep her close. But not too close.

Not yet.

-Yellow

Thirty-Two

Bianca & Mr. Yellow Get Debriefed

Location: *8:30 AM | Dr. Collins' Executive Office*

Mr. Yellow stood at ease, hands behind his back. Dr. Warren sat, sipping black coffee, as footage played behind him, silent clips from the night before. No audio. Just visuals. A robe is dropping. A mirror. A moment of stillness that said more than any moan ever could.

"She cried," Warren said. "She needed to," Mr. Yellow replied.

"She's been bulletproof since day one." Warren countered. "That was the problem," Mr. Yellow said calmly.

Warren tapped his pen twice against the table. "Was she manipulative?"

"No," Mr. Yellow said. "She was terrified." "Of you?" Warren asked. "No, of being seen."

Warren followed up, "Did you have any complications?"

Mr. Yellow's jaw tightened. "Naw."

"I'm not compromised; I'm precise. And she's finally at the edge of herself. One more push, and she'll either have a breakthrough or break completely," said Mr. Yellow; his tone was sharp for the first time.

"And if she gets attached?" he asked.

"She won't; I'm confident in that."

A beat of silence passed. Then, Warren nodded once.

"Good job. Report twice a week. No overnights without clearance." He nodded.

"One more thing," Warren added, "if you do start to feel something, I expect you to self-report before it becomes a problem."

Mr. Yellow nodded once. "If that happens, you'll be the first to know."

As he turned to leave, Warren said quietly, "She's a handful."

Mr. Yellow didn't look back. "She's worth it."

And then, he was gone.

Natasha Debriefs Bianca
Location: *9:15 AM | Natasha's Executive Office*

Natasha set check-in appointments with all the ladies who had been reassigned. She knew there would be some resistance.

Bianca walked in with her usual strut, but it was quieter than normal. Still polished and poised. But something about her felt stripped back. Softer, perhaps rewired.

Natasha didn't offer a chair.

"Stand," she said, arms crossed. "I want to see you. Something is different."

Bianca replied, "He didn't try to own me. He held up a mirror. I was the one who laid myself bare."

"So, he cracked you," Natasha said coolly. "Emotionally?"

"No. He opened me. I cracked myself."

Natasha narrowed her eyes. "Are you compromised?"

"You mean, am I falling in love?" Bianca smirked

"Or lust," Natasha snapped. "Same danger in this place."

Bianca smiled. "No. I'm clear, and I'm also not the same woman who walked in here yesterday." Natasha replied. "Good. Because the old you was headed for a fall."

"I thought being wanted made me powerful," Bianca admitted. "Turns out, being known is the real drug."

Natasha raised a brow. "And what will you do with that knowledge?"

Bianca's lips curved. "I'm going to stop performing. And start becoming."

"I love to hear you say that. I think Mr. Yellow is good for you," Natasha said. Let's see what he helps you build."

"And if I fall?" Bianca asked. "Then fall with your eyes open," Natasha said.

Thank you, Natasha. I'll keep you posted.

Then, Bianca turned and left.

THIRTY-THREE

Summer & Mr. Blue

Location: *10:02 PM | The Jasmine Room*

Summer entered the Jasmine Room like a runway model with somewhere more important to be.

Hair bouncing. Skin glowing. Walking, slow, calculated.

She was a woman who didn't beg. She baited.

She scanned the room: sleek lighting, velvet drapes, and low jazz playing from invisible speakers. And in the center, seated like a god carved out of discipline and dust, was Mr. Blue.

6'3", mocha chocolate, rippled muscles, smooth and clean with a fresh bald fade, a small beard trimmed close, and light brown eyes. He was fine and cold enough to freeze a woman in place.

She smirked. "You must be Mr. Blue. They said you were intense. But you're kinda delicious."

He didn't move or crack a smile. And he didn't return the flirt.

"You may speak," he said evenly. "But understand this: your words are not currency here."

Summer blinked. Tilted her head. That was new.

"Oh, baby. I don't pay. I earn. And I always get what I want."

Mr. Blue rose slowly, towering without even trying.

"Then this will be your first lesson in denial," he said. "Because you don't get me until I choose to give."

Summer chuckled low. "You think withholding makes you powerful?"

"No," he said. "I know it does. Just like your seduction is your crutch."

That landed. Her smile slipped half an inch.

"I don't need seduction to survive."

"Then stop using it like armor," he replied, circling her now, hands clasped behind his back. "You flirt to create confusion. To keep control. But that's not control. That's fear, dressed up in lingerie."

She whirled around, eyes flashing. "Excuse me?"

"You heard me," he said, stepping closer. "And here's your first task."

He handed her a small silk blindfold.

She took it, confused. "You want me to wear this?"

"No," he said, calm as ever. "I want you to choose to wear it. Big difference."

Summer stared at him, then at the blindfold.

She hated this.

Being put on the defensive.

Not knowing the next move.

He was unreadable. Calm. Domineering, but not controlling.

That unnerved her the most.

"What happens if I don't?" she asked, testing him.

He stepped into her space, chest nearly brushing hers.

"Then this session ends now. You can go back to Mr. Black and get fucked like a brat. Or you can stay here and learn what it means to be truly known."

Her breath caught.

It wasn't a threat. It was a promise.

She didn't want to submit. She wanted to win.

But she also wanted to understand why this man wasn't falling into her usual rhythm, why his restraint was turning her insides out.

After a long beat, she raised the blindfold.

And tied it. Tightly.

Mr. Blue smiled, just barely.

"Good. Now kneel."

She froze.

He waited.

And for the first time in years, Summer submitted. She dropped to her knees. Not for control. But for curiosity. And, for the first time, growth.

The floor was cold beneath her knees. Plush carpet, sure, but not soft enough to distract from the tension crawling up her spine.

The blindfold pressed against her lashes. Her breathing was louder than she wanted it to be. Everything else? Silent.

She hated this.

She hated how it made her feel like prey, as if she were waiting for something instead of being in control.

"Say your name," Mr. Blue's voice came, somewhere to her right.

She flinched. Just slightly. "Summer."

"No," he said. "Say it like it's not your weapon."

That burned.

"Summer," she repeated, this time in a quieter voice.

"Better," he replied. "Now tell me what you feel."

She swallowed hard. "Controlled."

"By?"

"You."

A pause.

"No," he said, strolling behind her. "Try again."

She bit her lip. Thought about it and blurted, "Felt."

"...by me," she whispered.

"There it is," Mr. Blue murmured. "The real you. The one under the performance."

His fingers never touched her. But she could feel his heat behind her, steady, calm, and *in charge*.

"Why did you come to Freak School, Summer?"

"To master control," she answered.

"Lie," he immediately jumped at her.

"To prove I can't be broken."

"Half-truth," he jumped at her again.

Then, after a brief silence. She said, "I came here because I'm scared that if I ever stop performing, there'll be nothing underneath." And just like that, the air changed.

He knelt beside her, not touching but present, and whispered into her ear like a confession:

"There is something underneath. And she's the version of you I want to meet."

A tear slipped out from under the blindfold before she could stop it.

She hated that.

But she didn't move.

Because for the first time, someone saw past the silk and seduction and said, I'm still here.

And the crazy part? She was relieved.

That's enough for tonight; let's reconnect tomorrow.

Mr. Blue's Reflection
Instructor's Audio Log: *2:14 AM I Subject: Summer*

Summer is dangerous.

Not because she disobeys. Because she uses desire as a distraction.

I saw it in her file: she's a model type. Tall, lean, light-skinned, long-haired, and gorgeous with an Ivy League degree. Total arm charm chick. The kind of woman moguls or ballers want to take care of and provide the soft life for. I am sure she's gone through a trail of men who thought they'd "won" her.

I bet the man she's engaged to doesn't really know her at her core. Or if he ever asked her who she was under her skin. She's been holding back her true sexual desires for a long time.

Tonight, she cracked and shed a few tears, and that's when I knew I had her attention.

She didn't kneel for long. But she will remember that she chose to kneel.

I don't want her blind obedience; that is just playing a role for her.

I want her stillness—that rare, unguarded moment when power and vulnerability blur.

That's when she'll be ready for me.

Until then, I'll wait.

-Blue

Thirty-Four

Summer & Mr. Blue Get Debriefed

Location: *10:00 AM | Natasha's Executive Office*

Summer arrived late, on purpose. She wore yoga gear with sneakers and had her hair in a ponytail. She walked in with a sway that said, "I'm still in control."

Natasha didn't look up from her tablet. "Please sit." Summer smirked. "No good morning?" "That depends," Natasha said coolly, tapping through a file. "Did you come here to report like a grown woman or flirt like a confused girl?"

Summer's smile faltered, but only slightly. She sat, legs crossed, shoulders back.

Natasha finally looked up. "Tell me how last night went."

Summer leaned back, exhaling slowly before she spoke. "It was intense." "Define 'intense,'" said Natasha.

Summer paused. "He made me kneel." Natasha arched an eyebrow. "And you did so?" "I chose to." Summer insisted.

"Mm," Natasha hummed. "Big difference. But not the one you think."

Summer narrowed her eyes. "What's that supposed to mean?"

"It means choosing submission doesn't make you powerful," Natasha said sharply. "It makes you human. You're not broken because you bent, Summer. But you are exposed, and I want to know how you're handling that."

Summer looked away. "It was just an exercise."

"No, it wasn't. Everything here is done with intention." Natasha said, her voice sharp now. "That was the first time you let someone past your surface without seducing your way through it. You let go. And that scares you more than being rejected."

Summer's throat tightened. "He got in my head."

"No, sweetheart," Natasha said, leaning forward. "He got under your mask. The one you've been hiding behind for years."

A long silence followed.

Then Summer whispered, "Why does that feel worse than just getting fucked?"

Natasha's expression softened. "Because when you're getting fucked, you're still in control. But when are you seen? That's when the real work starts."

Summer blinked fast, then uncrossed her legs, like the armor was slipping off without permission.

"What happens now?" she asked, quieter this time.

Natasha stood and walked to the door. "You stay with Mr. Blue. He's your match. Not because he wants to tame you, but because he won't chase the version of you you're trying to sell."

Summer stood, her voice low. "And what if I'm not ready?"

Natasha looked over at her. "Then you'll keep seducing people who never satisfy you. Your choice."

Summer didn't say anything else as the door shut behind her.

Mr. Blue was a mirror, not a blindfold.

Thirty-Five

Summer and Mr. Blue

3:15 PM | Audio Message: Natasha →Mr. Blue

Blue,

Proceed with a second engagement tonight.

She's leaning toward surrender, not out of desperation, but curiosity. Her journal reflects emotional clarity. You've pulled her from the safety of performance into self-awareness. Excellent work.

Tonight, make her feel what it means to be taken, not because she's irresistible, but because she's ready.

– N

Mr. Blue had a handwritten note delivered to Summer by her butler, Ron.

Meet me at the Velvet Lounge at 9 p.m. tonight
-Mr. Blue

Summer meets Mr. Blue
Location: *9:04 PM | Velvet Lounge*

Summer stood at the threshold again, this time without armor.

No lipstick. No lashes. Bare feet. The robe opened slightly at the collar.

Mr. Blue waited for her in the center of the room. Same posture. Same presence. A still ocean. "Come in," he said, without rising.

She entered quietly. Like a student ready to learn.

"Blindfold?" she asked softly.

"Not tonight," he said. "I want you to see everything tonight."

She nodded and approached. Stopping two feet in front of him.

"I thought about kneeling again," she said, voice trembling slightly.

"You don't have to," he replied. "You've already yielded the way I needed you to."

She swallowed. "And what part is that?"

"The part of you that thinks love is a performance," he replied softly.

He stood now, slowly, walking around her. "You're not here to entertain me, Summer. You're here to experience yourself."

She turned to face him. Eyes locked. "And what if I want to be touched this time?"

"Want," he repeated, as if tasting the word. "Not manipulate. No offer. Not teasing. Want." She stepped closer.

Suddenly, he grabbed the back of her neck and pulled her close. This kiss was aggressive and consuming, igniting a fire deep within her. She melted against him, the weight of her past lifting as she lost herself in the moment.

Summer felt her senses heighten as his lips moved against hers. His touch was confident, lighting a fire inside her that she hadn't felt in a long time. As his hands glided down her back, she moved in closer, feeling the warmth radiating from him. In this intimate moment, she realized she craved not only his lips but also the freedom to fully embrace her own desires without holding back. He lifted her effortlessly onto the bed, her robe slipping away as he laid her gently against the sheets.

Mr. Blue didn't rush in. He began his exploration with slow, deliberate kisses, starting behind her ear, savoring the soft skin there before trailing his tongue down to her neck. He gently licked, sucked, and bit her neck. He took his time, making her feel every sensation. Then he traveled lower, sucking her breasts and kissing her stomach until he brushed her inner thigh with a tenderness that made her gasp. That made him smile with a wicked grin.

When his lips nestled between her legs, the air was charged
as he teased her with gentle licks to her clit. His mouth worked
magic on her; she felt as if she were floating. He savored her
taste, every moan urging him on. Every flicker of his tongue
and gentle suck drew her closer to the edge. "Feel everything,"
he murmured against her skin. And she did finally tip over the
edge, her whole body consumed by her orgasm.

Even though she was breathless and trembling, he kept
stimulating her, blowing on it. He dipped his thumb in her
pussy to get it wet, then reached underneath her and used his
thumb to start rimming her peach ring. The sensation drove
her crazy. He kept licking her and sucking her thighs. She was
convulsing for another 20 minutes before she came into his
mouth again.

When he finally emerged from between her legs, he looked
at her with a hunger that sent shivers down her spine. "You
ready?" he asked. "Yes," she breathed, and with a swift, fluid
motion, he lifted both of her legs above his shoulders. As he
entered her, his body pressed against hers with an intensity
that stole her breath away.

He started slow, allowing her to adjust to the sensation,
but it wasn't long before he built a rhythm that sent waves of
pleasure coursing through her. Each thrust was powerful and
deliberate; it made her feel alive in every sense. She could see
the fire in his eyes as he pressed deeper. He was thick and long,
and his strokes left her gasping to breathe. His body glided
against hers with a perfect rhythm that made her body ache
for more. With each thrust, he seemed to reach deeper, hitting
places within her she didn't know existed.

She surrendered completely. His strokes were
overwhelming, a storm of sensations that crashed over her,
her body arching to meet his, every nerve ending alive and
tingling with desire. "God, you feel incredible," he groaned,
his breath ragged as he quickened his pace. She could feel
her tension building, drawing tighter and tighter. "More," she
urged, pushing her hips against him, craving the connection
that was igniting every part of her. He responded eagerly, the
sounds of their pleasure filling the room as he drove into her

with increasing intensity. As the tension reached its peak, he leaned down, capturing her lips with his in a heated kiss that sent sparks flying. With a final, deep thrust, she cried out, and he followed suit, the intensity of their climax leaving them breathless, but Mr. Blue didn't lose his stroke or hardness.

"Roll over; now I'm going to hit it from the back," he said. She turned onto her stomach and rose on all fours. He reached down and applied some CBD lube to her and himself to make sure his love muscle was super slick. With a firm grip, he pulled her hips back toward him, aligning himself perfectly. "You ready?" he asked, his voice low and sultry. "Yes," she breathed, her heart racing as she felt him slide into her again. This angle allowed him to get even deeper this time. He was immediately hitting all the right spots, sending fresh waves of pleasure coursing through her. As he began to groove steadily, his hands gripped her hips to set the rhythm. With each thrust and moan, he knew he was commanding her pussy. Then, she started giving it back, pushing it back on him, squeezing him; she wanted him to feel every inch of her. The powerful dance of bodies left them both craving more. As she edged him, he responded by spanking her and quickening his pace. The sound of the room was filled with their bodies slapping and their moans.

She could feel another release starting to rise. "Don't stop," she urged. Blue moved even faster. He was loving tearing up her pussy. He even leaned down to her ear and said, "Summer, what's your favorite color?" She grinned and yelled, "Blue." "Exactly," smacking that ass again and stoking her deeper. Then he said, "Repeat it in Spanish." "Azul es mi favorita," she yelled. "You know it is," he chuckled. His breath was hot against her back, and each deep thrust drove her wild. The way he spoke to her only intensified her desire. As he continued to rock her kitty, she felt herself teetering on the brink. She could hear his ragged breathing. "Almost there," he murmured. After a few more strokes, they melded into a stunning crescendo that left them both spent.

Mr. Blue held her close in the aftermath of that incredible experience. As she lay in his arms, he reminded her of his role.

He whispered, "You're not mine. In this moment, you belong to you." Then, he got the towels to clean them up. Afterwards, she curled against his chest, her breath still shaky. He looked at her softly. "You didn't let me have you. You chose me."

THIRTY-SIX

Summer and Mr. Blue's Reflections

Summer's Reflection Journal Entry:
2:12 AM | "Me and Mr. Blue"

I can't remember the last time I felt so comfortable with a man. After he completely wore my kitty out, I didn't rush to leave; I just stayed there in his arms, staring at the ceiling like it had answers.

I always thought about sex like a competition and sometimes a disappointment. But this wasn't about winning. It was the ultimate release.

Mr. Blue didn't try to tame me or break me. Now, he did try to make a core memory, and he certainly did that. I'm definitely going to be sore tomorrow based on how he beat this pussy up.

He fucked me with reverence, power, and patience. He didn't treat me like I was fragile. He came at me like he was on a mission to please me. There was no performance. I didn't arch my back on cue. I didn't cry out to give him applause. I just let my body respond to him. I truly let myself go with him.

And when I came four times, it was pure ecstasy.

I hadn't seduced him, and he still wanted me, not despite my rawness, but because of it. That's what broke me. He didn't need me to be more for him to love me like that. Performance is exhausting.

Now, I'm the one who can't forget his hands, his mouth, or the mirror he held up and refused to allow me to turn away from.

He showed me the power I've spent my whole life

faking was already mine.

Now, I must stop hiding from it.

Mr. Blue's Reflection
Instructor Audio Log: *3:06 AM I Subject: Summer*

She didn't seduce me tonight. She surrendered. It was about self-return, and I focused on her pleasure.

She walked in more softly. She was more honest. Her eyes weren't bait. They were searching for release.

She asked for the blindfold, but she didn't need it. She didn't want to be hidden.

She wanted to see everything and survive it.

When she said, "I want you," it wasn't a strategy. It was an invitation. She chose me. Tonight, that moment came when she stopped reaching for control and started reaching for pure pleasure. She didn't perform. She breathed. She held on. She came without shame.

And after? She stayed still. That was the breakthrough. She didn't rush to recover power. She didn't leave to reclaim the upper hand.

She laid there and cuddled. No pretense. Just herself. Fully present.

And I felt something unfamiliar. Not attachment. Not neediness.

Respect.

Not for her beauty or her talent at manipulation.

But for the courage it took to stop performing and being the version of herself the world always rewarded.

She is far more dangerous now.

Because a woman who has nothing to prove is a woman no one can control.

Not even me. And I won't try.

I'll guide and even challenge her. But I will not shape her.

She's not meant to be sculpted.

She's meant to emerge. And I have the privilege of witnessing it.

-Blue

Thirty-Seven

Dr. Collins Debriefs Mr. Blue

Location: *9:01 AM | Dr. Collins' Executive Office*

Mr. Blue entered precisely on time.

Dr. Warren Collins was already seated, reviewing footage on a silent screen. He didn't look up.

"Have a seat." Mr. Blue nodded and sat.

Warren clicked a button on his tablet. The screen behind them lit up with surveillance footage of Summer, post-session, lying in bed with Mr. Blue. Naked. Still. Unarmed.

"You fucked her well, I see," Warren said flatly.

"I received her fully," Mr. Blue replied.

Warren smirked. "Always with the semantics."

"She offered herself," Mr. Blue continued. "No performance. No manipulation. That wasn't sex. That was her stepping out of the costume."

Warren turned to face him now, folding his hands. "And how do you plan to handle her moving forward?"

"She's still a risk," Mr. Blue said calmly. "Not because she's unstable. Because she's used to being in control of the narrative. Now that she's not... she'll want proof that the connection was real."

Warren nodded. "So she'll test you."

"I expect a pullback. A shift. Maybe even a seduction attempt just to see if she can win back the upper hand."

"And what's your strategy when she does?"

Mr. Blue leaned forward slightly. "I will hold the line. I won't chase. I'll wait for her to come to me."

Dr. Warren studied him carefully. "You're not worried she'll retreat?"

"I'm counting on it," Mr. Blue said. "It'll force her to decide if vulnerability was a fluke or a new foundation."

Warren tapped the table thoughtfully. "And if she regresses?"

"She's out," Mr. Blue said without hesitation. "I don't tolerate drama from women in my care."

Warren leaned back. "You know, some of the other instructors think you're too philosophical."

"I'm not here for consensus," Mr. Blue replied. "I'm here to create internal rewiring. If they want theatrics, they can stay with Mr. Red or Mr. Black."

Warren chuckled. "Fair."

Mr. Blue added, "I get to witness the moment a woman stops selling herself and starts owning herself."

Warren stood and extended a hand.

"Keep going," he said. "But keep your boundaries. If she compromises your presence, I'll reassign her again."

Mr. Blue stood and clasped his hands firmly. "If she compromises my presence, I'll send her back to you myself."

They both smiled and nodded.

Thirty-Eight

Emily & Mr. White

Location: *8:30 PM | Velvet Lounge*

The velvet lounge was distinct from the other training rooms: soft lighting, jazz playing, and a scent of clean cedar and bourbon in the air.

Emily entered with a smirk already loaded on her face, hips swaying, and robe tied just tight enough to suggest rebellion.

She was still pissed about being reassigned. Mr. Green had been easy. Handsy, eager, starry-eyed. She could twist him up with a smile and ride his ego until he forgot his own name. That was safe.

This? Was not. Mr. White didn't stand when she walked in.

He didn't stare or scan her curves. Or even blink in her direction.

He was seated, his ankles crossed, forearms resting on the arms of a leather chair, as if he owned time itself.

She hated that.

"Emily," he said. His voice sounded like velvet over steel. "You must be Mr. White," she replied, injecting sarcasm into her walk. He nodded once. "I am. Were you expecting a frat boy with a savior complex?" I didn't know what to expect. "I was hoping for someone I could wrap around my finger."

He chuckled. "I'm not here to be manipulated, sweetheart. I'm here to unwrap you."

Her eyes narrowed. "You think you know me?"

"I'm interested in getting to know you. I'm a good listener," he said, walking toward her with a quiet confidence that felt like warm water rising. Here's what I see so far. "You talk fast to keep people from asking questions. You laugh so they don't look too closely."

He stopped inches from her.

"And that ring on your finger?" His eyes dropped to her hand. "That's a decoy. You don't really want the man who gave it to you anymore. You are torn between the version of you that promised him you would be his wife and discovering who you are for yourself."

She went still.

"How do you know that?" she asked, her face showing surprise. "I pay attention."

He walked past her now, toward a small table set with two tumblers and a single bottle of whiskey.

"You're not broken, Emily," he said, pouring two fingers. "You're just tired of being everyone's good decision."

She swallowed hard.

He offered her the glass. "You can stop performing now."

She took it, her hand trembling just slightly.

"This is going to be different, isn't it?" she whispered.

Mr. White smiled, slowly, knowingly. "Very."

"I read your file and your journal entries. I am not falling for the version of you in your file or the one that spun out Mr. Green," he said, voice low and measured.

Her smile cracked at the edges.

"I read between the lines, Emily. Between the elegant lie and your desperate truth."

She raised her chin. "You think I'm desperate?" "No, I think you're exhausted," he replied.

She let out a nervous laugh. "You're over-loved but under-held, Emily." He was so close now that she could smell the cedar scent on him.

"Your smile is a shield. You wear the ring like it's a muzzle." She stiffened. "You don't know anything about my engagement."

"I know that you are so insecure about your impending marriage that you felt like you needed to come here to get some skills to keep him," he said. "I know what it looks like when a woman's body is present, but her soul is shrinking."

Silence. His words hit her hard.

She felt rage; she wanted to leave. Or slap him. Or kiss him. She didn't know which.

"What are you supposed to be?" she asked. "A therapist in disguise?"

"No," he said. "I'm here to help you stop lying to yourself. Does a man who makes you feel like that even deserve you?"

Her breath caught. Tears started to fall; he was telling her the truth, and deep down she knew it. He stepped even closer. Still not touching her.

"I'm not here to fuck you, Emily," he said softly. "Not until you tell me who you really are?"

She flinched. This time, visibly. Then he reached into his back pocket and pulled out a small mirror. Simple. No frame. Just glass.

He handed it to her.

"Strip if you want. Or don't. But sit in that chair, look at yourself in this mirror, and name five things you see that aren't about beauty."

Her hand trembled as she took it.

"This isn't Freak School's fantasy hour," he said. "This is where the truth gets loud."

And then he walked away from her.

Not out of the room.

Just far enough that she had space to decide what she was looking at.

The mirror felt heavier than it looked.

It was just a smooth oval of glass in a small frame; it wasn't made to flatter, just reflect.

Emily sat down slowly, sinking into the deep velvet chair Mr. White had motioned her toward. The robe stayed on, but her heart thumped beneath it, fast and frantic.

She glanced toward him.

He wasn't looking at her anymore. He had retreated to his chair in the far corner, flipping through a notebook, as if he hadn't just shattered her foundation with a few sentences.

Emily took a deep breath and turned the mirror toward her face.

Her lips parted. She almost spoke, then stopped.

The woman staring back in the mirror wasn't smirking. She looked tired.

Her eyes looked like they'd been holding up walls pretending to be perfect for too long.

She exhaled shakily.

"Okay," she whispered to herself. "Five things."

She let the silence settle around her like fog. Then, she started:

"One... I see fear. Not the kind that screams. The kind that smiles through dinner parties and says everything's fine, when it's not."

"Two... I see a girl who learned to make men fall in love so that she wouldn't have to fall in love with herself." She blinked fast. More tears fell as her throat tightened.

"Three... I see someone who got engaged because "it was time," not necessarily because it was the right time."

She glanced at the ring now, like it was a trophy from a race she never wanted to run.

"Four... I see anger." She swallowed hard. "I'm mad at myself for making 'my purity' pledge my most valuable trait. I thought it would protect me from being forgotten."

She took another breath, sharp and shaky.

And then, quietly:

"Five... I see a woman who doesn't know who she is... but for the first time, wants to find out."

The silence after that was unbearable. She didn't cry. But her shoulders dropped. The performance was over.

She looked up. Mr. White was watching now, not with lust or judgment, but with support.

He didn't speak. He just walked to her, bent down, kissed her forehead, and said, "I'm proud of you. I know that was hard."

Nothing more. No reward. Just presence.

And in that moment, living in her truth didn't require being pure or perfect.

Natasha Debriefs Emily

Location: *9:00 AM | Natasha's Executive Office*

Emily entered without the usual flair.

No lashes. No red lips. Her hair was pulled back in a soft ponytail

She didn't speak first.

Natasha watched her. "You're softer today," Natasha said, her tone low and gentle.

"Don't get used to it," Emily replied, though her voice lacked the bite.

"I heard Mr. White didn't fuck you at your first meeting."

Emily sat slowly. "No. But he messed my head up. So it feels like he did."

Natasha leaned forward. "Explain."

Emily hesitated. "He gave me a mirror. Told me to name five things about myself that weren't about beauty."

"And?"

"I did," she said quietly. "I saw things I didn't want to say out loud. But I said them anyway."

Natasha nodded. "And now?"

"I feel like a fraud who finally took her mask off... and I'm scared everyone will see what's underneath."

"You think we didn't already see through it?" Natasha asked.

Emily looked away.

"I'm not as strong as I thought I was."

"You're stronger, actually," Natasha said. "Because you're finally not hiding."

Emily swallowed. "Why him?"

"Because you would've seduced anyone else just to stay in control," Natasha replied. "Mr. White doesn't play control games. He only deals in truth. And your truth is the one thing you never prepared for."

Silence.

Emily whispered, "What if I can't go back to who I was?"

Natasha's gaze was steady. "That's the point, isn't it?"

Emily nodded slowly. "I'm not sure I'm ready for what comes next."

"Good," Natasha said, standing. "That means you're actually growing. Your undoing has just begun. You'll have another session with him tonight."

And just like that, the debrief was over.

THIRTY-NINE

Emily & Mr. White

Location: *6:45 PM | Emily's Suite*

Emily was waiting when he arrived.

No robe. No lashes. Just jeans, a black tank top, sandals, and the kind of quiet that felt unfamiliar on her.

Mr. White didn't greet her with a compliment. He just looked her over once, subtly, and said, "Ready?"

She nodded. "We're going on a little adventure," he said. They walked down a stretch of historic brick-lined streets. The sun was dropping behind the murals and warehouse galleries, casting long shadows across the sidewalk.

"I was expecting ropes and blindfolds," she said, glancing over.

"You're not ready for that," he replied.

She blinked. "Excuse me?"

"I said what I said," he answered, "You're not ready to be touched until you've decided you're worthy of honestly feeling our feelings."

Emily looked away. He always flipped her reflexes upside down.

He stopped in front of a building that looked like an old bookstore. Inside, it was an artist's studio, with high ceilings, warm lights, and a jazz trio playing quietly in the corner. There were canvases everywhere. Some blank. Some half-done. Some beautiful paintings, too.

She turned to him, confused. "This is our training session today?"

"This is your first assignment," he said. "Paint. No rules. No references. Just expression."

"I don't paint." She snorted. "You do now," he replied.

The assistant walked over with smocks, paintbrushes, and

two small plastic grooved trays she had prefilled with seven different colors. Then, they walked to two open easels and got set up. He explained, "This is a free paint session, meaning you can paint anything; there's no class right now." He grabbed his brush and started by dipping it in red and grazing the canvas a few times.

She just looked at him in annoyance. "Why are we here?" she asked. "Because before I touch your body," Mr. White said gently, "I want to see what your soul does when no one's watching."

That did something to her. Frustrated, she grabbed her brush and started painting.

At first, it was messy, lines and colors with no form. Then, it became angry. Then, when she calmed down, it became coherent.

Mr. White didn't hover. He focused on his own painting, but he did watch her, though, to track her range of emotion. Once she got over being annoyed, she got into it and lost track of time.

When she finally looked up, she was breathless, and her hands were covered in paint splatter.

All the raw emotions came streaming out of her. She was so wound up that her hands shook.

"I don't know what I just made," she whispered. "You made a map," he said, walking over. "For what?" she asked. "For me to follow. When you're ready."

They stood and reviewed their canvases together. Mr. White painted a woman holding a flower. Hers was more abstract. Emily joked, "You should get me to sign this. It could be worth something one day."

He didn't touch her, but his presence wrapped around her like a robe she chose to wear.

"Next time," he said, voice low, "we'll begin with touch."

Emily looked at him. She didn't smile. She didn't flirt. She simply nodded.

For the first time, the idea of being touched didn't scare her.

When they walked back, Emily decided that she didn't want the night to end so early, so she invited Mr. White to her suite.

When they got back, Emily said, "Give me 30 minutes to try to get this paint off, and then come up."

Emily's Late Night Creep
Location: *10:34 PM | Emily's Suite*

The door opened before he knocked.

Mr. White stood in the hallway. He had showered. He had on a white linen shirt and slacks.

Emily stepped back to let him in. She wore no makeup. No robe. Just a soft cotton tee and shorts. She no longer feared him, seeing her completely vulnerable.

"You didn't have to come," she said quietly. "I didn't," he smilingly replied.

She paused. "But I'm glad you did." He nodded, stepping inside.

Her room smelled like lavender and vanilla. The R&B music played softly in the background. The lights were low. No candles or setup. Just her, in her natural environment.

She didn't offer wine. Didn't start a conversation.

Emily walked over to the bed, her heart racing with a mix of anticipation and liberation. She sat down, looking up at Mr. White with steady, resolute eyes, shedding the layers of expectation that had cloaked her for so long.

"I want this," she declared, her voice firm and clear. "Not to prove anything. Not to win. I need touch, and I have chosen you to share this experience."

He exhaled slowly. The energy between them shifted, electric and palpable, as if the air itself was charged with the weight of her truth.

"I need to hear it clearly," he said softly, stepping closer to the bed, his presence exhilarating.

"Touch me," she said, her voice unwavering. "I want to know what it feels like to be unwrapped, without the mask I've worn for so long."

He nodded, a silent commitment to honor her desire. He knelt in front of her, drawing her close, pressing the side of his face against her stomach, his warmth soothing against her skin.

He let the weight of his presence envelop her, creating safety so she could relax.

"Say stop whenever," he whispered, his breath warm and inviting. His fingers began to slide up her thighs slowly, tracing the soft skin. He kept his eyes locked on her face, capturing every nuance of her emotion.

She didn't close her eyes. She breathed deeply, embracing the freedom of her genuine emotions.

When his hands reached the hem of her shirt, she paused, allowing him to pull it over her head. Her hands moved down, lowering her shorts and panties, exposing not just her body but also her sweet Susie, waiting to be touched.

He stood and leaned in, kissing her just below her collarbone, a soft and anchoring gesture that felt like a promise. "I see you, Emily," he said, his voice low and reassuring.

She looked at him, her eyes shimmering with newfound courage. "I've never done this without the performance," she whispered.

"That's because no one's ever earned you," he replied, unclasping her bra with deliberate care.

Her breath caught, not from nerves, but from finally being seen. He took his time, worshipping her in silence. His mouth reverently kissed her body. Each kiss rewrote the narrative of her past, transforming her into the woman she had always wanted to be.

When he finally kneeled between her legs, he savored every inch of her, relishing the taste of her pleasure. After what felt like an eternity with him rubbing, licking, and sucking her, he let her cum in his mouth, with a skill that left her breathless and completely alive. When Emily climaxed, he kept licking and teasing her, drawing out her pleasure until she was completely trembling with sensation.

Yearning to reciprocate, Emily leaned down and pulled him up. "You need to undress and get in this bed with me." Her heart raced with anticipation of tasting him. The warmth of his skin against her lips sent a thrill through him, and she reveled in the sensation. As he laid back, she positioned herself under him and sucked the tip slowly at first, then she took him into her mouth, swirling her tongue, savoring the way he hardened at her touch. She watched as his eyes closed in pleasure and his breath quickened. Encouraged, Emily took him deeper, filling her mouth as she moved rhythmically, her head bobbing in a steady motion, her hands cupping his lower shaft. The taste of him was intoxicating, and with each suck, she felt a fire igniting within her that fueled her desire.

With one hand, she gripped the base of him, while the other explored his balls, teasing and caressing them as she worked her mouth. She could feel his muscles tense, and the low groans escaped his lips. She picked up the pace, her lips wrapping tighter around him. She was determined to give him everything she had to offer.

It was blowing his mind how good she was. Emily could sense his yearning, so she hollowed her cheeks and pushed herself further, taking him deeper until she felt him ready to burst. She pulled back for a moment to catch her breath. She looked up at him mischievously and said, "Are you ready for more?" Her voice was sultry and inviting. Mr. White could only nod, yes. She had him breathless. With renewed determination, she dove back in, her head moving faster now, a perfect blend of passion and eagerness. Each moment brought him closer to release. With one final surge of effort, she focused all her energy on the tip, applying just the right amount of pressure with her lips while she quickened her movements with her hands. The combination of her mouth and hands pushed him to his limit.

"Emily…" he let out a guttural groan, his climax crashing over him like a wave. He filled her mouth. Emily swallowed it all, the taste of him overwhelming her senses. Once he caught his breath, all he wanted was to feel her insides.

He reached for the lube and applied some to himself and her and entered her slowly, inch by inch. He knew he was bigger than her previous instructor, so he was attuned to how her body responded to him. He was engulfed in the sensation;

her tightness almost made him scream out. He had to think about math problems to calm down and not bust too quickly.

As he pushed deeper, she realized she was in trouble; it started to hurt a bit. He was thicker and longer than Mr. Green, and his rhythm left her breathless. When he picked up his pace, she felt incredible pleasure and pain. "Talk to me? Is it good for you?" he urged, his voice a low, sultry whisper.

"Yes, just take it easy on me," she gasped, her body arching in response. "I love how I feel inside you," he breathed. He slowed his pace a bit, but he did want to stretch her. And Emily was feeling every inch of him and squeezed from the inside. Then, he asked her, "Do you think you want to ride me?"

Then, she climbed on top of him, and he did most of the work underneath her, rolling his hips into her. When he found her sweet spot, their movements synchronized, and he rode that spot until she came so hard it felt like a revelation—and as her wall contracted, she took him over the edge with her, but he wasn't done.

With a playful grin, he gently urged her to slide off him, her body still humming with bliss. "I want to see you on all fours," he said, his voice low and sultry. He guided her into position, spreading her legs slightly apart, allowing him to admire her gorgeous young body and juicy pussy. As he positioned himself behind her, he leaned forward, brushing his lips against her back, sending shivers down her spine. "You ready?" he asked, his breath warm against her skin. "Yes," she said.

With deliberate slowness, he slid back inside her. He began with light, measured strokes, allowing her to get used to the depth. "You're so damn tight," he gasped. The way he angled himself sent waves of pleasure through her, yet each movement was hurting some, too, but she didn't want to stop. He stroked her a little more, but he felt her tense up and realized that she wasn't enjoying it as much as he was, so he switched things up again. "Roll over on your back; I want to finish looking at you."

As soon as she got on her back, he reentered her. He also leaned down and kissed her all over her face as he stroked her; soon, she felt more relaxed. The angle of his thrusts sent sparks through her body. "I'm so close!" she cried, then, with a few more quick thrusts, she shattered, her body trembling as she cried out. It felt like a floodgate had opened, and she felt him release at the exact moment. They came together. The experience left them breathless and connected in a way Emily had never experienced before. She held him as if he were a truth she had never thought she'd be able to feel.

Afterward, as she laid on his chest, his fingers were tracing a lazy pattern across her shoulder. She cherished the moment of connection. When she finally spoke, she simply said, "Thank you." Mr. White faintly smiled and said, "I enjoyed you," and kissed her cheek and squeezed her gently, acknowledging her and the transformative journey they were on.

FORTY

Emily & Mr. White's Reflections

Journal Entry: *1:42 AM | "My encounter with Mr. White"*

I feel transformed, and it wasn't even the sex.

During my encounter with Mr. White, he made space for me before he ever touched me. It was the silence before the kiss—the eye contact and how he listened to my body, adjusting to me.

I didn't feel like a prize. I felt like a person. And not the version I usually present to be worthy.

I didn't fake anything. Not my breath. Not my pleasure. Now, it hurts a little. I'm still new at this, and Mr. White is very well-endowed and skilled. I frankly wasn't ready for that, but I liked it. The part I can't stop thinking about is how he didn't dominate me.

He saw every part of me. He waited for my rhythm. He also didn't make it about his pleasure.

And he's a white boy who was smoother than any other man I've dealt with, and then he honored me.

It was the first time I've ever had sex where I didn't feel like I was giving something away. I felt like I was pleasing myself.

And if he never touches me again, I'll still be grateful. Because now I know what I deserve. And I will never accept less again.

-Emily

Mr. White's Reflection
Instructor Audio Log: *2:03 AM I Subject: Emily*

She invited me into her space, not with lingerie or language, but with presence.

Now, I haven't had a 24-year-old pussy in many moons, and Lawd, it's so tight. I do see now how Mr. Green got caught up. But Emily has matured even in the few days since she transitioned to my care.

I was proud of her for vocalizing her needs. When she said she was ready, she meant emotionally, not just physically. That distinction changed everything for her. I didn't rush. I didn't take it. I simply received what was offered.

She didn't default to performance; she also stripped away her approval-seeking self.

What I touched last night was her new sexual identity. She said she wanted touch, and then I pleased her. She was fully present, breathing and open.

That kind of sex isn't about climax. It's about completion through release.

She is transitioning out of performance mode. I suspect there will be regression—it's natural, but she knows what real feels like now.

That will be dangerous for anyone who tries to give her less.

This mission is working.

-W

Dr. Collins Debriefs Mr. White
Location: *9:03 AM | Dr. Collins' Executive Office*

Warren reviewed the data on Emily and Mr. White, including the body language footage, journal entries, and audio logs.

He didn't look up when Mr. White entered.

He glared over his glasses. "You crossed the line, White," Warren said.

"I don't think so." Mr. White replied calmly. "She invited me in."

"You fucked her last night in her room," snapped Warren.

"Yes. We connected physically with consent, clarity, and control. But Warren led the scenario. I just followed her lead."

Warren looked up sharply. "She's not supposed to be in control of scheduling training sessions, White."

"She wasn't. She made the request, and I didn't want to reject her. You know how fragile she is."

Warren tossed a file on the table. "You've trained six women here. None of them moved like Emily. What makes her different?"

"She's been so repressed," Mr. White said. "She wanted to try on this new persona of controlling her own pleasure as a grown woman."

Silence.

Then Warren stood. Walked to the edge of his desk, arms crossed.

"She's going to be trouble now."

"Emily was already trouble; you saw what she did to Mr. Green. That man is love-struck," Mr. White said.

Warren nodded.

"You're keeping the assignment. But any signs of emotional dependency, and I'll pull you."

"I'm not attached," Mr. White said firmly. "You sure? I saw what she did to you with her mouth." Warren asked. "You looked like a man praying when you held her."

Mr. White smiled. "I won't lie, I had an amazing time with her last night. There's something about young, new pussy that's incredibly captivating." Warren raised an eyebrow and smirked. "Let's keep it classy, White."

"Yes, sir."

FORTY-ONE

The Private Brunch—Summer, Bianca, and Emily

Location: *10:30 AM | Private Dining Room*

The room smelled like citrus and honey butter. Soft R&B drifted through hidden speakers. Summer, Bianca, and Emily sat at a round table set with linen and drank mimosas to catch up.

It was Bianca's idea for the ladies to meet.

She showed up in sleek loungewear, hair twisted up, with light makeup, always the diva. Summer wore a black jumper and no makeup. Emily sat in a soft cream t-shirt and leggings.

Bianca broke the silence, swirling her mimosa glass.

"So… Does anybody else feel like we've been spiritually bitch-slapped since our instructors were changed?"

Summer hollered, laughing. The kind that cracked something open. "I thought I was coming here to sharpen my edges," Summer said, reaching for a croissant. "Turns out, I had to lose them first."

Emily nodded slowly. "I thought I was just here to get my freak on; now I need to figure out if I still want to marry my fiancé."

Bianca raised a brow. "And?"

"I don't know yet," Emily admitted. "But for the first time, I'm really thinking about what I want. Not what looks right. Or what my parents expect. Not what Kenny needs. Just what feels right to me."

Bianca set her drink down. "Mr. Yellow didn't ask for my body. He asked for my truth. And I didn't even know I wasn't ready. He's helped me face some things, and he fucked the shit out of me."

They all giggled.

Summer tilted her head. "I didn't realize how much energy I've spent trying to be irresistible...the perfect arm charm... But true intimacy is not performance. I didn't like Mr. Blue at first; he didn't fawn over me, like most men do. He disarmed me and made me get real. But I must say, he's fine; he does and his stroke game "Ladies," she took a deep breath and banged her hand on the table three times, "it is quite impressive."

Emily shared, too, "Listen, y'all, my new instructor is this well-hung white boy. They call him Mr. White, and he was exactly what I needed. He made me get real. With Mr. Green, it was like we couldn't get enough of each other. Once he broke me open, I figured out that I like sex. It was like that high school phase I never got to have. But Mr. White has taught me about real intimacy." He said, "Intimacy means they could reject who you really are. But only if they meet the real you..."

They all took a minute to soak that in. Then, Summer chimed in, "I think it's called growth, ladies."

Bianca's eyes were softer. They all had empathy for each other, and they acknowledged their transformations.

"I used to walk into a room needing to be seen," Bianca said. "Now I walk in, checking if I want to see what's in the mirror."

Summer sipped her coffee. "Mr. Blue didn't break me. He waited for me. And that's what broke the part of me that always needed to be in control."

Emily looked at both of them. "I've been performing for so long, operating on other people's agendas. Now I am deciding how and when I want pleasure."

Summer leaned in. "So... who are we becoming?"

Bianca smirked. "Women who are truly sexually fulfilled."

Emily smiled. "Works in progress, I think."

Summer raised her glass. "To not be who we were."

Bianca clicked hers. "To become who we actually are."

Emily raised hers last. "To the men who are witnessing our transformations."

They clinked glasses and drank to celebrate.

Natasha's Reflection
Location: *12:02 PM | Natasha's Penthouse Suite*

The feed from the lunchroom played on the screen in front of her. Just three women bathed in morning light, laughing, listening, and leaning in.

Natasha wished that she could have participated in the conversation.

She lounged on her velvet chaise in her penthouse, her legs crossed at the ankle, sipping on a chai latte. Her eyes stayed glued to the monitor.

She was so thrilled to overhear this conversation and made a few observations:

> *Summer, once the control freak who seduced like a reflex, was now leaning into interacting with men without dominance. No more power games or competitive sexual energy.*

> *Bianca has realized that endlessly striving for perfection made her miss the signs that she wasn't connecting. She used to drink validation like champagne before we got her barefaced and centered. Now, she was laughing and genuinely enjoying herself. She wasn't performing for anyone.*

> *And precious, pristine Emily had grown the most. No longer Daddy's perfect virgin. She is determined to operate under new rules, and she means it.*

> *A slow, satisfied, goddess grin rolled across Natasha's lips. The Freak School process works, she thought.*

> *She set her coffee down, stood barefoot, and walked toward the screen.*

> *"These ladies are blooming," she whispered, beaming with pride.*

She watched as the women raised their glasses. "Y'all finally get it," Natasha said to the screen like a mother watching her daughters move on to the next step in life. She chuckled and tossed the fig into her mouth.

"It was about who they had to become to finally love

themselves enough. She clicked the remote, pausing the screen on a still frame:

Bianca, Summer, and Emily are all smiling at each other. "This is priceless," she thought.

Natasha took one last sip of chai and smiled, too.

Forty-Two

Drama in the Instructor's Lounge

Location: *4:38 PM | Instructor's Lounge*

The lounge was sleek: leather couches, a pool table, inset lighting, a wall of lockers, personal showers, a snack station, a fridge full of alkaline water and energy drinks, and a few pieces of exercise equipment, all wrapped in testosterone energy. No alcohol. No women allowed.

Mr. Blue leaned against the wall, arms folded. Mr. Yellow sat on the armrest of a chair, reading a dossier. Mr. White nursed a cup of black coffee, flipping through his handwritten notes like scripture.

The doors swung open, and Mr. Green, Mr. Black, and Mr. Silver walked in. The air immediately changed.

"I guess emotional therapy's the new foreplay," Mr. Black muttered, heading straight to the fridge. Mr. Silver chimed in, "Y'all got 'em writing journals and painting now?"

Mr. White looked up. "Is that jealousy I hear, or just the sound of irrelevance?"

"Ouch, did that hurt, guys?" Mr. Yellow smirked.

Mr. Green tossed himself onto the couch, fake-laughing. "Y'all act like you're saving souls. Meanwhile, Emily used to moan my name. Don't tell me White turned her into a nun."

"Quite the opposite, she moans her own name now while getting stroked correctly." Mr. White replied, dead calm.

Mr. Green's jaw tightened. "Let's not forget who cracked her open first," he said coolly.

Mr. Blue heard enough and leaned off the wall to jump on Mr. Green. "You know, Green, you cracked her ego, but White cracked her illusion. There's a big difference. This is not about getting notches on our belts; our job is to guide these women into sexual self-discovery."

Mr. Black laughed. "You boys talk like poets. But let's see how long these women stay transformed once you stop whispering sweet empowerment in their ears."

Mr. White raised his gaze towards Mr. Black. "They won't stay transformed for us. The transformation is for themselves. That's the difference between what we built and what you guys broke."

Silence.

Mr. Black slammed his locker hard. "This place used to be about control and slaying these ladies. Now it's group therapy?"

"No, actually, this place has always been about control. You guys just didn't realize you were the pussy-whipped knuckleheads being controlled," added Mr. White.

That comment really pissed off Mr. Green. He loved Emily, and he believed she would always be loyal to him.

Mr. Black had a comeback: "Yeah, right, you think they're not going to come looking for us again?"

Mr. Yellow chimed in. "I doubt it, but if they do, they'll be different. And since you haven't evolved, they won't stay." Then, he left the lounge.

Mr. White and Mr. Blue also headed for the door, like prophets walking away from a burning altar.

Mr. Green muttered under his breath. "Fuckin' philosophers."

Mr. Black sat down. Jaws tight.

Mr. Silver just sat there trying to figure out how to get back on the roster. He wondered what it would take to become the kind of man they'd come back for now.

Forty-Three

Mr. Green's Meltdown

Location: *11:47 PM | Emily's Suite*

Later that night, Emily was in bed, satin wrap tied, writing in her journal, when she heard a knock at her door.

"Emily, it's Mr. Green. Will you open the door?"

Her heart stuttered at the sound of his voice. She wasn't expecting him. She considered ignoring him. Then, she got up, untied her hair, threw on a long robe, and opened the door just enough for him to see her face.

"Emily. Hi, can I come in and speak to you?" She didn't move. "You know you're not supposed to be here, Mr. Green."

He smiled. Same boyish grin. The same eyes that used to make her feel like a prize.

"Em, I know. But I couldn't leave things the way they are."

"They're fine; I'm good actually," she said flatly.

"You look a little different," he said, his eyes scanning her, slower this time. "Softer, somehow."

Annoyed, she snapped, "Or maybe I was never hard to begin with; maybe you just weren't patient enough to see past the surface."

He blinked. "I didn't know what you needed."

"No," she said. "You knew. You just liked having sex with me. You liked me, sprung and easy to manage." "That's not true, Emily," he protested.

She tilted her head. "Why are you here now?"

Mr. Green stepped closer. "Because I miss you."

Emily let out a soft, dry laugh. "You miss the version of me who didn't know herself."

"I could give you more," he pleaded. "I've been thinking about how I handled things. I moved too fast. I didn't listen. But I can change."

Emily wasn't moved. "Mr. Green, you're not a bad person, but you were lazy with me."

"I needed someone who listens. Someone who waits, watches, and honors the experience."

"Like Mr. White," he said bitterly. "You think he's perfect?"

"Well, yes," she said. "He understands me, and he earned my intimacy."

Green sighed. "You're not going to give me a second chance."

She gave him a devastating look. "I gave you my body and my attention way too easily. I need something else now."

Green's jaw clenched. "So that's it?" "Unfortunately, yes, we are completely done," she said.

As she started to close the door, Mr. Green cried out, "I'm sorry, Em, I love you. I care so much for you."

She shook her head and shut the door. She did feel sorry for him, and she didn't have plans to take him back to Richmond, so his outburst was crazy to her.

After Emily shut him down, devastated, Mr. Green headed to the Instructor's Lounge.

He paced the locker room, shirt half-buttoned, eyes wild. He felt distraught.

He sat on the edge of the workout bench, elbows on knees, breathing hard.

Mr. White walked in, sipping water. "Tough night?" he asked, eyebrows raised.

Green didn't answer. "She dissed you, huh?" Mr. White continued. "Thought so. She's glowing these days. You can smell the healing on her."

"Fuck off, White," Green snapped.

Mr. White held up his hands. "Hey, I'm just saying, you had her, and you fumbled."

"She was different back then," Green said.

"No, you were actually," Mr. Blue said, overhearing from the hallway. "She's always been who she is. You just weren't deep enough to see it and help her grow."

Green stood up fast. "Don't act like you're better than me."

"I don't have to," Blue said. "Your results say it for me."

Green, with his 5'8" self, got up in White's 6'0" face, yelling. "Fuck that. I was one of the top trainers in the last cycle. You think you're saving these women? You're turning them into what exactly? Self-righteous vixens who don't need men at all."

Mr. Blue added his two cents. "When they don't need us anymore, that means we've done our job."

Green balled his fists. "You make me look bad to Emily."

"No one has to try to defame you," said Mr. White. "You did that all on your own."

Green snapped.

He lunged at Mr. White, fast and sloppy, his anger evident.

Blue, a martial arts expert, stepped calmly, catching him by the shoulder, flipping him down onto the padded floor to diffuse the situation.

Green wheezed, stunned.

A slow clap echoed in the room. It was Natasha.

She stood in the doorway, arms crossed, with a complete bitch face.

"Well," she said. "That was... informative."

The room fell still.

Green slowly stood, chest heaving.

Natasha stepped forward. "Mr. Green, get your ass up!" Security called me about you going to see Emily Jackson earlier. I came to look for you, and now I see this. You broke three principal codes tonight.

One: Unauthorized communication with a reassigned student.

Two: Physical aggression toward a fellow instructor.

Three: Demonstrating emotional instability without self-reporting."

She looked at the other men. "Anything I missed?" Everyone was silent.

Natasha turned back to Mr. Green.

"I had high hopes for you. You have been here for years; you have the look, presence, and charm. But charm without depth is just manipulation."

He said nothing. She extended a black envelope from her pocket. Here is your last month's pay. Effective immediately, your contract with Freak School is terminated. Go to your suite and pack your things. Security will escort you off the grounds within the hour.”

Green’s mouth opened, then closed. He hung his head and walked out. Someone from the security team was waiting in the hallway to escort him to his suite.

The room was silent.

Natasha looked at them all and said, “When a man refuses to grow…he doesn’t belong in a place built for transformation.”

The Culture Shift Begins

Location: *8:15 AM | Instructor's Lounge*

Three days after Mr. Green's termination, the mood was different.

The usual haze of testosterone and cocky banter in the instructor's lounge was replaced with stillness. Mr. Blue, Mr. Yellow, and Mr. White were in sessions with their clients. The rest of the instructors were trying to make sure they weren't next.

Mr. Black poured himself a cup of black coffee. He sat on the couch in the lounge, writing in his journal.

Mr. Silver came in, poured himself a coffee with a ton of cream, and sat across the room at a table. His phone was in his hand, and he was reading.

Mr. Silver asked Black, "Man, did you hear what happened?"

Mr. Black knew what he meant. "Yeah, Natasha fired him and kicked him out of the hotel."

"They made him pack up his shit, and security walked him off the property. All he really left with from here was his Freak School hoodie."

Mr. Silver reacted, "Damn, man. I heard he tried to see Emily to apologize. She slammed the door on him, and security called Natasha."

Mr. Black added, "They took everything. He's got no job. No place to stay. And no woman. Man's out here raw."

Then Mr. Silver leaned forward. "You wonder if that could've been us?"

Mr. Black looked at him, concerned. "Hell, man, it still could be us, man." Silver raised an eyebrow.

Mr. Black continued. "I built my whole identity here on

control. Tone. Tempo. Obedience. But Green's mess wasn't about that girl. It was about his own worth being tied to how much power he thought he had over her. He got comfortable and took too many liberties. He was videotaping his unauthorized sessions with her, I heard."

Mr. Black sat back, thoughtful. "We're trained to lead, to take control, to blow their minds with our mouths, our hands, our presence. We know how to read breath and how their bodies respond to touch. But there's a deeper kind of listening... one that makes a woman feel safe. That part? Some of us never learned. We need help."

Mr. Silver got up. "I wonder if Warren's office door is open?"

Mr. Black nodded once.

They left their mugs and walked down the corridor, quietly, with purpose.

Mr. Silver & Mr. Black
Location: *8:50 AM | Dr. Collins' Executive Office*

Warren looked up as Mr. Silver and Mr. Black stepped in, unannounced but expected.

"Gentlemen," he said. "I was wondering how long it would take before one of you came to see me." Mr. Silver closed the door behind them. "We don't want reassignment." Mr. Black stepped beside him. "We want realignment." Warren leaned back, intrigued.

Mr. Silver spoke first. "We know how to seduce, guide, and even dominate women to ignite their sexual awakening, but what we're realizing, maybe too late, is that we've never really understood how to hold *space* to lead a woman's transformation."

Mr. Black added, "We're watching the new engagement model work. Blue. White. Yellow. Even Bronze does this, and their clients are responding well. It's not just about discipline. It's depth that I think we lack. And we want to learn these techniques too."

Warren steepled his fingers. "So what are you saying?" Mr.

Silver looked him dead in the eye. "We want to grow. What happened with Green was terrible, and we do not want similar fates." Mr. Black nodded. "Please teach us how to lead with presence, not power plays... and we'll make sure we're thinking development, not domination, going forward."

Warren quietly stood and walked to his file cabinet, pulling out two black folders with gold lettering. *Advanced Masculine Facilitation Phase I.* He slid them across the desk to each of them. "You want to stay?" he said. "Earn it."

Mr. Silver smiled. Mr. Black took a big, slow breath in relief.

And just like that, two men who once confused control with worth are on their way to becoming someone worth following.

Forty-Five

Mr. Blue & Mr. Black

Location: *9:20 AM | Instructor's Training Room*

Mr. Black agreed to be mentored by Mr. Blue as part of his training. Now, Mr. Blue was training him to serve a new client, one who won't fall for anything in his former repertoire.

Mr. Black sat at the edge of the sleek leather chair, bouncing one knee. The air in the room was cool. Mr. Blue stood at the wall, arms crossed, watching him like an instructor about to give an exam to a student who used to cheat his way through school.

"You're about to work with someone new," Mr. Blue said finally. "Her name's Zuri."

"What's her profile?"

"She's a graduate student in clinical psychology. Former foster care kid. Hyper-independent. Doesn't respond to sexual energy. Doesn't engage in flirtation. Doesn't care about your tone, your tempo, or your record of breaking women open." Mr. Blue explained.

Mr. Black raised a brow. "So...what does she respond to?"

"Nothing," Mr. Blue said. "Until she feels safe." He slid a tablet onto the table in front of Mr. Black. Onscreen: footage of Zuri, in a plain black hoodie, with headphones in, completely unbothered after her intake interview.

"She's not trying to impress anyone," Mr. Blue said. "And she sure as hell isn't waiting for a man to lead her. She's watching, studying, and waiting for the moment someone tries to use emotion as a manipulation tactic."

Mr. Black shifted. "So how do I connect?"

Mr. Blue didn't answer right away. "You don't. Not right away." Mr. Black stared at him in confusion. "You build a container," Mr. Blue continued. "You let her test it. You let her walk around it. You never invite her in. You just leave the door open and tend the space."

Mr. Black's throat tightened. "So this isn't about disarming her?"

"No, not at all." Mr. Blue said. "This is about not making her feel like she has to arm herself in the first place."

Mr. Black nodded slowly. "OK, you think I'm ready?" Mr. Blue paused and said, "I think this will be the first time you realize the woman in the room is smarter than you, and that's not a threat. It's a gift."

"So what is my goal tonight?"

Mr. Blue smiled slightly. "Learn how to hold tension without needing to resolve it."

Forty-Six

Zuri & Mr. Black

Location: *9:01 | Training Room 2*

The door swung open, and Zuri stepped inside, her presence commanding attention without demanding it. Her tight bun framed her face, and the clear glasses perched on her nose gave her an air of sharp intelligence. She wore a pink crop top that contrasted with her black joggers, a casual outfit that spoke to her comfort rather than her desire for attention. In her hand, she clutched a notebook, the pages likely filled with thoughts and ideas she wasn't afraid to express.

Mr. Black stood by the window, his hands clasped behind his back, silhouetted against the soft glow of the afternoon light. He was tall and composed, his posture exuding confidence and calm. Zuri took him in quickly, her gaze assessing, but he remained passive, providing no cues for her to read.

"You're the one assigned to me?" she asked, her tone flat and devoid of inflection.

"Yes," he replied.

She walked over to the small table and sat down, crossing her legs with an air of defiance. Opening her notebook, she flipped through the pages, not bothering to look up at him. "You should know I don't do power games," her voice firm. "And I don't need fixing."

Mr. Black's lips curled into a slight smile. "Good," he said, his tone even. "I'm not here to fix you."

Zuri paused, her pen hovering over the page as she looked up, a flicker of surprise crossing her face. She had expected a different response, one laden with judgment or condescension. Instead, she found a calm understanding in his eyes.

"I'm here to learn what kind of space you need to expand,"

he continued. "And to stay out of your way until you invite me in."

Zuri blinked, processing his words. Just once, she allowed herself to absorb the sincerity of his statement. It was a refreshing take, one that piqued her curiosity. She nodded slowly, a hint of respect creeping into her demeanor.

"Alright," she said, her voice softer now, yet still resolute. "Let's see if that's true."

Mr. Black took a step closer, the distance between them shrinking just a fraction. "What does expansion look like for you?" he asked.

Zuri leaned back slightly, contemplating the question. "It's not about what you think I need," she replied, her tone regaining its edge. "It's about what I want to create. I'm not looking for someone to dictate that process."

He nodded, acknowledging her point without argument. "Fair enough. I want to understand your vision, what drives you, and what inspires you. So I can support it."

Zuri studied him for a moment, intrigued by his willingness to listen. "Okay, but I won't hold back," she warned. "If you're not ready for honesty, you might want to reconsider."

"Honesty is what I'm after," he assured her, his expression earnest. "I believe it's the only way we can truly connect and collaborate."

She felt a spark of interest ignite within her at his words. "Then, let's get to it," she said, flipping her notebook open wider. "I have ideas to share, but I need someone who can keep up."

Mr. Black grinned, clearly intrigued. "I'm all in. Show me what you've got."

As Zuri began to speak, her passion for her ideas igniting, Mr. Black listened intently, ready to dive into the depths of her vision. In that moment, a new dynamic was forming, one built on respect, curiosity, and a shared commitment to explore uncharted territory together.

Zuri's Reflection
Journal Entry: 11:03 PM | "Day One – Mr. Black"

Session #1. Subject: Instructor Black.

Observed behavior: restraint.

He didn't flirt. Didn't posture. Didn't perform.

I counted.

Zero compliments.

Zero attempts at charm.

One direct statement of intent: "I'm here to learn what kind of space you need to expand."

Which means one of two things:

1. He's been coached. Thoroughly.

2. He's finally humbled enough to listen.

Either way, it's interesting.

His energy wasn't empty, but it wasn't invasive. He didn't ask about trauma. He didn't try to dig. He simply held still.

That stillness felt almost like a challenge.

Not to surrender, but to be seen without having to flinch.

I didn't expect that.

I also didn't expect to want a second session.

But I do.

That alone is worth noting.

-Zuri

Natasha & Mr. Blue Debrief Mr. Black
Location: *9:00 AM | Freak School Observation Room*

Mr. Blue stood by the one-way glass, arms folded. On the monitor: Zuri, post-session, back in her suite, reviewing her notes. No tears. No reaction. Just intense concentration.

Natasha leaned back in a leather chair, one ankle crossed

over the other, watching him.

"Well?" she asked.

Blue exhaled through his nose. "He held the line."

"That surprises you?"

"I expected him to try not to seduce. What surprised me is that he didn't even think about it."

Natasha's eyes flicked to the screen. "She tested him."

"Three times," Blue said. "Subtle. Brilliant. Most men would have leaned in. He leaned out. Let her hold the tension." Natasha smiled. "So he's learning."

"He's transforming, slowly. But genuinely. She doesn't need a man to lead her. She needs a man who won't take it personally when she doesn't need him at all." Blue replied.

"And you think Black can handle that?" Natasha asked.

"I think if he can't, she'll show him the version of himself that still thinks his worth is measured by impact," Blue said. "And that alone could finish what Green started."

Natasha stood and walked toward the panel.

"Keep him on her," she said. "Let's see what happens when a man learns to be a mirror instead of a performance."

She paused, then smirked. "And if he breaks?

"Then, she'll be the one to fire him," Blue said.

They both smiled. And watched.

Forty-Seven

Teri & Mr. Red

Location: *6:21 PM | Prep School Charity Auction*

Teri is the one student who is local to Charlotte. There was a summer charity event to support her school that she needed to attend. She asked the instructor, whose real name is James Redd, to come as her +1; Natasha approved of them going out for the evening.

The night of the charity event, Teri felt a mix of excitement and nerves. This was her opportunity to not only support her school but also to showcase the new chapter of her life. She had invited Mr. Red to escort her.

Teri stood in front of the full-length mirror in her suite, adjusting her black cocktail dress that hugged her curves in all the right places. The soft fabric flowed gracefully, giving her a sense of confidence. Tonight, she wanted people to forget her ex's public betrayal.

When Mr. Red arrived, she could feel her heart race. He looked dapper in his tailored suit, exuding a casual charm that made her smile. "Ready to make an entrance?" he asked with a grin, his eyes sparkling with mischief.

"Absolutely," she replied, feeling a rush of excitement as they headed out the door together.

As they entered the venue, familiar faces greeted her, and she felt a surge of pride as she introduced James to her colleagues. As they mingled and chatted, Teri felt like she was finally stepping into her own skin again. However, just as she began to relax, she spotted her ex-fiancé across the room.

He was charming a group of people and standing close to a striking man who clung to his arm. The sight sent a wave of unease crashing over her. "Hey, are you okay?" Mr. Red asked, noticing her sudden change in demeanor. Teri forced a smile.

"Yeah, I'm fine. Just surprised to see him here." "Do you want to leave?" he asked. "No," she said, "I can handle this."

As they continued to mingle, Teri's ex approached them with a hint of smugness. "Teri! Long time no see," he said, his eyes darting to James. "And who's this? Your new toy?"

Mr. Redd straightened and reached for his hand. "Actually, I'm James Redd, her new man." Her ex raised an eyebrow with a smirk. "A younger guy, huh? You always did like to chase after trends."

"I'm doing just fine, thanks. James takes excellent care of me," she said, her voice steady.

Mr. Redd placed a reassuring hand on her back, grounding her, and "I'm lucky to be by her side," he said, his tone firm and confident. Teri glanced at him with a swell of gratitude. She could feel the confidence radiating from him, and it bolstered her own resolve. "Now, if you'll excuse us," said James as he led her away to another part of the room.

Mr. Red leaned closer, whispering in her ear, "That was amazing. You handled him to perfection," as he kissed her hand. Teri smiled at him, her heart swelling. "Thanks for having my back." He winked, a grin spreading across his face.

They moved back into the crowd, surrounded by laughter and conversation. Teri felt a sense of liberation wash over her as she realized that she had not only confronted her past but had also embraced her future. And with Mr. Redd by her side, she felt ready to take on anything that lay ahead.

When they got back to the hotel at the end of their evening, Mr. Redd was inspired to show her what taking care of someone is all about. "Hurry up and get out of that dress so that I can give you a happy ending," he shouted from her bathroom.

When he reappeared completely naked, she gasped when he came up behind her, and his fingers touched her hips.

He turned her around, kissed her deeply, and lowered her onto the chaise lounge at the edge of the bed. Her legs parted. Mr. Red dropped to his knees. And kissed her inner thigh like he'd missed her because he had.

His tongue moved with purpose. No teasing. He massaged

her with deep, rhythmic strokes that pulled moans from her belly.

Her hands gripped the chaise. "Teri," he growled. "You don't get to come until I say so." "Then say it," she begged. He didn't. He sucked her inner thigh and went back in. When she started to tremble, he finally spoke. "Now." She came hard, writhing, choking on her own gasp, but he wasn't done.

He stood, bent her over the chaise, and slid into her in one smooth stroke.

"Look at yourself," he ordered. The floor-length mirror was angled perfectly.

She saw her eyes, wide and wild.

She saw him pounding into her with long, steady strokes, his voice in her ear: "Teri, you're a force. And you only lose when you forget that." He showed out, grinding his hips, tearing up her pussy. Her second orgasm screamed out of her.

He covered her mouth. "Don't wake the others, baby." He came too with a low growl, hips locked tight to hers, sweat trailing down his back, like he had just cut an acre-sized lawn.

When they collapsed to the floor, all tangled limbs, he pulled her into his arms. Teri looked up at him, dazed but glowing. "You are so sexy to me. I loved representing you tonight, and coming home and eating the mess out of you, and stroking you."

"I love what you do to me, James."

Forty-Eight

Mel and Mr. Bronze

Mel's Reflection
Journal Entry: *10:12 PM | "Me & Sam"*

Sam and I have been spending lots of hours together.

We are doing our own thing—no scripts or touching beyond fingertips and holding hands and cuddling. We love to rest against each other like we've known each other forever.

My time with him means everything.

Sam doesn't ask for more. He asks excellent questions. He makes tea without me asking. He remembers what I say in passing. He watches my face the way other men watch my ass. He listens with his whole chest.

We haven't had sex in three weeks. And I've never felt more loved.

I don't know if we're allowed to talk about what happens after Freak School.

After rules, titles, and rooms with one-way mirrors.

But I want to. I want to ask him what it would look like to be his in real life, not as a project or performance, but as his woman.

And he might want that too.

God help me. I am falling for Sam.

I need the quiet, steady, present version of this remarkable man that I never expected to keep.

-Mel

The Conversation
Location: *10:06 PM | Rooftop Garden*

The sky was low and dark, stars barely cutting through the misty Charlotte haze. Mel and Sam sat on a cushioned bench under string lights.

She leaned into his side, his arm draped around her shoulders.

"Do you ever think about what happens after this?" she asked softly.

Sam: "Every day." She looked up. "Really?"

Sam turned to her, his brown eyes steady and unflinching. "Mel... I stopped treating this like an assignment weeks ago. I told Natasha and Warren that you are my last client ever."

Her breath hitched.

"I know I'm supposed to follow the rules. Maintain structure and distance. But I don't feel distant from you, woman. I haven't in weeks."

He shifted, facing her fully now. "You see me. Sam. Not Mr. Bronze. And I don't want to pretend like this connection isn't rare. You are such a special jewel to me."

She nodded, trying to steady her pulse. "I've been afraid to say it out loud, but I want to know if this... us... could exist outside of here."

Sam reached for her hand.

"Mel, I don't just want you in one of these training rooms. I want to walk into the world with you. Grocery stores. Coffee shops. Sunday mornings. The whole thing."

Her eyes filled with light tears. "So what are we saying?"

He smiled softly. "I think I'm saying... when this is over, we will not be over."

She leaned into him. "I want to be chosen. Not coached."

"You have been chosen, ma'am," he whispered.

And for once, she believed it.

Sam leaned in closer, his lips brushing against her ear as he whispered, "Let's not waste this moment."

Mel's breath caught at the intimacy of his words. She felt a rush of excitement and desire coursing through her. "What do you have in mind?" she asked, her voice teasing him.

He stood, gently pulling her up with him, leading her to a secluded corner of the rooftop where the soft glow of the lights created a halo around them. The city stretched out below. "Let's camp out over here," he said, his voice deep and inviting, as he turned to face him. "I want to savor you and take my time."

With a gentle push, he guided her to the low stone wall that framed the garden. She leaned against it, feeling the cool surface against her skin, contrasting with the heat radiating from her core. He stepped closer, his hands finding her waist, fingers grazing her skin as he leaned in, pressing a soft kiss to her lips.

Mel sighed into the kiss, her body responding instinctively, craving more. Sam pulled back slightly, his gaze searching hers, a mixture of hunger and tenderness. "Tell me what you want," Sam demanded. "I want you," she breathed.

With a smirk, he took a step back, admiring her for a moment as the string lights danced across her features, illuminating her beauty. "Turn around, Mel. I want to see you glow."

She hesitated for just a moment, then did as he asked, turning to face the garden, her heart pounding with excitement. Sam moved behind her, his hands gliding along her sides, feeling the warmth of her skin beneath the fabric of her dress.

"Just like that," he said, his voice low and sultry. "I want to feel every inch of you."

He slowly lifted her dress, exposing her thighs to the night air, the chill sending a delightful shiver through her. Sam's hands caressed her skin, sending waves of desire crashing over her, and she felt herself melting under his touch.

As he knelt behind her, he leaned in, pressing soft kisses along her back. "You're breathtaking," he murmured.

With a deliberate slowness, he entered her, filling her, his hands gripping her hips as he found that perfect rhythm. The angle was exquisite, and with each thrust, he pushed her closer to ecstasy.

She gasped, her body responding eagerly to his every move. He shifted slightly, hitting that sweet spot deep inside her, and she felt the pressure building, her body aching for release. "Yes, Sam, right there!" she cried, lost in the moment. He picked up the pace, each thrust sending shockwaves of pleasure coursing through her. "I want to feel you come for me," he urged, his voice low and sultry, driving her wild.

"I'm so close!" she gasped, the sensation overwhelming her as she surrendered to his powerful stroke.

"Let go, Mel, cum for me, baby," he whispered. Then, with one final thrust, she shattered, her body convulsing in pleasure as she cried out his name. Sam followed closely behind, his movements becoming erratic as he found his release, filling her with warmth.

They lingered in the afterglow, the night wrapping around them like a soft embrace. Mel leaned back against him, his arms enveloping her as they both caught their breath, the stars above twinkling as if celebrating their connection.

"I want to be wherever you are," Sam murmured against her neck, his voice filled with sincerity.

Mel turned her head slightly, looking up at him. "Then let's make it happen," she replied, a sense of determination and hope blooming between them.

In that moment, they knew they were ready to take on the world together.

Forty-Nine

Mel and Mr. Bronze Get Debriefed

Location: *11:15 AM | Natasha's Executive Office*

Two days after the rooftop conversation, Natasha asked Mel to meet with her for a quick check-in.

Mel sat across from Natasha, legs crossed, fingers gently tapping against her knee.

She wasn't defensive. She was settled.

That worried Natasha.

Natasha didn't speak right away. She studied Mel for a beat too long—enough to stir something uncomfortable.

"Is this the part where you warn me not to fall for my trainer?" Mel asked, voice soft but pointed.

Natasha didn't blink. "This is the part where I ask if you still remember why you came here."

Mel hesitated. "I came here to stop shrinking," she said. "To stop making myself a victim people felt sorry for." "Good," Natasha said, leaning forward. "And how are things going with that?"

Mel nodded. "With Sam, I feel seen, heard, and whole."

"That's not what I asked," Natasha replied, sharp as glass. "Are you making yourself small for him now?"

Mel was offended by the question. Natasha sat back, folding her arms. "Attachment and transformation can feel the same in the moment. But only one of them will follow you when he's not there."

Mel clapped back, "Natasha, a relationship rooted in conscious attachment can absolutely be a space for deep, lasting transformation."

Natasha said. "Agreed, but don't just fall in love. Choose yourself while loving him.

Silence.

Mel spoke softly, "I was grounded in self-love when I got here. Sam and I have something special. I felt loved by my late husband, but it is way deeper with Sam. I have never felt this kind of love from a man in my life."

Natasha nodded. "I'm not giving my love away," Mel said. "I'm offering my love with intention."

"Just keep your eyes open and your boundaries clear," advised Natasha.

Natasha stood, smiled, and said, "Sounds like things are moving right along. For what it's worth, I think he sees you. Not as a fantasy, but as a woman. And if he continues to show up like that when this is over, you may have found something worth keeping."

Mel exhaled.

And when she walked out of Natasha's office, it was not as a student but as a woman ready to love—without losing herself.

Dr. Collins Debriefs Sam
Location: *8:30 AM | Dr. Collins' Executive Office*

Warren looked up as Sam stepped into the room, dressed in a charcoal jacket, no tie, and a crisp white collar unbuttoned at the top.

He looked... determined.

Warren raised an eyebrow. "This is early for you."

Sam nodded. "I need to speak to you before the day starts."

Warren folded his hands. "Is this about Mel?"

Sam took a slow breath. "Yes. And more than that."

He reached into his jacket and pulled out a small black box.

Set it on the desk. Warren looked at it. Then at him. "Wow, you're serious."

"I've never been more sure about anything."

Warren leaned back. "She's still a student. You're still her instructor."

"She's graduating in another week, Warren, and when she does, I won't be her instructor. I'll be her choice, and she'll be mine," Sam said.

Warren studied him. "You know how rare this is. Most of

our instructors develop emotional bonds from time to time. Temporary attachment. Post-program fallout."

"I know," Sam said. "But this isn't chemistry. This is compatibility. The late-night tea we enjoy, the silence, and the inside jokes. This is emotional safety built day by day."

He paused.

"And I'm not rushing her. I'm not proposing at the graduation ceremony. I'm not making a spectacle of it. I just wanted you to know, when this is done, I'm going to ask her the real question."

Warren opened the box. Inside: a slender, rose-gold band featuring a brushed moonstone. "It's not flashy," Warren commented. "It's her," Sam said. "Beautiful. Quiet. Radiant."

"You prepared for her to say no?"

Sam smiled. "She won't. She's already said yes with every choice she's made since she stopped shrinking around me."

Warren tapped the box closed. "Then, you'd better be worth it."

"I already decided to be," Sam said. "Before she ever looked at me like I might be the one." Then Warren stood, handed him his box, and extended his hand. "Congratulations, Sam. Just don't fuck it up."

Sam clasped his hand, firm. "I won't."

Then, he walked out like a man with a plan and a future worth protecting.

Fifty

Dr. & Mrs. Collins

Location: *10:47 AM | Dr. Collins' Executive Office*

Natasha stood at the window, looking out at the inner courtyard. Warren sat at a sleek mahogany table in his office, nursing a black espresso. They were both in a good mood.

"He told you about the ring?" Natasha asked without turning.

"He did," Warren replied.

"And I believed him. He loves her completely."

Natasha turned now, eyes sharper. "You believe a trainer can fall in love without compromising his discipline?"

"I believe Sam stopped being a trainer the moment he started listening instead of leading," Warren said. "He didn't fall in love with Mel the student. He fell in love with Melissa, the woman."

Natasha moved to sit across from him. "We designed this place to push people into self-awareness through intimacy. Not...romance."

"I know," Warren said. "But this isn't romance. This is something else."

Natasha narrowed her eyes. "What?"

"Integration," Warren replied. "Mel isn't shrinking to fit into love, and Sam isn't performing dominance. They're both operating from wholeness. That's the difference."

Natasha let that sink in.

"Do you remember when we built the original framework?" she asked, softer now. "We said the goal was 'control through self-knowledge.' Not power. Not seduction. Just...truth."

Warren nodded. "And now, we're seeing what happens when someone uses the system not to manipulate others, but to meet themselves."

Natasha smiled faintly. "I used to think love was a side effect. A liability."

"And now?" Warren asked.

She tilted her head. "Now, I think it's a by-product of loving yourself...and being met there."

Warren leaned back. "It's funny, isn't it? We built Freak School to break patterns. But it's starting to create partnerships. The real kind. The kind the world rarely makes space for."

"I think this is what it looks like when the program stops being about training people to play the game better and starts teaching them how to walk away from the game entirely," Warren said slowly.

They sat in that silence.

Then Natasha chuckled. "Well, hell. Maybe we are building a legacy after all."

Warren lifted his cup. "To the ones who graduate with more than confidence and find the love they deserve." Natasha tapped hers against it. "To the ones who leave here free."

After the toast, Warren gave Natasha that look, and without a word, he stood from his chair to lock the door.

Natasha turned slowly, one brow raised, smirking. "Do you have time for a private session, Dr. Collins?"

He didn't smile. He simply crossed the room with that calm, commanding energy that had made her fall for him in the first place—the kind that said, 'I know exactly how to serve you.'

Warren leaned down, brushing his lips against hers. "I love how you lead in public and always let me eat and spank that ass in private."

She smiled and exhaled. "It's all about the balance."

He lifted her effortlessly onto the edge of his desk. Dropping to his knees, pulling down her lace panties with his teeth, his gaze locked onto hers with a smoldering intensity.

Then, without hesitation, he buried his face between her thighs, devouring her with a fervor that made her gasp. His tongue plunged deep, moving deliberately, licking and sucking on her clit with an unrelenting rhythm. Each stroke sent shockwaves through her body, pulling her closer to the edge, holding her there as her thighs trembled and her breath became a stuttered gasp.

When her orgasm finally hit, it shattered her completely. Her legs shook uncontrollably, and he clamped a hand over her mouth, but still, he didn't stop.

"Shhh, baby," he murmured, his voice low and teasing. "Do you want the staff to hear us?"

His mouth continued its skilled assault, and she shook beneath him, frantic, her fingers clutching his wrist as her eyes widened with pleasure. He waited patiently, allowing the waves of her climax to wash over her before he stood again, reaching into the drawer and pulling out a slim black leather paddle.

"Bend over the desk," he growled.

She obeyed, feeling a thrill of anticipation as he lightly tapped her ass. The sting sent a gasp escaping her lips, and he followed up with a firmer strike. Then, to soothe her, he knelt again. He rubbed, licked, and kissed her peach, his touch igniting her senses.

When he stood once more, he positioned himself behind her and began entering her slowly, deeply, and deliberately. "Mine," he growled into her ear, and she felt a rush of heat at the possessiveness in his voice. "Yes, baby," she moaned in response. "All yours."

They didn't just make love; they pushed each other to the brink, pouring everything they had into the moment, each thrust a declaration of desire, as they moved together, entwined in their passion.

When he finally reached his climax, she followed suit, the intensity of their connection sending them both spiraling. He collapsed against her spine, breathless and spent, their bodies still connected in the aftermath.

Natasha's voice broke through the haze. "You know what we need now? The shower," a playful smile dancing on her lips.

"Let's go to The Penthouse," Warren suggested, his eyes glinting with mischief as he helped her off the desk.

As they stepped into their suite, Natasha kicked off her heels and headed *straight* for the bathroom. Warren watched her with that hungry gaze, already loosening his tie and unbuttoning his shirt. "Where are you going, Mrs. Collins?"

She called over her shoulder, "To prepare my body for the shower."

Inside their spa bathroom, the lights were dim, the floors were warm, and the custom shower was precisely as she had designed it, complete with a built-in bench, an adjustable rain shower head, a hand-held wand, six full-body wall jets, grip bars along the walls, and a stool in the corner.

She pulled off her dress and twisted her hair up tight, like a woman who had plans after the storm. Warren leaned in the doorway, with clothes off. "You done getting fine for me, baby?"

"Oh, I'm already fine," she said, walking toward him in nothing but her smile. That was it.

He grabbed her waist, walked her backward into the shower, and sat her down on the bench, the water already misting.

"You know what happens when you give a man tools and no supervision?" he asked, dropping to his knees. "Show me," she said.

And he did. He used the wand first, warm pulses of water against her inner thighs, watching her squirm.

Then he put his hand on her thigh, pushed them wide, and placed his mouth between her legs. His tongue danced on her clit, teasing and slurping with a delicious urgency. As she reached her peak, he guided her to stand on the bench, facing the grip bars, a mischievous glint in his eyes. With a firm, yet gentle grip, he parted her cheeks and began to explore her ass, savoring every moment.

Slow. Deep. Unbothered. "Warren," she gasped, the pleasure overwhelming her senses.

When she tried to get down, he pressed her back up there and kept eating.

And when she cried out, "Daddy, I need some dick now."

"Keep gripping that bar, Mrs. Collins. Daddy's not finished."

Then, he helped her step off the bench, and she leaned against the shower wall, as if under arrest. Her hands were on the tiles, and he placed his hands over hers to anchor her.

Then, he mounted her again, plunging deep and unrelenting. The entire shower seemed designed for this moment. Once he started bouncing his dick inside her, he growled, "Whose pussy is this?" "Yours, Daddy!" she screamed, lost in the sensation.

He returned her enthusiasm, as he reveled in the primal connection and raw intensity they shared. She arched her back, twerking her ass against him, driving him wild as she squeezed him from the inside, pushing him closer to the edge. "Baby, I love you so much, and I love fucking you too," he murmured, his breath hot against her ear as they lost themselves in each other.

After an intense session, they finally reached their peaks together. Her body trembled from waves of pleasure, and he released himself, coating her ass with his cum. He got on his knees to lick her clean with a hunger that made her gasp.

His voice, low and possessive, whispered, "Your ass is mine." A sharp smack followed; as always, her response was, "Yes, Daddy."

After they left the shower, they snuggled in bed. Natasha had a satisfied smile on her face as she laid on her husband's chest.

"You know, after everything we've built together, Ren, I can't help but feel grateful. This life we've created—it's more than I ever imagined."

As Warren rubbed her hair, "I feel the same way, Tasha. Freak School has become such a beautiful journey. It's incredible to see our clients awaken to their desires and truly connect on a deeper level."

"It's not just about control and mastery; it's about celebrating vibrant, unapologetic intimacy. We're teaching them to be adventurous lovers, but more importantly, we're helping them get their needs met."

Warren kissed her cheek. "Thank you for being my partner in this journey. Together, we're making a difference—one freak at a time."

A Love Built to Last

Location: *5:20 PM | Marbella, Spain*

Mel stood barefoot on a white stone beach on the Costa Del Sol, the gentle waves lapping at her feet, creating a soothing rhythm that matched the fluttering of her heart. The air was fragrant with the scent of flowers and the ocean breeze. An arch of blooming jasmine flowers framed their ceremony spot on the beach. She wore a bronze dress and a small pillbox veil that was carefully tucked into her natural hair, which perfectly caught the light of the setting sun.

Tears glistened in her eyes as she held Sam's hand. They stood together, unbothered by the absence of a crowd. This was their wedding ceremony, celebrated in a sacred place just for them, where vows could be exchanged with honesty and love.

"I never saw you as something that needed fixing. Instead, I saw your strength, your passion, and your beautiful spirit, and I fell in love with every part of you. I just want to build with you—together, as partners, as equals. I want to create a life filled with laughter, adventure, and deep connection. I want us to face the challenges that come our way hand in hand, lifting each other through every storm and celebrating every triumph. I love you with all my heart, Mel. You are my best friend, my confidante, and my greatest treasure. I promise to stand beside you for the rest of my life." Sam's eyes softened, with a smile across his face, as he slid the custom wedding band onto her finger as a tangible reminder of the promises they were making.

"Sam, from the moment we met, you saw me for who I truly am. You stripped away the layers of expectation and taught me to embrace my authenticity. I stand here today, ready to commit my heart and soul to you. I promise to celebrate our love every day, to be your partner in all things, and to cherish every moment we share. I vow to support you, lift you when you feel weary, and stand beside you in times of joy and sorrow. Together, we will navigate the world, creating a life filled with laughter, love, and adventure. Then, she slid the ring on his finger and gave him the warmest smile.

Their first kiss as husband and wife was deep, rooted in the love they had cultivated over the last few months. It was real, a reflection of their journey from instructor and student to soulmates ready to face the world together.

As they walked hand in hand, the sun dipped below the horizon, casting a golden glow over the beach, sealing their vows in the warmth of twilight.

Before leaving for Spain, Sam took a six-month sabbatical from the history department at Whitmore, dedicating himself entirely to his new bride and the life they would build together. The first step was their three-month honeymoon cruise around the world, to deepen their bond and explore the world as a married couple. The cruise departed from Spain in three days, but Sam had a surprise in store for his bride on the wedding night: a private yacht pulled up with a staff of six to attend to their every need. As they stepped aboard, the gentle sway of the yacht rocked them into a world of luxury and intimacy. Candlelight flickered softly against the polished wood, and the aroma of gourmet dishes wafted through the air. Sam smiled at the look of wonder on his bride's face as she took in the stunning sunset over the horizon. "Tonight is just the beginning," he whispered, pulling her close. With a bottle of champagne in hand, they toasted to their future, laughter and love echoing around them as they embraced the magic of their first night together as husband and wife.

Later that night, they devoured each other, their bodies intertwined like the waves crashing against the shore, each touch igniting a fire that burned brightly between them. They spent all night and the next day exploring the depths of their connection, savoring the exploration of not just each other's bodies but also their souls.

The next evening, Mel leaned against the railing, gazing out at the calm waters, where the sun melted into the sea. Sam wrapped his arms around her, resting his chin on her shoulder. "I never imagined I could feel this way, but you've changed everything for me." She turned to face him, her heart swelling with affection. "You've changed everything for me, too. I was always the one trying to fit in with everyone else's mold. But with you, I feel free to be myself." Sam cupped her face. "And you're perfect just as you are, Mel." "I can't wait to see what the future holds for us," she said, her voice filled with hope.

"Whatever it is, we'll face it together," he promised, pulling her close as the night enveloped them. Their journey started at Freak School and blossomed into something beautiful and profound.

Freak School for The Fellas

Location: *9:06 AM | Freak School observation room*

The room was minimal by design, stripped of distractions, a blank canvas for transformation. One chair, one man, one mirror. No desk to create barriers, just the palpable weight of anticipation hanging in the air.

Dr. Warren Collins sat across from each applicant, his voice low and steady, slicing through the silence like a scalpel. There were no papers to shuffle through, only the raw power of his presence, commanding and unyielding.

Behind the two-way glass, Natasha observed every second, her gaze unblinking and unforgiving. She wasn't just watching what the men said; she measured the subtle shifts beneath the surface, the flickers of truth and deception that danced in their eyes.

The application process had already done its first job. Of the dozens who had applied, only 16 had reached this pivotal moment. They submitted essays, underwent psychological assessments, completed STD screenings, and paid a $500 non-refundable application fee. They had survived two rounds of virtual interviews, facing questions that cut to the core of their being.

This was the final test: did they have the capacity to grow?

Dr. Collins leaned forward, with intensity in his eyes as he posed a single question.

"When was the last time you considered keeping a woman safe?"

Some men stammered, their confidence cracking like brittle glass. Others lied, oozing performative charm. But a few paused, inhaling deeply, allowing the weight of the question to settle in. Those were the ones that piqued interest and gave authentic answers.

At the end of the week, only twelve men will be selected.

These men weren't just enrolling in a course; they were stepping into a tantalizing crucible, a forge meant to awaken their deepest potential and transform their very essence. Freak School for the Fellas isn't about mending broken pieces or merely enhancing their skills in the bedroom, though there's plenty of sexual training involved. This program is focused on embracing their unfiltered masculinity and undergoing a profound transformation.

Book 2: Freak School For The Fellas...Where Real Men Transform!

Order today at Freakschoolnation.com